DemonWars

DemonWars
THE FIRST KING

R. A. SALVATORE

TOR®

A Tom Doherty Associates Book
New York

DEMONWARS: THE FIRST KING

Copyright © 2014 by R. A. Salvatore

The Dame copyright © 2009 by R. A. Salvatore

The Bear copyright © 2010 by R. A. Salvatore

Maps by Joseph Mirabello

Chapter opening illustrations by Shelly Wan

A Tor Book
Published by Tom Doherty Associates, LLC
175 Fifth Avenue
New York, NY 10010

www.tor-forge.com

Tor® is a registered trademark of Tom Doherty Associates, LLC.

ISBN 978-0-7653-7618-3 (trade paperback)

Tor books may be purchased for educational, business, or promotional use. For information on bulk purchases, please contact Macmillan Corporate and Premium Sales Department at 1-800-221-7945, extension 5442, or write specialmarkets@macmillan.com.

First Edition: November 2014

Printed in the United States of America

0 9 8 7 6 5 4 3 2 1

To Diane,
for her kind words and constant support of DemonWars.
Her love of the series brought me back here
to further explore this world.

Everything I write is for Diane.
Everything I write is for my family.

I have to give an extra shout-out in this one, though, to Tom Doherty
and Mary Kirchoff. Thank you both for helping facilitate this return
to my beloved Corona. It's been a wonderful journey.

But mostly, this one's for you, Julian. I found out about you as I hit
the home stretch in writing The Bear. *After so many years and so*
many books, sometimes it's hard to look ahead and remember that
there's plenty of road yet to travel. You reminded me of exactly that,
and turned my eyes to the road ahead, with great anticipation.

Pops loves you.

Contents

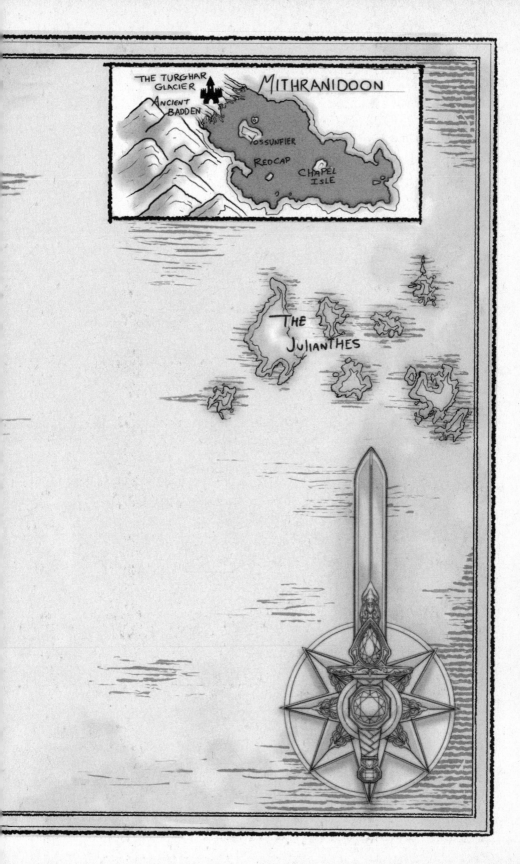

The Dame

Prologue

B rother Pinower hooked a finger inside the collar of his brown woolen robe and jerked it back and forth, suddenly feeling uncomfortably warm. And itchy, so itchy, as if a thousand little insects were crawling across his skin. But it wasn't the sun or the wind that had this young and healthy rising voice in the Abellican Church squirming. He knew that he should leave the wall immediately to report the dramatic and troubling sight before him, but he found that his legs would not answer his call. He couldn't turn away but was mesmerized, as were the other brothers of Chapel Abelle who were working on the main wall this day, by the long lines of ghastly wounded men.

Ghastly wounded and with many dead along the road behind the lines, no doubt.

"Someone inform Father," another dumbfounded monk managed to remark.

The sound seemed to break Pinower's paralysis. "Set them up in the courtyard," he instructed his many juniors. "Gather servants with blankets and fresh water and brothers with all the soul stones we can muster." He cast a pensive glance down the long slope to the southeast, to the seemingly endless line of casualties. He tried not to think about the many excruciating deaths he would witness that night.

When he climbed down from the wall, the horrible vision mercifully lost to him, Pinower found his footing and his purpose, and he sprinted across the wide courtyard, past the lower buildings of the gigantic chapel complex to the main keep and the office of Father Yurkris Artolivan, the oldest man in the Order of Abelle.

Artolivan looked every bit of his more than eighty years that day, slumped behind his desk, his skin sagging, his eyes dull and weary. Even his sparse, white hair seemed thinner and lifeless. He glanced up, as did his attendants, when Pinower rushed in unannounced.

"Wounded arrive from the battles," Pinower said, gasping for breath. "Many."

Artolivan exchanged concerned looks with his attendants.

"The rumors of the fighting in Pollcree?" one of those younger brothers remarked, for indeed they had heard only a few days before that two great forces were closing in on the small village from opposite ends and were sure to meet in bloody battle. Pollcree wasn't far from Chapel Abelle, barely a day's hard ride, and if these reports were to be confirmed by the arrival of the wounded this day it would mark by far the closest any of the heavy fighting had come to Chapel Abelle.

"Many?" Father Artolivan asked.

"More than all of those wounded we have seen cumulatively," Brother Pinower replied. He could not be certain if that was technically true, but it certainly seemed so from the view on the wall.

The old man rubbed a hand across his weathered and wrinkled face and with great effort pulled himself up from his chair. The nearest attendant brother offered an arm of support, but the proud Artolivan brushed it away and moved from around his desk.

"If there are men of Pollcree among their ranks, it would not do to keep them here," Brother Pinower reasoned. "I know our agreement, but they are too close to home. I would fear retribution or attempts at escape."

Artolivan paused and nodded, flashing a yellow smile at young Pinower. "You look better since you were put in charge of handling the prisoners," he said, a rare compliment from the man known as the father of the Order of Abelle. "Some of that paleness is at last retreating from your cheeks."

Pinower shifted uneasily from foot to foot, not even beginning to know how to respond.

"So, too, have you realized a confidence to speak of such policy in a room full of your superiors," said Artolivan.

Brother Pinower's shoulders slumped, fearing that he had overstepped his authority here. He glanced around at the older monks, all of whom were staring at him.

"We need such confidence in these dark times, Brother Pinower," said Artolivan, and several of the others cracked smiles that put Pinower at ease. "I have watched you grow beyond my expectations through this time of crisis."

Pinower felt his face blush fiercely.

"Crisis," Artolivan repeated, suddenly sounding like he was tired. So very tired. Artolivan and the warring lairds had worked out a compromise to allow the various chapels of the Order of Abelle, particularly the immense Chapel Abelle, to be used by both sides in the ongoing and escalating war between Laird Delaval and Laird Ethelbert as a neutral repository for the many prisoners taken on the field and, of course, as a point of medical care for all the wounded of either side. That was the best role for the Order of Abelle, Artolivan had rightly decided, a way to bring some manner of order and peace to a land ravaged by continuing war.

Thus, Chapel Abelle had become a dumping ground for prisoners from both the warring lairds, Ethelbert of the southeasternmost Holding of Honce, Ethelbert dos Entel, and Delaval, the most prominent and powerful laird in all the land, who ruled the strategic and fortified city at the southernmost navigable spot on the great river, the Masur Delaval. Scores of prisoners, hundreds even, had come into the increasingly vast complex of Chapel Abelle over the last months.

Brother Pinower had been the one assigned to oversee them, to heal their wounds, to put them to work, and to ensure that this encampment of opposing sides had remained secure and peaceful. His work had earned him praise from Artolivan and many of the other older brothers, and the young Pinower had felt as if his contribution here had been in the truest spirit of the tenets of Abelle. He used those thoughts to bolster his courage at that moment, for he knew that this day would be different. Of the prisoners who had come in before today, few had been seriously wounded. The battles had been so far-off that any soldiers grievously injured had not survived the long and arduous journey. Thus, before today, most coming to Chapel Abelle had suffered only minor wounds or no wounds at all. They were simply prisoners, who, in return for their lives, had taken an oath that their stake in the fighting had ended and they would serve out the end of the war in hard labor. Instead of killing their Honce brothers who happened to be fighting on the side of the other laird, Delaval's men would toil for the monks and their never-ending construction on this, the greatest chapel, perhaps the greatest complex, in the known world.

"Which banner, Ethelbert or Delaval?" Artolivan asked, his voice slurring, as if he had been drinking. He had not.

"I could not discern, Father. But likely both, I believe, by the sheer number of men involved."

Artolivan and the senior brothers exchanged looks again, but this time of doubt. Someone had won and someone had lost, and while many of the wounded would no doubt be men of both lairds, the prisoners who would remain behind in civil captivity would be of one faction or another.

On the ball of one foot, the small and lithe brown-skinned woman slowly pivoted. She stayed in perfect balance, ultimate grace, as she brought her other leg up teasingly, knee bent at first, but then straightening to become perpendicular with her body.

At the same time, the soft, silken robe she wore slid away from her smooth flesh, revealing her delicate foot and calf, her smooth thigh all the way to her hip.

Though deeply entranced in her dance, moving with the precision of a warrior and the discipline of a Jhesta Tu mystic, Affwin Wi still managed to glance from the corner of her large, dark eyes at the old man sitting and watching.

The septuagenarian, Laird Ethelbert of the southeasternmost Holding of Honce, gave a great sigh at that alluring turn and revealing movement of the woman's soft clothing.

Affwin Wi smiled a little bit outwardly and a great deal inwardly. She heard the longing and the love in the old laird's sigh, the wistful dreaminess in his still sharp eye. She entertained him, but she was no harem piece, no subservient or helpless creature.

She was, or had been, Jhesta Tu. She could outfight any man or woman in Ethelbert's army, and he knew it. She carried great power and great independence, and she was here, dancing before him, because she chose to be and not because he had ordered her.

And that gave her power.

She danced on and on, to one sigh after another from the man who wanted to consume her in passion but no longer could.

Gradually, Ethelbert's eyes closed, a look of great contentment on his face. Affwin Wi danced over to him and slid down onto the arm of his throne beside him, hugging his face against her small breasts until he began breathing in the deep rhythms of pleasant sleep.

Smiling still, Affwin Wi left the room, to find Merwal Yahna, young and strong, his virility shown in his hardened warrior muscles and exaggerated by the imposing profile of his shaven head. He wasn't large and bulky like so many of the greatest Honce warriors, who required such brawn to swing their gigantic swords and axes, but lithe and taut, a warrior of the desert and the fighting arts favored there, where speed and precision overcame bulk.

"I do not like that you dance for him," said the man, whom she had trained in the ways of the Jhesta Tu, her finest student.

She laughed dismissively.

"He loves you!"

"He cannot make love *to* me," Affwin Wi reminded as she reached up her hand and gently stroked Merwal Yahna's chiseled shoulder and upper arm. "He desires it but is too old."

"But you would let him if he could," the man accused.

"Your jealousy flatters me," Affwin Wi replied playfully. "And excites me."

She moved toward the man alluringly, but he grabbed her by the upper arms and pulled her back to arm's length.

"You would!" Merwal Yahna growled.

With a subtle roll of her arms, Affwin Wi brought her hands up, under, and then back out over Merwal Yahna's grasp, her elbows breaking his hold. She caught a grip on his forearm as she pressed his arms wide, and let her hands slide up until she had him firmly by the wrists.

A movement subtle, gentle, and effective, as was Affwin Wi.

"We are here to fight," Merwal Yahna reminded her. "We are paid as mercenaries, not whores!"

Affwin Wi laughed disarmingly. "We are employed by Ethelbert."

"To fight!"

"And so we have and so we will. His warriors look upon us with awe," said Affwin Wi. "He pays us well, but is there nothing more?"

Her conniving grin gave Merwal Yahna pause, and he stared at her curiously.

"Ethelbert is the ruler of a great city and land with wealth to rival the sheiks of Jacintha," she said. "He has no heir."

Merwal Yahna, not even fighting her hold, could only sigh at the ever-pragmatic attitude of his lover. Affwin Wi had no shame about her body or about lovemaking. To her, all of her physical being was merely a conduit to help her attain the emotional and spiritual goals—or in this case, the simple power offered by her alliance and dalliances with Ethelbert.

She had never pretended to be anything other than a woman who would have her way. No man—not Ethelbert, not even Merwal Yahna—could ever possess her.

"I grow warm and hungry when I dance," she purred, her voice suddenly husky. "Are you going to disappoint me?"

Merwal Yahna tugged his hands free and pulled Affwin Wi in for a crushing hug and passionate kiss. He tried to bend her backward to slow-drop her to the thick pillows spread about their room, but with an easy step and a twist of her pretty feet it was he, not she, who went down on his back.

Merwal Yahna was not disappointed.

Two banners preceded the lines into Chapel Abelle's courtyard soon after, one of Laird Delaval and the other of the third great city of Honce, the port of Palmaristown. The pennants came in side by side, a curious arrangement in these times, when the arrogant Laird Delaval was claiming unequivocal kingship of the whole of the land. But when Father Artolivan, no stranger to Palmaristown, noted the man riding the armored chestnut stallion before the banners, he surely understood.

The large warrior held up his hand to stop his entourage, then trotted the chestnut stallion over to the group of monks and dismounted with great ease, a man obviously accustomed to riding in full and decorated bronze armor.

"Prince Milwellis," one of the brothers greeted when it became apparent that Father Artolivan was struggling to recall the young warrior's name. "How fares your father, Laird Panlamaris of Palmaristown?"

"Well, Brother . . ." the man replied and motioned as if he, too, could not remember a name.

"Jurgyen," the monk explained.

"Indeed, and I do recall seeing you at my father's court."

"And this is Father . . . ?"

"Artolivan, yes, that name is known to me," said Milwellis. "A fine day to be in such company, Father." He bowed low in respect.

"A fine day?" Father Artolivan replied. "You have many outside who might not agree with your description."

"The battle was won, and that is no bad thing."

"Won at great cost."

"Pollcree?" Brother Pinower asked, and Milwellis snorted.

"It once was," the warrior replied. He pulled off his helm and shook his great shock of red hair, which bounced thick about his shoulders.

The flippant response brought a sour look to the faces of some of the brothers, Artolivan included, but that only made Milwellis snicker even more. Brother Pinower decided then and there that he didn't much care for this one.

"I did not know that Palmaristown had joined in the fighting," said Father Artolivan.

"We threw in with the claims of Laird Delaval long ago."

"Yes, yes, of course, the brothers of the Chapel of Precious Memories so informed us," Artolivan pressed. "But I did not know that your army had marched."

"No choice to it," Milwellis explained. "Laird Ethelbert has procured the allegiance of the many holdings along Felidan Bay and even on the Mantis Arm," he explained, referring to the long stretch of rocky coastland of easternmost Honce. "They had claimed neutrality, but no more. Ethelbert the dog has raised the stakes in this war."

"Many of those same seaside holdings have been sailing for Laird Delaval, have they not?" Father Artolivan interrupted with startling forcefulness, the man clearly tired of all this seemingly pointless warfare.

"They would have been wise to hold with their first choice, then," said Milwellis. "Their march to Pollcree was no more than an act of the deepest desperation by Ethelbert. Laird Delaval has established the center around the Holding of Pryd, commanding a line from that crossroad all the way to the Belt-and-Buckle in the south. Desperate Laird Ethelbert thought to flank that line and strike at Palmaristown, but rest assured that the tactic has failed."

"I will rest assured when this war is at its end, and not before," said Father Artolivan.

"We near that day!"

"So we have been hearing for many months. And yet, the wounded and the prisoners come in at greater pace each week."

"Many wounded today, I fear," said Milwellis, and he turned to glance back at the gate, where his soldiers were bringing in dozens of injured men.

"They will fill the courtyard and more," Brother Pinower dared to interject.

"Nay, that is the lot of them," said Milwellis.

Pinower wore a most curious expression. "Surely there is many times that number! I saw them from the wall."

"Mostly Ethelbert's men," Milwellis explained. "They will not enter the chapel courtyard until all of my men are fully attended. Every scratch."

"Prince Milwellis, that is not the agreement of the church," Father Artolivan reminded, but the man from Palmaristown was hearing none of it. He stepped forward and rose up tall, towering over the old Artolivan and making him seem small indeed in that moment—a realization that did not sit well on poor, shaken Brother Pinower!

"Here is the new agreement, old Father," Milwellis calmly explained. "You are to immediately and fully tend to my men, the men who serve Laird Panlamaris, my father. The dogs that run to Ethelbert's whistle will wait."

"And if Ethelbert's general brings in the wounded and the prisoners next time, are we to follow a reversed edict from him?" Artolivan shrewdly asked.

"No general of Laird Ethelbert will reach Chapel Abelle, unless as a prisoner," Milwellis assured him. "You will do as I instruct."

"And if we do not?"

The man smiled and lifted an eyebrow, a clear measure of threat in his posture. "That would not be wise."

"Nor would your stubborn and determined effort to drive the Order of Abelle from the side of Laird Delaval, which is surely the end result of your insistence," Father Artolivan replied with an evenness and strength in his voice that those around him had not heard in years, one that impressed and amazed Brother Pinower. "We have remained neutral, to the gain of both warring lairds and, more importantly, to the benefit of the people of Honce. If we are forced to break that neutral posture, I assure you that we will break against the laird applying that pressure. Rethink your position, Prince of Palmaristown, or I expect that Laird Delaval will come to blame Milwellis for the great loss of the brothers and their healing stones!"

The prince seemed almost to deflate at that, albeit slowly, as he gradually rolled back onto his heels. He kept his eyes narrow, though, and his teeth gritted, and he did not blink for many heartbeats.

"Brothers," Father Artolivan went on, "go through our gates and retrieve the wounded Ethelbert soldiers. Prepare the triage in the courtyard, as according to our agreements with both of the warring lairds. And when you do, be sure that there are no indications, on clothing or jewelry, of those poor unfortunates to determine allegiance to either laird. Those most wounded are to be tended first, regardless of allegiance, as is our way."

"These men are my prisoners!" Milwellis roared.

"And when you leave them here, they fall under the protection and responsibility of the Order of Abelle. As was agreed, Prince. Look around you at the nonclergy working on our walls and structures! Nine hundred and more have been sent here, and nearly half are men of Laird Delaval, captured by the forces of Ethelbert! Many came here wounded, many whole but as prisoners. They are out of the fight . . ." He paused as Milwellis whirled away and leaped back up onto his horse.

Without another word, the Prince of Palmaristown spun his mount around and galloped through the gate, his personal guard sweeping up in his wake.

"That one is trouble," one of the brothers remarked.

"It will come to this in the end, I fear," said Father Artolivan. "As the stalemate inevitably deepens and the common folk begin to grumble and stir in revolt, their families decimated by the continuing war, we will be forced into choosing a side."

"And how will we choose?" Brother Pinower dared ask.

Father Artolivan had no answer.

"They break and turn!" came a cry from the wall.

Artolivan led his entourage to the open gate, to look down upon the field, where indeed Prince Milwellis and the bulk of his forces had turned away.

"Abelle save us," Brother Pinower whispered as he sorted through it, for while one group of Palmaristown soldiers hustled the healthy Ethelbert prisoners toward Chapel Abelle, no doubt to hand them off and be rid of them, the main Palmaristown group led by Prince Milwellis took with them the wounded men loyal to their enemy, Laird Ethelbert! They were not going to allow the monks to heal those enemy wounded.

"The fool has just assured that there will never be peace in Honce, whether Ethelbert or Delaval proves victorious," Father Artolivan remarked.

"What will they do to them?" Brother Pinower dared to ask.

"Nothing," Father Artolivan said bitterly. "Prince Milwellis will simply let them die of their wounds."

Pinower looked over to another of the brothers, who merely shook his head and shrugged, and in that moment, Brother Pinower came to know the dark truth of Father Artolivan's prediction.

PART ONE

Aftermath

*W*hat do I owe?

To myself, to those I love, to my community around me and to the world, what do I owe? This is the essence of the question Dame Gwydre put to me when she insisted that I would not flee her beleaguered Holding of Vanguard in its time of darkness. Her contention, her belief in me—not in my fighting abilities but in the essence of who I am as a person—has shaken me profoundly.

Vaughna, Crait, Olconna . . . they're all dead now. And Brother Jond has been horribly wounded, his eyes taken by the fine edge of the sword I carry as my own. We five traveled together, we fought together, and I am alive only because of their efforts. With my gemstone lost, they all but carried me the many miles to the glacier, where, if I had simply fallen to the ground along the way, our troll captives would have put a painful end to me. When Ancient Badden, that most vile creature, discovered the truth of my sword, Vaughna claimed the blade as her own and died horribly in the maw of Badden's monstrous pet.

When Badden tried to kill me, Cormack and his powrie friends, who knew me not at all, rescued me. Cormack and Milkeila healed my wounds and gave to me a soul stone, that I might again become this alter-creature they name the Highwayman.

What do I owe?

I have been given a great gift from my parents, Abellican monk and Jhesta Tu mystic. I have seen both these respective transformative powers, the wisdom of the book my father penned and my mother practiced and the undeniable strength of the Abellican gemstone magic. Despite my infirmities—nay, because of them!—I have found a deeper truth and a more profound strength.

When I left Pryd Town those months ago, I could fight as well as Laird Prydae's champion, the legendary Bannagran. Now I believe I have only grown stronger. Without the gemstones, I find moments of greater clarity than ever before; I can align my ki-chi-kree for short bursts of tremendous energy and power, as I did when Ancient Badden threw me from the edge of the high glacier. I do not know that any man alive, other than an Abellican monk with the proper stones or perhaps the greatest of the Jhesta Tu mystics, could have survived that fall, but I did, and did so without the crutch that is a soul stone.

I have found the alignment of life energy, the perfect harmony of mind-body union, for those short moments in that highest crisis.

And as I have grown stronger without the soul stone strapped firmly to my forehead, so too have I grown with the stone. We are as one now; I can hold it in my hand and seal the line of life energy in place almost as well as if I had it upon my forehead, the top point of ki-chi-kree. The transformation from Stork to High-wayman, from drooling and staggering cripple to fine warrior, is nearly instanta-neous now, and without conscious thought. And that transformation is far deeper and far stronger. Every muscle movement, every swing of the blade, every antici-pation of an opponent's strike or parry crystallizes without a moment of consid-eration, and my appropriate response is launched before a thought need be given.

If I battled Bannagran now, I would defeat him, and with little difficulty. I say that with the full humility and understanding that such a truth brings upon me a call for responsibility.

And thus, the ultimate question hangs heavy over my head: What do I owe?

It's always been an easy question for me regarding those I love. I would have died for Garibond and would die now for Cadayle or Callen. I would fight for Jond and must admit that even Cormack and Milkeila and the powrie pair have become beloved companions in the manner of Vaughna, Crait, and Olconna.

I could have parted ways with them on the rocky rise above the glacier, but I did not. No one was more surprised than I when my feet hit that ice, when I rushed down to join in the fray against Ancient Badden's multitude of minions. By all rights, I could have turned south and gone all the way back to Dame Gwydre, and I do not doubt that she would have granted me my freedom for the trials I had already faced.

But I went down and fought, all the way to Badden, beside these compan-ions (dare I hope, these friends?).

I owed them.

Dame Gwydre speaks of responsibility to people she does not even know, to her people across Vanguard. Is it just the truth of being a ruler, I wonder, that demands such a sense of community, or is it that we all owe one another in this greater community?

I have Badden's head in a sack; I will be freed of my indenture when we re-turn to Dame Gwydre in a couple of weeks' time. I can then gather Cadayle and

Callen and hold the promise that Gwydre will sail me wherever in the world I want to go. I can go on my way and let the world go its own, I can forget the battles here in Vanguard and the continuing strife between the too-proud lairds Ethelbert and Delaval in the south.

Or can I?

What do I owe?

—BRANSEN GARIBOND

CHAPTER 1

Six Cogs One

She felt his calloused but gentle touch on her shoulders and neck, rubbing the stress away with oft-practiced perfection. Dame Gwydre sat staring out her window in Castle Pellinor, looking to the cold north. She had cut her brown hair quite short, but there was nothing mannish about her appearance, for the cut only accentuated her fine, thin neck and slender shoulders. And even under all the duress of the recent months, and even well into middle age, Dame Gwydre's face featured an eternal youth and vigor and sensuousness that belied the icy strength and determination ever in her eyes.

Gwydre sighed.

"We'll know soon enough," Dawson McKeege, the only man in the world who could be massaging Dame Gwydre, said to her.

She craned her neck to glance back at him, gray stubble prominent on his grizzled leathery face. Dawson was only a few years Gwydre's senior, but, having spent most of his life at sea, he looked much older. How well Dawson knew her!

"What makes you believe that I am thinking of them?" Gwydre asked.

"Because ye haven't been thinking of anything else since you sent that band after Ancient Badden," Dawson said with a laugh, and he kneaded Gwydre's shoulder as he spoke, bringing a wince of both pain and pleasure from the woman. "And you're all in knots under your skin."

It was true enough and he had seen right through her attempted dodge. Gwydre led Vanguard, and that vast wilderness holding was enmeshed in a brutal war, one that was taking a terrible toll on Gwydre's hearty subjects. Desperate times had forced a desperate gambit, and so Gwydre had enlisted some of the elite warriors of her land and sent them north to behead the beast that had arisen against her, the priest leader of an ancient and brutal religion.

"Why do we fight, Dawson?" she asked her dear friend.

"I've got no fight with you."

"Not us," Gwydre replied in exasperation. "We, men and women, all of us. Why do we fight?"

"Now or all the time?"

Gwydre half turned as her friend backed away and offered him a shrug.

"Now we fight because Ancient Badden's afraid that his Samhaist Church is being pushed aside, and so it is. He can't let go of that power without a fight, as we're seeing. He'll do anything to hold it."

"And so he has inflicted misery across Vanguard," said Gwydre. "To those loyal to me, and to those loyal to him. Great misery."

"They're calling that 'war,' I'm told," came the sarcastic reply.

"And why is the rest of Honce, all the holdings south of the Gulf of Corona, now in the grips of war?" Gwydre asked.

Dawson chuckled, seeing where this was going and having no answers.

Gwydre, too, gave a helpless laugh. Up here, the folk of Vanguard were embroiled in a brutal war with the monstrous minions Ancient Badden and the Samhaists had enlisted as mercenaries. Down south, across the far more populous holdings of Honce proper, it was brother against brother, laird against neighboring laird, as the two most prominent rulers battled to unite the land under one king for the first time in known history.

"They fight for the same reason we fight," Dawson said quietly, and in all seriousness (which was a rarity for Dawson McKeege). "They fight because one man, or two men, decided they should fight."

"Or one man and one woman?" Gwydre asked, clearly implicating herself in Vanguard's troubles.

"Nah," the sailor said with a shake of his head. "You didn't start this. This is Badden's folly and fury, and you've no choice but to defend."

"Thank you for that," Gwydre replied, and she patted her hand atop Dawson's, which was still on her shoulder. "In the southlands, Laird Delaval and Laird Ethelbert have decided that one and only one should rule over all the holdings, and because of that rivalry, thousands and thousands of men and women have been trampled under the march of armies. So is it just them, Dawson? Just those two men? Or do the armies marching for them want to fight?"

Dawson's face screwed up with puzzlement. "Many are believing in their leader, not to doubt," he said.

"But do they want to go to war?"

"Milady, I doubt any man's looking for more war after he's tasted war. It's an ugly thing, to watch your friend writhing on the muddy ground after his guts have been opened by a sword."

"So it is the pride and ambition of two men driving the insanity," said Gwydre.

Dawson shrugged and nodded. "As up here, it's the pride and ambition and anger of one, Ancient Badden."

With another sigh, Dame Gwydre turned back to stare out her northern window, and Dawson immediately moved nearer to her and began rubbing her neck once more—not because he had to, but because, as a friend, he wanted to.

"My father would not have gone to such a war," Gwydre remarked off-handedly.

"That's why the people of Vanguard loved Laird Gendron," said Dawson. "That's why the whole of Vanguard cried with you when he fell from his horse that day and didn't recover. And Pieter wouldn't have thought to fight such a war, either," he added, referring to Gwydre's husband, whom she had married while still a teenager, after Laird Gendron's death. "You picked a good one there."

"I miss him, Dawson. It's been more than a decade and a half, and still I miss him."

"You miss him more when Ancient Badden's pushing you, I'm thinking."

"I hate this," Gwydre admitted. "The suffering and the blood and the simple worthlessness of it all."

"There's nothing worthless about defending Vanguard against Ancient Badden and his monster hordes."

Gwydre patted his hand again. "And in the south?"

Dawson snorted derisively. "Who can be saying? Tough days in Vanguard, to be sure, but when we win—and we're to do that, don't doubt!—I'll be glad that we're a hundred miles of water or a hundred miles of wilderness away from those armies."

"I pray you are right," Gwydre said softly, and she stared to the north, the empty north.

I ain't a'feared o' fighting," said the tough little powrie Mcwigik. He plopped his bloodred beret on top of his wildly bushy orange hair and rubbed it into place as if he was adjusting a helmet. "In truth, I'm liking it, and likin' it more when we're talking o' fighting trolls. But if ye're asking me and Bikelbrin to go down there to fight that mob, and ye're thinkin' o' keeping one back here to watch over no-eyes there, then ye're thinking wrong. We're just five, ye dopes!"

"Six," corrected Brother Jond, the man Mcwigik had called "no-eyes." Dressed in his brown woolen Abellican robe and weather-beaten sandals with cloth wrapped inside their black straps to keep his feet warm, the monk shifted in his sitting posture to better face the sound of the dwarf's voice. He did nothing to hide his torn face, both eyes and the bridge of his nose lost as a prisoner of the wretched Ancient Badden; indeed, Brother Jond strained his neck to better demonstrate the wound to his companions.

"Bah, ye're a blind fool, and that's not a mix I'm wanting to fight beside," Mcwigik argued.

"I can use gemstones!" Brother Jond retorted.

"And put a lightning bolt up me arse!" roared Bikelbrin, Mcwigik's powrie companion. The two looked like bookends as they stood bobbing side by side. Both were tall for powries, five feet at least, and seemed as solid as the stones upon which they stood. And both had never met a blade suitable for trimming either hair or beard, it seemed, which gave their heads an enormous appearance.

"The soul stone!" Brother Jond argued. "I can send healing energy."

"To the trolls, ye twit!" said Mcwigik.

Similarly dressed in Abellican robes, though he had fallen from the order, and a powrie beret won in a fight with one of Mcwigik's former clan's dwarves, Cormack cast a nervous glance at his wife, Milkeila.

"If you do not lower your voices, the fight will come to us," Milkeila warned them all. The weight of the tall woman's words was not lost on any of the three arguing. She stood as tall as Brother Jond, a foot above the powries; there was nothing delicate about Milkeila. She had been raised among the shamans of Yan Ossum, a barbarian tribe on the Lake Mithranidoon. She had seen battle both magical and physical since her early days and had lived a life of discipline and dedication—and her defined and strong muscles bore testament to the fact. By any measure, human or powrie, she was handsome, even beautiful, her wide and round face showing a range from feminine wiles to warrior ferocity. The sparkle in her dark eyes promised passion or battle, and anyone engaging in either with this formidable woman would enter the fray tentatively, to be sure. She kept much of her brown hair braided, but it was obvious that she didn't fret with it for the sake of vanity.

All of that—her size, her obvious strength, her sheer intensity—brought gravity to Milkeila's words. Even the stubborn powries lowered their volume as they continued their argument, which again wound along the same path to Bikelbrin claiming emphatically, "Ye'll put a lightning bolt up me arse!"

"No, he won't," said the sixth of the party, a smallish man wearing an exotic outfit of black silk, a wide farmer's hat, and a fabulous and intricately detailed sword on his hip.

"Then he'll heal the damned trolls!" Bikelbrin fumed.

"No, he won't," the man, Bransen Garibond, said with a confident grin and a wink at the blind Jond—a wink that brought a chuckle to the blind brother's lips. What a ragtag group they were, Bransen thought. Outcasts all, except for Jond, they had banded together in common purpose to bring about the end of Ancient Badden. For the others, it had been a personal battle—the powries, Milkeila, and Cormack were defending their, and one another's, communities on the warm Lake Mithranidoon below Ancient Badden's glacier, and Jond had come north with Bransen at the behest of Dame Gwydre of Vanguard, in an attempt to decapitate the enemy by killing the vile leader. Bransen considered himself the biggest mercenary here, when he thought about it. He was not personally invested in the Mithranidoon communities, or in Vanguard, a land to which he was a stranger, and he had been tricked into the service of Dame Gwydre. He had come hunting Badden to earn freedom, for himself and for his wife and mother-in-law, reparation for his actions as the Highwayman that had outraged many of the Honce lairds. Now they were all traveling south from the defeated Ancient Badden's fortress, back to Dame Gwydre with their gruesome trophy. There was nothing left up here for the powries, Cormack, and Milkeila, and wounded Jond wanted to go home to Chapel Pellinor, and Bransen just wanted to get back to Cadayle and Callen.

Bikelbrin and Mcwigik both started arguing with Bransen, but Milkeila interrupted, and all turned to her to see her looking from Bransen to Jond curiously. "How did you see that?" she asked the blind monk.

"I saw nothing. I see nothing."

"You reacted."

"I agree with Bransen."

"To the wink," Milkeila insisted.

Jond's smile widened. "I felt it."

Both powries, Cormack, and Milkeila stared long and hard at the blind man.

"Ye felt the wink?" Mcwigik said with obvious doubt. "I got a great fart coming—ye feelin' that, are ye?"

Bransen drew his sword suddenly, pulling all attention his way. With a shrug, he poked its fine tip into his palm, drawing blood. "I am wounded!" he said to Jond, and before the monk could react, the agile Bransen silently shifted around to the other side of the group, behind the powries.

Brother Jond lowered his head and lifted a hand from his pouch, his fist clenched around a small hematite, a soul stone, which Milkeila had given him from her necklace of various magical gems.

Bransen, remaining perfectly silent, held his hand up for all to see, and sure enough, a wave of magical energy from Jond sealed the small wound.

"How is that possible?" asked Cormack, formerly Brother Cormack, who knew well the properties of the Abellican stones. "How did you anticipate his move?"

"We are all joined, connected," Bransen explained.

"Only a great shaman can sense such movements through the earth," Milkeila protested.

"Or a Jhesta Tu," said Bransen. "Brother Jond and I have formed a bond. He can heal me, and will heal me, unerringly, as we do battle with the trolls we spied on the road ahead. He will not heal the trolls by mistake."

"And I'll cast no bolts of lightning, I promise," said Brother Jond.

"And how're ye to keep the trolls off yer torn face?" Mcwigik asked. "I'll not be looking over me shoulder to protect yer arse when I'm fighting for me own!"

"Nor would I ask you to," said Jond.

"We'll find a place for him, near the fighting," said Bransen. "Near enough to throw a healing spell, at me or at any of you who can find a similar bond."

Cormack was nodding with obvious appreciation, and so was Milkeila, and after a moment of looking at each other, both dwarves said, "Well, all's the better then!" and the issue was settled.

"Six cogs one!" Mcwigik proclaimed, an old powrie expression of a team of warriors working in unison toward a single goal. "Now, let's go kill us some trolls, just because it's a fine day and there's no better way in all the world to spend it."

Bransen held his breath as he watched the approach of the troll mob, some dozen or so of the creatures pushing and shoving and growling as they made their way along the path, windblown free of snow, that served as the main road into Vanguard from southern Alpinador. The young warrior couldn't help but remember the last time he had been in a situation just like this, when he and a few friends had attacked a troll caravan in an attempt to free the humans they held as prisoner. Crait, a warrior of great legend and stature, had died in that fight, and Bransen and the remaining of his band had been taken captive.

The trolls had surprised them with their tenacity and with sudden reinforcements.

That would not happen again, Bransen, the Highwayman, had decided, and so, before he and his new friends had come to this point, he had circumvented the troll mob and ensured that this time there would be no reinforcements following closely along the road.

Still, the Highwayman could not deny the nervous sweat that made his sword less tight in his grip. He glanced back to Brother Jond and Cormack, to see them engaged in the same type of bonding that he and Jond had used to allow the blind monk to sense Bransen's proximity. Milkeila had already done so, but the stubborn powries would have none of it.

Bransen had seen Mcwigik and Bikelbrin in battle. He flashed a much-needed grin their way and figured that those two wouldn't need any help from Brother Jond.

Mcwigik noted his glance with a nod, then held up six fingers, clenched his hands together, and then held up one finger.

Six cogs one.

With an exaggerated wink, Mcwigik slapped Bikelbrin on the shoulder and the pair ran off around a ridgeline to the west.

So much like Crait and Olconna, Bransen thought, for in that earlier tragic battle those two had similarly separated themselves from the main fighting band in a flanking maneuver. This was not the same thing, Bransen reminded himself quickly. Mcwigik and Bikelbrin had concocted this plan and insisted upon it.

"Only to get themselves right in the midst of it," Bransen whispered, trying to lighten his own mood.

Bransen took a deep and steadying breath, falling into the state of the warrior, the state of the Highwayman, as Cormack and Milkeila came up to either side of him, as the trolls below neared the designated spot. All three of them turned to the ridge west of the approaching trolls and sucked in their breath as one when they heard the opening cry of Mcwigik.

Over the ridge came the rambling powries, their short, powerful legs seeming more to roll than to pump, but propelling them surely and rapidly at the surprised trolls below. The dwarves hardly seemed to be paying any attention to their foes, but were looking back and yelling warnings of approaching enemies.

For powries and trolls, though not on the friendliest of terms, were not mortal enemies (outside of Mithranidoon, where all who were not troll did war with trolls) and had often banded together in Badden's assault on the men of Vanguard.

"Great, now they're ready for us," Cormack muttered.

"Ah, but with a pair in their midst," Milkeila said as the dwarves moved into the welcoming troll group.

"And looking the wrong way," added the Highwayman, and he flipped off his farmer hat and pulled his black silk bandanna down into a half mask, holes cut for his eyes. "Be quick!"

Cormack stood a foot taller than the Highwayman, and most of the difference seemed to be in the length of his legs. But he couldn't begin to pace the explosive speed of the silk-clad warrior. Fast as a hunting cat and silent as its shadow, the Highwayman closed the ground to the trolls far ahead of his two charging companions. As he neared, he heard Mcwigik yell, "Here they come!" and smiled as the dwarf pointed at the ridge over which he and Bikelbrin had run.

And the trolls were looking exactly that way when the Highwayman came spinning into their ranks from the other side, his fabulous sword of wrapped silverel, a Jhesta Tu sword crafted by his mother, slicing troll flesh as easily as it would dry parchment.

And the trolls were still looking that way when the two powries pulled stone axes from their belts and began chopping at them with abandon.

And the trolls were still looking that way when Milkeila's shamanistic magic reached out to a nearby tree and coaxed down one of its branches to grab a troll about the neck and hoist it, flailing pitifully, from the ground.

The Highwayman cut through the first rank, took a fast stride at the dwarves, and then kicked off suddenly, throwing himself into a forward-diving somersault. He landed lightly on the other side of the pair, running still, and a slash to the right, a reversed backhand, behind-the-back stab back to the left had two more trolls down.

Cormack came in almost at the same time the bulk of the trolls finally grasped what was happening and tried to form some semblance of defense. Three of them fell into a skirmish line, just hoisting crude spears when the former monk flew at them, turning his body horizontal as he leaped. He beat the spears to the spot and sent all three trolls tumbling.

As the pile unwound, though, one of the beasts managed to re-angle its spear enough to stab at the man, tearing a painful gash on his hip. He squealed in pain but gritted through it and, still on his knees, unloaded a barrage of short and heavy punches into the troll's face, crushing its bones and dropping it to the cold ground.

Milkeila was beside the man, then, and nearly as formidable in melee as in magic, the shaman cracked her staff hard on another troll's head.

"Are you all right?" she called to Cormack as he came up beside her, but when she glanced at him, she found him strangely grinning. He led her incredulous gaze down to his wound, showing her that it was already on the mend—the magical mend.

Brother Jond. Six cogs one.

In a matter of heartbeats, the powries gleefully went about dipping their bloody caps into troll blood, and coaxed Cormack, who understood well that there was powerful and beneficial magic in a powrie cap, to do likewise.

"Not much of a fight," Bikelbrin lamented.

"Yach," Mcwigik agreed. "Someone find me a giant to kneecap!"

"We fight only when they're in our way," Bransen reminded them as he wiped his bloody sword on a troll vest. "Our goal is to the south, to Vanguard and Dame Gwydre."

"To yer lady Cadayle, ye mean," said Mcwigik.

"No less substantial a cause, then," Cormack remarked with a wink at Milkeila.

Bransen cut short the conversation by nodding his chin back to the north, where Brother Jond was making his way along the road, tapping his walking stick before him.

"He healed me from afar," said Cormack.

"Might be that he's worth keepin', then," said Mcwigik. "But I ain't standing watch over him!"

"No one asked you to," Brother Jond answered from afar. "To be blunt, I feel safer knowing that no powries are hovering over me."

That erased a few smiles.

"Six cogs one," Bransen reminded, and he knew in looking at his mismatched companions that it would be an oft-repeated litany if they were to make it across the miles to the more hospitable reaches of civilized Vanguard.

Of course, once they arrived at the court of Dame Gwydre, a host of other problems would certainly emerge, Bransen knew, and as Cormack and Jond also certainly knew, in trying to explain Mcwigik and Bikelbrin to folk who had never known the bloody-cap dwarves as anything but mortal enemies.

CHAPTER 2

The Center of Gravity

"They were smashed!" cried Yeslnik, the foppish Laird of Pryd and favored nephew of Laird Delaval, who proclaimed himself King Delaval of Honce. He flailed about as he spoke, his voluminous sleeves and leggings flapping and tightening over his limbs just often enough to remind those in the room of how delicate and stick-limbed this excitable man truly was. Not that any would remark on the man's erratic movements, for Yeslnik was also widely rumored to be the heir apparent to Delaval's expanding holdings.

"The son of Laird Panlamaris sent the traitors running back to the Mantis Arm! Oh, but we'll make them regret their decision to take Ethelbert's gold!" As he spoke, he danced around the circular chamber that marked the bottom floor of Pryd Keep, punching his fist into the air and smacking his hands together as if engaging in a battle with some imaginary foe.

His soft skin reddened under the blows.

A few of the men in attendance, Yeslnik's entourage from Delaval City and a pair of young brothers of Chapel Pryd, grinned stupidly and became animated at the less-than-inspired performance, but the true center of weight in the room, a muscular middle-aged warrior with long black hair just beginning to show a bit of salt with its pepper and a face that seemed carved out of stone, showed not a hint of emotion.

He did glance to the side, to exchange looks with Master Reandu of Chapel Pryd, the highest ranking of the village's brothers, who was serving, quietly, as leader of the chapel due to the failing condition of Father Jerak, who was by all reports beyond sensibility. Ever doubtful of the brothers of Abelle, Bannagran had nonetheless found himself growing closer to Reandu over the last few weeks, particularly with Yeslnik and his insufferable wife, Olym, bouncing about incessantly.

Still a young man, barely into his thirties, Reandu had played an important role in the dramatic events of Pryd Holding. He had halted the hand of his superior monk, Master Bathelais, when Bathelais might have struck dead the Highwayman, right before the Highwayman had crashed into Laird Pry-dae's room, initiating a fight that had cost Prydae his life. Soon after, it was Reandu who had spoken for the Highwayman, and favorably, and had convinced Bannagran to spare the life of Bransen Garibond and allow the outlaw to leave Pryd.

With all the tumult of the growing war, the investigation of Master Bathelais's death by Chapel Abelle had never come, and, indeed, the brothers up north had seen fit to elevate Reandu, the next highest-ranking brother in Pryd, to Master, giving him leadership in Chapel Pryd.

That promotion hadn't bothered Bannagran in the least. To Reandu's credit, by Bannagran's estimation, the monk seemed quite unimpressed by Yeslnik's proclamations and performance. Master Reandu shrugged at Bannagran with obvious resignation, as if to point out that they had to suffer the idiot.

"You do not view this as a great victory?" Yeslnik shouted at Reandu, his tone full of consternation and indignation.

"The Church of Blessed Abelle is neutral in the conflict, Laird Yeslnik, per agreement with both lairds Ethelbert and Delaval," Reandu replied. "Your claims of great battle mean to us only that we will witness more suffering."

Yeslnik stopped suddenly, as if some marionette strings had simply fallen limp around him, and his face seemed indeed to be made of wood or stone.

"The Decree of Neutrality by Chapel Abelle is well-known to both warring factions," Reandu reminded. "And accepted, and was even advised by your mentor, Laird Delaval. We do not ask the allegiance of a wounded man when we prepare our blessed healing."

Yeslnik gave a little, deprecating snort. "The situation is changing, Brother," he calmly—too calmly—explained. "A nimble church survives, while one set in the ways of the past can easily find itself marginalized."

Bannagran closed his eyes at that and tried to tune out of the conversation. Rumors had been spreading from both lines, Ethelbert and Delaval, that as the war had grown more furious, as the stakes had crystallized, pressures had been exerted on the brothers of Abelle in chapels behind each of the respective lines to tend only to those wounded supporting that region's ruling faction. The lairds were playing a dangerous game with the people, Bannagran knew from long and bitter experience, for the enemy wounded were too often friend and family to the peasants living about the chapels where they were brought for healing.

Peasants could be pushed hard—Bannagran had seen that from his friend and former laird, Prydae. But peasants also had the capacity to strike back hard when pushed too far.

In his mind, Bannagran saw again his errant throw, his axe spinning end-over-end, sailing above the wretched Highwayman and planting itself deep in Laird Prydae's chest. He saw again his friend's blood explode from that wound, saw again Prydae thrown down to his back with such force, the fountain of lifeblood spraying high above his horizontal form. Bannagran shook himself from the awful memory.

"The brothers of Abelle should be aware that Honce is changing," Prince Yeslnik was saying when Bannagran tuned back in. "The shameful Ethelbert has no sense of the community of Honce! He is not worthy of the title of laird, and many of the folk of his rogue holding bear more allegiance to their brethren south of the mountains than to their fellow men of Honce!"

"You speak of Honce as if it is a united kingdom," Bannagran couldn't help but interject.

"And it will be!" Yeslnik barked back at him. "And King Delaval will rule it!"

The answer was perfectly expected, of course, but Bannagran always liked hearing the insistence with which it was pronounced, particularly by this ambitious young man, who had everything in the world to gain if his fantasy came to fruition.

"But it will never be united under Ethelbert, and this the brothers of Abelle must know," Yeslnik went on, and he was flailing his arms again and turning and storming this way and that, as if little bolts of lightning were exploding through his limbs. "Nay, under the wretch Ethelbert, the Holdings of Honce will become subservient to the needs of the desert kingdom of Behr to the south!"

A couple of attendants gasped at that—so perfectly on cue, Bannagran thought.

"Will our women be sent south around the mountains to serve as whores for the sheiks of the desert wastes?" Yeslnik asked. "Will our children be indentured as water-carriers to mule the precious element from the few springs and ponds to the cities?"

Bannagran had followed Prydae into the court of Laird Delaval and thus against Laird Ethelbert, and his loyalties rested there, to be sure, but he could not help but be amused by the rapt expressions on the faces of many in the room. The bigger and more outrageous the tale, the more it intrigued, it seemed. For Bannagran knew Laird Ethelbert, or had known him a decade before, when the men of Pryd and Ethelbert had fought side by side in the east against the powries. On two occasions, Ethelbert had entered a battle in the nick of time to save Prydae, Bannagran, and their men. When war had later broken out between Ethelbert and Delaval, Prydae had initially sided with Ethelbert, in spirit if not in action. Laird Ethelbert, with no living children, had hinted strongly that he would name Prydae as heir. It wasn't until it became apparent that Prydae, because of wounds he had suffered in those previous powrie wars, was also the last of his line that Ethelbert had moved away from that course. He would not name Prydae as his heir, and so Prydae had thrown in with Delaval, who was offering the better deal to the young laird.

Part of that deal, though, had ceded Pryd Holding to Laird Delaval upon the end of Prydae's line, and that end had come prematurely at the end of Bannagran's thrown axe.

Now Bannagran was stuck with little Laird Yeslnik.

He sighed and pushed the frustration away, ever the good soldier, and tuned in to the continuing conversation. To his credit, again, Master Reandu seemed unfazed by the outlandishly dire exaggerations Yeslnik was spinning regarding Ethelbert's relationship with Behr.

"What say you?" Yeslnik finished, rushing right up to within a few fingers of Reandu and staring at him hard.

"I am a servant of Abelle," the Master from Chapel Pryd replied. "My course is determined not by my own emotions, not by the pleasures of a laird or prince, but by the edicts of the father of Chapel Abelle. You appeal to the wrong man, Laird and Prince Yeslnik. Your passion would better serve you in the north, where Father Artolivan's pen proclaims the actions of all in his clergy."

Yeslnik continued to stare at him for many heartbeats, and gradually Yeslnik's face softened into a cold chuckle. "Practiced in the art of diplomacy, I see," he said. "Well done! You have successfully delayed—not avoided, but delayed—the inevitable confrontation. But take heart, for I am certain that your Father Artolivan will choose wisely, when choose he must. Delaval is for Honce, Ethelbert is for Behr, and the beasts of Behr are no friends to the brothers of Abelle. Their gods precede yours and reject yours, and their God-Voice, the father of their religion, has put more than a few of your missionaries to the stake."

It was true enough, Bannagran knew, but remained quiet. Many of the missionary brothers of Abelle, those nagging and unrelenting proselytizing prigs, had indeed ventured into Behr and never returned, by all reports. Bannagran knew one exception, however, a monk from Pryd who had come back from the deepest reaches of the southern desert, along with an exotic wife, no less, when Bannagran was a young man, serving his friend Prydae and Prydae's father, Laird Pryd. The brothers of Chapel Pryd had not treated that monk very well, Bannagran recalled.

The standoff between Yeslnik and Reandu, neither of whom was blinking, ended when a man crashed into the room, huffing and puffing, and breathlessly announced, "They come."

"Ah!" exclaimed Yeslnik, turning to the man. He rubbed his hands together eagerly and flexed his fingers as if he couldn't wait to wrap them around a sword hilt (which amused Bannagran, since he had seen this one in "battle" before).

"So it will begin as we expected right here in Pryd Holding," continued Yeslnik. "Ethelbert's move in the north was crushed by Milwellis of Palmaristown. He knows that Milwellis will now march east and then south along Felidan Bay, then south from there, sweeping up in his wake villages formerly in Ethelbert's pay. Thus, Ethelbert did not retreat—he cannot retreat. Not this time, or he will be pushed into the sea. So he comes with all that he has left to strike at the heart and center of King Delaval's gains."

Yeslnik clenched his fist, his eyes sparkling with diabolical glee. "Never could you have guessed that your humble little hamlet of Pryd would become the center of the world! For all the world is drawn to this place, as if the weight of Pryd Town pulls in the armies, compels them to this place in this time to finally, undeniably decide! Never could you have guessed this, eh, Bannagran?"

Not in my darkest nightmares, the warrior thought but did not say.

L aird Ethelbert slowly sauntered on his mount toward his tent, as if neither he nor the beast could handle a swifter pace. Palfry, his devoted attendant, rushed up to help him dismount. Glancing around to ensure that no one else was watching, the proud old man accepted the helping hand.

He was just into his seventies now, his once bulky frame wilting and thinning about his arms, while thickening about his waist. He was glad for the comfortable robe he wore, a gift from a Jacinthan merchant. The men of Behr were so much more practical in their dress than the men of Honce.

"You must have ridden under a low branch, my laird," Palfry said. He brushed a leafy twig from what remained of Ethelbert's hair. Once thick, black, and curly, now it was thin gray fluff. Ethelbert's eyes, though, were still the steel blue of an ocean under clouds, still hinted at a great depth behind them, and still held the sparkle of a dancing wave.

"Bah, more likely a squirrel threw the branch upon me," Ethelbert replied somewhat churlishly. "Every creature in this part of Honce is against me, I say!"

Palfry smiled, so in love with this man who had become like a father, though Ethelbert had no living heirs. The laird had made it clear to Palfry that, though he was not in line for Ethelbert's title, neither would he be cast from the court of whomever ruled the great holding. Ethelbert had seen to that.

"Where are my commanders?" Laird Ethelbert asked.

Palfry turned and nodded his chin toward a distant clearing, where three warriors sat on logs around a tree stump, a parchment spread upon it. Ethelbert started for them, Palfry at his heels.

"My laird," the three commanders said together, standing as one.

"The soldiers were pleased that you rode their line, no doubt," said Kirren Howen, the senior of the group.

"Huzzah for Laird Ethelbert!" added Myrick the Bold, champion of Entel, the name given to the port regions of the city of Ethelbert.

Ethelbert hushed him with a waving hand and a snicker. "It is the least we owe them and less than they want, I am sure," he said. "They want to be done with this foolishness and go home, as do I."

"Our cause is right," said Tyne, a young and promising leader, a man Ethelbert had attached to his elite guard right before the advent of war.

"Righter than Delaval's, to be sure," the more seasoned Kirren Howen added.

"The claim of a dactyl demon would be more right than that of Delaval," Ethelbert said with a derisive snicker. "And I'd sooner my one daughter, were she still alive, marry the dactyl!"

Ethelbert's joke prompted an uncomfortable laugh around the tree stump, for all knew that Laird Ethelbert spoke only half in jest, revealing his deep wounds over Laird Delaval's treachery. In times past, the two greatest of lairds had worked together to build Honce's network of roads. With those roads connecting the many holdings, marauding powries and goblins had been more easily driven away. Trade had blossomed, and a sense of unity had spread across the land. Citizens thought of the notion and nation of Honce more than a particular holding.

All that changed abruptly when Laird Delaval struck, and struck hard, declaring himself King of Honce.

Laird Ethelbert had lived too long, had fought too many battles, and had worked to bring too many warring lairds to common ground to allow such a thing. And thus the current war began.

"What news of the son of Panlamaris?" Ethelbert asked now.

"He has not turned south," said Kirren Howen.

"To the east, still," said Myrick.

"He will turn," Ethelbert assured them. "Milwellis's win in Pollcree has convinced Delaval that this push to the center is our last, desperate try. And not without reason," he admitted.

"Had that battle turned differently . . ." Kirren Howen started to say, but Ethelbert cut him short.

"It could not have. We did not understand the true strength of Palmaristown or how deeply Laird Panlamaris had entrenched himself with Delaval. Panlamaris is seeking the favor of the man who claims the title of king, no doubt, so that Palmaristown can control all of the seaborne merchant trade in this new kingdom Delaval proposes. Our friends from the Mantis Arm peninsula could not match Prince Panlamaris's ground forces."

"I do not consider this to be our last and desperate try!" Myrick exclaimed.

Ethelbert's chuckle calmed him. "I am more interested in what our enemies consider it. In recognizing their thoughts may we act appropriately. Fear not, my fearless Myrick"—his joke on the man's title brought a bit of laughter from Palfry, Kirren Howen, and Tyne—"for I am not desperate, I assure you, and while I mourn the loss of so many allies at Pollcree, I have no doubt that the fierce peninsula warriors handed the son of Panlamaris great losses in the battle. He is stung, surely, and his soldiers, who have never marched across the land, are already missing their homes, I am certain. Their legs are built for ship planks, not cobblestones. We are not as wounded as they believe, of course. We have other allies and other methods, and I can only hope that the apparent victory in the north has served to foster a feeling of invulnerability among Delaval and his followers. None fall harder than the confident, after all."

"And no one's fall is more relished than the defeat of he who thinks himself invulnerable," said Tyne, the youngest of the group, to approving nods from Kirren Howen and Laird Ethelbert.

"Young and proud Milwellis will turn south," Ethelbert said. "Delaval and his commanders have come to think this our last stand. The son of Panlamaris, hoping to secure a prominent seat for his father and his town, will not be left out of the victory."

"And when he does turn?" asked Kirren Howen. "How long do we hold?"

"We know the terrain east of Pryd Holding," Ethelbert explained. "Laird Delaval does not. His generals are not well versed in the eastern reaches of Honce. The same is true, even more so, of Milwellis of Palmaristown."

"As long as we can, then," Kirren Howen replied, and Laird Ethelbert smiled and nodded, fully confident in these men who served him. Kirren Howen would not allow Ethelbert's army to be smashed by the bulk of Delaval's forces here in the middle of Honce; they were not here for that purpose.

"We hold faith that our journey to central Honce will not be in vain," Myrick the Bold asserted, and there was nothing but supreme confidence regarding Laird Ethelbert and these unknown ulterior motives in the old man's words. He bowed low, as did Tyne and Kirren Howen, and Ethelbert took his leave, signaling for Palfry to remain here with the commanders.

In another clearing not so far away, the Laird of Ethelbert dos Entel met with a second group of warriors, a half dozen men and two women of darker skin and black hair and blacker eyes. It was no secret among his ranks, or among his enemies, that Ethelbert had hired mercenaries from the deserts of Behr, but this group was another matter altogether. Their leader was a petite woman with deceptively soft facial features, a disarming wide, white-toothed smile, and dimples that could melt a man's heart at the same time that her sword—or even her bare hands—could dismember him. And, oh, how she could dance, Ethelbert mused, the turning and weaving of those supple limbs enough to melt an old man's heart.

Her name was Affwin Wi, the Eyes of Bursting Sunrise, given to her by her masters at the Walk of Clouds, home of the Jhesta Tu. Affwin Wi had been known among that order not as a creature of introspection or quiet meditation but rather as something akin to the sudden explosion of light when the sun peeked above the eastern horizon, an excitable and impetuous sort. These characteristics had gotten her into trouble among the introspective ascetics who sought to teach her. Jhesta Tu was an art of mind and body: Affwin Wi's masters feared that she possessed too little of the former and an abundance of the latter.

She had left the Walk of Clouds as a young woman, only a few years before. Again, contrary to Jhesta Tu teaching, Wi had taken on the role of teacher for the similarly fiery men and woman standing around her.

"Laird Delaval continues his advance?" she asked Ethelbert now.

"He cannot surrender the center, and Pryd Town is the center," the old laird replied. As Ethelbert spoke Merwal Yahna walked over to stand beside Affwin Wi. Ethelbert noted that the rest of Affwin Wi's disciples, amazing warriors all, shrank back as this one passed. He wasn't a large man, and the loose fit of his soft black silk clothing did not reveal his tightly packed muscles. Only his clean-shaven head could perhaps be construed as imposing—that and his eyes, narrow, small, and intense.

Watching the sureness of the Behrenese man's stride and the pure grace of his movements reminded Ethelbert of the value of this gift of deadly mercenaries the Sheik Kali-kali-si of Jacintha had given to him.

"Laird Delaval intends to meet me on the field with every warrior he can spare, and he can spare them all, so he believes."

"But he has not arrived to join them in this glorious victory?" Merwal Yahna asked, his voice measured. The deference Affwin Wi showed him by allowing him to speak was yet another testament to the man's rank.

"He is not well, by all word, and desires to heap praise and stature upon his buffoon of a nephew. No, my warrior, Delaval will not be on the field."

Merwal Yahna's small eyes lit up, and he gave a slight nod. A quick glance around by Laird Ethelbert told him that he need say nothing more, that the plan was understood and now in action.

Ethelbert bowed to these fearsome disciples of Affwin Wi and took his leave.

He would sleep well that night.

CHAPTER 3

Out of Their Element

He stumbled through the blinding storm, the cold wind whipping his cloak wide, the persistent snow rushing in around his armor. He stumbled and nearly fell, but knew the group behind him, nearly ninety men, depended on his continuing forward against the harsh elements. He shielded his eyes, futilely, and leaned forward against the wind, driving on.

But the ground gave way before him as he walked right over the edge of a chasm he could not see. His cry diminished as he dropped fifty feet to where the snow and ice cushioned his fall enough so that he did not die immediately. Twisted and broken, unable to draw in enough breath to scream out, he tried to hold faith that his brothers would get to him with their healing stones.

He died alone that night.

"He's gone over!" a monk had cried when Brother Juniper fell. "Ropes! Brothers! A stone of levitation!"

"Turn east and trek the length of the gorge!" Father De Guilbe ordered, his tone accepting no debate. "Brother Juniper is lost to us, and many more will perish if we do not find shelter from this accursed storm! East, I say, and with all haste!"

They did find shelter, meager though it was, amidst a tumble of boulders and a few thin evergreens. With frozen fingers, the servants of the brothers moved about the area, digging out any piece of wood they could find, breaking branches from the trees. Brother Giavno held his hands in front of his face and blew into them, trying to get feeling back into his fingers. He stood at the back of the camp, a wall of rock climbing up high behind him to the north. Before him, the servants dumped their thin loads of kindling.

Giavno waved the next brother in line over to the latest pile and presented him with two gemstones, serpentine and ruby.

The younger brother placed the ruby down and clutched the serpentine close to his chest, offering prayers to Blessed Abelle and reaching into the gemstone magic until an aura of bluish white light glowed about him. Shield in place, he bent and retrieved the ruby, then thrust his hand into the kindling pile and called forth its fiery properties.

The fingers of pine branches exploded to flames, but they didn't last and could not fully take hold on the thicker, wet wood. The brother called upon the ruby again and again until finally the flames caught. Still holding the serpentine shield, he left the ruby for Brother Giavno and carried the burning pile to his appointed section of the encampment.

"There is little shelter for the light of our fires," Brother Giavno warned his only superior among the group, Father Cambelian De Guilbe, a giant of a man, larger than life, standing well over six feet and weighing nearly three hundred pounds. De Guilbe's girth seemed all the more remarkable because the rest of their group had thinned considerably during the years away from Vanguard and Honce. De Guilbe was almost a decade older than the middle-aged Giavno but possessed of no less vitality. Indeed, with Giavno's own head more skin than hair, many who regarded the pair could not be certain which was the older. "The hill behind us blocks a view to the north. The chasm to the south perhaps protects us from attack, but the flames we need to stave off the cold this night will be seen for a long way."

"Yes, yes, I know," an obviously impatient De Guilbe replied, his tone revealing that this decision had weighed heavily upon him. When word had come of Ancient Badden's designs over Mithranidoon, a plan that would have wiped out all the communities living in the many islands scattered about the warm waters, De Guilbe determined that this fight was not his. He turned from the barbarians and powries, long his enemies, and their call for unity against Badden and decided that the time had come for his missionary group to return to the south, to Vanguard and the civilized lands of Honce. Away from the warm waters of Mithranidoon for more than two weeks, with no knowledge of what had happened in the brewing fight with Badden, the band of monks had wandered the rugged and broken terrain of Alpinador without much success. They had expected to be in Vanguard by this point, back in Chapel Pellinor, at least, but more than once they had lost days of travel by wandering in circles.

And worse, they had lost ten men to the elements and to monsters. Brother Giavno's warning recalled a dark night only a week before, when a host of ice trolls had descended upon the band. With magic and fighting skills, the brothers and their servants had driven the foul creatures off but at a cost of three lives and many wounds—so many that the entirety of the next day had been spent using the healing magic of the soul stones.

"Our food stores run low," Giavno said. "When the storm abates, we must form hunting parties and send them out."

"You are a beacon of hope on this miserable night," Father De Guilbe scolded. Brother Giavno went respectfully (and fearfully) silent.

"You still carry the weight of guilt that we did not follow Cormack up the glacier to do battle with the Samhaist ancient," De Guilbe accused him. "Or is it that you still carry the weight of guilt for the flogging you delivered to the traitor?"

"No, Father," Giavno denied, his eyes averted.

"Yes!" De Guilbe shot back. "Let it wash downstream, Brother Giavno. Cormack was condemned by his own actions. Your arm struck not from personal vengeance but from the demands put upon us as brothers of our beloved Abelle. You struck with righteousness."

"He was once my friend," the humble Giavno said simply.

"Of course it pains you, but our road is not easy. Spiritual purity and devotion are oft the harder roads, but it is a course we walk with pride!" He glanced around and gave a helpless little laugh. "Although I admit this Alpinadoran road is at least as confusing! Would that we had an Abelle of a different sort, yes?"

Brother Giavno's eyes widened at the apparent blasphemy, but Father De Guilbe patted him on the shoulder and chuckled his concerns away. "It is not an easy road we have chosen," he repeated, "not in body, not in spirit."

Before Giavno could respond, a brother along the western perimeter of the encampment called out, "Intruders!"

De Guilbe and Giavno rushed down, as did every other member of the group until De Guilbe impatiently waved them back to their posts.

"In the trees!" the monk explained to the leaders when they arrived. He pointed to a small copse of deciduous trees and a few evergreens about twenty yards from the boulder tumble.

De Guilbe stared hard for a short while, believing he noted a form slip through the trees, though he could hardly identify it. He waved several brothers over and handed each a smooth gray stone, a graphite, the stone of lightning.

"All at once," he explained and held his own hand forward, clenching the largest of the graphite stones. "If it is a troll or goblin scout, then let our barrage ward any others from thinking to come so near. On my count of three."

"Perhaps it is an ally," one of the monks replied. "Brother Cormack, or—"

Father De Guilbe fixed him with a withering stare. He most certainly did not want to hear that name with the reverent word *brother* before it.

De Guilbe looked back to the copse and began counting down. As he finished, ten bolts of lightning reached from the monk line, slashing through the trees, thundering into the snow-covered ground.

"Whoa, now!" came a cry from the north, up the hill below which Giavno and De Guilbe had just been standing. All in the camp turned with a unified gasp to see a man sitting calmly halfway up the rocky, seemingly unclimbable rise. He was dressed in deerskin, a thick brown cloak about his shoulders and upper chest. A tricornered hat, small feather in one side, adorned his head. A stick of some sort, perhaps a bow, rested easily across his lap.

One of the monks near De Guilbe lifted his hand toward the man, as if intending to loose another bolt of lightning.

"Whoa, whoa, young one," the stranger said, waving his hands defensively and wearing a smirk that showed no fear at all, that almost seemed to mock the impetuous man.

Father De Guilbe slapped the monk's hand down and stalked up to the stranger, Giavno in his wake. "Who are you, and what business have you with us?" the leader demanded.

"You boys seem a bit lost," the man replied. "Been watching you for a couple of days now, and I'm guessing that you haven't any idea where you're going."

Father De Guilbe bristled. "We are on our way to Vanguard and Dame Gwydre," he announced stiffly.

"Oh, I'm not doubting that you know where you want to go," the man replied. He slapped his hand on his knee and stood up, hooking the bow, for it was indeed a bow, over one shoulder. He eyed the decline before him, then skipped down nimbly and sure-footedly across the snowy and icy stones.

He was not a young man, clearly, his short hair and thick mustache long gone gray, but he moved with the grace of a twenty-year-old. He kept his upper body incredibly still while he moved down the broken path, and his legs seemed too long for his body. He was thin but not skinny and exuded an aura of great strength and power. Monks and attendants shied away from him when he got down from the hill.

"I said that you haven't an idea of where you're going," he finished, coming up before De Guilbe.

"I asked you who you were."

"I could be asking the same of yourself, since you're the ones who are out of place here."

"This is your home?" De Guilbe asked, looking about with mocking doubt.

The man shrugged. "As much as any place could be called that, I expect."

"And your name?"

The man laughed. "Jameston Sequin," he replied. "Not that it should mean anything to you."

"I have never heard of you," De Guilbe concurred.

"And that pleases me," Jameston replied. "The fewer of your church who know my name, the happier I am."

De Guilbe's face further tightened. "You are a Samhaist."

"Not in this life, not in the next, if there is a next," Jameston said with a snort. "And not in the one after that."

"Then—"

"Then nothing," Jameston said with finality. "I'm a hunter, and I know this land better than any man alive. You say you want to go to Gwydre, and that's where I'm going, so you should be glad to see me."

De Guilbe glanced over at Brother Giavno, who shrugged, unable to deny that they could indeed use some help in navigating their way from this inhospitable land.

"I'll take you, monk," Jameston offered. He looked over at the copse of trees, one of which was still showing small flickers of flame from the lightning barrage. "But only if you promise to stop scarring my home."

Just a few miles to the west of De Guilbe's group, Bransen's band of six unusual characters settled in for the night. They had found a small hollow between two large stones. The two powries of the team had gone to work immediately widening it, mudding and blocking any creases, cracks, and openings. Now the six—three men, a woman, and the powrie pair—settled in quite comfortably. The industrious dwarves had even constructed a chimney of sorts to keep the smoke out of their impromptu chamber.

They had left the glacier above Mithranidoon a full week after the departure of Father De Guilbe and his monks, after the fall of Ancient Badden and the sorting that needed to be done in the aftermath. Little fighting had been required after Badden's fall, for most of his minions, including the many Samhaist priests who had come into his call, had fled at his demise. These six, along with Milkeila's barbarian tribe and the other powries of Mithranidoon, had remained in the ice castle the ancient had constructed, awaiting an attack. No other priests of Badden's Samhaist order had arrived, however. The trolls, giants, and goblins brought together under the power of the great and evil man had simply dispersed to the mountains with his fall.

Still, there had been much to do. Ancient Badden had constructed his grand ice palace through the earth magic of Mithranidoon, digging a deep well to access that power directly. Day after day after his fall, the shamans of Milkeila's Alpinadoran tribes had worked tirelessly to close that conduit of power, to heal the wound Badden had inflicted upon the glacier, the lake, the earth itself. There also remained the disposition of Badden's prisoners, of which Jond had been one. Of the others, more than fifty in number, some had seemed capable of making the journey south with the winter coming on in full, but others obviously could not have survived.

And so it had been decided that just this one band of outcasts, unaffiliated any longer with the church or the tribe or the clan, would make the arduous and dangerous trip to Dame Gwydre in the hopes of securing a rescue caravan in the spring. Until then, the other survivors of the ancient's insanity would live on Chapel Island, the now vacated land where Cormack's Abellican brethren had built their home.

It fell on this group, now taken to calling themselves Six Cogs One, to relay the tidings to the people of Vanguard and to find the resolution.

"You should return with the caravan in the spring," Bransen said to Milkeila as they discussed the tasks before them again that night in the hollow.

The woman shook her head.

"Don't overestimate the generosity of Yan Ossum," Cormack answered for her, using the proper title of Milkeila's tribe. "They understand that in agreeing to bring the refugees from Vanguard to Chapel Isle they are threatening their very way of life."

"Longer than our memories have we lived on Mithranidoon," Milkeila added. "Only rarely have outsiders come to our shores, as with the brothers of Abelle a few short years ago. Now we have invited strangers to settle upon our waters, perhaps to learn our ways, and then they will be allowed to leave. I am amazed that Teydru and the others agreed to this—I think it an impulsive decision made in the glow of Ancient Badden's fall."

"The fall and, therefore, the salvation of all who dwell on Mithranidoon," Bransen reminded.

"Yach, but that Badden would've washed them all away," Mcwigik put in.

"All true, but there is no doubt in my mind that the shamans and elders will come to recognize the danger of their decision," said Milkeila.

"You do not believe they would hurt the refugees?" Bransen asked.

"No," Cormack insisted before Milkeila could answer. "They are honorable to a fault. They would not bring such dishonor and treachery upon themselves."

"But they will not be pleased at the arrival of the caravan from Vanguard in the spring, should it ever actually arrive," said Milkeila. "And I would not have myself associated with that troubling spectacle any more than I would now. I will not return to Mithranidoon, likely not for the rest of my life."

Bransen, having no argument, simply nodded.

"But me and me friend're going back, and might be in the spring," Mcwigik said. "Soon as we find a place for our kin away from that lake, we'll go and fetch 'em."

"Yach, and hopin' it'll be a place back on the Julianthes," Mcwigik's powrie sidekick Bikelbrin added. "Back to the dark sea, at least."

"Where to, then, for any of us?" Cormack asked, drawing all eyes his way. "You, Bransen, will find your wife, and Gwydre promised you that her Writ of Passage will allow you to go wherever you will, but what's in store for Milkeila and me? What for the powries, whatever their desires? We know where we are going now, to Dame Gwydre, but what about tomorrow's journey?"

"Wherever the Father of Chapel Pellinor tells me to go," Brother Jond said with a little laugh.

Bransen tightened up at the reminder that his friend Jond had ties greater than their road-sewn bonds.

"It is so much easier when you bear no responsibility for your road, true?" Cormack asked playfully. Bransen noted that the former monk was looking directly at him as he spoke.

"Sometimes, Broth . . . Cormack," Jond corrected himself, echoing that helpless laugh. "And sometimes it is a burden, truly."

"Perhaps our roads will stay as one, then," said Milkeila. "I would enjoy that."

"Not mine," Bransen said immediately and definitively. "With the fall of Badden, my indenture is ended and my road is my own to choose."

"And you would not choose to be with us?" asked Jond. "You wound me, friend."

"No, it is not—" Bransen started to explain, but he noted Jond's mischievous grin and knew the blind man was playing him here. "I miss my wife," he finished simply.

"I can understand that, certainly," said Cormack, who was now staring at Milkeila intently, a look Bransen understood, recognizing that he wore that same mask of desire and longing whenever he looked upon Cadayle.

Cadayle! She filled the young man's thoughts then, more fully than any time since his departure for Alpinador. His anticipation grew by the moment as he sat there in the comfortable hollow. All he longed for was to be in Cadayle's arms once more.

Soon, he knew. Soon.

I left the injured woman with some friends in Alpinador," Jameston Sequin explained to Dame Gwydre only four days after he had met with De Guilbe's party. With the scout leading them, the troupe had made great time moving into Vanguard and to Gwydre's castle in Pellinor.

Eager for news from the front, Gwydre had wasted no time in summoning Jameston to her court. When he had arrived, Gwydre had immediately shuffled Father De Guilbe and Brother Giavno, along with the other brothers of Abelle in attendance (including the father of Chapel Pellinor and her own lover, Alandrais), off to the side of the room.

Her smile had drooped with Jameston's every word as the man recounted his short time with her strike force, ending in a disastrous fight with a troll prisoner caravan, when, seemingly, it had all come undone. When, Jameston believed, Bransen and Jond and the others had been fully defeated.

By Jameston's grim account, it seemed certain that Ancient Badden had won.

"I went back toward the glacier, but just a few miles," Jameston explained. "Badden surrounded himself with many powerful minions—giants, even. I couldn't get near the place."

"But you do not know if they are dead?" Gwydre asked, obviously uncomfortably. Beside her, Dawson McKeege put a comforting hand on her shoulder to steady her.

"Only poor old Crait, and a fine fighter he was," said Jameston. "And that strange younger fighter, the one in black."

"Bransen," said Gwydre. "The Highwayman."

Jameston nodded. "Not sure if he's dead, but it seems as if he got hit on the head, and hard. He could hardly walk as the trolls led them off. I doubt he made it alive to the glacier."

"That'd be a terrible loss for us," said Dawson, who had brought Bransen to Vanguard to fight for Gwydre's cause.

"He is alive, or was, when we left Lake Mithranidoon," Father De Guilbe interrupted. It was obvious that the man had been waiting for an opportunity to jump in ever since Jameston had entered the room.

"What do you know of it?" Dame Gwydre asked.

"As I was explaining before we were sent aside," De Guilbe began peevishly, "we left the lake because word came to us of the designs of this very same Ancient Badden. Word from this man, this Highwayman, as you call him. So, yes, Dame Gwydre, he survived to the glacier, at least. If we're to believe the word of our fallen brethren, he also survived a fall from the glacier."

"The Highwayman came to enlist you against Ancient Badden?" Gwydre asked incredulously.

"He came to warn us that Ancient Badden meant to destroy everyone living on the islands across the lake," Father De Guilbe carefully equivocated. "And so we left, as my directives clearly demand."

"You did not go and do battle with Badden?"

De Guilbe bristled. "It is not my place."

"So who or what are we to blame for this new alliance between Abellicans and Samhaists?" Dawson McKeege asked sharply.

"Alliance and enmity have degrees in between, friend," said De Guilbe. "And we were ignorant of your current struggles with Ancient Badden and his followers, or of any edict from Father Premujon of Chapel Pellinor or Father Artolivan of Chapel Abelle decreeing that the Brothers of Abelle were at war with the Samhaists. We have been on the roads of Alpinador for years. It was not my place to go and start such a war."

"Surely you could have found your answers from the Highwayman!" Dawson protested.

"Who came to us with a traitor to our order!" De Guilbe shot right back.

"Who came to you with information enough to send you running to the south!" said Dawson.

"Enough!" Dame Gwydre interrupted.

"Makes me miss the birdsong and chirping toads," Jameston mumbled. Gwydre shot him a sly twinkle to let him know that she didn't disagree, for she, too, would surely have preferred a walk in the forest to this inane bickering.

"So at least we know that the Highwayman survived the ordeal of the troll capture," Gwydre recounted to Jameston. "To your great surprise."

"I'm not arguing."

"And he returned to do battle with Badden?" Gwydre asked De Guilbe.

"As far as I know," he said stiffly.

"Could you elaborate?" There was no missing the sharp edge creeping into Gwydre's tone or her weariness at De Guilbe's annoying verbal dance.

"He went with the traitor to our order and his woman, a barbarian girl," the large monk grudgingly explained.

"Ah, then, not to wonder why you kicked him out of your church," Jameston interjected. Gwydre hushed him with a look.

"Her people were joining in the battle, as were the powries of Mithranidoon," Brother Giavno interjected. Father De Guilbe shot a threatening glare of his own to back the monk down.

"Truly?" asked Gwydre. "Then there is hope."

"They are all dead," De Guilbe stated flatly.

Gwydre arched an eyebrow. "You know this? Or you presume?"

The large monk shrugged impatiently.

Gwydre nodded and turned back to Jameston.

"Any odds for armies going against Badden aren't good odds," the scout reminded.

"But the Highwayman had already been up there, so he knew . . ."

Jameston's laugh cut her short, and she stared at him, seeming less than amused.

"Your pardon," the scout said with a low bow, even bringing his hat down to arm's length to sweep it across the floor. "I'm always enamored of Dame Gwydre's optimism. Sure but you are a warm ray of sunshine on a dark forest trail."

"Take care in how you address the Dame of Vanguard," Father Premujon warned, which only made Jameston chuckle harder.

"Then we can hope," said Gwydre. She put her hand familiarly and warmly on the strong shoulder of tall Jameston Sequin, much to the annoyance of Premujon and every other Abellican brother in the room. "Then we can hope."

"Always that," Jameston replied.

They didn't have to wait long for their hopes to be fulfilled, for word rang out later that same afternoon of more travelers coming down the northern road. The alarms sounded loud and clear long before this second group neared the town, for among its ranks were reportedly at least two powries and a tall man wearing the beret of a bloody-cap dwarf.

Many people went into the streets to await the arrival, and Dame Gwydre and her entourage moved to the front of that throng. Soldiers and scouts slipped out all about the town perimeter, watching, their elm bows drawn and ready.

The approaching band came into view at last, over a rise to the north, and many in the crowd gasped, "powries," at the unusual sight. But Dame Gwydre was not looking at the bloody-cap dwarves. She was smiling, her eyes on Bransen the Highwayman and on Brother Jond beside him. She led the gathering right out of the gates, doing all she could to stop herself from breaking into a full run at the very welcome sight.

"We feared you dead!" she said when she stood before the band of six. Gwydre gasped then, and so did others around her, noting the garish wound on the face of the beloved Jond. Immediately a group rushed from Father Premujon's ranks to attend to the man.

"Yach, but so did we," said one of the dwarves, and he and his fellow laughed.

"Ancient Badden hoped that to be the case, I assure you," said the Highwayman. He rolled his sack off his shoulder and dumped its gruesome contents— the ancient's head—onto the ground before Dame Gwydre.

More gasps arose and several wails of protest.

"Remove that wretched thing!" one man demanded.

But Gwydre held up her hand to silence them. "Truly, I have never seen a more beautiful thing in all my life."

"Let it thaw a bit so ye can enjoy the stink of it, as well," advised the same powrie. Again he and his friend exploded into laughter.

Dame Gwydre looked from one to the other curiously, then stared hard at Bransen.

"We have a lot to talk about," the Highwayman admitted sheepishly.

CHAPTER 4

Throwing Down the Torch

Bannagran stood at the top of the main keep of Castle Pryd, staring to the east. He could make out the light of some campfires, seeming to twinkle on and off as the many trees waved in the evening wind. The savvy leader had set the torch on the wall near to him so that any milling about the streets of Pryd would see him up there in his shining bronze breastplate, cut to accentuate his solid and muscular form. He wore no overcoat and his arms were bare, showing the man's powerful muscles. Bannagran leaned forward so that his strong features reflected the torchlight. He kept his visage solid and determined, to direct the gaze of any onlookers to the plumed bronze open-faced helmet he had also set on the stone. How many times had the men and women of Pryd Town seen Bannagran adorned in that helm, his oft-broken nose crookedly protruding from the single line of bronze that ran down the front below his brow? They had seen that inspiring sight not once in the course of defeat, only in victory.

This was his role, he knew, and he had been taught well by his friend Prydae. As mighty as he was in battle, his biggest role was to serve as inspiration. "Better to kill one enemy loudly than ten silently," Prydae once said to him. He had to look and act the part of leader. If the warriors didn't trust in him, they could be routed and turned at the first sign of defeat, leading any one of a battle's ebbs and flows into a self-fulfilling prophecy of disaster.

So Bannagran wore his decorated bronze breastplate on the tower top that night. He was too far up for any below to make out the details of that crafted suit, of course, but just seeing the shine would remind them of the craftsmanship, of the line of carved silver wolves running across the chest and the multitude of jewels inlaid above and below that bas-relief. Bannagran was a simple man and had never been overly fond of such finery but, again, he knew his role. He hadn't come up here simply for appearance, however.

"What are you doing, Ethelbert?" he asked quietly, for something here was not quite right. Laird Delaval's forces were gathering around Bannagran in Pryd Town, with more streaming in every day. Surely Ethelbert knew that. No scout could miss it.

Milwellis had won in the north and was in position to swing to the south and press Ethelbert hard. Surely Ethelbert knew that.

So why hadn't he attacked Pryd a week before, as soon as Milwellis had handed his Northern forces the defeat at Pollcree?

Pryd Town swelled with soldiers. Even now Bannagran had at his command more men than Ethelbert could put on the field. That number only grew in Bannagran's favor with more of Delaval's warriors streaming in every day.

Bannagran looked past Ethelbert's distant camp then swung his gaze to the south, looking for some hint that Ethelbert had another force moving in to support him. The night was dark, unbroken by fires beyond the known encampments. Bannagran had scouts wide and far south and east of Ethelbert. There seemed no reinforcements on the horizon.

So, with the balance obviously shifting day by day to Pryd's favor, why hadn't Ethelbert already attacked?

And now, with the full weight of Delaval congealing around Pryd Town, why hadn't Ethelbert turned and flown the field, back to the east and the south where he could rally more allies?

Bannagran knew Ethelbert and had seen him in battle years before against the powries. He was a capable commander, a fine tactician who knew when to strike.

"A fine night," came a voice behind Bannagran. He couldn't stop his reflexive wince at the familiar nasal whine of Prince Yeslnik. Bannagran leaned more heavily on his hands, his fingers pressing tightly against the stone of the tower crenellations.

Yeslnik walked up beside him and followed his stare to Ethelbert's campfires.

"They are many," Yeslnik said.

"Not so many. Not nearly enough."

"I will defeat them," Yeslnik said, and by "I" he meant "Bannagran."

"If we can catch them and engage them, then we—you—will prove victorious, yes," Bannagran promised. "More so if Prince Milwellis pivots his force to the south."

"I prefer to let Milwellis run to the coast to put those wretched lairds of the Mantis Arm to the fire."

A tactical blunder, both militarily and politically, Bannagran knew, but he also knew that voicing such a concern wouldn't do much to dissuade the stubborn Yeslnik and, indeed, might prompt an even more stupid response from the impetuous and spoiled young man. Let the lairds of the Mantis Arm hold their loyalties to Ethelbert for now, Bannagran silently reasoned, for once this fight was decided and Ethelbert routed, those lairds would quickly realign behind the victor. They had no ideological and deep-felt belief in this war, after all, and were simply trying to figure out which laird's victory—Delaval or Ethelbert—would benefit their respective holdings the most.

"Do I need Milwellis?" Yeslnik asked. "Have I not given you enough to properly deal with this old sot from the south?"

"Yes, my laird, I mean, no, you do not need Milwellis, and, yes, you have more than enough men already gathered in Pryd Town to destroy Ethelbert's force."

"Then why are they not yet destroyed?"

Bannagran summoned his patience. "Because time works against Ethelbert. He is ill-supplied, and our numbers grow daily."

"But I can beat him now."

"A difficult fight."

"So?"

The callousness of that remark was not unexpected by Bannagran. Yeslnik didn't care how many men and women, his own as well as Ethelbert's, he sent to the grave as long as he achieved his victory.

"If Laird Ethelbert comes at us, we hold a defensive posture and he will be utterly destroyed," Bannagran tried to explain. "That would be the sweetest victory for you of all. If we must fight him in the open, then we will still win, though I fear that Ethelbert himself and many of his warriors will escape. If we must find him, we will win more decisively with every passing day. It is not just the victory, Laird, but the extent of the win that is important."

"I grow tired of the waiting," Yeslnik sighed. "March tomorrow morning."

Bannagran managed to avoid Yeslnik's gaze as he rolled his eyes.

"What will Ethelbert do in that event?" Yeslnik pressed. "He will see my strength and know his doom."

"He will likely flee the field," Bannagran replied, thinking it through as he spoke. He started to explain to Yeslnik that Ethelbert assuredly already knew of their strength, but the words caught in his throat and he stared back to the east more intently and with obvious alarm.

"What?" Yeslnik demanded anxiously, and he, too, looked that way. "What do you see?"

"Ethelbert is a shrewd commander. He knows he cannot win this fight,"

Bannagran pondered, more to himself than to Yeslnik. "He will flee. He seeks no more, perhaps, than to draw us out or to keep us occu—" Bannagran cut himself off and shook his head with slowly blossoming concern.

"That is a good thing, is it not?" the confused Prince Yeslnik asked as Bannagran wheeled away from the wall and started for the ladder leading back into the keep.

"How protected does Delaval City remain?" Bannagran asked.

"Behind her high walls?" the oblivious Prince replied.

"You have emptied her guard?"

"To fight Ethelbert," Yeslnik said, somewhat defensively, without knowing why.

"It is a ruse," Bannagran explained. "A feint of the highest order. He does not sit there intending to fight but only to keep us occupied, to keep us gathering our forces for a decisive battle that will not commence, not here, not soon."

"Then go and get him!" Prince Yeslnik cried, not catching on to the cause of Bannagran's alarm.

"Why is he here?" Bannagran asked.

"What puzzles are these?"

"To bring us here," the general from Pryd answered his own question. "Why does Ethelbert wish us here? Why does a swordsman invite a parry?"

Yeslnik stared at him blankly.

"Because such a parry will not defeat his true intended attack," Bannagran explained, and when Yeslnik at last seemed to be catching on, he repeated, more grimly, "How protected does Delaval City remain?"

Yeslnik's wail confirmed Bannagran's fears. The seasoned soldier rushed into the keep, Yeslnik dithering in his wake.

G uard Captain Rubert was widely considered the toughest man in the service of Laird Delaval. He had grown up on the streets of Delaval City, literally fighting for his every meal. His knuckles carried the scars of a hundred fights, a hundred crushed faces, and he wore a necklace of teeth he had knocked from the mouths of his opponents.

His reputation served him well, with an appointment to Delaval's own elite guards and a climb to the rank of captain, and in this latest adventure, where most of the soldiers had been sent from the city on the miserable hike to Pryd Holding, Rubert had escaped the call.

He was too tough, too valuable to Laird Delaval, the would-be King of Honce.

"Ah, but there's a cold wind coming down the masur this night," he lamented, tightening his cloak against the frigid breeze rushing down the great river, a harbinger of the approaching wintry season. "And I'm out o' weed for me pipe and got not a striker pad to light it up. Be a good sport," he called to his fellow sentry atop the wall encircling Laird Delaval's main keep. "Put a light up and a pinch."

As he neared, the man stood up and shrugged off the guard cloak. Even in the dim light of the quarter moon Rubert knew at once that this was not his companion. For that moonlight shined off a bald head, where his companion wore a thick mop of black hair, much like Rubert's own.

"Who are you?" Rubert called, his hand going to his finely crafted sword.

The imposter strode calmly toward Rubert. He carried no weapon that Rubert could see, and he was not a large man, certainly not near to Rubert's two-hundred-fifty-pound muscular frame.

"Far enough!" Rubert warned, drawing forth his sword, its dull metal gleaming in the moonlight.

The stranger continued toward him.

"You have been warned!" said Rubert. Heart pounding, he retracted his arm and thrust his blade at the man's chest.

But the man was no longer standing before him, having somehow moved enough to the side so that the blade slipped harmlessly past. Rubert felt a slight thump against his throat. He fell back, slashing his sword at the stranger, who by then had retreated safely out of reach.

"What are you about?" Rubert said, or started to say, or tried futilely to say, for no sound moved past his lips, though he did hear a wheeze a hand's width below them. He brought his free hand up to his throat and moved it before him into the moonlight, feeling the warmth of his own blood on his fingers. He started to protest, to ask the man another question, but again nothing came forth but a wheeze.

Another form scrambled over the wall behind his attacker, then more behind him. The original assailant grinned at Rubert and calmly walked by. Rubert meant to strike at him with his sword. He really did, except that his arm wouldn't heed his command to lift the weapon; indeed, he heard the sword, as if very distantly, clang against the tower's stone roof.

The stranger walked past, along with his companions. Rubert stood there, staring ahead, only vaguely aware that he was perched on the precipice of death's dark pit and falling forward without reprieve.

Only vaguely did Rubert feel his nose and cheekbone shatter against the hard and cold stone of the tower roof. Only vaguely did he hear the shuffle of light footfalls go past him. He didn't think of Laird Delaval, the would-be King of Honce, then. He didn't think of anything at all, just the inviting, irresistible blackness.

Laird Delaval was not a young man, and he surely felt every day of his nearly sixty years that evening. Winter was coming on in full force, with frost every morning and several snow flurries already. Delaval wasn't looking forward to it. He had hurt his knee in battle three decades earlier, thrown from his horse when some impudent peasant had stabbed his mount in the flank. Though the laird's wounds had healed—he was back to fighting form within a few weeks—the knee used every day of inclement weather, whether rain or the constant ache in the cold winters, to remind him of that long-ago fall.

"If my nephew can be rid of that troublesome Ethelbert in the coming battle, I just might winter in Ethelbert dos Entel this year and every year thereafter," Delaval said to Genoffrey and Tademist, his personal attendants and generals. Genoffrey had been with him since the early days, before Delaval had even been named successor to his father, the laird. A large man, his muscles not slackened in the least by the passage of the decades, Genoffrey wielded a claymore of extraordinary weight. More than once had he taken down heavy warhorses on the field of battle with a powerful swipe, and he had one time slain three men with a single swing, a feat that was still much discussed across the holdings of western and central Honce. Tademist, half the age of Delaval and twenty years Genoffrey's junior, had only recently joined the inner circle. Tall and lanky, the young warrior had not yet thickened with age. Where Genoffrey won with sheer power, Tademist was more of a finesse fighter, wielding a short sword and a long dirk, a rare two-handed fighting style, with cunning and unmatched speed.

The two men glanced at each other with obvious skepticism.

"I know, I know!" Laird Delaval said with a wave of his hand and a snicker. "Prince Yeslnik is not known for his martial prowess."

"But he has Bannagran, the Bear of Honce, with him, my king," said Tademist, who, along with Genoffrey and all the others of Delaval's inner circle, had started referring to Delaval by the title all in Castle Delaval considered inevitable.

"You know this one?" Delaval asked.

"I know that his reputation is well earned, by every account," Tademist replied, and Genoffrey nodded. "As is his title. They call him the Bear of Honce because of his great strength and size, and when he enters the field, the enemies flee."

"I have seen him in battle," the elder guard said. "Both when he was beside Pryd's son, Prydae, those many years ago, and in our most recent fighting south of Pryd Holding. If anything, his prowess in battle and in commanding his forces is greater than the whispered huzzahs. The Bear of Honce, indeed, in strength and sheer power, but he is more the fox in cleverness. Prince Yeslnik is well-served by that one and will win every day if he heeds the instincts of Bannagran of Pryd."

"That is good to know," Laird Delaval said, nodding. He started for his armoire, unbuckling his sword belt as he went. He knew that Genoffrey and Tademist were glancing at each other again behind his back, both of them concerned by his pained hobble. "I plan to live a hundred years, my friends."

"You will, my king, of course!" said Tademist.

Delaval laughed. "But these are dangerous times, and I fear that I've abused my body over the decades. Too many battles, too many hunts, too many women, and too much strong drink!"

Tademist started to protest, but Genoffrey cut him short. "I hear no regret in your voice," he said slyly.

Laird Delaval laughed again more heartily. "You were there for much of it," he replied, turning to face his oldest friend. "Do you believe that I should hold regrets?"

"Ah, but if our lives are twenty years shorter for the games of it all, then we'd have lived more than any man deserves!"

Tademist looked at his companion with horror that he would talk to the king so casually, and then both Delaval and Genoffrey laughed.

"You've been here for more than two years, young swordsman," Genoffrey said to Tademist.

"Do you not yet understand?" asked Delaval.

"Understand what, my king?" the poor young man stammered.

"That when it is just we three, you need not call me that," Delaval replied with obvious exasperation.

"But—"

"Oh, shut up," said Delaval, laughing once more, or still, actually. "All the formalities are for those out there," he explained, waving his hand at the closed door of his private chambers.

"And out there, never forget your place or his title," Genoffrey added.

"But in here we are friends," said Delaval. "Genoffrey was by my side when he was just a boy, a groom. As he grew, he trained with me and then became my constant companion in the wars. We saw men die, and often."

"Too often," Genoffrey grumbled.

"Aye, and we've killed men, and goblins and powries, side by side," Delaval continued.

"I am blessed to be here, my king—" Tademist said with a bow.

"Nonsense!" said Delaval. "You earned it with your skills! You remind me of a young Genoffrey, and I assure you, that is no small compliment."

Tademist, who considered himself fortunate in his daily sparring with Genoffrey on those rare occasions he even earned draw, didn't doubt that for a moment. He looked to his companion and smiled.

A knock on the door interrupted the conversation.

"Speak!" Delaval called.

"Your hot towels, my king," came the familiar woman's voice of Maddie Macabee, another of Delaval's personal attendants.

"Hot towels for aching bones," Delaval said with a sigh, and he nodded Tademist toward the door.

But a sudden and sharp cry from outside the closed door froze Tademist in his tracks. "What are you about?" Maddie yelled, followed by a thump and a scream. Not just any scream. Delaval and Genoffrey knew such a keen quite well, the dying shriek, the final wail of a man or woman as death descends.

Tademist knew it, too, and drew his weapons as he rushed to the door. From over his shoulder Genoffrey pulled out Spinebreaker, his legendary claymore, and Delaval slid his fine blade from its scabbard and let the belt fall to the floor.

The door burst open before Tademist got to it. In rushed Maddie Macabee, though not of her own accord. She was already dead, her chest gashed open. She flew forward, tumbling before the dodging Tademist, who did well enough to ignore the shock enough to prepare for the man following Maddie into the room.

Behrenese, judging by the color of his skin, the man held a fine, slightly curved sword in both hands. He entered in a fast and steady walk, perfectly balanced all the way to Tademist, where he launched a sudden thrust, then retracted his blade with amazing precision and speed, launching it into a downward diagonal swipe that would have taken Tademist from shoulder to hip had he not been focused solely on defense.

Tademist twisted away from the thrust and backed out of the downward cut then responded fast with a sudden thrust of his own sword, a stab of his dagger as he retracted the sword, and a second thrust. He advanced as he attacked, thinking to drive the man back, for other Behrenese appeared at the doorway.

But the man was suddenly not in front of him. Luck alone saved Tademist as he happened to turn the correct way in trying to find his too-quick opponent and happened to have his sword at the proper level to barely deflect another thrust of his opponent's fine blade.

A man went by the combatants to Tademist's right as he squared back up with his opponent. A woman entered next, as sounds of fighting erupted in the hallway, the castle guard rushing to their leader's aid.

Tademist faded right as the woman, a fine sword in her hand as well, moved to pass him on the left. He wanted to intercept, but his opponent kept him dancing, kept him dodging.

As the woman passed, she smiled at him, and such an awful grin it was! Tademist felt his knees go weak, as if she had just withered him to his core. In that smile he knew—somehow—that he and his beloved King Delaval were surely doomed.

G enoffrey was used to missing with his first swing. The claymore wasn't wieldy, after all, and Genoffrey never took pains to disguise his first attack. The blade came lumbering down from on high and the warrior before him easily and gracefully leaped back and to the side.

Genoffrey hid his grin, purposely seeming to overbalance as Spinebreaker thumped against the thick carpet. He even appeared to stumble.

The warrior rushed forward to the side of him, pivoted fast, and came in with a straightforward thrust, but just as he started the turn, so too turned Genoffrey, dropping his foot back as he lifted and re-angled his blade, putting it right in line to pierce the charging warrior.

He thought he had a win, and the necessary quick one so that he could go to the side of his beloved Delaval. But the warrior leaped up high, front somersaulted above the level claymore, and landed in a run past Genoffrey. The soldier tried to turn to keep up and felt the burn in his side, felt the warmth of his blood spilling from a long and deep gash.

To his credit Genoffrey grimaced through the pain, completed the swinging turn, and would have scored a hit on the retreating man had not that man, almost as if he had long anticipated this reaction, dived into another roll, this time along the floor.

This Behrenese warrior was two plays ahead.

W ell, come on then and be done with it," Delaval said to the dark-skinned, slight woman, although he had no way of knowing if she even understood him. She just smiled and circled, her curved and decorated sword down low before her, its tip nearly cutting the threads of the carpet.

"I need not ask who sent you," said Delaval. "Long have we known that the traitorous Ethelbert favored the beasts of Behr."

"You leaders of Honce slaughter your people with impunity," she answered, surprising Delaval with her command of the language. "And yet, we of Behr are the 'beasts'? Tell me, you who would rule the world, how do you measure such a title?"

She came forward suddenly, her sword flashing left, right, and center with three separate thrusts that seemed almost as one to the Laird of Delaval. To his credit, he managed to pick off the first and back out of the reach of the second and third.

She wasn't done, though, quick-stepping forward and turning a complete circuit—something few warriors would ever dare try—bringing her sword in fast at Delaval's side, then doubling the complexity of her form by changing its angle mid-swing.

Somehow, and he knew luck to be a part of it, Delaval managed to block.

"How much is he paying you?" he asked, trying hard to keep the nerves out of his voice. In just those two routines, the man feared he was outmatched. "I will double it!"

"Shallow principles," the woman chided. "We are beasts."

"You intervene where you do not belong!" Delaval growled at her. "You risk a war with all of Honce!"

"Idiot Delaval," she said, and she came again, in a vicious flurry of swings and thrusts that left Delaval dizzy, that left Delaval retreating.

That left Delaval bleeding.

"You do not command all of Honce," the woman finished.

Tademist did not hear Laird Delaval's gasp as Affwin Wi's blade punctured his belly. The young warrior heard nothing but the near constant ring of metal as he and his shaven-headed opponent exchanged vicious and furious flurries. Sword hit sword, dirk hit sword, and so fast was the man from Behr that even as Tademist intercepted his thrust with the dirk and perfectly executed a responding thrust with his sword, he found it fully parried.

If that weren't impressive enough, the man from Behr then immediately launched another thrust routine, left, right, right again, and then right a third time.

Tademist blocked the first three, but his anticipation had him sliding his blade across to block a thrust angled left that never came. He felt the stab in his shoulder, felt his dirk arm go weak, and heard the weapon hit the floor.

G enoffrey did hear Delaval's gasp, a sound he had heard only once before, in a far-off and long-ago battle in the Belt-and-Buckle mountains. He reacted with a sudden and brutal straightforward rush, stabbing his sword then slashing it, then reversing it with a powerful backhand. He didn't get close to hitting his opponent, but he wasn't actually trying for a kill there. He drove the man back, back, and then he turned and charged across the way, behind Tademist and toward Delaval.

He registered that Tademist was in trouble, but there was nothing he could do at that time, for before him the woman was into another wild exchange with Delaval, their blades ringing and screeching with hits and slides, and Genoffrey's fine eye told him that his friend was too slow here, that the woman was outmatching him, strike for strike. He watched her setting Delaval up with every stride he took, and indeed, he felt as if he was running in deep mud, as if everything before him was just out of his reach. She brought Delaval's sword to the right, then a bit farther to the right, and then again, with three short, quick stabs, then she flipped her blade across to the left, actually tossing it to her waiting left hand.

"No!" Genoffrey cried in dismay as Delaval futilely tried to re-angle his own sword. To the laird's credit, he did manage a central thrust, but the woman stepped away from it, farther to his left, and turned as she went, rotating her hips and shoulders, lengthening her thrust and putting great force behind it.

Genoffrey felt a slug in his lower back—he knew it to be a stab from his pursuing opponent—at the same time he watched the Behrenese woman's sword slide deep into King Delaval's chest.

It occurred to him that it was appropriate that he and his dear friend would die at the same time.

He finished his charge, unable to interrupt his own momentum, slashing Spinebreaker down hard against the woman's blade, but too late, of course, for that only jarred the impaled laird.

Genoffrey stumbled forward, taking Delaval with him hard into the far wall. The king crashed in without any attempt to cushion the blow, slammed face first into the stone, and bounced away, crumbling to the ground. Somehow Genoffrey managed to hold his footing and hold his blade, turning about with his back against the wall. He saw the woman, in obvious distress, looking down at her sword, nearly half its blade snapped off.

Whatever comfort that might have given Genoffrey, though, ended as she thrust her arm at him and launched the remaining piece of her weapon, flying spearlike, spinning sidelong in the air.

Genoffrey heard it hit the stone wall behind him.

It took him a moment to realize that it had gone through his throat.

He slid down to a sitting position. The woman approached him, while the man who had been his opponent, his sword red with Genoffrey's blood, turned toward Tademist.

Genoffrey heard Tademist's cries, one after another, as the two men stabbed at him. Every now and then came the ring of metal as valiant Tademist managed a block, but mostly Genoffrey heard the sickly sound of metal puncturing flesh.

He didn't see any of that desperate last stand, though, for he could not take his eyes off the slight woman walking toward him. She bent low before him, stared into his eyes, and gave that wicked smile once more, then yanked her broken sword out of his throat.

She started for Delaval, but calls from the hall turned her.

She crossed Genoffrey's field of view, running back toward the exit. He wanted to turn to Tademist, wanted to turn away from the sight of his fallen friend, Laird Delaval.

But he couldn't. He hadn't the strength, and even the slightest movement sent fires of agony tearing through his body. He couldn't even manage to close his eyes, and so was forced to watch Delaval's lifeblood pouring from him, pooling around him as he lay so very still.

To Genoffrey, that was the cruelest trick of all.

CHAPTER 5

Six Cogs Scattered

The lines of allies couldn't have been clearer to Dame Gwydre as she listened to Bransen relay his tale of capture, escape, and ultimate victory over Ancient Badden. Beside Bransen stood the fallen monk Cormack and the barbarian woman Milkeila, with a pair of powries behind them.

Across the way to the left side of the room sat Father De Guilbe and his entourage, including Brother Jond, who Gwydre knew was the link between these wildly disparate groups. Jond was a good man, an honorable man, who put moral duty first and foremost. Gwydre hoped that to be the case, for De Guilbe had made no secret of his loathing of Cormack.

"We had enough allies to get through the ancient's defenses," Bransen remarked, throwing a sour look Father De Guilbe's way as he spoke.

Gwydre sighed inwardly. Why did things always have to be so complicated?

"It was not our place to go!" Father De Guilbe protested. "I could not know of your predicament, Dame Gwydre!"

"We have already been over this, good Father," Gwydre calmly replied. "No one holds you or your brothers at fault for the choice you made in retreating from the glacier."

"No one?" De Guilbe asked sharply, his glare landing on Bransen.

The man in the black silk clothing grinned, something Dame Gwydre did not miss. "And you slew Badden?" she asked Bransen.

"It would do great injustice to those around me, these four and two other powries, for me to make such a claim, Lady," Bransen replied, managing another sly grin at De Guilbe as he did. "It was my blade that took his head, yes, but only through the sacrifice and efforts of those around me."

"However it was done, it is appreciated," said Dame Gwydre.

"It was done for a price," Bransen reminded, and all in the room widened their eyes at that rather callous announcement, a reminder that stole the joy from the room. "And now, good Lady, with your generosity, I would ask that you extend that reward."

Beside Gwydre, Dawson McKeege and another advisor began to protest, but Gwydre held up her hand to silence them and bade Bransen to continue.

"I would have my Writ of Passage," Bransen demanded. "I will go and collect my wife and her mother and travel Honce as a free man as I was promised."

Gwydre nodded.

"And I insist upon a similar writ for Cormack and Milkeila," Bransen added.

"No!" shouted Father De Guilbe, leaping to his feet. Beside him, Brother Giavno tried to grab his arm, but the large, older man tugged free of his grasp and stormed toward Gwydre. "Cormack does not answer to the laws of the lairds but to that of the Order of Abelle."

"Are you saying that Chapel Abelle will not honor my wishes?" Gwydre asked. If the cool and calm woman was shaken in the least by the sudden and violent outburst she didn't show it.

"I beg you not to do this, Dame Gwydre!" Father De Guilbe said. "Brother Cormack betrayed us!"

Despite the heightened tension, Gwydre smiled at De Guilbe's clever and selective use of Cormack's title. He only called Cormack "brother" when claiming church jurisdiction, it seemed. She waited for De Guilbe to finally stop his march, just a few feet from her chair, then she turned to Cormack.

"Have you anything to say in your defense?"

"I followed my heart," Cormack replied. "Everything I did, I did because I believed it to be the will and manner of Blessed Abelle, the calling of my order."

"Betraying us to the barbarians?" rasped De Guilbe.

"Ending a needless slaughter," Cormack corrected. "You held the men of Milkeila's clan prisoner. You—we—had no right!"

De Guilbe started to shout back, but Dame Gwydre silenced him and bade Cormack to continue.

"The Alpinadorans of the neighboring islands would all have died at the base of our chapel before surrendering our captives to us," the young man explained. "I could not tolerate that slaughter. There was no need for it."

"So what did you do?" Gwydre prompted.

"I freed the four men and showed them the way out of our dungeon to rejoin their people. The Alpinadorans left our island. The battle ended, and so ended the death—the death of Alpinadorans and of monks."

Dame Gwydre turned to De Guilbe, her expression cold.

"A simplistic review," the monk said.

"Then do elaborate."

"The men we held were not captured, they were rescued. Rescued from certain death and healed of grievous wounds through the power of Blessed Abelle, by the brothers of Blessed Abelle."

"That does not give us the right to hold them as prisoner!" Cormack argued. "You cannot so coerce fealty to faith!"

Gwydre looked from Cormack back to De Guilbe, her expression caught somewhere between disbelief and outrage.

"Our manner is of no concern to Dame Gwydre," Father De Guilbe said to her. "My orders came from Father Artolivan of Chapel Abelle. To him alone do I answer."

"True enough," Dame Gwydre conceded. "But a writ is mine to give, and so I do, to both Cormack and this woman, Milkeila, though I would like to speak at length with you both before it is finalized."

"Yes, Dame Gwydre," Cormack said, and Milkeila graciously bowed.

"I would ask for writs for the other heroes of the fight," Bransen interjected then.

"Bloody caps?" Dawson McKeege gasped behind Gwydre, and, indeed, the Lady of Vanguard, too, seemed more than a bit disconcerted at that suggestion.

To the side Father De Guilbe laughed loudly, as if mocking Gwydre and this path she now walked.

"Go back to your brothers," Gwydre said to him and waved him away.

He complied, but continued his mocking laughter.

"Come forward," Dame Gwydre bade the powries.

"Name's Mcwigik," said one. "And me friend's Bikelbrin. Come from the Julianthes but spent a hunnerd years on that lake, Mithranidoon, with our friends."

"And your friends are still there?"

"Yach, still on the rock."

"You do not wish to rejoin them?"

"Seen too much o' that smokin' lake," Mcwigik replied. "Not for going back, unless going back's for taking them off with us."

"Yach, but more than a few're wanting off that rock," Bikelbrin added.

Dame Gwydre sat back in her chair, and Dawson McKeege immediately began whispering in her ear, his great concern more than obvious.

"You ask much of me, Bransen Garibond," Gwydre said a few moments later.

"I . . . we gave much to you," the Highwayman replied. "At great risk."

Gwydre frowned. "I cannot grant powries the writ to walk freely through the lands of men."

Bransen stood up very straight and crossed his arms over his chest.

Gwydre sighed and looked at the dwarves. "Were I to grant you passage, free of battle, throughout all of Honce, would you agree to lay down your arms?" she asked.

Both Mcwigik and Bilkelbrin began shaking their arms and looking at the limbs curiously. "They're attached to our shoulders," Mcwigik answered. "Ye sayin' we got to cut off our arms to stay with ye?"

Gwydre and the others, even Cormack, chuckled at that. "Your weapons," she explained. "Were I to grant you passage, do I have your word of honor that you will not take up arms against any man or woman? That you will not do battle with any men?"

"Even them that's deservin' it?" asked Bikelbrin.

"Even them. No battle. Not ever. If I am even to consider giving you the writ Bransen desires, then you must promise me that you will not—not ever!—again spill human blood. Can you make such a pledge?"

"Don't hear ye whining that we spilled Badden's blood," Mcwigik retorted. "Last time I looked, he was human. Headless, but human."

"Aye, and we dipped our caps in his blood, and mines shinin' all the better," added Bikelbrin.

"Where we come from, them needing a crack get a crack," said Mcwigik.

"That is not the way among men," said Gwydre.

"Bah, but them men with money and land and power—and them women with such—they get to pick them needing a crack," said Mcwigik. "And when the crack's given, what?"

Behind and all about Gwydre, men bristled at the obvious insult, but Gwydre remained calm, reassuring them all.

"It is by the law, good dwarf," said Gwydre. "The law is bigger than men and women."

"Bigger than most," said Mcwigik. "Not bigger than the lairds and the priests, from what I'm hearing. Even a powrie might walk free, what, if a laird or lady says so."

"I do not know," Gwydre answered honestly. "My writ for you might hold no weight beyond Vanguard."

Mcwigik spat upon the floor.

Dame Gwydre looked at Bransen and shook her head. "This is beyond my power to grant."

Bransen narrowed his eyes.

"But I will offer this. When the weather breaks and the winter is no more, I will send you both back to the lake," she told the powries, "with wagons laden with supplies and with a map to take you and your kin to Brinewind, a port in eastern Vanguard. From there, I will supply you with a boat and star charts so that you can sail for your distant home."

Mcwigik and Bikelbrin looked at each other for a few long moments. Mcwigik stepped forward and fell to the floor, where he sucked up his spit.

More than one person in the room groaned.

Mcwigik stood up straight and smiled at Gwydre.

"I am not sure what that means," she said, caught between revulsion and laughter.

"Means I ain't spitting at yerself anymore," said Mcwigik. "And means me and me friend're liking what ye're saying."

Gwydre watched as Bransen looked at Cormack and Milkeila, both of whom (apparently more familiar and comfortable with the ways of powries) smiled and nodded.

"You would turn them free on the coast to lay waste to innocents," Father De Guilbe said from the side.

"They did not kill me, though they surely had the chance," Cormack argued. "When Father De Guilbe cast me adrift, beaten and dying, the powries took me in."

"More the reason to hate them," muttered the unrelenting De Guilbe, who had only gone as far as the doorway.

"Enough," Dame Gwydre warned him. "Father De Guilbe, you weary me."

"And you overstep your province with Cormack and now with these two little . . . murderers," the monk replied. "I assure you that Chapel Abelle will hear of this, all of this!"

"At the same time they learn of the death of Ancient Badden, no doubt," said Bransen. "And learn that Dame Gwydre has led them greatly in their battle with the Samhaists."

Father De Guilbe looked at him curiously, as if he couldn't believe what he was hearing from this strange man. "Who are you?" he asked.

"The man who helped save the life of one not worth the trouble, it would seem," Bransen replied.

Now Father De Guilbe's eyes went very narrow, a look of absolute loathing and threat.

Bransen grinned at him.

"Perhaps you should not be so secure of Dame Gwydre's writ, Highwayman," De Guilbe said.

Dame Gwydre stood up suddenly, her eyes flashing as she scowled at the obstinate monk. "If you would counsel Father Artolivan to ignore my writ, then you would counsel him badly," she warned in an even and deathly serious tone.

"You war with the Samhaists and you would war with the Brothers of Abelle, too?"

"Chapel Pellinor, all the chapels of Vanguard, exist by my grace alone," Gwydre retorted. "Do not ever forget that."

Behind Gwydre, Dawson McKeege groaned. Behind De Guilbe, Brother Giavno did likewise.

You are satisfied with her decision?" Cormack asked Mcwigik and Bikelbrin when they were alone with Milkeila.

"She didn't attack us, and that's something," Mcwigik replied.

"She assured you safe passage," Milkeila reminded.

"Yach, and we're knowin' it," said Mcwigik. "And we're not thinkin' bad of her."

"She did good by us. We're knowin' that," Bikelbrin added.

"Don't mean we won't kill her one day and dip our caps in her blood, though," Mcwigik said, and when both Cormack and Milkeila's eyes went wide, the two dwarves enjoyed a good laugh at their expense.

"We'll be taking the wagon and the boat, and off we're going back to where we're belonging," Mcwigik proclaimed.

Cormack reached up and grabbed his cap, pulling it from his head. "Will you want this back?" he asked.

"Are ye wanting to give it back?"

Cormack thought for a moment, then shook his head. "I wear it as a reminder of some unusual friends," he explained. "I wear it to remind myself not to be hasty in judging others until I know them."

"Fine words," said Mcwigik.

"To get ye killed to death," added Bikelbrin, and the dwarves laughed at Cormack again.

"We let ye live to put a burr in Prag's fat arse, ye dolt," said Mcwigik. "Weren't for him and ye'd've been gutted on the beach that first day."

Cormack fell back as if slapped.

The powries laughed again.

"How am I to know when you're speaking true and when you're speaking in jest?" the former monk protested.

"Ye're not," Mcwigik answered. "Not now, and not ever."

"Are you friends, Mcwigik and Bikelbrin?" Cormack asked.

"Been friends for a hunnerd years," Mcwigik assured him.

"To me!"

The dwarves looked at each other. "If we're ever in the forest or on a boat and we see Cormack or Milkeila in trouble, then know we'll help ye," Mcwigik said for both, for Bikelbrin nodded his assent through every word of it.

"And we'll be thinking many times o' the one human wearing a powrie cap and glad how he came by it," Bilkelbrin added. "Kicking Prag's ugly face!"

Cormack patted each on the shoulder appreciatively as he left with Milkeila to go to their room across the hall. "I will miss those two," he said to his wife.

Milkeila nodded, hand on the knob. "The world seems less . . . colorful already." As she finished, she led Cormack's gaze down the hall, where several grim-faced guards stood ready with long halberds and armored all in bronze.

"Dame Gwydre did not err in granting them passage," Cormack said.

"You speak to convince yourself, not me."

Cormack looked at his wife carefully and glanced over his shoulder at the closed door of the powries' room. He wondered if he was a fool, for had he been in charge he would have trusted that pair of dwarves, would have given them a Writ of Passage.

"No other laird would have honored that writ," Milkeila said as if reading his mind.

"You know nothing of Honce," Cormack replied.

"I saw the looks on the faces of those here in Pellinor," Milkeila said. "Mcwigik and Bikelbrin would not have much of a life in the lands of your people. What life, I wonder, might Milkeila find there?"

Cormack put his arm about her shoulder and pulled her close as he guided her into their room. "A fine one," he promised, but he glanced back over his shoulder again as he closed the door. He would indeed miss his powrie companions, his powrie friends.

I have little desire to be caught up in the endless drama that so marks your church," Bransen said to Brother Jond.

"You know little—"

"I know much!" Bransen interrupted. "I spent years as a slave in service to the Brothers of Chapel Pryd."

"A slave? Surely you exaggerate!"

"I lived in a hole in the floor and spent my days emptying chamber pots. True, in exchange, they gave me bits of miserable, cold food, and my dungeon wasn't open to the snow and the rain." Bransen gave a little snicker, his eyes looking past Jond and, indeed, into the past, as he remembered those many days he had spent with Father Jerak and Brother Bathelais and Brother Reandu . . . ah, Brother Reandu! Blind Brother Jond couldn't see the confusion on Bransen's face at that moment, of course, but he did tilt his chin in apparent curiosity at the man's pause.

Bransen's mind whirled back to his days as the Stork, living in a tiny, one-room cellar at Chapel Pryd. He almost felt ashamed at the way he had described his time there to Jond. For all the discomfort and for all his outrage at the brothers for what they had done to Garibond, the brothers at Chapel Pryd had not been cruel to the young and wounded Bransen, who, because of his affliction, was known then as Stork. Brother Reandu in particular had often shown him affection and sympathy and, indeed, had aided him in his last desperate fight with Laird Prydae, at the cost of Master Bathelais's life.

"They let me go," he said finally.

"The brothers of Chapel Pryd?"

"Chapel Abelle," Bransen corrected. "They let Dawson McKeege take me here to serve Dame Gwydre, though they knew that Delaval and that pathetic excuse of a man, Yeslnik, would have rewarded them greatly had they turned me over for execution."

"But instead, you were pressed into service you did not desire."

Bransen shrugged. "Aren't we all? I do not think Dame Gwydre wanted this war. Nor did Crait and Olconna and Vaughna. Nor Brother Jond."

The blind monk smiled widely at that, as if he saw something Bransen could not.

"What is it?" the young warrior asked.

"It does my heart good to hear you speak like that, my friend," he explained.

The door swung open to the room, and Father De Guilbe and Brother Giavno entered.

"What are you doing here?" De Guilbe asked Bransen.

"He is here at my invitation," Brother Jond answered. "I have known this fine young warrior for many weeks now. We have shared the road of adventure."

"You speak for him?" De Guilbe asked rather sharply.

"I do."

"He befriends Cormack," De Guilbe warned.

"Cormack who saved the folk of Mithranidoon from certain doom, your chapel and clergy among them," Brother Jond reminded.

Bransen noted the big man tense up at that, and so he smiled widely, just to make De Guilbe even more uncomfortable.

"Beware your actions," De Guilbe warned him.

"Cormack helped kill Ancient Badden," said Bransen. "While you ran away, he battled the greatest foe of your order and of Dame Gwydre's holding. Perhaps it is Father De Guilbe and his fleeing monks who should beware their actions."

"Leave this place," De Guilbe commanded.

Bransen looked to Brother Jond, who needed no prompting. "Stay!" the monk from Chapel Pellinor argued.

"Brother!" De Guilbe fumed.

"Good Father, I serve Father Premujon of Chapel Pellinor," Brother Jond answered, remaining very calm. "I name this man as a friend, for he has stood beside me in my trials."

"As you helped me after our capture," Bransen replied.

"I'd no more abandon him than I would abandon my beloved Abelle, Father De Guilbe," said Jond. "He is a man of good heart and great courage, a man we should coax to the ways of Abelle, not a man to be shunned."

Father De Guilbe wore a strange, wicked smile as he replied, "And Cormack? Have you made an assessment of the former Brother Cormack?"

Jond shook his head. "Should he appeal to Father Premujon for reinstatement in the order, I will speak honestly of that which I know regarding the man."

"And you believe that I was wrong in excommunicating him?"

Again Jond shook his head. "I make no judgments of that which I do not know, Father," he said. "I know little of this man, Cormack, but I will speak honestly to that which I have seen . . . heard. His work against Ancient Badden was no small thing, but whether that absolves him of his actions on Mithranidoon is not for me to decide."

"Those actions should absolve him," Bransen insisted. "Particularly since he did nothing wrong on the island on the lake."

"Be gone from this place!" Father De Guilbe insisted, and again Brother Jond started to argue. But this time, Bransen put his hand on Jond's shoulder to quiet him, more than happy to be out of the company of the irascible De Guilbe.

De Guilbe didn't even look at him as he walked past, but Brother Giavno gave him a look that seemed regretful, almost heartbroken, almost apologetic.

Bransen chuckled as he walked from the room, thinking of how much that reaction by the younger brother reminded him of the same sort of conflicts he had seen in Chapel Pryd regarding the young man known as the Stork.

He got into the hall, pulling the door closed behind him, and heard De Guilbe explode at Brother Jond. Bransen just shook his head. He certainly had needed no further confirmation of the many reasons he was no fan or friend of the brothers of Abelle.

Exhausted from the squabbling in her audience chamber, from the incessant complaining of the unlikable De Guilbe, from having to deal diplomatically with powries—with bloody-cap dwarves!—exhausted from her own excitement and anticipation of the possibilities now that Ancient Badden was dead, Dame Gwydre wanted nothing more that night than to fall into the arms of Alandrais, the brother of Chapel Pellinor who had become more than a friend to her.

The moment she entered her private chambers, where Alandrais was waiting, she knew something was wrong.

The man hadn't dressed down into his nightshirt but was still wearing his heavy brown robes and hadn't untied his uncomfortable sandals. He half stood, half sat on the edge of Gwydre's desk, his strong arms crossed over his chest, his expression stern.

Thinking him distracted by something extraneous (or hoping that to be the case), Dame Gwydre walked over and reached up to stroke his face.

He was looking right at her when he stiffened away from her touch.

"What is it?" she asked, afraid she knew.

"Father De Guilbe is a powerful man in the Order of Abelle," Alandrais replied.

"So is Father Premujon."

"Who supports Father De Guilbe. And Father De Guilbe has the ear of Father Artolivan."

Dame Gwydre stepped back from the man. "I have not spoken to Father Premujon about the new arrivals from Alpinador, nor does it matter much concerning my own words—"

"You should not diminish him or contradict him, particularly on matters relating to the order," Alandrais scolded. "As with the man, Cormack, it is not your concern."

Gwydre nodded her head as she mulled over those words for a few heart-beats. "Cormack, who helped defeat Ancient Badden and thus may have saved my people?" she asked. "That man, Cormack? That hero, Cormack, is not the concern of Dame Gwydre, who rules Vanguard?"

"His disposition in the church is a matter for the Order of Abelle."

"When have I said that it is not? My argument with De Guilbe stemmed from his remarks to my man, the Highwayman."

"Your threat to him, you mean."

"Aland, what is this about?" Gwydre asked, coming forward in a concilia-tory manner, again reaching to stroke his bearded face.

This time, he stood straight and turned his back on her.

"Alandrais?"

"Dame Gwydre . . ." he started, and then he took a deep breath and turned around to face her directly. "Gwyd," he restated, using his pet name for her. "I am a brother of Abelle. I will always be such—my first and foremost love is forever my church and my prophet."

"I have never asked you for more than that," Gwydre interrupted.

"Haven't you? When you threaten the very chapels of my order, as you did with Father De Guilbe, you place me in an uncomfortable—"

"And I am the Dame of Vanguard!" Gwydre cut him off. "The people of this land depend upon me for their welfare, as they depended upon my hus-band before me and my father before him. I will always be as such, and first and foremost in my heart is my responsibility to the people of Vanguard. I have never asked you to betray your order, to place me before Abelle in your heart, and yet you are doing just that to me, right here and right now."

"Your words to Father De Guilbe—"

"Were not an idle threat, I assure you," Dame Gwydre snapped.

Brother Alandrais stared at her hard, but there was no blink coming from the woman, no backing down in the least.

"You should leave," she said after many moments of unsettling silence had passed.

Brother Alandrais started to reply but stopped short, looked to the side for a moment, then nodded and walked past Gwydre, out of the room.

The Dame of Vanguard winced when that door slammed closed. She took a deep breath, wiped away whatever tears were daring to form in her eyes, and walked across the room to her private stock and poured herself a large glass of boggle, a rare and precious wine, rumored to be made by woodland elves or some other such faerie folk.

It had been a long day.

Indeed.

CHAPTER 6

The Opportune Moment

Laird Ethelbert couldn't hide the smile widening on his face as the scouts offered their reports. So it was true: His assassins had killed Delaval.

Yeslnik had fled to Delaval City, taking much of his entourage with him, including his elite, well-armed, and bronze-armored warriors who had been so devastating to Ethelbert on the battlefield of late. Many of the support groups surrounding Pryd Holding were apparently peeling away as well, falling back to guard Delaval City or falling off simply out of confusion.

Ethelbert had beheaded the beast, and the beast's body was flailing without purpose or direction.

"Yeslnik will become Laird of Delaval Holding," he whispered, nodding. He looked up as he finished to see all his scouts and generals and advisors staring at him, hanging on his every word. "This boy, Yeslnik, who has no understanding of warfare and who has never bloodied his blade on a living opponent."

His emphasis on the word "living" brought a derisive laugh, for it was rumored that the Prince of Delaval had oftentimes wiped his sword on the bodies of fallen enemies to make it look as if he had gallantly struck many mortal blows. The joke among Ethelbert's men and even among the fighting warriors of Delaval's ranks was that Yeslnik must have extraordinarily long arms to reach the battle from his favored position, far in the rear.

"We have accomplished all that we hoped," Kirren Howen remarked, bowing in admiration for his laird's cleverness.

Ethelbert nodded but then addressed another of the scouts who had not yet offered his report. "What news from the north? Has Milwellis pivoted?"

"No, my laird," the man replied, stammering nervously. "I mean, yes, my laird, but not toward us. He went north to Chapel Abelle and the coast. From there, he marched east but then back to the west as if unsure."

"And now?"

"Back east of Chapel Abelle, along the north reaches of Felidan but still west of the Mantis Arm," the scout replied. "He has not sought engagement since his victory at Pollcree."

"Because he thinks his legacy safe," said the smiling Ethelbert. "And thinks the war nears its end. He paused because he expected the battle to commence here, an obvious rout for Delaval. And while I was in retreat to the southeast, Milwellis could move east with ease, against holdings unsure of their allegiance to my, obvious losing, cause."

"Obvious, my Laird Ethelbert," said Kirren Howen, and several others snickered. "But the battle will not commence here, as Milwellis anticipated. And our withdrawal will not be retreat."

Ethelbert was nodding, but his expression did not show agreement. "Delaval's forces slide away. They are confused and demoralized."

Kirren Howen looked at the man slyly.

"Perhaps the battle should commence here, and now," Ethelbert said, grinning at his old general. "We had thought to make the attempt and withdraw posthaste, but since we have been more successful than we ever deemed possible, is it possible that Pryd Holding is within our grasp?"

"They maintain a sizable garrison, but they are in confusion," said Myrick the Bold.

"Do we dare?" asked Kirren Howen.

"Do we dare not to seize the opportunity?" Ethelbert replied. "What might be the gain, I wonder?"

"Pryd Holding," said Myrick the Bold.

"And Prince Yeslnik suing for peace on our terms," added Kirren Howen.

"And Bannagran," said Ethelbert, nodding, his eyes gleaming, for he knew that one well and suddenly understood the potential prize here. "Can we do it?" he asked his most trusted soldier.

Kirren Howen didn't answer. He looked around questioningly at the scouts. "I can know by this very evening," he finally assured Ethelbert.

"Calculate then," Ethelbert bade him. "We must act quickly if we are to act at all. Before Yeslnik's advisors—Laird Delaval's old competent warriors—mitigate their confusion and protect their flanks."

Ethelbert grinned widely at Kirren Howen as he finished. "I believe we can do this. We have struck a mortal blow, but only if we press the wound before it is tended."

Kirren Howen nodded and bowed then went fast to the scouts, and not a man or woman on that field thought for a moment that they would not attack Pryd Holding within the next two days.

Y ou see their eyes?" Lady Olym asked her husband as they were hustled
through the streets of Delaval City, toward the main keep, where Laird
Delaval lay in state. "They revere you."

Prince Yeslnik had indeed noticed the many stares—hopeful, pleading,
wounded all at once, their intensity nearly stealing his breath and the strength
from his legs. Laird Delaval, King Delaval, was dead. Only then did the implications of that reality truly hit Yeslnik, the favored nephew, the Laird of Pryd,
the Prince of Delaval's Honce.

Now they all looked at him. No, not at him, but *to* him!

He carried in his every step the hope and desperation of a wounded people.
His words now, his every word, would hold great importance and power. His
every whim would become edict; dozens, scores, hundreds would clamor to
fulfill his every wish.

A smile and squeal of joy would not be appropriate, so the prince managed
to hold his somber demeanor as he continued on his way, reminding himself
that the weight of Delaval's office, the reality of the war and all the rest, now fell
upon his shoulders.

His private giddiness turned to terror when he entered the audience chamber, the hall of state, to see his mentor, Uncle Delaval, laid out upon a stone
sarcophagus. The man appeared serene in death, his face chalky but relaxed,
arms crossed over his chest.

"I wish for more privacy," Yeslnik said, and immediately the guards began
clearing everyone from the room. Yeslnik didn't wait but staggered over to the
body and fell to his knees beside it, overwhelmed. He had never thought of
Delaval in any terms other than the good the man could do his fortune and
ascent to power. He couldn't deny his feelings of guilt now as he knelt by the
corpse of the man who had treated him as a son. Never before had the self-
absorbed Yeslnik allowed such feelings to invade his consciousness. Never before had he troubled himself with empathy or guilt.

Now it hit him like a shield bash, a great jolt to his sensibilities, a shocking
intrusion into the bubble that was his private domain, and it carried with it a
rush of emotion the man had never before felt, a great wave of regret, as if his
whole life had been a meaningless thing.

He fell over Laird Delaval, weeping. He grabbed his uncle's hands and
squeezed the cold flesh. Delaval's robe opened enough for him to see the wound,
still torn open, for in cleaning the man the dried blood had been washed away.

Howling, Yeslnik slapped his hand over the open gash and then pulled it away with a start and a yelp. He stared at his hand in horror, seeing a cut on his palm, his own blood dripping from the wound.

"It is the sword tip, my laird," explained one of the attendants, rushing over with a cloth.

Yeslnik's eyes went wide with shock. "You left it in him?"

The attendant colored. "It is customary to disturb the body as little as possi—"

"You left it in him?" Yeslnik repeated, standing up tall. "The sword that killed him? Take it out! Take it out this moment!"

"My laird," said Pendigrast, the father of Chapel Delaval.

"Take it out!" Yeslnik yelled at him, pointing at the ugly wound.

Pendigrast glanced around nervously. "This is hardly the time, my—"

"Now!" Yeslnik demanded and stamped his foot. "Now! Now! Now! Take it out of him! Now!"

Pendigrast saw the horrified expressions worn by the people still in the room. The father of Chapel Pellinor moved hastily but awkwardly to the body of his fallen laird. He looked around again, his gaze settling on the still-fuming Yeslnik, and then he focused on the wound, working his fingers to widen the gap in the torn skin. He felt like he was pulling against tough leather, but he managed to wriggle his hand inside enough to grasp the back edge of the broken weapon.

He started to pull, but it would not come free. Sweating now, Father Pendigrast glanced anxiously up at Prince Yeslnik again. The man stood resolute and unblinking.

Father Pendigrast took a deep breath and moved his hand in more forcefully to get a stronger grip on the blade. Understanding now the stubbornness of the unyielding flesh and bone, he pulled with all of his considerable strength.

A sickly, crackling sound accompanied the slide of the blade. Pendigrast grimaced, as did everyone in the room, with more than one in attendance giving a horrified gasp. But the monk didn't relent. An edge of the jagged blade cut him, but he continued to pull the item forth.

Finally he freed it and moved quickly to use his voluminous sleeve to try to mitigate the mess on Laird Delaval's chest. He turned at the sound of Yeslnik's approach, showing the obstinate prince the blade as he did.

The slightly curving, etched, and decorated blade.

Prince Yeslnik's eyes went wide and he found himself gasping for breath, his eyes locked on the bloody spectacle. Misreading him, Father Pendigrast moved the blade away, or started to, but Yeslnik reached out and grabbed him by the arm, holding it fast. Ignoring his own wound, an action which in and of itself would have astounded anyone who knew the oft-whimpering man, Yeslnik grabbed the blade, taking it from the surprised father's grasp.

Yeslnik held it up before his astounded eyes. He wiped it fast on Pendigrast's sleeve then held it up again to study it, his expression dumbfounded.

"What is it, my prince?" Pendigrast asked.

"I . . . I know this blade," whispered Yeslnik, twice the victim of the man called the Highwayman.

Castle Pryd loomed above the tree line behind them. They had been pushed back to the very edges of their town, their backs literally to the walls of their outlying farms.

One after another, the defenders of Pryd glanced back at that keep, their last refuge, and it seemed to offer little hope against the ferocity of the advancing men of Ethelbert dos Entel.

And on the southerners came, roaring in anticipation of victory, charging across the snow-covered field with abandon. A few stray arrows and spears reached at them but proved inconsequential and did nothing to slow them.

A group of defenders took a position at the corral rail up on a bluff. "Hold that spot at all costs!" they had been ordered by the field commander, who had then promptly retreated past the farmhouse and across the back field.

Grim-faced, knuckles white as they gripped their weapons, the proud and battle-seasoned warriors of Pryd Town intended to do just that. This would be their glorious stand to turn the tide against the surprising and ferocious charge of Ethelbert.

The first force came against them, a disorganized mob of Ethelbert's leading line, seemingly oblivious to the defenders crouched behind the bluff. They came on almost casually right to the fence.

Up jumped the defenders, spears stabbing wildly, and behind them came a cheer from the men of Pryd Town. In a day of constant retreat, these warriors had held; the men of Ethelbert scrambled away or fell bleeding to the mud and snow.

Before those retreating few had even crossed the field, however, Ethelbert's main line came out of the trees across the way. Now with the defenders' position clearly defined, the attackers gathered in a tight group in the center and sent out lines to flank, left and right.

Without delay, they came on.

The defenders of Pryd Town kept glancing left and right, kept looking for support, for if the invaders passed their position, where might they flee?

Many broke and ran. Those others who stood their ground held for only a few moments as the full weight of Ethelbert's center came against them, pressing and stabbing and slashing. The attackers dislodged the rails and tossed them aside, then pressed over the bluff, driving the valiant defenders of Pryd under the sheer weight of their numbers. Splashing through mud and blood, they came on.

Across the back field the next line of Pryd defenders looked on in dismay, knowing that they were next.

"Fight them from the trees!" the field commander yelled, though neither he nor the men he led were sure of what that meant. They had few range weapons, few arrows and spears, remaining.

On came Ethelbert's hundreds, seeing the tower of Pryd before them, not so far, seeing victory, not so far.

The men of Pryd Town broke ranks and ran.

The men of Ethelbert shouted all the more eagerly and ran ahead even faster.

"Where is Bannagran?" one fleeing defender cried. "Will the Bear of Honce come to our aid?"

"Where is Laird Yeslnik? He has deserted us with his army and now we are doomed!" cried another. Many of those in full retreat made it to the road and turned fast for Pryd Town with men coming from the trees along either side, scrambling and stumbling, terror clearly stamped upon their faces.

Ahead of them all, the shouting started in the town. Alarm and confusion echoed from the walls, followed by shrieks of surprise.

Among those retreating along the road arose fears that Ethelbert had a second force pressing Pryd from the north. What else could incite such commotion in the town so far ahead of the retreat?

What else, indeed.

Out of the gates of Pryd Town, he came, dressed all in bejeweled bronze armor and driving the chariot of Prydae, a cart of war not seen since the former laird's demise. A rack of spears beside him, his legendary great axe waving high above his head, Bannagran came on in splendor, unafraid, eager for battle. Behind him surged the rest of Pryd's garrison, some on chariot, most just running and waving pitchforks and clubs, rallying to the call of Bannagran.

Those on the road parted as he neared, for he showed no sign of slowing. "Charge ahead!" he cried, his voice strong and resonant. This man, so long the hero of Pryd, the champion of its lairds, shamed those who would flee before Ethelbert.

The road behind him crowded with soldiers, now running back to the south, back toward Ethelbert's approach. All along the sides, among the fields and the trees, cheers went up for the Bear of Honce. "Charge! Charge!" replaced the fearful "Run away!"

Bannagran rushed in front of it all and showed no sign of slowing the fabulous chariot and his mighty team. Ethelbert's leading line loomed before him now, but he didn't make any move to veer or halt. To those before him, he seemed in the grip of suicidal glee, but to those behind him, he appeared as the heart of Pryd, the champion, the warrior.

Ethelbert's men in Bannagran's path set their spears for his charge, digging them in to skewer the team.

But Bannagran dropped his axe to the flooring beside him and took up a spear, veering his team as he neared and letting fly one missile after another. As one man fell mortally wounded and a second lurched aside, Bannagran turned the chariot back in line and plowed ahead. For now the integrity of the block was gone, and now the armored team and the spike-wheeled chariot crashed through, scattering men. Another spear flew from the driver, another of Ethelbert's men spiraled down to the ground in agony.

Bannagran had his axe in hand in a flash and chopped across to drop another man, then stabbed its pointed tip back to fell yet another. He turned his chariot, rambling right off the road, crashing through brush and men alike, the horses trampling everything in their path.

So great was the spectacle that few of Ethelbert's men remained focused on that which followed Bannagran, the weight of Pryd's garrison charging with renewed hope and eagerness.

The chariot crashed through a thicket and nearly broke apart as the wheels caught on some roots. Never slowing in the least, Bannagran merely leaped from the cart, great axe in one hand, spear in the other. He rushed at a group of ten men and noted which was giving the orders. That commander fell, Bannagran's spear deep in his chest.

In leaped the wild warrior, his axe slashing with great and powerful strokes. No man would stand against him; his roars stole their strength, his axe sheared their limbs and crushed their bones and let their blood. He ran back toward the road, calling for his men to rally behind him, cutting down enemies with every step, it seemed.

The center of Ethelbert's line collapsed; the men of Pryd, working in a wedge formation with Bannagran at their tip, pressed through, widening the breach, splitting Ethelbert's forces asunder.

Bannagran kept looking for their leaders, kept listening for their commanders. Whenever he spied one, he rushed that way, cutting his path to the man. Enemies struck at him from the side but from afar, throwing stones or knives or small spears, with none daring approach the man, the possessed and crazed warrior.

A dozen wounds marked Bannagran's body, but if he felt any of them he didn't show it. Every hit of stone or knife seemed to spur him on further, more furiously, as if the pain was only granting him greater, almost supernatural strength.

And the spectacle of Bannagran, the great Bear of Honce, commanded too much attention of the men of Ethelbert, allowing the charging forces of Pryd to cut deeper, to gain more strength and momentum.

It was Ethelbert's line that broke that day, the old laird and his forces retreating fast to the south.

Ethelbert knew his folly as he fled. He should have waited for Affwin Wi and the others to return to him before making his move against Pryd Town. He should have had some counter to the strength of this demon warrior from Pryd, a man he had seen in battle a decade before. He had gambled to gain the center and strengthen his hold, and he had lost, but he was not forlorn as he and his forces regrouped that night, several miles south of Pryd Town, with no intention of turning back to the north.

For his greatest foe, Laird Delaval, this man who would be king, was dead.

CHAPTER 7

Abelle's Win

Silent as the shadow he crossed, Jameston Sequin moved along the line of pines, circumventing the drifts of snow with practiced ease. He knew this place, this tended grove, and knew, too, that he was likely being watched. He knew the watcher, though, and had come to see that very man.

Still, he kept his caution and covert manner, unsure of who might be gathered around the one he expected was more than aware of his presence.

A large raven flopped onto the branch of a nearby pine, looked right at him, and cawed loudly.

Jameston straightened and stared at the bird, smiling knowingly.

The bird hopped down and before it ever landed on the ground transformed suddenly and with a bright flash of light into an old man, bald and with a beard braided by clumps of dung, dressed in light green robes, a heavy fur cloak, and open-toed sandals. Only a Samhaist priest could keep his feet from freezing to black with those feeble shoes.

"One day I'll catch you unaware," Jameston said to the man.

"Or I'll grow tired of your trying," the Samhaist replied, but Jameston knew it to be a good-natured threat. Despite all their differences, despite Jameston siding with Gwydre against the troll and goblin hordes of Badden, despite Jameston's obvious disdain for the Samhaist religion, Wisterwhig was not an enemy. Not a friend, perhaps, but not an enemy.

"So, Badden's gone," Jameston said.

"Killed by Dame Gwydre," Wisterwhig replied. "And by his own arrogance."

Jameston raised a bushy gray eyebrow at that startling admission, to which Wisterwhig merely shrugged.

"He did find Mithranidoon, and that is no small thing, of course," the Samhaist said.

"You disagreed with his war?"

Again Wisterwhig, a man Jameston found quite reasonable compared with most of his Samhaist brethren, merely shrugged and then said, "It was not my place to agree or disagree. I do not remember Badden ever asking my opinion."

Jameston snorted. "I love the hierarchy of learned men."

"Spare me your incessant sarcasm, scout," said Wisterwhig. "You come on behalf of Gwydre, I expect."

"Indirectly," Jameston admitted. "As much for my own curiosity as for her needs. There's less activity now. I've seen no sign of goblins or trolls moving south."

"Winter is on in full force in the northland," said Wisterwhig dismissively.

"They fought through the winter last year," Jameston reminded. "Ice trolls favor that season."

The old Samhaist made no move to respond.

"Winter favors them in battle, but your folk aren't sending them to Vanguard," said Jameston.

"If you have all the answers, why do you bother me, scout?"

Jameston leaned back and grinned. "I have all the suspicions. I'm looking for the answers."

"You ask that I would ease Gwydre's mind?"

"Ease the minds of lots of folk," Jameston replied.

"You presume that I have a responsibility to people who have turned their backs on the old gods."

"No," Jameston answered slowly, measuring his words. "I just think you're a decent enough fellow despite those robes you wear."

Wisterwhig laughed. "You're quite wise for an idiot, yes?" he said, imitating Jameston's even tone. Jameston laughed with him. "Or quite the decent murderer, don't you think?"

"I've never hid my feelings for your church or th'other one."

"You have never hidden your feelings on any matter," said Wisterwhig. "Which is why I tolerate you."

"Just tolerate? Should I be insulted?"

"We could banter like this all the day, I fear."

"We have before."

Wisterwhig surrendered with an upraised hand. "I am glad the war is over," he admitted, a startling revelation to be sure.

"Is it?"

"You will not take my word to Dame Gwydre," the Samhaist said.

"I can tell her enough without it," Jameston agreed. "But I'm glad to hear it."

Wisterwhig's nod showed that they had a mutual understanding and agreement here.

"Who'll be the next ancient?" Jameston asked, grinning widely, for he knew that he wouldn't get much of an answer to that one. "Wisterwhig?"

"That is for the old gods to decide."

"And will the one they name then start the war anew?"

"You speak of something a decade removed," answered the Samhaist. "We are not as impatient as the brothers of Abelle. The successor will not be named this year, possibly not even next year, and, after that, he will have many months of work ahead of him in just informing the groves and calling in his disciples."

"You surrender Vanguard to the monks?"

"Not so," said Wisterwhig. "We know that the brothers of Abelle will fail in the end. Their baubles are impressive until the deathbed, and there they have no answers. Just empty promises. Those who follow them pass on unprepared for the judgment of the old gods."

"And those dead ones will come back and discredit the monks?" was Jameston's sarcastic response.

"The ghosts speak to us. To all. In the end, we Samhaists, not the monks, hold the answers most needed. If I did not have faith in that I would not wear these robes."

Jameston conceded the point with a nod.

"Patience," Wisterwhig added. "It is a necessary virtue and one, perhaps, that Badden lost in his last years. Events prompted change in Vanguard, and he wished that errant course corrected before his passing. We do not consider our ancient to be the sole proprietor of godly wisdom, scout. You know that much, at least."

"So, many disagreed with Badden's war?"

"Or thought it an unnecessary provocation. In the end we will win, and we'll need not enlist goblins and trolls and powries and barbarians to achieve the victory. Because we are right, scout—because our gods are true—we will win."

Jameston had been kidding earlier when he had asked if Wisterwhig, not a leading member of his religion by any means, might be named as the next ancient, but truly, Jameston wished that a possibility.

This Samhaist priest, at least, was reasonable and decent enough.

The scout's step as he left Wisterwhig's grove was much lighter than the footfalls that had brought him to this place. Jameston never feared a good fight and was always happy to kill a goblin or a troll, but he knew that the folk of Vanguard had suffered far too much already.

The weather here was trying enough without adding the burdens of a war.

Dawson McKeege tried to stay seated, but he couldn't manage it. He kept getting up and pacing around the thick carpet, his eyes scanning the closed door at the side of the room. He knew what was going on in there. Gwydre had asked him to stay with her this evening because she had discerned the tone of Brother Alandrais when he had arrived earlier that day, and Dawson trusted her instincts implicitly.

"Come on, then," he whispered, eyeing the door. He glanced across to a cabinet on the other side of the room where an hourglass drained away; he had upended it almost immediately after his friend had gone to meet privately with Brother Alandrais. She'd been in there nearly a full hour.

Dawson licked his lips. Perhaps things weren't going quite so bad?

The man straightened as the door opened and Dame Gwydre came through. One look at her told McKeege that his hopes for some reconciliation had been in vain.

She stared into his eyes, her face very tight, and she nodded curtly, as if giving any further movement would cause her to dissolve.

Like telling someone when a loved one had passed, Dawson thought. "He's a fool, then," the crusty old sailor said.

Dame Gwydre walked past him and patted him on the shoulder as she moved to sit stiffly on the divan, eyes unseeing. Dawson was quick to her side.

"For the best," he said, putting his arm about her. He was the only man in the world who might tell Gwydre that, he realized.

Gwydre was glad of it at that moment. She slumped at long last and put her head on his shoulder, turning to bury her face in his shirt, her shoulders bobbing with sobs. After just a few brief moments she composed herself and sat back up straight, sniffling away the tears. Then she gave a cleansing sigh and even managed a little laugh at herself as she wiped the moisture from her eyes.

"It's for the best," Dawson repeated without thought. As soon as the words left his mouth he heard them as incredibly inane.

But Gwydre just laughed and nodded. "I would have ended our love affair if he had not," she said. "It was too much trouble now."

"Now that the war's looking to be over, and ain't that the irony?"

Gwydre frowned. "With Ancient Badden looming, I had no time for quibbles with the brothers of Abelle. Now that Badden is gone, I expect that I and the church will face some trying moments of disagreement."

"Alandrais wasn't man enough to keep them separate," Dawson accused.

"He'd've kept jumping in at you whenever you took a stand against his masters. As with De Guilbe."

Gwydre nodded. "All true."

"If he loved you—" Dawson started, but Gwydre put her hand up to stop that line of thinking short.

"Once, he did love me," she said. "And I loved him. It was not convenience that brought us together. Indeed, at the time we started this relationship I thought it the least convenient thing in all the world."

"But did he?"

Gwydre eyed Dawson curiously.

"I mean, there's no doubt the brothers of Abelle gained greatly through the relationship," Dawson clarified. "Their fight with the Samhaists added a powerful ally because of Brother Alandrais's loins."

"Dawson!"

The sailor shrugged but didn't retract.

"I would not have sided with the Samhaists in any event, and that much was clear before Alandrais and I fell in love," Gwydre insisted. "As their grip on southern Honce eroded, Ancient Badden grew ever more demanding and desperate and vicious."

"Aye, I know," Dawson admitted. "And Alandrais loved you. I know that, too, though I'm wanting to punch the fool in the nose right now."

"You can't blame him for . . . this," said Gwydre. She reached up and stroked her friend's grizzled face. "It's been a long time in coming, and it is for the best."

"Still would feel good to punch him."

Gwydre managed another laugh. She pulled herself to her feet and began to pace in much the same manner as Dawson had earlier. "I am quite the fool," she muttered. "To get involved with a monk at a time such as this—nay, to get involved with a monk at all! Oh, what pain have I brought upon my people? I have betrayed their trust for the sake of my own selfish needs."

"You betrayed nothing!" Dawson shouted and leaped from the couch. "'Twas Badden who betrayed you, who betrayed us all. He held Vanguard hostage to protect his losses in the south. He demanded of us—of you—that which you could not do! Were you to deny the folk the blessings of the monks' gemstones? Were you to let the sick and injured die because Badden didn't want the monks praying over them with the soul stones?"

"The situation wasn't so bad before my tryst with Alandrais."

"Before the war in the south turned the folk of Honce away from the Samhaists, you mean. Wasn't about you and wasn't about your monk lover. Badden's desperation came from knowing that his priests were being chased from half the holdings of Honce, and even where they stayed in their groves, the lairds weren't listening to them. Delaval and Ethelbert have the whole of Honce in flames, and the folk're suffering. In that suffering they've turned to the brothers of Abelle and their gemstones and away from the Samhaists."

Gwydre considered the reasonable rebuttal for a few long moments, then nodded and smiled her gratitude at this man, her friend Dawson. Dawson took his leave and went back to his own rooms, pleased that he had been able to help his friend through her trying night, for surely Dame Gwydre was as a beloved sister to the old sailor, a woman he would gladly die defending.

Dame Gwydre continued to pace the room long after Dawson had gone. She did feel much better than when she had walked out of her meeting with Alandrais. Dawson was a valuable friend to her, unafraid to speak to her as a friend and not as his liege lady.

Truly he was a shining gem to Gwydre. He kept her grounded, kept her humble, and she knew that his love for her was unconditional, that if she were thrown down the next day from her position of authority and cast penniless into the street, Dawson McKeege would treat her no differently and no less affably.

Some of his honesty that night had stung, though, she had to admit. She didn't think that Dawson had mentioned the gains her tryst had brought to the brothers of Abelle simply to make her feel better. There was a ring of truth in his claim.

Too much, she decided, and so, instead of going into her private chambers to don her bedclothes, Gwydre, Dame of Vanguard, went into the cold winter night.

The brothers of Chapel Pellinor had just finished their evening prayers when she arrived at their door. Father Premujon did not deny her request for an audience. Nor did he say anything when she entered the room and told his attendants, who included Father De Guilbe, to leave them.

"May I help you, Lady?" Premujon said when they were alone. "This is most unusual."

"I was visited by one of your brothers this night," she said.

"I see," Premujon mused. "And who—"

"I'll not speak around it," Gwydre said. "You know well of my relationship with Brother Alandrais, and you know by now that the relationship ended this night."

"Dame Gwydre, I am not—"

"Father," she prompted in an exasperated tone.

The man sighed in surrender. "I know. Of course, I know."

"As you knew of it when it commenced."

The father tilted his head and eyed her curiously.

"Before it commenced, perhaps?" she asked slyly.

"Now how would I have known that?"

"Because you blessed Brother Alandrais's decision, this night and those months ago when first we began our relationship."

Father Premujon sat back very straight, as if he had been slapped. "Good Lady, what do you imply? Do you believe that I sent Brother Alandrais to your bed?"

"Our relationship benefited Chapel Pellinor greatly."

Father Premujon considered that for a moment and conceded the fact with a nod. "Indeed, you were a mighty ally in our struggles with Badden's Samhaists, but I expect that you would have supported us over him in any case."

"A cool war of words and not a fighting battle."

"True enough," said Premujon. "So now you fear that I orchestrated your relationship with Brother Alandrais, that I sent him to you hoping you would fall in love for the sake of Chapel Pellinor?"

Gwydre didn't answer the charge.

"I did not," Premujon stated flatly. "When Brother Alandrais became smitten with Dame Gwydre, he came to me and confessed in full, and he was a man in terrible conflict. He understood the implications of any advances he might make, both for the church and for his continuing role in the order. What would you have had me say to him, Dame? Generally, my order frowns on such relationships, of course, but we often make exceptions, or merely let the situation quietly run its course."

"Quietly?" Gwydre asked sarcastically.

"Such situations do not usually involve a laird or a dame," came the dry reply.

"And in this case?" Gwydre asked. "Which course did Father Premujon prefer?"

"That you and Brother Alandrais would find love, and that such love would bring benefit to Chapel Pellinor and help us rid the land of the vile Samhaists," the man admitted without hesitation.

Dame Gwydre fell back a step, surprised by his forthrightness.

"What would you have me say?" the Father of Chapel Pellinor asked. "What would you have had me do? I saw the gain to my order, to be sure, and did not dissuade such a beneficial outcome." He rose from his seat and walked over to Gwydre, placing a hand on each of her shoulders and looking her straight in the eye. "But milady, good Dame Gwydre, not I nor any of my surrogates sent Brother Alandrais to court you. In no way. We simply decided not to interfere with nature's course. And now, this evening, no one here bade Brother Alandrais to bring an end to your relationship."

Dame Gwydre didn't doubt him. Somehow, the truth he had just spoken hurt her and comforted her all at once. Her love affair with Alandrais had been real. Of course, that meant that the end of that love was real, as well.

Gwydre reached up with her right hand and pulled Premujon's hand from her shoulder, grasping it tightly. "It is my friendship and trust with you that placed me on the side of your order against Badden's Samhaists, you know. My love for Brother Alandrais did not determine my actions."

"But it spurred many of Badden's," the monk replied. "To the great benefit of Vanguard in the end."

Gwydre nodded. "Thank you," she said softly and took her leave.

She spent a long night thinking of her many days with Alandrais, days in the sun and in the snow. She laughed and she cried that night; she let the light and the darkness have their play in her emotions.

For the next morning, Dame Gwydre had to let it all go, had to be again the leader of her people in a time that was far from settled and far from safe.

CHAPTER 8

Writ and Rebuttal

"The nearest Samhaist's grove is empty, they say," Cadayle said to her mother, Callen Duwornay.

"How would they know, for who would go?" Callen replied.

"They went before the snows," Cadayle insisted, struggling to bite back the desperation she heard in her own voice.

"So before the snows the Samhaist went away."

"And he hasn't returned."

"They're not knowing that," said Callen.

"They're whispering that the war is over."

Callen moved a step away from the blazing hearth. "Every hope to hang on," she said, a common criticism she had thrown her daughter's way these last few weeks. Bransen had been taken from Cadayle to go and fight in Gwydre's war, and each passing day had weighed more heavily on the poor young woman's mind.

She knew that her mother was only looking out for her with her constant words of caution, and she knew, too, that all the people in this new town, Tanadoon, were hanging desperately onto any bit of hopeful information. They were all refugees here, all displaced from a place they had once called home, and all with family serving in Gwydre's army against the terrifying onslaught of the monstrous minions of Ancient Badden.

A few weeks before, word had gone out that the local Samhaist had deserted his grove, and the people of Tanadoon had taken it as a sign that the war had ended. But new reports of goblin or troll incursions had continued to surface; the war had rolled along. Three of the families in Tanadoon had lost loved ones soon after the initial reports of the deserted grove had begun to raise the hopes.

But over the last three weeks, the reports of battle had slowed to a stop, and no news of further tragic losses had been delivered to Tanadoon. That lull had added life to the excited whispers that maybe, just maybe, the tide had turned.

"There's been no smoke over the grove," Cadayle said. "In the cold, even a Samhaist would need a fire."

"So it might be that he's not there," said Callen. "Might be that he's dead, and you won't ever see Callen Duwornay crying over the death of a Samhaist!"

"They're whispering that the war's over," Cadayle dared again.

"They've been whispering that since we got here," said Callen. "And we're all wanting it so bad that we're listening to every word."

"I miss him," Cadayle said, her voice barely a whisper. She brushed back her long, wheat-colored hair, showing more clearly the redness and moisture rimming her large brown eyes, so much like her mother's. "More and more each day. I know he'll come home to me, but I fear he's lying dead on a snowy field. And then I feel as if I'm betraying my love for doubting him! I don't know—"

"I do," Callen interrupted. "I know that what you're feeling is what I'm feeling. Don't you doubt that I love that husband of yours—he saved my life as his mother and father saved my life. And yours. Keep your faith in him. Bransen has overcome greater trials than most men, and it will take more than a goblin to kill him."

Cadayle managed a smile at that, and a nod, and she turned from her mother to the cabin door, thinking to go out and retrieve more wood for the fire. She pulled her meager shawl about her as she went through the front door into the driving storm, her mother's scolding voice echoing in her ears. For weeks, Callen had been telling Cadayle that she needed to eat more, to put some fat on her body for the coming winter. But Cadayle hadn't found her appetite in a long while and had lost quite a bit of weight since Bransen had departed. She went to the wood pile on the side of her porch and bent to retrieve some, but as soon as she reached for the logs a gust of wind flapped the shawl back over her shoulder. She instinctively went to grab at the flap but froze in fear, feeling another hand at the shawl's edge, pulling it back over her shoulder.

"A woman, poorly dressed and vulnerable," came a whisper behind her in tones suggestive and even lewd.

Cadayle felt her heart pounding, felt her pulse thrumming in her temples. She considered grabbing a log and spinning about to thump the intruder across the head. She considered screaming, or running away.

Callen shouted for her, though, and the cry "Bransen!" almost sent the overwhelmed Cadayle spinning to the ground.

But the hand on her shoulder clasped more tightly and spun her about—spun her to face her husband, standing right behind her, grinning like a happy fool.

The most beautiful fool Cadayle had ever seen. She threw herself upon him, squeezing him to her and kissing him all over his face. She felt the moisture of her tears on her cheeks, felt as if her head would simply explode from excitement and joy.

Callen ran onto the porch and joined in the hug. Bransen extended an arm to bring her in closer and to loop his cape over her against the freezing wind.

"How? When?" Cadayle stammered, but Bransen hushed her by putting a finger over her lips, and he ushered both of the women back inside. He went out and retrieved a few logs, then came back in and closed the door tightly.

As soon as he placed the kindling down on the hearth, Cadayle wrapped him in another crushing hug. "Tell me that you're home," she whispered in his ear. "That you're really home. That your days in the war—"

"Are over," Bransen confirmed. Cadayle sobbed with joy and hugged him even tighter. Back in her seat at the side of the hearth, Callen put a hand over her mouth, her cheeks streaked with happy tears.

"I killed him," Bransen said simply, pushing Cadayle back to arm's length, and looking at both women as he explained. "Dame Gwydre knew that to win meant to cut off the head of the serpent. I did that. I killed Ancient Badden, who led the Samhaists, who sent the hordes against Vanguard. He is dead by my hand, and there is hope throughout Pellinor that the war is dead with him."

"Hope, but we do not know," Cadayle said with some obvious doubt.

"It is over for me," Bransen said. "By Gwydre's own word." He reached to his belt and pulled forth a rolled parchment. "She told me to kill Badden for the reward of my freedom to go wherever I would go with her Writ of Passage in hand."

Cadayle looked at him, confused, then turned to Callen, who now had two hands over her mouth, as if afraid to make a sound and disturb these wonderful developments.

"We are free, all crimes forgiven," Bransen said calmly when Cadayle turned back to him. "We can go wherever we want."

Cadayle grabbed him again, one hand on either side of his face as she locked his gaze with her own. "Do not ever leave me again," she said with intensity that widened Bransen's eyes in surprise. "Promise me that you won't ever leave me again."

"I won't—" Bransen started to say, but, surprisingly, Callen cut him off.

"Don't make promises you cannot keep!"

"The war in Vanguard is no longer my affair," he said evenly. "I am done here. I am done with war. I am done with running from guards. We'll find peace now. We'll live in peace, we three. I am at peace and in love," he said directly to Cadayle, now reaching up to similarly place his hands on her soft face. "And happy with you beside me. The fighting is done."

Cadayle could hardly keep her eyes open, so overjoyed was she with that proclamation. She didn't resist when Bransen pulled her closer for another, deeper kiss, and at that moment, both of them felt as if everything in all the world was right.

I have scrubbed it and scrubbed it, and still I cannot remove all the blood-stains," Yeslnik said with disgust. He held up the broken blade for Banna-gran to view. "But enough so that we know this blade."

"It looks like the Highwayman's," Bannagran admitted, slurring his words just a bit, for the side of his face was still swollen from a well-aimed and well-thrown rock during his daring and heroic charge that had sent Ethelbert fleeing.

"It is the Highwayman's!" Yeslnik declared, and he ended with a strange sound that seemed a cross between a growl and a whimper and threw the sword blade to the floor. "I knew that beast would prove nothing but ill to Honce! I implored my uncle to hunt him down and kill him."

Bannagran rubbed his face, fearing where this might be going.

"Oh, would that he had never been allowed to walk out of Pryd Town!" Yeslnik yelled. "With Laird Pryd's blood on his hands!"

"It is not as simple as that," Bannagran dared say.

"Isn't it?"

"No," said the champion of Pryd, the man who, indeed, could have exe-cuted the Highwayman quite legally. He chuckled helplessly as he thought back to that terrible time after the fall of his dear friend. The people of Pryd had verged on revolt; if Bannagran had not banished the Highwayman and had executed him instead, the streets of Pryd Town would have run red with blood.

Yeslnik growled again and shook his head forcefully, as if throwing all this turmoil to the side. "You have redeemed yourself in any case."

Bannagran bowed.

"I am the Laird of Delaval now," said Yeslnik, "and the King of Honce. All the holdings will accept that as soon as we are rid of the troublesome Ethelbert. He is on the run to the south—in no small part because of the exploits of Ban-nagran the hero, the Bear of Honce, I am told. You do smell like a bear, I am sure." He gave a little derisive snort and chuckle.

"Laird Ethelbert backed us into a corner with his bold attack," Bannagran explained, ignoring the insult and reminding himself that if Prince Yeslnik had ever actually been close enough to a bear to smell it, he would have then smelled of his own piss. "Truly, I did not expect that he would move so decisively."

"But you turned him, broke his line and sent him fleeing."

"We had no choice in the matter. Charge and win, or die. We chose to fight."

"No, Bannagran chose to fight, and his choice dragged along the men of Pryd and those Delaval soldiers I left behind," said Yeslnik. "That is the essence of a leader, and I intend to reward it."

"As you will, my king."

"I will name you Laird of Pryd," said Yeslnik. "No more the steward, but the laird, who will pass the ownership and title down to his own children."

"I have none."

"Then make some, dolt!" Yeslnik retorted. "Or name a nephew as an heir, as did—as wisely did—King Delaval. I will see this done, as soon as we attend to pressing needs."

"To finish off Ethelbert," Bannagran reasoned.

"I will see to that. I have sent emissaries to Laird Panlamaris and his cowardly son Milwellis to dispatch his forces to the east and then south along the inner coast."

Bannagran wisely hid his wince at the adjective Yeslnik had attached to Milwellis. To hear the foppish pretend warrior calling Milwellis a coward strained credulity to be sure!

"I doubt that any will stand against them, but neither shall Ethelbert find his escape in that direction. We will push him right back to his city on the sea this time, and there will be no escape. The lairds of the Mantis Arm will join with me now. Their ships will blockade Ethelbert. There will be no escape, and I will push the imbecile right into the Mirianic!"

"The men of Pryd will march with you, my lai . . ." Bannagran paused, somewhat confused at how to properly address Yeslnik now.

"King," Yeslnik insisted. "The coronation is a mere formality. Honce is mine."

"My king," Bannagran finished.

"And Pryd is yours, Laird Bannagran," he said. Bannagran bowed. "The men of Pryd will march with me indeed. But not all of them. Not Bannagran, the new Laird of Pryd."

The Bear of Honce looked at him curiously.

King Yeslnik bent and retrieved the broken sword, then handed it to Bannagran. "Find him," he ordered. "Find the Highwayman, Bannagran of Pryd. Find him and kill him. You can serve your king no better way than to serve me the Highwayman's head on a banquet tray. Do that, and Pryd Holding is yours and your family's forevermore, with borders we will expand."

Bannagran eyed the sword more closely, remembering when he had done battle against the man who wielded this very blade.

"Find him and kill him," King Yeslnik said again.

The Bear of Honce, champion of Pryd, nodded.

CHAPTER 9

Stubbornly Entrenched

There is talk that he will be put in line as heir to the lairdship of Vanguard!" Father De Guilbe shouted and waved his arms frantically.

Father Premujon sighed and shook his head. "Cormack is not even of Vanguard. Dame Gwydre would do no such thing as that."

"I heard it!" De Guilbe protested. "Do you deny that he has been named a hero of the holding?"

"All who participated in the battle with Ancient Badden have so been named," remarked Brother Jond, sitting on a bench at the side of the hall. "Except the powries, of course. Dame Gwydre made up some other title for them, one that carries no consequence."

"And you agree with the bestowment?" asked De Guilbe.

"For the powries?"

"For Cormack!" De Guilbe shouted.

Poor Brother Jond appeared uncertain. "Speak freely," Father Premujon coaxed him.

"Why, yes, I do," Jond blurted, with such enthusiasm that those who knew him, Premujon included and perhaps most of all, then realized that his tentativeness had been designed to elicit exactly this explicit permission from his Father Premujon. "Of course I do."

"He betrayed your brethren!" said De Guilbe, and he even took a step toward Jond before Brother Giavno caught him by the arm.

"Dame Gwydre is not of our order and does not answer to us," Jond explained. "Her titles are secular alone. Despite your hatred for the man, you cannot deny that he bravely battled Ancient Badden. Had it not been for him, it is unlikely that Badden would have been overcome—and his fall is to the benefit of us all."

"And if Cormack becomes Laird of Vanguard?" De Guilbe asked. "What then for Chapel Pellinor and the Order of Blessed Abelle in his Vanguard?"

Father Premujon just shook his head at the ridiculousness of the premise.

"I bid you, Father, for your own sake, to search this hatred you hold for this man, Cormack," Brother Jond dared to say, drawing more than a few gasps from around the room. "I have known him but a short time, true, but his character seemed to me in alignment with the precepts of the order."

"Brother!" more than one voice shouted, loudest of all, that of Father Premujon.

But somehow, Brother Jond seemed above them all at that moment, as if he held some insight they could not share, as if the badges of honor he wore—the one from Gwydre's recognition and, more importantly, the garish scar across his face—allowed him to speak truth to power with impunity.

"He betrayed the Blessed Abelle to the barbarians!" De Guilbe roared.

"Did he?" Brother Jond's question, asked so innocently, took the steam from the large man. "Or was it Father De Guilbe, frustrated after years of wandering the terrible environ of Alpinador, who clung to stubbornness beyond all reason and morality?"

"I will not be spoken to in such a manner by a brother!" Father De Guilbe shouted at Father Premujon.

"Enough, Brother Jond!" Premujon said sharply.

The blind monk settled back on the bench, seeming quite pleased with himself.

"I will not have this," De Guilbe continued. "You will punish this brother severely. And I will have Cormack punished, as well."

"He is in Dame Gwydre's charge," Father Premujon reminded.

"Then demand of the Dame," said De Guilbe. "Cormack parades around in a powrie cap, arm-in-arm with a shaman of Alpinador. He mocks us openly and with impunity. You cannot allow this to stand. His mere presence will erode support for us here in Vanguard and will diminish respect for Blessed Abelle."

"It was Father De Guilbe who demanded of Cormack that he always wear the cap," Brother Jond remarked.

Father Premujon motioned to a pair of younger brothers to take the blind troublemaker out of the chapel.

"And she is a most lovely woman, this Milkeila of Yan Ossum," Brother Jond said as the brothers helped him to his feet and began escorting him from the room. "Calm in temperament, generous in heart, and fierce in battle. I need not see with my eyes to know that she is most beautiful."

"Brother, go in peace," Father Premujon bade him, begged him.

"Our order would be enhanced greatly if we could coax her to us," Jond managed to get in before the younger monks pulled him out of the chamber.

"No more so than if we purchased a mule," Father De Guilbe muttered.

"This Milkeila is rather like a domesticated animal, don't you think? And with the appearance of one."

No one but De Guilbe himself chuckled at his joke.

"I would ask you again to exact punishment upon Cormack," De Guilbe stated flatly.

"He is not Brother Cormack any longer," Father Premujon reminded. "He is not of our order."

"He was of our order when he betrayed the emissaries of Abelle," De Guilbe replied. "He was meant to die for his treason. Only through unfortunate circumstance does he still draw breath."

"But he did not die, and so he was banished from your island," said Premujon. "Appropriately so!" the father of Chapel Pellinor added with enthusiasm to erase De Guilbe's growing scowl.

"It is different now," De Guilbe said.

"What would you have me do?"

"Take him from Gwydre to be judged by his peers. Take him in chains as a heretic."

Father Premujon looked around the room for support. He knew he was in a corner here: Father De Guilbe was no small player in the Order of Blessed Abelle and had been hand-picked by Father Artolivan, a personal friend, to lead the missionary team to Alpinador. The man's obstinacy, so clearly on display, offered little room for compromise.

And the man's power would demand of Father Premujon that he make a stand one way or the other.

He has suffered his entire life," said Master Reandu. Into his thirties now, Reandu's face showed the strain of the last couple of years. Father Jerak of Chapel Pryd had declined to a point of incoherent babbling, and Reandu had to take up the reins in these most trying times with all of the responsibilities but none of the imprimatur of the office. No small part of that burden came from the fact that Reandu's actions had led to the death of Master Bathelais, who would have succeeded Father Jerak. No action had been taken against Reandu for that confused and tumultuous fight—even Bannagran, who had been battling the man Reandu had saved, had forgiven him.

"And he suffers to this day, I am sure. Every step comes with the grimace of the pained Stork," Reandu finished.

"The Stork who killed Prydae," Bannagran reminded.

Reandu smiled knowingly, sadly. The Stork hadn't directly killed Prydae, after all, but had simply ducked Bannagran's thrown axe, which had then struck down the laird. Bannagran's anger as he spoke Bransen's nickname was rooted in deep guilt, Reandu knew, much as his own guilt over Master Bathelais gnawed at him, and that was never a good thing.

"Bransen has moments of . . . surprise, I agree," said the monk. "But you know his life story as well as any. The loss of his mother and father, of Garibond Womak . . ."

He stopped there, seeing Bannagran's eyes narrow dangerously. The fate of Womak was not a good subject to bring up around Pryd Holding. For the sake of Prydae's manhood, through some ridiculous Samhaist assertion of virility restored, the man had suffered castration. And for protecting the belongings of his friend, Stork's father, Garibond had been burned at the stake.

"He carried chamber pots—it was all he could manage," Reandu said, referring to Bransen's stay at Chapel Pryd as a servant. "He lived in a hole."

"I do not envy him his miserable existence," Bannagran interrupted. He reached to his belt and pulled forth the broken blade of a fine sword. "Do you recognize this?"

"Is that Bransen's blade?" Reandu asked.

Bannagran shrugged. "It would appear. How many like this could there be? This blade was pulled from the chest of King Delaval. How many like this one, Reandu?"

"In Behr?"

"In Honce!"

"We know that Ethelbert has many ties to Behr, where such blades—"

"Enough!" Bannagran commanded. "Our own Stork was a party to the group who murdered King Delaval. So says King Yeslnik, and so it is true."

"I know," Reandu admitted. "Yeslnik came to Chapel Pryd this morning." He paused and shook his head. "King Yeslnik?" he said with obvious disdain.

"I would remind you that your tone will hold consequences, Master Reandu," said Bannagran.

"You approve of his ascension?"

"It is not my place to approve or disapprove. It simply is. I am a subject of Pryd Holding, which is indebted to and in alliance with Delaval Holding. We threw our fealty to Laird Delaval, who proclaimed himself king, and his successor was his choice alone."

"You didn't answer my question."

"There is no answer to such a foolish question," said Bannagran. "Yeslnik is King of Honce, by Yeslnik's word. Laird Ethelbert will try to foil him, but Laird Ethelbert will fail."

"And since the King of Honce would see Bransen dead, so Bransen is condemned?" said Reandu.

"Yes."

Master Reandu took a deep breath, saddened by the decision but with no recourse.

"What do you know of his whereabouts?" Bannagran asked.

Reandu shook his head and sighed.

"Brother, I insist," said Bannagran.

"There is word that he traveled through Palmaristown, heading generally east, in the direction of Chapel Abelle. I do not know if he ever made it there, for there has been nothing more. I do not even know if he truly made it as far as Palmaristown, for that has never been confirmed by the Chapel of Precious Memories."

"When was this?"

"Months?" Reandu said with little certainty, indeed with a shrug of his shoulders. "A couple at least. Not long after his departure from Pryd Town."

Bannagran sighed, and Reandu studied him carefully. "Why do you care?" the monk asked.

"Because the king told me to care."

"You're charged with catching him and killing him," Reandu accused.

"I should have done that long ago, for the death of Laird Prydae."

"No," Reandu replied. "No, you chose wisely. The people of Pryd love you all the more for the mercy you showed . . ."

His voice trailed off as Bannagran held up his hand, begging silence.

"Bransen is not an evil man," Reandu finished.

"That is not my decision. He is complicit in the murder of the king, so he is guilty of treason against the throne. So says Yeslnik, and so it is."

Reandu started to argue, but Bannagran interrupted with finality when he growled, "It simply is."

Cadayle stiffened reflexively, her breath coming in gasps when she heard the horses rambling into town outside her door. The last time she had heard such a ruckus her husband had been taken from her.

Bransen gave her a hug and assured her that all was well. They went to the window together, where Bransen pulled the curtain aside.

They recognized Dawson McKeege immediately, riding a horse with an escort of several grim-faced soldiers and a single, empty wagon.

"To take us where we wish to go," Bransen insisted when they pulled up outside his door.

"With winter coming on strong?"

"Trust in Dame Gwydre," said Bransen. "I have her word."

Cadayle motioned toward the window then. Bransen turned to see Callen, who had gone across the road to borrow some spices, moving over to speak with Dawson, who smiled widely at the sight of her and tipped his floppy hat.

Cadayle started for the door, but Bransen held her back and bade her to watch the exchange—the undeniably pleasant exchange. Dawson hopped down from his horse and even kissed Callen's hand. Suddenly the men around him didn't seem quite so grim-faced any longer.

The young couple went onto their porch.

"Greetings!" Dawson said upon sighting them, his crooked smile still wide.

"Have you found another battle to which to drag my husband?" Cadayle asked sarcastically.

Dawson paused as if confused, then said, emphatically, "Oh, no, no, good lady. Your husband's heroics in the northland seem to have ended all that!"

"The war is truly over?" Bransen asked.

"What we're hoping, at least," Dawson replied. "No fighting, no goblins, no trolls, and no Samhaists that we can find. I'm thinking that Dame Gwydre's gamble did its work, and wouldn't that be a grand thing for all of Vanguard?"

"It would, indeed," said Bransen. He paused and considered it all for a few moments, then added uncharacteristically, "I hope it's true."

"Then why have you come?" Cadayle asked.

Dawson stepped back as if slapped.

"I mean, you came here for us, didn't you? For Bransen, at least, but it can't be time to sail the gulf."

"Oh, I wouldn't be putting my *Lady Dreamer* out now, so late in the season! Not if all the demon dactyls were chasing me!"

"But here you are, with an empty wagon."

Dawson laughed and bowed. "Guilty, my lady," he said. "We came for you—all three with an invitation from Dame Gwydre for you to winter at Castle Pellinor."

Cadayle looked at Callen, who nodded hopefully. Then Cadayle turned her confused expression to an equally confused Bransen.

"Back to Pellinor?" he asked. "Why?"

"It is more comfortable than here, of course. You've earned that at least," Dawson answered, but Bransen knew better and shook his head in reply.

"There's trouble," Dawson admitted.

"He's done fighting for you!" Cadayle insisted.

"Not that kind of trouble," Dawson said hastily. "I weren't lying to you when I said that all was at peace, good lady. No fighting to be found and none asked of Bransen. Nay, this trouble's with the brothers of Blessed Abelle."

"A group for which I care little," said Bransen. "I put them not so far above the Samhaists, to be honest."

"Brother Jond?" Dawson asked, and Bransen perked up at that. "He calls you his friend."

"I am."

"And Cormack?"

"He's no longer of that order."

"But the order isn't letting him go so easily," Dawson explained. "Father De Guilbe is a fiery one, full of anger, anger aimed at Cormack. Cormack's been arrested."

"Father Premujon put him in chains?" Bransen asked.

"Dame Gwydre took him," said Dawson. Bransen gave a little hiss of disappointment and dismay.

"She had no choice in the matter," Dawson continued. "Father De Guilbe demanded it of Father Premujon—the big idiot De Guilbe apparently has some power in the order and with Father Artolivan, who leads them all. He put Premujon in a tight corner to be sure. Dame Gwydre had no choice but to give in to De Guilbe's demands and arrest Cormack for trial. She's got him, but rest assured he's comfortable and outside the influence of his former brothers."

"To what end?" asked Bransen. "Is he to be sentenced? He risked everything for Vanguard and fought with courage and strength. Without him Ancient Badden would have won the day and your war . . ." He stopped when he noted that Dawson was nodding with his every word.

"There are rumors that he is to be tried before both court and church," Dawson explained. "If it comes to that, it will be fair, I promise. Dame Gwydre will preside and will surely mitigate any demands of the brothers upon Cormack with her knowledge of his heroics in ending the war."

"What of Milkeila?" Bransen asked. He turned to Cadayle and reminded her, "The barbarian woman, wife of Cormack."

"She is well, and within Pellinor with Cormack. They are not ill-treated, I promise you. I came to relay all of this and to extend Dame Gwydre's invitation. I hope you will agree to join us in Pellinor. Your presence would be a great boon to your friend Cormack."

"I have already said everything on his behalf. What influence could I possibly bring to such a trial?"

Dawson glanced back at his men, and they all laughed at that.

"You still do not understand, do you?" Dawson asked. "You, who dropped the head of Ancient Badden at Dame Gwydre's feet, do not understand the power of your mere presence. You're a hero, boy! Your name is being whispered through every vale in Vanguard. To have you there, at Cormack's side, will surely carry great weight. It will bolster Gwydre's hand in this argument and diminish De Guilbe. You shame him, Highwayman, for you went where he would not, and you did what he could not. Cormack's stature rises with the Highwayman beside him. I beg you to join me. You will find Pellinor comfortable for the winter, and you will do a great favor to this man you call a friend."

Bransen turned to Cadayle, who nodded.

"My ma, too?" she asked suddenly of Dawson.

The man turned his smiling face to Callen Duwornay and gave her a playful wink. "Ah, but that I insist upon," he answered.

Callen's blush was not lost on Cadayle.

CHAPTER 10

A Church on Trial

I can go back, but it's getting cold and I'm getting old," Jameston Sequin said, starting the conversation on that note as Dame Gwydre walked into the room.

"Do you need to go back?" the woman asked.

Jameston shook his head. "It's done and over."

"You have met with Samhaists directly?"

"A couple. One, I trust. The other . . . well, he's a Samhaist, but I don't see why he'd lie to me. The stories were consistent. This was Badden's stand. He wanted to take Vanguard as his own since his order has lost southern Honce to both the warring lairds who just love those monks and their baubles."

Dame Gwydre stiffened at that comment, a curious movement. Jameston looked at her quizzically.

"The brothers of Blessed Abelle have powerful magic, you know," she said, and Jameston nodded. "They can deliver messages over far distances in a hurry, it would seem."

"I'm no expert on Abelle gemstones," Jameston admitted.

"They can," Gwydre replied. "Not an easy task, apparently, and not without danger to the courier. So they reserve this practice for the most urgent messages alone."

"Sounds like you have something important to tell me."

"Laird Delaval is dead, murdered by Laird Ethelbert," said Gwydre.

Jameston shrugged as if he hardly cared. "One of them had to go."

"But while Laird Ethelbert's assassins were killing him, Laird Delaval's men were chasing Ethelbert's army back to the south."

"They'll keep fighting without a laird leading them?"

"They've a new laird and not a promising one from what I could discern. The war rages, escalates even."

"Idiots," Jameston muttered.

"Beyond all reason, Father Premujon told me. This war is to the death."

"Oh, it is," Jameston agreed. "To the death of Honce."

Both paused and sighed at that harsh reality. "Southern Honce," Gwydre added at length. "Vanguard has found peace, it would seem."

"It's true," Jameston assured her. "No goblins or trolls or barbarians to be found. Most of Badden's priests weren't too happy with his decision to employ mercenary monsters. The priests are split now and fighting among themselves, and that's always a good thing. It'll take them a year and more to put a new ancient in place. I expect before that time, you'll be hearing from many Samhaist priests who want to make peace. They'll be asking you to allow them to hold their groves and tend to their followers."

"Do they think they will have any followers in Vanguard after the misery Badden has loosed upon us?"

Jameston shrugged. "Prideful bunch, and I never thought much of the intelligence of the average man or woman."

Gwydre gave a little chuckle at that, a helpless one. "Vanguard knows peace on the battlefields, perhaps, but not peace of mind."

"I'll go out on a thin trail of old turds here and guess that the Abelle crowd is causing you misery."

Gwydre laughed again and held up her hands helplessly. "They wish to try Cormack for heresy. They demand it."

"Cormack? The tall one who went to the glacier and helped kill Badden?"

"The same."

Now it was Jameston's turn to laugh at the sheer absurdity of it all. He stopped when he noted that Dame Gwydre was staring at him intently.

"How well do you know him?" she asked.

"Cormack? Don't know him at all. Heard about him. Talked to him once."

"How well do you know Bransen?"

"The Highwayman?"

Gwydre nodded. "He arrived in Pellinor this morning at my request."

"I traveled with him for a short time," said Jameston. "Good fighter, that much I know."

"Not unlike Jameston in skill or in temperament."

"I don't think I ever fought like that," the scout replied. "Not that well, but I hope I had better sense than that one even when I was a young man."

"Not unlike Jameston in his disdain for the Samhaist and the brothers of Abelle—oh, and for the lairds of Honce."

"I'm liking him all the more."

"Spend some time with him," Gwydre bade Jameston.

"That an order?"

"A request. I think that you might counsel him well."

"Ah, you mean that you want me to make sure that he likes Dame Gwydre more than he likes the other lairds."

Gwydre smirked at him, and Jameston couldn't suppress a return smile.

"You've earned that much from me, at least," the scout said. He took Gwydre's hand and kissed it. "Since you're th'only one worth a dactyl demon's damn."

"My husband was a good man."

"You do well by his memory."

"You loved my father," Gwydre added.

"Hard man not to love," Jameston admitted. "Were more lairds like him, were more people like him, I might spend less time in the forest."

"Then you'll spend some time with Bransen?"

"For you, pretty lady? Of course."

Dame Gwydre leaned forward and kissed Jameston on the cheek then walked past him and out of the room.

For the first time in several days her smile was genuine.

He stood alone in the center of the circular room, but he did not bow his head. Nor did he remove his powrie beret, even after Father Premujon, after whispering with Father De Guilbe, ordered him to do so.

Instead, Cormack calmly looked over at Dame Gwydre and asked, "Is it required of me, in this, your chamber, to remove the cap?"

She shook her head. Cormack didn't even bother to glance back at the monks.

From the front of the room, near the door (which was open so that many of Pellinor's citizens could view the proceedings), Bransen watched it all with a grin and a growing respect for Cormack. The man was cool-headed, unconcerned, as if the monks could not truly touch him. They had whipped him near to death and cast him away in a rickety boat to die, and yet he had survived. Perhaps Gwydre was the source of his confidence—maybe she had told him that she would stand with him in these proceedings—but more likely, Bransen thought, Cormack would have acted no differently were this trial in the chapel and governed only by the two fathers.

They couldn't touch him. Not truly. Even if they burned him at the stake, they couldn't touch the soul of Cormack.

Premujon called upon Father De Guilbe to open the trial with an explanation of the man's alleged crime. Bransen listened intently through it all, hearing of the battle at Chapel Isle, where the monks had "rescued" and were "saving" three wayward Alpinadorans when the barbarians came against them viciously. After days of successful defense and another prisoner taken and, De Guilbe declared, with the barbarians ready to break and retreat, Cormack had snuck into the room and ferried the Alpinadorans away, betraying the brotherhood, scorning his superiors, and condemning the four Alpinadorans to eternal damnation.

It was a rousing recanting, Bransen thought, if one were inclined to believe such things. Many in the room, monk and Vanguardsman alike, called for Cormack's head. Of course, to Bransen the courageous actions only made Cormack more the hero.

Dame Gwydre wasted little time in quieting the ruckus and made it clear that she would tolerate no mob mentality here.

"Father De Guilbe," she said, "it would appear that Brother Cormack—former Brother Cormack—did no more than to grant men their freedom. Were they, the Alpinadorans, incarcerated for any particular reason? Had they committed criminal acts against Chapel Isle?"

"They owed their lives to us," said De Guilbe. "To Blessed Abelle. Only through the power of the gemstones did they draw breath, for we found them adrift on the lake, grievously—nay, mortally!—wounded."

"But they wished to leave after you saved them?"

De Guilbe squared his shoulders and did not reply.

"Do you consider their incarceration their cost for your efforts, then?" Gwydre calmly asked.

"I had my charge from Father Artolivan of Chapel Abelle," the man replied staunchly. "My Alpinadoran guests would have come to our way—perhaps they would have then become emissaries of the good word to the rest of their heathen folk. That is a more important healing than the closing of any physical wound."

"The captured Alpinadorans would have come to Blessed Abelle?"

"They were not captured! They were saved! And yes!"

"Never!" a woman cried from the back of the room, directly opposite Cormack, and all eyes went to Milkeila. "Not like that," she added quietly, speaking directly and in apologetic tone to Dame Gwydre.

"It is not your place to speak here," Father De Guilbe said through gritted teeth.

"Unless Dame Gwydre requests it of you," Dame Gwydre added, throwing a disdainful glance at De Guilbe. "And she does, Milkeila of Alpinador, so please, continue." With a steadying deep breath and a nod at her husband, Milkeila stepped tentatively from the gathering.

"What do you know of this incident?" Dame Gwydre asked her directly. "Were you there?"

"I was among those attacking the chapel," Milkeila admitted, and she looked to Cormack again. "Even as the man I love was defending it."

"You admit to a crime punishable by death?" Father De Guilbe demanded.

Bransen put a hand near his sword without even thinking. As he considered his reflexive movement, he realized that if the monks moved against Milkeila here he would indeed draw on them and defend her.

"Continue without fear of retribution," Dame Gwydre bade the woman. "You are charged with no crime and"—she paused to glower at De Guilbe— "you will not be."

"Among the prisoners was a very powerful shaman of my people," Milkeila explained, "one who would not even willingly accept their gemstone magic, even at the price of his own life."

"And you, too, are a priest of that barbarian religion," De Guilbe accused.

"No longer," said Milkeila. "Like Cormack, I have come to see that neither side is right."

That brought more than a few whispers around the room, particularly from the grumbling monks, but Gwydre again was quick to calm them.

"Father De Guilbe is wrong when he said that we were nearing the end of our assault," Milkeila insisted.

"We were slaughtering you at our wall!" accused De Guilbe.

"We would have kept coming, to the last," said Milkeila, talking directly to Gwydre and ignoring De Guilbe altogether. "Those prisoners were our brethren. We would not abandon them, whatever the cost. It is not our way. Which is why, when Bransen came to us with word of Ancient Badden even though I was out of favor with the leaders of Yan Ossum, all the tribes came together to defeat the wicked man." She finally did turn to look at De Guilbe. "Unlike the brothers of Abelle, who ran away."

The room seemed as if it would erupt.

And yet, again, the power of Dame Gwydre calmed it. She turned to De Guilbe. "Have you anything else, Father?"

"The disposition of the Alpinadoran converts is not your concern," De Guilbe said firmly. "Nor are my orders regarding our stance against the tribes of Mithranidoon—we were at war with them for years before this incident. I saw the men we rescued as perhaps a mediation of that continuing conflict. But again, I need not explain myself to you in this matter. I was sent to Alpinador, a place outside Dame Gwydre's province, by the Order of Blessed Abelle, acting upon lawful commands issued by Father Artolivan whose sovereignty in these matters Dame Gwydre and all the lairds acknowledge."

De Guilbe leveled his gaze on Gwydre. "This man betrayed my orders, the lawful orders of the Order of Blessed Abelle, and by doing so endangered us all. It is as simple as that," he insisted.

Bransen shifted uncomfortably as he studied Gwydre then, for he saw that the woman had little argument against the simple logic, however she might feel about the larger situation.

"Have you anything to say?" she asked Cormack. It seemed to Bransen as if she was begging the man to give her something, anything, to back down Father De Guilbe.

"Father De Guilbe was wrong and immoral in his actions," Cormack replied without hesitation. "We had no right to hold the Alpinadorans."

De Guilbe started to shout in protest, but Gwydre hushed him immediately.

"Father De Guilbe's decision to hold the men in our dungeon brought actual war to us," Cormack explained. "It is true that we had battled the barbarians on the lake for many months, but not lethally. Our fights were more gamesmanship than serious conflict, until that point. After the prisoners were taken, we were killing them at our wall and they were killing us—not as often, but we had fewer to spare. It wouldn't have ended until one side or the other had been completely destroyed. I could not allow that insanity to continue. If the cost of that is my life, then so be it. I already accepted such a judgment from Father De Guilbe, delivered to me by a brother who was as a mentor to me. I could not allow the killing, senseless and without gain to either side, to continue. I freed the prisoners, as Father De Guilbe charges. In the same situation I would do it again."

Murmurs erupted about the room, some complimentary, some calling for Cormack's death. Truly, Dame Gwydre seemed at a loss.

She was trapped here, Bransen realized. To go against the powerful Order of Abelle so openly as to intervene in their private matters would surely bring disaster to her holding.

"Would anyone else speak?" she asked, a plea if Bransen had ever heard one. He was about to answer that call when blind Brother Jond tapped his cane on the hard floor.

"I will," he said. "I, who know you well, Dame Gwydre, and who went to Alpinador on your behalf to end the carnage of Ancient Badden."

Gwydre's smile showed her appreciation. "Please do."

"I was not at the island, of course," said Jond. "But I watched..." he chuckled at his choice of words, and many in the room joined him awkwardly. "With my ears I witnessed the efforts of Cormack against Ancient Badden: He was nothing short of courageous and valiant, fighting for Vanguard and for the good of us all. In the weeks that followed, I had many opportunities to speak with the man—brother to brother—and I find him to be of exemplary character and human decency."

Reading De Guilbe's furrowed brow, Bransen figured that if the father could have gotten away with it, he would have leaped upon Jond at that moment and choked the life from him.

"And with all respect to your office and judgment, Father De Guilbe," Brother Jond added, "my heart grows heavy indeed to think that our beloved order has cast out a man of such fortitude and character."

De Guilbe exploded, shouting at Brother Jond to remember his place, sit down, and shut up. Several monks joined in that chorus, filling the room with the buzz of excited titterings and whispers.

"I will speak for Cormack!" Bransen heard himself yelling above the din. The room quieted instantly, all eyes falling on the Highwayman, on the man who had killed Ancient Badden and delivered them from a horrendous war, on the man who had dropped Badden's severed head in the road, a gift to their beloved Dame Gwydre. "I will echo Brother Jond's words to a one, except to add that it does not surprise me to see the Order of Abelle so confused and wrongheaded regarding the disposition of an honest and decent man. Such a monk is a rare thing, I fear, and one who does not fit their tenets."

Of course, that brought only more shouting and tumult, until finally Dame Gwydre managed to calm it down.

"You have no standing in this, Dame Gwydre," Father De Guilbe pronounced once more. "This matter happened beyond Vanguard and within the domain of the Order of Blessed Abelle. Cormack is ours to discipline."

"Cormack helped Vanguard win a war," Gwydre reminded.

"Nonetheless, you know that I am correct."

The dame rubbed her face, and Bransen held his breath. This was her place to take a stand, a brave one, or to fail, the Highwayman knew, and he sorely hoped that Gwydre would prove herself better than the typical self-serving coward he had come to expect from a laird.

"I will speak for Cormack!" exclaimed another voice, an unexpected source indeed. All eyes in the room, most notably those of Father De Guilbe and Cormack himself, fell to the speaker, Brother Giavno, Father De Guilbe's second.

"This is madness wrought of foolish pride," Giavno said to De Guilbe. "As our stand against the Alpinadorans was madness, and murderously so!"

"Brother!" De Guilbe shouted.

Giavno whirled to address Father Premujon. "Our time in Alpinador was trying," he explained. "We lost men and good brothers to the weather and the beasts and, yes, to Alpinadorans. Worse still, we knew by the time we had arrived on the lake called Mithranidoon that our mission was futile. We were not going to convert any souls in that barbarian land." He looked to De Guilbe and repeated, "We weren't.

"I do not know if Cormack was right or wrong in what he did," Giavno said in more humble and muted tones. "I do not know if Father De Guilbe acted wisely or acted the fool in keeping the Alpinadorans against their will. We punished Cormack for his betrayal. I beat him near to death with a scourge, and we cast him adrift on the lake to die. But he did not die. And how did he repay us for our punishment? By returning with that man, there"—he pointed to Bransen—"to warn us of impending doom. Were it not for them and for Milkeila and her people, Ancient Badden would have succeeded in dropping the edge of a great glacier into our lake, washing us all away to our certain deaths. Enough, please, Father Premujon. Let Cormack go."

He looked to Cormack as he finished, tears in his eyes. "I am proud to say that this man was once my friend and sorry to admit that I failed him miserably."

Again the whispering erupted, more muted and with many heads nodding. Bransen, as surprised as any, watched Dame Gwydre intently. She looked to Father Premujon; the two shared telling nods.

After a long while, Gwydre asked, "Are you satisfied, Father Premujon?"

"I am," he replied.

"Father De Guilbe claims this situation a matter of the Order of Blessed Abelle. Despite my strong feelings here I am forced to agree," Dame Gwydre admitted.

Many around the room gasped, but Bransen grinned and nodded, fully expecting what was forthcoming.

"Then I would argue that Cormack is no brother of the Order of Abelle, that his title was lawfully stripped by a man empowered to do so," said Premujon. "When he was put in that boat and cast adrift he became the charge of Dame Gwydre and not of Father Artolivan or his emissaries."

"But I defer to you, for your guidance, at least," said Gwydre.

With a look to Father De Guilbe that was part apology, part exasperation, Father Premujon said, "We have had our justice on the brother, Cormack. It is up to Dame Gwydre to decide whether his actions merit further punishment or celebration. I have witnessed the cost of this war with the evil Ancient Badden for many months now, my good lady. I would counsel you to leniency at the least."

"Go free, Cormack," Dame Gwydre pronounced immediately. "With my great, great appreciation for your heroic efforts against the most evil Ancient Badden."

The room exploded into cheers, but Bransen watched Father De Guilbe. He even walked among the throng swarming Cormack, veering to be near to De Guilbe so that he could hear the man say to Premujon, "Father Artolivan will hear of this."

"Oh, he will, indeed," the father of Chapel Pellinor replied.

Bransen laughed, and both men regarded him. He almost mentioned that more monks like Premujon, Cormack, and Jond might make him rethink the value of the Order of Blessed Abelle, but he merely tapped his finger to his black bandanna—his head wrap which held the soul stone Cormack had given to him (and the irony of that pleased him all the more)—and turned and walked away.

The snow fell heavily in spurts this day, but there was little breeze and the temperature was pleasingly moderate, leaving the air dancing with large, lazily drifting flakes. Unlike most winter Vanguard storms, it was not a day where one had to remain huddled beside a fire, though surely many chose that route.

Dame Gwydre, wrapped in a dark blue shawl, was glad to be out, feeling very much like a little girl in a friendly snowstorm. Walking beside her, Bransen was similarly at ease. He had known much snow in Pryd, of course, but there was something very different about the Vanguard winter, something . . . cleaner. In Pryd, the snow came and melted and left a muddy mess repeatedly, but up here, once the snow landed on the ground, it stayed throughout the winter season.

"I trust you are enjoying your stay at Castle Pellinor," Gwydre said. "I have been so busy of late that I have had little time to look in on you and your lovely family."

Bransen continued to look at his companion curiously for a short while, still unsure of why Gwydre had bade him, in no uncertain terms, to come outside and walk with her this afternoon. "We have never been more comfortable, of course," he answered, but with clear hesitancy in his voice, which drew a knowing grin from Gwydre.

"Always expecting *the mule's arse rent*, yes?" the Lady of Vanguard teased.

Bransen stared at her, mouth hanging open as if he had no idea of how to respond.

"You don't know that old saying?" Gwydre asked.

"The mule's arse rent?"

Dame Gwydre laughed at him. "Mules are frustrating creatures, particularly if you have one you don't know well. The mule's arse rent is the extra and unanticipated cost of renting such a beast when it is returned with boot prints on its arse."

Bransen just stood there, gaping.

"An old saying, is all," said Gwydre. "Or is it my use of the crude term that surprises you?"

"You constantly surprise me, Lady Gwydre."

"Good!"

Bransen laughed helplessly.

"To my point, though," Gwydre continued, "you fear that I have some ulterior designs in bringing you here—even above hoping that you would speak for Cormack at Father De Guilbe's spectacle."

Bransen arched a brow. "The possibility has crossed my mind."

"You do not trust me."

"I . . . it's not . . ." Bransen stumbled.

"You have every right to be suspicious," Gwydre conceded. "My man Dawson deceived you initially to trick you to Vanguard, and I demanded of you that you fight on my behalf."

"I understand now that you had little choice," said Bransen. "After meeting Ancient Badden, I better understand your desperation."

"And you forgive me?"

Now it was Bransen's turn to laugh. "Forgive you? You saved my life in tricking me here. I understand that."

"So we are friends?"

"Of cour—" Bransen started to say, but he suddenly felt as if he was walking into another trap here. He stopped abruptly and stared hard at Dame Gwydre, who burst out laughing.

"Oh, but you are insufferable, Bransen Garibond!" she said. "You owe me nothing, of course. I did not demand that you return to Castle Pellinor, did I? Nay, Dawson explained Cormack's time of need. We trusted that you would do the right thing."

"Perhaps I am growing tired of doing the right thing."

"You say that because you suspect that I brought you out here for something other than a friendly conversation."

Bransen shrugged, not denying it.

The dance went out of Dame Gwydre's step, and she said in all seriousness, "I wanted to tell you what is happening in the world, the good news and the bad. You, above many, should know."

"I, above many, hardly care."

"I don't believe that," Gwydre replied. "But even if true you should be told, and I owe it to you to tell you myself."

"I do care about Cormack," Bransen admitted.

"That is part of it," said Gwydre. "Part of the good news, I am happy to say. Brother Giavno's outburst at the trial has caused a great furor in the Order of Abelle. Father De Guilbe is outraged to this day, of course, but he finds few allies. He is a friend of Father Artolivan, so it is said, but still, Father Premujon, at the urging of our friend Brother Jond, has decided that he will travel beside Father De Guilbe to Chapel Abelle in the spring on Cormack's behalf. There is even talk that Father Premujon—who is a good man, I assure you—will ask that Father Artolivan overrule Father De Guilbe and offer Cormack reinstatement in the order. This is a fight that will grow within the ranks of the monks, and it is a fight long overdue, I think."

"Anything to alter their smug faces would be a good thing and, yes, is long overdue," Bransen agreed.

"Worth witnessing, you believe?"

That brought a suspicious, even knowing scowl to Bransen's face, and Gwydre laughed all the more.

"Jameston Sequin assures me that our war here in Vanguard is over," she said. "My plan was borne in desperation, I admit, and yet, because of you and your companions, it appears to have worked. The Samhaists have no stomach for continuing the fight, and without Badden guiding the monsters from the north, they have not been seen in weeks."

"What would you have me say?"

"That this news pleases you," Gwydre replied. "That you care, at least."

Bransen's pause was telling. "I do," he admitted. "Do you think I feel no pain when I see others torn and broken? Do you think me so selfish that I care not at all for the people who are mere victims in the plays of those who seek power above all?"

"You wanted no part of this fight, or of the fight in Honce."

"Because it is a fool's errand," Bransen replied. "Do I kill for Delaval or for Ethelbert? For Prydae, who ruled my home holding and who brutalized his own people? Do I kill for the sake of the Order of Abelle, who would hold a man as flawed and vicious and ultimately wrongheaded as Father De Guilbe in such high standing?"

"So we are all alike, we laird and ladies and fathers and priests?"

"I have seen little to convince me otherwise."

"You wound me to my heart."

Clearly uncomfortable, Bransen shifted and reached toward Dame Gwydre as if to pat her on the shoulder. But even in that, he failed and flailed, so at a loss.

"I understand!" Gwydre said with a good-natured chuckle. "I, my man at least, deceived you and sent you off to a war of which you wanted no part. You do not offend me with your honesty, Highwayman. Far from it. I find you refreshing. Only one other man would speak to me in such a manner, and he, Dawson, I consider my closest friend."

"You humble me and shame me for my harsh words," Bransen said, dipping a slight and awkward bow.

"I appreciate you," Dame Gwydre clarified. "For what you did and for who you are."

"Then accept this as an apology of sorts," said Bransen. "Were you to wind back the days to my arrival in Vanguard and offer me a choice to go after Badden or to leave, a choice and not a bribe conditioned on your writ, I would fight for you. Of my own volition. I would go to Alpinador and again deliver the head of that foul creature."

Dame Gwydre's smile widened, genuine and nearly taking in her ears. "You have no idea how happy I am to hear those words from the rogue known as the Highwayman."

"Don't take it as an invitation to press me back into service of your court," Bransen quipped, and Gwydre laughed again.

"The war is over—do keep your blade in its sheath. I ask nothing more of you, but I wish to make you an offer. Father Premujon and the others, including Cormack and Milkeila, will sail to Chapel Abelle as soon as Dawson deems the gulf safe for passage."

"Cormack should not do that."

"He is safe—his trial is ended and cannot be redone," Gwydre assured him. "And I intend to go with them, so long as the peace holds up here and I am not urgently needed in my court. I would like you to sail with me—you and your family, I mean. I don't know that I will be needed at Father Artolivan's chapel. I expect not, truly, but there are other matters in the southland I wish to discern, not the least of which the disposition of my Writ of Passage for Bransen Garibond, Cadayle, and Callen.

"Laird Delaval is dead, Bransen," she added as the man mulled over her offer. "But Laird Ethelbert cannot claim victory, since he and his army are being pushed back to his holding in the most furious fighting of all. I do not know what will transpire across Honce, but the situation is obviously dangerous."

"Dangerous and none of my business," said Bransen.

"You say that now, as you said it when first you came to Vanguard," Gwydre reminded.

"Would you have me save the world?" Bransen answered with obvious sarcasm. "Is there another Badden to slay?"

"I know not what needs to be done, nor do you. I go to learn and to see if there is any way in which I might use my standing to help the people who suffer because of the prideful fighting between two powerful lairds. Do you not wish to learn the same? Do you not wish to learn if you are truly free to walk the lands of Honce? You owe that much to your wife, I would expect."

Bransen sighed as if cornered.

"And to Cormack, as your friend, if there is anything you can contribute to his argument against Father De Guilbe."

"I will go," Bransen said suddenly, silencing her further comments. "I know not how long I will stay, and I intend to hold you to your promise that I will be delivered to a location of my choosing."

"Our agreement holds," Gwydre assured him.

Bransen looked at her with a sly smile. "You believe that I will wish to entwine myself in this fight," he accused.

With a light laugh Dame Gwydre turned away. Bransen watched her dance off through the continuing snowfall. Was she asking too much of him?

Or, he wondered, was he demanding too little of himself?

The world, his world, was on fire. How far could the Highwayman run?

PART TWO

The Wider World

*T*he woman has shaken me to my core, has taken my expectations and twisted them into unrecognizable knots.

I am not unused to such unsettling realizations of the true nature of the powers of Honce. From Father Jerak and the brothers of Chapel Pryd to that horrid Prydae who so disfigured Garibond, my father, I came to understand that many of the qualities that put a man in power in the first place seemed also to disqualify him from properly tending the flock in practice. So much had this axiom become a mantra for me that I was hardly surprised by the idiocy of Prince Yeslnik, who is truly an exaggerated collection of every flaw I had ever seen in those who had attained power. Yeslnik, so much a caricature, did not surprise me in the least and did not shake me (other than to make me shake my head in resignation).

I had known minor exceptions, of course—Brother Reandu comes to mind, and even Brother Bathelais had moments of great decency. But truly, Yeslnik the liar, the fool, the pretend hero, the hapless lover (judging from his wife's desperation), and, ultimately, the coward, embodied the extremes of my expectations of a laird. How appropriate, it seemed, that he who would stand above the lairds would be even more the fool than they.

But now I have come to know Dame Gwydre. I hardly know how to speak to her, to view her; I have to admit that she frightens me. I don't believe her to be secretly sinister and conniving. Quite the opposite! The idea that there is no underlying deception and selfish intent about the woman is a notion foreign, one that mocks me in my certitude and endless petulance.

Nay, she doesn't frighten me, except that she makes me afraid that she will shame me. For if this perception of goodness I believe of Gwydre is indeed the truth of Gwydre, then who am I? No hero, certainly.

When the snow fell deep this cold winter in Vanguard, the people of Pellinor struggled to retrieve enough wood to keep warm. With the drifts piled high, the forest was not safe for individuals or small groups to venture. So Gwydre, as she has apparently done many times before, held a grand ball in Castle Pellinor, with

*all invited. All! Every person about the town of Pellinor. And with the great cel-
ebration came a feast that lasted for days. And during that time, at Gwydre's
behest, Dawson and her soldiers ventured often into the forest and retrieved piles
of wood for the folk of Pellinor to take with them as they at last departed the
castle.*

*And Gwydre ate with them and danced with them and led them in song.
I looked upon her and wished that she were not so atypical a laird, that all the
people of Honce, of all the world indeed, could be so blessed to live under the care
of such a ruler.*

*She shames the callous heart of the Highwayman. She frightens me because
she did something to me. Dame Gwydre made me, at long last and against all
expectation, hope.*

*Hope. She made me hope. She made me believe that the world could change.
But hope is not as easy an emotion as is surrender. For that is what I have done,
Dame Gwydre has shown me to my great discomfort. When the Stork became
the Highwayman, the Stork surrendered.*

*I care not for the war in the south, so I declare. I cared not for Gwydre's war,
so I declared. I fought only because of Gwydre's deception and blackmail. Beyond Cadayle and Callen and my own needs, I declared myself removed, uncaring, not responsible.*

She shames me, and the hope I feel when I look upon her scares me.

*Who would I be had I been raised in Pellinor instead of Pryd? I doubt that
the Highwayman would exist, and that is a notion that bothers me profoundly.
But how might that persona of the Highwayman have grown in such a climate as
Pellinor? Would Father Premujon have treated me as the brothers in Chapel
Pryd treated the Stork? Would Gwydre have allowed it?*

*No. Not up here. Up here, even the relationship between Castle Pellinor and
Chapel Pellinor is a very different one than that I experienced in Pryd Town.
Back home, the brothers were terrified of the laird and would not go against him
even when they knew he was wrong. But here Premujon and Gwydre are friends,
and she supports him in his work most of all when his work is benefiting the
people, the common folk. Both Gwydre and Premujon act as if they serve the folk
and not as if the people were put here as pawns for their pleasure.*

*Perhaps it is the harsh climate of Vanguard and the simple pragmatism the
difficult environment demands. Up here, the folk stand as one, or die alone.
Would the common folk suffer the selfishness so typical in the southern lairds and
nobles? Would they sit idly by, freezing and dying, while their leaders of castle
and chapel hoarded the winter supplies?*

I doubt they would ... but as I reflect on this matter, I realize that I am applying a pragmatism to my observations of character that is unfair to Dame Gwydre. I so clearly see her heart in the way she dances in a snowstorm or sings to the people of Pellinor.

She would be a good leader of good heart wherever her holding. And had he grown among the pines of Pellinor, the Highwayman would not exist.

And Garibond Womak would still be alive. Alive and friend to Bran Dynard and Sen Wi.

So it is not Gwydre I fear in the end but the hope she lights in my heart and soul, in the way she forces me to feel responsibility beyond the boundaries of my own needs.

Had I known the light that is Gwydre before, I wonder what I might have answered when she came to me with no threat or deception and asked me, for no reason other than the good of the folk of Vanguard, to go north and do battle with Ancient Badden.

She has shaken my beliefs to the core.

—BRANSEN GARIBOND

CHAPTER 11

Just As the King Had Planned

W e're driving them hard," shouted Erolis, a nobleman from Pryd who had so distinguished himself in the fighting that Bannagran had given him one of the ten chariots in his elite team.

Bannagran could only nod as others chimed in above the din of pounding hooves and rolling wheels. They had started to the north on the hunt for the Highwayman, as Yeslnik had demanded. That alone had bothered Bannagran more than a bit, given the Highwayman's reputation among the commoners. Indeed, Bannagran had let Bransen go after the death of Prydae for just that reason, a potential revolt among the people of Pryd Holding.

Word had caught up to them after their departure, though, that King Yeslnik was soon to be engaging the forces of Laird Ethelbert far to the east of Pryd, along the western banks of Felidan Bay, the long inlet that separated Honce proper from the large peninsula of the easternmost regions known as the Mantis Arm. Yeslnik had recalled Bannagran with all speed.

And so the good general had followed his orders, wheeling his group of ten back to the south and then east, rumbling to the limit of the horses' strength along the cobblestone roads. They were getting close, Bannagran knew, and that was a good thing, for more than a few of the twenty horses drawing the war chariots would need to be replaced.

"Smoke in the northeast," Erolis called as they neared an intersection in the road.

"Stay east," Bannagran replied. He knew this land—he and Prydae had battled powries throughout this region, driving them to the sea, years before.

"Some town is burning," one of the others said.

"Good enough for them," another added.

Within a half hour, they came upon the stragglers of Yeslnik's rearguard and, they learned, southern flank.

"Ah, but never have me eyes looked upon a more blessed sight!" cried one man—a man from Pryd, Bannagran knew.

Bannagran pulled his chariot up beside the beleaguered footman. "You are Farmer Grees?"

"Ah, Laird Bannagran," the man replied with a low bow.

Bannagran scowled at him from the chariot for using that title, one not yet officially proclaimed. "Where is King Yeslnik?"

Grees halfheartedly waved generally north.

"The town and smoke?"

"Nay," Grees answered. "That'd be Milwellis, we're hearing. The king's due north of us—might even be back to the west a bit."

Bannagran didn't have to probe further to get the hidden meaning there, that Yeslnik, as usual, was safely to the rear of the fighting.

"Can ye go to him?" the man asked suddenly. Bannagran looked at him with surprise.

"Might I be speaking without getting yer spear in me chest?" Grees asked, his voice low.

"What are you about?"

"About to die, I'm guessing," Grees answered.

Bannagran scowled; behind Grees several other footmen shifted nervously.

"Go and tell King Yeslnik, I beg ye," Grees pressed.

"Tell him what?"

"He's got us spearheading straight east," Grees explained. "And the front groups're making great gains. The enemy're falling back before them." He sighed and lowered his voice as he added, "None to the south of us. None of us, I mean, guarding our flank. But there's a road there."

Bannagran looked to the east, then the south, trying to get a feel for the situation. Farmer Grees was a veteran of many battles, as were most of the men of Pryd. His tone spoke volumes more than his actual words.

"Mighty spearmen are the folk o' the Mantis Arm," Grees added. "Who spend their days harpooning the fishes."

"They've crossed the bay?"

"Aye, Prince Milwellis hit them hard in the north and cut them off from the mainland—he's built a fortress at the north tip o' Felidan to keep the men o' the peninsula on the peninsula. But aye, they've got boats a'plenty."

"You're being flanked to the south," Bannagran reasoned. "While the Felidan Bay villagers retreat, their allies from across the bay are sliding in beside and behind you."

Grees didn't have to answer.

"How many? How far west have they pushed? And how far east are the front runners of your surge?"

"I can't be knowing, but they're there. They're falling too fast afore us, let-ting us push east and stretch thin. These folk are no strangers to the way of battle—they've been fighting powries all their lives."

"Why are you men back here?" Erolis interjected, accusation heavy in his tone. "If your line advances with all speed, then why are you so far behind?"

Farmer Grees pointed down at his foot, which was heavily bandaged, but showing blood through the wrap. "All of us here been taking hits and can't keep up."

"And when you heard of the southern flank, you hesitated more," Bannagran remarked, and Grees and many others shifted uncomfortably.

"Good fortune that you did," Bannagran said even as Erolis started to launch another accusation. "And good fortune that you are rested." He turned to his charioteers. "We go south, and these men will run behind us. We'll cut the enemy off along the road." Turning back to Farmer Grees, he instructed, "Your men come in behind us and turn fast to the east. Our enemies will be in rout and retreating, so run among them and kill them."

"What of them that's already crossed the road?"

"The chariots will hold the road," Bannagran declared, loud enough for all to hear. He snapped the reins and his team leaped off, rambling across an open field to the road running south beyond.

"For the Bear of Honce!" he heard more than one man cry enthusiastically behind him. He hated that nickname, hated being compared to some animal, but he couldn't deny its power to rally men, and he surely needed that energy and hope at this time.

Flames hungrily ate the thatched roofs, billowing thick black smoke into the air. Men, women, and children screamed and rushed about in stark ter-ror as horsemen weaved through the village, launching torches onto the roofs, launching spears at the pursued, or just running down the smaller ones and trampling them under hoof.

Prince Milwellis of Palmaristown kept his horse running and couldn't stop laughing at the frenzy before him. This village, of no name worth remember-ing, had sent some men to the north to . . . to what, Milwellis still wondered. To parley? To defend? In either case, they had utterly failed, since Milwellis, eager to be the first to Yansinchester, the target city of King Yeslnik's diversion to the coast, just sent his large force swarming over them and into their village.

Out of the corner of his eye, Milwellis noted a man darting behind the corner of a building. He kicked his mount into a short gallop, spinning around the corner, spear ready, to find the man huddled with his back against the stone, his hands open and defensively against his chest and belly.

"Oh please, good sir, please don't kill me!" he cried. "I'm with no one, not Ethelbert. Just a fisherman, I am."

"Be at ease, good man," Milwellis said and lowered his spear across his lap.

The man straightened, his arms going down by his sides. "We're just simple folk," he started to say.

"Then no real loss," Milwellis interjected. He thrust his spear into the man's gut. The fisherman shrieked and doubled over as Milwellis tore his barbed weapon back out, taking along the man's entrails.

"I would carve the crest of Palmaristown in your forehead for your treachery against King Yeslnik, fool!" the merciless prince shouted as the man crumbled to his knees. "But I haven't the time!"

The fisherman fell flat on the ground, and Milwellis whirled his horse about, stomping over him as he went back to the fun at the village center.

A large group moving east-to-west," Erolis confirmed from his perch up in a tree. "Slipping in behind Yeslnik's line as they spearhead east."

"Heartbeats?" Bannagran asked from his chariot below.

"Hundreds, five hundred, perhaps."

Bannagran nodded and motioned his man down from the tree (and since the wind carried great bite this day, Erolis was more than happy to follow that order).

"You follow as swiftly as you can," Bannagran commanded Grees and the fifty other footmen he had rounded up. "We will turn them and send them running, and the quicker you are among them, the more confusion they will find. So, for your own lives, warriors, run!"

As soon as Erolis stepped up into his chariot, Bannagran set his own off along the road, the other nine quickly sweeping up in his wake. Bannagran kept the pace measured for a short while, trying to gauge his timing for maximum effect at the enemy crossing point.

As usual, his instincts proved perfect, and when he set his team into a full charge along the last span to the enemy crossing, more than three dozen warriors from various villages of the Mantis Arm were within striking distance of the road.

Bannagran's armored team and chariot roared down at the Ethelbert soldiers. The warrior led with a series of spear throws, plucking them from the stand before him, launching them with precision and great power, all the while aiming his team at the largest concentration. A couple threw spears back his way, but they were more concerned with trying to get out of Bannagran's path, and their missiles proved ineffective.

Men rushed about wildly, and some broke. Some who thought they had dodged the brunt of the charging horse team found their legs literally cut from under them by the great jagged blades protruding from Bannagran's wheels.

Screams echoed east and west of the road, including cries of alarm that the Bear of Honce had come. And from the north, where the other nine charioteers similarly pounded into Ethelbert's forces, the fifty footmen howled and hollered and ran on at full speed.

The road was cleared in moments. Bannagran pulled his team up to the side, took up shield and spear, and leaped away. None could stand before him. Indeed, his enemies knew him and shouted his name in terror as they broke and fled before him.

All that Bannagran had hoped came to fruition in short order. The concentration of enemies moving to flank the southern end of Yeslnik's line fell apart almost at once, and those who managed to escape the catastrophe ran back the way they had come, to the east.

Bannagran and his nine fellows gave short chase, launching spears, inciting further terror. Grees and the others swept by, cheering their leader, the great Bannagran, who had arrived to turn certain disaster into victory yet again.

"To your chariots," Bannagran ordered the nine. "Those who have already crossed the road will try to strike at us from the west. They are caught alone!"

As predicted, the peninsula warriors did come on from the west, trying to break through to secure their reinforcements. But this was Bannagran, the Bear of Honce, the hero of Pryd, the hero of Yeslnik's Honce. Their spears were met by brutal and unforgiving charges of chariots. At one point Bannagran even grabbed a handful of javelins, leaped from his chariot, and chased after a group of five who ran back to the west.

Not fast enough for one, who caught a spear in the back, and then another, who took one in the back of the thigh, and then a third, whom Bannagran hit with a flying tackle, burying him in the dirt.

Just before Bannagran cut that one's throat open with the serrated edge of his short sword, the man cried, "I surrender! Oh, but it's not my war! I've children!"

Bannagran held his slash, stood up straight, and hoisted the man to his feet beside him. He looked back to the man he had hit in the leg, thrashing on the ground, and to Erolis, closing in for the kill.

"All quarter!" Bannagran called, and Erolis nodded. "These, too, are men of Honce!"

"Hail King Yeslnik!" Erolis called back.

Bannagran scowled at his prisoner.

"Hail King Yeslnik!" the terrified man answered, and Bannagran nodded grimly and pulled him back toward the road.

Soon after, Grees and the others returned, full of cheer and bluster. "We ran them off for good!" the farmer asserted. "And many're down."

"Well done," Bannagran congratulated him. "Now we turn west and quickly. Those out there are cut off from their allies and families, and they know it."

"How many?" Grees asked, concern in his tone.

"It matters not," Bannagran assured him. "They'll have no heart for the fight."

Proud of his men and glad that he had again ably led them, Bannagran left the western fields of victory, driving for Yeslnik's position in the center of his extended line. As it seemed that the fighting had ebbed—all warriors he passed on his way told him that the enemy had retreated to the fortified coastal towns—Bannagran eased his pace, so that his charioteers and footmen and their hundred prisoners, taken in those western fields with hardly a fight, as he had predicted, could somewhat pace him.

He wanted them to arrive in view of King Yeslnik soon after he and the unpredictable young nobleman had begun their conversation. In dealing with Yeslnik, Bannagran knew, it was always wise to somehow gain an advantage.

He found the young king basking in luxury in a grand tent, surrounded by so many layers of sentries that Ethelbert's entire army, had it come at them, would not likely have gotten to Yeslnik. Inside, around a table set with lavish foods, Yeslnik and his field commanders dined and drank.

Bannagran wasn't surprised.

"Ah, but the great Bear has come," said Yeslnik.

Bannagran winced at the mocking tone.

"I expected your arrival this morning," Yeslnik went on. "You were seen not far to the west many hours ago. I told you not to tarry."

"I happened upon a situation that needed to be addressed, for the good of my king," Bannagran explained. "I had not the time to ride to you and to correct the breach in your defenses."

"Breach?" Yeslnik replied, his tone going higher and betraying his sudden anxiety.

Always the brave one, Bannagran thought.

"The success of your maneuver at your southern flank was obviously unanticipated," Bannagran carefully explained. "Huzzah for the men of Delaval, so obviously eager to please their new king!"

Yeslnik smirked at him, and Bannagran knew that the king understood the criticism behind the compliment. A buffoon in many ways, too prideful for his or his subjects' good, and possessed of ridiculous vanity and deceit, Yeslnik was nevertheless not a simpleton, particularly not in matters politic. Bannagran silently reminded himself never to forget that.

"The peninsula warriors made a fatal mistake," Bannagran went on. "They tried to flank your spearheading advance by secretly advancing to the south of the southern end of your line. But they stretched themselves too thin. They are more used to fighting on the sea, methinks, or at the seacoast."

They heard a commotion outside the tent, and Bannagran knew that his men had arrived with the prisoners—and not a moment too soon, he thought.

"They were desperate against your bold gambit in the south, and so they erred," the Bear of Honce finished. He led Yeslnik and the other commanders present to the tent flap, coming in view of Bannagran's forces leading the long line of captives.

"What is the meaning of this?" Yeslnik asked Bannagran, surprising the champion.

"It means that our enemy's gambit has failed," he started to answer, but before he could finish, before his group even fully entered the encampment, horns blew from the other direction and a great cheer went up among King Yeslnik's forces.

Yeslnik led Bannagran and the others from the tent to come in view of the new arrivals, Milwellis and his forces.

"They have razed a line from the neck of the Mantis Arm to here," King Yeslnik explained to Bannagran. "They have struck fear into the hearts of the fools who would oppose my reign. Never again will the men, what few remain, of the Felidan Bay villages take up weapons in support of Ethelbert. The region is nearly secured."

He turned to Bannagran. "Do you notice anything absent among Milwellis's ranks?"

Bannagran looked hard, but found no answers to the curious and curiously leading question.

"Laird Bannagran did not hear of your edict, my liege," one of Yeslnik's other commanders remarked. Yeslnik nodded.

Bannagran looked at them with puzzlement.

"The days, the months, nay, the years, of merciful war are ended," Yeslnik explained.

"Merciful war?" Bannagran echoed with confusion.

"Merciful?" Yeslnik spat. "The reason this uprising of Ethelbert continues is because of false mercy!"

Bannagran let the description of the war as the "uprising of Ethelbert" go without the obvious challenge. This war was more a matter of Laird Delaval's expansion of his substantive holding than anything else. As soon as the roads had been completed, Laird Delaval, with his large resources, had moved to unify Honce under his banner. Ethelbert, the second strongest laird, with the support of many other lesser lairds and with ties to Behr in the south, had opposed him.

"Only when the cost of their choice is clear to those who would oppose me will they cease in their folly," Yeslnik explained.

"What would you have me do, my king?" Bannagran asked, a bit tentatively, for he was truly afraid of where this curious conversation might be leading.

"Tell me what is missing from Prince Milwellis's grand entrance," Yeslnik replied, and loudly, so that the approaching Milwellis clearly heard.

Bannagran scratched his head, not wanting to answer.

"Prisoners," Yeslnik said with a hiss. "The day of false mercy is ended. We do not offer quarter."

Bannagran swallowed hard, his mind whirling through the myriad of troublesome implications of such a ruthless edict. Why would any of those loyal to Ethelbert ever surrender with such a fate before them? He wanted to speak out, to explain to King Yeslnik that his own victory that very day would have been hard to achieve and would have cost him dearly had not the disoriented and fearful warriors of the Mantis Arm surrendered in those western fields—surrendered, despite outnumbering Bannagran's forces two-to-one, because they knew there was no long-term solution to their dilemma.

"Execute them," Yeslnik instructed Bannagran, the king's words snapping at the champion like a jolt of lightning.

"I took them fairly, upon my word," Bannagran dared to argue.

"My word overcomes your word."

"Yes, my king," Bannagran stammered, "but you cannot take from me my honor if you wish me to remain valuable to your cause." His justification sounded inane to his own ears as he improvised the words, but he had to say something, anything, to dissuade Yeslnik from this course. Bannagran could kill any man or woman in battle without the slightest regret; he was a warrior and had been since his youth. But to kill unarmed, defenseless prisoners on such a scale, many of them simply folk caught up in the folly of lairds?

"Are you refusing me?" Yeslnik asked, the threat clear.

"No, my king, I am asking your deference in this matter."

Yeslnik stared at him hard.

"Oh, just kill them quickly and be done with it," said Prince Milwellis. "My liege, allow me," he added, staring at Bannagran as he spoke, as if this request was surely elevating him against the champion of Pryd, who many believed to be Milwellis's primary competitor for the favor of King Yeslnik. "As a reward for my efforts in the north."

Yeslnik looked from Milwellis to Bannagran and gave a little laugh, then motioned for Milwellis to proceed. The fearsome prince of Palmaristown eagerly climbed back upon his horse and motioned for a few of his most deserving and trusted comrades to follow.

"It would seem the situation here is well in hand," Yeslnik said to Bannagran in dismissive tones. "I expect that you are not needed after all. Take your charioteers and return to the hunt of the Highwayman."

Bannagran gave a curt bow and spun away, rushing to his chariot and motioning his nine to follow quickly.

"And do not fail me again," King Yeslnik said to him.

Bannagran snapped his reins and sent his team charging away, hoping to be far from this place before the screams of terror and agony filled the air.

No such luck.

CHAPTER 12

Moral Outrage

Bransen and Cadayle stood arm in arm by the prow of *Lady Dreamer* as she bounced and splashed her way through the springtime swells. The sky above loomed dark and foreboding, and some drizzle had filled the morning air, but Dawson McKeege had assured them and all the other nervous "stiffleggers" (as he called those who hadn't spent much time on a boat) that it wasn't much of a storm.

"Just a pall," he had called it. "Worse on the spirits than on *Lady Dreamer*." The couple knew his words to be sincere. After all, Dame Gwydre herself was aboard; Dawson would never take a chance with the life of his beloved Lady of Vanguard.

"Chapel Abelle," Cadayle mumbled after a long while of silence. "What will you say to them when we arrive?"

"Nothing," Bransen answered. "Unless they ask. Then I will ask them why they found the need to so torment my family. What threat was Brother Dynard, truly? Or are they afraid to learn, as Father De Guilbe was so fearful of the barbarians that he would kill them all before speaking with them honestly?"

"They will welcome you with open arms, then," Cadayle replied sarcastically.

"They should hear the truth, if they ask."

"You would not have waited for that invitation a few months ago."

Bransen looked at his wife curiously before nodding in concession. "Father Premujon understands—and accepted Cormack despite great risk." As he spoke, he glanced back across the deck, to the sails of the vessels trailing them. De Guilbe and his people were on one, with the notable exception of Brother Giavno. Giavno sailed on *Lady Dreamer* with Father Premujon and his closest advisors, including Brother Jond, and with Cormack and Milkeila, as well.

"Not so great a risk for the father," Cadayle corrected. "Not with Dame Gwydre by his side."

"This meeting at Chapel Abelle will be interesting, even for me, though I hardly care for the affairs of the Order of Abelle," said Bransen.

"The Order of Blessed Abelle," Cadayle corrected with a wry grin.

Bransen rolled his eyes.

"But you will still offer your opinion if asked," Cadayle said with her unending playful sarcasm.

"Your own mother was thrown in a sack with venomous snakes, then hanged by her wrists and left to die," Bransen reminded, stealing her giggle.

"Samhaist justice, not Abellican," she said somberly.

"The brothers of Chapel Pryd sat silent at her trial, at her sentencing, and at her intended execution," Bransen reminded. "And those brothers were more than passive in the death of Garibond Womak!"

Cadayle hugged him close. "I did not mean to upset you," she said.

"It is the way of a difficult world," Bransen replied, returning the hug.

"Where will we live?" Cadayle asked.

"If Dame Gwydre's writ is accepted, anywhere we choose."

"And where will that be?"

Bransen looked at her carefully, trying to weigh the wistfulness in her beautiful eyes—those same eyes that had steadied him and warmed him when the other children had tormented him in his youth. In looking into Cadayle's eyes, Bransen could truly see her soul, her gentle and kind and loving soul. The wonderful view brought peace to him then, on *Lady Dreamer*'s damp deck, and reminded him how much he loved this woman and how fortunate he had been to find her.

"Pryd Town," he said. Cadayle started in surprise, and then a telling grin spread across her beautiful face. "Home."

"I would like that."

"So would Callen, I think."

"And Bransen, who offers it out of his boundless generosity?"

"It was my home on the lake. Although I am pained by the ending Garibond found, I think he would like it if we built our home there, in his memory. Also, if Yeslnik is laird, I will like it all the more simply because I know that Dame Gwydre's writ will bring frustration to the dimwit every day."

"And how many times will you rob him?"

Bransen laughed and hugged her tightly again. "No more," he said, shaking his head. "Dame Gwydre says that all is forgiven: that is our freedom. Our time in flight from pursuing soldiers is ended."

"Have you thought of becoming a father?" Cadayle asked. Something in her tone gave Bransen pause for a few heartbeats. His eyes popped open wide.

She looked up at him and smiled, then slowly nodded.

The next hug was the tightest yet, and the warmest.

H e uses Laird Delaval's own seal overlaid with a *Y*," Father Artolivan observed as he held the rolled parchment to arm's length so that his failing eyes could make out the insignia.

"He names himself Yeslnik Delaval, King of Honce," Master Reandu, the courier, explained.

"He would, wouldn't he?" Artolivan asked with a snort. "And before I read this, good Brother, would you desire to forewarn me of anything?"

Reandu looked at him curiously. "King Yeslnik is in a foul mood," he admitted. "His beloved uncle was murdered, after all. Is there something you fear, Father?"

Artolivan chuckled and looked around at his attendant, Brother Pinower, who seemed equally as sadly amused.

"We had a bit of a disagreement with Prince Milwellis of Palmaristown regarding our role in the disposition of prisoners," he explained. "I expect that the young man of hot humor complained to Yesl . . . to King Yeslnik, who no doubt wishes to chastise us for our impertinence."

"If he could think past the gains of the next day, he would understand Milwellis's posture to be one of disaster," Brother Pinower added. "I have little affection for the coldhearted prince of Palmaristown, I must admit."

"More than I," Artolivan mumbled.

"The events in the south move quickly," Reandu said. "Since the murder of Laird Delaval, Laird Ethelbert tried to assault Pryd Town. He was turned back by the brave men of Pryd and a great champion whom I name as a personal friend. The battle has turned vicious and furious. King Yeslnik will see this through, whatever the cost."

Father Artolivan held up a hand for him to pause, then broke the seal, unrolled the parchment, and began reading. Almost immediately his jaw went slack, his eyes went wide, and he began to shake his head.

He passed it off to Pinower, who truly seemed as if he had been slapped in the face as he read it and gave a yelp of protest.

"King Yeslnik demands the release of all the Delaval prisoners held at Chapel Abelle and at any other chapels," Father Artolivan explained to the concerned Reandu, taking the scroll back from Pinower. "And he wishes us to serve as executioners for those captives of Laird Ethelbert's army."

"Impossible," Reandu started to argue, but Artolivan thrust the scroll into his hand, and he couldn't deny the meaning of the words on the parchment.

"What are we to tell our brethren at Chapel Entel in Ethelbert? Or at any other of our chapels in holdings under the domain of Laird Ethelbert?" Master Reandu asked.

"To barricade their doors and pray," Father Artolivan asked as much as stated, so ridiculous was the answer.

"This is insanity," Brother Pinower dared declare.

"It is the unbridled vengeance of a man answerable to no one but himself," Artolivan said. "The old graves of Honce are filled with the results of such folly." He cast a sympathetic glance at the obviously uncomfortable Reandu. "Speak freely, brother from Pryd," he bade. "What do you think of King Yeslnik's designs?"

Reandu swallowed hard and shook his head. "I do not . . . I don't," he stammered, shaking his head again more forcefully. "I must reflect on it, Father."

"Truly?" asked Artolivan with evident surprise.

"I . . ."

"Be at ease, Brother," Artolivan mercifully said. "We are all caught by surprise. We must all reflect. I will write and seal my response for you to take on your return to Father Jerak and Chapel Pryd."

"Thank you, Father Artolivan," Master Reandu said with a bow.

After a long and uncomfortable silence, Father Artolivan, who thought their audience at an end, looked at the younger man curiously.

"There is one more matter," Reandu explained, "though I hesitate to even mention it in light of the gravity of the previous issue."

"Come out with it," Artolivan bade him. "I am old, but my heart is strong enough for your surprises."

Reandu smiled and nodded, obviously appreciating the levity. "There is a man traveling the roads of Honce. His name is Bransen Garibond, a man of my home holding."

Behind Artolivan, Pinower shuffled nervously.

"He is known as the Highwayman, a great warrior, but he also travels in the guise of an awkward and damaged man often called the Stork," Reandu explained.

"Yes," Artolivan prompted.

"He is charged with the murder of Laird Delaval," Reandu explained. "It was his sword that slew the great man."

That news, of course, confused the two monks of Chapel Abelle. As far as they knew, the Stork was still in Vanguard, a long way from Delaval City. They both did well to hide that fact, however.

"If you find him and capture him, King Yeslnik will be pleased, no doubt," said Reandu, who couldn't hide his grimace as he spoke.

"You are pained by the prospect," Artolivan observed. "You know this man?"

"For many years."

"And you believe that he killed Laird Delaval?"

"He is capable of great anger. It is not unexpected, given the tragedy of his life," Reandu explained. "The evidence seems strong, though I am surprised that Bransen would go to the lengths of murder. I . . . I simply do not know."

"He was seen west of here, along the road to Palmaristown," Father Artolivan said. "Though that was before the onset of winter. I have heard reports that he went to Vanguard."

"Those reports must have been in error," Master Reandu said.

"Or it wasn't his sword."

Reandu paused at that. It seemed to the others as if a dark cloud left his face, however briefly. "I will report that back to King Yeslnik as well," he assured them.

Father Artolivan let that sit for a few moments before nodding. "Is there anything more?"

"No."

"Good," said Artolivan. "You have given me more than enough, I am sure. Allow me now to reflect on King Yeslnik's demands so that I might properly fashion a response. But do tell me, how fares Father Jerak?"

"No better, no worse," Reandu replied.

"Your service in his stead is not unnoticed, Brother," Artolivan assured him.

Reandu swallowed hard.

"With the accidental death of Master Bathelais the chapel will likely fall to you in full."

Reandu shifted from foot to foot, too overwhelmed to reply.

"Father Jerak is an old and dear friend of mine. I am glad that he trained such competent successors," said Artolivan. "I am sure that your work would please him, as it pleases us. Go with grace, good young Master Reandu."

Reandu breathed a sigh of relief, bowed, and quickly took his leave.

"You need to reflect?" Brother Pinower asked Artolivan, his tone full of doubt.

"On whether or not it would be politic of me to publicly spank this young twit who thinks himself King of Honce," Artolivan replied.

"What are we to do?" Pinower asked.

"We are not to free the prisoners sent to us in good faith by Laird Ethelbert and his commanders," Father Artolivan insisted. He took a few deep breaths, but far from steadying him, he seemed to grow more agitated as he continued, his voice reflecting a deep-seated outrage. "To do so would be to betray our word to the people we serve. And of course the brothers are not going to act as executioners for a young king drunk with power! The Order of Abelle was founded as a gentle alternative to the vicious Samhaists. We have won over Honce's people with the utility of our blessed gemstones, true, but also with our determination to reduce the suffering of men, not to play as the Samhaists in inflicting misery. This is who we are. We are not murderers and executioners!

"This is madness!" he roared, though he quickly calmed and lowered his tone, suddenly fearful that Reandu was not far enough away and might hear. "Tell no one of this edict."

"Of course, Father," Pinower replied.

"Oh, what a week of ecstasy and agony," Father Artolivan lamented. "To hear the grand news of Dame Gwydre's victory and now to see the truth of King Yeslnik laid bare."

"Perhaps Dame Gwydre will aid us in our conflict with King Yeslnik," Brother Pinower offered. "Surely she will not agree with his brutal tactics."

"How far out is *Lady Dreamer*?" Father Artolivan asked, for only a day earlier, the advance ship from Vanguard had slid into Chapel Abelle's long wharf with news that Gwydre was on her way.

"Three days. Perhaps two. The weather has held across the gulf, we believe. She departed only four days behind the advance ship. No one is faster across the dark waters than Dawson McKeege."

Father Artolivan reflexively turned to glance out the window of his room, overlooking the dark waters of the Gulf of Corona. "Write our response immediately," he instructed. "Advise King Yeslnik—all proper respect in the use of his formal title!—that we will take his edict under advisement."

"Delay," Brother Pinower reasoned.

"Better that than to invite immediate war," said Artolivan. "We will indeed enlist Dame Gwydre in this trouble, should she be willing."

"Then the longer we take in replying the better."

"No, write it immediately—not with our decision, but with a promise that our decision will be forthcoming in short order. I want Master Reandu as far from here as quickly as possible, before he is even made aware of the impending visit of the victorious Lady of Vanguard. Reandu is spoken of in the highest terms, and he seems a man of mature and moderate temperament despite the unfortunate incident that led to the loss of Master Bathelais. But I'll not have our true feelings revealed beyond this room."

"Yes, Father."

"Let us hope that Dame Gwydre offers a solution," Artolivan said.

"Perhaps the solution will come from within," Pinower replied. "From the heart of Father Artolivan, who is closest to the spirit of Blessed Abelle."

He and Father Artolivan exchanged a long reflective look as the gravity of that statement weighed upon them.

Master Reandu left Chapel Abelle the next day, bound for his home of Pryd and bearing Father Artolivan's rolled and sealed response, which, of course, wasn't really a reply at all. Brother Pinower spent most of that day and the next two on Chapel Abelle's high wall, staring out at the gulf. When at last the sails of Vanguard ships appeared in the distance, he rushed to Father Artolivan and then down through the winding tunnels and stairways descending through the hundreds of feet of rocky cliff upon which sat their home. Much of Chapel Abelle lay within that mountain now, as the monks continually fashioned the deep limestone caves into chambers grand and humble. From the lowest chambers the two entered a long tunnel, its sides sculpted like the ridges of a clamshell, its air thick with brine and torch smoke. The fortified back door of Chapel Abelle, hundreds of feet below the main structures, opened onto a small beach in a deep, secluded bay.

With *Lady Dreamer* clearly in sight, Pinower rushed along the wharf past the brothers gathering up lines. He spotted Dawson, who often docked here. Beside him, to his sincere relief, stood Gwydre herself.

The young monk felt a sense of great elation at that, relief that she, this woman who might be the only hope against the insanity of Yeslnik, had indeed made the journey south from Vanguard.

"Praise Abelle, for he must have guided her heart," Pinower said with a hopeful smile. He looked back to the approaching ship and his smile became a look of concern, for moving up beside Gwydre came another distinctive figure dressed in black silk.

"Aye, but there's that Highwayman fellow," one of the wharf hands remarked.

"We should put him on a boat right back to Vanguard for his own sake," another added. "Afore Yeslnik hangs him, I mean."

"We know now that he could not have participated in the murder of Laird Delaval," said Pinower. "Unless he found some blessed spirits to fly him to Delaval City in the south and back again."

"Blessed?"

"Cursed spirits, then."

"I am not so certain that our new young King Yeslnik will accept any evidence contrary to the notions that fill his mind, given Master Reandu's description of him," said Pinower.

The ship moored alongside the long wharf then, monks and sailors fast tying her off, and soon the impressive procession moved down the plank to join Pinower and the other monks working the docks. Pinower was glad to see his old friend Father Premujon disembark beside Gwydre.

"All news from the north is good," Premujon said after the formal greetings, where Dawson did all the introductions.

"And so we have brought an eclectic entourage," Dame Gwydre remarked. "Brothers of the order and a priestess of Alpinador. A man of legend," she said, looking at Jameston Sequin, whose name was known along the southern coast of the Gulf of Corona, "and one in the making," she added, looking to Bransen.

"And of course, the hero of Vanguard and all of Honce, the lady who has renewed hope in our order with her victory over Ancient Badden," Brother Pinower said as they all began walking toward the doorway and the many staircases that would bring them back to the top of the great cliff. "It is a grand day in Chapel Abelle, indeed!"

"A day of hope," Gwydre agreed.

Pinower's expression flashed with both concern and tempered hope at that, but he said no more.

CHAPTER 13

Cornering a Snake

Every village along the Felidan Bay is ablaze," General Kirren Howen reported to Laird Ethelbert. "We will find no allies from that direction. And the villages of the Mantis Arm have been cut off from the mainland."

"They have many boats," the laird replied.

Kirren Howen shook his head, his expression grim. "They have been battered, laird. I doubt they'll come forth and leave their families to the mercy of merciless Milwellis of Palmaristown."

"But Yeslnik has broken off and moved back inland," Ethelbert remarked.

"Leaving Prince Milwellis of Palmaristown and his vile forces free run of the inner coast," the general reported. "Now the both of them, Yeslnik from the northwest and Milwellis from the north, would seem to have entered into a race to see who might arrive at our gates first."

Laird Ethelbert poured two glasses of shinaba, a potent liquor distilled from tart roots from the steppes of To-gai, a brutal land of horsemen and vile beasts to the west of the deserts of Behr, south of the Belt-and-Buckle. "To a good try, then," he said, handing one to Kirren Howen.

"I am not yet ready to surrender Ethelbert dos Entel to that putrid Yeslnik," the general said as he took the drink, then quaffed it in a single gulp. With Ethelbert's nod of approval, the man moved across the room to pour another.

"Surrender?" Ethelbert echoed incredulously. "Not Yeslnik or Milwellis will see the streets of my Entel, unless it is through the eyes of a disembodied head."

"A good try, you said. You speak as if we have lost."

"And we have, though we have stung our enemies profoundly," Ethelbert replied. "I fear that we haven't the resources to again march north and challenge for Honce, nor would I deign to put the people of the holdings through a continuation of this . . ."

He stopped when he noticed his general staring at him hard and disapprovingly.

"Your men fight because they love you," Kirren Howen declared. "You fought, not out of self-gain, but because you were the only one who could slow the thievery of Laird Delaval. Most men of Honce understand this."

"You are too kind, my old friend," Ethelbert replied. "And I do not doubt your loyalty or love, or that of many others like Myrick and the warriors of my holding. But for many of the others, the men and women of other holdings whose lairds decided that my gold was better than Delaval's, there is only misery and blood and agony and death. They hold my name no higher than the name of Delaval, or Yeslnik now (though I dare to believe that he will be less loved than either I or Delaval could ever have been). They fight because they are told to fight. They die because they cannot escape. They hate us all, no doubt, and hate their own miserable lives almost enough to make death a welcome alternative."

Kirren Howen didn't disagree, but the look on his face was one of utter dejection.

"We are not surrendering," Laird Ethelbert assured him. "And not Yeslnik or Milwellis will march into Ethelbert dos Entel. That much I promise. We are now the great biting turtles of the Belt-and-Buckle's end stones." He brought his hands together, fingers interlocked, and drew them tighter. "We close ranks and fight from positions where ten men might fend off a hundred. And whenever our enemies carelessly venture near our point, we bite at them and teach them pain.

"And we are more than a huddled turtle," he continued, a sinister smile coming over him. "We have vipers to send forth, a most venomous group."

Kirren Howen considered the words for a few heartbeats, then grimly nodded. "And when the vipers poison the attackers and send them reeling?" he asked. "Do we march forth and drive our enemies before us?"

"Eager for another try at the Bear of Honce?" Ethelbert asked slyly.

"A worthy opponent!" Kirren Howen replied. "So, yes."

"I do not like battling that one," Ethelbert admitted. "I fought beside him and Laird Prydae those years ago."

"I remember it well. Would that Bannagran—Laird Bannagran, I am told—had decided to ally with Laird Ethelbert!"

"Would that Laird Prydae had kept his loins, and then his life," said Ethelbert with a great sigh as he considered the tragic events that had ultimately driven Prydae and Pryd Holding from his side. He noticed Kirren Howen looking at him curiously.

"I thought to name Prydae to my line," Ethelbert said, surprising the general.

"He was a good man," Ethelbert explained. "But he lost his ability to continue his line, his balls taken by a powrie. Still, I blame myself for not acting forcefully enough to enlist him and his important holding, a holding become all the more important by the rise of the Bear of Honce." He ended with a profound sigh, one that had Kirren Howen nodding his head in agreement.

"To the vipers, then," Kirren Howen said and handed a second glass of shinaba to Ethelbert, who drained his first, then brought the other up to tap the general's, a toast they were both glad to acknowledge.

A re you ready, my prince?" asked Dimitri Raetu, holding back his obviously eager horse. The scouts ahead had reported confusion and terror in the ranks of their enemies, with most fleeing south. This next charge, back to the east and the Mirianic, would take the rocky hill anchoring the southern bank of a large bay just north of the city of Ethelbert dos Entel. That strong position would ensure that no ships could put in and off-load soldiers right behind their lines and would also serve as a fine vantage point for the short run to Ethelbert's city.

Milwellis, victorious all through the morning and all the day before, beamed with glee. Was he ready to win yet again? How could he not be? "King Yeslnik is still two days from Ethelbert City, and we'll be at her gates by evening."

"Is this a bad thing, my prince?" asked Harcourt, another of the commanders. He was the oldest of the generals who had set out from Palmaristown with Milwellis those weeks before. He also had fought with Panlamaris, Milwellis's father, in the powrie wars and in many sea battles when Panlamaris had seized control of the western reaches of the Gulf of Corona, thus ensuring Palmaristown's place among the most highly prized and important ports in all of Honce.

Milwellis looked at him curiously, not understanding how the prospects before them could possibly be considered as such. Still, his father had made it clear to him to heed well the advice of the veteran Harcourt. "You fear that I will outshine the king? Do you think me impolitic?"

"No, of course not, and we . . . you have earned all honors," the old general answered. "Your march south will be remembered throughout Honce for generations to come—already the bards are writing their songs of Milwellis's great victories—and never will a Palmaristown ship be out of reach of a friendly port, since you control them all now, from the river through the southern coast of the gulf and down the length of the Mantis Arm. All glory to Milwellis. Young prince, you've done your father proud, and no easy task that!"

Milwellis's stare took on a harder edge. "But . . . ?" he prompted.

"King Yeslnik is new to the throne, and the throne itself is new," Harcourt replied. "As such, he is no doubt unsure."

Several of the other Palmaristown knights, splendid in their shining suits of bronze, shuffled uncomfortably on their horses and looked to Milwellis, seeking to gauge his response to the possible affront.

"Unsure and insecure," Milwellis added, nodding his approval at the blunt-speaking Harcourt, which reassured the others. "So we are faced with a dilemma. I desire credit to Palmaristown's brave warriors for the taking of Ethelbert dos Entel, but I fear to walk too tall above Honce's new king, to whom my father has pledged fealty. What am I to do?"

The way he had asked, grinning from ear to ear, told them that he had already sorted out the solution, and so the knights just glanced at each other with confident nods and waited for Milwellis to explain.

"I will take my leave of you now," he told them, "riding west to King Yeslnik's line and camp. You proceed as we had planned. You will have no trouble smashing to the city's gate. And when I arrive, King Yeslnik will find his path clear to victory, Ethelbert dos Entel, the greatest prize of all, presented to him by my minions. All glory to Yeslnik for leading the march into the city, but all the men of the king's many holdings will know that it was Palmaristown and Milwellis who truly won the day."

He looked to Harcourt, who was nodding with approval. "Aye, but your father has raised a son who will well lead Palmaristown and more," the general said.

With a stern look Milwellis dismissed the others. As they walked their mounts away, he brought his horse up very close beside Harcourt.

"You find me too forward in front of the others?" the general asked.

"I have never heard such compliments flowing from the lips of Harcourt," Milwellis answered. "I find them unsettling."

"Perhaps you have never deserved them before."

Milwellis sat up straight as if the man had slapped him.

"I promised your father that I would counsel you and protect you," Harcourt pressed. "And protect you particularly from yourself. This is not easy business—oh, killing our enemies is simple enough, and a task you've learned well."

"But the politics of it," Milwellis reasoned.

"Trickier by far," said Harcourt, and he lowered his voice as he added, "And more so given that our new king is a man of exceeding vanity and unworldliness. Would that Laird Delaval had known an heir as worthy as Milwellis."

"You say so only because you fear you have angered me."

"I speak only because I do not fear to anger you," Harcourt answered without hesitation. "My loyalty is to Laird Panlamaris first, and I was fighting beside him before you were born. He charged me with fulfilling his own role beside you, to criticize when needed and to counsel always."

"And to praise?"

"Only when deserved. As now. There are two men in particular making names in this war, yourself and Bannagran, the champion of Pryd."

"He is a peasant."

"The warriors love him, and Yeslnik has named him Laird of Pryd."

"That does not change his peasant blood," Milwellis said with a scowl.

"And the warriors love you," Harcourt was quick to add. "And you have the advantage, young prince, for they fear you, as well. All who watched the burning of the Felidan villages understand well the severity of Prince Milwellis, and fear is a tool that will serve you well in the days after Ethelbert's certain defeat. As King Yeslnik sorts out his new and vast domain he will wisely and warily defer to you."

"All Honce's coast for Palmaristown, eh?"

"That is your father's greatest wish, one that you have made possible, even likely."

"My choice in going now to Yeslnik?" Milwellis asked. "Wise?"

"Brilliant beyond your years," Harcourt answered.

"Ride with me?"

"With honor, Prince of Palmaristown."

Aye, General Dimitri," one of the Palmaristown's knights replied with striking emphasis on the man's newfound title. The others, peers all until this point, laughed at their new commander's expense.

Dimitri Reatu laughed with them. This was his first command, handed to him by Prince Milwellis himself when Milwellis and Harcourt had departed. The mission seemed straightforward enough. The armored horsemen had a clear run to the hill and a clear trail up it. The fact that their enemies held the higher ground seemed inconsequential and had been to this point. For the Ethelbert defenders hadn't bows strong enough or spears heavy enough to inflict any real damage against the bronze plating and hadn't the heart to continue the fight anyway, having been in retreat for days now. A few stubbornly (or under orders) kept their positions along the hillside, a few light spears had reached Dimitri's band, and an enemy occasionally climbed on rocks, sword or long spear in hand to block the way.

But the Palmaristown knights had ridden right through the diversions, ignoring the flimsy missiles and cutting low the peasants, who wore no armor, who carried shields of ill-sewn leather, and who wielded weapons that bronze armor easily turned. In a gallop more often than a trot, Dimitri Reatu led his men up the side, with the top, the goal, clearly in sight.

Through the slit in his full helm, Dimitri hardly noted the Behr features on the shaved-headed man who appeared among the branches of a tree to his right or his strange black clothing.

Just another peasant to ignore or, if he ventured too near, to slay, so the new general thought.

Only one of Dimitri's band of ten even noted the stranger's sudden movements, his leaping from branch to branch with the grace of a squirrel, bounding to the top of a small pine just ahead and to the side of the lead rider. The knight called a warning, but his voice was filled more with curiosity than alarm.

The stranger disappeared into the thick boughs of the pine.

The knights charged forward.

The pine tree leaned over suddenly, as if to grasp at them. It was the black-clothed stranger, holding its top branches and leaping to the side, his weight and momentum taking the tree down with him in his descent. He came across Dimitri's horse, both men disappearing in a swirl of green.

And the knights gasped in unison as the tree swung back up, a flailing Dimitri affixed to it, the stranger sitting in Dimitri's saddle, hoisting the general hard to help the recovering tree gain momentum.

The nearest knight leaped his horse ahead and readied his sword to slash at the attacker, but as if he had anticipated that very movement, as if Dimitri's horse was no more than an extension of his thoughts, the stranger slapped the mount and it reared on cue, bucking and double-kicking back, slamming the charging horse in the chest. The jolt sent the knight tumbling from his seat to crash hard at the side of the trail.

The stranger whirled Dimitri's mount around and produced a strange weapon: two black poles as long as a forearm fastened end to end by an equally long length of dark leather. He held one of the poles and sent the other spinning as he brought his horse in line to pass by the next charging knight.

That man yelled, veering in and leveling his sword.

But the spinning pole went about that sword and wrapped it. A quick twist by the black-clothed warrior snapped the blade in half and freed the strange weapon in the same instant.

The knight tried to turn in closer, to stab with his suddenly shortened half sword, but the stranger veered his horse opposite, keeping just out of reach. As they passed, that curious twin-poled weapon snapped in against the back of the knight's bronze helm with such force that the back plate buckled in hard against his skull. The knight howled and reached up with both hands to clutch at his aching head, caring not that he had let go his reins, thinking only to get his cracking skull out of the bronze prison. Half mad with explosions of agony, the man never let go of the sides of his helm even as he toppled from his mount, even as he hit the hard ground headfirst, all of his weight crushing down upon his neck, pulverizing his spine. He flopped on the ground and rolled, coming to an awkward rest, having no control, no strength to straighten himself out.

The warrior from Behr turned to bring himself straight between the next two knights in line, and they adjusted their swords accordingly, thinking him mad and foolish despite his impressive display.

Just before the three horses passed, the stranger leaped to stand upon his saddle and sent his leather-tied sticks into a whirling display, moving them from hand to hand, over one shoulder then behind him and back under the other shoulder and all about his head with amazing precision.

The two knights tried to ignore the diversionary movements, tried to focus on taking the warrior's legs out.

The horses passed, the knights stabbed repeatedly, and the stranger from the southland danced and leaped and worked his sticks into a spin, into a forward rolling action before him. He caught the flying pole tight under his right armpit suddenly, leaped the stabbing blades and landed sidelong, pulling hard all the while on the other pole with his right hand, building tension against his own lock. He back-kicked his left foot just as he released the trapped pole from under his arm. It snapped forward like a To-gai viper with such force that it drove right through the knight's bronze helm and through the side of his skull.

The knight across the way fared little better, the back-kick hitting him with a force he could not have anticipated and at just the right angle to lift him from his seat. He went over the far side of the horse, his left foot still caught in the stirrup, and that tether twisted him underneath the galloping beast. Hooves pounded against him, which only frightened the horse more. It ran off across the hillside, the knight bouncing along the stones behind it.

The other horse continued to run as well, its rider quite dead, slumped over its neck.

The trailing knights, wanting no part of this southern creature, tried to turn aside, but other southerners appeared from the brush, leaping at them, kicking at them, stabbing them with long and thin poles. Only one managed to turn about completely, thinking to ride away to warn Prince Milwellis. He broke free and fought hard to balance his mount, refusing to relinquish the gallop even though he was in a steep descent. As the sounds of fighting receded behind him, he gradually relaxed and tried to ease his horse, but he realized his folly when he noted movement within the brush to the side of the path.

Another black-clothed warrior, a woman.

She closed in a confusing blur, springing to her hands, then over to her feet, then up into the air in a dizzying spin, landing again on her hands and springing away once more. With stunning speed she moved toward the trail, and the knight knew that he could not get past this somersaulting demoness.

Hands down, feet down, full airborne somersault, she came on, and he aimed his sword to the side at her as he crossed before her on the path.

But she just sprang higher in her next leap, climbing far above the sword, and the knight could only gawk.

She came out of her curl as she descended, her muscles and momentum driving her extending legs out to crack against the knight's shoulder and neck. He jolted down, then bounced back up and didn't even realize that he was clear of his saddle and mount and flying free to the ground, didn't even realize that the horse this black-clothed demoness from Behr was now astride was his own. He hit the ground, and all consciousness flew away.

The woman now riding paid him no heed, charging instead up the hill. Almost all the knights were down by the time she arrived, rolling and fighting, but one man remained in the saddle, and one of her warriors lay bloody on the ground beneath him.

Outraged, the former Jhesta Tu charged right for the man, who turned to meet the charge.

Except that suddenly she wasn't there! The horse remained but was riderless. By the time the knight understood that the woman had tucked her legs and leaped away and was now descending across his own mount, it was too late. The graceful woman barely touched the horse's back as she crossed over and flew away. The knight started to cry out a warning to his companions.

But he could not yell, could not make a sound, other than the gurgle of bubbling blood. He reached up to grasp his throat, flung aside his heavy gauntlet to get his fingers under his helm. To feel the warm blood, his throat slashed from side to side. He glanced back at the woman and saw a small, decorated sword barely more than a long dagger in her hand and stained with his own blood.

As he fell, he realized that it was not a dagger but a broken sword. In the last moments of his life he recalled that a sword had been broken in half in the chest of King Delaval.

The same sword, he knew with dying certainty. No comfort as the darkness closed.

———

U nworthy enemies," Merwal Yahna complained when the battle had ended.
Affwin Wi, her broken sword dripping with blood, glanced around,
her gaze focusing on the one of her warriors who was writhing on the ground.

"Not so unworthy," she argued.

"It was not their worthiness, but Ti'ragu's own error," Merwal Yahna
assured her. "His leap fell short of his target."

Affwin Wi nodded, then indicated Merwal Yahna's bloody nun'chu'ku, the
two poles tied with leather.

With a grim nod in reply, the fierce half-To-gai-ru, half-Behrenese warrior
walked over to his badly wounded companion and again sent his weapon into a
spin, catching the flying pole under his arm. His muscles bulged and strained as
he pulled against the hold, taking sure and merciful aim at the base of Ti'ragu's
skull.

All of the other Hou-lei gang began to hum in a low and somber key.

Merwal Yahna released the trapped nun'chu'ku pole, and it snapped forward to devastating effect.

Ti'ragu lay very still.

C aught in the top branches of the swaying pine, Dimitri Reatu rolled
around just in time to see the execution of the wounded Behrenese warrior. Somehow that cold-blooded act, killing one of their own with such impunity, brought the first-time general to a new plane of terror. His fingers turned
bloody as he desperately forced them under the rim of his helm and under the
fine silk rope tied about his neck and hanging him from the trunk.

All of his knights had been slain within moments, the black-clothed southerners moving about them with deadly precision. He dared hope that maybe they
had forgotten him or believed him already dead. He closed his eyes, tightened his
neck muscles as much as possible to fight the choke, and tried to go very still.

He knew their laughter was directed at him before he even opened his eyes
again.

The one who had caught him, the tall one with the shaved head and the
strange weapon, moved to the low boughs right below him and pulled forth
from them a silk rope—the other end of the one binding him, Dimitri understood, just a moment before the southerner tugged it and the clever knot unwound and the young general crashed and bounced to the ground in the midst
of his laughing, victorious enemies.

Prince Milwellis and Harcourt did not receive the greeting they had antici-pated when they at last came to King Yeslnik's encampment. Traveling through the tree-lined dells of the region, they had not seen the developments in the east along the shore until they crested the tall hill to stand beside Yesl-nik and his commanders.

Milwellis noted immediately that the king's eye was not turned to the southeast and the city of Ethelbert dos Entel as he had expected, but to the northeast.

"You are here?" Yeslnik blurted with surprise when the Prince of Palmar-istown rode up beside him.

"What is this about?" Milwellis demanded, sliding down from his mount and running to the edge of the hillock.

"Your army is being routed," one of Yeslnik's commanders remarked.

"And you are here!" Yeslnik added.

"Routed? They should be at the gates of Ethelbert by now!" Milwellis de-clared, and he began stomping about like a caged beast.

"They've lost a league of ground," Yeslnik grumbled.

"Did Ethelbert come at them with all his force? Even then, we should have routed—" Milwellis stopped when he noted Yeslnik's generals shaking their head.

"Our scouts saw no sizable force moving from the city gates," one said. "Are you certain that your men simply did not retreat?"

The scowl Milwellis gave him was all the answer he needed and more than enough to silence that notion.

More scouts went out from Yeslnik's camp soon after, and more came in, with reports of dead Palmaristown soldiers and the main force in fast retreat. Milwellis wanted to ride to them, but Yeslnik would hear none of that.

"He's more interested in making sure that he's surrounded by strength," Harcourt dared to mention to Milwellis as they wandered about the encamp-ment.

Milwellis looked at him incredulously but finally nodded, glad again that his father had thought to put this candid and seasoned warrior beside him.

Long after the sun had set, the riddle of the retreat was finally solved, for some of Yeslnik's scouts returned with a pair of Milwellis's men, both wounded.

"Demons!" one insisted. "They walked invisible through the trees!"

"Demons?" Yeslnik and two of his commanders said in unison.

"Not demons," the other said. "Men, sure enough—and women!

Southerners. Beasts of Behr. Ah, but they're demons when they're fighting, none should doubt!"

"A sizable force?" Yeslnik asked.

"A handful."

"Backed by?" Milwellis asked.

"Just a handful," answered the soldier. "And our knights're all gone."

"Gone?" asked Yeslnik.

"Dimitri Reatu?" asked Milwellis.

"All gone," the soldier answered grimly. "They went up the hill—"

"And the demons came down," the other soldier added.

King Yeslnik lifted a hand to silence the plethora of questions the others started to ask. "You saw them? Up close?"

The soldiers nodded.

"What weapons did they wield?"

"Strange ones for some, swords for a couple," one answered.

"And one used a half sword," said the other.

Yeslnik looked at him curiously.

"Broken, maybe," the man explained. "But half a sword and with a jagged tip."

King Yeslnik looked as if he might topple over. He turned to regard his commanders and Milwellis.

"What is it, my king?" the Prince of Palmaristown asked when it appeared as if Yeslnik couldn't find his voice.

"The assassins who killed King Delaval," one of the commanders explained.

"Where are these enemies now?" Yeslnik demanded of the soldiers. Even in the dim light it was obvious that the blood had drained from the young king's face.

The two looked to each other and shrugged, then turned back sheepishly to the king. "The fighting has stopped, my king," one of Yeslnik's scouts said for them. "The enemy disappeared into the hills, likely exhausted."

King Yeslnik began glancing around, eyes darting nervously from shadow to distant shadow.

"And so the war continues," he said, his voice cracking and uneven. "Ethelbert has averted disaster—we cannot push him into the sea."

"A full attack, north and west, my king," one of the commanders offered. "A few assassins will not stop the prepared lines of our army!" He looked to Milwellis accusingly as he spoke.

"No, no, no," Yeslnik replied, shaking his head and walking about in circles. "No, we should not remain here. Not now. Ethelbert has turned the tide against us. He is wounded and battered and will not come forth. And so we can go, quickly."

"Go?" the commander asked.

"To lands more familiar and more to our liking," Yeslnik explained. "Yes, that is the course. We will retreat to Pryd Town, or to Delaval."

"Delaval was no defense against the assassins before," the commander dared to remind him.

"But we will be more vigilant!" Yeslnik screamed. "We will back away—and parley. Yes, parley. Perhaps Ethelbert will stay in his city and we can go. We can take the rest of Honce. Yes, yes, I must consider our course. But not here. Not now. Break the camp, and be ready to depart."

He walked off as he spoke, and it did not escape Milwellis and Harcourt that more than one of King Yeslnik's commanders rolled his eyes.

"He is a man of great courage," Harcourt whispered to Milwellis as they rode from the camp soon after, heading back to where the army of Palmaristown had regrouped.

Milwellis didn't bother to reply to the sarcasm. There was no answer.

CHAPTER 14

Aimlessly Wandering

A dejected Master Reandu walked into the small village of Eskald three days' north of Pryd Town. An inconsequential place, Eskald had no chapel and only a tiny keep, barely more than a stone house atop a cleared hill, to serve as the castle for its laird.

The day was young, and Reandu thought to travel right through Eskald and continue on his way home. There was another community, Chud, a cluster of huntsmen's houses several hours farther to the south. As he passed along the main road through the bulk of the houses, though, the monk saw that the people were all astir, and he knew that their agitation was not on account of his arrival.

He turned a questioning gaze on one young woman whose response was a chin nod toward the laird's house on the hill. Following that look, Reandu noted a familiar sight: the chariot of Bannagran.

With a sigh of relief—perhaps he could ride south with the man—Reandu moved up the hill. He didn't even have to tell the lone guard to announce him to the laird, for Bannagran was coming out the door even as he approached.

Reandu thought that a good thing, for the Laird of Eskald, a man of great mouth and little repute by the name of Mackwok Boln, was one of the most insufferable and self-absorbed men Reandu had ever met. A visit with him would involve hours of time, listening to the man recount the exploits of his long-lost youth, how he rode with Prydae in the powrie war (which wasn't true, though the pompous laird had probably claimed as much to Bannagran, who had led Prydae's forces in that very conflict), and how Laird Ethelbert had not come to attack Eskald out of respect, nay fear, of the heroic Mackwok Boln. Reandu had heard it all before and on several occasions, including the first steps of his journey north to Chapel Abelle.

The look on Bannagran's face, like it was locked in a permanent sigh, told Reandu that his friend had not been spared the recounting.

"Has he saved the world this day?" he greeted.

Bannagran laughed at that. "Twice, methinks."

"I did not expect to see you here," said Reandu. "I've been told that the fighting has moved south."

"All the way to Ethelbert dos Entel."

"And you are north of Pryd. On the hunt for the Highwayman?"

"I've been tasked with that," Bannagran reminded. "King Yeslnik has determined that his finest general should don the mantle of bounty hunter, and this at a time when his greatest enemy might soon be pushed into the sea." His voice trailed off as he noted that Reandu was smirking at him. "What do you know?"

"His finest general?" Reandu echoed with a wide grin.

Bannagran snorted at him, waved his hand and walked past, heading for the chariot.

"I am just unused to such aggrandizement from you, about you," Reandu explained, hounding him every step.

"Be at ease, monk," said the warrior. "Else I will show you the truth of the claim."

Reandu laughed at the empty threat.

"What news of our masked friend?" Bannagran asked.

"He was seen on the road to Chapel Abelle," said Reandu. "He passed through Palmaristown but did not arrive at Chapel Abelle."

"One of the villages to the west of that place, then? Or did he pass to the east by the chapel and move along Felidan Bay? If that is the case, then he is likely dead. Milwellis offered little quarter to the people of the holdings who joined with Laird Ethelbert's cause."

Reandu blew a deep sigh, certain that Bannagran would not be pleased with his information. "The whispers claim that our friend Bransen went to Vanguard before the winter."

"The whispers are wrong, then," Bannagran said, and he nodded his chin to the spear bucket set on the chariot, in which stood the broken half of the sword blade that had been taken from the chest of King Delaval.

"Or that is not Bransen's sword," Reandu replied. "He went to Vanguard before the winter, they claim, and claim with some confidence. It is rumored that Bransen joined with Dame Gwydre in her struggles against the Samhaists. We both know that Bransen had no love for that cult."

Bannagran suddenly appeared more tired, and he rubbed his face.

"You believe that King Yeslnik will send you there in pursuit?"

"If the Highwayman is there, then he will," Bannagran replied. "Without doubt. He wants our friend dead. More than anything in the world, he wants the Highwayman slaughtered."

"If Bransen is in Vanguard, then he couldn't have killed King Delaval," Reandu said plainly. "The distance is too great, and the seas and land impassible through the winter months. Surely King Yeslnik will understand this and will rethink the best course for his finest general."

Bannagran shook his head through every word. "It would hardly matter. Yeslnik's hatred of this one was strong before the evidence of the Highwayman's complicity in King Delaval's death, before King Delaval had even been killed. Twice now has our little friend robbed him, and both times shaming him in front of his insuffera . . . his wife. To a man like Yeslnik, that is a more egregious crime than murder."

"A vain man like Yeslnik, you mean, and with an insufferable wife."

"Your words, not mine, and words to get you slain."

Reandu just shrugged. "King Yeslnik has invited great strife within the Order of Abelle. Father Artolivan cannot do what he has demanded of us."

Bannagran looked at him curiously.

"To free all prisoners loyal to Delaval who were sent to the keeping of the brothers," Reandu explained. Bannagran nodded as if he did not think that so egregious. Reandu let that notion sink in just a bit more before adding, "And to kill all loyal to Ethelbert."

Bannagran's face screwed up for a moment, but then he just shook his head and snorted, as if hardly surprised, as if nothing Yeslnik did would ever surprise him.

"He will send you to Vanguard?" Reandu asked, and Bannagran nodded.

"To the edge of the world and over it," he replied. "Our young king is not in good humor. He is wounded by the death of Delaval."

"And he is afraid," Reandu dared to say, and again Bannagran nodded.

"And he is frustrated by Ethelbert's stubbornness and fight," the warrior added. "Yeslnik is focusing all of those emotions on the Highwayman now, as if he is the source of all the prince's ills. He will not rest until he has the head of Bransen Garibond."

"So you are certain and will head straightaway to Vanguard?"

"No, and I hope that I am wrong!"

"You are returning to Pryd, then?"

Bannagran nodded. "Though I fear my rest will be short."

"And you will offer a brother a ride in your fine chariot?"

"No, but I am sure that Reandu is so forward that he will take one anyway." He moved up to his driver post. Grinning, Reandu stepped up behind him.

They made Pryd Town the next day, just as the first advance scouts of King Yeslnik's army were arriving with news of the stinging reversal at the gates of the southern city. The news that the war was still on in full, that Ethelbert had stayed the seemingly inevitable conclusion, was not as unwelcome to Bannagran as it was to Reandu. At least for Bannagran, it offered some hope that he wouldn't be sent to the cold north of Vanguard.

CHAPTER 15

That Which Is Right

"They'll not be any quicker because of your pacing," Cadayle said to Bransen later the very same day that *Lady Dreamer* brought them to Chapel Abelle. Sitting beside her on the long bench in the antechamber, Callen gave a laugh.

"He's blazing a fine trail across Father Artolivan's rug," she said.

Bransen did stop his pacing momentarily to regard the women. They had been waiting in the antechamber to Father Artolivan's audience hall for more than an hour, expecting to be called in to speak on behalf of Cormack, who was in front of the Court of Chapel Abelle facing the impassioned appeals of Father De Guilbe.

"He's got Father Premujon speaking for him, and Brother Giavno, even," Cadayle reminded. "And Dame Gwydre herself. She had to preside neutrally over the court in Vanguard, but here she makes no secret of her support for Cormack and Milkeila."

"I've seen too much of the likes of men akin to Father De Guil—" Bransen started to say, but he stopped fast as the door swung open and Father De Guilbe stormed from the audience chamber. Brother Giavno came close behind the large and angry man and tried to speak.

De Guilbe turned suddenly and snapped, "Do not follow me, Brother, else I will be spending my next days inside Chapel Abelle's dungeon!"

At first, Giavno looked as if he had been slapped, but as De Guilbe stormed from the antechamber and across the open courtyard the monk just sighed and shrugged at the three witnesses.

"I'm guessing it went well for Cormack and Milkeila," Cadayle said with a grin.

"Beyond anything I could have hoped," said Cormack from the door. Arm in arm, he and Milkeila moved from the audience hall.

"Father Artolivan would like to sanction our marriage formally," Cormack explained.

"Then you are forgiven," said Bransen.

"And offered a return to the order," Milkeila said.

Bransen's face twisted uncomfortably at that. "You'll not go back," he said.

"I've made no decision," said Cormack. "But it was good to be asked."

From inside the audience hall Dame Gwydre called out, "Hurry along, then!"

"They would see you now," said Milkeila.

Bransen and the two women exchanged surprised looks, for they thought they had been brought here solely to speak on Cormack's behalf, which was apparently no longer required. With a shake of Cormack's hand and a hug for Milkeila, Bransen entered the audience hall, his wife and Callen close behind.

"I had thought to be speaking for Cormack," he said as he walked to the center of the carpet. He faced a long table, behind which sat Father Artolivan and Father Premujon, Dame Gwydre, several other monks Bransen did not know, and, surprisingly, Jameston Sequin and Dawson McKeege. He couldn't help but feel as if he were standing before some kind of inquisition, though he took faith in the friends seated at that table.

"It was not necessary," Father Artolivan replied. "Cormack's character was well presented and represented."

"We have heard news of you, young man," Artolivan continued before Bransen could ask why he had been summoned if not for Cormack. "Information regarding the Highwayman."

"It is good to be famous." Bransen's sarcasm didn't brighten the grim faces staring back at him, which didn't bother him so much concerning Artolivan, but Dame Gwydre seemed equally uneasy.

"You are hunted, friend," Artolivan said, "accused of a crime against the throne of Honce."

"I did not know that Honce had a throne," Bransen replied, all glibness gone from his voice. "Just a bunch of petty lords with petty concerns and not a care at all of who they destroy to see their desires fulfilled."

Father Artolivan smiled and glanced at Dame Gwydre.

"A notable exception to the rule," Bransen quickly added, bowing deferentially to the Lady of Vanguard.

Dame Gwydre waved it off and seemed hardly to care, but Father Artolivan cleared his throat, bringing the conversation back on topic. "You are accused of a serious crime, Highwayman."

"That I robbed that idiot Yeslnik in Delaval City?" Bransen replied. "Of that I admit my guilt. I robbed him as well in Pryd right after I rescued him from certain death at the hands of marauding powries. I have already admitted my past deeds, though in my heart I fear that my biggest error was in saving Yeslnik from the dwarves." He bowed as he finished, and when he came up, he saw the principles at the table all exchanging somber and concerned looks. Bransen looked back to Cadayle and Callen, and then all three of them shared confused shrugs.

"Dame Gwydre's Writ of Passage was offered with knowledge of those thefts," Bransen said somewhat more defensively than he had intended.

"Laird Delaval—King Delaval—was murdered in the same tower where you robbed his nephew," Father Artolivan said.

"At the same time?"

"No. Recently," said Artolivan.

"While you were in Vanguard," Dame Gwydre added.

Bransen held up his hands, not quite understanding. "I am sorry?" he asked as much as stated.

"King Yeslnik—" Father Artolivan started, but Bransen interrupted with a cry.

"King?" he blurted.

"He proclaims himself King of Honce as the rightful heir of Delaval, who similarly demanded the title," Artolivan explained.

Bransen snorted with obvious derision.

"He believes you complicit in the death of his uncle, King Delaval," Artolivan explained.

"My arms are not that long," Bransen quipped, but he saw Gwydre, grim-faced, shaking her head at him. "I did not know the man. Why would I want to kill him? And if I haven't killed the loathsome Yeslnik, then why would I go out of my way to kill his uncle?"

"Your contempt for the new King of Honce is noted," Artolivan said dryly. "As is your proclamation of innocence."

"I have been in Vanguard throughout the winter," Bransen replied, growing more animated with every word. "With him." He pointed to Dawson. "And with Brother Jond, and Cormack after him. How could I have been involved in a murder in Delaval City?"

Father Artolivan held up his hands to calm the man. "We are not your judge and jury. We know that you could not have been involved in this tragedy. But King Yeslnik will not be so easily swayed, I fear, given all that I have heard of him."

"What does that mean?"

"It means that my Writ of Passage to you may not be enough," Dame Gwydre answered. "It means that you and Cadayle and Callen should remain here or perhaps even sail back to Vanguard with me when I go."

Bransen stared at her hard, angrily, suspiciously.

"I honor the Writ of Passage," Father Artolivan was quick to say, "and will not detain you in any manner. You and your family are welcome at Chapel Abelle."

Bransen never blinked and never stopped staring at Gwydre.

"Yeslnik claims that Bransen, the Highwayman, killed Delaval," Gwydre said.

"We know otherwise," said Bransen.

"We do," Gwydre agreed. "But he does not. Nor do the lairds who do his bidding. It was Master Reandu of Chapel Pryd who delivered the news, only right before we arrived here."

Bransen's face brightened at the name.

"You know him?" Gwydre asked.

"Quite well, I am told," said Artolivan. "And if it means anything to you, young man, I think that Master Reandu doubted in his heart the claims against you."

At that moment the words meant nothing, for suddenly the weight of it all came clear to Bransen. He felt as if the walls were pressing in on him. He could hardly remember to draw breath. He had no response to this surprising news or to the involvement of Reandu, his old . . . what? Friend? Mentor?

"We will work to clear your reputation," Dame Gwydre assured him.

"If Yeslnik is King of Honce, then your work will be in vain. Know that he will always hate the Highwayman," Bransen finally replied. "As much because of his own failings as a husband and a man as because of the robberies."

Behind him, Cadayle gave a little yelp of surprise.

"His wife was rather taken by a man who would fight against enemies instead of sniveling inside the coach," Bransen explained to her and turned back to the table. "If Yeslnik is your king, then, as much as I would have thought it impossible, my estimation of the nobility and leadership of the Honce Holdings has sunk even lower. He is a fool and a fop, a vain and preposterous coward, and—"

"Enough, Bransen," said Artolivan. "We will work to clear your name as Dame Gwydre insisted. We are interested in justice."

"That is not my experience with laird or brother."

"Enough," Artolivan bade him. "We ask that you remain here for your own sake and the sake of your family until we can clear away all this confusion."

"Or we will be sailed to Behr," Bransen said, staring again directly at

Gwydre, then sliding his gaze to take in Dawson McKeege, who was nodding his agreement.

"Give us time," Gwydre said. After a stone-faced moment, Bransen nodded.

"And now you will excuse us," Father Artolivan said. "For we have other matters to discuss."

Before Bransen and the two women turned to go Dame Gwydre interjected, "No, I wish Bransen to sit with me as we discuss the situation."

Father Artolivan looked at her with surprise and something less than enthusiasm.

"He has earned it," Gwydre insisted. She turned to Bransen and motioned to an empty chair at the end of the table. "He may be quite important as this goes forward. The Highwayman is not unknown in Honce and not unloved by many of the people we seek to serve."

After a moment Artolivan sighed. "Would the two of you please excuse us then?" he said, indicated Cadayle and Callen. Cadayle moved up and kissed Bransen on the cheek and squeezed his hand, then took her leave with her mother.

For all his bravado, Bransen felt quite unsure of himself as he moved to take the seat between Jameston and Gwydre. He sat quietly as the group began discussing Yeslnik's new edict regarding disposition of prisoners. He wasn't surprised by the foppish, self-proclaimed king's lack of simple morality, of course.

"And you will react how?" Dame Gwydre asked after Artolivan had explained every detail regarding Yeslnik's demands for the prisoners entrusted to the Order of Abelle and his further demand that the church declare allegiance to him in his struggles with Ethelbert.

"We must refuse this man who calls himself King of Honce," Father Artolivan declared. All the monks around him nodded and whispered their agreement.

Bransen arched his eyebrows in pleasant surprise.

"And I will support you, of course," said Dame Gwydre. "Let us hope that King Yeslnik will listen to reason on this matter."

"He won't," Bransen interrupted, surprised at himself for saying that aloud. Everyone turned to him, so he continued, "He is stubborn and vain beyond description."

"In that case we will be faced with more difficult decisions still," said Father Artolivan. He sighed and seemed very old and tired at that moment. "But we will forge our way through the obstacles as they are presented to us. For now King Yeslnik awaits our further word on his edict regarding the prisoners.

He will not be pleased, but we must follow that which is right and just and in concert with the teachings of Blessed Abelle."

For some reason the decision and declaration of the father of the Order of Abelle unsettled Bransen even more than the unsurprising news of Yeslnik's continuing and escalating stupidity. He left the meeting much later on, his thoughts spinning, both for himself and his family and their place in the world and for the larger issues of Honce and this new king who could be nothing more than a catastrophe.

The couriers went from Chapel Abelle soon after the meeting had adjourned. While watching them depart, still surprised by the continuing actions of the church, Bransen heard a familiar voice call to him.

"How do you fare with the new order of the world?" asked Cormack.

Bransen turned and greeted him as he approached. "I am not surprised by the actions of Yeslnik, to be sure. I have encountered the man a couple of times in the last months. Neither meeting has left me impressed with his wit or his wisdom."

"I mean regarding Bransen," Cormack clarified. Bransen stared at him curiously.

"You expected to walk Honce a free man," said Cormack.

"And so I shall."

"By your stubbornness and your sword? Is there not the matter of your wife and her mother to consider?"

"Dame Gwydre—"

"Is powerless against Yeslnik at this time. Her Writ of Passage will not be honored for a man believed to be the killer of King Delaval. And, honestly, it would be foolhardy to not rescind the order. If you go and present that document, then she, too, will be complicit in the killing of King Delaval."

"I had nothing to do with that. I was beside you, was I not?"

"And you believe that matters?"

Bransen gave a helpless laugh. "No," he admitted.

"So what will you do?"

"I don't know. Dawson McKeege has pledged to sail me wherever I wish to go. Perhaps to Behr."

"Jacintha?"

Bransen furrowed his brow in puzzlement.

"The principle city of the desert kingdom," Cormack explained. "Just south of the city of Ethelbert dos Entel around the Belt-and-Buckle mountains, whose rocky spurs jut into the Mirianic as if god himself did not want the men of Honce and of Behr to mingle."

"Jacintha, then."

"It is a strange place with strange ways," Cormack warned.

"A fine choice you offer," Bransen replied.

"Father Artolivan will not expel you or your family, nor will he turn you over to Yeslnik's soldiers if they come."

"So you offer me imprisonment in a chapel of a faith I do not hold true or a journey to a strange and dangerous place," Bransen reasoned. "Shall I thank you for creating great contentment within my tumultuous soul?"

Cormack couldn't suppress a laugh at the deserved sarcasm. "Vanguard," he said a moment later, and again he drew a puzzled look from Bransen.

"It is a wondrous place," said Cormack. "Full of freedom and personal responsibility. It is the perfect location for one who wants no part of the politics and intrigue of Honce, or of Behr, I am told."

"Will Cormack be there?"

"And Milkeila. Dame Gwydre speaks of dividing up her vast holding into smaller duchies and has hinted that she will offer one to me."

"And you would like the Highwayman as a subject," Bransen said dryly.

"Or as a neighboring duke."

Bransen laughed all the more, and all the more helplessly. "I thought you just said . . ."

"I did, and I hold to it," Cormack replied. "I only mean that if you wished more for yourself and Cadayle, then you will find an ally in Dame Gwydre, do not doubt. She expressed deep gratitude to me when we spoke quietly about a possible appointment, though she counseled me to consider Father Artolivan's offer to return to the Order of Blessed Abelle."

"And will you?"

Cormack shrugged, and Bransen knew that the man was truly uncertain here, truly torn. "I would be a liar if I said that I was not intrigued. Great healing might be accomplished between the Order of Abelle and Milkeila's shaman brethren and between Vanguard and the Alpinadoran tribes. Father De Guilbe did great damage on Chapel Isle. Our battle with the many tribes of Mithranidoon Lake—"

"And De Guilbe's refusal to join in the common cause against Ancient Badden," Bransen interrupted, and Cormack nodded solemnly.

"Perhaps I can do some good," Cormack finished.

"As a monk or as a duke?"

"That is the question, is it not?"

"Why not as both?"

It was Cormack's turn to wear an expression of surprise, which shifted to one of intrigue. He paused for a few moments, then took a deep and steadying breath and looked back to Bransen. "But what for you?"

Again, the young warrior shrugged. "I wish at some point to travel to Behr—I must. But Honce is my home, and I do not count that lightly. And there is another matter . . ." He stopped just short of telling Cormack of Cadayle's pregnancy, deciding instead to remark, "Honce is Callen and Cadayle's home, as well, and they should be free to remain here and wait for my return— particularly Callen, who long ago grew weary of the road."

"You would trust Yeslnik to honor the Writ of Passage for them and not imprison them to use against you?"

"Of course I would not."

"And so we are back where we began."

"I will go to Pryd Town to test Dame Gwydre's Writ of Passage," Bransen decided then and there. "And if it is not to be honored, I will do what I need to clear my name and to demand the commute of any claims made against me. I served honorably under a bargain from a Honce Lair . . . Lady. I expect, when the truth is known that I could not have participated in the murder of King Delaval, that my covenant with Dame Gwydre will be respected."

"You will march south and demand all that?"

"I will journey south more quietly, and learn and adapt," said Bransen. "I am the Highwayman, have you not heard? And the Highwayman has many friends in Pryd Town."

"And many enemies?"

"That is what I intend to learn."

She knew.

That truth permeated Bransen's thoughts as he navigated the corridors and courtyards of the sprawling complex of Chapel Abelle. He had tried to hide his decision from Cadayle for the time being—out of cowardice, he admitted to himself—but she had seen through him, and his tenuous and halting answers, stuttered even though he had the soul stone firmly tied against his forehead, had led Cadayle to more incisive and determined questioning.

By the time Bransen had managed an appropriate dodge to the larger question of his intentions, Cadayle had already confirmed her suspicions.

She knew, Bransen believed, that he was planning to leave her once again despite his promises to her in Vanguard.

The look on her face as he had walked out of their room that morning, a combination of resoluteness and sadness, had nearly made him change his mind, had nearly turned him toward a different course—perhaps back to Vanguard with Cormack.

But now, as he walked the ways of the great chapel complex, as he heard the familiar dialect of the many men hard at work, Bransen understood that he must go at once to Pryd Town, to confront Reandu with the hard evidence, the letters of proof from many reliable affiants. He had to believe that somewhere, somehow, even in the holdings of Yeslnik, the truth would ultimately win out and he would be exonerated and that Gwydre's Writ of Passage for him and for his family would be honored.

If there was any justice in the world, this course would be the correct one to walk.

But Cadayle knew.

His inner tumult slowed his steps as he neared Father Artolivan's chambers, and he slowed further as he came to hear loud arguing from behind the solid oaken door. Growing up as the Stork, where so many people had thought him an idiot and had spoken about him and about important matters right before him, it didn't even occur to Bransen that he shouldn't eavesdrop.

Right before the door, the words became clear, as did the voices of fathers Artolivan, Premujon, and De Guilbe.

"You would have me kill them," Artolivan shouted, "these men who were given to Chapel Abelle and put under our care on condition that for them the war had ended?"

"We must choose between Yeslnik, who will win, and Ethelbert, who hides in the south," De Guilbe argued. "The greater movement of the kingdom is beyond our control. Delaval won and gave his winnings to Yeslnik, and thus Yeslnik is the King of Honce."

"That simply?" asked Premujon.

"Yes! Unless you know of some great army stirring to oppose him."

"His victory over Laird Ethelbert seems assured, by last reports," Father Artolivan unhappily agreed, speaking lower so that Bransen had to move right up and put his ear to the door to understand.

"Then we are to recognize Yeslnik as King of Honce," said De Guilbe. "What other choice is before us?"

"Recognition with precondition," said Artolivan. "Perhaps. We can force King Yeslnik's hand on this and other matters, promise our fealty, but only to a goodly king."

De Guilbe snickered loudly. "You think yourself the king," he accused.

"Father De Guilbe!" Premujon scolded.

"If Yeslnik is the King of Honce, then the decisions are his to make," De Guilbe continued, undaunted. "We cannot say that we agree here and disagree, and therefore will not abide, there. Is he the King of Honce or is he not? And if he is, then we are bound to honor—"

"I will not murder unarmed prisoners!" Father Artolivan cried.

"Then you should not have involved our order in this secular business of war!" Father De Guilbe scolded.

"Father!" Premujon shouted again.

"It is true!" De Guilbe shouted right back at him. "We heal the wounded for both sides. That is a good thing, and all the chapels agreed. But then you agreed to turn our most holy and important monastery into a prison?"

"A prison that sent men to the aid of Vanguard!" Premujon reminded.

"That matters not at all! Father Artolivan took it upon himself to involve the order in matters where it did not belong. You cannot make such a stand and then decide at a later date that you don't like the outcome."

"We retained our neutrality," Father Artolivan argued, and De Guilbe snorted as if the notion was absurd.

"Until one side or the other gained the advantage," De Guilbe said. "For surely, had Ethelbert won the field, his demands upon you would be equally harsh and distasteful."

"I do not believe that, nor do I believe that Laird Delaval would be possessed of such . . . cruelty."

"Then you are a fool," said De Guilbe. "And you have softened to the point where your leadership is a danger to the Order of Abelle."

"Father!" Premujon shouted again, but De Guilbe shouted back at him to shut up.

"I demand a Council of Fathers," De Guilbe said.

"Denied," said Father Artolivan.

"You cannot deny it alone!"

"Denied," echoed Premujon. "Two to one, then. Find more fathers of similar humor to yours and make your request at a later date."

"And until then, know that I will not execute the men of Laird Ethelbert, taken under honor and sent here under promise of my protection," Father Artolivan assured him.

"And the men of Laird Delaval?"

"Are here as agreed. King Yeslnik will not have them turned free to serve his cause until the war with Laird Ethelbert is settled."

Father De Guilbe began to laugh, a chuckle that rang of little mirth in the ears of Bransen.

"Our order has gone soft," he said. "As with Cormack, who betrayed us."

"This was about Cormack all along," Premujon accused.

"It is about a church that forgets the harsh lessons of the wider world," De Guilbe replied, but calmly now—and that seemed far more imposing to Bransen than his fiery rant of a few seconds before. "A church so steeped in false hope and idealism and tolerance that it ensures its own inevitable collapse."

"If I gave you a sword and the order from King Yeslnik, would you kill the prisoners with your own hand, Father De Guilbe?" Father Artolivan asked.

"Yes," the man replied without the slightest hesitation.

Bransen did well to hide his own gasp as both Artolivan and Premujon issued theirs.

"Because I look beyond the lives of a few and the immediacy of our current situation," De Guilbe clarified. "War is cruel, and need be, to end it swiftly and to make the mere thought of it cause men to piss in their breeches."

"You sound like a Samhaist," said Premujon, his voice subdued now as if De Guilbe's stark admission had simply broken his will to argue.

"You are dangerously wrong in your decisions, Father Artolivan," said De Guilbe.

"If you believe that, then find enough support among the brethren to force your council," Father Artolivan wearily replied. "Truly you tire me. I sent a man of spirit and hopefulness to Alpinador those years ago, a mission that I thought De Guilbe might accomplish in bridging the differences between our ways and those of our northern brothers. This man who returns to me these years later hardly resembles the one I knew."

"Because I am wiser."

"Because you are hardened, and stubborn."

De Guilbe snorted, and Bransen heard heavy footfalls coming his way. He managed to jump back a couple of steps and tried to appear as if he was just arriving when the door was flung open and the large monk rushed out. With only a cursory glance at Bransen and a dismissive shake of his head, De Guilbe stormed away.

"Greetings, Bransen Garibond," Father Artolivan said—to Bransen's back, since the Highwayman had turned to watch the angry De Guilbe's departure. "To what do I owe the pleasure of your visit so early in the day?"

Bransen turned about. "Your pardon, Father," he said with a bow. "I have made a decision and wished to inform you first of all."

"A decision? I did not know that you were faced with a question."

"Concerning my destination and my place in the world."

The monk nodded and waved for Bransen to enter the room.

"I will take my leave of Chapel Abelle this day," Bransen explained. "With Dame Gwydre's Writ of Passage in hand, I will go to clear the name of the Highwayman."

"King Yeslnik will kill you," Father Premujon remarked, but Bransen merely shrugged.

"Yeslnik seems not to be a reasonable man," Father Artolivan added.

"I know him well," Bransen assured them both. "And I do not disagree regarding his temperament. But there are others I know to be reasonable and just."

"You will build support for your cause?"

"That is my hope," said Bransen. "And I hope that Father Artolivan will lend that support." To the side, Father Premujon shifted uncomfortably, as did Brother Pinower, who had walked into the room behind Bransen.

"I will speak truthfully to that which I know, of course," Artolivan said. "What more would you have from me?"

"A second Writ of Passage."

Artolivan looked at him incredulously, while Premujon and Pinower said no in unison.

"You cannot ask this of Chapel Abelle," Premujon elaborated against Bransen's obvious disappointment. "We are in difficult straits with King Yeslnik as it is."

"And with some in your own ranks?" Bransen asked, and Premujon didn't disagree.

"You appreciate the difficulty I have in openly defying King Yeslnik at this time, on this issue?" Father Artolivan asked.

"I do."

"I cannot offer you any imprimatur that would serve you against the king's men," Father Artolivan said. "But perhaps I can fashion some writ to add my voice to Dame Gwydre's, some imprimatur to ensure those favorable to your cause that I witnessed Dame Gwydre's testimony on your behalf and found it credible." He looked around as he finished and both Pinower, who had moved up to stand beside him, and Premujon nodded their agreement, albeit with some obvious reservations.

"That would be most helpful," said Bransen.

"Your wife and her mother are welcome to remain here at Chapel Abelle," Artolivan added. "I trust you will not be bringing them along on your undoubtedly perilous journey."

Bransen sighed deeply; the thought of being away from Cadayle again after only a few short months together gnawed at him. Thoughts of traveling to Behr flickered through his mind once more, along with a nagging feeling that he should sail north again with Gwydre and Dawson and make his home in Vanguard. It had been a fine winter, the most peaceful and enjoyable Bransen had ever known. Beside Gwydre and Dawson and Cormack and Jond and even Premujon, Bransen and his family had felt as if they were truly among friends.

"Bransen?" he heard Artolivan remark, and realized that he had fallen deep within himself and had missed a question or two. He shook the doubts away and looked at the leader of the Order of Abelle.

"Your wife?" Artolivan asked.

"I have to go," Bransen said, as much to himself as to the others. "If Yeslnik is to be King of Honce, then I have to clear my name and regain the freedom I earned from Dame Gwydre."

"King Yeslnik is a stubborn one," Father Artolivan warned. "He will not be easily swayed."

Bransen, knowing Yeslnik better than any in the room, nodded, but he smiled as he did, and in a flash drew out his magnificent sword. "For the third time, I will put him at the tip of my sword," he promised, and he didn't fight that mischievous, almost reckless, smile from widening on his face as he went into a sudden slash and thrust move, ending up in a powerful pose, sword forward. "I suspect that while his eyes are seeing the sharpened edge, his heart will see the truth of Bransen."

Brother Pinower looked horrified, and Father Premujon cleared his throat uncomfortably, but Father Artolivan let forth a great squeal of laughter and clapped his hands. "Brilliant!" he congratulated. "I only hope that Honce will forgive you for stopping short your deadly blade."

"Father!" Pinower and Premujon said together, but Artolivan waved them away and walked up to Bransen, patting the young man on the shoulder.

"I would like for you to stay, Highwayman," he said. "Though I know you cannot. Return to me, if you find the time."

"To retrieve my family, of course."

"And to sit with me! I have only heard small stretches of the history of Bransen Garibond and this hero known as the Highwayman." He paused and looked at Bransen as if seeking permission, before finishing, "And of the Stork. I would like to hear the whole story."

"Ask Cadayle," Bransen replied. "She can tell it as well as I, since she was there for most of my steps, even the awkward ones of the Stork, that as often as not left me face down in the mud."

"Sometimes in the mud of Chapel Pryd, with buckets in hand," said Artolivan, and Bransen looked at him, surprised that he knew so much.

"Small stretches of your history," Artolivan assured him. "And there is one more thing." He reached up and touched the front of Bransen's black bandanna, tapping right atop the soul stone hidden beneath it and secured to his forehead.

Artolivan turned to Pinower and pointed to the desk, and then pointed more emphatically when the younger monk hesitated.

"I have had a long discussion with Brother Cormack," Artolivan said, and it took a moment before Bransen realized that Artolivan had added the church title to his friend's name.

Pinower walked over with a small, decorated box. With obvious reverence, he handed it to Artolivan, who held it before Bransen as he slowly opened its hinged lid.

Bransen's eyes widened as he stared at the contents: a small star-shaped brooch, no more than a fingertip across at its widest point, centered with a soul stone and containing in its five tips other stones of various colors. He recognized the ruby at its top point, flanked left and right by malachite and a particular type of agate known as cat's eye. The striated stone set in the bottom left point he thought to be serpentine, and the other he knew as quartz, but a cloudy variety whose properties Bransen did not know.

"This was made for Laird Delaval's grandfather, ironically," Artolivan explained, "in the early days of the Order of Abelle. To Father Abelle's surprise, the laird refused it, despite its obvious powers, since we were not as accepted back in those days, when the Samhaists dominated Honce." He lifted the brooch and slowly turned it so that Bransen could better see its wondrous craftsmanship, including small hooks and pins on the backing. "It is fashioned of silverel, the same metal as your unusual sword, and edged in graphite, the stone of lightning."

"What does it do?"

"Separately, the gems are each possessed of their own blessing."

Bransen, who knew of the gemstones, of course, nodded. "They are all enchanted?"

"It is a fine item," Artolivan confirmed. "It was crafted to be sewn to the chest, above the heart, but perhaps on your forehead . . ."

Bransen reached up and touched his bandanna. "To the cloth?"

"To the skin itself," said Artolivan, and Bransen's eyes widened in surprise and a bit of trepidation. He calmed quickly as he remembered the fight on the road with Dame Gwydre's raiders, when his bandanna and stone had been knocked away and he had been helpless against the troll enemies.

"I have spoken about you at length with Brother Jond, as well," Father Artolivan explained.

"Women in Behr wear gemstones in such a manner," added Brother Pinower. "They call it tikka, and it is considered quite beautiful."

"And those are simple and mundane jewels," said Artolivan. "Magically speaking, I mean. You will find these stones useful in other ways."

He handed the brooch to Bransen, who slowly lifted it to his forehead with one hand, slipping free the other soul stone as he slid the new one in place. He closed his eyes and fell within the flux of energy offered by the gems.

His *ki-chi-kree*, his line of life energy, remained straight and strong, as with the other soul stone. And other possibilities flitted through his thoughts, a jumble at first, but gradually sorting themselves out.

Possibilities.

"You would give this to me?" he asked, opening his eyes to stare hard at Father Artolivan.

"An extraordinary gift for an extraordinary man," Artolivan replied. "It does my old heart good to see that brooch, so long in the coffer, upon your forehead."

"And it looks quite good," Father Premujon added with a smile.

Bransen left Artolivan's quarters with his bandanna in his hand, and he walked with the sure gait of the Highwayman, not the awkward stumble of the Stork.

You hate me," Bransen said solemnly after a long and uncomfortable pause. Cadayle looked up at him; across the room, Callen laughed.

"For a hero, you're sure for saying some stupid things," the older woman remarked. "She's no more for hating you than you are for her, and you should be able to see that clear enough in her eyes by now."

"Of course I don't," Cadayle added, and she hugged Bransen close. "But I am afraid, and I'll miss you dearly, as I did in Vanguard those weeks you were gone from me."

Bransen hugged her back even more tightly. "I know. But I have to do this. My name is clear, as Dame Gwydre agreed."

"We'd be free enough in Vanguard," said Cadayle.

"I've spent most of my life trying to figure out how and where I belong," Bransen replied. "Honce is our home—Pryd is our home. Even if we choose not to live there, we should be able to return at our leisure."

"When we left, you left a dead laird behind," Cadayle reminded him.

"But even that is forgiven by Gwydre."

"By Bannagran?"

"I don't know, but I will find out." He paused, his next admission coming hard. "I want Brother Reandu—Master Reandu, I mean—to know the truth of it, to know that I am no criminal and that his order, at the very highest level, has deigned to honor and accept me."

"Because of your life at Chapel Pryd. Because of the way Reandu and the others treated you."

Bransen couldn't deny the obvious truth of Cadayle's observations, so he just slid back from her a bit and shrugged helplessly.

"If Bannagran or Yeslnik catches and kills you, I'll never forgive you," Cadayle said, ending with a spreading grin.

"Then you don't hate me?"

Callen let out a great burst of laughter.

"I know you have to do this. I only wish I could go with you," said Cadayle.

"Not now."

"I know."

"Here, you hero," said Callen and she took a couple of steps toward Bransen and tossed him his bandanna, which she had been sewing. He caught it and examined it, then slipped the now thin eye-mask on.

"The dashing Highwayman," said Callen.

"They know who I am," Bransen replied. "And now I need not hold a gemstone in place. There is no point to the disguise."

"Yes there is," said Callen.

"The common folk of Pryd know the Highwayman more than they know Bransen Garibond," Cadayle agreed. "Your reputation is your advantage against Bannagran."

Bransen's step was sure-footed but much less animated as he walked out of Chapel Abelle that afternoon. He was confident that his course was correct, and that he had justice on his side, but the thought of leaving Cadayle for an extended period yet again—even though he expected to be gone from Chapel Abelle for no more than a couple of weeks—wounded him. He glanced back to see Dame Gwydre and Dawson McKeege watching him from the wall, Gwydre nodding her approval.

Cadayle was not there, though, and Bransen was glad of it, for had his beautiful wife been watching, he would have turned and rushed back to her.

He sighed and laughed at himself for his own weakness, then adjusted his hat, brim low to cover the gem-studded star set in his forehead, and hoisted his pack higher on his shoulder and moved on his way. He stayed mostly to the side of the road, moving along the brush and trees, enjoying the solitude and the sounds of a world awakening in the full bloom of spring.

He let his guard down—who wouldn't in so idyllic and peaceful a setting?— and so he was caught by surprise when a voice called out, "You've got a longer road before you if every step forward is taken with half a step backwards!"

Startled, Bransen jumped back, his hand going reflexively to the hilt of the sword set on his hip. He relaxed when the speaker, Jameston Sequin, walked out of the shadows.

Bransen glanced all around and back the way he had come, back toward Chapel Abelle, which was long out of sight by then.

"What are you doing out here?" he asked.

"Been a long time since I've walked the ways of Honce."

"Vanguard is part of Honce," Bransen said, but Jameston, like most Van- guardsmen, dismissed that notion with a snort and a wave of his hand.

"Haven't been here in more years than you've been alive," he continued. "Thought this'd be as good a time as any to reacquaint myself."

"Heading where?" Bransen said suspiciously.

"You'd know that better than myself."

"I am going to Pryd Town."

"I am going to Pryd Town," Jameston echoed.

Bransen put his hands on his hips and stared at the man. "Dame Gwydre believes I need a bodyguard?"

"Doubt that, since she sent you against Badden."

"But she asked you to come with me on my journey."

Jameston shook his head. "Was my idea."

"One she thought wise."

"I'll give you that much. But I do want to walk the ways of Honce again, and I know more than a bit about staying out of sight and out of notice. I think you'll find that helpful."

"I am no novice."

"Could've fooled me with the way you were dancing down the path. And if I was one of Yeslnik's men, one with a bow, you'd be lying dead in the brush."

Bransen just stared at him hard.

"Oh, but quit pretending," said Jameston. "You know I'll be helpful, you know I won't slow you down, and you know you don't want to walk alone. You also know, but you're too proud to admit it, that you might learn from my long experiences. Sure, you know how to fight—you're as good as any I've ever seen, and I've seen many!—but you could learn a few things about when to fight and where to fight from, I'm thinking."

Bransen didn't reply, but his visage did soften.

"You know you don't want to go alone," Jameston said with a grin under that outrageously thick mustache of his.

Bransen couldn't resist that smile, and returned it.

"Good thing we've got a long road ahead of us," Jameston said, moving beside Bransen as he walked by. "Because you've got a lot to learn and I've got a lot to teach you."

Bransen didn't reply, other than to widen his smirk. He had spent his life in learning, from the Book of Jhest his father had penned, from the brothers of Chapel Pryd, and, more recently, from Dame Gwydre. He wasn't about to let foolish pride get in the way now, not with the likes of Jameston Sequin offering him the lessons!

CHAPTER 16

Moments of Private Clarity

Young Brother Pontitious huffed and puffed as he ran along the road to the west, his precious cargo, the edict from Father Artolivan, set in a scroll case and slung over one shoulder. Until that morning, he had been jogging along with three other brothers, but they, with their scroll cases, had turned down the southern road for other destinations.

Pontitious's pace was much greater that day, for he hoped to reach Palmaristown, his goal, before sunset. Suddenly he felt very vulnerable there alone on the road with so important a letter, and those feelings only increased when he heard the clip-clop of a horse and the rattle of coach wheels behind him. Pontitious veered off the side of the road, moving down into a gully behind some brush, where he crouched and looked back the way he had come.

He relaxed when he saw the horse, adorned in a bridle that showed the evergreen symbol of Chapel Abelle and his beloved order. He knew this horse, and recognized the small wagon it pulled. He scrambled back up to the road, waving for his brethren.

"Ho, Pontitious, Brother," hailed the driver, a man named Josaul, and he slowed the horse to a stop. "I'd hoped to find you on the road. You've made a fine pace!"

"Would that Father Artolivan had decided to afford me a coach all the way from Chapel Abelle," Pontitious said, moving to climb up beside Josaul. "My feet are sorely bruised."

He reached up, but froze in place when the coach's door flew open and Father De Guilbe leaned out, lifting his head over it and scowling fiercely at the young courier.

"Father," Pontitious stammered and fell back.

"I do not recall hearing an invitation for you to ride with us," De Guilbe said.

Josaul started to say something, but Pontitious spoke over him. "No, Father. I assumed that a coach from Chapel Abelle would afford a brother a seat."

"You deliver Father Artolivan's message to Laird Panlamaris?"

"That is my duty, yes, Father."

De Guilbe offered an unsettling grin in reply. "Do you know Laird Panlamaris, boy?"

"No, Father. But I met his son when Prince Milwellis passed through Chapel Abelle."

"And your impressions of the young man?"

Pontitious realized that his expression and body language were giving away his feelings for the brutish man, none of them positive. "I . . . I . . . I didn't know him well."

Father De Guilbe laughed at him, and he knew that he needn't say any more. The large and imposing father then motioned toward the bench seat beside Josaul. "Do join us," he said in a tone as unsettling as that wicked smile. "I wish to see the look on Laird Panlamaris's face when you deliver to him the notification of Father Artolivan's treason."

Brother Pontitious swallowed hard and never stopped staring at Father De Guilbe as he made his way onto the seat beside Josaul. Behind them, the door closed, and Josaul urged his horse back into motion.

Pontitious looked at him with concern, but he just shrugged and shook his head helplessly.

They made the great port city by midafternoon, and, with Father De Guilbe guiding Josaul, for the father was obviously quite familiar with Palmaristown, the Chapel Abelle coach soon rambled right up to the coach house of Panlamaris Keep.

Ordering Josaul to stay with the coach, De Guilbe escorted Pontitious into the castle, and, again, this time as a diplomat and not a navigator, had them at their destination in short order, standing before the throne of old Laird Panlamaris.

"De Guilbe, young fool, is that really you?" greeted Panlamaris, a grizzled old man, still thick and strong and carrying the scars of a thousand fights.

"Not so young anymore, laird," De Guilbe replied.

"Aren't you supposed to be in Alpinador, converting barbarians to the light and the stones?"

De Guilbe waved the notion away. "Too stubborn and stupid a lot for that," he replied jovially, for these two were obviously old friends (which of course made Pontitious even more nervous). "I could not convince them, so I killed a bunch instead."

Laird Panlamaris laughed heartily, as did the many attendants in the room, as did Father De Guilbe. Only Pontitious, so obviously and painfully nervous, did not join in.

"Your order is better for it," Laird Panlamaris said. "I've met a few Alpinadorans in my sailing days. Not one worthy of civility. Fierce warriors, though, huh? So I count those among my finest kills!"

Another round of laughter made Pontitious want to crawl into a crack in the floor. Never in his young life, not even on his first day at Chapel Abelle, had he felt so out of place.

"So what brings young De Guilbe to my humble city?"

"Not so young, though I wish I were, and there is little humble about the grandeur that is Palmaristown. I do believe that your fine city has grown as powerful as I have grown old."

"A flagon of mead for that man!" Laird Panlamaris called to an attendant, who scurried from the room. "And, aye, we have prospered under the fine friendship of King Delaval, may the old ones see fit to seat him at their table."

"Aye!" Father De Guilbe agreed, while Brother Pontitious winced at the reference to Samhaist, and not Abellican, tradition.

"And you must know, De Guilbe, that everyone in the world seems young to me," Laird Panlamaris added with a laugh.

"Father Artolivan?" De Guilbe said slyly.

Laird Panlamaris snorted and waved his hand dismissively. "No, perhaps not that one. The gods don't want him so they make us keep him."

Brother Pontitious's eyes widened at that, and he looked to Father De Guilbe for some guidance but found instead the man smugly smiling at him. Brother Pontitious knew at that moment, beyond all doubt, that Father De Guilbe had injected Father Artolivan's name into the conversation to elicit exactly that response.

"Your pardon, brothers," Laird Panlamaris said with obvious insincerity. "I do not suffer that one well."

"Your son would agree," said De Guilbe, and Panlamaris nodded.

"The rebuff of Milwellis will be remembered the next time Father Artolivan calls upon Palmaristown's fleet for transport or supply or defense," Laird Panlamaris promised.

Smiling all the wider, Father De Guilbe reached around Brother Pontitious and removed the slung scroll case. "I expect none of those to happen anytime soon," he explained, handing it to Panlamaris.

An attendant rushed up and took the case, popping off one end and rolling wide the scroll. He read it quickly, bending low and reciting its contents into the ear of Laird Panlamaris.

The man sat stone-faced. Another attendant came in with Father De Guilbe's flagon of mead, and the monk took his first swallow just as the reader finished, stood straight, and stepped back.

"You would drink with me after delivering this?" Panlamaris said, his voice calm but in a manner that promised violence. Brother Pontitious took a step away from the throne.

"I?" De Guilbe replied. "Not I. Brother Pontitious here delivered the note. Would that it had never been penned, but Father Artolivan would not heed my advice."

"You know what it says?" asked Panlamaris, his tone growing stronger and darker.

De Guilbe nodded.

Panlamaris fixed a withering gaze on poor Pontitious. Not a large man to begin with, the young brother seemed to melt into the floor.

"He is a courier and nothing more," De Guilbe explained.

"Then get out of my chambers!" Laird Panlamaris yelled. Pontitious began stammering and stuttering and looked to De Guilbe for guidance.

"Get out," De Guilbe quietly advised.

Bowing with every backward step, mouthing words though no sound came forth, Brother Pontitious executed a graceless departure.

"Has Artolivan gone mad, then?" Panlamaris asked when the young brother was gone at last.

De Guilbe shrugged and sighed.

"Yeslnik wins—has won!" Panlamaris insisted. "Ethelbert is pushed to the sea and will not break out. More of Honce's holdings pledge fealty to Yeslnik daily."

De Guilbe nodded.

"This . . ." Panlamaris fumed and reached over and tore the scroll from his attendant's grasp. "This is treason."

It occurred to De Guilbe that he could diffuse the situation at that point by mentioning the extraordinary nature of Yeslnik's request regarding the disposition of the prisoners and the awkward situation it presented for the church. But the wounds regarding Cormack were too raw for the man who for the first time in his life had miserably failed his mission—a failure he still believed was due to Brother Cormack's treachery.

"It is far worse than you think," he heard himself saying. "They harbor not only the prisoners from Ethelbert's army, they hold in chains not only the men loyal to King Yeslnik, but there is another in their chapel who is much sought after."

Panlamaris, fist clenched up beside his strong, bearded jaw, leaned forward in his seat, eyes locked on De Guilbe.

"They harbor the Highwayman," De Guilbe announced.

Panlamaris's eyes popped open wide, and he mouthed, "He murdered King Delaval."

"Dame Gwydre has provided him with a Writ of Passage, forgiving all crimes."

"She forgives the murder of the king?" Panlamaris roared, and De Guilbe saw no reason to clear up that little matter and merely shrugged.

"How many brothers are at Chapel Abelle?" the Laird of Palmaristown demanded.

"Less than three hundred."

"How many prisoners of each side?"

"I know not the exact count. A couple of hundred of Yeslnik's men, perhaps twice that of Ethelbert's."

"Would that my son were returned from the Mirianic coast," Panlamaris muttered. "He has many of my finest commanders and warriors with him."

De Guilbe looked at the man curiously, for only then did it occur to him that his words might be escalating this incident above the level of parley and disagreement. "What do you mean?" he asked as Panlamaris rose quickly and forcefully from his throne.

"Ah well, then," the man said. "It wouldn't do for Milwellis to have all the fun, would it?"

"What will you do?" De Guilbe asked, but Panlamaris wasn't listening to him.

"Since Yeslnik's decree I've got more men free of duties, what with fewer prisoners to watch," Panlamaris said, nodding his head as he worked through the details. "Couple hundred monks, a few hundred others . . ."

"Dame Gwydre is there with four ships of men."

"Skinners and drunkards, no doubt. She won't follow the course of Artolivan. She's nobody's fool, from all I've heard. She'll get on her boat and go home. This isn't her fight."

That last word resonated in De Guilbe's thoughts, at first uncomfortably. As he considered the wheels that seemed to be turning here, however, the fiery monk grew more and more at ease, coming not to regret at all his decision to tell Panlamaris of the Highwayman.

Good enough for Father Artolivan, he thought but did not say.

"You've got to know what they see," Jameston explained. "If you were up on that rock, where would you be looking? What movements would catch your eye?"

Bransen squinted in concentration as he followed Jameston's pointing hand.

"Or over there by the stream in that stand of oaks?" the scout asked.

"There are a million places to hide, and surely there is no path invisible to all of them," Bransen replied.

"Am I telling you anything different than those who taught you to fight?" Jameston retorted, his expression finally showing that he was growing weary of Bransen's constant arguing. "Is there any perfect defense? Or a swing that can't be parried?"

"Measure your enemy," Bransen admitted. He laughed at himself then and waved his arm wide. "So where would enemies most likely hide in wait? What vantage points are most likely and how to avoid them?"

"You couldn't have admitted that an hour ago and saved me my talking?"

Bransen started to reply but stopped short and laughed instead.

"Pretty wife you left behind," said Jameston.

"It's been a long road," Bransen admitted.

"We just left!"

"Not from Chapel Abelle," Bransen started to explain, but he realized that Jameston had been playing with him with that last comment. "For so many years my life moved in a slow and straight line," he explained, as much to himself as to his companion. "Everything around me was solid as stone even when I wasn't."

"When you were this Stork fellow, you mean?"

Bransen nodded. "Even as I began to find those moments of escape from the Stork, there were so many constants. It was as if the world was there, one place known to me, and I could play with it as it amused me. But now there is so much tumult, so many things changing."

Jameston shook his head. "Now you've got others depending on you," he said with a knowing grin. "That's the only real difference."

Bransen stepped back as if he had been slapped and let the scout's words sink in.

"I've seen it happen a thousand times," Jameston said. "You've got your wife, now with child, and her mother all needing you."

Bransen sighed as he considered the truth of the statement.

"So you're more careful with every step and smiling less because you've got something to lose. For the first time in your life, you've got a lot to lose."

"Thank you for pointing that out," Bransen sarcastically replied.

"And you're making the biggest mistake of all," said Jameston, slipping past the sarcasm. Bransen went silent. "You've got more to lose because all the world—all your world—is better, but you're smiling less. You're letting those bad maybes bury the good that is."

"What?"

"Lighten your step!" Jameston scolded. "I spent many hours with Callen on the boat. She told me of a masked man who challenged the Laird of Pryd and defeated him. She told me of a masked man who leaped from a Samhaist bonfire to slay a powerful priest. Of a masked man who saved Yeslnik, then robbed him and stole his powdered wife's heart at the same time. Oh, and then robbed him again in his own castle for no better reason than to witness the foolish expression on his face."

"It does seem as if everyone is prying into my past."

"Everyone but yourself," said Jameston.

"What does that mean?"

"It means you're forgetting to remember where you came from and how far you've walked," the scout replied. "It means you're losing your joy in your worry. You see powries raiding a coach and take them on, then take on the men in the coach when you're done with the dwarves. You see a high castle wall and decide to climb it for treasures you don't even want. Now there's a man I want to walk beside."

"I'm right here."

"No. Wish that you were." Jameston finished and walked down the path, leaving Bransen to ponder his words.

They were apart for nearly half an hour, Jameston continuing along the road south, when finally a voice came out of the trees to Jameston's right not so far away.

"If I was one of Yeslnik's bowmen, you'd be lying dead in the brush."

Jameston froze at the sound of his own words coming back at him. He slowly turned to regard Bransen, sitting easily on a branch, his legs dangling, his mask down over his eyes low enough so that the star-shaped brooch showed clearly on his forehead.

"And how did you know to be there instead of up on that rock?" Jameston asked.

"Because I know that you know what your enemies are likely to see and from where they're likely to be watching." He pointed across the way to a thicket up on a bluff on the other side of the stream. "They can't see you from there. You were careful to make sure of that."

"Good to know that you listen to me, boy," said Jameston.

More than you realize, Bransen, who was smiling widely inside and out, thought but did not say.

Father Malskinner and Brother Honig of the Chapel of Precious Memories entered the keep of Laird Panlamaris somewhat tentatively, expecting an angry berating from the volatile man. Brother Pontitious had stopped by the chapel of Palmaristown before his return to Chapel Abelle to inform the monks of the stern and defiant message he had just delivered on behalf of Father Artolivan.

"Ah, good," Laird Panlamaris greeted warmly. "I always count on Father Malskinner to be on time."

His apparent good humor had the three monks visibly relaxing.

"I trust that your son is well?" Father Malskinner said.

"Since your church has taken its stand he had better stay away from Ethelbert's swords," came the rather sharp reply.

"The brothers would not refuse to care for any man's wounds," Father Malskinner replied.

"Yes, any man of either side. Under Father Artolivan, your order has perfected the art of—"

"Neutrality," Father Malskinner finished.

"Cowardice," corrected Laird Panlamaris. His arm sliced to his side. Immediately a dozen men dropped their halberds level with the monks and closed in on them in a nearly complete and inescapable circle. The two monks were herded together as sharp bronze spear tips prodded at them.

"Laird Panlamaris, I protest!" Father Malskinner said.

"I expect you would!"

"What is the meaning of this?" Malskinner demanded.

"Your Father Artolivan has declared opposition to King Yeslnik,"

Panlamaris calmly explained. "So it follows that he has declared his opposition to me, loyal to Yeslnik as I am. If your leader is going to declare war you would be wise to be better prepared than to walk into your enemy's castle."

Malskinner bristled impotently. "I demand that you release us!"

Panlamaris laughed at him and motioned to the guards. The prodding of halberds quickly had the two monks moving toward the room's side door.

"Take their gemstones," Panlamaris instructed.

"I demand you release us to the Chapel of Precious Memories!" Father Malskinner cried again.

"Where my guards are even now collecting the rest of your treasonous band," Panlamaris declared. "Your chapel is my chapel now, monk. I will have your inventory of gemstones and all the gold you have taken from the people of Palmaristown these last decades. Your welcome in my domain is at its end."

Father Malskinner started to protest but stopped walking as he did and got stuck hard in the arm by one of the long weapons. He yelped and clutched at the wound then reached reflexively for the small pouch of stones he had hanging on a sash at his left side.

The tip of a halberd pressing against his throat stopped that movement. A second guard produced a knife, stepped in to cut the pouch free.

"You and your flock will remain as my guests," Panlamaris said. "For as long as I decide. Perhaps you will know freedom again. Perhaps not, but I assure you that any actions you take against me, my people, or my king will be returned with . . . vigor."

Brother Fatuus had spent many of his days down at the dock section of Palmaristown and so knew the group of men who walked into the Chapel of Precious Memories. These were the dock masters, even the harbor master himself, tough and disciplined and loyal to Laird Panlamaris.

They were armed, though they came in with their weapons sheathed, but Fatuus felt the hairs on the back of his neck tingling. He alone among the brothers of the Chapel of Precious Memories had been to Chapel Abelle in recent months to warn them of the approach of the Highwayman, and so he appreciated the gravity of Father Artolivan's declaration perhaps most of all. He had seen the prisoners of both Ethelbert and Delaval and understood the insanity of King Yeslnik's demand that one group be freed and the other executed. These men and women worked side by side at Chapel Abelle; the lines of loyalty had been blurred to nothingness. And not one of them by Fatuus's estimation would prefer to be sent from Chapel Abelle if that meant going back to the front lines of the awful war. Even offering complete freedom and land, Dawson McKeege had been unable to convince more than a handful to sail with him to Vanguard!

Thus King Yeslnik's declaration had been a fool's writ. But for Father Artolivan to make such a bold response, as relayed by Brother Pontitious, was no small thing.

Brother Fatuus knew Laird Panlamaris well, too. He had watched the man swell with pride over the last few months as his son scored great victories across the land in the name of King Delaval and now King Yeslnik. Panlamaris remained unwavering in his support for King Yeslnik.

These armed loyalists were not in the Chapel of Precious Memories by accident or coincidence, nor was the sudden and unexplained absence of Father Malskinner and Brother Honig a coincidence.

"Tell the brothers to quietly slip into the streets," Fatuus whispered to a nearby pair of monks. "Move to the eastern gate with all haste and with as many gemstones as can be carried."

"Brother?" one of the monks asked incredulously.

"With all haste," said Fatuus. "And beware the men in the nave."

"Laird Panlamaris's men," one of them said, as if that fact should be reassuring.

"Shed your robes and go dressed as common folk," Fatuus added. "Go now."

When the pair hesitated, Fatuus shoved them hard, launching them on their way. Then he took a deep breath, recognizing his duty here. Accepting his lot as the highest-ranking brother within the chapel, Fatuus went to the nave to greet the visitors.

Less than half an hour later, Fatuus was dropped in chains before Laird Panlamaris's throne. Throughout the rest of the day, he watched as brother after brother, often severely beaten, was brought in and dropped unceremoniously on the floor.

The next day, Laird Panlamaris's dungeons swelled with monk prisoners, for only a handful of the fourscore brothers of the Chapel of Precious Memories had managed to escape the city.

CHAPTER 17

Saving Future Allies

Jameston Sequin was not a sound sleeper. Living most of his life alone in the wilds of Vanguard and southern Alpinador, the man had trained himself to react to the slightest of sounds or movements.

His eyes opened wide this dark night, and he was surprised indeed when he looked to the side to see that Bransen's bedroll was empty. Jameston silently congratulated the young man; escaping Jameston unnoticed was no small feat!

The scout lay very still for a few moments, allowing his sensibilities to fully adjust to the darkness. He rolled silently to his side, tucked and set his foot under him, then just as silently rose up tall and gathered his bow and quiver. He heard another sound then, a slight shuffle, and followed it to a small clearing.

Bransen stood in the middle of the lea, working his fine sword furiously through a series of practice cuts and blocks, a brilliant dance of perfect balance, which again reminded Jameston of just how good a fighter this young man truly was. Jameston rested the tip of his bow on the ground beside him and leaned on it, enjoying the show.

Bransen turned in one mock attack to the side and then spun all the way around, looking right at Jameston.

Jameston knew that he had been seen, and that confused him and unnerved him more than a little. For the night was not bright—only a few stars twinkled above—and he was fully engulfed in the darker shadows of a stand of thick spruce. Bransen couldn't have seen him from that distance, not viewing from the lighter open lea to the darker shadows.

But Bransen had seen him. Of that Jameston was certain.

The scout shook his head and continued to watch as Bransen finished with a flurry, moving from a series of defensive poses and blocks to a sudden and violent forward movement, sword thrusting. The young man ended by lifting that magnificent blade high to his right. To Jameston's astonishment the blade erupted in a sudden burst of flames!

"How the . . . ?" Jameston stuttered, compelled to walk forward. His surprise only heightened as Bransen, seeming as surprised as Jameston by the flaming sword, reached over with his free hand and felt the burning blade.

"They're not hot flames, then," Jameston reasoned as he walked up beside Bransen. He reached toward the fiery sword, snatching his hand back immediately. An all-too-real fire danced on the shining metal of that beautifully etched sword blade.

Bransen looked at him with puzzlement and shrugged.

"I never saw your sword do that before," said Jameston. "I never heard of any sword doing that before!"

"It's not the sword," Bransen replied. He pointed to the star set on his forehead, three of the gems—ruby, serpentine, and the agate—twinkling. "The ruby gave me the fire. The serpentine shielded me from its heat."

"Nice brooch."

"I grew up among gemstone users in Chapel Pryd," Bransen explained. "My connection to the stones and their powers is considerable." He paused and smiled widely. "The cat's-eye let me see you as clearly as if you were standing in the midday sunlight." He looked at his sword as he spoke, and with a thought, winked out the fires, leaving the silverel blade unscarred.

"Full of surprises," Jameston remarked.

"Even to myself."

"And what else can you do with that toy you've got stuck on your head?"

Again Bransen shrugged. "I don't know—yet. But I will find out."

Jameston stared at him for a few moments then headed to the campsite. "Long walk tomorrow," he said without looking back. "And not many hours left before we start it."

Bransen nodded, though Jameston wasn't watching him. The young man didn't immediately follow. Instead he stood under the stars, staring at his sword, trying to sort out the unexpected benefits the brooch had shown him, and wondering what more might yet come.

They were off early in the morning, Jameston setting a swift pace. Signs along the road indicated a village not too far in the distance, and Jameston wanted to get there before they set their next camp. "Maybe we can try out that writ of yours," he said. "Or you can just wear the deerskin coat and pants and keep a hat on your head."

"No," said Bransen. "My clothing suits me. I am Bransen the Highwayman. I will not hide who I am. Dame Gwydre says I need not."

"The man who calls himself King of Honce says you do."

Bransen couldn't help but snort at the reference to Yeslnik. "I expect that I will have to visit with the man who calls himself King of Honce, then."

"To convince him?"

"To take his money. To make his wife swoon for no better reason than to see the anger on his face."

"Then he'll want you dead even more."

"Then I'll have to kill him and hope his successor is more reasonable."

Jameston stopped abruptly and stared at his companion, who was grinning and obviously enjoying the banter. "Took my advice, did you?"

In response, Bransen hopped and skipped lightly, landing in an exaggerated heroic pose. Jameston enjoyed the best laugh he had known in many years.

"I should thank you," Bransen said.

"Oh?"

"You don't have to do this."

"Dame Gwydre's a friend, and she's better served if you learn to keep your head on your shoulders."

Bransen, smiling all the more widely, shook his head through every word. "This isn't about Dame Gwydre. Not entirely, at least. So I thank you for teaching and most of all for reminding me."

"You do have a way of talking in riddles, boy."

"Reminding me to smile," Bransen said. "And to enjoy this, as trying as it may be."

"Well, what's the point otherwise?"

"There is none!" Bransen gave a little laugh and dropped a hand comfortably (surprising to both) on Jameston's shoulder. "And so I thank you, Jameston Sequin. Because of you I have remembered my past and what I have overcome to get to this point."

Jameston gave an exaggerated deep bow.

"I've been in love with Cadayle since I was a boy, you know," Bransen said.

"Good taste."

"But I never, ever dared believe she could love me in return."

"Because you were the broken boy, the Stork?"

Bransen stared at him and couldn't respond past the lump in his throat.

"You figured she loved you after you found a way around that infirmity?"

Jameston asked. Bransen's tight expression turned into a perplexed look. "So now you doubt that she—"

"Never!" Bransen retorted. "I doubt nothing about Cadayle."

Jameston's smile relaxed him a bit. "And you shouldn't," the scout said. "Easy enough to see in her eyes. Cadayle loves Bransen, not the Highwayman. Cadayle's always loved Bransen, but she probably wasn't sure that he could ever love her. Could you?"

"What do you mean?"

"When you were the Stork, could you have loved Cadayle?"

"I did!"

"And you would have married her, even if you hadn't found the answer to your problem in that gemstone you wear on your head?"

"Jameston, of course! I have loved her . . ." Bransen paused then and assumed a pensive pose, truly asking himself that question for the very first time. If he was still an infirm and unsteady creature and Cadayle professed her love for him, would he have accepted her proposal?

"No," he answered at last. He looked at the scout, dumbfounded, and shook his head. "I would not have let her marry me."

"I know. And I know that she wouldn't have let your condition stop her from wanting to marry you. Don't ever let yourself think that you weren't good enough for her, boy. You're still the Stork, and he's still you, and Cadayle loves you."

The two men stared at each other for a bit longer before Jameston complained about needing sleep. He patted Bransen on the shoulder and walked back to their camp, leaving Bransen with the realization that the Highwayman wasn't the only one full of surprises this night.

Bransen was still considering the conversation of the previous night when they broke camp the next morning. His gratitude to Jameston Sequin had only grown as he had pondered the great gift the man had given him. Jameston had seen into his soul, it seemed, and had offered a salve to a wound that lay there, one that Bransen had never even openly acknowledged to himself.

There was a new spring in Bransen's step. He was feeling quite good about himself, about the possibilities of the gemstone brooch, and about the woman he had left behind in Chapel Pryd. That step did slow as the sun lowered in the west, however, as he and Jameston moved down the cobblestones into the heart of Eskald.

They heard the whispers coming at them from every direction as they entered the town.

"The Highwayman!"

"That's him!"

"The Highwayman has come!"

"You've made quite a name for yourself, boy," Jameston said.

"We're not far from Pryd Town," Bransen whispered back. "And, yes, something important happened there of which I was more than a small part."

"They appreciate it," Jameston observed.

Bransen didn't reply, but his smile showed that he was not so far above basking in the compliments. Jameston liked seeing that from the young and exotic man. Though he had been a loner, nearly a recluse in recent years, Jameston Sequin was no neophyte in recognizing and understanding the foibles of men and women. Bransen's acceptance of the complimentary remarks with such inner satisfaction reinforced the depth of Bransen's humanity in Jameston's mind. No man or woman, not laird nor dame nor general nor cobbler nor blacksmith, could work for the betterment of others without some measure of personal pride. Many people viewed that as a failing, as hubris, but Jameston knew it to be a simple and acceptable truth of human nature. Charity came from the heart, and accepting the compliments only reinforced the notion that such charity was correctly given.

If Bransen had not been smiling, if Bransen had not quietly acknowledged the whispers of the villagers around him, Jameston would have worried that Bransen's actions—the very actions which had inspired the awe-filled whispers—had not been taken for their benefit.

The pair made their way to the village's common room, where all eyes turned upon them as they took seats at a small, round table. The serving girl began to move their way, but the tavern keeper, an older and severe-looking woman with short hair curling tightly to her rather square forehead and a small but tight frame, held the serving girl back and went to see to the guests herself.

"Ye got some belly for walking in here open," she remarked.

"A fine day to you, too, good lady," said Jameston.

"It could be," she replied curtly.

"Would you prefer that we leave?" Bransen asked.

"Makes no nevermind to me. Go where ye want, but go looking over yer shoulder if ye got any sense between yer ears."

"I have a Writ of Passage from a Honce laird . . . err, lady," Bransen said, holding it up.

"One loyal to Ethelbert or Yeslnik?"

"I do not really know."

"Best be hoping it's Yeslnik and that he's listening," the tavern keeper said. "So are ye eating or drinking or both?"

"You would still serve us?" Jameston asked.

"Am I looking like a soldier to ye?"

"A little bit, yes."

That brought a chuckle from the woman. She told Jameston of a fine stew and a finer brew, and that seemed like just the thing for the road-weary duo.

When she went to get their meal, Jameston kept up the small talk, chattering to Bransen about the weather and other nonsense. So out of character was the man of few words that Bransen looked at him strangely.

"I thought that squirrel was going to jump down and bite your neck," Jameston said.

Bransen's jaw hung open at the gibberish.

"What with them two by the door staring at us like that," said Jameston. "More than a furry-tailed rat can take."

Bransen's mouth started to form the question "What?" when Jameston's words began to register. He began laughing, a bit too much, and used the hopeful distraction to get a look at the men by the door.

That quick glance confirmed Jameston's concern as valid: grim faces staring intently—too intently—at Bransen.

He turned back to Jameston and began talking about a squirrel chasing a skunk, the pair by the door enough in view out of the corner of his eye for Bransen to see them depart.

"Trouble," Jameston said seriously.

"Do we eat or do we leave?"

"If you leave, I'll just eat yours, too."

Their meal went off quietly. One of the too-curious men who had left returned to his previous seat by the door and did a poor job pretending that he wasn't staring at them.

"Try not to look too intimidating, and we'll have a bit of fun," Jameston remarked as they rose to leave.

The pair passed right near the spy as they exited the tavern. Jameston dipped the tip of his tricornered hat to the tavern keeper. Bransen tossed a mischievous wink at the seated man. Outside they found the street strangely empty, the long shadows stretching into a wider darkness as the sun fell below the western horizon.

"We should not remain here through the night," said Bransen.

"Thought you wanted to test that writ Gwydre gave you."

Bransen considered that for a moment but shook his head. "Not here in some village whose name I hardly know. Pryd Town is only a few days march south of here."

"Got more friends there?"

"And probably more enemies," Bransen admitted. He let his thoughts slip back to his last days in his hometown as he and Jameston set out, moving off the road as soon as they were out of sight of Eskald. He thought of Bannagran and Laird Prydae and the look on the warrior's face when his thrown axe had spun right over the ducking Bransen to dive deep into the chest of Prydae, mortally wounding the nobleman. How Bannagran had wanted to kill Bransen for that!

But the people wouldn't let him. They marched on the castle, demanding the release of the Highwayman.

Bransen nodded as he replayed it all, remembering that the final brokers in the standoff had been the monks of Chapel Pryd, mostly Reandu. Where would they stand now, and was Bransen acting the fool to begin to believe that they would do the right thing? Was he deluded, drunk with optimism, because of his unexpectedly positive experiences with Dame Gwydre and Chapel Pellinor and with the brothers at Chapel Abelle?

This was the church that had burned his beloved Garibond at the stake, he reminded himself.

"Best get your thoughts back to what's around you," Jameston whispered, drawing him from the inevitable memories inspired by being so near to Pryd. Bransen perked up immediately but gave no indication that he and Jameston were on to whomever might be watching them.

Bransen began using the techniques Jameston had shown him. If there were men in the area watching him, where would they be? And if they were watching the road and not the two men walking in the brush to the side of it, then where?

Bransen felt his blood pumping, felt the rush of adrenaline coursing his veins. The brooch on his head called to him then, a confusing jumble of possibilities.

And a pathway, he saw suddenly, an invitation. He grabbed Jameston's shoulder and motioned for him to stop, then closed his eyes and let his spirit fly free of his corporeal form, sliding through the brooch into the open air. Invisible, propelled by will without constraint, the disembodied spirit of Bransen Garibond darted all about the area impossibly fast.

He passed near one would-be ambusher, crouched in a tree, and marked the spot, thinking to move along. He sensed the man's thoughts completely and honestly; as expected, he was here hoping to catch or kill the Highwayman. The man was thinking of the bounty, of the glory, of how King Yeslnik and Bannagran would reward him when he brought in the Highwayman's head.

Not surprised, Bransen again started to move along to will his spirit back.

But he couldn't. Suddenly Bransen felt a compulsion he had not known before. Unable to mount a defense or argument against it, he found himself sliding into the ambusher's body.

A wall of outrage and denial came up against him, the man instinctively battling against this awful intrusion, this invasion into his very being. He flailed mentally and physically, and the movement cost him his balance and he tumbled from the branch, crashing through the tree to land in a shocking jolt against the hard ground.

The jarring landing expelled Bransen's spirit instantly. A wave of disorientation overwhelmed him and left him lost in the ether. He saw one spot of light, warm and inviting, and instinctively made for it, not realizing until he had passed through it that the brooch was showing him the way home.

Back in his own body, Bransen nearly swooned and fell over. He started to talk, but a hand slapped over his mouth and held him fast then pulled him to the ground. He realized where he was when he was finally able to open his eyes and see Jameston staring at him incredulously. Bransen could only shrug in response, since he wasn't even really sure what had just happened.

Commotion began to grow around them. The fallen man howled in pain; Bransen had felt more than one of the poor fellow's limbs breaking. Others nearby shifted in the branches and the brush, wondering if battle was upon them.

"They're here to kill us," Bransen silently mouthed.

"Well, yes," Jameston replied, rolling his eyes.

Jameston held up four fingers and pointed toward the noise. Bransen somehow understood and nodded, slipped his mask down over his eyes, and started that way. The scout pulled and strung his bow in one fluid motion, then moved off the other way, disappearing into the brush.

Circling wide of the fallen man, keeping him between them and the road, Bransen noted more movement. After his spiritual flight he knew exactly where to look. He made out one man creeping toward the writhing victim, another in the tree, as well as a third.

Another man appeared along the road the way Bransen had come. The man started to call out, "He just fell—"

The whizzing sound of an arrow slicing through the tall grass cut him short and stole his breath as he suddenly lurched over.

"I'm shot!" he managed to cry, tumbling from Bransen's view.

"Where?" called a man from across the road.

"What direction?" shouted another from the tree above the first to fall.

A second arrow cracked into the wood at that location, a perfect shot that pinned the speaker's hand to the branch.

"Down! Down!" the man in the next tree yelled. "To the northwest!" He leaped to the ground beside his fallen friend.

"And here!" Bransen added, springing into their midst. Swords rose against him, but he was already past their range, rushing between the men and turning as he went, cutting a downward stroke across the back of one man's legs. The second man cried out and thrust at him, but Bransen's powerful blade picked off that thrust with enough force to send the sword flying from the man's hands.

He wouldn't have been able to do anything with his weapon anyway, for Bransen, far too fast for him, sent his fine sword slashing across, but purposely high of the mark. The man yelped and instinctively ducked, and Bransen continued his sword's movement, turning around and stepping forward. He threw his left arm up high as he spun, still coming forward. His elbow hit the man hard in the nose, shattering it and snapping his head back. Bransen planted as the man recoiled and hit him with a vicious right cross, pommel in hand.

This time the man's head snapped to the side. He staggered only a step before falling face down with a groan.

Bransen paid him no heed, knowing the man to be out of the fight. He turned instead on the man he had slashed, still standing exactly as Bransen had left him, reaching back to grasp his torn leg. Two steps brought Bransen directly behind him. He stepped again to gain momentum, then leaped and laid flat out, his legs tucked tight.

His double kick sent the man flying to the ground. Bransen, too, fell flat, and a pair of arrows soared past above him. He landed lightly and sprang back up just as the man Jameston had shot in the hand dropped to the ground before him. His right hand bloody and tucked in tight, he brandished a dagger, waving it frantically at Bransen, grimacing in pain with every movement.

"You would make me kill you?" Bransen asked, punctuating his question with a sudden thrust that left the tip of his sword resting under the man's chin.

The man gave a little squeal, and his dagger fell to the ground.

Bransen dove away, another arrow coming at his position. The knife man cried out and stumbled away. Bransen let him go, focusing instead on the two archers who had a bead on his position.

One archer, he corrected silently, as Jameston's next arrow took one through the upper arm. He fell onto the branch and managed to hold tight. To Bransen's relief, the second man turned and let fly to the northwest. He sent off another arrow, ducking as one cracked into the tree by his face.

Bransen let it go, leaving the man to Jameston, as three more men appeared directly across the road and coming hard for Bransen, two brandishing shields and swords, the third a shield and bronze-tipped spear.

"I arrest you, Highwayman!" one cried.

Bransen met their charge with one of his own and hit them with a barrage of thrusts and slashes, his Jhesta Tu sword slamming against bronze shields, slapping against one sword then the other, severing the spear tip when his opponent stubbornly brought it back to bear. He leaped and rushed left and right, sword working every step as he moved to defeat the integrity of their line, to push them apart enough so that he could get between them.

But these were not simple peasants seeking a bounty. They had obviously known battle and carried the scars of many fights. Still the Highwayman of fame kept all three on their heels with his speed and side-to-side movements, his sword finding any opening they presented or just slashing hard against a shield, digging deep grooves.

He slid to the right in fast steps, stabbing hard to make the man on that flank fall back, then went to the left, flipping the blade to his left hand and stabbing with equal precision and speed.

Bransen cut the second course short with a sudden stop and complete turn, tossing the sword to his right hand. The three men skidded to their own short stops. Bransen used the moment to heed the call of his brooch, though he knew not what it was saying. Driven by some subconscious thought, he thrust his arm and the blade high to his right and felt the ruby tip of the brooch tingle.

His opponents widened their eyes in obvious shock and fell back in unison.

Bransen heard the crackling and managed to glance up at his blade.

At the flames dancing about the carved silverel blade.

Grinning, he slashed the sword down and across. The defenders exaggerated their dodges, trying to stay far from the fiery weapon. Using those wild and erratic movements against them, Bransen slashed left at one man, then back at the man standing to his left. Both yelped and faded far from danger, opening the path the Highwayman sought.

Bransen jumped between them, and his brooch screamed new possibilities. He grabbed the half spear of the man to his left, neutralizing any immediate attacks, and sent his sword in a down and around parry at the sword coming at him to his left. He caught the blade with his own and continued his movement, sending both weapons up high, then turned and snapped off a succession of quick elbow smashes above the off-balance man's shield, cracking him one, two, three in the face.

The spearman bull-rushed from the right, or started to, but Bransen quickly let go of his spear, planted his hand against the leading shield, and let the power of the brooch flow through him. Before he even realized what he had done, he noted the spearman flying backward, as if he had been thrown from a catapult. The man landed hard on his feet but staggered back a couple of quick steps and fell to his bum, where he sat, scorched shield before him, hair dancing wildly at its ends, a confused and dazed look in his unfocused eyes.

Bransen spun fast to see the swordsman he had elbowed rolling on the ground, the one remaining foe coming in hard.

Again the Highwayman invoked the power of his new brooch, and the attacker stopped suddenly and turned, slashing with abandon. He kept on, fighting as if against some unseen demon.

Jameston walked up to Bransen and looked at the swordsman with puzzlement, then back to Bransen. The Highwayman merely shrugged, took a step forward to the side of the fighter, tapped him on the shoulder, and when the man finally glanced his way, smashed him hard in the nose with the pommel of his sword.

"What was that about?" Jameston asked.

Bransen pointed to the tip of the brooch holding the smoky quartz, the gemstone of illusion. "I guess his eyes were crossed," he said somewhat sheepishly.

Jameston shook his head and sighed. "Gather them that aren't dead and disarm them," he instructed.

Bransen started to round up the rogues, slapping them up to the road with his sword, when he noticed the first man Jameston had shot in the gut curled on the ground, groaning softly.

"That one's near dead," Jameston explained, leading two more from across the way, one with an arrow halfway through his bicep, the other leaning on him and limping badly with two arrows stuck deep into the back of one leg.

"Watch them," Bransen said, rushing past Jameston to the mortally wounded man. He eased the man onto his back, wincing at the gruesome sight, the arrow deep into the man's belly, his guts all torn up.

"Shh," Bransen soothed him, putting one hand up to his brooch and setting the other firmly on the man's stomach, the arrow shaft tight against the crook between his thumb and forefinger.

"Shh," he said again, sending waves of healing energy into the man, almost anesthetizing him with a blast of concentrated warmth.

Bransen yanked the arrow out, the man howling in agony. The others cried out in surprise. Bransen held the wounded man down and put his hand immediately back to the ghastly wound. Gradually, the injured rogue eased to lie flat and his breathing improved. Many heartbeats passed, Bransen holding the pose, continuing the flow of healing magic. He found the man's line of *ki-chi-kree* fluctuating wildly; he used the connection of the soul stone to coax it back to straight. Drawing some of the man's agony into himself, Bransen winced and clenched his jaw.

After many minutes, the man's *ki-chi-kree* finally settled. Bransen leaned over him and whispered into his ear, "The Highwayman is not your enemy." Repeating it a couple of times, Bransen straightened on his knees and turned to regard Jameston and the prisoners.

"The Highwayman is not your enemy!" he proclaimed. "Now be quick and get your friend to a warm bed. Care for him, and he will live." Bransen leaped to his feet and walked back toward the group.

"Go on, then," Jameston said above them. "And go fast, before I slip with this bowstring and put one of you down to the dirt!"

They scrambled at that, past Bransen, who seemed not to notice.

"Good choice," Jameston said to him as he approached.

"I couldn't let him die."

"He tried to kill you."

"He didn't know any better. But now . . ."

"Now what? Now you don't know, and the whole group might come back at us in a day or two."

"You said it was a good choice," Bransen protested.

Jameston grinned slyly. "Yep. And I think I figured out why that pretty Cadayle fell in love with you."

Bransen just shook his head and, with a glance back at the group, followed Jameston into the brush.

"If you're thinking this to be a clean war of minor wounds, then you're the fool," Jameston warned. "I hope you've got the stomach to kill a man when you need to."

"I know a couple of former Samhaist priests, a young thug, and a former laird who would vouch for me on that point."

Jameston nodded and held his knowing grin. "Glad you can do it," he said. "And gladder still that you don't prefer it that way."

Bransen nodded.

So was he.

CHAPTER 18

In the Arms of My Loving Mother

las, Brother Fatuus," Brother Pinower said as his fellow monk from the Chapel of Precious Memories was shoved before the imposing line of Laird Panlamaris's considerable force. Pinower leaned on the crenellated wall of Chapel Abelle's gate tower roof, along with all the principals of the mother chapel and the visiting dignitaries from Vanguard, including Cadayle and Callen.

Hands bound behind his back, poor Fatuus couldn't hold his balance and fell hard to the ground.

A few feet behind the battered monk, sitting astride a large gray mare and dressed in splendid bronze armor, Laird Panlamaris didn't blink, and none of his attendants moved to help poor Fatuus back to his feet.

Panlamaris said something to the man standing beside his horse, who sprinted across the field to the man who was positioned not far below Chapel Abelle's imposing wall.

"Your answer to King Yeslnik's edict is unacceptable," that courier relayed.

The brothers of Chapel Abelle weren't surprised by the appearance of the Palmaristown soldiers that morning, for a handful—just a handful!—of Palmaristown's monks had managed to get to Chapel Abelle with word of the takeover of the Chapel of Precious Memories by the angry Laird Panlamaris.

"You will release the prisoners loyal to King Yeslnik!" Panlamaris's courier shouted. "The others, and the Highwayman, will be turned over to Laird Panlamaris!"

"The Highwayman?" Brother Pinower remarked. "How could he know . . . ?"

"De Guilbe," Brother Giavno reasoned, shaking his head.

"Good, they think he's here," Cadayle couldn't help but whisper, and her mother pulled her close.

"It saddens me to see how far my old friend De Guilbe has fallen," said

Father Artolivan, who seemed very weary and old indeed that day. "And all because of foolish pride."

"What say you, Father Artolivan?" the courier demanded. "My laird grows impatient."

Artolivan started to reply, but Dame Gwydre begged his indulgence and stepped up beside him. "I, too, rule a Holding of Honce," she called down. "A large one and no enemy of, or stranger to, the sailors of Palmaristown. Make your Laird Panlamaris aware that an attack on Chapel Abelle at this time is also an attack on Dame Gwydre of Vanguard."

The relay man looked to the courier, who nodded. He ran back across the field and the dame's words were told to Laird Panlamaris.

His answer came back immediately, for he obviously had known that Dame Gwydre and her contingent were present in Chapel Abelle.

"My Laird Panlamaris offers you sanctuary, good Lady of Vanguard," the courier explained. "You and those loyal to you may leave Chapel Abelle now by ship or through the front gate. This is not your disagreement."

"My fight, you mean, for you come with swords."

The courier had no response. Gwydre looked around at the monks, who were all staring at her with breath held, and smiled her assurance.

"There your laird errs, my friend," she called down. "This is my . . . disagreement. I and my Vanguardsmen will not leave Chapel Abelle at this time. Tell Laird Panlamaris that Dame Gwydre and Vanguard stand with Father Artolivan as guests in his good house. Explain that your laird, too, is welcome here, where we may speak of these pressing issues before rash decisions are made that cannot be undone."

Laird Panlamaris's response came back in mere heartbeats. "Father Artolivan's decree of disobedience to the throne, if it stands, thus does end all discussion."

"It stands, and I stand with Father Artolivan," said Gwydre. "Pray tell your laird that he should consider very wisely his next actions."

The proclamation, so final and clear, lifted the hearts of all the brothers.

Word went back and came forward, and the courier's pause as Panlamaris's response was whispered into his ear foretold ill.

"We have prisoners, Father Artolivan," he said with a backward motion. On Panlamaris's responding wave, a dozen or so captured brothers from the Chapel of Precious Memories were shoved forward to stand beside the kneeling Fatuus.

"Surrender the prisoners loyal to King Yeslnik," the courier demanded. "Or these men who would not denounce you, your brethren, are declared guilty of treason against the throne of King Yeslnik and shall be punished accordingly."

"Treason?" Father Premujon shouted before Artolivan could reply. "They have done nothing!"

"They refused the leniency of Laird Panlamaris and the choice of the new father of the Chapel of Precious Memories, Father De Guilbe," the courier said. Gasps sounded all along the wall.

"This is my Laird Panlamaris's last word," the courier finished. "Release the prisoners loyal to King Yeslnik at once or witness the consequences." He bowed and ran across the field to join his companions.

"I cannot do this," Father Artolivan lamented. "But am I to witness the executions of innocent men?"

"Perhaps we should let them go," said Gwydre.

"And then he will demand that we turn over the men of Ethelbert for execution as King Yeslnik has decreed," said Artolivan. Gwydre had no answer.

But across the field, Brother Fatuus did.

"Abelle!" he cried, his voice clear, unafraid, slicing loudly through the windy day. "My prophet, my saint, oma tula mere!"

"Saint?" said one monk down the wall. "That is heresy. The beatification has only just—" Others hushed him.

Brother Fatuus rolled over and managed to slip his bound hands around his tucked feet to bring them in front of him. He flipped up from his knees to his feet and began walking toward Chapel Abelle, repeating that cadence every step, his voice strong and without a quiver. "My prophet, my saint, oma tula mere!"

"Oma tula mere?" Brother Pinower and others asked.

"He's got Vanguard blood, he does!" Dawson McKeege explained. "Oma tula mere—in the arms of my loving mother."

"What is he doing?" asked Brother Pinower.

"He is giving his soul," Father Artolivan replied, his eyes growing moist.

Cries of "Halt!" resounded from Panlamaris's line, to which Fatuus merely lifted his arms and eyes to the sky and continued his march and his chant.

Panlamaris motioned a spearman to his side and pointed emphatically at Fatuus.

"My prophet, my saint, oma tu—" Fatuus gasped as a missile hit him square in the back. Everyone watching from the chapel walls and tall buildings—monks, Vanguardsmen, and even the men who had been sent to Chapel Abelle as prisoners—gasped when the point of that spear drove through the monk's back and out his belly.

Fatuus dropped to his knees, arms still high, gasping for breath. Somewhere, somehow, he found a moment of great strength and wrenched his hands apart, loosing the bindings. Fatuus found his voice again. "Oma tula mere!" The wounded monk miraculously regained his footing, impaled though he was, and resumed his march, his arms high and wide.

A furious Laird Panlamaris summoned other spearmen; a barrage of missiles soared at Fatuus. Again and again the spears violated his flesh, plunging into his shoulder, his back, his calves.

Fatuus kept walking, kept chanting, now more like singing to a beloved. "My prophet, my saint, oma tula mere!"

"Stop him!" Laird Panlamaris howled, but those soldiers around him seemed frozen, awestruck, as were the witnesses within Chapel Abelle.

"My prophet, my saint, oma tula mere!" Brother Fatuus sang, joined by a dozen other prisoners of Laird Panlamaris, who began to walk toward Chapel Abelle.

Spears reached for them. Riders broke from Panlamaris's ranks, running down the brothers, cutting them down with heavy bronze swords. But not one stopped chanting until the moment of his death. Not one cried for mercy or in pain.

Ahead of them Brother Fatuus, impaled by seven heavy spears, kept walking and singing. A rider bore down on the monk.

"Shoot him dead!" Father Artolivan shouted.

"Stop him!" Cadayle screamed.

"We can't reach!" Brother Jurgyen cried in reply. All winced at the expected moment of Fatuus's death.

Suddenly the rider's mount stopped and bucked, then spun about, hurling him to the ground. The horse began pawing the ground wildly, kicking and neighing as if it had gone mad. The swordsman crawled away, dragging a broken leg.

"My prophet, my saint, oma tula mere!" Brother Fatuus cried in glory and passion.

"Open the gate! The gate!" men shouted while others ran for the huge beam that sealed Chapel Abelle's massive doors.

When at last it opened, there knelt Brother Fatuus, a look of complete serenity on his pale face. "Oma tula mere," he rasped.

And then he died.

Across the field Laird Panlamaris began his charge, hundreds of Palmaristown soldiers churning the ground beneath their running feet and the hooves of their mounts and chariot teams.

The monks dragged Fatuus inside and scrambled to close and secure the gate. All eyes turned to Father Artolivan.

"Turn them," he grimly instructed. "With all the power of beloved Abelle—nay, of Saint Abelle, for we have seen now his miracle, turn them!"

Grim-faced, the brothers began sorting their gemstones, holding back until Brother Pinower gave the call.

A barrage of lightning reached out from Chapel Abelle the likes of which had never before been seen in Honce. When at last the flashes ceased and the ground stopped shaking and the spots no longer danced before their eyes, many men were down, crawling, writhing, burning. The charge had turned to retreat.

"You are besieged!" Laird Panlamaris cried in outrage. "You shall never leave!"

Old Father Artolivan, feeling strangely alive at that terrible moment, did not reply, silencing any responses from monk or Vanguardsman. He watched Panlamaris for only a moment before his reverent gaze shifted below to where brethren and prisoners from Ethelbert and Delaval alike knelt around Brother Fatuus in shared prayer.

Your allegiance in the face of Laird Panlamaris has renewed my hope, Lady of Vanguard," Father Artolivan said to Gwydre as the group of leaders made their way across the courtyard toward the main chapel. Across the field Panlamaris's army was at work setting tents, though many, including the laird himself, had moved down to the small town of Weatherguard.

"The inspiration for this day belongs to a monk I do not know," Gwydre replied. She nodded her chin toward the courtyard, where Brother Fatuus lay wrapped in a decorative shroud of the type used for a church father.

A large group had gathered on the far side of the courtyard. It seemed as if all the prisoners were there. Before them a pair of their ranks stood speaking with Brother Pinower.

"I would ask one more thing of you, Dame Gwydre," said Artolivan. "Laird Panlamaris will not be foolish enough to assail your ships, so your way home is all but assured. I ask you to take these men, Laird Ethelbert's at least, so that they may be spared the fate King Yeslnik has decreed. They deserve better."

Dame Gwydre turned to stare directly at the old father. Everyone else stopped as well, hanging on her every word, confused by the wry smile she wore.

"Good Father Artolivan, I would ask a favor of you," she said. He looked at her curiously, which seemed to please her greatly, as if she wanted this to be a surprise.

"Privately," she added.

"Of course."

The group moved toward the gathered prisoners and Brother Pinower.

"What trouble, Brother?" Father Artolivan asked.

"None, Father. This is Malcombe of Delaval City and Elefreth Pavu of Ethelbert dos Entel," he said, indicating a sturdy man with piercing blue eyes and curly black hair, the classic Delaval specimen. The other was a swarthy man, no less striking or imposing, obviously of the south and perhaps with a bit of Behrenese blood in him.

"Of course. Greetings to both of you this troubling day," said Artolivan. "The events have unsettled you, no doubt."

"We know of King Yeslnik's demands," Malcombe said.

"Yes."

Malcombe straightened his shoulders. "I was a knight in Laird Delaval's army," he said. "Among the elite warriors who rode with Delaval himself."

"This, too, is known to me," said Artolivan. "I am not so old as to have forgotten your pomposity on the day you arrived here at Chapel Abelle, all broken and outraged."

That seemed to shrink the proud warrior a bit, but he managed a smile. "Broken and near death, and, save the work of your brothers, I would surely have gone to my grave."

"Praise Abelle that you did not."

"I do," said Malcombe with a simple sincerity that added great weight to the statement. He nodded at Artolivan, then turned to his fellow Delaval prisoners watching from afar. To a one they signaled their agreement with him, with whatever pact had brought him to stand before Artolivan at this time.

"I—we—ask that you do not turn over my friend Elefreth and the other good men of Laird Ethelbert," Malcombe said.

More than a few of those with Artolivan gasped.

"Most of us have been here for more than a year, some for nearly two," Malcombe explained. "We have been treated well by the brothers, and we have come to know one another as friends and companions, not as enemies."

"We will fight one another no longer," said Elefreth with a heavy Entel accent.

"I expected as much and am glad for you that you have found your way from the darkness," Father Artolivan told them. "I was just now arranging with Dame Gwydre passage for all of you, or at least for those condemned by King Yeslnik's wrongful order, to Vanguard and freedom."

Malcombe and Elefreth looked at each other, a flash of hope fast giving way to looks of grim determination.

"I would let my men make that decision," said Malcombe.

"And I mine," Elefreth agreed.

"But this is my home, and I will not leave it now," said Malcombe. "Particularly not now."

"What then?" asked Father Artolivan. "To return to your respective lairds that you may be once more pressed into battle?"

"Nay, never that," said Malcombe, Elefreth nodding with every word. "For too long we've been fighting and bleeding and dying for the wants of the lairds."

"And you are weary of the battle, understandably so," said Artolivan. "But what, then? Do you ask to live out your lives here in Chapel Abelle?"

Malcombe straightened again, as did Elefreth, and behind them, all the prisoners, hundreds of warriors, stood as one and at rigid attention.

"Not weary of the battle," Malcombe corrected. "Weary of the cause."

"There is no cause in their battle," Elefreth agreed.

"But we're ready to fight if that's what is needed," said Malcombe.

"To fight? For whom?"

"For ourselves!" a man shouted from the ranks, and others cheered and agreed.

"To fight for you!" said another. "And for those monks, and for that one, Fatuus, who just showed us a good way to die!"

The cheering erupted at that, so sudden and heartfelt that Artolivan's eyes, and those of all around him, grew wet with tears.

"We are here at your call, trusting in your judgment," said Malcombe. "If you arm us and send us forth, we will crack open Laird Panlamaris's siege. Perhaps we could go out as if freed and chase them from the field as they naively welcome us into their ranks."

Father Artolivan was emphatically waving his hands to stop the line of thinking, for it was all too sudden for him and too overwhelming. He looked to Dame Gwydre for support.

"You are men I would be proud to have in Vanguard," she said. She and Artolivan retreated fast for his private quarters, with Dawson and Brother Jond in tow.

I t is all so unsettling," Callen said as she sat with Cadayle, Cormack, and Milkeila. "This day, I mean."

"We have witnessed the depths of treachery, the horror of inhumanity, the miracle of faith, and the hope of men's souls in the span of a single hour," said Cormack.

"I have seen it before, on a warm lake in the north," Milkeila added, tossing a wink at her husband, who nodded his agreement. "I am no longer surprised by the potential and the depths of the hearts of men."

"What will it all mean?" asked Cadayle. "How will it end?"

Brother Pinower walked over as she spoke. He regarded the four before nodding his chin toward a small window in the tower of the large chapel. "They are seeking the answers to that question even as you speak," he said.

"You know Father Artolivan well," said Cormack. "What will he do?"

"You know Dame Gwydre. What of her?"

Cormack smiled and pondered the question for a few moments, then smiled with confidence. "She will not abandon Father Artolivan to the whims of King Yeslnik. Of that I am sure."

"Perhaps the whole of our church will flock to Vanguard, and southern Honce be damned," said Brother Giavno.

"And what would you do, Brother, if it were up to you?" Cormack asked him pointedly. For a brief moment, all felt the tension in the air. This man, a disciple of Father De Guilbe, had whipped Cormack to within an inch of his life on De Guilbe's command.

"I would not have left Mithranidoon, save to follow Cormack and Bransen to the glacier and Ancient Badden," Giavno replied. "Or at least I pray that had the decision fallen to me I would have had the courage of Cormack and Milkeila." Embarrassed by the reminder of his previous failures, he bowed then and started away.

But Cormack called him back. "Sit with us," he bade the man who had once been his mentor, who had once been his friend, who had nearly been his executioner. "Let us solve the problems of the world and muse on the miracle of Brother Fatuus."

A look reflecting both gratitude and great sadness flashed on Giavno's face, and he did indeed join them for a discussion that nearly mirrored that taking place behind the window in the tower.

I ask that you allow me to remain here at Chapel Abelle and that my ships can sail north and return, laden with soldiers," Dame Gwydre said flatly, her tone indicating no sway in her position.

"Soldiers? To what end?" asked Father Artolivan.

"To the defense of Chapel Abelle," Dame Gwydre replied. "To the support of your courage. I had not thought this war of southern Honce to be the affair of Vanguard, but I see now that I was wrong. This is no petty fight between warring lairds. It is a battle for the soul of Honce. And a fight whose victory or loss will determine the future of Vanguard, I do not doubt. For if he wins here, Yeslnik—a man who claims a throne that does not even exist—will turn his eyes and his armies north."

"Because you were here when Laird Panlamaris was humiliated, both by Brother Fatuus and by the complete rejection of his assault," Father Artolivan reasoned.

"It would not have mattered," Gwydre said. "Unless I promised fealty to Yeslnik."

"There remains that option."

"At the cost of my soul. For how could I give credence and fealty to a man who would murder the men of Ethelbert you hold here? How could I keep my own soul if I were to ally with a man like Panlamaris after what he just did to the innocent brothers of the Chapel of Precious Memories? I will not abandon principle and what is right for political expediency, Father Artolivan. I did not do so when Ancient Badden demanded freedom to continue his reign of terror against the folk of Vanguard. A sorry and false woman I would be to turn my back on my fellows to the south."

"This is truly an unexpected day," said Artolivan. Weary, he moved to his chair. "A day that will echo in the songs of the bards for lifetimes hence, perhaps. Or one that will quickly spell our utter doom. I do not know."

"Aye, and that's where a measure of courage is needed," said Dawson Mc-Keege. "And without that measure"—he gave a snort to reflect complete disgust—"then what's worth singing about, anyway?"

Father Artolivan looked at the man incredulously, but then gave a much needed chuckle of agreement.

"Do you understand now why I keep him around?" asked Gwydre.

"Do you understand the magnitude of what you are proposing?"

"I will annex Chapel Abelle for Vanguard, but fear not, for you will continue with all freedom to do as your heart instructs," said Gwydre. "My action will be only to reinforce Vanguard's commitment to you and your brothers."

"You will be declaring war with Delaval City and Palmaristown, both of which can muster a garrison much larger than Vanguard's."

"Then we will fight better," said Gwydre.

"Or die better," Dawson added. "Like Brother Fatuus. I'm not knowing how long they will be singing of our choices this day, but the grandsons of the grandsons of the grandsons will be singing of Brother Fatuus. Of that I am sure."

"For Brother Fatuus, then," Gwydre proclaimed. "It is a good way to die!"

After many nods and hopeful smiles, Father Artolivan said grimly, "There is one more thing that must be done this day. De Guilbe will no doubt begin a rival order in Palmaristown—it has already happened, I am certain, since many brothers were not among those executed on the field. Laird Panlamaris will seek to justify his stand here, in any case."

"Your reasoning is sound, I fear," said Gwydre.

"We have seen the miracle," said Father Artolivan. "All of us. The strength of Brother Fatuus, the turning and bucking of the horse when Fatuus was surely doomed before he reached the gates of Chapel—" He paused there to smile.

"You will finalize the beatification of Abelle!" Father Premujon cried in joy.

"Blessed Abelle," said Artolivan. He paused again, his mind still sharp, still weighing every possibility, working fast behind his sparkling eyes. "From this day forth let it be known that we are the Order of *Blessed* Abelle, the Abellican Church, and that this place will be named St. Abelle—no!" He paused again for effect, grinning so widely that it seemed as if he would explode into joyous laughter. "St. Mere Abelle!" he finished.

Dame Gwydre and Dawson McKeege cheered, and Father Jond wept with overwhelming good spirit.

CHAPTER 19

The Impetulant

ere, then," Master Reandu said to Bannagran. He handed the man a long knife. "Do it yourself." Beside him a pair of younger brothers stiffened.

From the sill of a high window in Chapel Pryd, Bransen listened carefully to every word. A short while earlier, the monks had spoken of King Yeslnik's edict that all prisoners of Delaval be released and all those taken from Ethelbert's ranks be executed. Bransen was glad of their reaction, particularly the angry foot stomping of Reandu. For some reason he did not quite understand, Bransen needed to believe the best of this man. He remembered a day when Reandu had helped him finish his chore of lugging chamber pots to the dumping area, when Reandu had subsequently washed the filth from him. There had been tenderness there, once, though it had been suppressed under the orders of severe Bathelais and the even more severe Father Jerak.

Bransen shrank back when Bannagran had stormed into the chapel, full of unfocused anger and agitation.

"Do not try my patience," Bannagran warned. "My road has been long and wearying. I've no tolerance for your stubbornness this day."

"I have released the Delaval prisoners," Reandu calmly replied. "Against my better judgment but for your own sake."

"That was half the edict."

"You would have me murder helpless captives?"

"King Yeslnik did not demand that of you."

"Of course. I am simply to turn them over to you so that you might employ some valorless and immoral cad to stab and beat them," Reandu said, his voice thick with sarcasm that surely spelled defiance. "How easy it is for King

Yeslnik to make such a demand, his own hands clean of the blood. How easy it is for Bannagran to follow such a command . . ."

Up above, the Highwayman could hardly believe that Reandu was showing such independence, such . . . humanity. This was the man who had declared Garibond's heresy, which had doomed the innocent man to the fire.

"Silence!" Bannagran yelled.

"Then bloody your own hands, warrior!" Reandu spat back in his face.

"Do you think these hands clean?" the Bear of Honce roared, holding his large, strong paws up before him. "In this war and a dozen before! Do you think I have not killed many men?"

"These are helpless prisoners!"

"Many men undeserving? Men whose only crime was to serve the losing laird? So stained are these hands that your own Abelle could not wash the blood from them! There is no place in your heaven for Bannagran!"

"Then take this dagger and murder the five men of Ethelbert held within Chapel Pryd," said Reandu. "Cut their throats or stab their hearts." He held the dagger again, and Bannagran narrowed his eyes and stared at him angrily.

"Because you cannot!" Reandu lectured and pulled the dagger away. "You are a warrior, not a murderer!"

"This is an execution of the convicted, no murder," Bannagran said.

"Murder!" Reandu reiterated. "These men have committed no crimes."

Bannagran seemed to gasp for breath for a few moments before replying, "They are to be turned over. All loyal to Ethelbert are to be executed by order of King Yeslnik."

But Master Reandu was smiling by then, the Highwayman noted from far above. "You'll not kill them," he said with confidence.

"Their loyalty to Laird Ethelbert dooms them," Bannagran answered.

"You cannot ask a man to exchange his loyalty to an opposing laird," said Reandu. "You know as much." Reandu paused, and it occurred to Bransen that both he and Bannagran had known all along where this conversation would lead, almost as if they had choreographed it beforehand.

"But if they expressed loyalty to a third party, one neutral in the war, perhaps," Reandu posited.

"None who don the robes of the Order of Abelle fall under the edict of King Yeslnik, certainly," Bannagran replied. His guards looked at him curiously, as did all the monks in the room, except Reandu standing before him.

"Of course, because then they will serve the order and not Laird Ethelbert," Reandu said. "It is curious that you mention that, new Laird of Pryd, for this

very morning, all five of the remaining prisoners expressed just such an interest. I happen to have several extra robes that will fit them well."

"I will see them dressed as such, and this very day," Bannagran warned.
"Else they will face the wrath of King Yeslnik."

Master Reandu, who looked quite pleased with his cleverness, bowed.
Bannagran and his soldiers left the chapel.

D o not hesitate," Yeslnik said to his brutish guard. "It is imperative that
you react as soon as I indicate, true and fast."

"Me pleasure, me king," said Brawnwin, a three-hundred-pound behe-
moth of a man. He carried his great axe casually on one shoulder and could
wield it with one hand as easily as most men could wave a short sword. Brawnwin's head was shaven and looked as if it had been melted on atop his massive
shoulders, large rolls of skin falling down the back of that neck and great jowls
that seemed to grow out of his collarbones in the front.

"They may come to his defense," Yeslnik warned. "Their magic is potent."

"One cut, me king," Brawnwin assured him.

Drawing power from the imposing brute so readily at his command, Yeslnik stepped a little more lightly as they ascended the long stairs of Chapel Delaval. Until recently, this church of the Order of Abelle had been known as the
Chapel of Weeping Brothers, a name dating to the slaughter of the first monks
in the city, who took their own lives rather than denounce Abelle in the great
tragedy of Cordon Roe. Many of the brothers currently in Chapel Delaval still
referred to the place by its older name, a more fitting title this dark day.

Yeslnik and his entourage of a dozen armed and armored guards shoved
past the brothers who answered their knock on the heavy wooden doors.

"Father Pendigrast, immediately," Yeslnik commanded. "And bring forth
all the prisoners delivered to you who have not yet been ushered north to
Chapel Abelle."

"The prisoners, King Yeslnik?" a young monk asked.

"At once! All of them, and in chains!" He waved the young monk away
emphatically, giving him a shove with his foot when the monk didn't move
quickly enough. The hapless monk flew several feet before he stumbled and
crashed into the side wall.

In moments, Father Pendigrast appeared with three of the higher-ranking
brothers. He was one of the younger fathers in the order, not yet forty, pro-
moted because of the untimely death of the father before him and the man's
two expected successors, all taken by the same bout of the grippe that had

swept through Delaval City. There was no missing the trepidation on Pendigrast's face as he moved into the nave and walked along the worn fabric of the carpet that led between the chapel's center pews. Pendigrast had obviously expected this visit. How could he not, given that Father Artolivan's edict of disobedience had reached Delaval City that very morning?

"I sent one of your young brothers to fetch Ethelbert's men," Yeslnik said as the man approached. "To save you the trouble, of course."

Pendigrast glanced to his monk companions, closed his eyes briefly, and breathed deeply to steady his obviously frayed nerves. "You have seen the edict of Father Artolivan of Chapel Abelle, who rules my order," he said quietly.

"Of course," said Yeslnik. "A meritless writ I will ignore, as will you. Where are the prisoners?"

Pendigrast swallowed hard. "King Yeslnik, Chapel Delaval serves at your pleasure, as it served at the pleasure of Laird Delaval before you."

"King Delaval," Yeslnik sharply corrected.

"Yes, of course. King Delaval. But we serve Father Artolivan above all."

"Get the prisoners," Yeslnik interrupted.

"My king, I cannot," said Father Pendigrast.

Yeslnik gave a bored glance at the giant Brawnwin, who came forward suddenly and with a single chop of his axe cut Father Pendigrast apart from shoulder to hip. The man's legs crumbled beneath him, blood spewing for just a few heartbeats before Pendigrast fell sideways, quite dead. Monks cried out, but Yeslnik's guards were among the most fierce and violent in all the city. Brandishing their weapons they formed a defensive ring about the king, spear tips thrusting to keep Pendigrast's entourage back.

Yeslnik looked up. "Who is the new Father of Chapel Delaval?" he calmly asked. The monks all stammered and stuttered until finally one pointed to a man about the same age of Pendigrast.

"Congratulations, Father," Yeslnik said to him. "Now send your minions to retrieve the prisoners." Never taking his withering gaze from poor, frightened, newly appointed Father Dennigan, Yeslnik watched as a dozen ragged men were led into the nave in chains.

Yeslnik smiled widely, a most wicked and pleasing idea coming to him. He reached to Brawnwin's belt and pulled the man's bronze short sword from its sheath, then tossed it on the ground before Dennigan.

"You kill the first one," he instructed. "Then hand the blade to the next most superior brother and on down the line."

"I am no warrior, King Yeslnik," Dennigan stammered.

"Kill him. Now," said Yeslnik. "Or explain your failing to Father Pendigrast."

Hands trembling, Dennigan picked up the sword and moved on shaky legs to the nearest of the prisoners, a young man barely out of his teens. The boy pleaded with his superior to be spared.

"Do it!" King Yeslnik cried.

Dennigan leveled the blade at the prisoner's throat and whispered that he would try to make it clean. The boy began to cry. Dennigan dropped the blade to the floor and vomited.

"Pathetic," Yeslnik said. "All of you!" With a flick of his white hand he motioned to two guards, who rushed to the chapel doors and flung them wide. More soldiers charged into the chapel.

"Arrest the brothers and drag those miserable wretches from Ethelbert into the streets," Yeslnik commanded. He turned to Brawnwin. "I trust that you will find ways to execute them that will amuse me."

He led Brawnwin's gaze over to Dennigan, on his knees now, shoulders bobbing violently with great sobs. Yeslnik gave a derisive snort. "Wound him," he whispered to the brute. "But leave him with enough to make the journey to Chapel Abelle bearing my response to Father Artolivan."

"And yer answer will be?" Brawnwin asked eagerly.

"The brother who delivered Artolivan's treasonous writ," said Yeslnik. "Put his head in a sack."

Brawnwin's grin nearly took in his ears.

The next morning, Brother Dennigan felt a heavy boot kick against his back, shoving him from Delaval City's north gate on the eastern side of the great river. In his hand he held a sack that bore the severed head of Brother Piastafan, the courier from Father Artolivan, his mouth locked wide open in a final, horrified scream. As Dennigan pulled himself from the mud to a kneeling position, a wagon rolled out of the gate and splashed beside him. Brawnwin came forth and grabbed him by the collar. With tremendous strength the brute lifted Dennigan over the side of the wagon and unceremoniously dumped him in.

"With all haste to Chapel Abelle," instructed King Yeslnik, sitting astride his mare just inside the gate. "And you, monk, tell your Father Artolivan that when I am soon finished with Ethelbert, the Order of Abelle will be held accountable for his treason. This is our time of great need, the moment of triumph for the line of Delaval, and I will never forget that Artolivan and your church did not stand with me."

Dennigan managed to shift to a sitting position and looked back vacantly at the young tyrant.

"Oh, about that boy you were too weak to kill," Yeslnik said to him. "We stripped him naked, bound his hands, and put him in a sack with some poison-ous snakes this morning. Perhaps you heard his screams. They lasted a pleas-ingly long time."

Dennigan closed his eyes and shook with silent sobs.

I knew that Yeslnik was an impulsive child, but this surprises me," Bransen said to Jameston when they regrouped in the woods behind Chapel Pryd after both had witnessed the conversation between Reandu and Bannagran from opposite windows high on the side of the nave.

"You knew he had done as much," said Jameston. "We heard this at the other chapel, and you said then that Yeslnik's murderous mind didn't surprise you."

"Not Yeslnik," Bransen corrected. "Nothing bad that comes from him would surprise me. The reactions of Brother Reandu and Bannagran, however . . . I never thought them so possessed of moral boundaries," Bransen explained and Jameston nodded. "Especially not Bannagran."

"Is that the reason?" asked the scout. "Or are the both of them weary already of King Yeslnik?"

It was Bransen's turn to nod. "Could it be that King Yeslnik is so far beyond the moral boundaries that even the always callous lairds will be put off by his demands?"

"Or it might be that these callous lairds you speak of have a bit of sense and know that they can only ask so much of those they dominate before they find the tines of a pitchfork aimed their way. It didn't take much convincing by Gwydre to get the people of Vanguard to turn and fight against Ancient Badden."

"Yeslnik is an idiot."

"An impetulant one, for sure," said Jameston.

Bransen nodded, for the word sounded right. After a moment's reflection, though, Bransen screwed up his face curiously and echoed, "Impetulant?"

"Aye."

"I don't know that word," said Bransen.

"But you know what it means."

"Impatient? Impetuous? Petulant?"

"Yes."

Bransen gave a helpless laugh.

"It's from an old hunter's song," Jameston explained. " 'The Herstory of History.' "

"Herstory?"

"You can figure that part out."

"True, but why?"

"When you live alone in the forest you learn to speak little and listen a lot," Jameston explained. "Putting words together to make a quicker point saves you breath."

"Crazy V would have had a herstory," said Bransen.

Jameston laughed. "And a good one! And more than a few who knew her would be embarredassed by the tales told of V."

"Embarred . . ." Bransen started to echo, then he could only chuckle. "Redassed? What did you call him?"

"Who? Yeslnik?"

"Impetulant?" asked Bransen.

"Fits him, don't it?"

"Better than any. King Yeslnik the Impetulant. We should put it on his headstone. Soon."

"Then let us start the carving of king and stone."

Jameston paused and let the moment slip aside, watching Bransen as the young man glanced back toward Pryd, the town that had been his home for so many years.

"You are proud of the laird and the monks," Jameston remarked. "Their actions in dodging Yeslnik's verdict give you hope."

Bransen considered that for a few heartbeats. "I cannot deny that. My relationship with Brother Reandu is . . . complicated."

"He's the closest thing you've got to family after your wife and mother," said Jameston. Bransen didn't argue with that assessment. "Is it time for us to go see him?"

Bransen nodded but did not move. Jameston stepped aside and motioned him to lead the way, but Bransen still made no move.

"You think it harder to test that Writ of Passage now," Jameston reasoned. "Now you're hoping they might honor it, and now, with such hopes, you're more afraid of how you'll feel if they don't."

Bransen took a deep breath.

"Put your mask down over your eyes and walk openly through the town," Jameston advised. "The people here will remember you. They saved you once. Maybe once again?"

Bransen took off his farmer's hat and his mask and shook his hair out, which parted it in the middle and showed the star-shaped brooch set on his forehead. His deerskin coat fell to the ground with the hat, and he tied the mask on securely. He looked different from the Highwayman who had left Pryd Town months before. His dark hair was longer, and, of course, he now wore the brooch. His bandanna, once a mask and hood, was now rolled so that it was just a thin strip across his eyes. But the black silk outfit was unmistakable, with one sleeve long, the other torn off at the shoulder, and with a black strip tied about his otherwise bare upper bicep.

The gasps of recognition and whispers of "The Highwayman!" began as soon as Jameston led him from the forest and onto the main road far across the way from Chapel Pryd. The pair moved toward Chapel Pryd, with many people following in their wake.

They knew the Highwayman here in Pryd Town. And they loved him.

Chapel Pryd was close to Castle Pryd, and as the monks obviously heard the approach of the Highwayman and his considerable entourage, for their courtyard gates opened before Bransen even approached, so too, he figured, had some in the castle heard.

He didn't think about that as he walked through the chapel's outer wall, a flood of memories greeting him the moment he stepped again onto Chapel Pryd's courtyard. Up the white stone path, the doors to the chapel proper were also opened, brothers peering with obvious apprehension.

Bransen moved into the large foyer, Jameston beside him, and before he could even ask the astonished young brothers standing there to see the leaders, Master Reandu appeared flanked by several others.

"Bransen!" Master Reandu blurted. "What are you doing here? Are you mad? You left under condition of a strict penalty."

"Good to meet you, too," Jameston muttered so that only Bransen and a couple of nearby monks could hear.

"And I return to insist that the condition be revoked," Bransen said.

"Are you a madman?" Reandu repeated, apprehension growing on his face.

Bransen reached over his shoulder and produced Dame Gwydre's Writ of Passage from the scroll tube he had tied diagonally across his back. "On the contrary, Brother Reandu," he said, handing it over.

"Master Reandu," one of the monks behind corrected sharply.

"I find this to be a most glorious day," Bransen announced. He offered a smile before finishing, "Master Reandu."

Before the monk could respond, a shout came from the courtyard. "You!" came the resonating voice of Laird Bannagran.

"The Bear of Honce!" the monk behind Reandu breathed with obvious terror.

"It would have to be, would it not?" Bransen asked as he turned. But any intention he had of parleying here, of letting Dame Gwydre's writ carry any weight for him, disappeared as he swung about.

Great axe in hand, a look of sheer outrage on his face, Bannagran didn't seem to be in any mood for talking. The laird charged with a roar, his axe upright before him, not tipping his hand about the intended angle of his initial cut.

Jameston moved for his bow, but Bransen, drawing his sword with his right hand, pushed Jameston to the side with his left. His sword came out in the blink of an eye, which seemed to surprise Bannagran. He kept coming, though, his axe head slipped over his left shoulder. He turned his foot in with his closing step at the Highwayman, also to the left.

A lesser fighter would have cringed and braced, and thus been cut in half, but the Highwayman anticipated every movement. When Bannagran went into his sudden spin, axe flying to arm's length, Bransen was already moving. He shifted to his left, dancing past the retreating Jameston. When Bannagran came around, axe slashing powerfully, he hit nothing but air. Too fine a warrior to leave himself open despite the daring move, Bannagran recovered almost immediately, stopping short his swing as soon as he realized the Highwayman's dodge. Reorienting himself, he squared up with his opponent.

"Are we to do this dance again?" the Highwayman asked. "And who will die this time when you throw your weapon at me in frustration?"

That last question made Bannagran narrow his eyes with anger. He stepped forward fast, chopping down left to right, right to left, and back to the first strike. The Highwayman swayed to his left, to his right, and to his left again, causing three near but complete misses. He countered with a sudden stab of his sword, but Bannagran threw his hips behind him, less gracefully than the Highwayman had dodged the axe swings but effective nonetheless.

The Highwayman thrust again. Bannagran, his hands wide on the handle of his great axe, drove his weapon down to deflect the blade low, then stepped ahead and threw forward his right hand, the lower on his axe, punching the handle at the Highwayman's face.

Bransen dropped under it and came on lower this time. Bannagran had to throw his feet out behind him wildly to save his shins. He staggered and scrambled as the Highwayman pressed the attack, stabbing at one leg, then the other.

"Read it!" the Highwayman shouted to Master Reandu, the Writ of Passage still rolled in his hand.

The Highwayman duckwalked in a crouch, his sword prodding faster and faster to keep the retreating Bannagran off balance, to keep him working furiously with his feet and his weapon so that the great warrior of Pryd Town could not begin a counterattack.

"I did not return to Pryd to fight you," the Highwayman said to him.

"I told you to stay away," Bannagran growled in response. "Forevermore!"

"Things have changed," the Highwayman insisted.

"The worse for you!" Bannagran shouted as he leaped up and forward, clearing the Highwayman. The warrior landed in a forward roll and came up and around with a great sidelong slash designed to keep the Highwayman far away.

But Bransen was right beside him as he turned. The sword blade hit the axe handle before Bannagran could build any momentum. The Highwayman slid it right up to slam hard at the crook between axe handle and head.

The Highwayman grabbed Bannagran's chest with his free hand. "I don't want to fight you!" he yelled in Bannagran's face.

"Hold, Laird Bannagran!" cried Reandu, who had finally recovered his wits enough to read the scroll.

Bannagran pulled his left hand free of his trapped axe, retracted immediately, and moved to slug the Highwayman, a heavy and powerful punch that would have surely crushed the young warrior's face. But Bannagran flew backward before he had barely begun the swing, jolted by a blast of lightning-like energy. He landed on his heels but stumbled down to a seated position on the floor some ten feet away, his long black hair flying wildly.

"You cheat with the gemstones!" Bannagran growled through chattering teeth.

"He has a Writ of Passage from Dame Gwydre of Vanguard!" Master Reandu shouted, "Forgiving him his crimes of theft and praising him for the great victory in the north!"

"What?" Bannagran scrambled to his feet, giving no indication he intended to abandon his battle.

"I fought for her," the Highwayman explained. "I killed Ancient Badden of the Samhaists and freed her people from the grip of horrible war."

"That means nothing to me." Bannagran hoisted his axe as if he meant to charge again.

"In return, Dame Gwydre has pardoned me for my past . . . difficulties," the Highwayman said.

"A Writ of Passage," Master Reandu said again.

"Does that include your murder of King Delaval?"

"My what?"

"I thought not!" Bannagran said and charged again. He came in furiously, his axe working brilliantly in short strokes and stabs with its pointed iron top. Almost any other warrior in Honce would have been cut repeatedly by that barrage, and all in the room gasped and winced, expecting the Highwayman to fall to the floor in pieces.

But to the Highwayman, it seemed as if Bannagran was moving in slow motion. Bransen easily worked his sword, tip up, tip down, left and right, to slap against the axe every time and always before the powerful Bannagran could gain momentum behind his swing.

Silverel rang against iron and tapped against the wooden handle. The Highwayman's hand moved in a blur before him, perfect aim, perfect angle. The exchange went on for what seemed like an eternity, though it was not more than a score of heartbeats. More gasps echoed in the nave of Chapel Pryd.

Bannagran came in hard, swinging left to right. The Highwayman chopped a shortened downstroke, sliding his sword again along the blade to hook the axe under the head. He continued his rotation through the backhand, high over their heads, then down to the left and low to the right, where an extra shove of that sword nearly swung Bannagran around.

The Laird of Pryd fought to hold his balance but didn't even recognize that the Highwayman had disengaged and turned his sword with such precision and speed that the tip was in at Bannagran's throat before he had begun to move his axe again.

All in the room gasped to see the great Bannagran, the Bear of Honce, defeated. But Bannagran wasn't quite finished yet. With a suddenness that startled everyone except the always cool Highwayman, Bannagran threw himself over backward. At the same time he used his tremendous strength to bring his great axe sweeping up from the side so that as he pursued, the Highwayman had to suddenly retract his blade or have it raked aside by the axe.

Bannagran hit the ground in a roll, throwing himself over and stumbling fast back to his feet, slashing his axe the rest of the way to his right, then back again to the left.

Fast and balanced, the Highwayman rushed in as the axe went to Bannagran's left, stepping quickly past the man's right. He flipped his sword to his left hand and stabbed behind his back to the right. Bannagran turned and lurched in a desperate dodge as Bransen ran by him. Though the fine sword did whip past, it seemed to all that he had avoided the blow.

He turned and the Highwayman continued back a couple of steps, then spun to face him directly once more, tossing his sword back to his main hand.

A curious expression crossed Bannagran's face, and he slyly slipped one hand behind his hip to feel his torn tunic and shirt under the back of his breastplate. He looked questioningly at the Highwayman.

Bransen half shrugged, half nodded to confirm Bannagran's suspicions: He had lost this fight not once but twice, for in both the movement that had removed the sword from under his chin and in his dodge from the Highwayman's charge, the only thing that had saved him was Bransen's mercy. Twice in the span of a few heartbeats, the Highwayman had beaten him.

"Are we to continue this folly all the day?" Bransen asked. "Read the Writ of Passage."

"You murdered King Delaval!" Bannagran snarled.

"His sword is whole!" Master Reandu cried in sudden realization.

The Highwayman glanced back at him curiously, then looked to his magnificent blade.

"He repaired it!" Bannagran insisted.

Bransen snapped his sword down beside him and retreated three fast steps. "What are you talking about?" he demanded. "My sword, my mother Sen Wi's sword, has never been broken."

"The sword that slew King Delaval was broken in half," Reandu explained.

"In the man's chest," another monk added.

"Surely not a blade like this," said Bransen, presenting his sword before him.

"Exactly so!" Reandu replied pointing to Bannagran. When he looked to the laird, Bransen saw Bannagran draw the top half of a delicately curving blade from a sheath on his hip, a scabbard that Bransen had thought for a long dagger and empty since no hilt had shown there.

"The blade that killed King Delaval," Bannagran said, holding it up for Bransen and all the others to clearly view. "So much like your own. Too much like your own!"

Bransen turned his blade over up before his eyes, noting the unmistakable similarities. "Where did you get that?" he asked, finding it hard suddenly to even draw breath as the implications of that blade—unmistakably a Jhesta Tu blade—began washing over him.

"From King Delaval's chest," Bannagran answered. "And for it, King Yeslnik has declared you guilty of murder."

"But it is not my blade," Bransen protested, turning his own over again to accentuate his point.

"It is too similar, possessed by one of like mind and training as you," Bannagran said.

Bransen had no answer other than to shake his head. Eventually, he managed to say, "I was in Vanguard when Delaval was murdered. Dame Gwydre will confirm my claim. Last time I was in Delaval City was before the winter, and Laird Delaval—"

"King Delaval!" Bannagran corrected.

"King Delaval," said Bransen, not wishing to argue such points. "He was very much alive when I left, and I have never returned. That is not my sword, and I have never seen another sword of this type in my life until just this moment!"

Bannagran stared at him hard. If he was softening at all to Bransen's reasoning, he wasn't showing it.

"Does the truth not matter?" Bransen asked.

"Not to King Yeslnik," said Bannagran.

"What is this insanity that has gripped all of Honce?" Bransen asked as he spun around, sheathing his sword in a single fluid movement to address all in the chapel. "Is there no limit to the misery these lairds will inflict for the sake of their own gain?"

"Enough of your speeches!" Bannagran yelled at him. He turned his gaze wider. "All of you be gone!" he demanded. "Now!" Brother, soldier, and peasant alike scrambled to escape the volatile man's wrath, leaving only Bransen and Jameston, Reandu, and a pair of Bannagran's guards in the wide nave.

"You have seen Dame Gwydre's Writ of Passage," Bransen said when the commotion died away. "She offered to me and my family a full pardon in exchange for my actions on her behalf against Ancient Badden. Will you honor her decree?"

Bannagran paused and continued to stare at him. "Your family? Callen Duwornay and her daughter, you mean."

"Yes."

"For them, yes," said Bannagran. "For you, no. Not until you clear your name with King Yeslnik, and I think that unlikely."

"And if I do? Am I to be welcomed back in Pryd with Callen and Cadayle beside me?"

Bannagran looked to Reandu, gave a deep and profound sigh, and then stated, to Reandu's obvious surprise and to Bransen's, "Yes."

"Bannagran?" Reandu asked.

"Yes," the Bear of Honce said again more forcefully and confidently. "I'm sick of it all."

"I did not mean for you to kill Prydae," said Bransen. "But I went to his tower to protect my love and would do so again!"

"Silence," Bannagran warned. "I have given you what you desire and all that I can. Ask no more of me. Understand, Highwayman, that I'll not tolerate any of your indiscretions should you ever return."

"I will return."

"King Yeslnik will never agree."

"But, my family? You said—"

"They can return to Pryd Town at their leisure," Bannagran assured him. "That poor woman, Callen, never deserved the sack, though her sniveling lover surely did. The Samhaists are long gone from Pryd Town, so I care not if the Duwornays walk here openly. But you remain another matter."

"I will clear my name," Bransen said.

"I am tasked with killing you," Bannagran admitted.

Bransen laughed. "Care to try again?"

"Bransen!" Reandu and Jameston scolded in unison.

Bannagran held up his hand to silence them and assure them that all was calm here. "Be gone from my town and my holding."

"I ask two things of you before I leave."

The Bear of Honce put his hands on his hips and stared at Bransen hard, thinking to question the young man's nerve in making requests. However, remembering their fight and noting that the young warrior did not flinch or back down, Bannagran merely waited.

"First, I would speak with Master Reandu."

"You have until the noontime hour."

"And, second, allow me that broken sword."

"It is not mine to give."

"Let me study it at least," said Bransen, desperation creeping into his voice. Bannagran, Reandu, and particularly Jameston looked at him with surprise.

"Please," said Bransen. "I believe that to be a Jhesta Tu blade."

"Like your own."

"Perhaps."

Bannagran tossed the blade to the floor at Bransen's feet. With trembling hands the young man picked it up and turned it over and over, pointing it away from his eyes so that he could study the break.

Wrapped metal. Just like his own sword. Only the Jhesta Tu were known to create such blades. Bransen could hardly draw breath. He closed his eyes and considered the possibilities here, if the Jhesta Tu mystics had truly come to Honce. That long road, that long-avoided road, now loomed before him, within his grasp, as never before.

"Then Laird Ethelbert has hired Jhesta Tu mercenaries from Behr," Bannagran remarked.

Bransen blinked out of his contemplations. "No," he said as he tried to sort through Bannagran's claim. "No."

"It is such a blade," said Bannagran.

"Jhesta Tu are not mercenaries. They cannot—"

"That blade slew King Delaval. The wielder of that blade, part of a small band by all reports—and dressed as you are, by all accounts—scaled the castle walls and defeated King Delaval and his elite warriors in short order."

Bransen couldn't doubt the claim, but he did not understand the concept of Jhesta Tu mercenaries. If they were fighting for Laird Ethelbert, which seemed likely, then it was for philosophy and preference and not for coin. The notion shook the young man profoundly. "May I keep this?" he asked.

Bannagran held out his big hand. Bransen reluctantly set the sword blade in it.

Bransen turned to Master Reandu. "In private?" The monk nodded and started for a side room.

"Noontime," Bannagran reiterated as Bransen walked past. "Then be far from Pryd, and return not other than on pain of death unless King Yeslnik has declared your innocence and freedom."

Bransen didn't bother to respond.

Master Reandu's visage and posture changed noticeably when he and Bransen were away from Bannagran and alone in a side room of Chapel Pryd. His face brightened and his step lightened, and his smile seemed truly genuine.

"My heart warms at seeing you walking so tall and straight," he said.

"You saw it before I left, when you took me to kill Laird Prydae," Bransen replied curtly. Reandu stiffened and took a step back at the grim reminder of that fateful day.

"But that was because of the soul stone."

"As is this," said Bransen. He brushed his long hair aside and indicated the brooch set in his forehead.

Despite his reservations at the initial sharp retort, Reandu moved closer, eyeing the marvelous piece of jewelry. "Yes, but even so," he said, reaching up to touch the brooch. "You seem more comfortable and stable."

"I am."

"All the gems . . . are they magical? Where did you get such a marvelous piece?"

"They are, and this was put upon my forehead by Father Artolivan of Chapel Abelle," Bransen answered.

Reandu fell back another step and looked at him incredulously. "Father Artolivan gave that to you?"

"I just said as much."

"It is . . . unexpected."

"That he would offer it, or that I would take it?" Bransen asked.

"Both!"

Bransen chuckled. "I served Dame Gwydre in exchange for her Writ of Passage. I dealt a great blow to the Samhaists when I took Ancient Badden's head from his shoulders. Father Artolivan knows that I am no enemy to him or his church. Does Brother Reandu?"

"Of course!"

Bransen eyed him doubtfully, then smiled as he produced a second parchment, the writ from Father Artolivan. He handed it to Reandu, who read it with eyes so wide that they seemed as if they might roll from their sockets.

"I understand your actions here, Bransen. Perhaps better than anyone. I saw the punishments you endured at the hands of the people of Pryd, at the demands of Laird Prydae, at—"

"The punishments my innocent father endured?" Bransen interrupted. "At the hands of the Samhaists and Laird Prydae?"

"And at the hands of Chapel Pryd," Master Reandu admitted without further prompting. "What am I to say, my old friend? I did not approve of the treatment of Garibond, nor do I think the treatment offered to your mother and father fair or wise, though I was not involved in those decisions. I was not a voice of power within Chapel Pryd. . . ."

Reandu's voice trailed off when Bransen put up a hand. It occurred to Bransen then just how much of the upper hand he had gained in the last few months. Here was Reandu, Master Reandu, the acting leader of Chapel Pryd, stuttering and stammering excuses to him. Bransen did well to hide his amusement for Reandu's sake. He reminded himself of Reandu's commitment to him, such as it was, in the dark days.

"I am glad that you were not punished for your actions at Castle Pryd," Bransen said, referring to Reandu's intervention against Master Bathelais when Bathelais had sought to stop Bransen with a blast of lightning.

"Master Bathelais did not recover from his fall," Reandu said, his voice low, his guilt all too clear. "I am not proud of how I attained my current position, but I am grateful to Father Artolivan and the masters at Chapel Abelle for their understanding and faith in me."

"I have not forgotten the sins of your chapel," Bransen said. "But neither have I forgotten the day you helped me with the chamber pots or when you washed the filth from me. I am not your enemy, Master Reandu."

That proclamation brought a profound sigh of relief from the brother. "It does my heart good to see you standing so straight and tall," he said once again after a few heartbeats of slow and steady breathing. "I do not lament the passing of the Stork."

"Even if in his stead comes the Highwayman, whom King Yeslnik hates above all?"

"King Yeslnik is wrong," said Reandu.

The startling words had Bransen lifting his eyebrows.

"And more the fool for the edict he issued to Father Artolivan," Reandu said, trying to keep his voice low. "He would have our order act as executioners and go back on our promises. Does he believe that the holdings of Honce will rally to his flag when he would so callously murder the many men whose only crime was to serve the lairds they had known all their lives?"

"I watched your conversation with Bannagran earlier this morning," Bransen admitted, and Reandu looked at him curiously. "Regarding the disposition of the prisoners, who are now brothers, it would seem. I was in a high window overlooking the nave."

Though they were not in the high-roofed nave, Reandu reflexively glanced up before shaking his head and reminding himself to doubt nothing about this surprising young man.

"I would not have allowed the prisoners to be killed," Reandu said after he sorted through the startling information.

"You handed Bannagran the knife."

"Because he would never have killed them," said Reandu. "Bannagran is no murderer."

"Garibond," Bransen said.

Reandu shook his head. "His fire has dimmed with the wisdom of age. He has served the people of Pryd well as steward and now as laird. They have come to trust him and love him, and they follow him into battle."

Bransen shrugged as if he hardly cared. "I hope you are right, for the sake of the people of Pryd."

After a long and uncomfortable pause, with Master Reandu clearly caught between his hopes for Bransen and his growing loyalty to Bannagran, the monk asked, "Will you return to Pryd Town when you have cleared your name?"

Bransen replied with a grin that revealed . . . nothing. For only when he had heard that question had he realized that it hardly mattered. The entire reason for his journey to Pryd, to secure a home for his growing family, hardly mattered to him at that time.

The Jhesta Tu had come to Honce.

While Bransen was meeting with Master Reandu, Jameston Sequin walked out of Chapel Pryd and over to the next impressive structure. He was stopped at the gates of Castle Pryd by grim-faced guards, crossing halberds before him and looking very much like they would enjoy eviscerating him.

Jameston just laughed at them. "Go and tell your laird that a friend of Dame Gwydre of Vanguard would like a word with him," he instructed.

Neither guard budged.

"Would you deny the Dame of Vanguard access to your Laird Bannagran?" Jameston asked. "Without even asking Laird Bannagran? I've known more than a few presumptuous guards. They're all dead now, of course, but I admire their spirit."

The guards looked at each other for a moment, then one backed away and started into the castle. He picked up his pace almost at once, which amused Jameston greatly.

Soon after, Jameston found himself standing before Laird Bannagran.

"Jameston Sequin at your service, good Laird of Pryd Town," he said with a bow. "Come from Vanguard to your door."

"If you wish to ingratiate your Lady Gwydre to me you would have been wiser to come in to Pryd Town separate from the Highwayman."

Jameston laughed. "Wouldn't even have found my way to your town."

"You find this amusing?" Bannagran asked grimly.

"All of it, in a sad manner," Jameston replied. "Guess that's why I spend most of my time walking the forests of Vanguard and Alpinador."

"What do you want?"

Jameston nodded at Bannagran's short response. "I'm a good friend of Dame Gwydre and empowered to speak for her. I'd be a sorry emissary if I didn't pay a visit to the laird."

"A visit? Should I set a banquet table?"

"I'm not your enemy, nor is Dame Gwydre," said Jameston.

"The politics of the world are not my own to decide."

"Just yours to laugh at, helplessly," Jameston quipped. "Oh, I see that in your eyes, Laird Bannagran of Pryd. Tired of war, tired of stupid lairds and stupider kings and stupider reasons for men killing men."

"You pretend to know more than you do," Bannagran replied. "I have no time for your pointless banter. You came seeking audience, and, as you claim to be a spokesman for Dame Gwydre, I granted your request. Do you have anything of value to say, or are you just here to annoy me?"

Jameston laughed at that.

"Do not try my patience," Bannagran warned. "Other men who have done so have lost their heads."

"That wouldn't be a wise choice for you," Jameston replied. "Gwydre's got no fight with you, nor do I, and I doubt King Yeslnik would appreciate you starting a war with Vanguard."

"What do you want?"

"I want to tell you of Bransen, the Highwayman," Jameston replied. "He had nothing to do with the murder of King Delaval. He was in Vanguard, maybe even in Alpinador, at the time, and I've been with him every moment since he sailed south across the gulf with Dame Gwydre."

"Gwydre is in Honce proper?"

"Left her at Chapel Abelle," Jameston explained. "I'm not thinking she's pleased with what she's seeing here in the south."

"That is not my concern."

"But the Highwayman is."

"And?"

"He had nothing to do with the murder of Delaval."

"So you believe that matters a whit?"

"Not in your world," Jameston replied with a snort. "But I think it does to you."

Bannagran stared at him hard.

"He's a fine fighter, that one," Jameston said. Bannagran didn't blink. "He could have killed you."

"Your insults do not serve Dame Gwydre here."

"No insult, just observation," said Jameston. "You might have saved yourself when he had his blade at your chin, I suppose, but he had you when he went past you, and you know it."

Bannagran continued his unflinching stare.

"But he didn't stick you, did he? And he could have, in a fight you started."

"Do you have a point here, other than to insult?"

"No insult intended," Jameston said and bowed low. "I'm only saying so because I'm thinking you should take a closer look at this young man you call the Highwayman. There's more to him than you think."

"Thank you for your advice. I will inform Dame Gwydre that her observant emissary is a wise man."

Jameston grinned at the unrelenting sarcasm, seeing it for what it was. "Bransen had nothing to do with Delaval's death," he repeated. "That doesn't matter to King Yeslnik, but I believe it matters to you."

"Take care your words."

"Bransen's not the reason you're so mad right now," Jameston dared to press on. "I see the twist in your face, Laird Bannagran of Pryd. You know what is right and what simply is. When what simply is doesn't match with what is right, it sticks you harder than Bransen's sword ever could."

"You presume a lot, emissary."

"I've seen a lot, good laird," Jameston replied, bowing low again.

"Is there anything more?"

"I'll pass along your well wishes to Dame Gwydre when I see her again."

Bannagran just sighed as Jameston took his leave.

CHAPTER 20

Focusing Purpose

Dame Gwydre sat on the balcony of her lavish room at St. Mere Abelle, looking across the expansive courtyard to the front wall and beyond, where the first flickers of evening campfires began to sprout among the ranks of Laird Panlamaris's besieging force.

"Second thoughts?" Dawson McKeege asked her from the middle of her room. She turned to regard the man, managing a slight smile.

Dawson understood her dismay. News had come in a short while before of Prince Milwellis's rampage along the populous region known as the inner coast, the western banks of Felidan Bay, with many villages burned to the ground and many, many people killed. Devastation was reported all along the coast, with too many bodies to bury, including many warriors who had come from the wilder reaches of the Mantis Arm.

Yeslnik's victory seemed assured in short order. His apparently overwhelming win did not bode well for St. Mere Abelle and Father Artolivan, nor for Dame Gwydre and her decision to throw in with the monks.

"He says that he is the King of Honce, and so he may well soon be," Gwydre replied.

"We do not know how far south the prince managed to go," Dawson reminded her. "And some of the monks here who've been to Ethelbert dos Entel say that it's a formidable city."

"Let us hope. If Laird Ethelbert can hold back the tides of Yeslnik, then our chances here are greater indeed, but—"

"But if he comes against us with all he's got, then you're wondering if you chose right in standing by the monks, because we're sure to lose. But ye knew that, and didn't we talk about the songs they'll be singing when we're long gone from the world?"

"I know," Gwydre admitted, turning her wistful gaze to distant fields where campfire after campfire flared to life now.

"But now that it seems real, you're wondering about what your choice will mean for them that follow you," Dawson reasoned.

"Perhaps we should sail for Vanguard. All of us, with the monks and the prisoners, too."

"That'd take a lot o' boats."

"Or fast ships turning back."

"To what purpose?" Dawson asked. "He'll come for ye. For all of us."

"We know the ways of Vanguard. Yeslnik does not."

"I'm thinking his armies will cut new ways."

"It may be the wiser course. Perhaps the people of Honce will have no will to pursue. . . ."

"We'll not abandon St. Mere Abelle," said Father Premujon, entering through Gwydre's partially opened door with brothers Giavno and Jond beside him.

"Not for Chapel Pellinor?" Dame Gwydre asked.

Premujon shook his head. "Father Artolivan has made a bold stand, and we stand with him above all. Brother Fatuus has shown us the way."

"The way to die," Dawson deadpanned, but no one laughed.

"St. Mere Abelle is the most defensible structure in the world," said Premujon. "Both in natural blessings and constructs. The brothers have built and fortified this place over the decades. The only approach by land is up a steep hill, and a slow-moving army . . . we all witnessed the fate of Laird Panlamaris's charge. The small, narrow harbor is nearly unreachable by any who do not know the rocky reefs about it, and it, too, would be easily defended by merely a handful of brothers with the proper gemstones. A single sinking could prevent other sizable ships from even attempting the approach. And even if Yeslnik's sailors somehow gained the wharf area, the tunnels are easily defended or, if need be, easily shut down."

"You inspire confidence, Father," Dame Gwydre remarked.

"Look again to that wall, milady," Premujon went on. He, too, seemed to be gaining strength from his own words. "The wall of St. Mere Abelle is thicker and taller than any in Honce, and forget not that behind the wall wait scores of brothers well trained in the use of potent magic."

"I saw as much when Panlamaris dared approach," Gwydre admitted.

"Then we're decided," said Dawson. "St. Mere Abelle is part of Vanguard, if Father Artolivan agrees."

"He is on his way here this very moment," said Premujon. "To do just that, as he indicated when first you proposed it."

"And this chapel will hold strong against King Yeslnik, a safe harbor for any who want no part of his Honce," Dawson proclaimed, smiling widely at his beloved lady, knowing well that she needed his confidence in this dangerous hour.

"Would that it were that simple," Gwydre replied, though she did flash her own smile to show her appreciation to her trusted friend. "When Yeslnik is through with Ethelbert he will likely reinforce Panlamaris's siege."

"St. Mere Abelle can hold forever and longer," Premujon assured her. "They have access to all the water and food they would ever need."

He continued on, but Gwydre, not disagreeing, finally managed to stop him with an upraised hand. "I do not doubt the might of this sacred place," she assured the three monks. "When first I sighted Chapel . . . St. Mere Abelle from Dawson's boat, my heart leaped in awe. I do not doubt the strength of this place or the resilience of those who reside here. Of all my holdings, this one on the front line of the expected war and under siege even now is the one for which I least fear."

"Lady?" an obviously confused Premujon asked.

"While we are trapped here, what mischief will Yeslnik wreak behind us in Vanguard?" The others suddenly wore concerned expressions, as if that little matter had escaped them. "With a few of the great warships of Delaval or Palmaristown to blockade us, what might those still in Vanguard do against the approach of Yeslnik's thousands should he choose that route? To whom will they look to lead them with Dame Gwydre, Father Premujon, and so many of our finest warriors here south of the gulf?"

Beside Premujon, Brother Giavno gasped audibly, accurately reflecting the sudden trepidation of all in the room.

"Never said it'd be easy," Dawson muttered under his breath.

Almost as if to accentuate Dawson's point, Father Artolivan knocked on the partially opened door then and shuffled in, and old indeed did he appear. The great weight of the monumental events had taken a toll on him. It seemed that, as with Dame Gwydre, doubts had begun to surface.

"We are part of Vanguard," he announced without prompting. "St. Mere Abelle is within the domain of Dame Gwydre. That is my decision, though I do not come to it easily. Your generous offer is accepted, good lady, may Abelle watch over us all." He bowed slightly as he turned to leave again. "You will forgive me, but I must retire early."

Father Premujon nodded to Brother Giavno, who rushed to catch up to Father Artolivan and help him back to his private quarters.

"I worry for him," Premujon said. "These are difficult times, all the more so because of the decline of Samhaists, making this a time that should be the golden age of our church."

"It will be," Dame Gwydre assured him. "If good people stand strong."

"Stand strong and sail swift," Dawson added.

"That is indeed our plan and our need," said Gwydre. "We can hold St. Mere Abelle—of that, I have no doubt. But you must lead my ships with cunning and skill. We cannot allow Palmaristown to seal off the sea routes and control the coast. You have been beside me for so long, my friend Dawson, and now what I ask of you is no less than that I asked of Bransen, Jond, and the others in sending them after Ancient Badden. We must be mobile, quick, and strong. The fewer options we offer to King Yeslnik, the more likely he will be to accept any terms or compromise."

"Fair winds and following seas," Dawson replied with a wide grin and a look of sincere love for his dearest friend.

Callen Duwornay moved tentatively toward her bedroom door, surprised by the knock. She expected it to be Cadayle, of course, and feared that something might be troubling her daughter at this late hour, for indeed, the night was past its midpoint.

She flinched, her rich brown eyes going wide to see Dawson McKeege, his floppy cap in hand.

"What trouble?" she started to ask, but Dawson hushed her gently.

"No trouble, pretty lass," he said. "Or might be for me, but nothing to get yerself upset about."

"It is very late," Callen said, and she reflexively grasped the front of her loose nightshirt and slipped a bit farther behind the cracked door.

"Begging your pardon."

"Given, but what is the matter?"

"It's about you and yours going to Pryd to live," Dawson explained, his voice shakier than Callen had ever heard it. "That's what I'm hearing."

"That is the plan if Bransen can manage it."

"No water near Pryd."

"No water?"

"No sailing water—river or ocean, I mean."

Callen looked at him as if she did not understand.

Dawson, clearly uncomfortable, rubbed his stubbly, weathered face. "I'm sailing in the morning. Not knowing when I'll be back."

"Going home?" Callen asked.

Dawson shook his head and rubbed his face again. "I'll be on *Lady Dreamer* for all the season, until winter puts me in dock, either here or back in Port Vanguard. It's not what I'm wanting, but Gwydre needs me, and that's a call I've never let pass."

Callen smiled and nodded, though her expression drooped just a bit as she asked, "So you have come to me to say farewell?"

Dawson seemed to Callen as if he might cry. He shook his head. "I'm not wanting to, pretty lady. Not since the first time I saw you."

"Dawson!" Callen said.

"I know I'm not proper here, and I'm not knowing how to tell you otherwise, but I had to tell—"

He stopped then. He had to, for Callen Duwornay came through her doorway and wrapped him in a great hug and a passionate kiss.

She hadn't even realized how much she had longed to hear words like that from this man, hadn't realized the depth of her feelings for Dawson, so busy had she been in the teasing and lighthearted banter with him.

So she kissed him with passion she hadn't shown since the long-ago night when a wicked Samhaist and the people of Pryd Town had mutilated the one man she had ever dared to love and had thrown her in a sack with a snake for her crime of loving him.

Clearly nervous, and clearly not knowing what he was supposed to do next when Callen broke off the kiss, Dawson stammered and glanced around.

Callen tugged him into her room.

M a?" Cadayle asked, gently knocking on Callen's door. It was long past breakfast, and it was typically Callen who awakened Cadayle for their morning meal. Cadayle knew Callen to be a prompt and responsible woman, and her unusual tardiness this morning brought real fears to her daughter.

"Ma?" she asked again and pushed open the door.

To come face-to-face with Dawson McKeege.

"What?" she started to ask, when she noticed Callen, standing off to the side of the shade-darkened room, wrapped in a blanket and apparently nothing else.

"Ma?" Cadayle stammered, and then, "Oh, oh, oh!"

Callen started to call to her, but Cadayle didn't wait and reflexively slapped Dawson across the face. Then, in horror, Cadayle sucked in her breath and threw her hand over her mouth, her eyes darting from Callen to Dawson to Callen to Dawson.

"Why'd you do that?" a surprised Dawson asked.

"I don't know!" Cadayle cried, and with a final look at her mother, she gave a sharp yelp and ran off down the hall.

But by then she was laughing, giggling like a young girl.

"Ye've got yerself a strange girl there, Callen," Dawson muttered.

"Have you met her husband, then?"

"Can't wait to see their kids," Dawson said with a helpless chuckle. "Ye think the girl's sensibilities scarred?"

"I think her surprised," Callen admitted, walking over and reaching with her blanket-gown to wrap Dawson next to her naked form. "And I think her happy, because she's always happy when I'm happy."

"And ye are?" Dawson asked.

"Fool," Callen teased, kissing him, sealing his lateness for his meeting with Dame Gwydre.

B ransen stood with Jameston in the forest to the east of Pryd Town. Jameston leaned on his bow, watching the young man, who seemed confused about his next steps.

"You'll not find an easy path to clearing your name," Jameston remarked. "Back to the north and Chapel Abelle, then? Be good to see your family. Let Dame Gwydre take the lead in arguing your case with the idiotic Yeslnik. That's my advice."

"You go and do that, with my gratitude," said Bransen.

"What's that supposed to mean?"

"My road is southeast. To find the other half of a broken sword."

"You're thinking to kill the murderer and bring his head in to toss at Yeslnik's feet? Much like you did with Badden?"

Bransen shook his head through every word.

"Bring him in alive, then, so he can speak the truth that you weren't involved."

Still Bransen shook his head.

"Say it, boy," Jameston prompted.

"I'm not going to fight with the one who killed Delaval."

"Then how're you to clear your name?"

Bransen turned and looked at the scout directly. "I'm not sure I care any longer," he admitted. "So please tell Cadayle and Callen that they may have to remain at Chapel Abelle a bit longer."

"Bannagran said—"

"I would not trust their safety outside of Chapel Abelle, particularly if Yeslnik or his lackeys come to understand that I go to find he who killed Delaval not out of anger or for vengeance or for their perceived justice."

"Then why?" Jameston smiled as Bransen took a deep breath. "Because they're like you—like your ma, at least."

"Jhesta Tu," Bransen confirmed. "Long have I wanted to embrace the mystics of that which has guided me from Stork to Highwayman."

Jameston considered the words for a few heartbeats, then nodded and shrugged. "Your road to choose."

"And you will go north?"

"Only following your own steps. This is your journey."

"Because that is what Dame Gwydre asked of you, but now I travel for myself and not for Dame Gwydre."

Again Jameston shrugged. "Doesn't matter to me. I travel for myself and have been enjoying the road beside you. And that's the whole point of it, isn't it?"

"Enjoyment?"

"Aye."

"There is more than that," said Bransen.

"Never!" Jameston said with a grin.

Bransen knew better than to argue with the stubborn scout. Besides, though he wouldn't admit it aloud, he was glad for the company—particularly the company of this man, this friend. He took a deep breath and took a bold step to the southeast, toward Ethelbert dos Entel, toward this unknown Jhesta Tu who had slain Delaval the king, toward the realization of his greatest hopes or his greatest fears.

But he didn't slow.

Not this time.

The Meaning of His Gift

I met Jameston Sequin on a road east of Pryd Town. I had first been introduced to him on a winding trail in Alpinador, far, far away, when he had
intervened to help me and my companions in a fight with trolls. His reputation
preceded him by only a few sentences, mostly revealed in the wide-eyed admiration from that most unlikely source of such animation, Crazy Vaughna.

I had known Jameston Sequin for months and had spent many hours with
him and many alone with him before I ever truly met him. There was always
something about him and his unusual appearance and demeanor that had drawn
me to him and had made me glad indeed (though I wouldn't openly admit it)
when he had unexpectedly joined me on my perilous road out of Chapel Abelle. So
many extraordinary visual clues had revealed to me long before that this was no
ordinary scout, with his huge mustache and amazingly long-legged strides and
that distinctive hat he wore, named after him because its triangular design
served him as a sight for his deadly bow. Truly Jameston seemed larger than life,
a man, perhaps the first I had ever met, whose reputation was not diminished,
indeed was enhanced, by familiarity.

So I had known him, had traveled with him, had battled beside him, but it
wasn't until one morning a week out of Pryd Town, the smell of recent battles
heavy in the air, when I actually met Jameston Sequin, and all because the enigma
that was this formidable scout finally forced me to ask him a simple question.

"Why?"

He looked at me, and I knew at once that he understood the context and
the depth of my inquiry. Maybe it was my stance, or the tone I had used in asking, or the simple lack of context for such a question, uttered suddenly on a
faraway road. Whatever the reason, Jameston knew. I could see it in his eyes
and in that grin he often wore, a look that made anyone around him know for
certain that he, Jameston, knew more than they knew or at least understood
better.

"Where?" he flippantly replied. "When? Who?"

I wasn't letting him get away. Not then. I needed to know. He had surprised me by deciding to stay with me even after I had learned of the presence of Jhesta Tu and had proclaimed that my journey was my own and not for Dame Gwydre. To understand his decision, I needed to know the truth of Jameston Sequin. "Why?" I responded.

"Any answer I gave would work, I suppose, since your word works for any question." He grinned wider because he knew that I knew that he knew, if that makes any sense, and he was determined to play it out fully.

"Why are you who you are?" I clarified, though it certainly wasn't necessary. "Why a scout? Why do you spend your days in solitude?"

"I'm here with you."

My sigh made him grin all the wider.

"You are becoming predictable," I told him.

"When people think that, it makes me more dangerous."

"Or are you afraid to tell me? To tell anyone?"

Finally, I could see that I had hit his sensibilities, and hard. His expression changed, as if a cloud had passed overhead to darken the day. He moved off the road to a small grouping of rocks large enough to serve as seats, bidding me to follow. I saw weariness in his step that I had never before detected.

"You want to know why I went into the emptiness of Alpinador?" he asked me as he took a seat, still looking older than before.

"I want to know why you're here with me."

"That's what I said," he replied. Was he always one layer ahead of me in my thinking?

"Pride and money," he said then, and his smile became self-deprecating. "I went to Vanguard as a young man, younger than yourself. I was a confident one, almost as much as you are, and I was good enough to back it up. Things that seemed so simple to me, like how to hide and how to find someone else who's trying to hide, befuddled others. I understood animals—I don't know why or how, but everything about them and the way they were likely to behave just seemed obvious to me."

"And goblins and trolls and powries," I remarked, and Jameston nodded.

"With all that behind me, with all the folk of Vanguard looking north for furs and timber and exotic items, the road seemed obvious. I wanted to make a name for myself, boy, and make a fair amount of coin at the same time."

It all made sense to me, of course, but I knew, too, that the young man who had first gone out from civilization for those reasons was not the same person now sitting before me. As Jameston continued his tale of exploration and build-

ing his reputation and fame as a guide and hunter, one question became apparent: What had changed his mind?

"I had the coin. It came from the caribou moss, from leading teams to it, from protecting caravans, and from this hat!" He tipped his "sequin," that triangular cap favored by archers across Vanguard and even in northern Honce proper. "All the coin in the world, and nothing I wanted to spend it on," he answered, plainly and again with that self-deprecating chuckle, as if it had all been a bad joke he had inadvertently played upon himself. "The fame led to a line of the same questions being asked over and over again. To some I was a hero, but I wasn't any such thing. To most I was a curiosity, something to gawk at.

"Aye, that's what I was," he said, sadness in his tone. "And there was no point to any of it, so I went on without any sense of purpose."

"Even mocking those who claimed such purpose driving their own lives," I dared remark. Jameston's corresponding nod was more enthusiastic then, as if I had grasped exactly his point in telling me all this.

"My purpose was all for me when I was a young adventurer, looking to conquer the world," he said. "Then I had no purpose at all, and for a long time."

"And now?"

"Now? Dame Gwydre's father cut a new trail in front of my wandering feet. I didn't walk it, not far anyway, until I had to, many years later." As he finished, he looked up at me, locked gazes with me, and I knew then, in that moment, that I had truly come to know Jameston Sequin.

"When you met my group in a fight on the trail," I reasoned.

"That was part of it."

"You walk with me to find purpose in the life of Jameston Sequin."

My proclamation was met with a somewhat accepting and somewhat incredulous look. Finally, he shook his head. "You're just on the trail Gwydre's da cut for me."

Part of the bigger whole, he meant. Part of the purpose that was not self-centered, as was the one that had driven Jameston Sequin to the wilds of northern Vanguard and Alpinador, the one that had brought him fame and false fortune. It wasn't until he realized that his journey through this life wasn't about him alone, but about a greater sense of brotherhood and community, that Jameston Sequin had found a trail worth walking.

As I pondered that unexpected conversation throughout that day, I knew, too, why Jameston had shared it with me.

Dame Gwydre, like her father before her, had cut a trail, but it was one I was reluctant to walk.

And so it was that even as I directed our journey, to the east and the Jhesta Tu and my greatest question and challenge, even as I led, so I was being led.

It was . . . comforting.

—Bransen Garibond

CHAPTER 21

Let the Word Go Forth

A calm spread over St. Mere Abelle. Panlamaris's army remained entrenched across the field, but they would not come on. No monks were out to guide the many prisoners, who, suddenly, did not seem to be prisoners any longer. Their work was not diligent this day as they milled about, whispering about the grand changes that had come to the world and to their corner of it. Ethelbert man and woman and Delaval man and woman mingled effortlessly and without thought, their old boundaries and battles now, finally, fully left behind.

In every prayer room of the great chapel, the brothers did their work, those lesser monks assisting the more powerful as they used a soul stone to soar out from their bodies, to travel spiritually to every corner of Honce, to their brethren with the word of Father Artolivan.

Come gather in Chapel Abelle, the blessed St. Mere Abelle, their spirits implored their brethren. Or to Ethelbert dos Entel if you must, and pray for the mercy of Laird Ethelbert. Hide, brethren, from the fires and follies of King Yeslnik.

The finality of the decision, a frank admission that the Abellican Church had severed ties, had declared a complete and likely irrevocable break with King Yeslnik and thus the bulk of Honce itself, had weighed heavily on Father Artolivan and the others, but when Father Dennigan of Chapel Delaval had arrived, carrying the head of Brother Piastafan, what choice had been left?

"Let the word go forth," Father Artolivan had told his brethren, his voice thick with regret and sad resignation. And so the brothers went to their work this calm morning, their spirits soaring from their corporeal bodies and from St. Mere Abelle, flying to the distant chapels to the limits of their power, then entreating the brothers of the outward chapels to spread the word to the wider corners of Honce.

"This ability of the monks to spread the word wide and far is an advantage for us," Dame Gwydre said to Dawson, Cormack, and Milkeila at the windswept docks of St. Mere Abelle. "Should it come to war, our armies can remain in coordination. Our enemies might wait a week to hear word from a distant battlefield, but we can know . . ."

"You overestimate the power of spirit-walking," Cormack dared to intervene. "This is a highly unusual event—we did not dare try it even in those hours when our situation in Alpinador grew desperate. This is most extraordinary for Father Artolivan to command it, or even allow it."

"He did as much to relate to us the happenings in the southland when we were in Vanguard," Dame Gwydre protested.

"And paid a dear price. One of the brothers who came spiritually to Vanguard—"

"One of? There was only the one."

"Only the one who made it," Cormack corrected. "Out of a dozen who made the attempt. Most fell short, weary before they ever managed to float their spirits across the Gulf of Corona. Another never even made the gulf, having fallen to possess a poor girl he saw along the road. He has recovered from the shock of that ill-fated meeting, but she remains a stuttering fool. And another brother did cross the gulf, only to be drawn into the corporeal form of a dockman on the wharves of Port Vanguard. He did not manage a possession and was driven mad in the attempt."

"Why would they attempt such a thing as possession?" Milkeila had to ask, her eyes wide with shock.

"Aye, it seems an evil thing!" added Dawson.

Cormack nodded. "It is a compulsion that breaks the greatest of brothers, a temptation borne out of no rational thought and rarely controlled by rational thought. Spirit-walking is outlawed within the order, other than by specific exception. A brother trapped in the forest, freezing to death, would be violating church edict if he so used a soul stone to seek out aid."

Dame Gwydre started to argue against that reasoning, but stopped and swallowed hard and glanced back at the long tunnels that would take her back to the cliff-top structures, only then truly appreciating the enormous weight that had bowed the shoulders of Father Artolivan.

"They use it now, as previously to inform you of the great events in Honce, because of the magnitude," Cormack explained. "Even should a few brothers fail, even should a few bystanders be driven mad by an unintended possession, the cost is worth the gain, for Father Artolivan knows well that many of his brethren and the prisoners they shelter are in dire peril now, and he would not have them go to unwitting slaughter."

"His brethren, or your own?" Dawson asked, drawing a sidelong glance from Cormack. "You sound like one who's thinking the church a good place to be."

Cormack glanced at Milkeila, who grinned knowingly, not disagreeing with Dawson's assessment.

To that, Cormack merely shrugged.

"Sail swift and sail safe," Gwydre said to them. "To Vanguard, one ship, to Ethelbert dos Entel the other."

Dawson nodded, then stepped up and gave the woman a hug. "I'll be for Entel," he whispered. "So my journey's the long one."

"What will I do without Dawson beside me?" Gwydre whispered back.

"The right thing," he replied and squeezed her tighter. "I lost me heart last night," he whispered even more quietly. "And now I'm leaving her here under your own protection."

"Callen?" said Gwydre, loudly enough so that Cormack and Milkeila caught it and looked at the hugging couple curiously. She pushed Dawson back to arm's length. He didn't answer, other than to smile.

And Gwydre's own smile more than matched his own. How strange the fates could be! A deception to bring Bransen to Vanguard to serve in a war had brought Dawson together with a woman who stole his heart, an event that neither he nor Gwydre had ever expected would happen again.

"Sail swift and sail safe," she said, her voice breaking. "And come back to your lady, who will be by my side."

The good news carried Dame Gwydre back through the tunnels and stairs to the high ground of St. Mere Abelle. When she arrived, though late for a meeting, she did not go straight to Father Artolivan's audience hall. Instead she climbed the ladder of the back wall, overlooking the narrow bay that sheltered St. Mere Abelle's docks.

Lady Dreamer was just putting out, all lines away. A second ship was already out from the docks, awaiting Dawson's craft. The two would travel together throughout the first couple of days, moving to the middle of the gulf, before Dawson turned east to run the coast all the way to Ethelbert dos Entel at the end of the Belt-and-Buckle and the other went north.

The tide brought *Lady Dreamer* out a short ways, and one sail dropped open, Dawson tacking hard and expertly to turn his bow out to open waters.

Gwydre took comfort in the great confidence she held in Dawson Mc-Keege. If anyone could get to Laird Ethelbert and properly deliver her message, it was he. The comfort helped her to get past the great sadness that enveloped her as *Lady Dreamer* started away, for she missed her longtime companion already. He had become a true brother to her, a confidant and the one man who kept her focused on and honest to what was in her heart. How would she get through these trying days without him?

She made a mental note to look in on Callen and Cadayle. She was quite fond of the mother and daughter, and if Dawson saw so much in Callen, then Gwydre figured her positive impressions of the woman must be valid.

When she finally arrived at Father Artolivan's gathering, she found the elderly church leader with Father Premujon, brothers Pinower, Jond, and Giavno, and several other monks she did not know by name engaged in a heated debate about their next moves.

They stopped chattering as one when Dame Gwydre entered, Father Artolivan motioning for her to take a seat beside him on the raised dais that centered the gathering.

"My ships are out for Vanguard and for Ethelbert dos Entel," she explained. "Our break with King Yeslnik is complete." Several deep breaths, signaling fear and determination, came back at her. "We cannot turn back from our stance now, Father Artolivan," she pressed. "Yeslnik will not forgive."

"Let us hope your good man Dawson gets to Laird Ethelbert's side before Yeslnik pushes him into the sea," Brother Pinower remarked, and Gwydre winced at the proposition.

"King Yeslnik and Laird Panlamaris will not forgive, Lady of Vanguard," said Father Artolivan. "We must hold them off long enough to diminish their appetite for war. Perhaps then we might find some common ground upon which a peace can be enacted."

"Or we must win," said Brother Pinower, and all eyes turned his way.

Their expressions told Gwydre that this was exactly the argument into which she had walked.

"Yeslnik proclaims himself King of Honce and there seems to be no one who can stop him," Pinower explained. "But his actions have already wrought great disdain. Almost to a man and woman, the prisoners we hold here have pledged their loyalty to our cause. They will fight, though the option of sitting to the side of the battle is open before them without ill consequence. How many men in Yeslnik's army would be so willing and eager for more battle, I wonder?"

"How many of Laird Panlamaris's men did not look on in horror when our brethren were evilly murdered on the field outside St. Mere Abelle?" Brother Giavno agreed. "And if Brother Fatuus so touched and inspired us, what might be the effect of his determined march on those among Panlamaris's ranks who witnessed it?"

"Our hopes may prove correct and will aid us," Father Artolivan warned. "But they alone will not turn the tide against the power of Delaval City and Palmaristown and Pryd and all the rest."

"We sit and wait, and we fight if we must?" Dame Gwydre asked. She made it clear with her tone that she was not enamored of that passive course. "And we seek Ethelbert for alliance, though we know not what he has left to even continue in this war. Dawson might well arrive at Ethelbert dos Entel's docks to find Yeslnik's soldiers manning them. Or to find Laird Ethelbert helplessly trapped within his city, as we seem to be here."

Her grim assessment was met by blank stares, until Father Artolivan offered, "We are seeking other routes of resistance and alliance."

"Other routes? Surely any allies we could find would be welcomed."

"There are two names being spoken across the breadth of Honce behind those of the warring lairds," Artolivan explained. "Two men have distinguished themselves and have led Yeslnik to near-certain victory. Every prisoner in St. Mere Abelle, Ethelbert and Yeslnik man alike, knows of these generals: Bannagran of Pryd and Milwellis of Palmaristown."

"You wish to find alliance with Yeslnik's generals?" Dame Gwydre tried to keep the incredulity out of her tone. How desperate were they, truly?

"Not Milwellis, certainly," said Artolivan. "He is a man of ill temperament and great hubris. He holds no love for St. Mere Abelle."

"Particularly since we just sent his father scurrying away with lightning prodding his arse every step," Gwydre added.

Artolivan conceded that point with a nod and just a hint of a much-needed grin.

"Master Reandu of Chapel Pryd is a good and temperate man, and he has the ear of Bannagran, whom he considers a friend. Perhaps . . . ?"

"If Master Reandu still holds court in Chapel Pryd," Dame Gwydre warned.

"He does," said Giavno. "I went to him in spirit this morning, though I had not the strength to impart the message of Father Artolivan. Still, I sensed calm about that town."

"I doubt that King Yeslnik would force Bannagran to move against his friend Reandu, but should Yeslnik do such a thing it is possible that Bannagran would take great exception."

"It seems a desperate plan, but I see few other options," Gwydre admitted. "If we could turn this General Bannagran to our cause, then it would bolster our hopes, of course. But to what do we ask him to pledge his fealty? To Vanguard? That seems unlikely, at best."

The monks all glanced around at each other and Gwydre realized that she had touched upon the very heart of the debate into which she had intruded, the backdrop that had inspired the notion that they might "win."

"Yeslnik and Ethelbert have torn Honce apart with their war of greed," Father Artolivan began, his tone measured. "We have rejected Yeslnik and have little connection to Laird Ethelbert, though we seek him, not to serve him, but as an ally against our common foe. We will not serve King Ethelbert, Dame Gwydre. The Abellican Church will fight beside him, perhaps and if he is willing, but we will not serve him."

"He is very tied to the ways of Behr," Brother Pinower explained. "And to the religions of Behr. He is not hostile to our order, but neither is he a believer."

"So if we gain ground, if we can hold against Laird Panlamaris and even begin to move against King Yeslnik, then to what end?" Gwydre asked. "Am I to declare autonomy of Vanguard from Honce? Will the Abellican Church then become the Church of Vanguard?"

"Suppose we show the people of Honce a third way, beyond Yeslnik and Ethelbert?" Father Artolivan asked.

"And that would be?" Gwydre asked. "Compromise?"

"A queen."

"You are mad!"

"Perhaps," Father Artolivan conceded. "It is a difficult proposition."

"A desperate one, you mean," said Gwydre.

"And are we not desperate?"

Gwydre sighed.

"You saved Vanguard, Dame Gwydre," Father Artolivan said. "Can you save Honce as well? Two lairds hungry for power have driven the land to near ruin. Every family has been devastated now by a war that will not end."

"Will it not?" asked Gwydre. "It seems that Laird Yeslnik has a strong upper hand, by all the reports and your own admission."

"That result might prove the most disastrous one of all," said Artolivan. "Yeslnik is a merciless, privileged beast of the highest order. He would have me murder all the prisoners he has sent while freeing all the men sent by Laird Ethelbert, and both by treaty for honorable recusal from the war!

"Nay, Dame Gwydre, that outcome cannot be allowed. The Samhaists have been driven from most of their groves, Blessed Abelle be thanked, and now King Yeslnik has declared war with the Abellican Church. Indeed, I expect him to declare Father De Guilbe as Father of the Order of Blessed Abelle and to enlist his phony interpretation of the teachings of our Blessed Abelle as his official religion. You wish to sue for peace and to declare autonomy, but you know that this man, Yeslnik, will not agree and will not relent."

"Have you come to regret your words and actions against King Yeslnik and Laird Panlamaris, Father Artolivan?"

The old monk smiled more widely than ever before, and, for the first time in the meeting, serenity washed over his wrinkled face and his eyes twinkled with hope. "Not for a moment," he replied. "Though I have come to realize the difficulty of the road such principles demand."

"Cordon Roe," said Brother Giavno, surprising them all with the reference to a most terrible incident that had occurred in Delaval City in the early days of the Order of Blessed Abelle. "Brother Fatuus," he added, grinning, against the confused expressions. "We all will die, after all, be it now or in a decade or in several decades. Better to die contented. Better a life guided by principle, even a short one, than a century of misery wrought by the knowledge of personal cowardice."

"Queen Gwydre of Honce," remarked Father Premujon. "It rings of hope."

"It rings of presumption and arrogance," said Dame Gwydre.

"Perhaps it is the time for both, good lady," said Father Artolivan. "Perhaps it is time for both."

D awson stood near *Lady Dreamer*'s prow, his favorite place when his ship found a good wind and threw her spray up high. She opened her sails now, leaving the docks of St. Mere Abelle far, far behind. The slight splash of salty water felt good to Dawson, made him feel alive and gave him a burst of that brine smell that seemed to define his life. He came up here to be alone with his thoughts, to reflect on his life and the point of it all.

And today, Dawson needed that contemplative energy more than ever. The night with Callen Duwornay had thrown his emotional balance into a delicious swirl, a jumble of possibility. Terrifying possibilities, since Dawson had stepped away from his typical course. But that was the way of the world right now, was it not? Honce was at war with itself in a struggle that would dramatically redefine the old feudal holdings, however this insanity ended. And the roads! Dawson had long been among the most worldly of people in parochial Honce and even more parochial Vanguard. *Lady Dreamer* was his freedom, his transport to exotic lands. Until these last few years, only the sailors and the marching armies typically saw any of the world beyond their own home villages. The average person in Honce would spend the entirety of his or her life knowing only a few square miles of land and a few score, perhaps a hundred, other people.

While that no doubt remained the truth of the land, the roads connecting all the major holdings of Honce proper were taming the land and making possible many more journeys to Delaval City or Pryd Town or St. Mere Abelle. The world was changing, and the tumult of those monumental shifts was a big part of the reason for the war.

Now Dawson's world, too, was changing, had changed. He couldn't believe that he had found the courage to be so forward with Callen, couldn't believe his good fortune to find his feelings reciprocated. He could only hope now that he would be able to get to the city of Ethelbert dos Entel and back in time to realize the sweetness of his courage. Suddenly, he couldn't imagine his life without Callen.

Dawson took a deep breath. If Callen went home to Pryd Town, then was he to abandon his life at sea? How could he give up *Lady Dreamer*? How could he give up Callen?

"I say, Captain!" said an insistent voice from behind, in such a tone that Dawson realized he must have been hailed several times already.

"What? What, then?" Dawson stammered. He focused on the situation at hand, noting that they were fast closing on *Shelligan's Run*, the ship he had selected to deliver Dame Gwydre's message back to Vanguard. At first all seemed as it should, but Dawson's face crinkled a moment later when he noted the commotion on the deck of the other ship, with sailors running to the port rail and to the rigging.

"West, Captain," Dawson's crewman said.

Dawson looked that way and felt his heart sink.

Palmaristown warships, three of them, each twice as large as *Lady Dreamer,* sailed in tight formation. Their decks were full of crewmen, archers with their deadly longbows. Even from this distance Dawson could make out the distinctively high poop deck of a Palmaristown warship, for those craft had each been equipped with a large ballista, a gigantic crossbow set on a rotating platform.

Giant sails full of wind, the ships came on fast.

Dawson's thoughts whirled. Could *Lady Dreamer* tack fast enough and fill her sails with the westerlies quickly enough to outrun them?

He shook his head doubtfully. *Lady Dreamer* could get up to speed and outmaneuver anything on the water, true, but she wasn't even at full sail, and she couldn't straight-line outrun Palmaristown warships, the greatest vessels in all of Honce.

Dawson glanced back the way they had come, thinking that maybe they could turn about and get into the protection of St. Mere Abelle's harbor before the warships got in range and laid waste to his two ships.

And there, Dawson McKeege saw his doom, for he sighted two more Palmaristown warships running the coast.

He had sailed into a trap.

Five ships, fully manned and armed for battle, any one of which could probably defeat both *Lady Dreamer* and *Shelligan's Run*.

Two of the ships in the west continued their straight charge, while the third had veered to the north to cut off any attempt to flee into the open waters of the gulf.

There was nowhere to run.

He thought of Dame Gwydre then and how he had failed his friend. He thought about Callen. Once the notion of the beautiful woman entered his mind a great despair washed over him. He knew that the beautiful possibilities had just flown away.

Would he take comfort in the memories of his last night when the Palmaristown fleet put him into the dark water? he wondered.

CHAPTER 22

The Wake of War

Well, you know an army or two marched through here," Jameston Sequin said somberly—the only tone appropriate for the images around them. They were nearing the Mirianic coast now, far to the southeast of Pryd. Torn roads, burned forests, and carrion birds, so many carrion birds, greeted them at every turn.

A ground fog covered the region this day, thick with the smell of death.

Bransen had fought in several battles, most notably in the large and wild fight outside Ancient Badden's castle, so he was not unused to the aftermath of war. But this was different, darker and more sinister. For he knew that this time the smell of rotting bodies was not fully from, not even mostly from, the corpses of combatants, the soldiers of Ethelbert and Yeslnik who had fallen in their struggles. No, the air was thick with the smell of rotting, dead children and other innocents caught between the bloodlust of the warring lairds.

"You got no belly for it," Jameston said, obviously seeing the sour expression on Bransen's face.

Bransen looked at him hard. "You do?"

Jameston gave a helpless chuckle. "You're starting to understand why I live in the woods."

"And yet, here we are."

"I already told you . . ."

"I know, a purpose bigger than your own life," said Bransen. "Are you, am I, possessed of magic enough so that we can just lift a gemstone and utter a phrase and repair all of this?" As he finished, he swept his arm toward the south, where a trio of burned-out cottages stood. Even the animals on the small farms had been killed, and several cows lay on the field, covered with pecking birds.

"Not thinking that, and you're not either," said Jameston. "We'll find ways to help. That's something."

Bransen nodded, his expression grim. They set off again, heading east, and Jameston's words seemed prophetic soon after, when cries for help and of fear rent the heavy air.

The pair rushed through a stand of thick trees and around a rocky bluff, Jameston stringing his bow as they ran. With the sounds coming from over an old and crumbling stone wall—crumbling, but still taller than a tall man—Bransen reflexively called upon his brooch and his Jhesta Tu training, reaching into his concentration and the malachite stone simultaneously, instantly, instinctively. He leaped high. Too high. He felt weightless, the malachite working its magical levitation and amplified by his Jhesta Tu understanding. He had meant to grab a hold on the top of the wall and pull himself over, but he climbed into the air to the wall top and above, floating right over, almost as if he was swimming in the air.

He remained in control of his body and kept his wits about him as he crossed over the stone wall. From that bird's-eye view, the Highwayman witnessed the chaos. Before and below him poor peasants scrambled among several small cottages, while armed men chased them and beat them down. Out of one house rushed a young warrior, his hands full of bread, a peasant woman charging after him, screaming for him to stop. One of his companions stepped up from the side and cracked her across the back of the neck with a heavy club, throwing her face down to the ground, where she lay still.

The Highwayman noticed a bow aimed his way. He reached into the gem again, to the smoky quartz stone. The archer let fly, and the arrow missed cleanly but the bowman cheered, thinking his shot dead center, for it had surely hit the decoy image the Highwayman had created of himself.

Below, the man who had clubbed the woman lifted his weapon to strike her again as she lay in the dirt.

The Highwayman dropped to the ground before him.

"Wha—" the man managed to gasp before he was hit with a series of short punches and flying elbows that sent him spinning away. The Highwayman turned as the stealer of bread spun back and dropped the loaf, sword in hand.

The Highwayman's fabulous blade came forth, slashing across to cleanly intercept the warrior's thrust, parrying the enemy blade, a second then a third time. Any unwitting onlooker might have thought the warrior deftly picking off the attacks of this strange, black-clothed warrior. But Bransen and the warrior knew the truth of it: The poor warrior had no idea of the fast-changing angle of the longer and stronger sword coming at him and the only reason his smaller iron weapon was parrying was because this far superior swordsman was aiming for that iron weapon!

"Affwin Wi!" the warrior cried desperately. "Ethelbert! Ethelbert!"

The Highwayman knew the first words as a name, so much like his mother's own, but the stunning realization didn't slow his assault. He hit the iron sword again and again, sending numbing jolts up the warrior's arms, and finally he maneuvered the man where he wanted, at the same time using the noise of the fight to bring another pair of marauders charging at him.

His blade came across left to right, driving the iron sword out before it. The Highwayman stepped forward in a spin, elbow flying high to snap at the warrior's throat as he came around, sending the man gasping to the ground but leaving the Highwayman perfectly balanced and squared up against the newest two attackers.

One attacker, Bransen mentally corrected, as one of the charging enemies lurched suddenly and went staggering aside, an arrow deep in his hip.

The other man charged in, screaming, lifting an axe above his head for a powerful chop.

But in the blink of an eye the Highwayman was up against him and inside the angle of any strike. The sword slashed above the attacker, lopping the head off the high-raised axe even as Bransen's free hand grasped the handle. With the weighted head suddenly gone the attacker lost all balance. Bransen twisted his arm that held the axe handle, repeatedly slamming it down against the man's forehead.

The man stumbled, dazed. The Highwayman let go of the handle, grabbed the man by the front of his leather tunic, and again reached into the power of the Jhesta Tu and of the brooch, two properties together.

He used the malachite's levitation powers to lessen the weight of the man and the jolting power of the graphite backing to add lightning into his throw.

The warrior went flying away up high, over the side of the small cottage, to land on the thatched roof. He lay twitching in violent spasms that made him bite the tip off his own tongue.

The Highwayman looked to the fallen woman, blood running from her ear. Rage gripped him. He charged the center courtyard of the house cluster where several warriors had gathered, some setting a defense against him, others lifting bows and firing off to the north—at Jameston, Bransen assumed.

They were ready for him and too many, but he didn't care. The image of the peasant woman, her skull broken, haunted and drove him on. He lifted his sword, and the blade burst into flames.

An arrow shot out and struck him in his left shoulder.

Nearly blinded by rage and pain, the Highwayman yelled and charged all the faster. He grabbed at the power of serpentine, the fire shield, and then demanded more of the ruby firestone. Now flames covered not only his sword but his entire body!

Like a living bonfire, half-blinded by flames, and with agony biting him from the arrow deep in his shoulder, the Highwayman surged into their midst.

They ran, terrified, overwhelmed, and confused. The Highwayman caught one and cut him down. He heard the whizzing of arrows cutting the air nearby as Jameston Sequin took down a second and then a third.

Weariness and pain overwhelmed him. The Highwayman dropped the magic enacting the fiery cloak, then dismissed the serpentine shield and fell fully into the central gem of the brooch, the soul stone, seeking the warmth of its healing magic.

Bransen knelt in the dirt while all around him townsfolk cheered and screamed and cried. Glad he was to see the familiar boots of Jameston before him, to feel his companion's hand grasp him under his good shoulder and help him back to his feet.

"Pull it out," Bransen said through gritted teeth, meaning the arrow.

"I'll get whiskey and something for you to bite."

Bransen grabbed him hard as he started to turn away. "Now!" he demanded.

"Boy, you can't—"

"Now!" Bransen insisted, tugging Jameston's hand toward the arrow shaft. Jameston still resisted, so Bransen reached for the bolt himself and grimaced all the more as he tugged on the arrow.

"Push it through!" Jameston enjoined. He grasped Bransen's hand with his own, reversing the pressure.

Waves of agony assaulted Bransen, but he fell into his meditation and into the soul stone. A moment later he felt a sudden looseness in the wound as Jameston pulled the arrow from the back of his shoulder.

"You won't be using that arm anytime soon," the scout lamented. Bransen didn't even hear him, his thoughts fully immersed in his discipline and the gemstone magic even as his free hand grasped the wound.

The townsfolk gathered about them, clapping and nodding their appreciation, but Bransen's focus remained absolute. Jameston began talking to the people, but Bransen didn't hear. He stood straight and let go of his shoulder: No blood came forth. Jameston and the others looked on in amazement as Bransen reached down and retrieved his sword—with his left hand. He spun the weapon over and slid it expertly into the sheath on his left hip, showing only a trace of a grimace.

"I'll be using the arm sooner than you believe," Bransen said softly to his friend.

"How'd you jump that wall like that? How'd you throw a man onto a roof? How'd you do that with the fire?" Jameston came back at him, one, two, three.

Bransen smiled coyly, though in truth he really had no idea. Something momentous was happening here, some joining of his Jhesta Tu sensibilities and the powerful brooch upon his forehead. He had walked through flames before, stepping from the log pile of a Samhaist bonfire to strike down the evil Bernivvigar. His Jhesta Tu training alone had assisted him in keeping the flames from his body, but it had been a very temporary effect. This time was different. He had magically summoned the flames about his whole body and had hardly felt their warmth. Not a wisp of smoke now arose from his clothing. Skilled monks could use their serpentine to enact such shields against fire, of course, but the speed and completeness of Bransen's work with the gems at his disposal had surprised even him. Made him ponder what other wonders lay before him.

"Oh, but ye saved us!" one old woman cried, taking Bransen from his private thoughts. He looked around at the gathering of townsfolk then, noting the absence of men. This village was old and very young, but there was little in between, like so many of the other villages of war-ravaged Honce.

"Who were these marauders?" Jameston asked. "What laird do they serve?"

"Ethelbert's own," an old man answered. "And ain't yerself?"

Jameston's head shook most emphatically. "We serve at the pleasure of Dame Gwydre."

The old man looked skeptical. "But he's looking like one o' Ethelbert's," he said, pointing to Bransen.

The clothes, Bransen knew. He sucked in his breath at the reminder that there were Jhesta Tu about, that he was close to his goal, his last best hope.

"Not with Ethelbert—never met the man," Jameston assured them. "But these soldiers were from Laird Ethelbert's ranks?"

"This time," the old man replied. The resignation in his voice was not hard to hear. "Next time it'll be Delaval's men."

"Yeslnik's," a girl corrected, and the old man snorted as if that mattered not at all. It didn't, from the perspective of the poor villagers caught in the middle of violent chaos.

"They be all about the land, roaming like animals," another elderly man explained. "Prince Milwellis is fighting at the coast again, but in here there's just pieces of the armies, scattered and finding food where they can."

"And who do you serve, Ethelbert or Yeslnik?" Bransen asked to many a blank stare.

"Don't think they care," Jameston suggested in a whisper.

No camps, no food wagons, no one giving orders," Jameston elaborated as he and Bransen made their way out of the small village. "Just a bunch of broken soldiers, hungry and scared and with nothing to believe in. I've seen it before."

Bransen shook his head, not able to grasp it.

"They fell off the side of the armies—both armies," Jameston explained. "Or they ran off the side. There's a point where it's too much fighting. Drives a man blood-crazy, takes the point of it all from him."

"Was there ever a point to it?" Bransen asked. "More than the greed of a couple of selfish lairds, I mean?"

Jameston shrugged. "Pride of home, fear of not defending what's yours. Starts that way, might still be that way for many in the ranks of both armies, but for some there comes a time when they can't remember their home, at least not well enough to connect it to what they're doing way out here. Maybe some just have nothing left to fight for."

"So they slaughter defenseless villagers?"

Jameston shrugged again. "I'm not excusing it, boy. I'm telling you what is, not what should be."

"And it will only continue to get worse," said Bransen.

"Or so many will just be dead that there won't be enough left to make it worse," said Jameston.

"Your optimism inspires me."

"You don't care about it anyway, boy. Remember?"

Bransen shot him a cold look. "We should go straight to Ethelbert dos Entel," Jameson said, his laugh a pitiful sound.

"We?" Bransen asked. "I should go. Where Jameston goes is for Jameston to decide."

"Already told you I was following you."

"Have I told you that you needn't?"

"Every step."

"Have I told you that I don't want you to?"

"You'll get to that eventually," Jameston replied with a disarming grin. "But I'm here now, so I can tell you that you'd be quite the fool to walk into Ethelbert's city."

"How so? How am I to find the Jhesta Tu I seek? Should I just walk from village to village?"

"Going to Ethelbert's city might get you to meet them, indeed, but not in the way you're wanting."

"What are you implying?"

"I'm not implying, boy, I'm saying. There's a laird in Ethelbert dos Entel who might be thinking that it's past time to negotiate a truce. We're not far from his home, with nothing but the sea behind him. Wouldn't he have a treasure to offer King Yeslnik if the Highwayman walked into his midst?"

"But he above all must know that I was not involved!" Bransen protested.

"You're still believing that matters? After all this and all you've seen?"

Bransen considered it for a moment, then gave a helpless shake of his head. "No."

"What do you want?" Jameston asked him. "You want to meet these assassins Ethelbert's brought from Behr—"

"They are Jhesta Tu, not assassins."

"King Delaval would disagree. If he were alive, I mean."

"If they killed King Delaval . . ."

"You saw the sword."

"It was because they believed in the cause against him," Bransen stubbornly finished. "The code of Jhest is not mercenary, it is principle. If the Jhesta Tu have allied with Laird Ethelbert, then that speaks well of Laird Ethelbert."

"And if I give you that, will you answer my question? What do you want, boy?"

"First, I want you to stop calling me boy."

Jameston nodded. "What would be your perfect life? To live with Cadayle and your child, your children, and with Callen nearby? All in peace? To farm the land or hunt for food? To go to church and pray to whatever gods you find?"

"Yes, and no."

"What *do* you want?"

"I want . . ." Bransen took a deep breath and truly considered the question. "I want a home for my family, and peace, yes. I'm sick of smelling corpses."

"Are you sick of battle? Even when it means battling someone like Badden or that priest Bernivvigar before him?"

Bransen looked at Jameston as if the man had just slapped him across the face.

"You spend your hours working that sword and working your body through practice—practice for fighting," Jameston remarked. "You just found strength back there in that village that I've never seen before. Did you hate it, b . . . Bransen? Do you hate the fighting even when you're thinking the fight to be just?"

"Just? For which laird? They are two sides of the same ugly stone!"

"Forget that!" Jameston scolded. "Forget the greed and the pride behind it all and make it personal, just for now. Just so you can answer—to yourself and not to me. What drove you to rescue Callen and Cadayle? What did you feel when Badden's head flew from his shoulders? What do you want, Bransen Garibond? What do *you* want, Highwayman? Who is the Highwayman? Why is he the Highwayman?"

Every word stabbed at Bransen's sensibilities profoundly. He wanted to shout at Jameston that Dame Gwydre had obviously put him up to that line of questioning, so much had it echoed her more gentle nudging over the winter in Pellinor.

He knew what he wanted regarding Cadayle and his coming child—and more children, he hoped. For them, with them, he wanted peace and security and enough comfort to give them the room to love and enjoy one another.

But Jameston was right, he knew, though he wouldn't openly admit it at that strange moment. There was more to him than Bransen Garibond.

There was the Highwayman.

CHAPTER 23

From the Depths

"We might be able to get to smoother and deeper water," the helmsman reported to Dawson as he ran back amidships. "I'm betting *Lady Dreamer* can run from them warships when the swells ain't so tall."

"Aye, and what o' *Shelligan's*, then? She's not so fleet," another crewman reminded.

"What of her, then?" the first replied angrily. "If we're to fight beside her, then we're to drown beside her!"

"Enough o' that," Dawson implored. He turned to Cormack and particularly to Milkeila. "You've got some magic, I'm hoping."

Milkeila glanced at the vast and powerful ocean waters, then back at Dawson doubtfully.

"A few tricks?" asked Dawson.

Both the young fighters nodded reluctantly.

"And so we aren't leaving *Shelligan's Run*," Dawson declared loudly. He focused his gaze on the helmsman. "A sorry group o' friends we'd be and a sorrier commander by far for meself if we'd leave our friends to certain doom."

"But it's certain doom for them if we stay and fight, too," the helmsman stubbornly reminded.

"Aye, might well be, but we'll sting the Palmaristown dogs, don't you doubt. And we won't be sailing the seas the rest of our days remembering them we let die!"

That last statement had the crewmen gathered about pumping their fists with determination.

"Signal *Shelligan's*," Dawson ordered. "Fill the sails and start east and just a bit north. We'll split them wider as they try to box us, then turn back to fight two on two to start it up."

"Two on four, ye mean, since they're twice our size," the helmsman grumbled, but the man beside him slapped the back of his head and bid him shut his mouth.

Lady Dreamer signaled her sister ship and waited patiently as she readied her sails. All the while the five Palmaristown ships continued weaving their net, two to the south, one to the north, and two more coming straight in at the prey from the west.

"Go then!" Dawson called when *Shelligan's Run* signaled she was ready and began to tack, turning her prow east. "And don't outrun *Shelligan's!*"

The chase was on, seven ships crashing through the swells at full sails, oak beams creaking and groaning in protest, crewmen pulling hard on the ropes to try to keep the sails angled perfectly to make the most of the strong spring breeze. As the ships leaped away, it seemed like they were holding their own against the two in pursuit. Dawson briefly wondered if they might just try to keep running.

But the Palmaristown caravel in the north was too fast and would soon enough be able to turn south to cut them off and slow them enough for the two behind to catch and rake their decks with volleys of arrows and giant ballista bolts.

Dawson moved to the taffrail, Cormack and Milkeila beside him, watching the run, gauging the progress of the chasing warships and the one in the north. He had to make his dramatic turn before that one started south, or it would catch them before they could get in a straight run again.

He'd wait until the last moment, for that northern ship was outdistancing the two chasers, and the two by the coast were making no move to close, instead ensuring no escape to the coast and freedom.

"Did you see that?" Milkeila asked suddenly, pointing. Both Cormack and Dawson turned to her, following her finger to the north, to the Palmaristown ship. Angled strangely, her prow suddenly too much pointed northward, her sails slack, her momentum stolen.

"She hit a rock!" Cormack exclaimed, for indeed it appeared as if the ship had struck something, and hard.

"No rocks, no reefs this far out," Dawson muttered with certainty. He knew every bit of the gulf waters better than any man alive.

But the other ship was stopped. She shuddered again as they watched, her masts trembling violently, her sails whipping back and forth. They were too far away to make out any distinct movements on her deck, but they saw commotion there, sailors running about.

"What is it?" Cormack asked.

"I'm not knowing," said Dawson. "Break north!" he shouted to his crew. "And signal *Shelligan's* to the same!"

Heartbeats later *Lady Dreamer* leaned low to port, *Shelligan's Run* in her wake.

Yach, but they got her!" Shiknickel cried to his crew, a score of bandy-legged powries pedaling hard to turn the screw on their deadly, ram-headed barrel boat. "Cracked her wood and told the sea to come aboard!" The powries gave a cheer.

"Well, turn us to her, then, so's I can wet me cap in human blood!" one cried to the agreement of all.

"What ho now?" Shiknickel asked, glancing to the side out the one conning tower on the cylindrical, mostly submerged boat. "Two more coming to play."

"Two o' her friends, or the two they were chasing?" asked one of the crew.

"The runners. They're thinking the way clear, they are. Yach, but we'll show them the bottom!"

Others cheered, but two dwarves near the back of the barrel boat glanced at each other and stopped their leg pumping. One hopped up and made his way forward.

"What're ye about?" Shiknickel demanded as he came to the side of the sturdy captain.

"About seeing the flag on them new-coming boats," answered the dwarf, a recent addition to Shiknickel's crew.

"Well what're ye knowin', Mcwigik?" Shiknickel asked, showing great deference for this one, who had been hailed as the savior of a lost powrie band that had been missing for one hundred years.

Shiknickel stepped aside as Mcwigik moved to the small top port to climb the three-step ladder and poke his head out, staring to the south.

"Dame Gwydre's flag?" called Bikelbrin from the back.

Mcwigik strained to make out the pennant. "Aye!" he said at length. "Flying the flag we seen over Castle Pellinor."

"The Vanguard queen who sent ye back to fetch our lost kin?" Shiknickel asked.

"That don't matter!" one of the bloodthirsty crew protested.

"Shut yer mouth, or I'll be fillin' it with me fist!" Shiknickel barked at him, for indeed, three of the dwarves who had been retrieved from Mithranidoon, including gray-beard Kriminig, were of Shiknickel's own clan. Kriminig, whose

beret glowed as brightly as any dwarf's in all the Julianthes, had long been regarded as a (missing) hero of the dwarf captain's clan.

"Aye, it's Gwydre's boat," Mcwigik replied when the captain looked his way.
"And ye don't want us to hit it?"

"Not with bigger boats chasing it," Mcwigik reasoned, assured that he had
hit a good note when Shiknickel's face brightened. The captain pulled out a small,
reflective device to signal the other barrel boats in the water, moving past Mcwigik to the top. Shiknickel stopped Mcwigik when he started back for his seat.

"Stay beside me a bit," he ordered. "We'll be going close by them littler
ones, and if they're not what ye're thinking they'll be the first to drown."

More than one set of eyes focused on Dawson when the screaming started
from the Palmaristown ship to the north. Something terrible was happening there, and *Lady Dreamer* was sailing right toward it.

The warship shuddered again and her mainmast lurched over to port,
and, even from this distance, the crew of *Lady Dreamer* could discern that
it had cracked down by its base. The ship was taking on water, evidenced by a
pronounced list.

"What's hitting her?" more than one crewman asked, voices tinged with fear.

Dawson, too, was more than a little afraid of this course that would bring
them so close to whatever was destroying a great warship so efficiently, but
when he glanced behind, he saw the two Palmaristown ships in full pursuit.
To stop or even turn was to fight them; to fight them was surely to die.

"Powries." The almost breathless call came from a crewman working hard
at the rigging at the bow.

"Powries?" Cormack echoed beside Dawson. Cormack and Milkeila chased
him to the rail.

In the distance they saw the rounded wood and the small conning tower
of a strange craft, her barrel-like shape and terrible ram smashing through a
swell before settling into the dark water.

Blood drained from Dawson's face, and a million thoughts swirled in his
mind as he finally came upon a desperate plan: Join with the Palmaristown
ships against the even more ruthless powrie enemy.

Yach, but we're takin' her down, Gwydre's boat or no!" Captain Shiknickel
cried. "'E's wearing a powrie cap, he is! Double-time left!"

As calls for the righthand turn echoed the length, Mcwigik's eyes opened wide. "A powrie cap?" he mouthed. Gulping hard, he shoved his way back to the short tower to stand beside Shiknickel.

Below, the dwarves shouted and sang of getting to ramming speed, of dipping their berets in the blood of men.

Shiknickel's call of "Hold yer feet!" stopped them cold.

S hoot it dead!" one man cried, but Dawson held his hand to belay that order and to keep everyone calm as they stared at the powrie barrel boat, nearly stopped and splashing in the rough waters barely thirty yards off *Lady Dreamer*'s starboard bow. A red-bearded dwarf crawled from the conning tower, holding it fast as he settled his feet on the concave deck, waves rolling over the wood.

"Mcwigik," Cormack and Milkeila said in unison before Dawson could mutter the same.

"Yach, ye dogs, and know yer good deed's not been forgotten," the dwarf hailed them as *Lady Dreamer* fast closed on the barrel boat. "Ye keep on running with yer partner there, and we'll be giving a good poke to them two that're chasing ye, not to worry."

Dawson swallowed hard and looked to his companions.

"Good Mcwigik, and the best to yer kin!" Cormack yelled, taking the cue and moving up beside Dawson.

"Aye, and Bikelbrin's below!" the dwarf replied.

"How many boats have you?" Cormack called.

"More than a few, and good ones. Ye wanting them's wearing that flag as them's chasing ye put to the bottom? Hope ye do, because that's where they're going, don't ye doubt!"

"You will let the ships under the flag of Dame Gwydre pass?" Milkeila dared to ask.

"Aye, a debt repaid, and fun repaying!"

Mcwigik gave a great laugh then as *Lady Dreamer* glided past, a chuckle filled with such wickedness that Dawson, Cormack, and Milkeila were glad to have him on their side.

"We should tell them to be gone from the gulf," Cormack said quietly to Dawson.

"Aye, but that's giving the waters to Panlamaris, now ain't it?" the older Vanguard sailor replied.

Ahead, the Palmaristown ship keeled over, dropping sailors into the cold waters. Like sharks, a trio of powrie boats rushed the scene, dwarves scrambling on the decks, serrated knives in hand. Dawson and the others on *Lady*

Dreamer watched in revulsion as one poor woman was hauled up by the hair onto the side of the powrie boat, her throat quickly slashed open. Powries swarmed over her, slapping with their berets.

The three on *Lady Dreamer* glanced back to the boat carrying Mcwigik, already pedaling fast to the south to intercept the Palmaristown ships.

"Weren't a thing we could do to stop them, anyway," Dawson mumbled. Given the carnage just ahead, his justification rang hollow even to him.

"Every choice we make, every battle we fight, takes a piece of my soul," Cormack said and leaned heavily on the rail.

Lady Dreamer and *Shelligan's Run* continued to the northeast under full sail for a long time, long after the two ships giving chase broke apart under powrie rams, long after the screams of more Palmaristown men and women rent the early spring air, long after the remaining Palmaristown ships, hugging the coast, turned and fled west.

Finally, the two Vanguard ships dared to separate, *Shelligan's Run* turning north to deliver Gwydre's message to Vanguard, *Lady Dreamer* turning straight east on their critical mission to ally with Laird Ethelbert.

There was no cheering on either boat for their improbable escape. Nearly every sailor on both of the ships more than once uttered the justification that "the Palmaristown crews would've shown us no mercy."

They had to say that, and had to believe it, given the sight of powries with knives slaughtering helpless crewmen as they splashed about in the dark and cold waters. They had to say that, because they had left fellow men of Honce to the merciless, brutal dwarves.

They had to say that, and so they did, and like Cormack, every one of them lost a little bit of his soul.

The Center, the Flank

Prince Milwellis grabbed the man by the front of his threadbare tunic with one hand and hoisted him up to tiptoes. "And where did you find this food?" he demanded.

The man's eyes darted all about as if he was searching for an escape route. But the whimpering sounds that came from him showed that he realized there was no way and nowhere to run. A former soldier in Milwellis's ranks, he and a pair of his companions had been caught in the forest, settled around a substantial stash of food they had procured from area villages. Caught so completely by surprise, the poor fellow's companions were still sitting, soldiers towering over them.

"We didn't . . . we didn't know what we was to do," he finally blurted.

"You are a soldier of Palmaristown. I am your prince. What more do you need to know?"

"Please, lord," the man gasped as Milwellis pulled the tunic up a bit more, tight against the bottom of his chin. "When the demons came north—"

"The demons?"

"Ethelbert's demon warriors!" one of the other two blurted. The soldier standing over him kicked him hard in the ribs for daring to interrupt.

"Aye, them demons," the man in Milwellis's grasp quickly added. "We saw them come down from the hill. They killed the knights, and we were next. And we tried to fight—" His response was cut off into indecipherable garbles as Milwellis, outraged by the reminder of the loss of his elite warriors, tugged him up even harder, and growled as he did.

"Please, lord!" he gasped.

"You battled them?"

"Tried, lord."

"Tried?"

The man whimpered and Milwellis threw him to the ground, turning on the other two, particularly the one who had interrupted earlier.

"We couldn't fight them," the man stammered. "We couldn't see them.

Just men dying. Screaming and then dying. And they were above us in the trees! All about us—as if there were ten thousand of them!"

"Ten thousand? How many were there?"

"Just a few," the man he had thrown to the ground squeaked in response. Milwellis turned back on him, hands out in confusion.

"Demon warriors," the other one added.

Prince Milwellis took a deep breath. "Pull the lines in tight and strengthen the flanks," he instructed his commanders.

"Back to the north?" Harcourt asked quietly, moving by his leader's side.

Milwellis shook his head. "Back to Ethelbert dos Entel," he said. "Back to Ethelbert's lair."

"We've no support from King Yeslnik," Harcourt reminded. "He has left the field."

"More the glory for us, then."

"You don't fear Ethelbert's demon warriors?"

Prince Milwellis looked at him hard, and Harcourt chuckled.

"Do you disagree?" Milwellis asked honestly.

"Keep the lines tight," Harcourt recommended. "Laird Ethelbert has a few tricks, but in the end, the weight of the army will win out. It'd be a great thing for your father to put our enemy back in his box."

"And better for Palmaristown since Yeslnik fled the field," said Milwellis.

"King Yeslnik, my prince," Harcourt teased, and both men laughed.

Strong Prince Milwellis stroked the growing beard on his face and looked to the south where lay, five days' march away, Ethelbert dos Entel.

"Nothing," Bannagran assured Reandu one warm morning in Pryd Town. "Not an Ethelbert soldier to be found."

"And not a Yeslnik one, either," Master Reandu replied.

Bannagran gave him a look of mock anger.

"And that is a good thing," Reandu pressed on anyway. "The folk of Pryd have time to get their gardens and fields in, perhaps. It would do my heart good to see an easier summer this year than last."

"You're glad to have your young brothers home at Chapel Pryd," Bannagran said.

"And our laird, who is needed at this troubling time," Reandu replied.

Bannagran nodded, knowing well that Reandu's compliment was heartfelt.

"King Yeslnik was truly unsettled by the Behr assassins and their efforts against Milwellis's force?" Reandu asked.

"Terrified. And I'm not certain that I blame him."

"You said the field was won."

Bannagran shrugged. "It seemed as if the sides were closing in on Ethelbert. The outlaw laird had no escape, save the sea at his back. I believe that if we had come to his walls, both forces, Yeslnik and Milwellis, Ethelbert would have boarded his private ship and fled his city, leaving it an easy victory and an end to the war."

"And how much better that would have been for everyone," Reandu remarked, watching Bannagran closely as he did, suspecting a rather curious undertone here.

"Yes," the Bear of Honce replied more than a little unconvincingly.

"Would you measure King Yeslnik against your old friend, Laird Prydae?" Reandu asked. "Or against Prydae's father, Laird Pryd before him?"

Bannagran's expression became an open scowl then, and Reandu was quick to back off the explosive question. He knew that Bannagran was not enamored of young King Yeslnik, of course, particularly since Bannagran had offered Chapel Pryd a dodge to avoid Yeslnik's awful order that all Ethelbert men and women held prisoner were to be put to death.

"Compared with King Delaval, then?" Reandu pressed.

Bannagran's face remained very tight.

"What will Honce be like when King Yeslnik takes full control?" Reandu asked. "What will life in Pryd be like?"

Again Bannagran shrugged. "I cannot predict what will someday be, other than to tell you that I believe the war nears its end and that the forces of Delaval will prevail. You, too, have heard the news from Chapel Abelle . . ."

"The edict said St. Mere Abelle," Reandu corrected.

Bannagran nodded. "They have thrown in with Dame Gwydre, who, I am told, opposes Laird Panlamaris of Palmaristown and King Yeslnik."

"Will Bannagran lead the folk of Pryd on a campaign through the wilds of Vanguard, then?"

The question made the big man visibly shrink. The Laird of Pryd did not say that he would do as his king asked, as would be appropriate. "Let us hope for a peaceful summer, that the folk of Pryd Town can heal their wounds," was all he said.

T oo many," Harcourt said to Milwellis as the reports came in one after another regarding the strength of their opponents. "We will sweep the field of them, perhaps, but will not have enough might left to tear down Ethelbert dos Entel's tall walls. The city is well fortified, with many engines of war lying in wait behind her stone barriers."

Prince Milwellis rubbed his face. He knew that Harcourt was responding not only to the reports regarding Ethelbert but also to those concerning his own force. His men were growing tired and increasingly glancing back to the northwest. Attrition was already beginning to work against him, with men simply disappearing from his ranks, and the whispers said that it was from more than confrontations with Ethelbert's soldiers.

"Have the runners returned from King Yeslnik?"

"King Yeslnik is long gone from the field, my prince," Harcourt replied. "He is almost directly south of Delaval City by some reports. Others say that he and his private guards have gone back to Castle Pryd."

"We have Ethelbert in a trap from which there is no escape," Milwellis protested. "We have turned his desperate attempt to break out. It was a showy and dramatic response by Ethelbert, to be sure, but without the numbers to back up any change in the course of the battle!"

"All true," said Harcourt. "But King Yeslnik is not to be found, and I doubt we'll get him and his warriors back to the field in time to finish this grim business."

Milwellis blew a frustrated sigh.

"And Yeslnik's tactics work against him, and us, regarding such an event," Harcourt went on. Milwellis looked at him curiously.

"His retreat was marked by the scorching of the world," Harcourt explained. "Every village, every field of crops, every garden, and most every animal was trampled under boot. So fearful was he that Ethelbert and his assassins would pursue, he destroyed the ability of Ethelbert's army—of any army—to follow his route back to the west."

"He intended to put Ethelbert in a box of barren ground?"

Harcourt shrugged. "Likely he means to send the fleets of Delaval and Palmaristown to assault Ethelbert from the sea. Or perhaps he hopes to keep Ethelbert in his city while he solidifies his grasp on the rest of Honce, and by sheer weight of support force Ethelbert into a truce."

"A truce that would include no assassins from Behr, no doubt," Milwellis remarked with a knowing chuckle.

"Let us hope that he is wiser than he is brave," Harcourt dared to say, knowing that some levity was needed here, since Milwellis's dream of finishing off Ethelbert seemed suddenly an unlikely thing.

"Sweep the field," Milwellis ordered.

"My prince?"

"Chase Ethelbert's ragged band back into the city," Milwellis explained. "Let us see if the walls of Ethelbert dos Entel are as solid as you fear."

"And if they are?"

"Then we will turn back to the north."

"How far?"

"Let us follow Yeslnik's lead." He grinned as he added, "Around Felidan Bay to the Mantis Arm? A few fortresses under the flag of Palmaristown scattered about the Mantis Arm would serve my father's seaborne designs well."

Harcourt smiled and nodded his approval. "A wise leader has more than one road before him and keeps both trails open for as long as he can."

"And has wise advisors to help guide his course," said Milwellis.

The regrouping and advance was on in full that very day, Milwellis's army, promised a swift victory or a swift return to Palmaristown, marching with eagerness once more. They crashed through two of the villages they had already flattened on their first pass, and all the people of those hamlets fled before them.

They found only meager resistance from a couple of small Ethelbert encampments that were not fast enough in flight before them.

They arrived in Yansinchester yet again, the last sizable town before Ethelbert dos Entel itself, the high-water mark of Milwellis's advance. This time they found the town itself deserted; they knew the survivors to be in the one structure in Yansinchester that had escaped the first march intact, Chapel Yansin.

"Bring the wounded to be tended by the brothers," Milwellis ordered his commanders. "And harm no one in the chapel. Allow these peasants some manner of peace. Perhaps they will think Laird Panlamaris beneficent when our pennants snap in the strong coastal breezes above this land."

He and Harcourt got a laugh out of that order.

They were not laughing a short while later, however, when the first couriers from Laird Panlamaris's force arrived with news that Milwellis's father had marched and been met with a magical barrage outside Chapel Abelle and was besieging the monks of the mother chapel.

Milwellis's face twisted in anger at yet another dire turn in this unfolding drama.

"Trust in your father," Harcourt said to calm him. "He is as fine a general as has ever ridden the ways of Honce."

Milwellis chewed his lip, his dark eyes flashing dangerously, his hands clenching into fists at his sides.

"My prince?" Harcourt asked.

"Are we to battle for useless land in the name of a king who had not the courage to stand and fight on his own behalf while our brethren and my father and laird battle treachery near to our own home?" Milwellis blurted, his breath coming in ragged gasps.

Harcourt put a hand to his shoulder to calm him.

"Advise me," Milwellis demanded, pleaded.

"Do as our king," Harcourt said. "Turn and burn the land behind your march."

Milwellis began to nod. "To Chapel Abelle," he whispered, as if he couldn't put anything more behind his voice.

"Most of Ethelbert's minions are back in his city now," Harcourt offered hopefully. "We can run to the gates of Ethelbert dos Entel within a matter of hours."

"Tomorrow," Milwellis decided, his voice suddenly strong once more. "A fresh march. Let us get close enough to shoot our arrows at them and turn quickly enough to persuade them that we leave of our own choice. Perhaps we can even send a message to Laird Ethelbert, a warning that if he comes forth we will destroy him."

Harcourt nodded, glad to see that his prince was continuing to think on his feet, adapting, and wisely, to every new twist.

"Tomorrow," he echoed. "And today we camp here in Yansinchester?"

"We have unfinished business here," said Milwellis, turning his angry stare right at Chapel Yansin. "For here we discover enemies of Palmaristown."

They came within sight of Ethelbert dos Entel's northern reaches the following afternoon, staring down from the same hills where Milwellis had lost his knights. The carnage of the battle remained all too clear. Milwellis trembled with rage.

Harcourt did not miss that reaction. "My prince," he said comfortingly, drawing the volatile young man out of his fuming contemplations.

"Would that I had Ethelbert's head on the ground before me," Milwellis growled.

"But you do not, though take heart in that you have surely wounded him more profoundly than he you."

Milwellis looked up from the body of a Palmaristown knight—Erolis, he recalled, though the carrion birds had done too much to disfigure it for him to be sure—and offered a thankful nod to his honest companion.

"What can we do to sting Ethelbert one last time before we turn?" he asked. "What can we do to make him know that we are here, right before his wall, and that he daren't come forth?"

Harcourt grinned and nodded.

Under the cover of darkness, on that cloudy and moonless night, every archer in Milwellis's force crept down from the hill to the field before Ethelbert dos Entel's north wall.

They couldn't see their target any better than any defenders might see them, of course, but then, their target was the size of a city.

A hundred bows lifted to the sky and let fly. Then again and again and many more times after that until at last cries came from the city as Ethelbert's people realized they were under attack. The last volley was flaming arrows, five score streaking through the night sky to cross over the wall and seek further fuel within.

A response finally came, but by then the Palmaristown archers had turned and fled.

Several fires erupted within the city wall, Milwellis and Harcourt saw from the hilltop. Perhaps a few people had been injured or even killed, perhaps those fires, though surely quickly attended, would cause some damage. But none of that was the point, after all. Milwellis had just told Ethelbert that he was here in the dark within striking distance of the desperate laird's last refuge.

The next morning Milwellis's army moved back to the north, driving livestock and villagers before them, destroying the gardens and the fields.

And dragging with them the twenty-three brothers of Chapel Yansin bound for Chapel Abelle.

CHAPTER 25

Worthy

"They're running," Jameston remarked to Bransen. "Like deer before the wolves."

The pair stood looking to the east from opposite branches of a tree. Something was happening there, some fighting or other commotion, but they couldn't make out what, exactly, for a line of hills blocked their view even from the high perch. That was the nature of this ground along the southernmost Honce coastline, as if the towering mountains just south of their position, the great Belt-and-Buckle, had collided with the sea in days long lost to the world and had strewn great broken mounds all about the region.

Suddenly soldiers were scrambling past the trees as if the demon dactyl itself was close on their heels. Not far before them, one spearman stumbled as he headed down a slope, nearly thrown from his feet as the back quarter of his spear shaft collided with a tree. Finally orienting himself, he just threw the spear to the ground and continued his desperate run.

Bransen got Jameston's attention and pointed up above.

"Too thin," the scout replied, meaning the branches.

Bransen shook his head and started up anyway, falling into the malachite in his brooch. He lessened his weight greatly, his hands easily propelling him skyward. Within only a few moments he had climbed nearly twenty feet to the tree's tiny top (which wasn't bending under his weight in the least). He looked back to see Jameston gawking at him and shaking his head in disbelief.

Bransen suppressed his smile and looked to the east again. Though he still couldn't see as widely as he had hoped, the view proved enough to make out the pennants flying over a large force.

"Palmaristown," he muttered, turning his gaze south. The structures of Ethelbert dos Entel, built on steps up the mountainsides, were in clear view only a couple of leagues away. Was the war nearing its end? And what might this mean for his quest to find the Jhesta Tu? Bransen danced his way back down to Jameston and relayed the information.

"So these are Ethelbert's men," Jameston remarked, glancing down at the fleeing force. "They'll run all the way to the city, I'm guessing."

"Not all of them," Bransen determinedly replied. To Jameston's gasp of surprise, he leaped from the tree and floated—floated, not fell!—to the ground. He was running as he landed, scrambling through the thick copse to intercept nearby soldiers.

"I've got to get me some of them damned stones," he heard Jameston mutter as the man carefully and painstakingly worked his way back down to the ground.

The Highwayman slipped into a grove of pines, sliding silently through the dense branches. He followed a movement out of the corner of his eye to his left, and he glided as a shadow to intercept.

The man ran before him; the Highwayman's foot thrust out to strike the trailing foot of the fleeing soldier, kicking it behind his other ankle. The man tripped and tumbled forward, landing awkwardly in a skid on his knees and hands. Apparently still oblivious to the source of his fall, he started to scramble back to his feet.

A fine sword blade atop his shoulder, its sharp edge barely an inch from his neck, froze him in place.

"Please, sir, I've a family," he begged.

The Highwayman retracted the sword, grabbed him by the collar and hoisted him to his feet, turning him as he stood to look him in the face. The soldier gasped, eyes widening as he considered the black clothing and the unusual gemstone brooch.

"Affwin Wi?" he asked.

The Highwayman paused at hearing that name yet again. "You know Affwin Wi?" he asked.

"Of her all do," the terrified soldier replied.

"Let him go!" came a cry from the side where a pair of soldiers appeared, swords in hand. They advanced slowly toward the Highwayman, their blades raised threateningly.

"Oh, I'm not thinking that you're in a place to be telling him what to do," came an answer to the side of the newcomers, who both looked and blanched at the sight of Jameston Sequin, his bow drawn, arrow leveled.

"Easy," the soldier with Bransen instructed his companions. "He's one o' Affwin Wi's boys."

The other two certainly did relax at that.

"Praise the ancient ones," one muttered while the other gave the sign of the evergreen.

Bransen and Jameston exchanged glances, both of them noting yet again that curious combination and juxtaposition of the major Honce religions. The ancient ones were Samhaist gods, the evergreen the sign of the Order of Blessed Abelle.

"If ye're to sting him, then now's the time or never's the time," one of the newcomers remarked.

"Him?" asked Bransen.

"Prince Milwellis," the other newcomer clarified.

"Aye, that one came back mad because you and your friends stung him so hard the first time," said the first. "So stick him again, we beg, and this time stick his own body, if ye're getting me point."

"He's a dog what's killed a thousand mothers and more than that o' children," said the man standing beside Bransen.

"To see his blood staining the waters o' the Mirianic would do our hearts good when we come from Entel, and don't ye doubt that we'll be back," said one of the others.

"Where is Affwin Wi?" Bransen asked. "Has she returned to the city?"

The three soldiers exchanged shrugs.

"She's still out, I'm thinking," said the one near Bransen. "Not far from here, last I heard."

"Be gone," Bransen told his prisoner and the others, and they were happy to oblige.

Bransen fixed his gaze on Jameston, who nodded solemnly and slipped back into the thick grove of pines, with Bransen close behind.

Two other sets of eyes watched the exchange between the strangers and the soldiers, all the more carefully when they took note of Bransen's sword.

Merwal Yahna motioned to Pactset Va, and the two men slid away from the scene, no less silent than the black-clothed stranger carrying a sword he should not possess.

"Jhesta Tu," Merwal reported to Affwin Wi soon after. "There is no doubt."

"He wore our clothing," said Pactset Va, a young and strong specimen with small dark eyes and his hair bound in a topknot. "And carried a sword as your own traced with vines."

Affwin Wi drew her broken blade and rolled it over in surprisingly delicate hands that had many times driven right through the throat of an opponent.

She looked to Merwal Yahna with an expression that was not hopeful. The Jhesta Tu had hunted them in Behr, but they had thought their mercenary stint with Laird Ethelbert would allow them reprieve from their continual trials against Affwin Wi's former masters. Had they found her again?

Affwin Wi took some solace in the likelihood that this new mystic would be acting mostly alone; the Jhesta Tu considered the adjudication of the matter of a rogue like Affwin Wi to be a personal challenge for their disciples, whereas the Hou-lei traditions Affwin Wi had come to follow, much more forceful and warlike, called for as many warriors as needed, and then some more, for any given task. In simple terms, Hou-lei didn't fight fairly. Three times before the great warrior had helped her fend off Jhesta Tu.

Since the Jhesta Tu's companion in the woods earlier was surely not of Behr or Jhesta Tu, Affwin Wi had no reason to believe this time would be different.

Well, you do look like a southerner," Jameston quipped as he and Bransen made their way to the southwest, tracing a wide perimeter of Ethelbert dos Entel. "You've got the skin for it."

Bransen could only shrug. Though Jameston was teasing, his words were true enough. With his brown skin and jet black hair, the black clothing and his exotic sword, the Ethelbert warriors had thought him from Behr. And they understood the significance of his dress. "Affwin Wi," he mumbled, and he found it hard to breathe. They were close; the Jhesta Tu were close.

"And what are you planning to do when we find these folk?" Jameston asked as if reading his mind, which was probably not a difficult thing to do at that moment.

"Learn from them," he replied. "You cannot understand, but I am trapped in an infirm body."

"Are you, then?" the scout asked, his eyebrows rising along with the sides of his mouth as he put on an incredulous grin.

"Without this," Bransen explained, pointing to his brooch, "I am a helpless, babbling fool, the one you saw being dragged toward the glacier after the troll fight."

"Wasn't it a knock in the head?"

"A knock in the head that dislodged the gemstone," Bransen explained.

Jameston nodded and smiled. "I wondered on that. I saw you walking— being dragged, actually—and thought you knocked silly beyond any chance of regaining your senses."

Bransen lifted an eyebrow. "Thank you for the assistance."

"Told you not to fight the damned trolls."

Bransen let it go with a laugh, not willing to recount all those earlier questions at this pressing time.

"You think these strangers we're hunting will free you of that stone?" Jameston asked.

Bransen saw that the scout didn't understand. He was simply too edgy at that moment to go into great detail. "They will," he replied.

He turned to glance at Jameston and ensure that the explanation would suffice just as the scout froze in his tracks, his eyes locked.

"Looks like we're going to find out," Jameston whispered out of the side of his mouth. Following his gaze to a pair of thick pines across a small open patch of ground, Bransen saw a warrior, lithe and strong with tightly wound muscles. His brow, furrowed and pronounced with the dark, thin lines of his eyebrows, made his black eyes seem even angrier, fiercer, an imposing appearance that grew only more so for his shaven head. He was dressed in black silk clothing akin to Bransen's own and casually swung a strange weapon at the end of one arm, a pair of forearm-length solid wooden poles secured at their ends by a short length of leather.

"Nun'chu'ku," Bransen mouthed as he considered the very deadly weapon he recognized from his lessons reading the Book of Jhest.

The warrior said something in a strange tongue, and Bransen tried to unwind the words. He knew the language from the book his father had penned, but he had never heard it spoken before. The warrior repeated his phrase, a demand from the insistent tone.

"You know what he's saying, boy?" Jameston whispered.

"Something about Jhesta Tu," Bransen answered, shaking his head. "Asking if I am Jhesta Tu, I think, but I cannot be certain."

"Act certain, then," Jameston replied.

"Jhesta Tu," Bransen said loudly.

The warrior's dark eyes narrowed immediately, and he began to walk slowly to their left, putting himself more in line with Bransen.

"Wrong answer," Jameston said.

"Jhesta Tu?" Bransen asked this time, and he pointed at the warrior. That stopped the man in his pacing, and his expression turned more to curiosity.

"Who be you?" the warrior asked in the common tongue of Honce, though heavily accented in the dialect of Behr, a rolling and bouncing singsong effect of consonants bitten off and vowels exaggerated.

"I am Bransen Gari—" Bransen started, but he changed direction and said with confidence, "I am the son of Sen Wi of the Jhesta Tu and of Bran Dynard, trained at the Walk of Clouds."

"But you have de sword," the warrior said, his accent thick.

"I wield the sword of Sen Wi."

"You be Jhesta Tu."

Bransen shook his head, and the warrior snickered.

"You give me the sword."

Bransen shook his head again.

"You give me the sword now, and you go."

"And if I do not?"

"Then I take the sword from your body, yes." As he finished, the warrior sent his nun'chu'ku into sudden motion, spinning the bottom length in a fast rotation at his side, then snapping it across his chest so that it wrapped under his upraised arm and slapped flat against his back. It came back in front of him and to his right for another spinning display before going under his upraised arm and around his back. When he brought the wooden pole humming before him once more, he set it into a furious reverse spin before him, then worked it back and up beside his right ear. He slapped his left wrist across his vertical right forearm and caught the flying pole in his grasp, immediately tugging it across back to his left while letting go with his right hand so that the other pole now flew freely.

Back and forth he worked the amazing weapon, changing hands and perfectly moving the momentum from one pole, through the leather tie to the other pole, reversing the spins.

It ended as suddenly as it had begun, the man somehow turning the nun'chu'ku so that its spin tucked it neatly under his right arm.

"Awful lot of bluster for so few words," Jameston quietly remarked.

"Give me de sword now," the warrior said.

Bransen drew his blade in a fluid and powerful movement, snapping the sword before him, angled diagonally to the sky. He slowly folded his elbow, bringing the back of the sword blade in against his forehead. After only a very short pause he snapped the blade down and to the side with such speed that it cracked through the air. He ended, as the practice demanded, with the tip of his blade a hair's breadth from the dirt, angled down and slightly away from him.

Bransen kept his expression purposely grim, although he was beaming inside in confidence, bolstered by the Behr warrior's expression, which confirmed to him that he had executed the sword salute perfectly.

"I think not," he said, taking a slow and deliberate step forward. Jameston faded away from him a couple of short shuffles to the side, bow in his left hand, right hand positioned to grab an arrow from the quiver strapped diagonally across his back.

The warrior paid no heed to Jameston, his dangerous gaze locked on Bransen. He moved his right arm just a bit, the nun'chu'ku dropped free of his hold and unwound to its full length at the end of his grasp. He slid into a crouch, left hand coming up before his chest in a blocking position, his right arm sliding back just a bit. He gave a brief shout and stood from his pose. He never blinked and never stopped staring at Bransen as he took a couple of steps farther to the left and fell once more into that ready posture.

"What's that about?" Jameston asked.

"He is showing me that he is unafraid," Bransen explained.

"Should I just shoot him?"

"You wouldn't hit him."

"Hmm," was Jameston's doubtful response.

The warrior's eyes narrowed, and his lip twitched into a snarl as if the chatter was an insult to him, which Bransen realized it probably was.

The Highwayman saluted crisply with his sword again then slowly walked his left foot forward toward the warrior, falling into a wide-stance, forward-diagonal crouch. He crooked his right elbow and turned his right wrist so that his arm looked like a serpent as he brought it back up high, his sword pointing forward past his head. He gracefully lifted his left hand before him, palm out. The warrior from Behr sent his weapon into a spin and strode forward a step.

The Highwayman dropped his arm, stabbing his sword forward in an underhand movement as he stepped closer to his opponent. He came up fast, handing the blade to his left hand and striking a mirror-image of the pose from which he had started.

They were barely three strides apart and then only two as the warrior from Behr gave a shout and came forward, his weapon working a dizzying blur of spins before he caught it in both hands. He turned them so the poles snapped vertically, the leather tie drawing a horizontal line before his face.

The Highwayman tried to sort out a counter. His next movement would likely end the posturing and begin the actual fighting. He tried to remember everything he had read about nun'chu'ku and the techniques involved, tried to somehow link that book knowledge against the minimal display he had witnessed from the Behrenese warrior.

He simply wasn't sure of what he was up against here, of the limitations and strengths of this exotic weapon. A mischievous grin came to his lips and he thought himself very clever as he began to shift again very slowly.

Suddenly, thrusting his blade, turning it over so that its razor edge pointed skyward Bransen poked toward the warrior's face but pulled up short and slashed the sword for the sky, thinking to sever the leather tie of the nun'chu'ku. The warrior didn't try to pull the exotic weapon away; the Highwayman thought he had scored a clean hit.

But the man from Behr lifted his hands as the sword came up, absorbing most of the strike's energy. As the blade connected with the leather but without any momentum to cut through, the warrior crossed his hands before his chest then thrust upward with his right and pulled downward with his left, the resulting turn of leather and wood nearly tearing the sword from the Highwayman's grasp!

The warrior drove the weapons higher and stepped through, turning right-to-left suddenly as he went, his trailing left foot snapping out to kick the Highwayman squarely in the gut. Bransen had to grab his sword with both hands to prevent it from being torn from his grasp.

The Highwayman threw his hips back, absorbing the brunt of the sharp blow. As the warrior turned about before him, now driving the sword's blade back down, Bransen went forward a short step and leaped into a twisting somersault, still holding fast with both hands and now tucking his elbows in tight to try to gain control of the movements of the weapons. He thought he could tear his sword free with the momentum of the twist and take the leather tie apart in the process, but the Behrenese warrior, again one step ahead of him, simply disengaged as Bransen tumbled past. The sudden freedom of his blade nearly toppled Bransen as he came around to his feet.

The Highwayman moved instinctively, knowing that his opponent would expect an overbalance. Taking his sword in his left hand alone, he pivoted onto the ball of his right foot, spinning around and dropping a downward backhand parry perfectly in line with the flying end of the nun'chu'ku. The metal rang out in vibration from the heavy hit as Bransen came up square with his opponent, falling immediately into a defensive crouch, hands joining on the hilt of his sword before him.

Not an instant too soon. The Behrenese warrior, offering no opportunity for Bransen to move to an offensive posture, launched a sudden and furious routine, the nun'chu'ku whipping before him in a sidelong swipe, then going into a spin above his head, where he cleverly changed hands and came in from the other side.

Bransen barely blocked.

Again and again and again the wooden poles hummed through the air up high, down low, behind the warrior's back. He came in left and down, right across, right and down from on high.

The Highwayman was purely reacting, trying hard to follow the man's dizzying movements to get his sword out to block. Somehow he kept up, but he felt as if he were drowning, as if the water were rising too fast for him to stay above it.

He tried to block another swing from the right, but the warrior shortened the strike and the nun'chu'ku whipped past. The Highwayman understood as the man dropped low before him, still rotating. Instinct alone had Bransen leaping and tucking his legs, narrowly avoiding a cunning leg sweep that would have put him to the ground.

He couldn't leap fast enough, though, and he had to put all his weight to his right leg and lift his left, turning it to absorb the blow as the nun'chu'ku came around and smashed him hard against the side of his shin.

Bransen gritted through the hit and stabbed down hard. With no momentum left in the nun'chu'ku, the warrior let it go and caught it quickly with a reverse grip, then slapped the pole against the descending sword blade. Again he loosened his grip and shoved, pushing Bransen's sword away, turning his hand over as he went, using that sword as a fulcrum to throw the bulk of the nun'chu'ku beneath it. His left hand crossed under his thrusting right elbow, catching the free pole as he sprang from the crouch before Bransen. Momentum regained as he lifted his left hand up high and over then down and back across, the descending warrior got past Bransen's desperate defensive turn enough to send the flying nun'chu'ku pole hard against Bransen's right shoulder.

The Highwayman gasped at the explosion of pain and stumbled to his left, stunned by the sheer weight of the blow.

Jameston had seen more than enough. He had long ago taken a measure of the Highwayman as the finest young warrior he had ever seen, but he already knew that Bransen was ill-prepared to battle this fierce warrior. In a single fluid movement, Jameston's right hand snapped up and grasped an arrow, pulling it from the quiver, drawing it down over his right shoulder, and setting it expertly to the bow. Still moving in the same beautiful line, the scout drew back and lifted the bow, string coming against the side of his nose. He didn't have much space between Bransen and the strange warrior, but he didn't need much.

A form, a leaping and spinning, black-clothed warrior, flew in from the side and behind, just above Jameston. His bowstring lost all tension, the top of his bow snapping forward suddenly and awkwardly, arrow falling to the ground.

The scout cried out in surprise but kept his wits enough to grab his bow in both hands like a stave and swing to his left where the assailant had gone.

Had gone and was now coming back ferociously. Jameston turned that way. Smaller than the other opponent, a woman warrior came at him with clenched fists. She opened her left as she thrust it forward. Instinct alone prompted Jameston to pull his bow in close defensively. The small knife she had used to cut his bowstring stabbed into the bow and stuck fast.

At the last moment Jameston leveled his bow like a spear to fend the charging warrior. She did stop but slapped at the bow left and right, grabbing at the wood.

Jameston retracted and stabbed ahead repeatedly, trying to keep her at bay. He began rotating the staff's end in small, fast circles; when he had her attention there he cleverly charged and thrust forward. He thought he had her, would have scored a solid hit, but a second stave entered the fray, chopping hard from the side, turning down Jameston's bow-staff.

"What?" he cried, noting another black-clothed warrior to his left. He let go of his bow with his right hand and lifted it to block. Too late, for the warrior ran the staff up the angled wood above his lifting hand.

Jameston managed to turn so that he only took a glancing blow across his jaw, but when he looked back he saw the woman flying through the air at him, spinning a forward somersault. She straightened as she came over, her legs snapping forward, her black silk slippers poking from under the wide cut of her silken pants.

That's going to hurt, Jameston thought, as one foot crunched against his cheek and nose; the other slammed him hard in the collarbone. He went flying backward, arms and legs akimbo, and landed on his back, his breath blasted away. Before he could begin to even think about rising, the other warrior was above him, the tip of a staff in tight against the bottom of his chin, ready to drive through his throat.

Jameston lifted his hands in surrender.

The Highwayman tried to block out Jameston's troubles. He couldn't afford even to glance at his friend's precarious position while battling a man of such talent and speed. He was still reminding himself of that when the Behrenese warrior faked high and swept low with his legs, sending Bransen tumbling to the ground.

Even as he fell Bransen sought the malachite, lessening his weight. He landed lightly on his back, turned his legs under him and tightened his stomach, hoisting his shoulders with such force that he propelled himself right back to his feet with a suddenness that took his opponent by surprise.

The Highwayman went for the win, thinking to wound this warrior fast and spring away to help his fallen friend. He thrust out, a certain hit on the warrior's hip, but he shortened the strike, both because he had no desire to kill this man and because he was anxious, too anxious, to get to Jameston. And because the Highwayman simply wasn't used to fighting someone this quick and trained in the Jhesta Tu manner.

So when he expected his blade to penetrate flesh, he found instead a nun'chu'ku spinning an underhand block, pushing the angle of the cut wide. Worse, the exotic weapon wrapped up and around and the warrior grabbed both ends, locking the sword in place. The Highwayman reacted in time to prevent the sudden twist from snapping his blade in half by turning with the angle change, but the movement had him and his opponent in an awkward alignment, slightly askew of each other and both leaning away.

The warrior from Behr fell even lower, dropping his back, left leg into a deep crouch. Then he began kicking with his right leg, hitting the Highwayman in the shin and side of his knee, and then again in rapid succession.

The Highwayman fell into a similar crouch and responded with his own kicks, but his opponent had the advantage, the momentum, and the initiative. Feet circled and kicked forward and back, slapping and bruising as the two held tight to their entangled weapons.

For a few heartbeats, the Highwayman took two blows for every one he delivered. He gradually moved to more even footing and even managed a solid hit against the back of his opponent's outstretched thigh, his toes jabbing hard into the man's hamstring.

But that leg came up higher suddenly and clipped Bransen's chin, nearly sending him tumbling away. He moved in closer, and kicks became jabbing knees. Again the Highwayman took the worst of it. He knew the style of fighting well from his readings, but he had never engaged in it, had never even sparred with this technique, and he was up against a master.

A knee came in hard against the side of his thigh, bruising him sorely. He shifted away from the assault. The warrior from Behr promptly straightened his leg in a snap kick that left Bransen's left arm numb.

He wanted to retreat and regroup, but he couldn't pull his sword free, and he surely couldn't surrender it.

So the Highwayman went the other way, crouch-walking even closer to his opponent. He let go of his sword with his left hand, punching at the warrior, who easily shifted back enough so that, even if the punch landed, it could do no real harm.

But the Highwayman wasn't trying to punch the warrior. Instead, he grabbed the man by the front of his silken shirt and with a yell, threw himself forward so that they were tight together.

The warrior from Behr laughed—exactly the response Bransen had hoped to elicit, for it told him that the warrior had believed his move to be a desperate attempt to drive the trapped sword in for the kill. The warrior then snapped his head backward and forward viciously, his forehead crunching against the Highwayman's nose.

Bransen accepted the powerful hit, for he was already deep into the graphite of his brooch, bringing forth its powers. As the warrior from Behr snapped his head back again for another butt, the mighty jolt of lightning power kept him moving backward, had him flying backward, arms and legs flailing. He hit the ground and jerked about wildly.

The Highwayman stood and with a flip of his wrist sent the nun'chu'ku into the air where he caught it with his free hand. He hid well his grimace of pain as he straightened, for his knee, thigh, and hip were beyond bruised.

"Drop the weapons!" the woman shouted.

Bransen glanced to the side, where the man holding the stave on Jameston retracted it just an inch and popped it down hard against the underside of Jameston's chin, drawing a pitiful gurgle from the prostrate man.

In front of the Highwayman, the fallen warrior finally managed to stand—or tried to, at least, but his legs wobbled uncontrollably and he staggered back down to one knee. He cried out through chattering teeth in the tongue of the southern kingdom. Bransen understood enough of the words to recognize that he was calling for his friends to back away from Jameston.

In the common tongue of Honce, the Behr warrior added, "This one is worthy to wield that sword!"

Sweeter words Bransen Garibond had never heard.

CHAPTER 26

A Shiver of Sharks

He's a madman!" Laird Panlamaris roared, storming about and crushing the parchment in his powerful hand.

The courier from Delaval City shrank back from the wild man, eyeing the door of the tavern's common room as if searching for an escape route. He wasn't the only one; of the thirty men and women in the room, all seemed more than a bit unsettled by the powerful man's outburst. All save one dressed in monk's robes and sitting calmly at the same table Panlamaris had occupied when he had been handed the note—before he had leaped up, fuming.

"A madman!" Panlamaris said again and he kicked a chair across the room.

"He is the King of Honce," Father De Guilbe remarked. When the Laird of Palmaristown fixed him with a severe glare, he merely shrugged.

"Read it!" Panlamaris said, throwing the parchment De Guilbe's way.

De Guilbe didn't catch it, but rather, deflected it to the floor. "He demands that you attack Chapel Abelle," he said.

"Yes," Panlamaris replied. "He wants me to throw all that I have against those walls, with the monks hurling fire and lightning at us from on high."

"And with your finest warriors off rampaging in the far east," said De Guilbe.

"It is madness!" Panlamaris declared.

"Foolishness, at least," De Guilbe agreed. "King Yeslnik is a man who does not yet understand battle."

"Am I to write his lesson in the blood of Palmaristown's garrison?"

"Are you?"

"No!" Laird Panlamaris yelled. He took a deep breath and seemed to relax a bit. He even managed to grab a chair from a nearby table and take his seat across from De Guilbe. "We cannot go against such a fortress as Chapel Abelle.

Not with their magical powers and with my ships getting sunk by powries behind them. Powries! Of all the ill times to have powries in the gulf!"

"A remarkable coincidence, you believe?" asked De Guilbe, and in a tone that suggested that he thought it no such thing.

"Is it not?"

"Among those who did battle against Ancient Badden were a pair of powries," De Guilbe explained.

Laird Panlamaris and many others looked at the monk incredulously.

"It is true," De Guilbe insisted. "When the Highwayman dropped Ancient Badden's head at Dame Gwydre's feet, he was accompanied by the man Cormack, who betrayed me, by a barbarian woman, and by a pair of bloody-cap dwarves. He introduced those powries to Dame Gwydre as friends, and the powries wintered in Castle Pellinor."

"This cannot be," said Panlamaris, giving voice to what almost everyone in the room was thinking.

"But it is, I tell you," said De Guilbe. "They wintered in Castle Pellinor and were given free passage from the city as soon as the snows had calmed."

"Powries?"

"Ugliest little creatures I have ever seen."

Laird Panlamaris stroked his beard and stared through the tavern door and up the hill to the distant outline of Chapel Abelle. "You believe Dame Gwydre enlisted the little beasts?"

"I know that Dame Gwydre did not kill the two who came to Pellinor," De Guilbe replied. "I know that she released them, and that the one called the Highwayman named them as friends. Friends help friends, do they not?"

Laird Panlamaris stared off into nothingness for a long while, his eyes narrow, his nostrils flared. His defeat at the wall of Chapel Abelle had stung him profoundly, but the loss of three warships had positively infuriated him. Panlamaris had been a sailor throughout his youth, when his father had ruled the port city, and he had traced the Honce coast from Delaval City to Ethelbert dos Entel and from the Vanguard coast all the way to southern Alpinador. He had battled powries before, as well, out on the open Mirianic and in fact had been instrumental in devising ways to cripple the dreaded barrel boats, using ballista-launched weighted nets to drag the low-riding craft under the waves.

As with almost every sailor in Honce, Laird Panlamaris hated powries most of all.

And now—was it possible? The notion that these wretched little beasts had joined in with his enemies boiled his blood.

He slammed his fist down on the table so hard that the nearest leg creaked in protest, cracked, and nearly buckled.

"We attack, my laird?" one commander standing nearby asked with great enthusiasm.

"Shut up," Panlamaris said, then to De Guilbe added, "I will confront Dame Gwydre in parley. If she is in league with these beasts, then one day soon Vanguard will bow to the rule of Laird Panlamaris."

He stood up powerfully, his chair flying behind him, and called for a scribe. "Soon," he repeated grimly to De Guilbe.

P edal faster, ye mutts, or we're to miss all the dippin'!" Shiknickel cried out to his crew. Up in the squat tower, the powrie watched as a pair of barrel boats closed fast on a warship, another flying the colors of Palmaristown.

Below and behind him, the tough dwarves picked up their pace, the barrel boat leaping away across the dark waters. Shiknickel grinned but didn't openly applaud their efforts, preferring instead the inspiring, "Yah, but ye call that fast? Ye mutts, me dead mum could swim past ye!"

He was smiling wider as he finished, but his grin disappeared a moment later when the Palmaristown warship attacked. Deck-mounted ballistae, giant spear throwers, let fly at the nearest barrel boat, launching thick, weighted netting. Their shots weren't true but didn't have to be, for just putting the spears near to the boat, which was no more than twenty yards from the warship's broadside, sent the net over its tower, hooking fast and draping over the back half of the boat. The drag slowed the craft immediately, and, worse, the netting hooked the barrel boat's single propeller. Instead of charging in now at high speed to ram the warship, the barrel boat was suddenly adrift and tilting as the heavy weights pulled at her.

Spotters ran along the warship's deck, pointing out the second approaching barrel boat while the ballista crews reloaded. A host of archers appeared at the rail and began raking the trapped barrel boat even as some of her crew tried to climb to cut the netting free.

"They was ready for us," Shiknickel whispered. "Bah! Stop yer pedaling!" he shouted down to the dwarves. "Stop, I'm tellin' ye!"

Mcwigik came to the base of the ladder. "Gwydre's boat?" he asked.

Shiknickel motioned for him to climb up. "Palmaristown, still," he explained. "But they're coming out ready."

Mcwigik grimaced as he considered the scene. The trapped barrel boat was listing now, water splashing in through her tower. Dwarves tried to come up, and arrows cut them down.

The second boat had turned, but the warship, too, was tacking to give chase.

"They ain't seen us yet," Mcwigik remarked, and Shiknickel nodded grimly. "We got to be quick and hard."

Mcwigik smiled at him and punched a fist into his open palm.

Shiknickel lifted his signaling mirror and turned it behind the boat, where he knew three other barrel boats to be on the prowl.

"Lay quiet," he ordered Mcwigik. "They'll go by us chasing our friends. Almost." He ended with an exaggerated wink.

"They're turnin' inside us, are they?" Mcwigik asked.

Shiknickel smiled.

"Swing out wider?"

"Slowly," ordered Shiknickel. "They're lookin' th'other way, so keep our spray down and keep them looking th'other way."

Mcwigik went back into the hold and motioned for silence. Facing the crew, he held up his right hand while slowly turning circles with his left, and the right hand crew began a slow pedal, executing a left turn.

"Quarter," Shiknickel called down.

Mcwigik began a slow cadence of patting both hands and the crew began to pedal in unison at the easy pace.

As the Palmaristown warship continued its turn and gained speed, obviously unaware of Shiknickel's boat or those trailing, the captain called for a turn back to the right. When the angle was right he shouted down, "Full and fast, and get ready for a jolt!"

A powrie barrel boat was built for head-on collision, with a devilish ram leading its charge just below the waterline. Many buffers had been engineered around that ram, and, even without them, the thin planking of a typical surface sailing ship would have proven no match for the concentrated pounding of a barrel boat's solid ram. Slammed against a stopped ship, with only the power of pedaling dwarves, that ram would still break through to some degree. In this case, with the barrel boat coming in at an angle before a fast-sailing ship, the explosion knocked every dwarf from his seat and sent Mcwigik flying against the front inside wall.

But the dwarves were laughing, for they knew that their unsettling bounce had been nothing compared to what the unprepared crew of the sailing ship had just felt.

Indeed, the powrie ram drove a gaping hole in the starboard bow of the warship, and the momentum had lengthened that hole considerably, splintering planks near to midship. A man plummeted from the rigging, dislodged by the sudden and unexpected impact. Several others went flying over the rail, and all on the deck were tumbling, caught completely by surprise.

Without even being told, the powries rushed back to their seats and began pedaling in reverse. Wood creaked in protest, for the ram was fairly stuck, and the heavier warship dragged the barrel boat along as its momentum played out.

"Forward! Back!" Mcwigik shouted in succession, the reversals rocking the barrel boat and tearing apart more of the sailing ship's planking in the process. From above, they could all hear the Palmaristown sailors crying out, "Powrie boat!" and calling for nets and arrows.

That brought more laughter than anything else, for every powrie on Shiknickel's boat understood the damage they had inflicted on the warship, and all knew that the blustering sailors would very quickly be far more concerned with the fact that their ship was sinking than with the powries.

The barrel boat finally slid free.

"Put her back a dozen and watch the show," said Mcwigik.

"Can't see a thing," one dwarf remarked to the giggles of the others.

"Listen, then," Mcwigik replied. "Sure to be a song sweet to me ears."

They heard but didn't feel another loud crash.

"Tikminnik's boat," Shiknickel called down. "Get yer caps ready, boys, for she'll list over soon enough!"

Much cheering and rubbing of hands ensued.

Within a very short time, the Palmaristown warship lay on her side, most of her underwater. Men bobbed and splashed or hung on desperately to the rigging while the powrie boats circled like sharks.

Shiknickel led the way onto the deck, calling for gaff hooks as he went. Heartbeats later, the first third of the crew in rotation had climbed from the tower, long hooked poles in hand. The remaining dwarves pedaled slowly and turned to Shiknickel's call, bringing the barrel boat beside one floundering sailor after another.

"Please, sir, no!" one man cried desperately. "I've a wife and little girl!"

"And ye should've stayed home with them, eh?" a powrie replied. He slapped his gaff hook down hard, catching the man by the shoulder, and hauled him to the side of the rounded deck.

Other dwarves were fast to the spot, serrated knives in hand. They expertly opened up the best areas for a long and thick bloodletting. And so it went throughout the rest of the day, until the sharks arrived. The boats went to the aid of their netted kin then, helping them finish cutting away the pesky ropes and then holding tight to the listing craft, keeping back the sharks while the crew powries bailed her.

The next morning the seas were calm, the Palmaristown ship and all her crew gone from sight, with not even flotsam to be seen.

The powrie captains and their top advisors all sat atop their respective decks.

"Where to, then?" one asked. "Getting tired o' waiting for them fools to come out here in the open waters."

"From the west, always," another observed.

"Palmaristown," Shiknickel explained. "West and at the mouth of the river."

"And with most of her fleet down? And most of her men out fighting on the field?" Mcwigik asked slyly.

Half a dozen barrel boats started out to the west, a shiver of sharks.

Hungry sharks.

They were in range of Palmaristown's archers, but in range, too, of the monks on St. Mere Abelle's wall with their devastating gemstones.

Dame Gwydre and Laird Panlamaris rode from their respective ranks simultaneously, meeting on the field at a tent Panlamaris's men had set up. Beside Gwydre rode Father Premujon and Brother Pinower, and a pair accompanied Panlamaris, as well, including Father De Guilbe.

The sight of the large and imposing monk distressed Gwydre, but not as much as it unsettled poor Premujon. She felt naked out here without Dawson beside her. Reports magically collected by the brothers had reached her of his escape from the Palmaristown ships in the gulf. She was beside herself with relief but sorely missed the man she had leaned upon for so many years.

Given the events in the gulf, where Palmaristown warships had somehow been defeated, Gwydre eagerly accepted the invitation to parley with her opponents, hoping against reason that the impasse might be at an end. As she neared the tent and noted the expression on Laird Panlamaris's face, her doubts overwhelmed her optimism.

A table had been set inside the tent, three chairs on each side. Gwydre took hers in the middle, directly opposite Panlamaris.

"Lady, it is good to see that some among you have a bit of honor, at least," Laird Panlamaris began. "A very tiny bit."

"Good tidings to you, too, Laird Panlamaris," Gwydre retorted, "who came unbidden with his army to the gates of a chapel and stained the field before her with the blood of innocent men."

"Innocent?" Father De Guilbe growled, but Panlamaris silenced him with an upraised hand.

"You know Father De Guilbe," Panlamaris said. "And this is Captain Dunlevin Brosh, who commands the Palmaristown fleet."

"Father Premujon of Chapel Pellinor," Gwydre replied. "And this is Brother Pinower, who speaks for St. Mere Abelle."

"What?" De Guilbe noted, his brow furrowing. "Saint?"

"St. Mere Abelle," Dame Gwydre said again. "Until recently known as Chapel Abelle."

De Guilbe gave a wicked chuckle. "The fool Artolivan. Does he think that his symbolic gestures will help him against the inevitable fall? Will he hide behind a name—a name he dishonors with every treasonous action he takes?"

His voice grew louder with each question, his outrage bubbling over. "We will return to our mission when I am installed as the proper head of the Order of Abelle!" He slammed his fist on the table, trembling.

Gwydre and the two monks accompanying her looked to one another helplessly, incredulously. The dame turned to Laird Panlamaris. "You support this subversion?"

"Subversion?" the old warrior repeated. When De Guilbe began to bellow in protest again Panlamaris reached out and forcibly pushed the man back into his chair.

"Subversion?" he said again. "You would say that to me after what happened in the gulf?"

Dame Gwydre eyed him with confusion. "Your ships tried to attack—"

"You sent powries against my warships!" Now Panlamaris's voice began to tremble and rise with righteous outrage. "Powries! Bloody-cap dwarves working in concert with the ships of Vanguard!"

"My men plucked from the water and cut open so that the vicious beasts could brighten their berets!" Captain Dunlevin Brosh cried.

"You are mad to think I would—"

But Panlamaris cut her off. "It's a coincidence, then, that the ships of Vanguard were allowed to sail free while the ships of Palmaristown were sent to the bottom, all hands slaughtered? Am I to believe that a cruel trick of fate, Dame Gwydre? Or am I to call it what it is? You, and your church"—he added, poking his finger at both Premujon and Pinower—"have allied with powries against the men of Honce!"

"That is a lie!" Father Premujon leaped from his chair as did Brother Pinower, shouting with rage. For a moment it looked as if negotiations might turn physical.

But Gwydre calmed it all, standing tall between the brothers and her opponents. "Enough!" She turned a withering eye on Laird Panlamaris. "You requested a parley. For no better reason than to offer this slander?"

Laird Panlamaris forced both De Guilbe and Brosh to sit quiet. "Is it slander, Dame of Vanguard?"

"I know nothing of any powries in the gulf. I know only that your warships gave chase to my ships, unlawfully and without provocation."

"Without provocation?" Panlamaris howled, his voice thick with incredulity. "You have come here and stolen Honce land."

"I have offered support to the autonomous Abellican Church, which chooses secession before giving in to the heinous demands of the one who calls himself king. To murder men taken honestly in honorable battle! Shame on him, and shame on you if you agree with such a thing! Laird Panlamaris was known throughout Vanguard as a man of honor, but I wonder if that is still true, if you would agree with this vile edict of King Yeslnik!"

She accompanied her strong words with a wary eye on Panlamaris's every move. She'd clearly pricked his vanity when she mentioned his reputation throughout Vanguard, which was hardly true, given that few in Vanguard had ever heard the name before.

Panlamaris sat for many heartbeats in silence, never blinking as he looked across the table at his adversary.

"Reconsider your course," he finally said. "Come back into the fold of a unified Honce. And you as well," he added, addressing the monks. "Your Father Artolivan's time is passed, but we can salvage the remnants of your order. All can be forgiven—even Father Artolivan's reputation can be protected when he quietly retires—but only if you act quickly and wisely."

"And if we do not, you will storm the walls of St. Mere Abelle once more?" Dame Gwydre asked with obvious sarcasm.

"Or perhaps I will cede Chapel Abelle to you," he said, and beside him, Father De Guilbe winced. "And lock you in your walled prison. The waters of the gulf will be mine in short order despite your evil alliance with the dwarves."

"There is no such alliance!" Gwydre insisted.

Panlamaris snorted derisively. "Whatever the case may be," he said, "I will own the gulf. The Palmaristown fleet will find allies from Delaval City soon enough, and we will chase the vile dwarves from our waters. I will hold you in this prison of your making, your own little kingdom, while the armies of King Yeslnik debark in Port Vanguard and sweep your holding out from under you. How inviting will Chapel Abelle's walls seem then, good lady?"

Dame Gwydre didn't blink, though Panlamaris's words had indeed shaken her, for she saw their prediction as a quite likely prospect. Suddenly, it was a staring contest between the two, across the table, and it became apparent quickly that Laird Panlamaris wasn't nearly as confident as he sounded.

Still Dame Gwydre didn't blink.

The six rode away soon in opposite directions.

"So now we know how Dawson escaped," Brother Pinower dared say, walking his mount beside Gwydre's on the way back. "Powries. Powries! I cannot declare them god-sent, though I surely am glad that they chose their targets well!"

"It is a minor victory," Dame Gwydre warned. "As was our victory when we turned back Laird Panlamaris's charge. Neither offer far-reaching consequences or relief if the outcome across Honce continues in favor of King Yeslnik and his brutal lairds."

"And Father De Guilbe," Father Premujon said grimly. "He will fight us to the death, and more than a few brothers, I fear, will follow his angry call."

"It is going to be a long, dark summer," said Dame Gwydre.

Send out couriers to my son," Laird Panlamaris instructed Captain Dunlevin Brosh. "Runners across the land and a battle group of your fastest warships to run the coast in the hopes that he is near enough to see their pennants. Together Milwellis and I will drive the traitorous witch from her castle and right into the sea! And then we will win the waters of the gulf, as I promised, and will bring Vanguard under the rule of Palmaristown."

"Palmaristown?" Dunlevin Brosh echoed with surprise. He immediately swallowed hard, tipping his hand that he did not mean to blurt out his thoughts so freely.

"King Yeslnik will be so grateful to us for putting the Order of Blessed Abelle back into his fold under the fine Father De Guilbe, so grateful that we crushed the insurgent Gwydre, that he will allow me to expand my holding to the north all the way to the borders of Alpinador."

"Yes, my laird," Brosh replied.

"And even if he does not," Laird Panlamaris said with a snicker. "Simply killing Gwydre and Artolivan will be worth the war."

CHAPTER 27

By Their Rules

He felt naked before her. She was slight of build, with dark hair and brown skin and dark, darting eyes full of energy and life that scrutinized and drank in every inch of Bransen. She moved with incredible grace, as if her slippers weren't even disturbing the grass as she circled him. He wondered if she looked like his mother. Certainly she appeared similar to how Garibond had described Sen Wi. And her clothes were just like his, and thus, just like his mother's.

Had she known his mother? Bransen's eyes sparkled at the thought, but his smile didn't last more than a moment as he realized that Affwin Wi could not be much older than he, perhaps not even as old.

Perhaps, then, he wondered, Affwin Wi had heard of his mother. How he wanted to ask her, but her command had been uncompromising: Stand still and stand straight, look straight ahead only and say nothing.

This went on for what seemed like ages. It occurred to Bransen that Affwin Wi was testing his patience. A true Jhesta Tu, in tune with his surroundings and comfortable in his own contemplations, could stand silently and unmoving for hours.

"You carry sword of Jhesta Tu," Affwin Wi said suddenly from the side, just out of his line of sight and so somewhat startling him. Her heavy southern accent bit off every syllable, so it took Bransen a few moments simply to decipher her sentence.

"I do," he answered, taking her extended silence as a prompt for him to finally speak.

"You dress in clothes of mystic warrior."

"Yes," said Bransen.

"You are Jhesta Tu?"

Bransen turned his head to regard her—or started to before her widening eyes and upturning snarl warned him to look back ahead. "My mother, Sen Wi, was Jhesta Tu."

"Mother?" Affwin Wi echoed in surprise. Across the small clearing, Bransen saw the bald-headed warrior's apparent relief in his chuckle.

"Sen Wi of the Walk of Clouds," said Bransen.

"I do not know this name."

"She left many years ago, twenty-one years ago," Bransen explained. "She married my father and came to Honce with him."

"You do not look of Behr. Not full."

"My father was of Honce, a monk of a Honce church, who went to Behr and the Walk of Clouds, where he learned from the . . . from your masters."

"And they taught you?"

"I never knew my father. My mother died the day I was born."

"But you know!" There was no missing the accusation in her tone.

"From the Book of Jhest. My father penned a copy of the Book of Jhest."

"You taught yourself?" the bald-headed warrior called out incredulously from across the way.

From the corner of his eye, Bransen saw Affwin Wi thrust her hand to silence him. She stormed around to stand before Bransen.

"I did," he answered. "From the book."

Affwin Wi stared at him for a moment then laughed.

"Merwal Yahna"—she indicated the bald-headed man—"says you are worthy of the sword."

Bransen gave a slight bow, which he knew to be the proper acceptance of such a compliment.

"Why are you here?" Affwin Wi asked.

"I came to find the warrior who broke a sword in the chest of King Delaval," Bransen admitted, and the woman stiffened at the apparent threat.

"I came to find the Jhesta Tu to honor my mother and to learn," Bransen quickly explained.

"You were friends with this Delaval?"

Bransen snorted. "Hardly. His successor wants me dead."

Affwin Wi waited a few moments, even glancing back at Merwal Yahna, who offered a slight nod in reply. "You came to learn?" she asked.

"To confirm that I am correct in how I follow the Book of Jhest," said Bransen. "And to learn, yes. To learn more about this philosophy that has so guided my life. I have seen the broken end of your sword, and I knew it to be Jhesta Tu. So I came to find you."

Affwin Wi began to pace back and forth before him, occasionally glancing at him, deep in contemplation. "You are worthy," she decided. "You may join with me."

Bransen felt as if his heart would pound right through the front of his chest as he considered the implications, the great step forward he had just taken.

"Your friend will leave now," Affwin Wi stated.

The shock of that jolted Bransen from his whirling thoughts. Despite the orders placed upon him, he glanced back to the far edge of the clearing, where Jameston stood between the pair who had captured him.

"Begone," Affwin Wi ordered.

Jameston eyed Bransen.

"I care not where, but far from us," Affwin Wi said. "Now. Begone."

"I am supposed to watch over the boy," said Jameston.

"He is not a boy, he is a man," said Affwin Wi. "He follows Jhesta Tu. How are you, who are not Jhesta Tu, to watch over him?"

"I was—"

"You are not," Affwin Wi barked. "Only one more time I tell you, begone."

The threat in her voice clear to hear, Jameston looked in question at Bransen again. The young warrior took a deep breath and nodded.

Jameston met Bransen's eyes for a long moment before returning that nod in farewell and slipping off into the forest.

Leaving Bransen nervous and very alone and very naked indeed under the withering gaze of Affwin Wi.

H e is powerful with your stones. Are you not interested in protecting your Laird Ethelbert?" Affwin Wi asked succinctly and directly when Father Destros of Chapel Entel balked at arming his monks with sunstones in Laird Ethelbert's hall for the meeting with the strange Highwayman.

Father Destros swallowed hard. "Are you not confident of your abilities to protect my laird?" he asked. As soon as the words left his mouth he knew that calling out Affwin Wi on such a matter might be unwise.

The woman's hand snapped up quicker than Destros could react, her poking finger right before his eye, meaning that she could have jabbed that finger right through his eye had she chosen to do so.

"He uses your stones, priest," she warned. "And he fights as Jhesta Tu. You will protect your leader, and my people will protect him." She backed away but didn't take her eyes off the man until she was out in the hallway.

Father Destros had to remind himself to breathe. She was right, of course.

This wasn't about their growing personal rivalry but about the safety of Laird Ethelbert. He went to his desk and retrieved a sunstone, pocketing several others as well. When he entered Laird Ethelbert's audience chamber a short while later, he had the sunstone firmly in his grasp. Not only would the gem allow him to counter any use of magic, it would allow for detection of magic as well. Destros figured that he might learn more than a bit about this mysterious Highwayman; he only wished that Affwin Wi hadn't been the one to deliver the suggestion.

And certainly not the command.

Jameston Sequin picked up his pace. He knew that he had already been seen and was being followed, so moving stealthily really didn't help him much.

Perhaps they were just ensuring that he continued far from Ethelbert's holding.

Jameston wasn't one to leave things to chance, however, so instead of trying to find a way to hide or outrun them, which he almost certainly could not do, he sought instead a place to face them.

These were fine warriors, he knew from bitter experience, fast and deceptive. Unlike his usual confrontations, Jameston didn't believe that the chaos of a forest favored him. He needed something solid to narrow the field of battle.

He had passed this way the previous night, knew the lay of the area. So he moved quickly to a cluster of abandoned, mostly ruined cottages. Jameston picked a fairly concealed course and stealthily gained the door and slipped inside. He went fast to the far corner and put his back against the solid wooden wall, watching the door.

He hadn't long to wait. Within moments a black-clothed figure entered the dimly illuminated, one-room cottage.

Jameston smiled, thinking it the same woman he had battled earlier that day.

"You should relax and tell me why you're following me," the scout said.

Caught by surprise, the woman froze in place, slowly swiveling her head to regard the man and his leveled and ready bow.

She stood straight and turned to face Jameston squarely.

"Don't even think about trying to get back out that door," Jameston said. "You're leaving in front of me, in case your friends are about and curious. Now, tell me why you're following me."

The woman narrowed her eyes and took a deep breath as if contemplating her options.

"You won't get to me, and you won't get out that door," Jameston promised.

"And you won't get a dagger or some other bolt into the air before I let fly. I don't miss. So start explaining why you followed me."

"You are to be gone," she said in a halting command of the language.

"I was going. Do better."

The woman lifted her chin defiantly.

Jameston pulled back on his bowstring just a bit more. He hated the thought of killing a woman, or anyone for that matter. But he had done so before and would do so again if he had to. Saving his skin was an acceptable reason.

And saving Bransen's, he realized. If this woman had come out to kill him, what did that portend for Bransen?

Jameston's face tightened, and he drew back his bowstring further. "I'm going to ask you just one more time," he said grimly.

Bransen was not wearing his mask across his eyes as he paced into Laird Ethelbert's audience hall beside Affwin Wi, instead letting it hang loosely about his neck. They strode right up to the large chair on which sat the aging laird, a disarming smile on his face.

"So this is the Highwayman," Ethelbert began. "Yes, young warrior, I have heard of you even here. I was quite sorry to learn of the death of Laird Prydae."

Bransen took the jab calmly. "He was killed of his own actions by his own champion."

"Yes, yes, I know the sad tale."

"Do you know that he was trying to rape my wife when Bannagran's axe found his chest?" Bransen asked.

Affwin Wi's hand flicked out at Bransen's side, jabbing his thigh hard. He looked at her; she glared her reply. "Proper respect," she whispered.

"That is quite all right, my huntress," Laird Ethelbert said with a light-hearted laugh. "Better that this one speak the truth in his heart so I may better come to know the truth of him, yes?"

Affwin Wi gave a curt bow.

"And I do know enough of Prydae to acknowledge what you claim. Well, let us just say that he was not capable of such an act," Ethelbert said to Bransen.

"That did not stop him from trying," Bransen replied. "Or from falsely condemning her mother"—he glanced to the monk wearing the robes of a father and standing at Ethelbert's side as he finished—"to the Samhaists."

"I surrender, I surrender," Ethelbert said with a jovial laugh. "I will not replay those events and will not argue with one who was there when I was not.

I was saddened by the death of Prydae, a man I had known as an ally in battle. Whether he deserved it or not. . . ." He let it go at that with a shrug.

Bransen accepted that reasoning with a bow.

"And you are an interesting mutt, are you not?" Ethelbert said. "You wear on your forehead the gemstones of an Abellican monk, yet you fight with the techniques—and clothing—of the southern mystics."

"My father was of the Order of Blessed Abelle, my mother a Jhesta Tu," said Bransen.

"I know that," Ethelbert said. "I met your father and your mother on their return from Behr. They came through my city two decades ago, and I granted them an audience. It did not end well for them, I assume."

Bransen's face went from a sudden brightening to a dark cloud at the grim reminder of Bran and Sen Wi's respective fates.

"I warned your father that the brothers would not be as tolerant as he hoped," Ethelbert said.

Bransen felt as if the ground were shifting under his feet. He had come in here full of confidence and determination, and now Laird Ethelbert had maneuvered the conversation to a place that clearly had Bransen on edge. He wanted to hear more of Ethelbert's encounter with his parents, and he knew that such desire ensured that he would not.

Ethelbert read him perfectly and quickly deflected the conversation yet again.

"You know of my struggle with Laird Yeslnik?" he asked.

"I thought he called himself King Yeslnik," Bransen replied with enough obvious disdain to draw a large smile from Ethelbert.

"He can call himself God Yeslnik if it pleases him," Ethelbert replied. "Because when I kill him it will matter not at all."

Bransen didn't react.

"So I have met him as you desired," Ethelbert said to Affwin Wi, suddenly sounding very bored with it all. "What is the purpose? Is he friend, or is he foe?"

"He states that he is Jhesta Tu," the woman replied. "He will pledge loyalty to Laird Ethelbert."

Bransen looked at her in surprise.

"Because I am his superior," Affwin Wi clarified boldly. "And the decision is not his to make." She turned to regard Bransen directly. "Is that not true?" she asked, invoking a clear test of his loyalty.

Bransen paused, but only for a moment, before answering, "Yes."

"Is there anything more?" asked Ethelbert.

Affwin Wi studied Bransen for a few moments then said, "Speak your mind freely. This is your last chance to do so."

Bransen didn't know exactly what that might mean. "I am Jhesta Tu," he explained. "In part. But because of my heritage and my experience, I am more. I have found the promise of my father, the joining—"

Affwin Wi hit him so hard across the face that he was sitting on the floor before he had even registered the pain of the blow.

"You are Jhesta Tu, or you are not," she said while Ethelbert laughed. "Which are you?"

"I am Jhesta Tu," Bransen said, lowering his gaze to the floor.

M y arm's getting tired and I just might let go," Jameston warned.
      "You must be gone," the woman replied.

"I was going—" Jameston started to say, but he bit it off, suddenly realizing what she really meant. He had tracked them and had found them. He had fought this very woman and believed he was beating her when her friend had intervened.

He knew of them, which made him an intolerable threat.

"So that's what it is, is it?" he said. "You can't have me wandering on my way knowing what I know." He gave a little laugh. "Well, I know a lot more now, I expect. . . ."

He heard the pop behind him, a sharp bang and the splintering of wood, followed by what he thought was a hard punch in his back just behind his right hip.

Jameston instinctively glanced down, and then he knew. For the nun'chu'ku had blown right through the wall behind him and into his back with such force that Jameston's leather jerkin was pushed out in the front.

"Oh, now," Jameston muttered, realizing that the pole had gone right through him. Already the feeling was leaving his legs, and he was having a hard time drawing breath.

He looked up at the woman, who stood easily now, smiling at him.

Jameston managed a nod. Growling, he drew back and sent his arrow at her. She got her arm up with amazing speed, but the arrow bored right through her forearm and into her forehead. She was still smiling when she fell dead to the floor.

Jameston shuddered, a thousand fires exploding within him as the warrior with the shaven head—it had to be that one, Jameston knew—tugged the nun'chu'ku out of him and back through the wall.

Jameston was sitting when the fierce warrior came around the front and entered through the door. The scout wanted to put his bow up for one last shot, for one chance to kill this vicious man, but when he lifted his left arm, he only then realized that he wasn't even holding the bow anymore, that it was on the floor at his feet.

Merwal Yahna crouched over the dead woman, then rose and glanced at Jameston. He would come over and finish the job, Jameston figured, but surprisingly the man just snorted and turned away.

Jameston watched as the warrior cradled his fallen friend, then carried her out of the house.

And as he left, the darkness began to close in on Jameston Sequin.

CHAPTER 28

Bloodletting

Mcwigik leaned his elbows on the top of the small barrel boat tower, staring at the distant fires and candles twinkling in windows. So many lights. More than Mcwigik had ever seen, more than he had ever imagined possible. For a hundred years he had looked across the waters of Mithranidoon, where even a single firelight was an oddity. For many years of life before that, the largest collection of people together he had ever seen was the town of Hard Rocks on the Weathered Isles.

But even that place, once thought impressive, couldn't have been one-twentieth the size of this!

"Got to be Palmaristown," Bikelbrin said, coming up beside him. "We're at the mouth o' the river, and that's where Shiknickel said it'd be."

"We get ten of us boys together, and we call it a town," Mcwigik replied, shaking his hairy head. "Thirty and we call it a city, a hundred and it's a kingdom."

"Lot o' people in there," Bikelbrin agreed.

"Lot o' blood," his friend reminded.

"We get killed to death in there, and there's none to be burying our hearts."

"Bah, but we won't be knowin' that anyway!" Mcwigik said with a laugh, and he and Bikelbrin clapped each other on the shoulders.

The powrie shiver stayed offshore as the lights went down in the city, and only then did the eager dwarves resume their pedaling, moving very slowly and quietly. With a hundred thirty warriors among all the boats, they figured they'd find themselves outnumbered a hundred to one or more.

Dreams of berets shining brightly enough to light up the night carried them on their way.

B ransen sat on the roof of the inn in Ethelbert dos Entel, his legs tightly crossed before him, his hands on his bent knees and his eyes skyward, basking in the contemplative light of a million stars. His thoughts were out there and within himself all at once, a meditative state of serenity in the face of the great questions of purpose and being. To face the many questions of his future meant that he needed the cleansing experience of being fully in the present, of recognizing his mind-body connection and putting that in context with his greater connection to the universe around him. He needed to find that moment of perfect, unfettered clarity, that complete sensation of peace.

But the stunning revelations and twists of the last day stayed with him, nagging him with doubts, particularly on where Cadayle might fit into his new allegiance to Affwin Wi. She had dismissed Jameston out of hand; what might that portend for Cadayle?

Bransen took a deep breath and threw away that unsettling thought. He forced himself back inside his *ki-chi-kree*, his line of life energy, and then sent that line spiritually up into the dark and starry sky.

A different sensation tugged at him, though, and suddenly and unexpectedly, a feeling that something, somehow, was amiss.

Bransen interrupted his meditative journey to refocus on this disturbance, this ill feeling. It had direction, like a cry of pain, out in the dark night.

Bransen let his soul slide through the soul stone of the brooch and escape his corporeal form. He started away spiritually, but hesitantly, until he felt again that strange sensation that something was terribly wrong.

Then he moved with purpose, willing his noncorporeal form over the city's wall and out across the empty fields to the edge of a forest he had traversed that very morning.

T he docks were quiet, those few guards on duty either asleep or gambling, throwing bones against a warehouse wall. One or another would occasionally glance at the harbor to check the masts of the few ships in port.

Barrel boats didn't have masts.

The powrie craft came in slowly, their underwater rams prodding the sand below the wharves so that even as the dwarves climbed from their craft and slowly walked across the top arc of those rams, they remained out of sight to the distracted guards up on the boardwalk.

"Beat that point!" one gambling sentry shouted triumphantly as the bones rolled a strong number.

The words had barely left his mouth when a mallet cracked down atop his head, breaking his skull and shattering every bone in his neck.

"As ye asked!" a dwarf explained.

How the other four guards started to scramble! Started, but never even made their feet, as a score of powries, weapons flashing and swung with bloodlust, fell over them. They cried out for their companions on the docks but those sleeping or inattentive men and women were already dead, powries already wetting their berets in freshly spilled blood.

The dwarves methodically formed into six units, each crew as a battle group. They used the very bones the men had been rolling to determine which of the six would stay behind and watch the boats for the first forays.

"Not to worry," many told the losers. "Plenty to kill."

Five battle groups moved up into sleeping, unwitting Palmaristown, a hundred weapons, a hundred serrated knives to open veins.

Like a plague of hungry rats they roved through the town, sweeping through houses and tenements, at one point overwhelming a group still drinking and shouting in one of the nearby taverns.

They came in, and they killed. They dipped their bloody caps, and they moved on.

After a very brief while, the crew still on the docks realized that their companions were into powrie bloodlust now and would not be coming back, so they, too, went up into the city. As their friends had assured them, there were plenty still to kill.

It took nearly an hour, with hundreds and hundreds murdered, before Palmaristown even began to organize any semblance of defense against the intruders. Many, many more people died to powrie blades before the dwarves faced any real resistance. Even then, with armies of both Prince Milwellis and Laird Panlamaris out of the city fighting in the war, the fierce powries pressed on.

With Laird Ethelbert on the run in the south and his own mighty warships securing the gulf, Laird Panlamaris had never imagined such an attack.

The bloodbath went on throughout the night, a night that would be known in the region for decades hence as "the dark of long murder," and, when the powries finally did retreat, they set fire to every structure they passed so that, by the time their barrel boats pushed back out into the river, a quarter of the great city was ablaze.

By the time those fires finally died away days later, two of every three structures in the great city—the second largest in Honce—lay in ruins. One in every three residents within the city was dead.

Warships sailed fast for home as the word of the tragedy spread, but the powries, with their shining berets, slipped past them unnoticed into the open waters of the gulf.

U sing the cat's-eye gemstone set in his brooch, Bransen had no trouble navigating the darkness beyond the wall of Ethelbert dos Entel. He ran on light feet, falling into the malachite as well as the soul stone to provide added lift and distance to each desperate step.

Soldiers walking perimeter outside the wall called to him, but he ignored them and sprinted on. They couldn't hope to catch him with his magically enhanced speed, and even the few spears they threw out at him fell far short of the mark.

Bransen didn't look back, his focus squarely ahead as he tried to recall the exact route his spirit had taken as he tried to hear again the disturbance that had sounded so clear in his state of meditation.

His heart beat even faster when he entered the small forest. He nearly fell over with fear as he skidded to a stop before the small cluster of ruined houses. Behind him in the east the sky was still dark, still hours before the dawn.

Bransen tried to hear again the psychic cry, but all was silent. He summoned his courage and ran into the house, to find Jameston crumpled on the floor, blood pooled about him.

"No!" Bransen fell over him, reaching into the soul stone, bringing forth mighty waves of healing magic.

But Jameston was already cold.

Bransen dug deeper, seeking any flicker of life energy, any notion that the man's soul had not yet fled, seeking resurrection itself, something even the greatest of gemstone users had always believed impossible, something Abelle himself had never managed.

Because it was not possible. Jameston, this man he had come to know as a friend, as a teacher and mentor, as a father, even, was lost to him.

CHAPTER 29

Darkness Rising

A storm?" Brother Pinower asked. He stood on the wall with Brother Giavno, looking out to the west. The sun was not yet halfway down from its zenith to the horizon, but a dull pall had already settled on the land, a premature twilight.

Brother Giavno was shaking his head before Pinower even asked the obvious question. "No. Not a storm, not clouds."

Pinower looked at him curiously, and the man's grim expression, horrified even, had the young monk even more perplexed.

"Smoke," Brother Giavno explained.

"Smoke?" Pinower echoed, turning fast to regard again the strange phenomenon. "But that is too far . . . I see no flames. It is out to the horizon and more. . . ."

Brother Giavno didn't bother to respond. It was smoke, he knew. Somewhere far to the west something big was burning.

More monks came to the wall over the next few hours as the daylight waned and the gigantic cloud in the west grew darker and more ominous. Across the field the army of Palmaristown seemed equally engaged by the spectacle.

Many brothers stayed on the wall after night fell to view the sky three-quarters full of stars and one quarter, the western edge, an eerie combination of blackness built on the foundation of an ominous orange glow.

Dawn's light showed the cloud expanding still, and that morning everyone in St. Mere Abelle moved to the towers and the walls to view the spectacle, even Dame Gwydre and Father Artolivan.

The old father groaned at the site.

"What could it be?" Brother Pinower asked from behind him.

"Palmaristown," the old monk said with certainty.

T he Highwayman is still out there," King Yeslnik said to his perfumed wife. "And you think he is coming to slay you?" Lady Olym asked.

"Do not be flippant with me, wife!"

"He didn't kill your Uncle Delaval."

"You know nothing!" Yeslnik scolded. "We found his sword. . . ."

"There are many swords."

"Not like his!"

Lady Olym sighed and waved him away. "Perhaps he dropped it or someone took it from him."

"Plundered his corpse, perhaps?" said Yeslnik in a sneering tone that struck hard. "That would not please you, would it?"

"I do not know of what you are speaking," she said, but the possibility worded by Yeslnik had clearly knocked her off-balance here, and there was little conviction in her assertion.

King Yeslnik slapped her hard across the face. It was the first time he had ever done anything remotely like that. When she lifted her hands to try to deflect him, he punched her squarely in the nose. She staggered back and fell on her backside, staring at him in wonder.

"I will hear no more of the Highwayman from you. Ever," Yeslnik warned.

"You spoke of him first!"

"Ever!" he repeated threateningly. Wailing, Olym curled into a fetal position.

"Ever," King Yeslnik said again, leaning over close. "Bannagran will kill him. Kill him!" he shouted suddenly, and the startled Lady Olym jerked and wailed. Yeslnik whirled away from the pitiful woman and plopped into the chair at his desk, dropping an elbow on the arm and chewing at his nails.

Had he failed in fleeing the field before Ethelbert dos Entel? Should he have accepted the losses and pressed Ethelbert to the edge of the sea to be done with this foolishness quickly? But Ethelbert's assassins would have killed him!

He lurched to his feet and began pacing nervously. "Panlamaris will deal with those traitors at Chapel Abelle," he said to himself. "Why is this so hard? Why won't these fools just concede to the inevitable?"

"You are king," came an unexpectedly supportive voice. Yeslnik spun about to see his wife sitting up. He looked at her curiously, then more closely.

"You are the King of Honce," she said again. "Only the prideful laird of that miserable city in the south and the traitorous fools at Chapel Abelle refuse to see it. All the rest is yours."

Yeslnik continued to stare at her, but he felt compelled to move over to her. He fell to his knees, very close, and stared into her eyes, one swelling from his punch.

"Gather the lairds who follow you," Olym suggested. "The dozens who love you. Lend them warriors to extend their holdings to engulf all of those flattened by you in your glorious march and by Prince Milwellis. Take the Inner Coast and the Mantis Arm. Take all those communities along the Belt-and-Buckle. Take them all, and let Ethelbert in his city and the monks in their chapel watch from their walls as the world, as King Yeslnik's Honce, goes along without them."

Yeslnik's jaw hung open, for never had he heard such advice from this source. He was amazed that Lady Olym even knew about the march of Milwellis in the east or of the many communities he had run across and run over to Ethelbert dos Entel and back. He continued staring for just a few heartbeats. Slowly shaking his head with disbelief, he pulled her close and kissed her more passionately than he had in a long, long while.

Lady Olym pushed him back after a few more heartbeats. "They cannot come out against you, or you will destroy them," she said.

"Delaval warships will blockade Ethelbert dos Entel," King Yeslnik proclaimed.

"Yes!" Olym squealed.

"And Chapel Abelle!" said Yeslnik. "A prison of their own making!"

"Yes! Oh, yes!"

"And I will send Panlamaris by land and by sea into Vanguard, and Dame Gwydre will know her folly!"

"Lead them yourself! You are the King of Honce!"

Yeslnik tackled her, showering her with kisses all over her face.

"Take me, my king!" she cried. "Ravish me!"

Yeslnik nearly swooned, overwhelmed, for he had never seen his wife in such a state of passion aimed at him before. His confidence grew with every kiss and every caress.

It was good to be the king.

"Panlamaris," said the whispers across the wall as the lone rider stormed across the field toward St. Mere Abelle. "That is Laird Panlamaris himself!"

Some calls went out for archers or for gemstone assaults as the large and imposing Laird of Palmaristown drew closer to the wall, but those were few and without conviction.

That cloud of smoke rising in the west, that sign of Palmaristown burning, served as a white flag of temporary truce in the stunned sensibilities of all who glimpsed it. Although Palmaristown had come against St. Mere Abelle, even in the face of the executions of Fatuus and the other brothers, the image of certain horror occurring in the west allowed Panlamaris to make this ride unhindered, right to the base of St. Mere Abelle's high wall.

Behind him on the field a few other riders halfheartedly followed, but it was obvious that the laird's seemingly reckless ride had caught his own soldiers by surprise.

"To eternal flames with you, damned witch!" the man called when he came in sight of the Dame of Vanguard. "The blood of thousands, of mothers and children, stains your pretty hands. How will you wash it away?"

Dame Gwydre rocked back on her heels.

"She is here, as are those in support of her!" Father Premujon yelled down at Panlamaris. "Whatever ill has befallen your city—"

"Powries!" the fiery old laird interrupted. "Powries by the score. Powries set loose by the witch of Vanguard. What horror have you set upon the folk of Honce, wicked Gwydre?"

"I did no such thing," Gwydre managed to reply.

"As in the harbor with my ships!" Panlamaris yelled. "And now a cowardly assault on a sleeping city, to cut the throats of children and burn the buildings to ash! Eternal fires for you, I say! And, oh, but do not doubt that your precious Vanguard will feel the wrath of Palmaristown, of Panlamaris and Milwellis, of King Yeslnik and all the goodly folk of Honce! They will know you, powrie friend, and they will loathe you! I await the day when Dame Gwydre is dragged through the streets of Palmaristown that all may spit upon she who invited the powries back to Honce!"

He whirled his mount around and thundered away, and not an arrow or bolt of gemstone lightning reached out after him.

The siege of St. Mere Abelle ended within the hour, Laird Panlamaris and his army moving with all haste back to the west.

Later that same day Prince Milwellis's army appeared in the distant south, moving with great speed to the west, to home, to the ruins and the dead.

CHAPTER 30

No!

How had this happened? How was it possible that this man, so competent, so formidable, so seasoned, had been taken down? What manner of foe had come against Jameston to corner him and defeat such a warrior? Jameston had successfully battled trolls and powries and barbarians, even giants for decades. Who could possibly have brought him down?

There was only one answer. Jhesta Tu.

Bransen knelt over Jameston for a long while, cradling the man's head, trying to come to terms with his loss. The minutes continued to slide past and still Bransen sat, recalling his first meeting with Jameston in the wilds of southern Alpinador, when the scout had joined in a fight against a company of Ancient Badden's trolls. He remembered the look on the face of Crazy Vaughna when she realized that it was Jameston Sequin, *the* Jameston Sequin, who had joined in their cause.

Walking with Jameston these last weeks, Bransen had come to appreciate that awestruck expression of Vaughna's all the more, for truly this man more than matched his impressive reputation.

Now Jameston was gone.

How alone Bransen felt at that terrible, terrible moment. Not just alone but confused, consumed by the unsettling notion that he had played a role in this, that he had allowed Affwin Wi to dismiss Jameston and send him away. All those thoughts swirled and coalesced, first reducing Bransen into a battered and defeated shell, weak in the knees and unable to hold back his tears.

But the stretch of pity and self-pity and hopelessness lasted only a few heartbeats, replaced by a bubbling rage that turned Bransen's churning gut into a pit of pure acid. He gently laid Jameston's head back and jumped up to his feet, seeking focus, seeking an outlet.

He considered the hole in the wooden wall, punched through with tremendous force. He turned Jameston's body over a bit and noted that the same blunt force had hit him with enough power to skewer him. An image of Merwal Yahna and his exotic weapon flashed in Bransen's mind.

Jameston had been near the wall, his back to it when slain. Bransen turned to see what his friend might have witnessed at that moment and noted blood on the floor by the door. He went to it, following the clear trail of blood droplets to the back of the cottage, a short distance into the forest, where he found the remains of a makeshift pyre and the charred and shrunken remains of a person. He saw a black silk slipper and knew beyond any doubt. No simple soldier had taken down Jameston Sequin.

"Jhesta Tu," Bransen mouthed as he regarded that slipper, and knew from its size that it had been worn by the woman who had battled Jameston while Bransen had fought Merwal Yahna in their first meeting with Laird Ethelbert's assassins. At least those two Jhesta Tu had hunted Jameston Sequin. They could not have done so without the permission, indeed the command, of Affwin Wi.

Bransen felt his jaw go tight, the muscles in his arms and legs twitching in anticipation. It took him a long time to slow and steady his breathing, to find his center and his mind-body connection. He couldn't hold that connection for long.

Too overwhelmed was he, too betrayed and confused. And too angry. Only once in his young life had Bransen Garibond felt such rage: on that terrible day when Laird Prydae had abducted Cadayle for his sexual pleasure and given Callen to Bernivvigar to be murdered. That same terrible time when he had learned of the murder of his father, Garibond Womak. That rage had allowed him to sit within the branches of a bonfire and feel no heat. That moment had incensed him to kill.

Bransen turned to the east, toward Ethelbert dos Entel. Toward Affwin Wi. Sprinting nearly the entire way, Bransen reached the wall of Ethelbert dos Entel before dawn. The sky over the Mirianic glowed in predawn light, but stars remained clear in the west. The city was only beginning to awaken. The Highwayman used that slumber to his advantage. He could have walked in through the gate; Affwin Wi had introduced him to the guards there, and she carried great weight in the city, but something deep within, his Highwayman instincts, told him that stealth was his ally here.

He moved along the wall, listening carefully, until he came to an out-of-the-way corner where he could climb and keep the still-dark western sky at his back. There, he fell into the powers of the malachite and used his strength and training to easily scale the twelve-foot barrier. He peered over the wall, the cat's-eye allowing him to see as clearly as if the sun was up in the east, with complete confidence that the guard he then viewed a dozen strides away could not see him.

The Highwayman went over silently, the dark sky behind him presenting no silhouette for the half-aware sentry to observe. He could have killed that sentry—it would have been an easier course than slipping across the wall top and down the other side—but he dismissed that notion out of hand. Still utilizing the powers of the malachite to lighten his step, Bransen crossed over quickly, allowing himself to drop to the ground in near silence because of heightened balance.

Though he could see Castle Ethelbert, it took him a few moments to get his bearings and determine the best way to navigate the crowded city, time he didn't have to spare as more sounds of the city awakening filled his ears and the sky brightened a bit more. He started at a trot, quickly a run, letting that low but imposing castle guide him. Affwin Wi and her group were in a wing of the castle. In short order he could see the balcony from which his spirit had answered Jameston's dying call.

He could just go back in the room. It was unlikely the others knew he had left or had learned their terrible secret. Prudence called him to that plan, but anger prevented it.

"No," he said, shaking his head. This was no time for secrecy and plotting, for deception and caution. Or perhaps it was just such a time. Bransen, so consumed, didn't care. "No." He walked in the front door of the castle's far western wing, the complex afforded Affwin Wi's group.

"When did you go out?" Pactset Va greeted him immediately. "How did you get out?" Va shook his head, his topknot dancing with the movement as he called across the way to his companion Moh Li, noting Bransen's dark expression.

Moh Li responded quickly to the call, stepping through a hanging curtain to look curiously from Pactset Va to Bransen.

"You did not tell me that this one left," Pactset Va reprimanded.

"He did not," Moh Li replied. "Not while I guarded." Both men turned suspicious stares upon Bransen.

"I left from my balcony."

Pactset Va waved a finger at him immediately, the man's face screwing up into a stern look. "You cannot do this!"

The Highwayman smiled slyly and walked right up to that poking finger.

"You leave only on the command of—"

"Shut up," the Highwayman cut him off.

Pactset Va's eyes popped wide.

"Shut. Up." the Highwayman said again, biting off each word through his gritted smile.

Pactset Va slapped him hard across the face.

"Shut up now," the Highwayman clarified, smiling wider and staring at him, oblivious to the sting of the slap or his red face.

The man moved to slap him again, but this time the Highwayman used Pactset Va's incredulity to get inside the man's defenses. He opened up a sudden and furious barrage of punches, left and right, into the face of the man. Five short punches sent Pactset Va back hard into the wall. Va brought both his arms up high to block, but the Highwayman leaped and spun a complete circuit, kicking expertly right below the man's blocking elbows, scoring a hard kick into Pactset Va's belly.

The Highwayman landed softly and leaped and spun again immediately, bringing his foot around to connect solidly on the side of his lurching opponent's face, launching Pactset Va into a sidelong somersault. He landed hard on the floor, semiconscious and groaning.

"You will pay the price!" Moh Li cried.

Without even a glance at him, the Highwayman strode up to tower over Pactset Va. Still not looking at Li, the Highwayman drove his foot down hard on Pactset Va's throat.

Moh Li gave a cry that told the Highwayman the man was charging at his back. At the last possible moment, the Highwayman reached down and grabbed the sword on his left hip with a backhand grip so that he easily pulled it free and snapped it back out under his right arm, blade stabbing behind him.

Just as Moh Li leaped for him.

The man collided with the Highwayman, but not hard, for he was scrambling desperately to avoid impalement. The Highwayman's sword angled down, and Moh Li crumpled to the floor. The Highwayman pulled the blade free and spun to see him writhing in agony. Moh Li had come in with a flying kick and had taken the sword into the back of his thigh, a deep, deep wound. Screaming, he flailed around now, trying to stem the blood flow.

"Shut up," the Highwayman said to Moh Li, kicking him in the face, silencing him. Perhaps he would bleed out, perhaps not. The Highwayman didn't care. Perhaps Pactset Va would choke from the throat kick, perhaps not. Images of dead Jameston filled Bransen's mind, and he did not care about these men's suffering.

He stalked through the room and kicked open the opposite door into the small anteroom before Affwin Wi's large chamber entryway. That second door swung wide before Bransen crossed to it. There stood Merwal Yahna staring at him, staring at his bloody sword. No look of revulsion showed on Merwal Yahna's face, though. Indeed, the man's smile widened wickedly.

The Highwayman reacted with anger, leaping ahead, but Merwal Yahna anticipated the charge, for he was moving even as Bransen did. The warrior from Behr leaped backward and to the side, and the Highwayman went through the door in a rush, skidding to an abrupt stop, acutely aware that Merwal Yahna was not alone in the room.

"You act rashly, warrior," said Affwin Wi, standing in a corner of the room. "Jhesta Tu do not act in such a manner."

"But they murder without cause," Bransen replied through clenched teeth.

"He found his friend," reasoned Merwal Yahna.

Bransen turned sharply to Affwin Wi and started to ask why, but he bit it back. It didn't matter; he didn't even want to know. He presented his sword toward Merwal Yahna, inviting him to battle.

The warrior snapped out his nun'chu'ku in a dizzying, spinning blur, ending his fast movement with a battle shout. He held the poles straight before him, leather cord taut, the muscles on his arms tight under the black silk sleeves of his shirt.

At the back of the room, Affwin Wi similarly exploded into sudden motion, whirling her arms in wide circles as she leaped into a wide-legged, ready crouch.

"A'shin ti!" Merwal Yahna shouted at her. "Abidu a'shin ti!"

Bransen didn't know the exact translation of the phrase, but he recognized it as plea from the warrior that Affwin Wi allow him to fight this battle alone. From the corner of his eye, he watched Affwin Wi relax and stand up straight, bringing her hands together before her chest and offering a slight bow before stepping back.

Bransen's gaze shifted back to Merwal Yahna. The Behrenese's face was locked in a stare of absolute concentration and simmering eagerness. The man went into another flourish, releasing the nun'chu'ku with his right hand and sending it into a violent spin with his left, around and up, over his head and around, and around the back of his head, where he caught it in his right hand and continued the flow around the other side.

The Highwayman didn't let him continue his display. Bransen rushed forward with a sudden and ferocious stab, retraction, and slash of his blade. Neither came close to hitting the agile Merwal Yahna, who deftly reversed the spin of his own weapon to send it snapping out to intercept.

But Bransen leaped to his right, using the malachite to enhance the great jump and turning his hips to keep his shoulders squared to the warrior from Behr as he sailed past. He bent his legs as he came over a chair, planting one foot on the arm, the other on the back and riding it to the ground as it tipped over.

Merwal Yahna came in fast pursuit, but Bransen hooked his foot under the arm of the chair as it and he descended. He kicked out, launching the chair Merwal Yahna's way.

Merwal Yahna blocked the spinning chair with a straightened leg, then battered it aside with his nun'chu'ku, breaking off pieces with the mighty blows.

The Highwayman seized the moment and leaped at him, kicking and stabbing. Up came the nun'chu'ku, spinning and snapping. Bransen blocked with his foot, then with his blade, then again to the left and back to the right. He stabbed ahead and Merwal Yahna's weapon was there, wood slapping the side of the sword, and again a second time.

There was no thinking here, no movements other than instinct as the two warriors let loose tremendous volleys and counters, wood hitting metal, sword slapping nun'chu'ku, a leg thrusting forward to steal momentum from a swinging pole and absorb the blow, an open palm slapping flat against the side of the sword, turning the thrust harmlessly aside.

It went on for a long while, a furious explosion that rolled and rolled from one end of the room to the other. Only Affwin Wi, so trained in the ways of battle, witnessed it. To her, it was a thing of beauty, a dance of precision and discipline.

To any other onlookers, it would have seemed a thing of chaos, a blur of movement and a cacophony of discordant sounds. Untrained onlookers would have gasped through every heartbeat, thinking a kill to be had.

Affwin Wi just smiled, pleased that her lover was showing himself so well here and excited by the possibilities of this stranger who had taught himself the ways of the warrior.

Bransen stepped quickly back against a sudden burst of snapping nun'chu'ku thrusts, the pole popping forward in the air before him in rapid succession. He felt the broken chair behind his heels and jumped backward reflexively, landing lightly.

Over the chair came Merwal Yahna, leaping high in a spin. He landed with his right side facing Bransen and unrolled his right arm out at the Highwayman, the nun'chu'ku lashing out like an extension of his arm.

But Bransen had seen the movement in his mind before it had happened. As soon as Merwal Yahna had leaped the chair, Bransen had known the end of the play. More importantly, he knew that his opponent could not easily alter the ending.

Instead of backing away, the Highwayman went forward and leaped high above the swing of the nun'chu'ku. He threw his sword up past Merwal Yahna, a daring distraction. Bransen turned as he sailed and kicked out, scoring a stunning blow to Merwal Yahna's face, snapping the man's head back viciously. He landed close to the warrior, his chest against Merwal Yahna's outstretched hand. Without slowing, Bransen punched his right arm under Merwal Yahna's elbow, then stabbed it out across the man's back, planting his hand firmly against Merwal Yahna's opposite shoulder blade. At the same time, with his left hand he grabbed Merwal Yahna's weapon hand. As soon as he had executed this locking hold, Bransen drove forward and upward hard, throwing all his weight into the move. Merwal Yahna, dazed by the kick, still stuck in the momentum of his initial attack, couldn't begin to turn about appropriately to respond.

Bransen heard the pop of the man's shoulder coming out of joint, and he drove ahead again to accentuate the move and the pain. He released fast, unafraid of the nun'chu'ku at that point, and spun backward, lifting his foot in a circle kick that caught Merwal Yahna square in the chest, knocking him back several steps. To his credit the tough warrior didn't fall, but the Highwayman pursued, jabbing hard with a left-right combination, avoiding Merwal Yahna's attempt to block with his right arm and hitting him squarely in the face.

The Highwayman faked his next punch, half throwing a right before retracting with enough force to drive himself into a backward lean. From there he lifted his left leg up high, so high, straight over his head!

His leg came down hard, outstretched and atop the dislocated shoulder with tremendous force. For all his toughness, Merwal Yahna blanched and lurched to the side. Bransen waded in with another combination of heavy blows, positioning his opponent perfectly to drive his knee into Merwal Yahna's gut.

The Highwayman sprang back then leaped up in a spin, his flying foot catching the doubling-over Merwal Yahna on the side of the head with such power that it sent him into a sidelong somersault. He landed hard and awkwardly, growling with agony, and grasped his torn shoulder in a mighty grip, groaning through gritted teeth. He was tense and curled, but he couldn't hold it, and gradually, he melted back to the floor, his growl receding with his strength.

Bransen leaped over him in a crouch, left hand extended against Merwal Yahna's face, lining up a surely fatal blow from his cocked, right arm.

And a blow did fall, a hard one, but it fell against Bransen before he could finish Merwal Yahna. Affwin Wi's kick staggered him to the side, and he had to fall over into a roll and then come back to his feet, spinning to face this newest opponent.

"You murdered Jameston!" he accused.

"He attacked those sent to make certain he had left."

"No!" Bransen retorted. "Never! Not unless he were forced to defend himself!"

Affwin Wi settled back easily and began to laugh. "Foolish young man," she said.

"I came here as a fellow traveler in the way of Jhesta Tu!" Bransen shouted, and Affwin Wi laughed louder.

"I am not Jhesta Tu!" she shouted back, and the words hit Bransen much harder than her kick ever could have. "Hou-lei!"

Hou-lei? The title rolled around Bransen's head for few moments until he connected it to his reading of the Book of Jhest. Hou-lei, the tradition that had inspired Jhesta Tu, an old mercenary warrior class, a tradition of divorcing fighting skill from moral judgment, of preparing for battle under the will of whatever sheik or king paid most handsomely. A Hou-lei warrior was an instrument, a weapon, and nothing more.

Bransen stood there blinking in disbelief, but everything suddenly made sense. "You are paid assassins," he said.

Affwin Wi shrugged as if that fact should have been apparent long before. She came forward suddenly and viciously, her arms waving alternating circles before her, her hands set in hooklike fashion, thumbs tucked, fingers tightly bent at the knuckles.

The Highwayman dropped his left leg back and fell lower, his own arms up before him.

As they closed, Affwin Wi kept spinning her arms, occasionally jabbing forward. Bransen blocked those first few stabs easily or turned aside from them, eventually coming to the same rhythm as Affwin Wi.

She picked up the pace. He stabbed with his hands. Back and forth they circled and slapped, hands stabbing like striking snakes, hands striking hands. They went faster, more furiously. Affwin Wi dodged one of the Highwayman's punches and kicked her leg out right before her. Bransen's shin came up to meet it. They hopped about, each keeping a leg in the air, waving, kicking, punching, slapping like a pair of cranes battling over a frog in a crowded pond.

Unused to this style of fighting, Bransen could not keep up. He was hit by more blows than he landed. Every strike the expert Affwin Wi delivered was in perfect balance, her weight behind the blow, her angle precise.

Bransen knew he couldn't win this kind of fight. He suddenly threw himself to the side and into a roll, coming up with Merwal Yahna's nun'chu'ku in his hands. He put the weapon into motion—it had looked so easy in Merwal Yahna's hands—and nearly clipped himself in the head. Affwin Wi laughed at him and charged.

Bransen dropped the exotic weapon, reached into his brooch, and met her flying form with a lightning discharge that sent her flying back the way she came. She landed and stumbled, fell over and rolled, came back to her feet and stumbled again, her teeth chattering, her black hair jumping wildly.

The Highwayman focused on the image of Jameston, focused on his brooch, focused on the power of Abellican gemstones. He enacted a serpentine shield and became a living torch, using the malachite and his fury to hurl himself at the Hou-lei warrior.

She shrieked and tried to dodge, and Bransen knew he had her. He crashed into her, bringing both to the floor. Bransen closed his eyes, not wanting to watch the flames curl her flesh.

She laughed at him, punched him in the face, and wriggled away.

Bransen looked down to see that his flames were no more. He looked up at Affwin Wi to see her smiling smugly, her hand extended, a gemstone in her open palm. A sunstone. The stone of antimagic.

"I know your secret, Highwayman," she said.

Bransen tried to yell his fury, but his words came out garbled, indecipherable, Storklike. His thoughts rushed back to the moment on the trail in the fight with the trolls, when a blow to the head had dislodged his gemstone and left him stumbling and helpless.

No, he decided. This was not akin to that. This was a gemstone countering his own. Damn it! He would be the stronger! He reached more deeply into the brooch and this time felt the connection through the static of the sunstone. Bransen leaped to his feet with a growl and charged. Another furious exchange brought him around to the side. Still, he couldn't keep up with the speed of Affwin Wi, so he focused his blocks and counters to his right side.

Predictably, the Hou-lei warrior seized the opening and launched a left hook Bransen could not block.

He didn't try to, taking the hit and using the force of the blow along with his own sudden retreat to open the ground between them enough to scramble to the side and grab his sword where he'd dropped it. But the incredibly fast Affwin Wi was there to stomp on the blade. Bransen had to let go of the hilt and throw his arm up to block. To his credit, he did deflect her short left jab, but her right hand swept in from behind and above, slashing down and across.

The Highwayman fell back and tried to turn his head to make the hit a glancing one, and indeed, he was nearly out of Affwin Wi's reach.

But she wasn't trying to strike him. Her slender fingers caught the edge of Bransen's magical brooch and wrenched it with her as he fell away, tearing the skin, tearing away the magic.

He was the Stork again, so suddenly, so helplessly, blood running freely from his torn forehead. He somehow got one leg under himself and stumbled halfway to standing, but Affwin Wi was there, dropping a series of heavy and strategic blows, more to taunt and hurt him than to finish him.

Bransen felt himself falling. Affwin Wi caught him by the shirt and hauled him to his feet. Before he could determine if he had the stability to stand, she punched him in the face. He fell away, Affwin Wi leaping a circle kick that snapped his head to the side violently.

All the world was spinning. Bransen hit the floor facedown and helpless. Affwin Wi could finish him with a stomp to the back of his neck. He tried to turn and nearly got to his side when her foot slammed him in the gut, doubling him up. Then she kicked him in the face, straightening him out again.

With a sudden burst of energy, Bransen pushed up to his hands and knees and scrabbled away, Affwin Wi laughing behind him. He thought of Jameston, dead Jameston, and of Cadayle, whom he would never see again. He thought of all the promises of his road and his life, of his brooch and his consistent strength, of the hopes and dreams he had dared entertain. Of his unborn child.

"No!" Bransen heard himself cry from somewhere deep within, from a primal place of pure rage and denial.

"No!" to Jameston's murder.

"No!" to his failure.

"No!" to the sudden end of his road.

"No!" to his loss of Cadayle.

"No!" to the thought of never seeing his child.

"No!" to the return of the Stork.

Just "no!" A wall of utter denial, of utter refusal.

Affwin Wi walked up to him.

The Highwayman, with all the grace of a Jhesta Tu warrior, kicked his leg out behind him and hit her in the knee, locking her leg painfully. The Highwayman leaped up, spun about, and launched a barrage of punches and kicks that had the Hou-lei warrior backing desperately, her arms working in a blur to try to slow the onslaught.

Where had he found this power and coordination? He had no soul stone, but his line of life energy ran strong and ran straight. He charged as she backed, his barrage did not slow, and all momentum fell to him, to the Highwayman, the Jhesta Tu, the angry warrior.

Fury guided but did not consume him. He punched and kicked with rage but with all his strength and speed in complete control. He focused on the sheer wall of denial that drove him but never lost sight of his surroundings or of his opponent.

Thus, when Affwin Wi feigned a block and fell to the floor, rolling in to take him out at the legs, the Highwayman reacted by leaping straight up into the air so high and gracefully that it felt as if he remained connected to the malachite. He landed in perfect balance, so lightly and perfectly, now towering over Affwin Wi, who had to work doubly hard and at an awkward angle to try to fend him off.

The Highwayman stayed focused enough to detect movement to the side and to get his arm up just in time to block the sliver of silver flying at him through the air. Holding his torn guts with one hand, Moh Li lifted another missile with the other. The spinning, many-toothed disk flashed past the crouching Highwayman. He had to finish Moh Li quickly, he realized.

He glanced at Affwin Wi, thinking that he might have to fend her off fast and then make the run to her companion. She stood with his sword in hand.

Another disk, another *shur'a'tu'wikin*, a "sword hidden in the hand," as the clever weapon was known, flashed out at him. He couldn't dodge and had to block again, this time the disk slicing hard as it deflected off his hand, all but severing his little finger. His digit fell limply to the side, hanging by nothing more than a strand of bloody skin.

Bransen made a decision. He swung his hand around gingerly as he brought it in close, catching the swinging finger in his grasp and tucking his fist tight against his ribs. He broke into a run. With a great leap to the side, he crashed through the grated window.

He dropped to the courtyard on his feet and kept on running. Never looking back, blinded by pain and confusion and a profound sense of despair, the Highwayman ran through the Entel morning. He smashed his way through the market, upsetting carts, and rushed down an alley. He found the strength to lessen his weight and make a great leap to a low roof, then scrambled from there to the city wall.

Sentries and commoners alike yelled at him as he went right over, sprinting away, the bright morning light dazzling through the tears that filled his eyes.

To his surprise he found no pursuit, but he kept running because to stop was to face the awfulness that had found his life.

And he feared, too, that, as soon as he settled and took a full measure, his moment of clarity, of escape from the Stork, would be at its end, and he would become helpless once more.

Epilogue

Exhaustion finally caught up to Bransen on a rocky hill several leagues north of Ethelbert dos Entel. He stared at the crashing waves of the Mirianic for a short while, his mind racing every which way. His anger was gone, stolen by remorse, shaken by disappointment as profound as anything he had ever known. All that he wanted at that terrible time was to get back to Cadayle, to sleep in her arms, to forget the wider world.

He had lost everything.

But he knew that he would never forget Jameston Sequin. He was surprised by the magnitude of that loss. This man he had known only a few months, whom he had come to know only in the last short weeks, had become so important to him. A friend, a mentor, almost a father. And in his excitement in thinking that he had found Jhesta Tu, he had sent Jameston away.

It had been there all along, Bransen realized, as he slumped to the dark sand beside a ridge of black rock. He hadn't needed any tutelage from the Jhesta Tu. Was there anything they could teach him greater than the wisdom that Jameston had shown him along the road? Truly?

Because most of all, Jameston Sequin had reminded Bransen to look within himself, honestly and openly. Jameston had nudged him to consider the truth of the many roads before him and to come to terms with the responsibilities of his training and skill and that gemstone brooch.

The brooch!

Bransen's hand went up to the dried blood on his forehead, the torn skin where the brooch had been set. He tucked his legs back under him and stood up suddenly, then sprang to the ridge of lava stone, a leap of several vertical feet.

He had no soul stone.

No fury drove him.

What was this transformation? Had the gemstone's magic, so closely attuned to his line of life energy, cured him of his malady? Was the Stork lost to him forever and without need of a magical crutch? Or was it a temporary fix?

The thought haunted Bransen suddenly. He looked away from the dark waters of the Mirianic to the north and west, toward Chapel Abelle, where he believed Cadayle to be. He had to get there, to her and to Father Artolivan. He had to be near to a cache of soul stones in case this confusing clarity could not hold.

More than that, even without the stones, even if he became the Stork again forever and evermore—particularly if he became the Stork evermore—Bransen needed Cadayle's warm embrace.

He didn't know if the clarity would last.

He didn't know that King Yeslnik was even then summoning the lairds of Honce to begin a new and more determined offensive, to wipe the world of Ethelbert and Artolivan and Gwydre.

He didn't know that Palmaristown had burned and that the rage of much of Honce was even then refocusing against Dame Gwydre.

All that he knew was that he needed Cadayle, and fast.

He started away and didn't look back, so he didn't see the sails of *Lady Dreamer* gliding above the dark water behind him, nearing Ethelbert dos Entel and the meeting of desperate men that would become the last, best hope for the land of Honce.

The Bear

PART ONE

Despair

I'm not an old man. I'm barely a man! But I feel old and worn and as if the rest of my life will be no more than a long and empty wait to die. For I have failed; I cannot escape that truth.

The irony of that reality does not elude me. I have spent most of my life simply trying to find physical control, trying not to drool on those with whom I speak, or trying not to trip during the most basic activity of walking.

From the depths I ascended, beyond my expectations or highest hopes, to what I considered perfect physical and mental control. Even beyond that I incorporated gemstone magic as if it were a mere extension of my will and want. From the valley to the mountaintop I journeyed, and the point of my life was the climb.

The climb. The meaningless, self-delusional ascent to nothingness. . . . What is it worth to Jameston, dead because he walked beside me? What is it worth to the memory of my mother, Sen Wi, her prized sword taken from me by a Hou-lei warrior woman whose very philosophy is anathema to that which my mother and father held dear? What is it worth, truly, to Garibond Womak, the man who raised me as a son but was mutilated and died because of his defense of me?

What is it worth? What is any of it worth? I want to believe in something bigger than myself, in some higher, noble purpose. I want to believe that the words inscribed in the Book of Jhest, the words my father so carefully penned to relay the guiding philosophy of the Behr mystics, are more than a selfish mental exercise.

I want to believe that Jameston Sequin was right in leaving the woods to walk a path of greater consequence beside me.

But I cannot.

For a brief moment, I dared to hope. Under the brilliance of the extraordinary Dame Gwydre, I allowed myself to believe in something bigger and to hope for a better world. My steps south were light, my steps to the east even lighter, since I believed I was moving toward a more worthwhile destiny.

Now I know the truth, and my folly, and that the nature of man is not divine but selfish. As water seeks its level so, too, will the unscrupulous—those unbounded by morality or empathy, by their very lack of personal shackles—rise to dominate their more community-minded brethren. Worse, I live with the certainty now that any gain is merely a temporary illusion. Even in Vanguard, where Gwydre rules well, she will be replaced. Perhaps the line of honor and decency will hold through another generation, perhaps two, but in the end evil will prevail. The first time the line of good Gwydre is succeeded by a man of evil intent—or even a man without empathy—that last flicker of the light of decency will be snuffed to darkness. And once the darkness takes hold, it does not let go. Delaval begets Yeslnik, Laird of Pryd, begets Laird Prydae begets Laird Bannagran. The descent is evident in the first instance, and in the subsequent incarnations the moral line is level at best and will inevitably slide.

This is the sad nature of things: Unshackled and unbounded, evil men will surely rise. Hou-lei defeats Jhesta Tu because Hou-lei holds no honor. To Hou-lei, there is no fair fight, there is only victory or defeat, and the victors write the histories.

And so did Affwin Wi intervene when Merwal Yahna could not defeat me, when I was proving to be the stronger. Am I now to hold my head high and claim a moral pedestal elevating me above her treachery? How so? She has my mother's sword and the brooch of magical gemstones given me by Father Artolivan. My indignation seems a feeble weapon against the reality of her victory, and my indignation will not bring Jameston Sequin back to life!

Even if we battle on, even if we somehow win . . . win? Alas, I do not even know how to define such a term! Yeslnik or Ethelbert? Will the fate of Honce sit with Yeslnik the Fool and his brutal armies or with Ethelbert and his paid assassins?

There is no victory to be found there, at least not for the common folk of Honce. Whichever side wins this war, the cost has been far too high, and the outcome will offer little more than a temporary stay from the next bloodletting campaign. I do not want to believe it, but I cannot escape this conclusion.

That is my folly, my false hope, the trap into which I walked because of the seduction of a woman, Dame Gwydre, who truly is different from the many lairds who rain their selfish whims like the lash of a nine-tail on the backs of the common folk. I see no hope for a better Honce.

Jameston should have stayed in the forest, a place more civilized by far.

What is left for me, then? Where might I turn? To Cadayle, obviously, and our unborn child, and there is nothing more. This is not my war, because there is no victory of any positive consequence. Even if I were to accept that any goodly gain must be a temporary thing because of the nature of man, what goodly possibility do I see before me? The fop . . . or the laird who hires assassins? Vain Yeslnik or Ethelbert, who gives his gold to those who murdered Jameston Sequin?

Would that I could kill them both and be done with them, but even then I suspect that I know what would rise in their stead.

I feel old and worn and tired of it all.

—BRANSEN GARIBOND

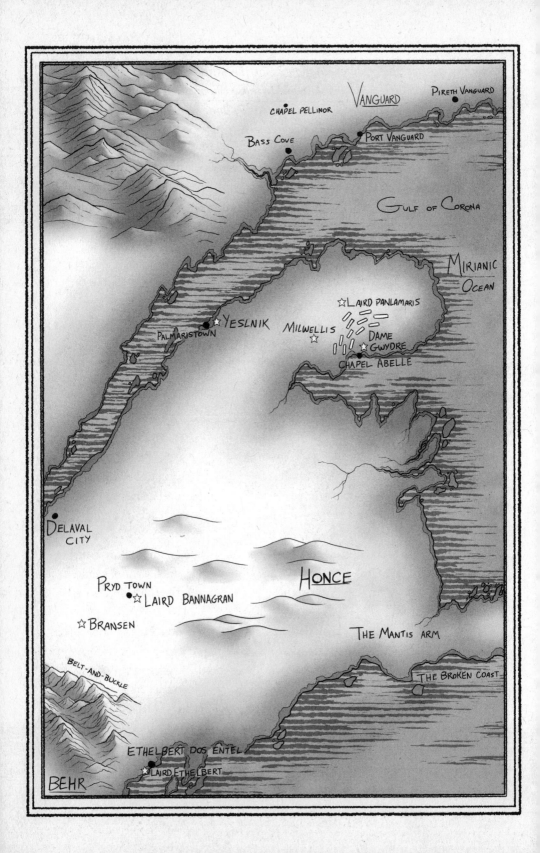

CHAPTER 1

Coward, You!

Every now and then he glanced at the rising sun just to ensure he was going north, though most of the time he would discover that he was not. He meandered aimlessly, not sure of where he was or who he was or, worst of all, why he was.

Bransen still wore his black silk pants, but he had taken off the distinctive shirt, replacing it with a simple shift he had found in an abandoned house. Gone, too, was his mask, the signature of the Highwayman. Soon after being chased out of Ethelbert dos Entel without his prized sword and gemstone brooch, Bransen had pulled the mask from his head and thrown it to the ground, thinking to be done with it, to be done with that persona forever. Almost immediately he angrily retrieved it. Fashioned from the one sleeve he had torn from the black silk shirt, that headband, like the rest of the outfit, had been the uniform of his Jhesta Tu mother, though he wasn't exactly certain of what that might mean anymore, given the beating Affwin Wi and Merwal Yahna had inflicted upon him.

However deep Bransen's despair, however lost he might be, he would not dishonor the memory of his mother.

He wandered throughout that first day after fleeing, finding water at a small stream. By late afternoon his stomach began to growl. He'd need a way to hunt, and so he started out, halfheartedly, to find implements—a stick he might fashion into a spear, perhaps. He got distracted rather quickly, though, as the smell of stew cooking wafted past on the breeze.

Bransen had no interest in meeting anyone, but his stomach wouldn't let him ignore the aroma that led him to lie on a knoll outside a small cluster of houses. In the center of the village burned a roaring cook fire with a large cauldron set atop it tended by a pair of old women. Bransen noted well the many inhabitants of the town milling about. Most were very old or very young; the only people near his age were women, many pregnant, probably from when the press-gangs came hunting. Like so many villages of Honce, this one radiated the unbearable pain of the protracted war.

The ridiculous, horrid reality of a world gone insane stung the young man anew, but it was, after all, just another in a long string of profound disappointments. He surveyed the area, looking for a way to sneak in, preferring to remain unseen and unnoticed. He glanced to the western sky, estimating another hour of daylight. The villagers were gathering to enjoy their meal. More and more would likely come out of those small cabins, and Bransen wondered how much of the meal would be left for him to pilfer.

He sighed and mocked his foolishness with a derisive snort, stood up, brushed himself off, and walked down into the village. Bransen was met by many curious stares. More than one person yelped in surprise, more than one mother pulled her children aside. Bransen understood their fear; he and Jameston had come upon several towns that had been ravaged by rogue bands of soldiers. He held his open hands before him unthreateningly.

"Far enough!" one old man said to him, brandishing a pitchfork Bransen's way. "Ye got no business here, so turn yerself about and be gone!"

"I am hungry and tired," Bransen replied. "I hoped that I might share some of your food."

"So ye think we've enough to be handing out?" the old man asked.

"I will work for it," Bransen promised. "Repair a roof, repair a wall, or gather wood. Whatever you need, but I could surely use a meal, friend."

"Which army are ye running from?" asked an old woman whose long nose hooked so profoundly that it nearly touched her chin, which hooked upward from her lack of teeth. She looked him over. "Yer voice sounds like Yeslnik, but yer clothes're more akin to Ethelbert. So which?"

"I found these clothes, as my own were too worn," Bransen explained, not wanting his distinctive pants to link him with Affwin Wi and her murderous band. Such a misconception might prove valuable to him in these parts, but still, the thought of anyone confusing him as a member of that Hou-lei troupe disgusted Bransen.

"Yeslnik, then," pronounced the old man. His snarl and the way he then gripped the pitchfork made Bransen know that he didn't think it a good thing.

"I serve no army."

"But ye did!" said the woman.

Bransen shook his head. "No. Not Yeslnik or Laird Ethelbert. I have come from distant Vanguard."

"Never heard of it," said the old man.

"Far to the north across the Gulf of Corona where Dame Gwydre rules with great compassion and love."

"Never heard of it," the old man said again. Those around him nodded their agreement.

It occurred to Bransen then just how parochial this and most communities of Honce truly were and how worldly he had become in so short a time. He thought back to his humble beginnings in Pryd Town, in the days when he could barely stumble the distance across Chapel Pryd's muddy courtyard. Never could he have imagined the road he had journeyed! The enormity of his travels only then began to become clear to him.

"I am no part of this awful war," he said.

The old woman's eyes narrowed. "I'm not for believing ye."

"And how'd ye get that tear on yer head, then?" asked the old man.

Bransen lifted his hand to touch the wound in the middle of his forehead where Affwin Wi had ripped the magical brooch from his flesh. "I . . . I ran into a low branch," he said.

"I'm still not for believing ye!" the old woman said with a hiss. "Now, ye turn about and be gone from here, or me old fellow here'll stick ye hard with four points o' pain."

"Aye," the old man said, prodding the pitchfork toward Bransen.

Bransen didn't flinch.

"Go on!" the old man insisted, thrusting the fork closer.

Unconsciously, the Highwayman reacted. As the pitchfork stabbed in, Bransen went forward and only slightly to the side, just enough so that the old man couldn't shift the weapon's angle to catch up to him. Once past the dangerous end of the pitchfork, the Highwayman moved with brutal efficiency, grabbing the shaft just below its head with his right hand, then knifing down his left hand with a swift and powerful chop. The handle shattered beneath that blow, leaving the old man with a short staff and Bransen holding the tined end of the pitchfork.

Bransen stepped back out of reach before those around him had even registered the move.

With a yelp of surprise, the old man took the stump of the staff and lifted it above his head like a club, stumble rushing at Bransen with something between terror and outrage.

Bransen dropped the broken end of the pitchfork and brought his arms up above his head in a diagonal cross just as the old man chopped down at his head. The Highwayman caught the club easily in the crook of his blocking arms and, with a sudden uncrossing, tugged the piece of wood from the old man's grasp. Bransen caught it immediately and sent it into a furious spin, twirling it in one hand, working it expertly behind his back and out the other side as he handed it off to his other hand. The old man fell back, throwing his arms up before his face and whining pitifully. No one else made a sound, transfixed by the dazzling maneuvers of this stranger.

Up over his head went the broken handle, spinning furiously. The Highwayman brought it down before him and around his right hip, then back out from behind his left hip. Bransen fell into the rhythm of his display; he used the moment of physical concentration to temporarily block out the darkness that filled his mind. Around and around went the staff, then Bransen planted one end solidly on the ground before him. One hand went atop that planted staff. The Highwayman leaped into the air, inverting into a handstand that brought his kicking feet up level with the eyes of any would-be opponents. He landed gracefully in a spin and used that to launch the staff once more into a whirlwind all about him.

Bransen's eyes weren't even open any longer, as he fell deeper into the trance of physical perfection, deeper into the martial teaching he had devoured in the Book of Jhest his father had penned. What started as a show for the villagers—a clear warning that Bransen hoped would prevent any rash actions leading to injury—had become something more profound and important to the troubled young man, a method of blocking out the ugly world.

Bransen's display went on for many heartbeats, spinning staff, leaping and twisting warrior, swift shifts and breaks in the momentum where Bransen transferred all of his energy into a sudden and brutal stab or swing.

When it finally played out, Bransen came up straight, took a deep breath, and opened his eyes—to stare into two-score incredulous faces.

"By the gods," one woman mouthed.

"Power," a young boy whispered, only because he could find no louder voice than that.

"Who are ye?" the old woman with the hooked nose asked after catching her breath.

"No one who matters, and no one who cares," Bransen answered, throwing the staff to the ground. "A hungry man begging food and willing to work for it. Nothing more."

"Begging?" a younger woman asked skeptically. She clutched a toddler tight in her arms. "Or threatening to take it if it's not given?"

Bransen looked at her closely, reading the anger on her dirty face. She might have been a pretty girl, once, an attractive young woman with blue eyes and wheat-colored hair. Perhaps once soft and inviting like a place to hide from the world, her hair now lay matted and scraggly, unkempt and uncut. The war had played hard on her; the only sparkle in her eyes was one of hatred, re-flected in bloodshot lines and weary bags. There remained no soft lines there, just a sharp and hardened person who had seen and borne too much and eaten too little.

Bransen had no answers for her. He gave a helpless little shrug. With a slight bow he turned and started away.

"Now where are ye going?" the old man asked behind him.

"As far as I need to pass beyond this war."

"But ye ain't going away hungry!" the old woman declared. Bransen stopped and turned to face her. "No one's to say that we folk o' Hooplin Downs let a stranger walk away hungry! Get back here and eat yer stew, and we'll find some work for ye to pay for it."

"Might start by cutting me a new handle for me fork," the old man said, and several of the others laughed at that.

Not the young woman with the toddler, though. Obviously displeased by the turn of events, she held her young child close and glared at Bransen. He looked back at her curiously, trying to convey a sense of calm, but the glower did not relent.

Repairing the pitchfork proved no difficult task, for there were other imple-ments about whose handles had long outlived their specialized heads. With that chore completed quickly, Bransen moved to help where he could, determined to pay back the folk equitably and more for their generosity in these dire times.

In truth, it wasn't much of a stew they shared that night, just a few rotten fish in a cauldron of water with a paltry mix of root vegetables. But to Bransen it tasted like hope itself, a quiet little reminder that many people—perhaps most—were possessed of a kind and generous nature, the one flickering candle in a dark, dark world. Reflecting on that point of light, Bransen silently chas-tised himself for his gloom and despair. For a moment, just a brief moment, he thought his decision to return to his wife and run away with her incredibly selfish and even petulant.

The people of Hooplin Downs didn't talk while they ate. They all sat sol-emnly, most staring into the distance as if seeing another, better time. Like so many in Honce, they seemed to be a haunted bunch. Their silence bespoke of great loss and sacrifice, and the manner in which each of them tried to savor every pitiful bite revealed a level of destitution that only reinforced to Bransen how generous they had been in allowing him to share their pittance.

Darkness fell and supper ended. The villagers worked together to clean up the common area about the large cook fire. As the meager and downtrodden folk of Hooplin Downs moved about the sputtering flames, Bransen felt he was witnessing the walk of the dead, shambling out of the graveyards and the bat-tlefields toward an uncertain eternity. His heart ached as he considered the condition of the land and the folk, of the misery two selfish lairds had will-ingly inflicted upon so many undeserving victims. His heart ached the most when he considered how futile his flickering optimism had been. Two men could destroy the world, it seemed, much more easily than an army of well-meaning folk could save or repair it.

Bransen sat before the fire for a long while, long past when the others had wandered back to their cabins, staring into the flames as they consumed the twigs and logs. He envisioned the smoke streaming from the logs as the escape of life itself, the inexorable journey toward the realm of death. He took the dark im-age one step further, seeing the flame as his own hopes and dreams, diminishing to glowing embers and fading fast into the dark reality of a smoky-black night.

"I don't think I have ever seen a man sit so still and quiet for so long," said a woman, interrupting his communion with the dancing flickers. The edge in that voice, not complimentary, drew him out of his introspection even more than the words themselves. He looked up to see the young mother who had questioned him sharply when he had first entered Hooplin Downs. The toddler stood now in the shadows behind her, which seemed to relieve some of her vulnerability, as was evident in her aggressive stance.

"All the work is done," he answered.

"And so is the meal you begged, uh, worked for," she added, her words dripping in sarcasm.

His eyes narrowed. "I did what I could."

The woman snorted. "A young man, very strong and quick, who can fight well . . . and here you sit, staring into the fire."

That description of his fighting ability tipped her hand.

"Your husband is off fighting in the war," Bransen said softly.

She snorted again, helplessly, angrily, pitifully, and looked to the side. "My husband got stuck to the ground by a Palmaristown spear," she said, chewing every word with outrage. "He'd likely be there still if the animals hadn't dragged him away to fill their bellies. Too many to bury, you know."

"I know."

"And here you sit, because your work is done," she retorted. "Here you sit, all whole and breathing and eating the food of folk who don't have enough to give, while men and women fall to the spear and the sword and the axe."

Bransen stared at her hard. She shifted and put her hands on her hips, re-turning his look without blinking. He wanted to tell her about Ancient Badden, how he had fought a more just war in the northland of Vanguard, how he and

Jameston had saved a village from marauding rogue soldiers. He wanted to blurt it all out, to stand and stomp his feet, to scream about the futility of it all. But he couldn't.

Her posture, her expression, the power forged by pain in her voice, denied him his indignation, even mocked his self-pity. He had his life and his wife, after all.

"What side are you on, stranger?"

"Doesn't matter." Bransen dared to stand up straight before her. "Both sides are wrong."

He saw it coming but didn't try to stop it. She slapped him across the face.

"My husband's dead," she said. "Dead! The man I love is gone."

Bransen didn't say that he was sorry, but his expression surely conveyed that sentiment. Not that it mattered.

"They are both wrong?" The woman gave a little helpless laugh. "You're saying there's no reason we eat mud and go to cold beds? That's your answer? That's the answer of the brave warrior who can dodge a pitchfork and snap its head from its handle with ease?"

Bransen softened. "Do you wish that I had fought and saved your husband?" He was trying to send a note of appeasement and understanding, but the question sounded ridiculous even to his own ears. His face stung when she slapped him again.

"I wish you had got stuck to the ground and not him!" She spun away from him, and only then did Bransen realize all the village folk had gathered again to hear the exchange. They looked on with horror, a few with embarrassment, perhaps, but Bransen noted that many heads were nodding in agreement with the woman.

"It's all a matter of chance!" The woman stomped back and forth before the onlookers. "That's what it is, yes? A hundred men go out, and twenty die! A thousand men go out, and more die." She turned on him sharply. "But the more that go, the more that come home, don't they? A thousand targets to spread the bite of Yeslnik's spears mean that each has more of a chance to miss that bite. So why weren't you there?" She launched herself at him. "Why are you here instead of showing yourself as a target to the archers and the spearmen?"

This time Bransen didn't let her strike him because he knew the situation could escalate quickly and dangerously for everyone. He caught her wrists, left and right as she punched, pinning them back to her sides. She began to wail openly, keening against the injustice of it all. He instinctively tried to pull her closer to comfort her, but she tore away, spinning about so forcefully and quickly that she lost her balance and tumbled to the dirt, where she half sat, half lay on one elbow, her other forearm slapped across her eyes.

Bransen's instincts again told him to go to her, but he didn't dare. He looked up at the many faces staring at him, judging him. He held his hands out questioningly, starting to back away.

A trio of women went to their fallen friend, one pausing just long enough to look up at Bransen and mutter, "Get ye gone from here." Her words sparked more calls. The woman's rant had touched a deep nerve here.

They weren't interested in his truth. All that mattered to them was the injustice that a young, obviously capable man was sitting here, seemingly untouched by the devastating reality that had visited upon all their homes.

Bransen took another step back from the outraged woman and held his hands up again, a helpless and ultimately sad look upon his face as he walked away.

When he was back in the empty forest, wandering the dark trails, Bransen's memory of his encounter in the village only reinforced his growing belief that he did not belong here . . . and perhaps not anywhere. He thought of Cadayle, the one warm spot in his bleak existence, and of their unborn child. Was he damning them both to a life of misery by his mere presence? Should he, after all, go the way of the younger Jameston Sequin, the way of the recluse, and not the way of the Jameston who had made the fateful and errant decision to come back into the wider civilized world?

What kind of husband would drag Cadayle and their babe into such an existence?

That question nearly drove Bransen to his knees. The implications were too harsh for him to even entertain their possibility.

Where would he fit in? How would he ever fit in?

And most important of all, why would he want to?

CHAPTER 2

The Inevitable Spiral

Prince Milwellis burst into the barn with a roar of defiance. Flames ate at one wall, but the mob battling within hardly seemed to notice, so desperate was their struggle.

The young, red-haired warrior prince rushed at one nearby fight, where a Palmaristown man lay bloody on the floor and two others tried desperately to keep up with the furious movements of the red-capped dwarves darting all about them. One soldier scored a hit with his sword, a solid stab, but the dwarf shrugged it off and returned with a smash of his spiked club that shattered the man's knee. Only Milwellis's intervention prevented a second and more devastating powrie strike as the soldier tumbled in agony.

The prince struck with his sword, a devastating slash across the powrie's chest that sent the dwarf stumbling back . . . but just a step. The ferocious little beast came on again with a snarl and a howl and a most wicked grin. Milwellis fell back, not willing to trade blows with the powrie. As he retreated he shoved his remaining comrade toward the dwarf.

That man, too, stabbed the dwarf hard, a strike that would have felled most opponents. In response the soldier got the club right between the eyes, a spike stabbing into his brain. His legs dropped from under him. As he fell he twisted the dwarf's club awkwardly, tying up the creature.

Milwellis stepped in. This time his clean strike at the powrie's neck finally finished the vicious little thing.

Milwellis jumped back and looked for the next opportunity. Beside him, the man with the crushed knee pleaded for help.

"Silence, fool!" Milwellis hissed, kicking the wretch to silence. "Crawl out of here!"

The fires reached across the ceiling, the barn surely lost. Milwellis and his men knew it and worked toward the door, but the remaining powries—the prince was shocked to see that there were only three others—fought on as if they hardly cared. Another Palmaristown man was pulled down and slaughtered and then another, though the last desperate swing of his sword managed to take one powrie with him.

Milwellis pushed his way through the door, tripping over the man with the shattered knee. The barn roof fell in behind them, sending sparks and embers flying into the night sky. Milwellis regained his footing and brushed the dirt from his clothes, storming about, cursing every step. "Only four?" he yelled in outrage. "Only four?"

For he had lost nearly a score of fighters in that barn, killed five to one by powries.

"Easy, my son," Laird Panlamaris begged a few moments later, the old man riding over at the sound of Milwellis's bellowing.

"Four, Father!" said Milwellis. "Four wretched powries held that barn for half the night and killed a score of my finest warriors."

"These are formidable foes," Laird Panlamaris agreed. "A bitter lesson I learned decades ago upon the sea."

"They are the curse of Honce," said another who rode up, a giant of a man, wearing the brown robes of the Order of Abelle. "Do not forget who loosed the evil upon us."

Prince Milwellis eyed Father De Guilbe squarely and nodded, his face locked in a hateful grimace.

"Dame Gwydre did this," De Guilbe said. "Dame Gwydre and Father Artolivan, the heretic who claims to rule the church."

"They will pay with their blood," vowed Milwellis.

"Not to doubt," agreed the Laird of Palmaristown, whose once-great city now lay before him in near ruin, the devious work of barely a hundred powries. "When Palmaristown is secured once more, the scourge of red caps driven into the Masur Delaval and drowned like the rats they are, I will sweep Gwydre's Vanguard into ruin."

"Do not forget Chapel Abelle, I beg," said De Guilbe. "If I am to take my rightful place as leader of the Order of Abelle, loyal to King Yeslnik and you, Laird Panlamaris, then I must be properly seated at the chapel that has come to be the center of power for my order. No replacement chapel, however grand, will suffice."

"Not even if King Yeslnik builds you the grandest one of all in Delaval City with a congregation numbering in the thousands?" the laird asked.

Father De Guilbe couldn't contain his grin about that intriguing possibility, though he quickly dismissed it. "Only if the rot at Chapel Abelle is cleansed," he declared. "A grander chapel would, indeed, be a step forward for the church, but only if the disease that has rotted its core, Chapel Abelle, is cleared from the land. Else that rot will continually spread, and the lies of Artolivan and his cohorts will undermine any of my efforts to bring the flock more in line to the edicts of King Yeslnik and the lairds who rule Honce. We cannot ignore Chapel Abelle!"

"And yet, friend, we would not again throw our men at those walls and against the gemstone barrage of a hundred brothers," Milwellis reminded him now. He looked to his father, whose face was locked in a grimace, his teeth grinding.

"*Look at your city nearly burned to the ground!*" De Guilbe shot back.

"We will trap them in their hole and take all the land about them," Prince Milwellis promised. "We'll keep them in and keep them silenced."

"We will bombard them until they fall upon their own knives out of madness and despair," Laird Panlamaris added, growling out every word. "From the field and from the sea! We will fill their walls with thrown stones."

Both De Guilbe and Milwellis thought the remark to be mostly bluster. To truly sack Chapel Abelle would require a vast army and armada at a price untenable with King Yeslnik's designs, particularly now that vicious powries had entered the fight on the side of their enemies. Certainly the wizened and seasoned Laird Panlamaris understood the truth of his words.

Prince Milwellis stared at his father and saw no hint of doubt in his steeled gaze.

"Come along," Laird Panlamaris told all around him, his voice still thick with simmering rage. "We've more powrie rats to catch."

The rocking of the ship across the currents and waves of the great river seemed much more acute belowdecks. Yeslnik expected that he would find his wife with her head out of their private chamber's porthole, "feeding the fish," as Captain Juront of his flagship (newly named *Grand Dame Olym* in honor of his wife) often called it.

He was pleasantly surprised to find that Olym was not at the window and didn't seem to be heading there anytime soon. Dressed in fine and revealing lace, her smile only adding to the obvious invitation, the Queen of Honce leaped upon her husband as he entered, wrapping his slight frame in her ample arms. Smothering him with passionate kisses, Olym reached over to shut tight the cabin door.

"There are powrie boats in the river," Yeslnik managed to say between kisses.

"We will destroy them," Olym rattled back in a single breath as she drove him back with a ferocious kiss and pushed him onto the bed.

"We will make Palmaristown in the morning," Yeslnik went on. "The city is in great disrepair. Hundreds were murdered by the dwarves."

"You will destroy them," Olym said without the slightest hesitation or reservation. She sat up and straddled him, pulling aside the folds of her garments. "You are the King of Honce. You are Yeslnik the Terrible, and all will tremble before you!"

She began clawing at his shirt, trying to undress him and herself furiously as the moment of passion swept her away.

"Yeslnik the Terrible," the foppish young king whispered to himself during the frenzy. He liked that. And he liked more the wild passion that had come over his wife of late! He had slunk back to Delaval from the far west, from the gates of the city of his greatest foe, Laird Ethelbert, in near despair, the promises of a swift victory slipping away. Emotionally flailing about, unsure of his next move or even of any point of any possible next move, Yeslnik had found strength in the least expected place: the arms of a wife who had cooled to him greatly over the last couple of years and, indeed, who had taken an obvious fancy to the rogue known as the Highwayman, the very same dog Yeslnik blamed for the murder of his uncle, King Delaval.

Even as Olym began to almost savagely ride him, Yeslnik recalled that the chasm between him and his wife had widened after Yeslnik's embarrassment on the road in Pryd a year before. His coach had been assailed by powries, and only the Highwayman's intervention had saved the day. Of course, the rogue had then humiliated Yeslnik and stolen from him!

Olym had turned from Yeslnik then and toward the knave! Yeslnik had been blaming the Highwayman for his conjugal troubles, but now, finally, pinned beneath his nearly frantic wife, he understood the truth. Power and danger drove this woman's hungry loins. She wanted—nay, demanded—a man who would crush the skull of an enemy under his boot with hardly a thought, a man who carried a sword more often than not bloodied with his enemy's entrails.

Lady Olym wanted a king, not a peasant! And this wild creature riding him to levels of pleasure and passion he had never thought possible deserved nothing less.

He was Yeslnik, King of Honce, and woe to those fools who did not drop to bended knee before him! He was Yeslnik the Terrible. Look upon him and be afraid.

Every time the people of Palmaristown believed they had rid themselves of the scourge that had crawled from the Masur Delaval in that awful night now called The Dark of Long Murder, another group of powrie dwarves reared its ugly head. And no matter the odds, those dwarves fought with their typical fury. The ratio Prince Milwellis had seen in the barn held pretty closely with each incident: Nearly forty powries had been killed or captured by the end of the second day, but the Palmaristown garrison had also lost more than two hundred warriors.

Back in his castle, which had mostly survived the fires, Laird Panlamaris took every report of powrie incidents with a heavy and resigned grunt, followed immediately by a slam of his large fist upon the armrest of his oaken throne. He waved away the newest crier who had come in to relate that a single powrie had killed eleven people in the market district before they had tied him down.

Panlamaris sank back wearily in his seat and muttered curses at Dame Gwydre under his breath, not wanting the guards in the room, their morale already low, to hear him.

His son, though, was not nearly as diplomatic. "Why are you not more outraged, Father?" Prince Milwellis rushed forward to stand before the throne. "How can you hear of these murders and not scream and thrash?"

Panlamaris's old eyes narrowed at his impetuous son. "To what end? We have shallow graves filled with hundreds of Palmaristown bodies. There will be more, many more, before this is settled."

"Eleven more now," Milwellis spat.

"You hold your sarcastic tongue," Panlamaris growled. He let his glower sweep the room, stealing any widening grins before they could begin. "I will not be mocked by anyone, least of all my son."

Milwellis looked about to argue, but he bit it back and bowed low in deference.

Panlamaris eyed him with amusement now. "You think me not outraged enough, my son?"

Milwellis could contain himself no longer, beating his chest with one fist. "*I* would go to Market Square and choke the powrie dead with my own hands," he replied through clenched teeth.

"A rather easy death for a powrie, then." Panlamaris gave a hateful little chuckle. "Perhaps I am more angry than you."

Milwellis and all the others in the room looked at the old laird curiously.

"How many powries have we in our dungeons now?" Panlamaris asked.

"Twenty-seven, my laird," one of the guards answered. "Twenty-eight if this latest survives the mob at Market Square."

"The rat'll live," another said. "Hard to kill the damned things."

"Prepare twenty-eight stakes," Panlamaris announced. "Tall stakes."

Prince Milwellis was about to learn much from his father in ways he had never expected.

I've spent many a day killing these little rat-dogs," Panlamaris explained later as the stakes were prepared to his specifications in the city square. "Not too sharp," was the order, for a sharp stake would cause such overwhelming trauma as to reduce the duration of the suffering.

"Never thought we'd have to fight them again," said Harcourt, hands on his old hips as he watched the construction. Panlamaris's trusted general had been in the east serving as advisor to Milwellis. "Never wanted to."

"We'll chase them off like we did on Durbury's Rock," Panlamaris promised. He turned to Milwellis, who, though listening, stood staring past the two old warriors toward the spectacle in the square before him. The first powrie prisoner had been dragged from the dungeon and stripped of his ratty clothing. Bound hands and ankles to four horses, the dwarf was naked and laid out spread-eagled in the square.

"Bah, what're ye doin'? O, ye dogs!" cried the powrie. His howls became indecipherable screams as a soldier pushed a stake slowly into the dwarf's rectum. The volume of his screams increased, surprising Milwellis, who hadn't thought it possible to so agonize a dwarf, as the intrusive pole tore through the creature's bowels and gut. Even the most bloodthirsty of the gathered throng on the square gulped and looked away.

The torturer kept going, though, and the screams became gurgles as the stake reached to the dwarf's throat. The horses pulled as instructed, and the bloody tip of the stake came right out the dwarf's mouth surrounded by bloody bubbles.

More soldiers cut the ropes and carried the dwarf to the docks where supports had been built. They hoisted the powrie up to hang high atop the stake some ten feet from the ground.

"How long?" asked Milwellis, very conscious that he was sweating.

Panlamaris shrugged. "Hours at the least. Seen some live for nearly a week."

Back in the square the next dwarf was dragged from the dungeon, the process repeated.

By the fourth powrie, the mob's squeamishness was gone, replaced by shouted reminders of the horrors the dwarves had inflicted upon Palmaristown.

As the sun settled in the west that day, twenty-eight powries rode high on stakes by Palmaristown's south and west gates and along her docks.

. . . Scarecrows warning their kin away.

King Yeslnik!" Captain Juront yelled in a tone that gave Yeslnik great pause. He knew they were nearing Palmaristown, finally, and was not surprised to hear Juront calling him, but the man's tone bespoke great uneasiness and concern. With a glance at his wife, Yeslnik rushed from his cabin, Olym scrambling close behind.

The young king climbed to the deck, the devastation of Palmaristown obvious immediately, with some areas of the city still shrouded in smoke. The sight initially brought relief to Yeslnik, who had feared that Juront's frantic tone was inspired by powries attacking *Grand Dame Olym*. He moved to the captain, who stood staring out to starboard and the Palmaristown docks, his first mate beside him, equally intent—so much so that neither man seemed to be drawing breath.

When he finally got into a position where he could follow Juront's gaze, Yeslnik, too, sucked in his breath with shock at the sight of dozens of powries on spikes in the harbor.

"Oike! What is that?" Queen Olym exclaimed as she came up beside the three men.

"Powries, milady," Juront managed to gasp.

"Ugly little things. Are they dead?" Even as Olym spoke, the flagship gliding in toward her waiting berth, one of the powries flicked his arm out to the side.

"Soon, milady," Juront promised.

"What is this?" Yeslnik asked.

"The vengeance of Laird Panlamaris, my king," Juront answered. "He is a fierce man of many battles. A man not known for mercy."

King Yeslnik tried to steady himself. He glanced at Olym, fearing the sight too raw for her delicate sensibilities.

But she was smiling, her eyes twinkling. "Fierce," she whispered with obvious admiration and interest. "He is a man to be feared."

Yeslnik cleared his throat and forced himself to stand tall. "Yes, well, the more of the dwarves he kills, the better it is for us all," he said.

Grand Dame Olym slid into her berth a short while later, the crack crew working fast to tie her off. Captain Juront led the procession from the ship, the royal guard spreading out quickly, marching to the docks to prepare the way for the king and queen. One of the staked powries hung just to the side of the gangplank. Yeslnik and Olym moved past and could hear the wretch groan and wheeze. A drop of blood splattered on the planks beside Queen Olym. The woman gasped, and King Yeslnik pulled her a bit to the side.

She wasn't horrified, however, as she revealed when she whispered into her husband's ear, "You must erect bigger stakes!"

A not-so-subtle growl, a promise of passion to come, reverberated behind those words. Yeslnik got her message and privately resolved to fell a forest of Honce's tallest trees.

"Hold quiet," Shiknickel implored his barrelboat crew. The small powrie boat bobbed on the waves of many crossing wakes, for they dared not put their strong legs to the pedals and drive the craft along. A fleet of tall-masted Delaval warships sliced through the water all about them, churning the river with the power of their passing.

Bloody-cap powries rarely ran from a fight, any fight. But if they revealed themselves in the midst of this fleet, Shiknickel and all the others knew, it wouldn't really be much of a fight. They might use their submerged battering ram to punch a hole in one ship, of course, but to what end? Typically, the ferocious dwarves would scramble to the deck as the ship listed and toppled, so that they could pull the sailors from the waters and cut them open to redden the powries' magical berets with more human blood. But even if they hit a ship now and tried to crawl out onto the deck, the archers from several other warships would cut them down in short order.

So they sat quiet, hoping their low profile—for the bulk of a barrelboat lay below the water—would allow them to remain unnoticed as the Delaval warships sailed past.

At the front of the seated crew, Mcwigik and Bikelbrin exchanged looks, at once wistful, resigned, concerned, and excited. They had spent one hundred years with a small group of powries trapped on the islands of a steamy northern lake, fed by hot springs, a place of teeming life amidst the harsh Alpinadoran tundra. Circumstance, unexpected friendships, and unusual happenstance had freed this pair and subsequently their kin from that soft prison only recently. Now fate had put them in this predicament on a river far to the west of the open sea that would take them to the Weathered Isles and their old homes, surrounded by enemies, surrounded by victims.

This, on the edge of disaster, was the rightful life of a powrie, the pair agreed with shared grins and nods, eagerness for battle overcoming any nostalgia for the safety of the island life.

"They're gone, one and all," Shiknickel announced to the crew.

"Fast for Palmaristown," one of the crew replied. He chuckled. "What's left o' Palmaristown!"

That brought a cheer across the ranks, for this group had been among the six crews who had quietly landed on the riverbank near the great human city and had gone in to lay waste, to let blood, and to stoke fires. Three of the six boats had gone back in for a second strike, unable to resist the seemingly endless supply of easy victims. Shiknickel, more comfortable on the water than on land and more conservative in his risk taking, had decided against that course.

"We really stung 'em good," Mcwigik remarked. "They're callin' to all the land for help, and all their misery's from just six crews."

His words brought more cheering.

"Aye, and if we can muster ten more crews we could take over the whole o' the place called Honce, I'm thinking!" another dwarf in the back blustered.

"Me cap'd get so thick and fat with blood it'd buckle me knees!" said another.

The backslapping and self-congratulating went on for a long, long while, each of the crew snickering and telling of his own mighty adventures in the night of carnage he had inflicted upon the unsuspecting folk of Palmaristown. Of course, since these were powries, each retelling spoke of grander battles, of more desperate struggles against legions of organized enemies, and of far greater kill counts.

It got so exaggerated that at one point, Mcwigik chimed in above the din with, "Bah, but if ye killed to death as many as ye say ye killed to death, and he killed half what he's saying, and him just half o' his, then I'm knowing them boats that just floated past us to be ghost ships or floatin' strays, because sure that there aren't any left alive in the whole damned place o' Honce!"

That pronouncement brought the greatest laughter and cheers of all, but it didn't slow the stories, which grew more outrageous as the barrelboat moved steadily northward, now far behind the north-sailing Delaval fleet, toward the mouth of the Masur Delaval and the open waters of the Gulf of Corona.

"Practice yer tales well, boys," Shiknickel said to them. "For ye'll be tellin' them to our mates on the Weathered Isles in just two weeks' time."

Yet another rousing cheer ensued, as loud as the dwarves dared with so many hostile warships not so far ahead of them in the river, followed by an old song of the rocky shores of the Weathered Isles.

Captain Shiknickel, however, did not join in. He looked back out the low conning tower of the barrelboat, then almost immediately turned to the crew, his shocked expression speaking volumes.

"What d'ye know?" Mcwigik asked and came out of his seat.

Shiknickel slammed his fist against the hard wall of the boat, shifting aside to give Mcwigik access.

"By a dead fish's stink!" Mcwigik yelled a moment later, and all remaining traces of the song died away, and more than half the dwarves jumped up from their seats.

"Staked them," Shiknickel explained.

"Aye, and at least the two nearest us're still alive," Mcwigik called. He spat on the floor and moved out of the way, allowing Bikelbrin to lead a procession of dwarves to view the gruesome sight of Palmaristown's dock, where a line of staked powries hung on tall poles. Every crew member spat after the viewing and grumbled all the way back to his seat, with most echoing the sentiment, "We got to go get 'em down and take their hearts for burying."

"Got friends there," one grumbled. "And I'll be seeing their kids born o' their hearts, don't ye doubt!"

Similar sentiments echoed up and down the line until Shiknickel finally hushed them with a reminder that they were very near to their enemies now and by pointing out that the humans likely had more stakes.

"Bah, but I ain't running!" one of the crew growled. "Not now."

"So that's how they're wanting to play it, are they?" Mcwigik said.

"I'm bettin' we can make a human scream louder than any of them boys up there when they got the stake," Bikelbrin added.

"And what are ye thinking?" Mcwigik demanded of the captain.

"I'm thinking that we're not to be seeing our home anytime soon," Shiknickel shot back. "Not now," he added, looking to the crewman who had earlier proclaimed the same.

"And not anytime soon," Mcwigik growled back at him.

"Aye, and we'll put word to them that's ahead of us, a line o' messages all the way to the Weathered Isles, and we'll put every boat we got into the water," Shiknickel proclaimed. "We'll take the gulf, we'll take the coast, and we're going ashore every time we see the chance to make the dogs pay."

"I'm thinking we're going back into Palmaristown in short order to take our boys down," said Mcwigik. Shiknickel nodded determinedly. "Get yer blood up, boys, and think o' ways we can make them hurt."

"I'm thinking that more than a few stakes'll be empty and waiting for us to put 'em to new use," said Bikelbrin.

Every dwarf on the barrelboat nodded grimly and vowed revenge—payback many times over for the horror inflicted upon their companions.

T he King of Honce arrives," Laird Panlamaris said to his son Milwellis, Father De Guilbe, Harcourt, and several other commanders.

"If he is everything I have heard him to be, I can hardly breathe for my anticipation," said Harcourt dryly.

Father De Guilbe blanched at the clear breach of etiquette—to mock a king in such a manner!—but Laird Panlamaris chuckled and patted Harcourt's strong shoulder. The two went back twoscore years to when they were young men, barely more than boys, sailing the high seas side by side, battling powries and pirates and doing a bit of pirating on their own. Harcourt had only recently traveled across Honce with Milwellis, advising the young general as he laid waste to the Mantis Arm and the coastal communities along Felidan Bay. If Panlamaris was to entrust the training of his promising son to the man, then surely they were familiar enough for a goodhearted jab, even one aimed at the would-be King of Honce. Neither Harcourt nor Milwellis had returned from the walls of Ethelbert dos Entel with a high opinion of the king, given that Yeslnik had turned tail and fled when victory seemed assured.

"He is a treasure," Panlamaris agreed. "As opposite his uncle Delaval as any man could be."

"And you loved Laird Delaval like a brother," Milwellis interjected, his sour expression showing that he, too, wasn't overjoyed at the unexpected arrival of Yeslnik's fleet. Indeed, Delaval and Panlamaris had been cut from the same cloth, one similar to Laird Ethelbert. Powerful warriors, brave in battle, stern in rule, and lusty with the spoils of their conquests, they exemplified an older code from when the world was wilder. Although none predated the Order of Abelle, all three had come to power under the harsh religious instruction of the Samhaists and at a time when the sword was more important than the notion of diplomacy.

"He is the King of Honce, by Delaval's proclamation," Father De Guilbe reminded them. "His bold actions regarding my order have set in motion long-overdue corrections against the weakness that has crept into the hearts of the brothers."

"Bold actions," Panlamaris echoed with a snort. He had seen the result of those bold actions firsthand when his army had charged the wall of Chapel Abelle only to be battered by a magical barrage the likes of which Honce had never before witnessed. "Has he made a new enemy where he might've found a friend, I wonder?"

Father De Guilbe's face went very tight, and he crossed his thick arms over his large chest and leaned back against the wall. He was a giant of a man, well over six feet tall and with wide and strong shoulders. The fact that he wore the brown robes of his order was the only thing that separated him physically from the burly and toughened warriors in the room.

"You would side with Father Artolivan now?" De Guilbe asked.

Panlamaris scoffed. "He has thrown in with the witch of Vanguard who brought powries to my shore. Bring me Artolivan, and I'll gladly hoist him on a stake as I did the powries."

"But you just implied—"

Panlamaris cut him off. "Yeslnik turned the church away, and so we are left with a monster." He paused for a moment and glared at the monk, who backed down. "To the docks," Panlamaris ordered them all. "Let us meet the king, though he is likely kneeling before the rail, reminding himself of what he ate for lunch."

They shared another laugh at Yeslnik's expense and went out of the room, Panlamaris leading.

Grand Dame Olym was already in her slip, her gangplank lowered, when Panlamaris and his entourage walked on the planks of the long wharf. Knights of Castle Delaval stood at silent attention in two rows upon the dock, halberds in hand, eyes staring straight ahead.

"Very impressive," Harcourt noted, grinning.

Laird Panlamaris, though, was not pleased. Upon the ship stood King Yeslnik, and there was something about his demeanor that immediately unsettled the fiery laird. Some confidence, he decided. The king started down the decline, his steps sure; he didn't even grasp the ropes on either side but descended quickly and steadily.

Behind him came more guards, then Queen Olym, followed by still more Delaval City warriors.

Yeslnik swept through the line of his guards, moving to stand right before the Laird of Palmaristown.

"You have reclaimed your city?"

"Of course. Powrie dwarves. Tough little ones, but they felt the bite of a stake up the arse." Panlamaris bit off the last word as Queen Olym rushed up to stand beside her husband.

No, not quite beside him, Panlamaris noted, but one step behind him to the left. It was a subtle shift from the norm for this couple, but sometimes, Panlamaris knew, the subtle indications would prove the most important.

"Dwarves loyal to Dame Gwydre, I am told." Panlamaris looked at Father De Guilbe.

"That will aid us," Yeslnik replied. "Gwydre remains in Chapel Abelle?"

"Aye, I've got three of my finest ships running the coast. There's no breaking out for a sail to Vanguard."

"But your ground army retreated back to Palmaristown, I am told," said Yeslnik.

"Retreated?" Panlamaris started rather sharply, but he calmed himself as Yeslnik stiffened and narrowed his eyes.

The young king was trying to claim the higher and more valiant ground here, Panlamaris realized, though the laird was having a hard time putting himself back in balance to properly respond.

"You left a nominal force, of course," Yeslnik said. "And runners to tell us if our enemies have broken out of their self-imposed prison."

Laird Panlamaris took a deep breath and stood up straight, his gaze darting all about. He didn't much like being spoken to in such a manner, particularly from a snot-faced boy like Yeslnik who had never bloodied his blade on a man able to defend against the strike. He could see his people shifting uncomfortably all about him but noted, too, the many heavily armed guards who had accompanied Yeslnik to the dock and the warships settled all about the long wharf, their decks lined with onlookers—archers all, no doubt.

He looked back to the young king and stared into his eyes. Panlamaris was quite surprised to see a measure of iron there that he had never before known, indeed, that contrasted starkly with everything that had ever been spoken of the foppish nephew of Laird Delaval.

"I've enough there to slow any attempt to break out of the chapel," Panlamaris finally answered. "But it's not something I'm expecting. Behind those walls Father Artolivan and Dame Gwydre stay alive, but if they come out they'll be caught and killed, and they know it. Oh, they can strike hard with their gemstones from the parapets while warriors scramble and try to bust through the heavy gates, but on an open field we'd kill them dead, and they know that, too."

King Yeslnik considered the words for a bit, then nodded, seeming satisfied with the reasoning.

"Good. I intend to keep them in their prison and to make their lives utterly miserable. We'll hold them there while our forces gather and march to the south, and this time Ethelbert will be pushed into the sea. How secure will Gwydre and Artolivan feel when they are fully isolated, the only resistance remaining against me in the whole world?"

"All the holdings?" Prince Milwellis asked.

"All," Yeslnik replied. "They will pledge fealty, or they will be razed to the ground without mercy."

The fiery, red-haired Prince of Palmaristown looked to General Harcourt. Milwellis's expression spoke volumes, a combination of frustration and anger. Hadn't he just marched across the land, battling all the way to the very gates of Ethelbert dos Entel? And after arriving there, only to promptly turn about and flee the field after Yeslnik had similarly retreated? The king took a southerly route while Milwellis had marched back along the coast, destroying every building in his path, to return to his father outside of Chapel Abelle's gates. And now, King Yeslnik was ready to repeat that futile and brutal march to the southeastern corner of Honce?

Staring at him for many heartbeats, his own expression one of amusement and absent surprise, King Yeslnik began to chuckle.

"You cannot blame the lad his apathy," Laird Panlamaris stated.

"Your son performed admirably," Yeslnik replied. Panlamaris beamed until Yeslnik qualified the statement. "Until the moment when he arrived at the gates of Ethelbert's city."

Milwellis shifted uncomfortably.

"And there he was chased away, and the foolish retreat of his army forced me to likewise abandon the field, to regroup and consolidate my power," said Yeslnik.

Everyone in the room knew that to be a falsehood; in a brief absence of Prince Milwellis, when he had gone to meet with Yeslnik, Milwellis's army had been forced back by an elite team of Ethelbert's assassins. But the prince had quickly returned and reversed that retreat and, indeed, had gone right back to the very walls of Ethelbert's city, even filling the night air with arrows long after Yeslnik's army was in full retreat across the breadth of Honce.

Milwellis shifted again uncomfortably and even growled under his breath, clearly agitated.

But King Yeslnik continued to smile and to let his daring stare drift from Panlamaris to Milwellis and back again.

Then and there, Laird Panlamaris knew that it didn't matter what had happened on that faraway field. All that mattered was what Yeslnik claimed had happened on that faraway field.

"You will not return to Ethelbert's gates," Yeslnik said to Milwellis after letting the uncomfortable silence settle for a bit. "To the people along the eastern seaboard your name has become . . . unfavorable."

"My king—" Milwellis started to protest, but Panlamaris was quick to put his arm up before his son to back him down.

"I hold the fact of your unpopularity in your favor," Yeslnik said, deflating the argument before it could begin. "You acted admirably in your march and in your return. Still, I would favor keeping you and your forces closer to home, particularly with powries running the coast. You will return to Chapel Abelle and invigorate the siege. Build great catapults and throw rocks at the monks day after day. Make them more miserable. Let none out and none in. When I and Bannagran of Pryd are finished with the fool Ethelbert, we will join in your efforts and end the threat of Dame Gwydre and Father Artolivan fully."

Milwellis seemed to calm at that proclamation. Panlamaris only looked on at the surprising King Yeslnik, trying to take a measure of the young man. It seemed obvious to him that Laird Delaval's old generals were advising Yeslnik, and while that might be a good thing regarding the disposition of the war it would surely make this fop harder to manipulate.

"We have much more to discuss," said Yeslnik. "We have two fleets to coordinate and three armies ready to march. But I am weary from my voyage and would spend some time in private, to rest and to plan. My generals will sit with you, Panlamaris, and help you to understand your role in the grand events unfolding."

The old laird didn't even bristle at the dismissal.

"You have my quarters prepared?" Yeslnik asked in such a manner that made it clear to Panlamaris that there could only be one correct answer to the inquiry.

Ye seen 'em?" Shiknickel asked his counterpart, the two standing on their respective barrelboat decks, bobbing in the river just north of Palmaristown.

"Aye, I seen 'em, and me and me boys're thinking we're to do something about them. Murky's boat seen 'em, too, and he's already in the gulf to pass the word."

"War," Shiknickel said.

"A thousand dead humans for every dwarf they staked," the other captain agreed. "We'll empty the damned Weathered Isles and bleed Honce until the rivers run red."

Mcwigik came on the deck beside Shiknickel.

"And we're not for letting yer friends sail free," the other captain called when he saw Mcwigik, for all knew of the deference that had been given to boats sailing under Dame Gwydre's flag. "Any boat what's not being pedaled is a boat what's being sinked."

Mcwigik rubbed his hairy face, but he couldn't disagree.

"Night's falling full," the dwarf captain of the other boat continued. "Yer-self for going in tonight?"

Shiknickel glanced back at distant Palmaristown with so many ships moored near her docks.

"Nah, too many," Shiknickel said.

"Some o' them boys're alive," Mcwigik protested.

"Aye, with a beam shoved through their guts. Nothing's to fix them holes."

"I ain't for letting them hang!"

Shiknickel took a deep breath and looked to his peer on the other deck.

"We go in quiet, then, just to cut 'em down," that dwarf offered. "Fast in, quiet in, and fast out."

The barrelboats emptied their crews on the riverbank just north of Pal-maristown long after midnight. More than one dwarf grumbled that he hoped their staked kin were scarecrows and not bait, for there were not more than twoscore of the powries charging into an enemy city of many thousands!

But, indeed, Palmaristown was secure in the notion that the powries had been run off and that the staked dwarves would keep them out. Few sentries were about the docks that night, and they were not an alert crew.

The powries ran over them, quickly subduing and muting those who sur-vived the rush with thick gags and mouthfuls of cloth.

They went to work methodically on both the stakes and their dead and doomed kin, finishing each dwarf with a swift blow to the head as they took him down and pulled him free of his pole. While some of the dwarves then went to work on the stakes and the prisoners, others cut the hearts from their dead kin, to be used in a ceremony and burial that would ensure descendants from these fallen fellows.

The barrelboats were back in the river soon after, pedaling hard for the Gulf of Corona, their precious cargo in tow. They would have to put ashore again the next day, they knew, to bury the hearts and perform their rituals.

The raid could be considered nothing but a terrific success, but all of those dwarves moved away from the city with heavy hearts. They had mercifully fin-ished a dozen of their kin and had retrieved four other hearts besides, exacting vengeance on twice that number of Palmaristown humans. But time and the layout of the city had worked against them: They had left other dwarves staked at Palmaristown's gates. They knew they had left friends behind.

"We'll pay them back a hundred times over," every powrie on those boats vowed, and it was not idle talk, as all of Honce would soon enough know.

The screams echoed over Palmaristown early the next morning, when the city awoke to find more than twenty men staked upside down, some doubled up, to the poles along the docks, a clear signal that Honce's long nightmare had just grown darker still.

Most looked to the river, faces drained of blood as if they expected a fleet of barrelboats floating up to empty an army on their docks. But when he arrived to see the newest of horrors, Laird Panlamaris turned his gaze to the other direction, toward Chapel Abelle.

Toward Dame Gwydre.

She had done this to him. She had unleashed the evil of the powries upon his beautiful city.

She, above all others, would pay.

CHAPTER 3

Promises and Puzzles

Rows of soldiers lined the docks, archers trained their bows, ready to sweep the decks clear. Dawson McKeege's *Lady Dreamer* came into the southeastern port of Ethelbert dos Entel under three flags: the crossed wood axes of Dame Gwydre's holding of Vanguard; the evergreen symbol of the Order of Abelle; and a universally acknowledged pennant of peace, a simple white affair. *Lady Dreamer* had picked up an escort a mile away from the city, a pair of Ethelbert warships, the best open-sea sailing vessels in Honce, with a high deck and three masts of multiple, billowing sails. As they had neared the city, the famed Entel longboats—giant shore-hugging vessels sporting only a single square sail with thirty sturdy oars to a side—had joined the armada.

One boat had rushed ahead to warn the city, and so thousands of people were out and about the hills overlooking the docks, staring down.

"Uncertain and afraid," said Cormack. Tall and long-legged with sinewy muscles, the former monk gave the impression that he was a much younger man, almost boyish, with a disarming smile and bright green eyes, a mop of shaggy blond hair on his head, and a scraggly beard such as a teenager might try to grow. Despite having left the Order of Abelle, Cormack still wore the signature brown robes, not so unusual a sight in Honce, but atop his head he sported a distinctive red beret: the bloody cap of a powrie. And so to all who did not know him Cormack surely seemed a walking contradiction—young and innocent, a bearded child as tall as a giant, wearing the robes of a beneficent order beneath a murderer's prized beret.

"Aye, all word's that they been pushed back inside their walls with nothing but the sea behind them," said Dawson McKeege, the old, grizzled sea dog. *Lady Dreamer* had put in to port only once since departing the great chapel of St. Mere Abelle, at a small town's single wharf along the outer reaches of the Mantis Arm, to gather supplies and catch up on the news of the day. News that had not shone favorably on the cause of Laird Ethelbert in his struggle against the allies of Delaval City. "Good that they're scared, I'm thinking, given what we're asking. If they thought their side winning, would they even have let us in to port? Nay, they'd've put us into the dark cold far up the coast."

He glanced away from the dock to look directly at Cormack, who directed his gaze to Cormack's wife, Milkeila, and the look of utter amazement on her wide, round face. Following her eyes to the city of Ethelbert dos Entel, it was not hard to fathom the source of her astonishment, given her background as a shaman among the tribes of rugged Alpinador. Ethelbert dos Entel was much larger than any city Milkeila had ever seen. More than that, the strange southern architecture—domes and slender towers and multistorey structures of angled walls and overhanging eaves—were as impressive in their own manner as the massive cliff and walls of St. Mere Abelle.

The woman shook her head in wonder, beaded black braids bouncing wildly about, framing her excited smile. Even Cormack, who had lived all of his youth in Honce proper and had heard many stories of this city and had even seen murals depicting it, couldn't help but giggle a bit at the exotic wonder of Ethelbert dos Entel.

Lady Dreamer slid into the slip readied for her, and Dawson, Cormack, and Milkeila went to the top of the gangplank while the crew and dockhands tied her in place. The three exchanged worried glances as they simultaneously spied archers at the ready lining the dock. Through them stepped a greeting procession comprised of monks amidst a swarm of warriors.

Dawson called down to them in his most charming voice. "We come from Chapel Abelle with word from Father Artolivan and Dame Gwydre of Vanguard Holding."

"St. Mere Abelle, you mean," answered the leading monk of the greeting party. "And glad I am to hear that!"

"You know?" Cormack blurted before Dawson could reply.

"Good word travels fast across the land, particularly when brothers are fleeing from the brutality of Laird Yeslnik and his armies!" answered the monk.

Cormack, Dawson, and Milkeila all breathed sighs of relief.

"Come along, and welcome!" the monk on the docks said. "I am Father Destros of Chapel Entel, sent to escort you to Laird Ethelbert."

"You mean, now that you're thinking you don't have to murder us," Dawson replied with a laugh and a glance around at the rows and rows of archers, bows still leveled *Lady Dreamer*'s way.

Destros's reply was to flash a disarming smile. Dawson led his two companions down to the docks.

"You are a long way from Vanguard," Father Destros said as the procession made its way to the streets and open markets of the remarkable city. It was no secret across Honce that Laird Ethelbert was quite fond of Behr, the desert kingdom to the south around the towering Belt-and-Buckle Mountains, upon whose northern foothills Ethelbert dos Entel had been built, and upon whose southern foothills lay the great Behr city of Jacintha.

"Dame Gwydre's no fool," Dawson replied. "She's seeing Honce tearing itself apart. Don't doubt that your troubles are to become Vanguard's troubles in short order."

"My Laird Ethelbert has no such designs upon the northern wilderness of Vanguard, I assure you."

"Word has it that your Laird Ethelbert isn't the one winning."

That remark jolted Destros to a halt, and all about them, soldiers and monks alike, gasped.

"I didn't come here for pretty words and pretend thoughts," Dawson said. "That might crinkle your nose a bit, but you'll be glad to see *Lady Dreamer* soon enough, I promise."

"Quite the diplomat," Cormack whispered to Dawson amidst the uncomfortable silence.

Dawson just chortled and gave a crooked-toothed grin.

Laird Ethelbert's palace was not a grand affair compared to the splendors of St. Mere Abelle, but it was quite beautiful and, like the city around it, filled with the colorful and exotic goods of the strange kingdom to the south. Painted screens and fans gave a myriad of angles to every room. The polished stones of the hallways prompted shiny and intricate designs of swirling colors and even a few small distinctive images that seemed like pieces of larger murals or teasing sentence fragments on an ancient and much-damaged parchment. The effect proved intoxicating even to grumpy Dawson.

A long time passed before Cormack and the others realized that Father Destros had slowed his pace considerably to let them bask in the beauty of Castle Ethelbert. He'd led them in a roundabout path to view it all, they realized, when at last they came into the wide audience hall of the laird.

There was no carpet leading to the marble throne and the old man seated upon it, but the patterns on the floor tiles showed them a clear enough path. A pair of delicate fountains stood to either side of that walkway, two-tiered and with graceful fish statues spitting water into the lower bowl and complementing beautifully the flow and grace of the mosaic tiles and the many screens and tapestries along the walls. Even the guards—dressed in red and blue and with wide flowing sashes as belts and sporting tassels along the length of their tall pole arms—seemed more decorative than utilitarian, though there was no doubting the strength of those iron hooks and axe heads they held fast!

Cormack, Dawson, and Milkeila took it all in, basking in the designs, but the former monk's gaze soon enough locked on a most curious figure, a small woman, her black hair and brown skin revealing her to be from Behr. She was dressed in black silks and carrying a sword that Cormack was certain he recognized. She stood to the right of the dais that held Ethelbert's throne, beside a man of similar heritage who was similarly dressed. Cormack instinctively understood the danger of these two, much more pronounced than the power of the laird's military advisors standing across the throne from them. It was hard to discern the musculature of the man, who was not of extraordinary height or girth, but Cormack knew that his muscles were tightly wound, like a coiled spring. His head was shaven, his eyebrows thick and black, and his dark eyes did not ever seem to blink, as if the lids dared not interrupt his intense stare.

"My laird, I present Dawson McKeege of Vanguard, emissary of Dame Gwydre," Father Destros said after bowing to Ethelbert. "And his companions, Cormack of . . ."

He paused and glanced back at Cormack and silently mouthed, "St. Mere Abelle?" to which the monk smiled and nodded.

"Of St. Mere Abelle, the Blessed Chapel," Destros continued. "And his wife, Milkeila of Alpinador. A most varied and unusual crew has come to our docks!"

That last flourish seemed lost on Laird Ethelbert, who stared only at Cormack with great interest.

"What are you wearing?" the old man said, and, indeed, he seemed ancient to the three newcomers, as old and tired as Father Artolivan himself.

"My laird?" Cormack asked.

"On your head," Ethelbert clarified. "Is that the beret of a red-cap dwarf?"

Cormack shuffled from foot to foot and cleared his throat. "It is, Laird Ethelbert," he explained. "Won in mortal combat."

"You killed a powrie and took his cap?"

Cormack thought back to that fateful day on a beach in far-off Alpinador, on the steamy, hot lake of Mithranidoon, when he had battled a nasty little dwarf named Pragganag. He hadn't actually killed the wretch, but he had won the fight. The other powries had then finished the job and had given him Prag's hat as a trophy as agreed upon before the duel.

"I defeated the dwarf and took his cap," said Cormack, trying to sound confident, "and by order of Father De Guilbe, who led my chapel, I am bound to wear it forevermore."

Ethelbert looked to Destros, but the young monk could only shrug, having never heard of such a thing before.

"Any man who can beat a powrie . . ." Ethelbert paused. "What weapon did you use?"

"No weapon," Cormack assured him.

The response brought a great guffaw of laughter from the old laird. "Any man who can beat a powrie—and with his bare hands no less—is a man I want by my side in battle!" the laird proclaimed, to many approving nods.

Ethelbert came forward in his chair suddenly, poking a finger Cormack's way. "But if you're lying," he warned, wagging that digit and wearing a scowl—but one that could not hold as he fell back and laughed again. "If you're lying, then I'd want you beside me anyway, to tell my tales as fancifully as you weave your own!"

Almost everyone in the room began to laugh, including the three newcomers, who looked to each other with great relief. Everyone, that is, but the silk-clad warriors, who were not even grinning.

"You've sailed a long way," Ethelbert said when the titter and chatter died away. "Do you mean to tell me why?"

"To tell you of the proclamation of St. Mere Abelle," Cormack said, "though it seems you have already heard the word."

"Even the church could not swallow the bile of the fool Yeslnik," said Ethelbert, his voice strained as he spat the cursed name.

"And we came because you've wound yourself into a tight spot," Dawson said bluntly. "And so have we, caught in the walls of St. Mere Abelle."

Ethelbert paused, his face growing very serious. All around him men tensed, a reaction similar to that out on the docks when Dawson had mentioned the state of the war.

"The Dame of Vanguard will not see Yeslnik win," Dawson quickly added.

"Dame Gwydre will support my cause?"

Dawson paused, frowning. "It's a bit more complicated than that, Laird Ethelbert." Dawson looked all around. "Perhaps in a setting more private," he continued in a lower voice. To the surprise of many in the room, and to the absolute shock of Father Destros, Laird Ethelbert nodded his agreement and told his attendants to arrange it immediately.

Dawson and Cormack exchanged quick, knowing looks: Laird Ethelbert's predicament was obviously as dire as they had heard.

In short order, the three visitors to the city sat in a small room before

Ethelbert, who was flanked by an older veteran warrior and Father Destros on one side and by the dark-skinned woman from Behr on the other. Unlike all the others in the room, she did not sit down, and her hand did not stray far from the hilt of the fabulous sword hanging on her left hip, a sword that looked exactly like the one Bransen carried.

"Choose your words carefully," Laird Ethelbert warned to begin the negotiation.

"We didn't sail halfway around the world, dodging Palmaristown warships and powrie barrelboats all the way, to dance pretty," Dawson replied.

"What does Dame Gwydre offer?"

"Not just Dame Gwydre, but St. Mere Abelle, as well," Cormack interjected.

Ethelbert shifted painfully in his seat, seeming even older than before.

"The war does not go well for you," said Dawson. "You've put a grand fight against Yeslnik and his uncle before him, by all accounts, but there's too many in Delaval and Palmaristown, and all along the river. Yeslnik can put fifty thousand in the field, and you've just a tenth o' that."

"We have heard proclamations of our defeat before," answered the veteran at Ethelbert's side. "Usually right before we chased Yeslnik from the field!"

"A grand fight," Dawson said again. "And no disrespect intended—far from it. Would that Laird Ethelbert had won the war outright, but 'twas not to be and is not to be."

"Then what?" asked Ethelbert. "I thought Dawson claimed that he did not dance prettily."

"True enough," replied the old sea dog from rugged Vanguard. "You cannot win, and you know you cannot win."

"I will kill him for you, great Ethelbert," the woman in silk promised in a thick Behr accent, leaning forward.

Ethelbert held up his hand to silence her. "What do you know?"

"Only what you know," Dawson replied. "And not to doubt that our own situation isn't much more promising, except that we're caught behind the tall and thick walls of the great chapel, with a horde of monks and magical gemstones to keep our enemies out. And not to doubt that we're not to win over Yeslnik's thousands, either."

"Not alone," Cormack explained.

"You've come for an alliance," said Ethelbert. "Ethelbert dos Entel and Vanguard, combined against Yeslnik."

"And the Order of Blessed Abelle," Cormack added. "Those who remain loyal to Father Artolivan, at least, for rumor spreads that Yeslnik has created a shadow church to subvert Father Artolivan's power."

Father Destros's face tightened at that, but he nodded to show that he was not surprised and, it appeared, to offer a bit of support for Artolivan.

"Then as I said out in the main chamber you have come to offer your support for my cause," said Ethelbert.

"Partly that," Dawson replied. "An alliance, but not fealty."

"Explain."

"Dame Gwydre is your peer, not your subject, and the church of Father Artolivan is something altogether different than those choices," said Dawson. "We need to work together to rid the land of Yeslnik, but not to place King Ethelbert in his stead."

That had all of those seated opposite Dawson bristling with outrage. Except for Ethelbert, who leaned back and rubbed a hand wearily over his old, wrinkled face. After some consideration, he shook his head.

"Vanguard separate, perhaps," he said. "But not the other holdings. It cannot be. After years of war and with the roads locked under the boots of armies, Honce cannot be as she was. The lairds must stand united."

"Aye, and not Vanguard separate," said Dawson.

"Then what?" Ethelbert demanded. "What does Dame Gwydre want?"

"Queen Gwydre," Dawson dared to correct, widening the eyes of the four across the room. "Ethelbert remains independent and supreme in his holding," Dawson quickly added. "Your city is your own, good laird, in gratitude from all of Honce for the battle you dared wage."

"Silence!" Laird Ethelbert shouted. "You come to my throne demanding fealty of me?"

"We come demanding nothing but offering our help in your struggle with Yeslnik."

"Mutual benefit?"

Dawson nodded. "Best kind."

"But to the end result of a Queen Gwydre?" Ethelbert asked incredulously. "Why would I agree to any such thing?"

"Because your only other choice is to be pushed into the sea," Cormack said, surprising everyone. "Or to remain trapped here surrounded by enemies. With a Queen Gwydre enthroned, Laird Ethelbert would be a man of the highest standing across the realm, independent within his own holding and in his dealings with others, like the sheiks of Behr. Such will not be the case with a King Yeslnik."

"But wouldn't that be the case with King Ethelbert?" the laird asked.

"We cannot prevail were those the terms," said Cormack. "Our only hope lies in turning some of Yeslnik's minions to our cause. The Order of Blessed

Abelle helps with that, but the name of Ethelbert is not held in high esteem in the lands of central and western Honce. You have dug deep trenches with your war, and not a family in Honce has been spared the grief. Such is not true of Dame Gwydre, who will be viewed as an alternative to the misery the common folk have known these last months and years. They will view her with hope, a savior from their pain, and will perhaps turn against their King Yeslnik and fight for her."

The old warrior to Ethelbert's side began to protest, but the laird cut him short with a snarling and derisive, "The common folk."

"All the men of Vanguard and all the men at your command combined would falter at the feet of Yeslnik's great army," said Dawson.

"And so you are in as desperate a situation as I," Ethelbert protested.

"Nay, for we can just sail home and be done with it," Dawson replied.

"The walls of St. Mere Abelle are impenetrable," Cormack added. "Forever and more can the brothers remain within. We are all quite above this war of yours if we so choose."

Ethelbert's narrowed eyes were his only response.

"Or it would have been, and still would be, a small matter for Dame Gwydre and Father Artolivan to broker a truce with Yeslnik in exchange for the autonomy of Vanguard, a land for which he cares little, and to which he cannot easily march or sail," Cormack added, though didn't quite believe. "But we choose this path."

"Because Dame Gwydre is no different than Delaval and Yeslnik," Ethelbert said with a snicker.

"So different you'd never think her a laird . . . err, dame," Dawson answered.

"Dame Gwydre and Father Artolivan choose this path out of generosity and duty," said Cormack. "They cannot abide the agony the common folk of Honce suffer because of the designs of an ambitious laird."

Ethelbert stiffened at that, and Cormack added, "We know that Delaval began this war, and that you tried to do as we now hope. And we have no love of Yeslnik or his second from Palmaristown, a brutal and wretched man. We would see Yeslnik defeated. This is the only way, and even this plan seems desperate."

"But you would do it for Queen Gwydre?" asked Ethelbert.

"We do it because it's right," Dawson answered. "Same reason we just fought the Samhaists in Vanguard."

"But you called it desperate and claim that you can sail away from it."

"A sorry bunch of heroes that'd make us," said Dawson.

"Heroes, yes," the laird replied with more than a little sarcasm.

"We have come as friends and allies, Laird Ethelbert," Cormack said, "openly and under a flag of truce. Our offer is one of cooperation and friendship and is yours to accept or reject."

"And if I reject?"

"We sail away to St. Mere Abelle."

"To Yeslnik's side?"

"Never," Cormack and Dawson said together.

Ethelbert managed a nod of acceptance at that. He waved them away, then. "Go to your boat or remain in the castle if you choose—my attendants will see to your room and needs. We will meet again when I have discussed this with my generals here."

The three rose, bowed, and turned to leave, but Cormack hesitated and fixed his gaze on the Behr warrior woman. "That sword," he said. "It is most marvelous."

The woman eyed him dangerously, unblinking.

"Affwin Wi is from the land of Behr, where such swords are crafted," Ethelbert answered.

"It is Jhesta Tu, is it not?"

"Speaking a name does not reveal understanding," the dark woman replied in her thick Behr accent, biting the syllables short and almost stabbing with the hard consonant sounds. "And does not impress. Speaking of what you do not know is the mark of a fool."

Cormack sorted out a reply, wanting to explore the origin of this particular sword a bit further. Instead he changed his mind and just smiled, bowed, and caught up with his companions, who had decided to go back to the security of *Lady Dreamer.*

Impertinent fools," said Kirren Howen, the general who had sat by Laird Ethelbert's side for the private meeting. Past middle age but not nearly Ethelbert's contemporary, the thick-haired, graying warrior took care with his tone to make his claim one of support and not absolute judgment.

Laird Ethelbert turned from the counter where he was pouring fine liquor for the two into delicate glasses he had recently received from Behr.

"Look at these," he said, holding them up for his friend. "You can see the tan liquid through their shining sides. So much more delicate and beautiful than a bronze mug, no matter how many wolves or dancing ladies you carve into one."

Kirren Howen cocked his head curiously. "Yes, laird." He took the glass as Ethelbert moved over and extended it to him.

"Yet another fine example of the idiocy of parochialism, do you agree?"

The general seemed not to understand.

"Beasts of Behr!" Ethelbert exclaimed with a laugh, explaining it all so bluntly and so simply, as was his wont. Certainly Kirren Howen caught on to the meaning immediately. For most of Honce, the desert kingdom south of the impassable mountains was a place of barbarians and beasts masquerading as men. But Laird Ethelbert and those of his court knew better.

"Have you ever seen Affwin Wi dance?"

"My laird?"

"You have witnessed her in battle, no doubt."

"Of course."

"As fine a warrior as ever carried a blade—though she would not even need a blade to kill most opponents."

"I cannot deny the truth of that."

"She is equally exquisite when she dances. A promise of love, delicate and beautiful, or dangerous, even deadly. She can twirl about on the ball of one foot slowly enough to kill a man with lust or break into a spin so fast that if she kicked out of it she could surely crush a man's heart with her foot. She is Behr, you see. So raw and pure, colorful and dark, delicate and deadly."

The door burst in then and two men, brawny warriors both, stumbled into the room, nearly tripping over each other.

"My laird," they said together.

"I can take their miserable ship right out of the water, Laird Ethelbert," promised one, Myrick the Bold, the ferocious and impetuous commander of Entel, the city's dock section.

"And I will deliver their heads to the gates of Chapel Abelle," said the other, an enormously strong man named Tyne.

"I thank the old ones and Blessed Abelle and the Sun God of Behr—whichever might be listening!—for you every day, Kirren," Ethelbert said to his older and calmer general. He tapped his glass against Kirren Howen's.

Another man, small of frame and hardly hinting at any warrior stature, rushed into the room. "Your pardon, my laird," said Palfry, Ethelbert's favorite attendant, like a son to the old laird. "I tried to slow them. . . ."

"I told you to summon these two, Palfry, not to excite them," Ethelbert said with a slight chuckle. "You know how hot run the humors of Myrick and Tyne!"

"Yes, laird," Palfry said, lowering his eyes.

"What do you think, Kirren?" Ethelbert asked. "Should we let Myrick sink this boat from Vanguard and just kill the emissaries, or cut off their heads as Tyne suggests?"

Kirren Howen's eyes went wide with surprise.

———

Quite the diplomat, are you not?" Cormack scolded Dawson again when they and Milkeila were alone in the captain's private room on *Lady Dreamer*.

Dawson snorted. "Speaks the man who told Ethelbert he couldn't win the war."

"What choice was I given after Dawson proclaimed Gwydre the Queen of Honce?"

"I didn't sail halfway around the world to parse my words, monk," said Dawson.

"His temperament might have been more calm if we'd brought Callen Duwornay," Milkeila suggested softly, not looking at them.

Both men gaped at her, then laughed aloud, the tension broken. The budding love between Dawson McKeege, Dame Gwydre's most trusted advisor, and Callen, the mother-in-law of the rogue known as the Highwayman, was, after all, the worst-kept secret on the Mirianic.

"It was a dangerous play," Cormack said after a bit, as Dawson broke out a jug of his rum and three wooden mugs.

"The world's burning, front to back," Dawson replied, handing Milkeila her mug first. It pleased him for some reason each time he remembered that this woman from Alpinador could drink the both of them under the table.

"A play no less dangerous than Cormack's follow," Milkeila said in her somewhat shaky command of the Honce tongue. She brought the mug up, dipped a finger into it, and closed her eyes.

"Now why do you do that?" Dawson asked. "A bit of barbarian magic to take the bite away?"

Milkeila merely smiled as she always did when Dawson asked that predictable question. She took a great swallow of the rum, nearly draining the considerable mug.

"She cheats," Dawson said to Cormack.

"At everything," Milkeila's husband agreed. "That's why I keep her by my side."

"Oh, I'm knowin' why you keep her by your side, monk. Too many days in a chapel full of men."

Both men looked at Milkeila as Dawson finished the crude remark, but both knew better than to expect a blush from this warrior, strong with the spear and her shamanistic magic and secure and comfortable in her skin.

"What I'm wondering is why she's keeping you," Dawson finished, raising his mug in toast to Milkeila, who smiled and returned the lift.

"For once we agree," said Cormack.

"Your words with Laird Ethelbert were correct," Milkeila said. "We should state our case openly with that one. He will see any deception, and he knows more about us than we believe."

"Now where do you get that?" asked Dawson.

Milkeila just stared at him hard, gradually directing his gaze to Cormack.

"The woman from Behr," Cormack explained. "Her sword."

"Looked a lot like Bransen's sword," said Dawson.

"Such swords are common in Behr, perhaps," Cormack offered.

"When we see her again, seek a vantage to peer beneath the left fold of her blouse," Milkeila advised.

"Why would I be doing that, aside from her obvious charms?" asked Dawson.

"I'm not sure," Milkeila replied. "Just a hint, perhaps, and a guess. Laird Ethelbert is no fool. He has survived the overwhelming force of Laird Delaval and several times seemed almost on the edge of victory."

"True enough," Cormack said. "He is cornered and in a desperate place, but let us not underestimate him."

"Or those around him," Milkeila added. "We have witnessed the fighting prowess of the Highwayman, and if Laird Ethelbert's bodyguards are of equal skill they will be formidable."

"If they're half as good as that one they could sink my ship by themselves," Dawson agreed and drained his wooden mug.

I would, laird," Myrick the Bold said. "At your word, my archers will sweep the deck. . . ."

He stopped under the mocking laughter of Laird Ethelbert.

"My laird?" he asked.

"Yes, yes, we should kill every one of them!" Ethelbert said with sarcastic exuberance, which melted into a self-deprecating, lonely chuckle. "They committed the greatest crime of all."

The three generals looked to each other with mounting confusion, and Kirren Howen finally asked, "Laird?"

"They told the truth," Ethelbert explained. He wasn't looking at them as he spoke, rather staring off into the empty corner of the room. "The greatest crime of all, to tell a laird the truth."

Another sad laugh ensued. When Ethelbert lifted his glass to his lips, his hand trembled severely. "Especially an old laird," he finished, looking back at the three.

"What would you have me do, laird?" an exasperated Myrick asked.

"Think," came the simple response.

Myrick and Tyne exchanged confused looks, but when they turned to Kirren Howen they saw that he understood. His expression revealed his sadness.

"So this is how we lose," Ethelbert said. "A much softer fall than we had expected, yes, Kirren?"

"Perhaps no fall at all," the general replied. "Do you trust their promises of autonomy?"

Ethelbert paused, then chuckled again, then shrugged. "Have I a choice? Truly?"

"Yes, laird!" said Tyne. "Send them away! Or send their heads away!"

"Our enemy gathers in the west," Ethelbert replied. "Our allies north along the coast have been ravaged. We'll find no reinforcements from Felidan Bay or the Mantis Arm. Yeslnik has razed those towns immediately west of us, so we'll find no support, supplies, or warriors should we choose to march. What is left to us, then? To wait here until the armies storm our gates once more?"

"A better deal with Dame Gwydre and Father Artolivan, then," said Kirren Howen.

Ethelbert nodded, looking very old. "More assurances, perhaps."

"King Ethelbert!" said Myrick the Bold.

The old laird laughed again but then steadied himself and straightened more fully than they had seen in many weeks. "It will not be," he replied, his voice strong. He held up his nearly empty glass. "Be of good cheer, my friends," he said, and he waited for them to return the toast. "For hope has come to us on a boat from Vanguard, and the fool Yeslnik has turned the church against his designs. No more do we fight alone!"

He drained his glass, then threw it against the stone wall, his old eyes sparkling as if reflecting the shattering and flying shards. "Go and retrieve our guests. Myrick, and Tyne, bring me Father Destros and Affwin Wi. Bid her to drag that angry Merwal Yahna along with her."

The two looked at each other in confusion, and Ethelbert said, "Go! Go!" and waved them away.

"Bid for better terms," Kirren Howen said when they were alone.

The old laird nodded, though he understood that he and Kirren Howen would not be in agreement over what those better terms might be. The wily old general was still thinking of Ethelbert as the King of Honce, as Ethelbert himself had been only a day before—assuming, of course, they managed to find some way to defeat Yeslnik of Delaval and his overwhelming garrison. With only oblivion or flight to Behr as the alternative to absolute victory, Ethelbert had held fast his dream of ruling the whole of the land. What would happen, after all, to his people, to Kirren Howen and poor Palfry, if anything other than that unlikely scenario came to fruition? No, losing to Yeslnik was simply unthinkable.

But now another possibility had rudely entered the equation, a third way, perhaps, and as if a great responsibility had been lifted from Ethelbert's tired old shoulders, the words of Dawson McKeege, crude and blunt as they had been, had invigorated his spirits.

At the same time, however, that new element had allowed Laird Ethelbert to physically slump. He could feel old again because the consequence of that inevitability was somehow not quite so dire.

Kirren Howen wanted him to bargain for greater power, a more prominent role, and perhaps even to fight for his well-earned right to the throne, should their alliance prove victorious, but Ethelbert, though he meant to play it out, was more concerned with those he would soon leave behind. A large part of him, the old and tired man, just wanted to agree to the terms the emissaries had brought and be done with it. But when he looked at Kirren Howen, so long his friend and companion, who had sailed with him and fought beside him for all these years, Laird Ethelbert had to nod his agreement.

He threw a wink to his general when the others began making their way into the room. "Better terms," he whispered so that only Kirren Howen could hear.

"Glad we are that you have arrived," Ethelbert said when all had gathered. "I admit to knowing little about your Dame Gwydre, though I am certain that you would regale me the day through with tales of her honor and strength were I to give you the chance."

"At least a day," Dawson said.

Kirren Howen and the other two generals grimaced at the interruption, but Ethelbert just laughed it off.

"I've not the time," he replied. "But pray do tell me, Dawson of Vanguard, is your lady as crass and irreverent as her emissary?"

For the first time it seemed as if Ethelbert had taken Dawson off his balance, as the old sea dog stumbled for a reply.

"Dame Gwydre is beloved by her people," Cormack dared say. "Her bloodline is long and true, good lairds all. Kind and generous."

"Not traits that will aid us against the wretched Yeslnik," said Ethelbert.

"But a demeanor that will endear many to her cause as we do battle," Cormack promised.

"Yes, you have already claimed as much," the old laird replied doubtfully. "I accept your . . . impatience as a call to action, but of course I cannot accept your terms as presented."

The three emissaries looked to each other nervously.

"You'd have us sail away?" Dawson said.

"If that is your choice. Did you really expect me to cede Honce to you before it is even won?"

"This is the choice of Father Artolivan, and if Honce is to be won it'll be no small part owed to his doing."

"And no small part to Dame Gwydre's, and no small part to the warriors of Ethelbert who have resisted the dominion of Yeslnik and Delaval before him for all these bloody months. More than ten thousand warriors from a multitude of holdings and fighting under my flag have given their lives for King Ethelbert. Am I to disrespect their loyalty and sacrifice?"

"You cannot win."

"I could take hostage emissaries from Dame Gwydre and Father Artolivan and use them to barter with Yeslnik. I doubt that he would give to me any less than Dawson of Vanguard has offered." Ethelbert let that uncomfortable thought hang in the air for a few heartbeats before breaking the tension with a smile. "But you see, friends, I hate Yeslnik more than you do. I prefer the alliance."

"We're not to turn the other lairds to the hoped-for flag of a King Ethelbert," Dawson reminded. "There's too much blood on the ground."

"Tell them to fight for Dame Gwydre or for the monks and Chapel Abelle," said Ethelbert.

Father Destros shifted uncomfortably.

"Your pardon, Father. For St. Mere Abelle," the laird clarified.

The monk bowed to Ethelbert.

"I care not of the promises you give to the minor lairds," said Ethelbert. "But they are not binding to me or to my generals or to my holding. Where was Dame Gwydre when Delaval declared himself King of Honce?"

"Warring with Samhaists, trolls, goblins, and barbarians in the north!" said Dawson.

"Only I slowed Delaval's march," Ethelbert went on as if Vanguard's struggles hardly mattered. "Only Laird Ethelbert dared step forth to oppose the tyrant. You say that some of the lairds loyal to Yeslnik may turn to our cause, to Dame Gwydre's cause, but how many of the lairds now fighting for good Laird Ethelbert will then desert to the more apparent winner?"

"So, please, good man Dawson, do not bluster and bluff. Your loyalty to your lady is commendable and speaks well of her and for her. We will need such conviction if we are to prevail over the dastardly Yeslnik. Let us join and complete that deed and then worry over the spoils that may remain."

"The other lairds—"

"Tell them whatever you would tell them to turn them against Yeslnik," Ethelbert replied sharply. "Most are not fools and likely hate the foppish pretender already. He is not half the man as his uncle, Laird Delaval. But I will not pledge fealty to your Dame Gwydre or to your church. I will, however, promise not to turn my armies against you once our common foe is defeated in exchange for your like promise."

Dawson, Cormack, and Milkeila exchanged concerned and confused glances.

"Perhaps you should sail back to St. Mere Abelle to deliver the terms," Laird Ethelbert said. "And then sail back here to tell me if they are agreeable to Dame Gwydre and Father Artolivan."

Dawson sputtered in response to that absurd notion.

"Then make a decision, Dawson of Vanguard," Laird Ethelbert demanded. "Here and now, or be gone from my docks."

Dawson's weather-beaten face scrunched up as he eyed the old man dangerously.

"Do you think that your Dame Gwydre will be pleased that her man let his wounded pride sever an alliance that we both need?" Ethelbert said simply. He paused for just a moment before adding, "Have we an agreement?"

"You're everything they said you'd be, old laird," Dawson replied, his face and posture relaxing. "And aye, we'll throw in with you to the death of Yeslnik."

"Palfry, my good lad," Ethelbert said to his attendant. "A feast is in order to celebrate this union. See to it."

The young page bowed and ran out of the room.

"Go and retrieve your crew," Ethelbert said. "A night of celebration and plentiful food will see them well on their way."

"I would stay, good Laird Ethelbert," Cormack said. "Along with Milkeila, my wife." He put his arm about the shaman.

"Your wife?" the old laird repeated with clear skepticism. How many times Ethelbert had witnessed such mixed marriages, although usually between one from Honce and one from Behr. Rarely had they succeeded.

"We will serve here, with your permission, as representatives of the Order of Blessed Abelle and of Dame Gwydre," Cormack offered.

"Well, indeed," said Ethelbert, and a sly smile spread across his face. "And given. But can you fight?"

"We can fight."

Ethelbert nodded and waved them away. Before they had even left the room he turned to Kirren Howen and to Myrick and Tyne, who drew very near. "Prepare a flotilla for Jacintha. I would advise my friends in Behr of the hopeful turn of events."

"Perhaps they will at last send us more warriors," said Myrick.

"It is possible," said Ethelbert, but with obvious skepticism. He looked to Kirren Howen, who nodded to show that he understood the true purpose here: to secure an escape route, should one be necessary, and to bring another possible ally into the mix should Ethelbert and Dame Gwydre prove victorious over Yeslnik.

True to Ethelbert's word, Dawson's crew ate well that night at a grand feast in the open market outside the doors of Castle Ethelbert. The laird and his generals attended, but only for a short time.

Long enough, though, for Cormack to finally get near to the woman warrior from Behr. He tried to strike up a conversation with her regarding her heritage and her sword, but she pretended not to understand him and just turned away.

In that turn, however, the former monk got a glimpse under the fold of her black silk blouse and was able to recognize a star-shaped, gem-studded brooch she had pinned to her chest. Perhaps there were more swords such as hers and Bransen's in the deserts to the south, but surely there were no other such distinctive magical brooches.

"It's Bransen's sword," Cormack later explained to Dawson on *Lady Dreamer*'s deck long after the moon had set in the west.

"How do you know?"

"She wears his brooch," said Milkeila.

"He's dead, then," Dawson said, his voice full of regret. "Might be that he was killed by Ethelbert. You two should sail with me, then."

Cormack shook his head. "Milkeila, perhaps."

"Not without my husband."

"Then, no," said Cormack. "We will be safe here. Father Destros is a man of fine reputation within my order. A man loyal to Father Artolivan."

"And you want to find out about Bransen," Dawson reasoned.

"We owe him that much at least."

"You had best walk with care and question in whispers," Dawson advised. "If it was Ethelbert who killed him, those answers might get you two tossed into the sea."

Dawson patted Cormack on the shoulder and gave Milkeila a hug before heading belowdecks to plot his course.

"This is a magnificent city," Milkeila said to Cormack, following him to *Lady Dreamer*'s rail.

Unexpectedly, a smile spread on Cormack's face, and Milkeila didn't quite understand until the man nodded his chin, prompting her to follow his gaze to the southeast. There, far, far across the dark waters of the great Mirianic Ocean, swirls of colors painted the sky, the legendary aurora that gave Corona its name, the heavenly ring of magical gemstones that God had shown to Blessed Abelle a century before. That gift had sustained the founder of Cormack's church on a distant deserted island and had returned Abelle to Honce, the blessed man walking on the ocean waters across the many miles. Cormack had heard of the equatorial aurora, of course, and had even seen hints of it from St. Mere Abelle on a couple of occasions, but never had he witnessed it so clearly. Never had its glory shone to him to so lift his heart as now.

"It is beautiful," Milkeila remarked with awe.

"The fruits of the ring did sustain Blessed Abelle," Cormack replied. "And so they will sustain us through these dark times."

He put his hand on the rail, and Milkeila put hers atop his. The lovers stared out at the aurora for a long while, then turned their eyes to each other and sealed the promise of the magic of God with a long and gentle kiss.

CHAPTER 4

Stark

He let the wind be his guide as he meandered across the lands devastated by war, paralleling the roads that had been viewed as a sign of hope and progress by the people of Honce. Those networks had been built to open trade, it was said, and to allow the lairds to move their armies to rid the land of powries. Few foresaw that those same roads would carry the engines of war to holding after holding as the two most prominent lairds, Delaval and Ethelbert, laid claim to a unified kingdom of Honce as their dominion.

Bransen avoided one battered village after another, having little desire to repeat the dialogue he had suffered with the widow from Hooplin Downs. Truly, after his encounter with the folk there, he didn't wish to speak with anyone, other than his wife, who remained so far, far away.

He did sneak into the clusters of farmhouses when he found them, though. In the dark of night the Highwayman made his way about the communities, pilfering food and drink where he could. With his great skill he was never seen or heard and was always well on his way long before the sun lightened the eastern sky. He tried to leave behind firewood or anything he could find to repay his unwitting hosts.

Each morning seemed to dawn a bit warmer as summer came on in full to this southernmost region of Honce. Still moving due west, Bransen kept expecting the road to turn north or to bend that way at least. But the towering mountains remained in clear view to his left, day after day. He was in lands unknown, for this was not the route that he and Jameston had taken from Pryd Town to Ethelbert dos Entel. In those first hours after fleeing the city, after his defeat at the hands of Affwin Wi, Bransen must have veered farther south than he had intended. Many times the battered young man considered backtracking to the coast and running due north until the coastline curved eastward, taking him to Chapel Abelle and Cadayle.

But Bransen found himself strangely transfixed by the scenes opening before him. He didn't know it, but he was following the route Yeslnik's army had taken when they had departed the field outside Ethelbert dos Entel's walls, the would-be king running from fear of Laird Ethelbert's strange Behr assassins. The same assassins who had murdered Laird Delaval and taken Bransen's sword and brooch. The same assassins who had taken from Bransen his hopes of a better Honce.

His travel became more difficult over the next few days, for there were no more farmhouses from which he could steal food—no standing ones, at least. And there were no chickens in any barnyard nor any living sheep or cattle or . . . anything. The crops had been burned and trampled, the ground torn and ruined. Bransen noted thousands of footprints and hoofprints and deep ruts caused by many passing chariots and wagons.

Bransen bent low to inspect the ground. Utterly, intentionally ruined, he realized to his horror. Most of it was simply black and red dirt common to the region, but Bransen also found white specks, as if someone had scattered something atop the trampled areas. He tapped his finger to one such speck and brought it up to sniff, then tasted it. Bransen's face crinkled, and he spat out the powerfully salty substance.

Some army had purposely done this. This was far more than the result of a march. One of the lairds—Ethelbert or Yeslnik—had devastated this region, had ruined the villages and the livelihood of the folk of southernmost Honce. Yeslnik, he figured, since the most recent tracks led to the west and since Ethelbert's army remained in his city on the eastern coast.

So Laird Yeslnik had crossed here in his retreat to Delaval City and had destroyed the farmland behind him. But where had all the residents gone?

Bransen's gaze went out to the north, toward where he approximated Pryd Town to be, and he imagined his former home overrun by bedraggled refugees, dirty and hungry and desperate. He sighed deeply at that probability but just shook his head and moved along.

Soon after, he came to a fork in the road, where one branch turned decidedly north and a broken signpost indicated it to be the road to Pryd. The other branch, continuing to the west, was marked for Delaval City. The army's passage, still due west, was clear enough to see, but the north road showed no fresh signs of any substantial passage.

Bransen went north for the rest of that day, moving near to the road, left and right, and searching for wagon marks or hoofprints of the slow, scraping boot marks of refugees. He found nothing recent.

The next morning he intended to continue north, knowing he would still have several days of walking before he reached Pryd Town, but he kept turning his curious gaze to the south. Without ever really understanding why, without questioning his urge, Bransen reversed course and headed that way, his pace swift all the way back to the signpost on the east-west road. He went right across the path, jogging across the despoiled fields and past the husks of burned-out houses. He happened upon one sizable community, or what had been, and found the scene of a ferocious battle. A small ruined keep sat on a hill at the southernmost point of the former town, its walls battered and torn down in many places, gray smoke still wafting out of its hollowed-out walls.

Bransen had to turn away when he moved up to the keep, or he would have vomitted the meager food he had scavenged over the last few days. For unlike the many deserted communities he had crossed, this larger one revealed to him the fate of its inhabitants. Their bodies covered the ground inside those keep walls, dead of arrows, hacked down by swords, charred by flames. A flock of crows lifted away when Bransen stepped inside, and a stench of death more powerful than anything the young warrior had ever imagined washed over him. This time he could not resist the urge to throw up.

They were all in there, men and women, old and young—very young. In one corner, Bransen found a dozen children, the largest among them surely not more than eight years, huddled together. Even at this state of great decay, with the crows having taken much, Bransen could see that their innocent bodies had been violated by many brutal chops of sword and axe.

How could any man bring himself to such depravity? What savagery had years of warfare brought to the participants, robbing them of their very humanity? He thought of the fop Yeslnik, for surely this was his doing. Bransen tried, unsuccessfully, to place this reality within the knowledge he had gained of the man during their previous encounters.

Was that weakling Yeslnik really capable of this?

The answer lay starkly before him.

Anxious thoughts crept around him like the black wings of the many cawing crows. He had to get to Cadayle and, with her and Callen, flee to Vanguard. They needed to be as far from this wretched and despoiled land as possible.

Bransen started to leave the ruined keep when he heard the distinctive whistling of an arrow cutting the air. Crouching low in the shadows, he scanned the area, using his skill and his magic, his inner *ki-chi-kree*, to propel himself up the rubble of the keep's southwestern corner. The roof in this section was fully gone, allowing Bransen to peer over the wall top. Spying three archers down a hill and across a field, he realized that the arrow had not been aimed his way. The men had a woman in tow, and one was pulling her along by the hair while the others took turns kicking at and spitting on her.

Bransen felt the blood running thick in his veins, felt his heart pumping strongly. His fingers tingled with anticipation.

"It's not my fight," he told himself determinedly, conjuring images of Cadayle, reminding himself that she was pregnant with his child. He had gone to Pryd Town to deliver his message and to Ethelbert dos Entel in search of a greater truth.

And he had failed. He had lost everything—everything except for Cadayle and their child and her mother. They were his responsibility now. That alone, and not some unknown woman being dragged away by ruffians in a land he did not know.

The stench of death continued to waft up about him, a pungent reminder of the awfulness of this place, a reminder that he could not stay here. Instinctively he looked west where the sun was low in the sky. He went back down the wall, exited the keep, and moved swiftly away to the north. He had almost made the road again, stubbornly telling himself with every step that this was not his fight and not his business.

But Bransen could not bring himself to cross that road. He turned about, to the south, in pursuit of the men and the captured woman. He turned his back to the north and to the responsibility he had proclaimed as his lone care and to the lie of dispassion.

As the miles rolled out beneath his feet he was surprised to find that those he pursued had not stopped with the setting sun but had continued on long into the night. Finally he spotted their campfire on a distant hill to the south. The ground was more broken now, for he had entered the foothills of the Belt-and-Buckle. Exhausted and hungry, Bransen still did not stop until he had drawn very near, almost to the base of the rounded hillock.

He heard the woman crying and screaming for someone to stop.

"Ye belong to me now, wench!" a man yelled back. "I'll take ye as I want ye!"

"Me husband," she pleaded.

"Dead and pecked by the crows!" the man shouted back. And she began screaming again.

Bransen crept up the side of the hill as fast as he dared, trying to remain silent and unnoticed. For there were others up there, he realized, and the top of the hill was bare of trees or any other cover he could discern.

Flat on his belly he crawled along, serenaded by the woman's soft cries and the grunts of her attacker. He peered over the hill and spotted them off to the side behind the two burning campfires where they lay behind a log, the man atop the woman, having finished his deed. But Bransen could hardly look that way, more surprised to see other women and children all about the place, some curled on the ground and sleeping, others milling about, their eyes vacant, their faces and hair filthy with soot and mud.

A pair of young boys began to fight, one quickly gaining the advantage. He knocked his opponent down and dropped atop him, straddling him and pummeling him mercilessly.

Those nearest adults seemed not to notice, and several other children just giggled as the beating continued.

The boy continued to rain blows on his victim, then, to Bransen's horror, reached out and picked up a small stone and smashed it down hard on his opponent's face again and again.

"Don't ye kill him," a man instructed. "Just hurt him."

Bransen found it hard to breathe. Across the way, the rapist stood and brushed himself off, then kicked the prone woman and spat upon her.

"Here now, don't ye do that," the man who had just spoken to the vicious lad called out. "My turn with her."

He headed over toward the log, opening his belt as he went, and no one seemed to pay him any heed at all.

"And if ye try to run again we'll do worse, don't ye doubt," said the man who had already had his way with the woman. He kicked her again for good measure and moved back to the main camp. One younger girl watched him with wide eyes, and he shouted at her, "Get me some food!" How she scrambled to obey!

Bransen couldn't comprehend the scene before him. He tried hard to keep his wits about him, to take a measure of the opposing force. He noted only three men—the ones he had seen from the keep wall—then he spotted a fourth coming up over the back crest of the hillock with an armload of wood.

This is not your fight, Bransen stubbornly reminded himself. *You can't save the world, fool. It's all beyond you. There is no point!*

He almost convinced himself to walk away. So despondent was Bransen that he nearly surrendered, there and then, to the darkness. Before he had even finished that internal battle, fate mercifully intervened, for a girl spotted him and let out a shriek, pointing and hopping.

Bransen probably could have melted into the forest at the base of the hill before any of them got a weapon drawn, but the sudden tumult shattered Bransen's pathetic justifications for leaving. He stood up and took a few steps toward the encampment, in full view then of more than twenty sets of eyes.

He noted the man behind the log scramble up from the beaten woman, hiking his pants as he went. He noted the previous attacker reaching down to grab a short bronze sword as the man with the armload of wood dropped it all except for two sturdy little clubs, one of which he tossed to the fourth man.

Bransen walked in. They obviously didn't recognize him as the Highwayman; he wasn't wearing his distinctive, one-sleeved shirt or telltale mask. Had he thought about it, he would have donned those clothes, using his reputation to his advantage. Too late now.

"Leave her alone," he said to the man still behind the log.

"What clan are ye?" the man with the sword demanded. "And what foolishness is in ye to think ye can walk into Clan Huwaerd? Get ye gone!"

"Clan?" Bransen replied skeptically. "I see four ruffians and a score of helpless prisoners."

Some of his bluster was lost as he spoke the words, though, as the young girl who had spotted him ran over to the man with the sword and hid behind him, calling him "father" as she went.

"What is this?" Bransen asked. He pointed back to the north, toward the distant, burned-out town and keep. "Was that your village?"

"He told ye to leave," said one of the men with the clubs, who, along with his partner, advanced menacingly.

"No, but he ain't going nowhere," said the other man, slapping his club into his open palm repeatedly. "He'll just come back for us with his friends."

The man with the sword moved toward Bransen's left flank. Of more concern, though, was the man who had just started with the woman, who reached down and produced a bow and arrow.

"Look to the trees for others!" the man with the sword ordered. All the women, save the one on the ground, and all the children rushed to different points along the hilltop and peered down into the darkness.

"Now ye tell us who ye are," the swordsman demanded of Bransen.

"And if I do tell you, will it matter?"

The man looked at him curiously.

"I am Bransen Garibond of Pryd Town, son of Bran Dynard of the Order of Abelle and of Sen Wi, who was Jhesta Tu. None of that means anything to you, I am sure, except that you know of Pryd Town—"

"You fight for King Yeslnik!" yelled one of the club wielders.

Bransen laughed at the absurd notion, but he bit it short as he added, "I fight for no one."

"I'm not thinking that's true," said the swordsman. He gave a slight nod at the archer, a movement Bransen caught clearly so that he was not surprised when the archer let fly an arrow. It came in true and fast, center of mass, but just before it stabbed into the center of Bransen's chest he snapped his left forearm straight up and ducked, deflecting the arrow high, where it flew away into the darkness.

Nothing happened for a few heartbeats, the four men gawking at him. But all at once the archer reached for another arrow and the other three charged.

The swordsman was closest, blade leading. As soon as Bransen turned toward him he cowardly skidded to a stop and fell back a step.

Bransen turned back to meet the two others, who were swinging their clubs with abandon and shouting wildly as if they meant to simply run him over. Bransen started to retreat, as seemed the obvious route, but he noted the pattern, side to side, of the respective clubs, and marked his opening.

The swordsman to the side slipped around to keep up with Bransen's retreat and started in again. Across the way, the archer leveled his bow.

Bransen darted forward, twisting and bending as he went to avoid the backhand from the man to his left and the forehand from the one to his right. He slipped in between those clubs, the men frantically trying to realign with him, punching out with their free hands, bringing the clubs back to bear.

Bransen stopped short and spun fast, then threw himself around backward and to his right, turning into the backhanded reverse of the club. He crashed into the attacker's leading elbow, hooking the man's forearm and jerking it out straight. Understanding the movement of the man who was now behind him, Bransen dropped down diagonally, turning and tugging as he went, throwing out his foot to trip up the man he had caught. That thug rolled down over his leg just in time to catch the swinging club of his companion.

The other man, to his credit, managed to pull his strength from his swing and didn't hit his companion very hard, but still the jolt shocked them both enough for Bransen to continue through with his move. He jammed his left hand against the man's elbow and yanked back hard with his right, painfully straightening the arm. He tugged right through it with his leverage and his deceptive strength, pulling the club from the man's grasp as he flipped him right over to the ground at the feet of his companion.

Bransen straightened, spun, and swung, smashing his club hard against the club of his opponent but down low enough to catch the man's gripping fingers in the process. How he howled! His weapon flew, and he grabbed at his shattered hand, stumbling backward.

Bransen turned fast to meet the charge of the swordsman. He heard the bow fire behind him and instinctively dove diagonally down and to the right, guessing rightly that the archer was aiming left, away from the approaching leader. Bransen went right through a roll and back to his feet, barely two strides from his enemy. Instead of lifting the club to block he tossed it up into the air, calmly saying, "Here."

The swordsman's eyes reflexively followed the ascent, and he looked back just in time to see Bransen lunging forward, close enough for him to stab certainly, except that he hadn't the time to react. Bransen rolled his shoulders, his right arm coming forward in a devastating, driving punch that hit the man in the face, just under the nose, and drove through, sliding up past the nose as the man's head snapped backward.

The swordsman's feet came right out from under him, and he dropped hard to his back. Even before the man tumbled Bransen retracted, shoving off his front foot to straighten quickly, gaining momentum as he powerfully reversed his spin so that as the next attacker—the man he had flipped to the ground—leaped in at him, Bransen's elbow shot out behind, smashing him in the face.

The man grunted and staggered, his legs going weak. He didn't fall, though, as Bransen whirled about, a long-flying left hook chopping the man across the jaw. That blow, too, would have knocked him sidelong to the ground, except that Bransen needed this man upright. He caught him firmly, lined him up, and drove forward with all his strength toward the archer.

After a couple of strides the dazed man started to resist, but holding him in both hands by the leather jerkin, Bransen jerked his arms out straight, then yanked them back in as he lowered his forehead and snapped his head forward.

The crackling sound and gush of blood showed this one's nose to be broken. Again Bransen bulled him across the hilltop at the archer.

The Highwayman recognized that he didn't have the time to reach the bowman, for the two behind him weren't out of the fight quite yet. As he neared the central fire, Bransen threw the man backward. He clipped the logs and fell over, still a few feet short of the archer. Bransen went down low, almost to all fours, cleverly scooping a stone. He came up straight again and looked at his foe's leveled bow.

"You have only one shot, of course," Bransen said and smiled and began to walk steadily at the bowman. "Perhaps you will kill me, though I think that unlikely."

He could see the man trying to steady his hands, clearly unnerved by the ease with which Bransen had just dispatched his three companions—and after Bransen had used his arm to deflect the first arrow away and had dodged the second with his back to the bow!

Smiling, mocking the man with a chuckle, Bransen hopped left, hopped right, and threw the rock.

The bowman cried out and let fly, but he was ducking as he did, thinking more about turning to run away than anything else. Still, his shot came dangerously close, whipping past barely a finger's breadth from Bransen's head.

He was too close, the arrow too fast. He never could have blocked that shot, and it occurred to Bransen that he had just come within an inch of death.

No matter. The archer was fleeing. The man he had head-butted writhed on the ground and seemed none too eager to try to get up anytime soon. Bransen turned.

That left only two.

The swordsman swayed as he stood there, his face bloody, his eyes already swelling from the brutal punch. The club wielder held his weapon in his left hand, the shattered fingers of his right hand tucked in tight against his side.

"Is this a dance you truly desire?" Bransen asked.

"Who are you?" the swordsman asked.

"I already told you."

"Why are you here?"

"Curiosity and disgust."

"Disgust?" asked the man with the club. "Have ye seen our homes? Have ye seen me kids, then, eight o' them, trampled dead under the spinning wheels of a chariot?"

Bransen had no answer to that. He lowered his eyes for a heartbeat and replied quietly, "I will go my way." Then he looked up and added in a much more sinister tone, "And if you try to stop me again or if I see you mistreating your own again like the dogs of war, I will kill you."

He was about to add that any who wanted to go with him would be welcome, but before he could speak he found himself reacting to a barrage of stones and sticks. He turned and blocked the most dangerous missiles, his eyes widening as he noted the charge.

The charge of children with sticks, some aflame, in hand. The charge of battered women, including the one who had been attacked behind the log. She came on most ferociously of all, throwing herself at Bransen, clawing at the air like a feral, rabid beast when he dodged aside. The look on her face, an expression locked in absolute denial, unsettled Bransen most of all.

A few stones hit him, though nothing serious, and the swordsman and club wielder hesitated, more than willing to let the children and the women begin the fight.

But it was no fight Bransen could accept. He darted for the side of the hill, catching the awkward swing of a youngster's stick. He shoved the child to the side as he sprinted past just to get clear of him. Bransen reached the lip of the hill, more stones and sticks following his every step, and he leaped and fell into himself, into his *ki-chi-kree*, mimicking the magic of the malachite gemstone. He flew, he floated, he leaped far into the darkness, out from the hill at such a height that he caught the branches of the trees below and half pulled, half ran along those intertwined elevated walkways.

By the time he dared stop, by the time he had ended the enhanced magical trance, the campfire in the hillock was a distant speck of light, the continued shouted protests a distant din. The troubled young man sat back against the tree trunk, shifting so that his vantage point gave him a clear view of the starry sky. He tried to digest what he had just seen, tried to play past the incongruity of the battered woman coming at him with such primal hatred and violence. He replayed what he had seen on the hillock and affirmed to himself that he had not witnessed it in the wrong light. She had been taken against her will and beaten into submission—of that, there could be no doubt.

Were these people so desperate, so out of sorts, that such behavior had become acceptable to them? Was their loss so profound to their sensibilities that any semblance of order, even if it was order under the stamp of a heavy and painful boot, brought a measure of security and comfort?

Bransen could hardly comprehend the reasoning behind it, but he quickly came to understand the reality of what he had seen: the ultimate breakdown of civilization itself. This was the result of war, taken to the extreme, the desperate and forced primitive order out of inflicted chaos and agony. This was the result of utter helplessness in the wake of complete loss.

He tried to sort it out, conjuring past experiences and knowledge. He thought of the Book of Jhest, with passages describing such atrocities. He thought of his own life in war. Towns in Vanguard had been similarly razed by the hordes inspired by Ancient Badden, but never had he seen anything akin to this!

The difference in Vanguard had been the faith the survivors held in Dame Gwydre and the other nobles. Even when all had been lost except life itself, those people in Vanguard knew that their larger constructs of society, the dame and her court, the Order of Abelle, remained and would be there to shelter them and to feed them and to help them build anew. The people on this southern hillock had no such comfort. To whom would they turn? Yeslnik had done this, but his foe, Ethelbert, to whom they had pledged fealty, could not come forth, could not protect them. Did he even wish to?

These people had lost many of their loved ones and their very way of life.

Because of the scorched earth and utter ruin, because of the absence of hope itself, they saw no way to reclaim it. As brutal as those four men leading the clan had been, they were the only measure of security and stability those poor folk on the hillock could hope to know. They were darkness, to be sure, but they were also the guides through the darkness, however wretched.

The young warrior knew that he could go back and kill those four and perhaps convince the others to then follow him. He could take them to Pryd, or even to Ethelbert.

He stared up at the stars and he shook his head at the helpless futility of it all.

He slept there, up in the tree, exhausted from his ordeal and from, most of all, the emotional battering he had taken in the shock of the cruel reality.

He awoke before the dawn, thinking to go straight off to the north to Pryd Town. Instead, Bransen went along the foothills of the Belt-and-Buckle. He avoided the hill where he had fought, but he looked for other clans. He found many of them scattered among the hills, desperate people living in caves or under overhangs or atop hillocks that provided them a defensive position. Bransen didn't get close to any, the bitter experience fresh in his thoughts, but he viewed them from the nearest vantage points, one after another, throughout the rest of that day. He ended by climbing as high as he could among the nearby mountains, a clear perch to widen the view below him.

Dozens and dozens of campfires dotted the night terrain, one or two at a time, mostly, but with one congregation of more than a score.

Bransen marked that spot and went there before the dawn.

He found the same situation as he had witnessed on the hillock, only many times larger in scale. This was the prime clan of the region, it seemed, with no fewer than fifteen armed bosses, men and women alike, brutalizing and commanding many others, young and old and infirm.

Soon after he left that complex of rudimentary dwellings built under the overhangs of red-rocked cliffs, Bransen came across the scene of a recent battle—probably one between the clan he had just left and a lesser group that had happened upon them.

Crows picked at the bodies scattered in the region, which included a few who might have fought back and a few more, very old, who would have no doubt been helpless in the face of the assault. There were no children to be found, however, except for the body of a single young girl. Bransen glanced back at the large clan and wondered how many among the children he had seen there were recent acquisitions.

The troubled young man did not sleep in that devastated region that night. He couldn't sleep. So he walked back out to the road and to the northern fork that would lead him to Pryd Town, and north beyond that, he hoped, to Chapel Abelle and Cadayle.

CHAPTER 5

Visions of Graveyards

"Not as secure as you insisted," King Yeslnik scolded Laird Panlamaris when the truth of the murderous night became evident across the city.

"What do ye know of powries?" the laird asked flatly.

Yeslnik stared at him for daring to so challenge the throne. Indeed, all about the pair, men and women of both courts shuffled nervously.

"You ever fight one?" Panlamaris went on, not backing down an inch. His voice grew thick, his accent flowing in and out like a master bard scaring a group of children about the bonfire with tales of goblins and ghouls. "You ever stick your sword into one's gut, tearing out its innards and thinking your battle done, only to have the beast laugh at ye and leap on ye?"

Yeslnik started to scold him but wound up merely swallowing hard.

"Aye, but it's a dactyl demon itself the witch Gwydre's put upon my city and upon us all," he said, standing up straight and casting his gaze all about the room. "Don't you doubt it, King Yeslnik. The powries are more than Palmaristown's problem."

He kept glancing away to the east as he spoke, toward Dame Gwydre's chapel prison. His thoughts turned to a vision of a charge against those walls, when at last they would be breached, when Dame Gwydre would kneel before him, begging for mercy.

"And what will you do about our problem?" King Yeslnik said—again, Laird Panlamaris realized when he turned his attention back to his present surroundings.

"Your city has a most important guest, the king himself," Yeslnik said. "And you allow these beasts to crawl in at night and cause such mischief?"

"No warships in port this night," Panlamaris said. "The powries come from the river, and so the river will be watched."

"See to it that they do not return until my own ship is long gone from your wharf."

"Aye, my king," the laird repeated absently, for his thoughts were again on Gwydre, kneeling before him, crying and begging until the moment he took her head from her shoulders.

They called it Sepulcher. To the powries this was procreation, and for hundreds of years it had been the only means of continuing their race. Mcwigik and Bikelbrin and the others took the hearts of their fallen comrades and buried them, then danced their magical movements and sang their songs invoking the healing powers of the world to breathe life into those hearts anew. In a matter of weeks a new powrie would emerge from the shallow graves, small at first but fast to grow into the image of the one who had provided the heart.

Mcwigik led the songs, the first of which spoke of times long past when the bloody-cap dwarves dominated Corona. Numbering in the millions, their kingdoms ruled supreme in every land from Behr to Alpinador and on the islands across the great Mirianic. Even those places now considered wilderness, like this very region across the Masur Delaval had been, according to powrie lore, once tamed under the armies of the dwarves.

But Sepulcher, for all of its rejuvenating magic, was a practice of inevitable decline; any dwarf lost whose heart could not be reclaimed could not be replaced. What's more, Sepulcher produced only male powries; even a female dwarf heart would yield a male child, one that looked much like its predecessor but was undeniably male. The dwarves had never been prolific breeders in the traditional sense, and, alas, there remained no female powries to be found in any event.

This was the lament of the songs as the dwarves, locked in a huddle, arms across each other's shoulders, moved to the second act of their ritual. The lament drifted to the recitation of heroic feats of heart retrieval, mostly at sea, as the determined dwarves steadfastly refused to let their race pass from the world. Among the powries no heroes stood taller than those who would dive into the cold waters to secure the lines to a sunken barrelboat and her lost crew.

The final act was a call to the powrie gods to grant a woman from the Sepulcher and was followed by the melodic and droning song of the warrior, the final, resigned acceptance.

Put me deep in the groun' so cold
I'll be dead 'fore I e'er get old

Done me fights and shined me cap
Now's me time for th'endless nap
Spill no tear and put me deep
Dun want no noise for me endless sleep
Done me part and stood me groun'
But th'other one won and knocked me down

Put me deep in the groun' so cold
I'll be dead 'fore I e'er get old
Spill no tear and put me deep
Dun want no noise for me endless sleep

"Aye, but they're coming," Captain Shiknickel informed the singers, and all eyes turned to the wide river. In an ultimate act of defiance, the powries had decided to create their mass Sepulcher directly across the river from Palmaristown on the western bank of the Masur Delaval and in full view of the city lights across the way.

"They'll find our boys," one dwarf lamented.

"Nah, but the dopes ain't for knowin' nothing about Sepulcher," Mcwigik replied.

"Yach, but what's yerself knowing about what they're knowing?" the other asked. "Ye been on a damned island for a hundred years!"

"I'm knowing that if they knew, they'd've cut the hearts after staking our boys. Cut 'em and burned 'em, and we'd be down a fair number o' dwarves."

"Aye," many others agreed, including Shiknickel.

"Mess it all up, then, and no cairns," reasoned Bikelbrin. "If they're not knowing that we buried something here, they'll not be looking."

"Summer's on, ground's soft," a different dwarf warned. "Not hard to see that the ground's been turned."

Bikelbrin grinned wickedly and looked to Mcwigik, and then the two of them turned to Shiknickel.

The dwarf captain laughed. "So we buried our waste, eh?" he remarked. "Dig them holes back halfway to the hearts. Had a hearty dinner meself. . . ."

That was all he needed to say. The dwarves excavated two feet of dirt. As was customary in Sepulcher, the hearts were down twice that. The dwarves did their business, laying a layer of shite into the holes once they were opened. They then filled the holes, scraped the ground, and tossed stones and branches about haphazardly.

"As fitting a cairn as any powrie'd e'er want," a satisfied Mcwigik announced.

"Boats ain't far. Arrows'll be flying in soon," a dwarf near the water warned.

The powries retreated up the riverbank to the north, where they had beached their barrelboats. They didn't immediately climb aboard and put back out, though, for the sailing ships didn't hang around on that side of the river for long. The dark of night favored the powries, who could see the silhouette of sails clearly enough against the starry canopy, while their barrelboats would be almost completely invisible to sailors on Palmaristown ships.

More than one of Shiknickel's boys pointed that out as they watched from a rocky point. They were hungry for revenge and eager to ram a few warships after burying the hearts of their fallen.

Shiknickel held them back. "Boats're already out, pedaling across the gulf," he reminded them. "Our boys'll be paid back in full order, and soon enough, when all the boats o' the isles come forth. Oh, but there's human blood to be spillin', don't ye doubt, and I'm tellin' me own shiver to know that they're killing more than any others."

The cheer was muted out of necessity, but there was no missing the enthusiasm from the powries at the proclamation. The Palmaristown stakes had gone too far; the folk of Honce, though they didn't really appreciate it yet, had declared war on the powries.

And to a one, the ferocious dwarves were more than happy to oblige.

You do wrong by me, King Yeslnik," Father De Guilbe protested at a private meeting between himself and the ruling couple. "To associate me with Artolivan and his ilk insults me profoundly."

"I have done you wrong?" Yeslnik replied, dramatically placing his open hand over his chest and setting the timbre of his voice to express surprise and injury, and, on a subtle level, a measure of a threat. Clearly, he was calling for De Guilbe to recant, but the priest, a veteran of battle and policy, a huge brute of a man who never shied from a fight and never spoke anything less than that which was on his mind, smiled and nodded.

"You look upon me with contempt, as does your wife," he said.

Queen Olym gasped in exasperation, even gave a little wail.

"I see it and I do not blame you at all, given the horrible treatment the Order of Abelle has shown to you," De Guilbe explained. "You scarcely looked at me on the docks, other than a single sneer."

"You would elevate yourself to the level of Laird Panlamaris, then?" the king asked incredulously. "Or that of his son, who conquered a third of Honce in my name? You believe that you, a monk who no longer even has Artolivan's ear, is as important to me as those two?"

"More important," De Guilbe said matter-of-factly, his barrel chest puffing out.

King Yeslnik seemed less than impressed. Queen Olym gave a bored sigh.

"An army might win a man's body by either breaking it wholly or forcing him to inaction," De Guilbe explained. "No doubt your great armies will sweep the land with the banners of King Yeslnik and Delaval City. But it is the church and not the state that keeps peasants truly in line. Would you have your entire reign be a matter of destroying one revolt after another?"

"You presume much."

"I have seen much. The folk of Honce—of any land—need the reassurance that their miserable existence will lead them to some better place. They need hope in eternal life and justice. The Samhaists provided that, albeit harshly, but they are of little consequence now. Because of the war, because of the healing powers of our gemstones, the Order of Abelle has become ascendant. We are the guardians of eternity and the partner you will need if you hope to keep the peasants in line."

"I mean to kill Father Artolivan. You do understand that, I hope."

"I would kill him myself if the opportunity ever arose."

Yeslnik didn't immediately respond, other than to tilt his head back and study the man more carefully. After a long silence Queen Olym remarked, "He wants Chapel Abelle for himself!"

"Ah," Yeslnik agreed, as if she had obviously hit the mark.

"We cannot wait for Chapel Abelle to fall," Father De Guilbe replied.

"We?" asked Yeslnik.

"You have already announced that you will march to Ethelbert's gates first. You will tame the land around Chapel Abelle to isolate Artolivan and Gwydre and their traitorous followers. You will not return before the end of summer, surely, and you will not camp your army on the field throughout the Honce winter. Nor do I expect defeating the chapel will come easily if you assembled a hundred thousand strong warriors for the task! Her walls are thick and tall and her brothers skilled at the use of gemstone magic, as Laird Panlamaris will surely attest."

"He doesn't believe in you, my great king," Olym remarked, but Yeslnik hushed her with an upraised hand.

"Your assault will not begin within a year, and I fear it may be several more before you finally break through those walls and expel the traitors."

Again Olym tried to protest and again Yeslnik silenced her by putting the back of his palm before her face.

"You do not have several years," said De Guilbe. "The peasants will need reassurance. They need to believe that their eternal—"

"Laird Panlamaris has already told me of your wishes to be instilled as an alternative father of the order," King Yeslnik interrupted.

"His wishes, as well. He understands the need."

"And I do not?"

"I would never hint at such a thing, my king. I am well-known among the brothers of Abelle. When I was selected to travel to Alpinador those years ago, every brother in the order heard my name, and they knew it even before that time, during the years when I was a leading master at Chapel Abelle. More than a few of my brethren understand, as do I, that Father Artolivan's decision to walk a neutral line in the greatest war Honce has ever known was a fool's errand. Wars have winners and losers, and it has been clear from the beginning that Delaval City would become the center of Honce, and her laird the new king of the land. I argued for such as soon as I returned from my adventures in the north. I told Artolivan to follow your edict to its fullest extent with great hope that the war would then soon end and you could assume leadership over the unified kingdom."

"Perhaps you were not as influential as you believed, eh?" Yeslnik said cleverly.

"Not with Artolivan's minions at Chapel Abelle and certainly not with Dame Gwydre and her followers," De Guilbe admitted. "If ever there was an argument against allowing a woman to preside over a holding, Dame Gwydre is it!"

The two men laughed at that declaration, but Olym didn't follow suit. Yeslnik, then De Guilbe, cut the laughter short with an uncomfortable cough or two.

"You need to give the brothers of the many chapels a choice apart from Father Artolivan," De Guilbe explained. "There will be debate in every chapel regarding the edicts of Father Artolivan, and it will oft be contested. If you present an alternative to Artolivan—Father De Guilbe of the Chapel of Precious Memories here in Palmaristown—then those arguments will be less conclusive. More and more brothers will cease to resist you as you sweep the land of all resistance to your inevitable rule." De Guilbe paused thoughtfully before adding, "Besides, my king, your ascent is obviously not without the sanction of God."

Yeslnik's eyes narrowed. "What do you mean?"

"Absent God's graces, no man may ever claim such a title," De Guilbe explained. "Thus, you are not merely King Yeslnik but Blessed King Yeslnik."

Yeslnik paused and looked to Olym, but she could only offer a shrug in response. "You really believe that?" Yeslnik asked.

"It matters not," said De Guilbe. "All that matters for your security and the strength of your kingdom is that the peasants believe it."

"Can I trust you, Father De Guilbe? I do not even know you."

"You can trust the judgment of Laird Panlamaris. You can know for certain that I left Chapel Abelle in disgust over Father Artolivan's refusal to admit the obvious: that Yeslnik is King of Honce and that we, his servants, are duty bound to abide by his edicts. That much, my king, you can verify and trust."

"Loyal to me?" the king asked. He held out his hand, a large jeweled ring sparkling in the room's torchlight. De Guilbe immediately fell to one knee, took up the slight hand, and kissed the ring.

"I may decide to move you to Chapel Delaval," Yeslnik said. "It would do well and wise for the seat of the church and state to be near each other, for we would need to converse often."

"I go where you command," De Guilbe said with a deeper bow of his head.

"For now that would be the Chapel of Precious Memories. Better that you are here, where the common folk are both weary and wary. I'll not return to Delaval City until the autumn at least, so I'll not need you there until then. My subjects of Delaval are very loyal."

"I am to claim myself as Father De Guilbe of the Chapel of Precious Memories?"

"I will make that claim for you, of course, and will also declare that the Chapel of Precious Memories serves as temporary seat of power for the Order of Abelle."

"Your faith in me is greatly appreciated," De Guilbe said.

"Faith?" Yeslnik snickered at him. "I will watch you in your new role. If I am pleased, I will formally appoint you the head of the Order of Abelle. . . ." He paused and considered the sound of that for a few moments. "Your first command from the throne, Father De Guilbe," he prompted. "Find a new name for your church."

De Guilbe looked at him curiously.

"It should have a reference to me in it somewhere," said Yeslnik.

De Guilbe's eyes widened, but he withered under the cold stare of Queen Olym and held silent.

"Yes, to the king," Yeslnik said, obviously thinking out loud. "The divine king." With a wide grin, a wicked grin, he looked at the stunned father. "Surely my ascent is more than accident," he reasoned. "You just said as much."

"I said that the peasants needed to believe in such—"

"You do not agree?"

"I . . . I, there is a difference between the secular and the spiritual, I be-lieve—"

"The Brothers of Abelle have long claimed a beneficent god, have they not? A shepherd overseeing the flock of man who blesses many with magical heal-ing and other divine gifts if they believe that he is the way to eternity?"

"Yes, but—"

"But? Father, if such a god exists—and you believe he does—then surely his will is involved in settling the outcome of this greatest of conflicts. Honce is uni-fied for the first time—or soon will be. A king will rule Honce for the first time, and that king will be me. If divine providence would play no role in that, then how are we to believe your claims of a god who cares about the plight of his flock?"

Father De Guilbe made no move to answer for, indeed, he had no retort against the outlandish claim.

"I am not merely a secular king, then," said Yeslnik. "I am a divine king. A divine king who deems your order misguided and nullified and who, by his graces, restores that order under the watchful eye of Father De Guilbe." He paused for a heartbeat before adding, "Perhaps."

The unambiguous qualifier stole any forthcoming debate from De Guilbe. Yeslnik made it clear with his tone and posture that De Guilbe was in a trial period here and that the impetuous king would think it no large matter to simply replace him.

"The Church of Divine Yeslnik!" Queen Olym blurted, clapping her hands together.

Yeslnik smiled at her but patted his hands in the air to temper her sudden enthusiasm. "Father De Guilbe will find the right notes," he assured her and warned De Guilbe at the same time.

"Indeed, my king," De Guilbe replied and bowed again, and he started backing out of the room before he even stood up straight again, for Yeslnik was absently waving him away. As he stepped out into the hallway, pulling the door closed behind him, he heard Olym say to her husband, "Brilliant play!"

The father sighed and stood upright, considering. He could do this, he sup-posed. What mattered the name, anyway? Still, for all his reassurances he found himself muttering curses at Father Artolivan as he headed for the castle exit. If only Artolivan had gone along with Yeslnik's demands! The Laird of Delaval had won the war, after all! Of that there could be no doubt.

Now to restore the church to any semblance of prominence De Guilbe would have no choice other than to give in to King Yeslnik's every self-glorifying demand.

"So be it," the man said, focusing his anger on the brothers he had left at Chapel Abelle and not on the rather pathetic King Yeslnik. He muttered a few possibilities before nodding as he said, "The Church of the Divine King."

Yes, De Guilbe thought, that one might be ambiguous enough to satisfy both of his needs.

Bludgeon them mercilessly," King Yeslnik instructed Laird Panlamaris and Prince Milwellis. "Fell every tree between here and Chapel Abelle to build your catapults and throw stones and livestock and peasants alike at their walls. Bring them pain. And do not let even one of them escape your web."

The Prince of Palmaristown nodded, quite satisfied with the task put before him.

"My ships will secure the river, let yours secure the gulf," the king said to Panlamaris. "Let us destroy any powries that may still be about and, more importantly, do not allow any to sail out of Chapel Abelle's docks."

"And none from Vanguard," Laird Panlamaris replied. "Oh, but we'll be paying Dame Gwydre's ports a visit or ten."

"As you will," Yeslnik said. "Your primary duty is to secure the siege of Chapel Abelle and to send the wretched powries to a cold and watery death. If you find the time to harass the minions of Dame Gwydre in Vanguard, then go with my blessing."

"We should destroy the wench now and be done with her and with those idiot monks," Panlamaris replied.

"One snake at a time," Yeslnik replied. "One snake at a time, and that snake now is Ethelbert. My army swells with the soldiers of the western holdings. I will gather Laird Bannagran in my wake and ride straight to Ethelbert's gates. His city will be mine before midsummer's day."

Yeslnik smiled, noting Prince Milwellis's uncomfortable shuffle. "Bannagran will know no more glory than the man who rains punishment upon the treasonous monks in Chapel Abelle," he promised. "Palmaristown will be the second city of Honce, behind Delaval, and it occurs to me that the great Laird Panlamaris's son should not wait for his father's death to find his own holding."

"Here now, my king!" Panlamaris protested.

"Ethelbert," Yeslnik explained. "When I have chased the scum laird into the Mirianic, his city will need a new laird. Perhaps your son will be that man, and what a glorious control that would afford the both of you of the long coast of Honce!"

Milwellis looked to his father with clear curiosity and excitement, but he found no such reciprocal expression. No, from Panlamaris there was only the unrelenting anger toward Gwydre and Artolivan, the curs who had loosed powries upon his beloved Palmaristown.

King Yeslnik remarked that he was tired and took his leave, but when he and Queen Olym reached their private room they were anything but weary!

"My king!" she tittered and swooned. "O, Divine King! Take me!"

She didn't have to ask twice.

Later, as the two lay in bed, Yeslnik asked, "Do you think I handled them accordingly?"

"You warned the monk, who was too independent, and you brought hope back to Panlamaris and his son," Olym replied. "Your wisdom knows no bounds and grows by the day. You will have everything you desire. Bannagran, more worthy than Milwellis by far, will lead your charge against Ethelbert. And with so fat a carrot dangled before their lustful eyes, know that Panlamaris and his son will not let Dame Gwydre and the monks escape their prison at Chapel Abelle. Your enemies have herded themselves into irrelevance, and Father De Guilbe, distasteful creature that he is, will frighten the other chapels to accede to your desires.

"Accordingly, my love?" she said mockingly. "Nay, masterfully. The world is yours, is ours, by autumn's turn."

CHAPTER 6

Dealing at Heaven's Door

He approached at night, for he wasn't certain if new residents had come to the house. He expected that some had, given what he had seen in the last miles of his trek. Only one year before, the hill upon which this house stood had been the outskirts of Pryd Town and afforded a view beyond the borders of civilization. But how the place had grown! Hundreds of new cottages had been constructed; an entire forest had been cleared away! And all for security reasons, Bransen realized. None had made a greater name for himself in the miserable war than Laird Bannagran of Pryd, whose garrison had chased Ethelbert's army from the field and rescued many towns from the crush of enemies.

When he had come through Pryd Town briefly with Jameston, Bransen had approached from the north and departed to the east, and in those places, though there were more cottages, the region seemed much the same. But here across the way, in the southwestern reaches of the holding, the explosion of residents was truly dramatic.

Bransen noted no candles burning in the house as he climbed the hill. So many memories followed him to the doorstep. The broken door and darkness beyond showed him to his surprise that the place had remained deserted, though whether out of respect for the former residents, fear of some curse because of their apparent fate, or simply because Pryd Town's traditional populace had been decimated in the many months of fighting, where so many of her men and women had marched off to battle, he could not tell.

This had been the home of Callen Duwornay and her daughter, Cadayle. Here Bransen, disguised as the Highwayman, had first courted Cadayle. Here on this very spot before the door marked where the Highwayman had killed his first enemy, a thug who had come here to do great harm to Cadayle and her mother.

Mixed emotions filled the young man as he stood staring at the spot where he had killed that young man. His actions had been justified—necessary even—for the sake of the women, and he felt no remorse for the thug. But in the larger reality of the world that had fallen like a boulder upon him, the sense of futility and ultimate despair colored his every thought. He couldn't escape the sense that the road he had begun that night at this door, the role he had taken on as a defender of some greater sense of justice, seemed the fool's errand.

Bransen walked away. He couldn't smooth the dissonance of his thoughts and feelings. He had done right in coming here to defend Cadayle and Callen on that long-ago night. Of course he had! But to what end? To what point?

He thought of Dame Gwydre as he walked across the rolling fields of Pryd Holding. The fighting had not come here, other than one small battle, and so the town itself appeared much as it had when Bransen had called it home only a year before.

Only a year, but it seemed like a lifetime to the young man. He could hardly believe the journey, physically and emotionally. He had walked from Pryd Town to great Delaval City and up the river to Palmaristown. From there, he had gone to Chapel Abelle and across the Gulf of Corona to Vanguard. Pressed into service to the Lady of Vanguard, he had traveled to the wild and frigid land of Alpinador.

And all the way back again, across the gulf to Chapel Abelle, south to Pryd Town and to the far eastern reaches of Honce to Ethelbert dos Entel. Despite the widening boundaries of its cottages and tents, how small Pryd Town looked to him now! Bransen had spent the entirety of his life here until that fateful night when, in rescuing Cadayle, he had also brought about the death of Laird Prydae. His road had begun with banishment, and in so short a time he had traversed the length and breadth of Honce and more. Was there a man alive more traveled than he?

That thought led him back to Jameston Sequin and reminded him of the man's tragic fate . . . and all for the crime of escorting Bransen to the east.

He paused on a hilltop, Castle Pryd and Chapel Pryd visible in the north, Cadayle's house behind him in the southwest, and the edges of a small lake visible across the way. There lay his first home, with Garibond Womak, before the ailing and aging man had put him in service to the brothers at Chapel Pryd.

So many memories flooded Bransen as he sat on that hill. He tried to put them in context with the new reality that he now understood. There had been very few pleasant times in the years of his youth, but those precious few struck him now. He thought of the many hours sitting by the lake with Garibond while the man fished for their dinner. He remembered as if it had occurred only the day before the first time he had opened the Book of Jhest, the tome copied by his father and protected from the outraged monks by Garibond.

He thought of Brother Reandu and his days at the chapel in a cellar hole. To keep his sanity then, Bransen had re-created the Book of Jhest, scratching the walls with a stone. His youth had been filled with long hours of grueling work, for even the simplest task had been brutally difficult to the boy known as the Stork, the boy whose muscles would not answer the demands of his mind. His youth had been filled with the torment of the other boys, often brutal and violent.

But in that youth, he had known the friendship and the courage of one young girl.

In the flailing hopelessness of Bransen Garibond, the image of Cadayle's hand, reaching down to help him to his feet, came to him again, reaching into the darkness of his heart and soul, the ache of his helplessness. Reaching for him and demanding that he take it.

He looked back to the southeast and envisioned the doorway at Cadayle's old house and thought again of that fateful fight when he, the fledgling Highwayman, had killed his first man. Bransen was not proud of that act, was not happy that it had been forced upon him, but he had done a good thing that day. He had acted for justice and for the defense of those who could not defend themselves.

"The call of the Highwayman," Bransen whispered into the predawn air, but he couldn't help but wince at the end of his only partly true proclamation.

Had it really been a selfless pursuit of wider justice? Bransen laughed softly, admitting to himself the truth of the Highwayman. Finding his power with his studies of Jhesta Tu and through the transformation offered by the soul stone—becoming the Highwayman—had been more a matter of personal satisfaction than any altruistic endeavor. He knew that and wasn't about to revise history for the sake of his pride. He had battled the tyranny of Laird Prydae because doing so afforded him a sense of control he had never experienced in his crippled youth. He was fueled and made powerful by the simmering rage that had flooded through him for all those years of torment, against the insults and the constant beatings of the bullies, against the softer but no less painful pity and disgust of the monks and many other condescending adults. How many times had Bransen heard the whispers that he would have been better off if they had just smothered him as a baby, when his infirmity had first been revealed? How many times had he heard the whispers that Laird Prydae or Father Jerak would do him a favor by putting him to swift death?

Anger, not altruism, had driven the Highwayman in those early days.

Bransen closed his eyes and pictured Cadayle's small hand reaching down to him, toward the Stork who lay in the mud after being decked by more ruffians. There, alone on the hill, he mentally took her outstretched hand and let it lift him once more from the darkness that had welled up inside of him since the disaster in Ethelbert, the murder of Jameston Sequin, the betrayal of Affwin Wi, the loss of his sword and gemstone brooch, and the horrors he had just witnessed in the ravaged southland.

He stood tall on the hill, tall and straight though he had no hematite, no soul stone, to support him. He felt his line of life energy, his *ki-chi-kree*, running solid and strong from his forehead to his groin. He was no more the Stork and would never again be the Stork. The world around him had gone mad, perhaps, and the terrible events and turmoil were beyond his control, but up there before the dawn, Bransen Garibond reminded himself that for most of his life this simple act of standing straight—of having a measure of discipline over his own body—was all that he wished in the world.

The notion brought a smile to his face, but only briefly. He was whole; it was not enough.

Because he was lost and he knew it. He had found a measure of senselessness to life's journey that mocked the very concept of purpose. He had walked the wider world and found it to be too wide, too uncontrollable, too much a cycle of inevitable misery and grief.

He started off the hillock heading for the lake, thinking to look in on the old stone house that had been his home for all of his youth. A small stumble, perhaps an honest trip, confused him and terrified him. He shook his head and started once more but veered almost immediately, turning toward the north, walking straight for Chapel Pryd. He needed to go there, needed to hear the counsel of Master Reandu. Bransen the agnostic sought some comfort.

Like all the communities of Honce proper in the summer season, the town of Pryd awakened before the dawn. Many people were out and about in the growing light as Bransen approached the large chapel, going about their chores before the hotter hours descended. Many sets of eyes fell upon him as he slowly and calmly walked the main road of Pryd Town, and he heard the whispers of "the Highwayman" following him. It was a more muted response than the one that had greeted him when he had come through here a month earlier beside Jameston Sequin. Bransen was glad of that. He didn't want any cheering; he couldn't bear the hopeful expressions that would inevitably come his way, as if he could do something to better the miserable reality of a peasant's existence.

Bransen didn't need that responsibility at this dark moment. He didn't want any responsibility for anything or anyone, even for himself.

He walked up the path through Chapel Pryd's gate. The front doors were open, a pair of brown-robed monks on the porch sweeping away the leaves. They stopped in unison and leaned on their brooms, watching Bransen's approach. One stepped toward the door and shouted inside for someone to get Master Reandu.

"You could just take me to his chambers," Bransen said as he neared.

"Better to meet him out here . . . at first, at least," the brother replied.

Bransen considered that for a moment, then glanced over at Castle Pryd and shook his head. "In case Bannagran comes running, you mean," he said, and the monk did not disagree.

"Well, it is a fine day anyway," Bransen said. "So better to speak out under the sun."

And so he wasn't surprised to see Bannagran rushing through the gates of the courtyard before Reandu even made his appearance. The man was not alone, flanked by a dozen warriors armored in bronze and with swords in hand.

Bannagran looked Bransen over dismissively. "I have received no word from King Yeslnik that you are pardoned," the Laird of Pryd warned.

Bransen didn't answer, seemed as if he did not care.

"I warned you about returning here."

"I had nothing to do with the death of King Delaval," Bransen said calmly. "I was in Alpinador and Vanguard and nowhere near to Delaval City."

"So you have claimed before."

"I know who killed him."

Bannagran stood up very straight and took in a deep breath, his massive and muscled chest straining the straps of his fabulously decorated bronze breastplate. He didn't blink as he held his penetrating stare over Bransen, who, caring about nothing in the world, was not intimidated in the least.

"Bransen," Master Reandu said suddenly from the chapel stoop behind them. Bransen turned about to see him. "What news brings you to Pryd? Evidence of your innocence?"

"No."

Reandu looked at him curiously.

"Where is your proof, boy?" Bannagran demanded.

"I didn't kill him. I was nowhere near Delaval City."

"Who killed him?"

"A woman—a woman from Behr."

"On what proof?"

"None but my word."

Bannagran paused for a few heartbeats, looked at Bransen, then to Reandu. He turned to his guards. "Take him."

"I came to speak with Master Reandu," Bransen said.

"If he resists at all, kill him on the spot," Bannagran ordered.

The soldiers fanned out around Bransen, iron swords in hand. They came at him with measured steps, each looking nervously to the man on his right and left, clearly intimidated, for some had witnessed the fighting prowess of the Highwayman and all had certainly heard the many stories of Bransen's martial exploits. Each step seemed a bit shorter than the one previous.

Bannagran growled, "Take him!" more ferociously. None of the soldiers needed a reminder of the power and severity of their laird. A soldier to Bransen's right lowered his shoulder behind his shield and rushed in suddenly, an obvious path and one that Bransen could have easily sidestepped.

But he didn't. He turned back to look plaintively at Master Reandu. "I need to talk with you," he said right before the shield slammed against him and sent him flying. He would have tumbled to the ground, but a second shield-rushing soldier hit him hard before he fell, jolting him upright. The man drove ahead as his companion from the other side continued to advance, pinning Bransen between them.

"With ease!" Master Reandu shouted. "He is not resisting!"

But the soldiers, as if considering the apparent submissiveness to be a dangerous ruse, came on in full. Several sheathed their swords as they huddled in, freeing up fists covered in metal gauntlets so that they could launch heavy punches at Bransen.

He curled up, protecting his most sensitive areas as the gang jostled him and slammed him, punched and kicked him.

"Bannagran!" he heard Reandu yell as he was smashed to the ground, but the monk's voice already seemed far, far away. Bransen curled up tight on his side, and a barrage of kicks battered him to semiconsciousness. He felt himself tugged over to his stomach, his hands wrenched behind his back and bound at the wrists with heavy, coarse rope. From that rope a second rope was strung, this one wrapping about the front of his waist, holding his hands fast and tight against his back. His captors slid a long pole under his elbows and across his back.

A man grabbed each end of the pole and roughly hoisted Bransen up from the ground. "Stand!" the guard leader called. Bransen stumbled to comply, but the man slugged him hard on the back of the head.

By then a crowd had gathered outside of Chapel Pryd's gate, and they began wailing and calling out in protest at the treatment of the Highwayman, the man who had brought such hope and justice to them in times not so distant. More soldiers appeared, and Bannagran faced the peasants down with an awful stare.

"Clear the way!" he ordered his soldiers and warned the peasants all at once. He turned to the crew, handling Bransen very roughly, punching him and tugging him, keeping him off balance as if they feared he would suddenly burst into motion and slay them all.

"He is not resisting, Laird Bannagran!" Reandu pleaded, but his words fell on deaf ears. The soldiers dragged and carried Bransen away, past Bannagran, who fixed him with a hateful stare.

Reandu rushed from the porch. "Don't kill the boy. He is just a boy," Reandu begged.

Bannagran moved to intercept him. "He said he knows who killed Delaval," Bannagran replied. "That is his only possible salvation."

"You will spare him?"

"It's not my choice to make."

"The people of Pryd will not forgive you, Laird Bannagran."

Bannagran looked at him as if it were foolish for Reandu to even believe that Bannagran cared.

But Reandu hit the laird with a different truth, one less easy to brush aside. "And you won't forgive yourself," he said.

Bannagran blinked.

"I will attend to him personally with a soul stone," Reandu offered.

"Once he is secured, you will have your chance to heal the outlaw."

Reandu seemed satisfied with that until Bannagran added, "The more you heal him, the more we can hurt him without killing him." The ferocious Laird of Pryd, the Bear of Honce, spat on the ground and turned away. As he neared the gate, many peasants still clustered before it, he barked, "Move aside!" How they scattered!

Master Reandu stood on the chapel walkway, rubbing his face wearily and trying hard to keep his breathing steady. Several brothers crowded behind him, assaulting him with a barrage of questions about why Bransen had come or whether he would really be executed. Reandu didn't answer any of them but just looked toward Castle Pryd. The sounds of the crowd informed him of the moment when Bransen was dragged through the strong iron gates and to the dungeons soon after, Reandu knew.

The cold and wet, filthy dungeons that smelled of death.

I trust that you are comfortable," Bannagran said to Bransen, a ridiculous question. The gaolers at Castle Pryd were well prepared to handle this dangerous man. They had the Highwayman chained by his wrists and ankles, the top chains lifting him a couple of feet from the floor by his arms, the bottom set securing his feet with just enough give to allow the ruffians to bow Bransen at the waist, wrapping him about a central beam. In deference to the man's inexplicable physical abilities, the gaolers had added a devious twist to the harness by cutting a ridge into the center of the beam where his belly rested. Into that ridge they slid a sword blade, edge out, then adjusted the chains to pull Bransen snugly into the beam, the blade tightly secured against his belly. Any struggling, indeed, even if he relaxed his weight onto the beam, would surely eviscerate the miserable prisoner. Hanging there, arms and legs locked at a forward angle, Bransen could only gain relief by sucking in his gut and turning back his shoulders so that the bottom of his rib cage hooked the edge of the beam and supported much of his weight. He couldn't hold that stressful position for very long, however, and the mere act of hanging there pushed Bransen to his limits of emotional and physical discipline.

The sun was nearing its high point in the day-lit world above, though Bransen was hardly aware of the time, when Bannagran at last entered the chamber. He walked around Bransen slowly, taking full measure. Bransen had been stripped to the waist. Bannagran nodded in apparent respect that the man had lasted this long without bloodying his belly.

"Have I thanked you for your hospitality?" Bransen asked, though he could do no more than whisper without inflicting pain.

"You appreciate your accommodations?"

"Eating will be difficult, but I have found some sleep already," the impertinent Highwayman replied.

Bannagran snorted and shook his head as he walked before the captive. He peered over the beam for a closer look at Bransen's midsection. "No blood yet," he said. "Impressive."

"You could always walk behind me and pretend I am one of your barnyard lovers," said Bransen.

Bannagran stared at him hatefully, then slapped him hard across the face. "This is no game, boy," he warned. "Your life's hanging by a rope."

"A chain, actually. Two!"

"And I hold the other end," Bannagran finished.

"Then let it go and be done with me."

"You pray that I'll make it that easy for you."

"You assume that I anticipate justice or fairness. I have learned to expect differently from Laird Bannagran."

The Bear slapped him again, a stinging blow that nearly pushed him onto the blade.

"Why have you come back to Pryd?" Bannagran demanded. He paused and looked past Bransen to the cell door to ensure they were alone. "Why have you done this to me?"

"To you?"

"I warned you, publicly, that you could not return here until King Yeslnik determined your innocence," said Bannagran.

"But you know I am innocent."

"That matters not at all!" Bannagran growled. "And you know it!"

"But it should matter."

Bannagran growled again.

"And if it doesn't matter, then nothing does," Bransen went on. "Nothing. And nothing that you can do to me matters one bit."

"Do not be too assured of that," Bannagran warned.

Bransen stared at him in response, his eyes flaring with intensity. He exhaled and relaxed suddenly, allowing his weight to come forward onto his waist against the sword. A line of blood appeared on Bransen's naked belly almost immediately, the sharp blade digging in.

But Bransen's expression didn't change; if he felt any pain at all, he didn't show it.

"I am Jhesta Tu," he explained. "My mind and body are one. I can deny pain, however much you choose to inflict. You cannot hurt me, Bannagran. You can slay me, but you cannot hurt me. I'll not let you."

"You are mad," Bannagran retorted, his voice full of revulsion. "Ever were you a strange creature."

"I am the Stork, remember? My whole life has been spent in misery—or was, until I learned to dismiss the pain."

"That easily?"

"That easily."

"If you wish to rethink that challenge, then do so now. For I will succeed in making you cry out for mercy, I warn."

Bransen didn't blink.

"Fool," said Bannagran. He moved over to the wall where a table was set with various torture implements. Reviewing them carefully, he lifted a long, serrated blade.

"You know the truth of it," Bransen said. "You know that any torture you inflict upon me will harm you. Every cut to me will be a cut to Bannagran's soul."

"You believe that I care at all for—"

"Yes," Bransen interrupted. "What were your words when first you walked in here?"

Bannagran closed his eyes and rolled the blade over in his hands. Then he looked at Bransen, and the young man knew, without doubt, that the game was over. Bannagran turned to him and lifted the blade and advanced—to kill him and be done with it and be done with him, once and for all.

Bransen considered his options. He had already tested the strength of the chains and the fit about his wrists. If he was to resist and attempt an escape, the moment was upon him. But did he even really care enough to try?

He grimaced away that ridiculous question with the image of Cadayle, pregnant Cadayle. The world might be worth nothing to him at that time, but Cadayle was worth everything.

Before Bransen could begin his desperate move, though, a voice from the doorway behind him interrupted the scene.

"Laird Bannagran, I beg!" said Master Reandu, his tone and his frantic, flailing arms full of horror.

"It is not your begging I seek, Reandu!" Bannagran stared hatefully at Bransen.

"What is this horror?" Reandu asked, coming around to better examine Bransen and the devious contraption that held him.

"None of your affair," said Bannagran.

"I protest."

"Go back to your chapel."

"No!"

Bannagran looked at him threateningly.

"Bannagran, laird, I beg of you. This man has done nothing to deserve—"

"The same could be said of most men and women my age in all of Honce," Bransen interrupted. "Deserve?" he laughed. "Have you been to the south where all hint of society has been replaced by savagery? Where the weak are slaves to the strong, the women chattel to be taken by any man who so desires? Where every decency has been sublimated to every urge?" He laughed again. "Deserve? Do any of us deserve the hubris of Delaval, now the idiot Yeslnik, and of Ethelbert? Or do we all deserve it because it is naught but a sad joke?"

"Bransen," Reandu scolded.

"You really do not care, do you?" asked Bannagran. "Would you grin as you died if I cut open your throat now?" The Bear of Honce smiled wickedly as he asked the question, lifting the knife as he approached.

Bransen smiled back and made no move to resist or protest at all.

"Spare him," Reandu begged.

"He must tell me everything he has learned," Bannagran demanded. "He has been to Ethelbert. He claims he knows who killed King Delaval. I will have every word."

"And then you will spare him?"

"If his words please me, perhaps," was all Bannagran would give. "But know that my patience is ended."

"Your blade will do no more than free me," Bransen said.

"Bransen!" Reandu scolded. "Tell him!"

Bransen looked at him incredulously.

"If you care not at all about anything as you claim, then what harm is there in telling Bannagran what he wishes to know?" Reandu reasoned. "What sense is there in offering your life? What are you protecting?"

The words gave Bransen pause, reflected clearly on his face, so clearly, in fact, that Bannagran lowered his blade and waited. Bransen thought again of Cadayle. He could not throw away his responsibilities to her!

"Laird Delaval was murdered by a woman," Bransen said. "Of Behr. She is Hou-lei and not Jhesta Tu."

Reandu and Bannagran looked to each other in confusion.

"Hou-lei, an older order than Jhesta Tu," Bransen explained. "With a philosophy that names a warrior as but an instrument, a mercenary. Her name is Affwin Wi. She leads a band of several followers. She broke her sword in King Delaval's chest and has claimed my sword as her own for replacement. If you fight her, Bannagran, she will kill you. So would Merwal Yahna, her escort, who is stronger but not as skilled."

Clouds of doubt crossed Bannagran's strong features.

"I have fought them both and have battled you more than once," Bransen said evenly. "Either would defeat you."

"These are Ethelbert's assassins?" Reandu asked, trying desperately to keep the conversation moving forward.

"Who came out of the city in the dark of night and turned back Prince Milwellis's army," Bransen said. Bannagran's eyes went wide, telling the young man that he had hit something important.

"Only a handful, though, you say?" Bannagran asked.

"One less, perhaps two less, by my hand," said Bransen.

"Why would you fight them?" Bannagran asked suspiciously. "Have you thrown in with King Yeslnik?"

"They disgust me," Bransen answered. "Ethelbert disgusts me. Yeslnik disgusts me, and you disgust me."

"Bransen!" said Reandu.

"You have ruined the world," Bransen continued, heedless of the frantic monk. "You trample children under your march and do not care. You have destroyed all expressions of civilized life in the south. You bring misery to every man and woman of Honce and care not at all."

"Bransen, please," Reandu begged.

Bransen didn't even glance at him, his steely gaze locked on the Laird of Pryd. "You ask me to fly a pennant from my sword tip. You, all of you, demand that I choose a side." He snorted derisively and did then look at Reandu. "When I was young and at Chapel Pryd, you might have asked me an equally relevant question, Master Reandu. You might have asked which chamber pot, which pail of shit and piss, I preferred: the one hanging from my right hand or the one hanging from my left."

Reandu put his hand over his mouth and fell back a step, turning to Bannagran as if he expected the ferocious laird to kill Bransen then and there. To his surprise, though (and to Bransen's as well), the young man's vicious words seemed to have a calming effect on Bannagran and even backed him off a step or two.

"So Bransen fights for no one except Bransen, then?" Bannagran asked.

"Bransen chooses not to fight at all," Bransen replied. "But should he have to, then yes."

"I will march to war soon," Bannagran said. "Bransen will march beside me."

The Highwayman looked at him as if the statement were preposterous, as if the Bear had lost his mind.

"Because if you do, I will ensure that you and your family will live in Pryd Town and live well. Callen Duwornay and her daughter will be welcomed back, and I will see to it that they are never in need again."

"I am Jhesta Tu, not Hou-lei," Bransen replied. "I am no mercenary."

"Why not?"

Bannagran's simple question struck him hard.

"You will be doing no more than emptying chamber pots by your own words," Bannagran continued.

"Nay, to do as you ask would be putting my skills against simple peasants pressed to service, who do not deserve my wrath."

But Bannagran was shaking his head. "Fight only this Affwin Wi creature, then," he said. "And her consort. Slay those who murdered King Delaval, and I am confident that King Yeslnik will forgive your every crime. He fears these assassins—it is why he fled the field before Ethelbert's gates. But now he is determined to return to the coastal city and be done with Ethelbert, and no doubt he will succeed. If in that process the Highwayman rids him of the assassins he most fears, then his gratitude will lead to pardon. And in return, I will let you and your family live in Pryd Town forevermore, as distinguished citizens in good standing. Choose your home among any standing, save Castle Pryd itself, and I will grant it."

Bransen made no move to answer, and his visage did not soften.

"Or, if you truly care not for anything," Bannagran added, "you can die here in this miserable dungeon." He seemed quite amused with his own cleverness as he continued, "Perhaps I will just let you starve and rot here in the mud, then leave you for the rats to devour. Or I'll have my most trusted guards drag your rotting body out into the woods, perhaps, to bury you where you'll never be found. Then I'll tell your lady that I know not what might have happened to you and let her live her life in misery, ever watching for your return."

"You would do exactly that, wouldn't you?" Bransen said with contempt.

"You claim that you do not care. But you know me, Highwayman, and you know that I care even less. I must go and face Ethelbert again. I plan to survive the journey, and if your blade helps me to do that then so be it. If you choose to be of no use to me, then you are of no use to me, and so I simply do not care for you."

"Accept the deal, Bransen," Reandu whispered breathlessly. "By Blessed Abelle, man, I came here seeing no hope for you. And now there is opportunity and hope. Perhaps you will help facilitate the end of this wretched war at the same time."

Bransen's thoughts were swirling; he had nothing to which he could attach them. No anchor, no reality. Bannagran had caught him completely off guard with the impromptu proposal. Was any of it possible? Was it possible that he would get his sword back? Or the brooch Father Artolivan had entrusted to him? And would Bannagran hold true to his promise? Would this action facilitate a better life for Callen and Cadayle and for his child?

His child.

Bransen found his anchor in that notion: his child.

He silently berated himself for this surrender, for this willingness to see the end of his life. How selfish he had become in his despair!

"How dare I?" he asked aloud.

"How dare you?" Bannagran echoed skeptically. "How dare you not? What wondrous gift have I just offered you, fool! I could kill you without question here and now—nay, I would be hailed as a hero to the throne for ending your life. And yet, I offer you another way."

Bransen's thoughts began to spin once more. The choice seemed obvious regarding the welfare of his wife and family, and, truly, what did he care if Yeslnik or Ethelbert won the day, so long as the miserable war found its end?

He tried to consider the implications to Dame Gwydre, the one leader he considered worthy of her domain. But what Bransen didn't know at that time was that Gwydre had thrown in with Ethelbert against Yeslnik, that she and Father Artolivan had repelled the attack of Laird Panlamaris and thus invoked the wrath of Yeslnik and of Palmaristown. He didn't know that Dawson McKeege had sailed to Ethelbert dos Entel or that Cormack and Milkeila were even then in Ethelbert's court.

"How do I know that you will be true to your word?" Bransen asked.

Bannagran smiled, obviously recognizing victory. "What do I have to gain by lying?" he asked. "If I cared whether you lived or died, you'd be long dead already."

"But if I succeed, you would have me living in Pryd Town."

"Expect no invitations to dine at Castle Pryd," the laird said dryly.

Bransen nodded. He felt as if he understood Bannagran fairly well. The man was callous and so ferocious as to be rightly considered vicious, but there was a measure of nobility there, a measure of honor. Bannagran had no reason to lie to him and no reason to fear him.

"I will kill Affwin Wi," the Highwayman declared. "And Merwal Yahna."

Bannagran smiled. "I will summon the gaoler to free you of your chains," he said. He walked up beside Bransen, hooked his hand under the band at the back of the man's trousers, and tugged him backward, forcing him away from the wicked blade. With his free hand, Bannagran slid that blade free of the beam and threw it forcefully to the side of the room.

"Yeslnik will not be pleased," Bransen warned as Bannagran moved behind him toward the cell door.

"Yeslnik is terrified of Ethelbert's assassins," the laird replied. "He will be thrilled."

"This brave and noble man you call king," Bransen quipped.

Bannagran paused before the door, even turned back in an initially angry reaction.

But what could he say?

CHAPTER 7

The Conscience Pangs of Pragmatism

I beg you to forget it," Father Destros said to Cormack and Milkeila. "For the sake of the wider world, leave your personal inquiries aside."

"The man was a friend and an important part of Dame Gwydre's designs," Cormack argued. "Am I to simply believe that he is dead and care not for how that came about? Is there to be no value or justice or account-ability to and for his death?"

Father Destros gave a long and weary sigh. "How many hundreds, thousands, have died as such?"

"But he was here," Milkeila said.

"Yes, this man Bransen, the man you call the Highwayman, was here in Ethelbert dos Entel, just a few weeks ago."

"And now Affwin Wi carries his sword," Cormack said.

"She had his sword when I was introduced to him, when she brought him before Laird Ethelbert," Destros replied. "He was very much alive and well at that time, and yet, Affwin Wi carried his sword as her own."

"And the brooch on his forehead?"

"That is why I and my brethren were brought to the meeting. We carried sunstones to counter any dangerous or devious magic the Highwayman might have tried to initiate at Laird Ethelbert. You must understand that we did not know his allegiance at that time, if he had any."

Milkeila put her hand on Cormack's arm. Affwin Wi wore that brooch, and neither of them could imagine Bransen trying to get along without it. They had both seen him in Alpinador on Mithranidoon without a gemstone assist-ing his movements. Absent a soul stone, the Bransen they knew was a helpless, stuttering creature.

"Might Affwin Wi have possessed another soul stone, Father?" Cormack asked quietly.

The monk shook his head. "None of which I am aware. Laird Ethelbert holds a few stones of varied powers, a soul stone among them, I believe. But again, I warn you not to ask him and not to bring this conversation beyond these sheltered walls."

Cormack let a few moments pass. "And Jameston Sequin?" he asked again. "A tall man with a great mustache who favored the bow and a tricornered hat?"

Father Destros shrugged and held his hands out helplessly. "Forget it," he advised again.

"If Affwin Wi played a role in Bransen's death—"

"Then you and Dame Gwydre," Destros cut in, "would be better off knowing nothing about it."

It seemed wrong to Cormack, against every measure of justice and truth that he wanted so desperately to cling to as a guide for his life. But there was merit to Father Destros's warnings. If he confronted Affwin Wi and his fears proved correct, she would likely attack him. Whichever proved victorious, Wi and her band or Cormack and Milkeila, the alliance he was working to forge between Dame Gwydre and Laird Ethelbert would be shattered.

"Laird Ethelbert loves the woman," Father Destros said, as he had declared at the beginning of their conversation. "He will support her, no matter her complicity in your friend's demise. And we do not even know that he is dead!" The monk continued hopefully, "More likely Affwin Wi, who claimed him as a subordinate in her warrior band, sent him on some mission. Her followers are among the few scouts leaving the city of late, the eyes and ears of Laird Ethelbert, a most vital role. She would probably demand much of the Highwayman before accepting him fully into her elite band."

Cormack and Milkeila could do little more than nod their agreement with the reasoning, whatever they suspected differently. They took their leave of Chapel Entel then, Destros smiling and waving to them every step as they exited his audience hall.

The father's expression turned much darker the minute they were out the door, however, for he hadn't told the couple everything. On the last day Bransen had been seen in the city, Destros had been summoned by Affwin Wi to use his gemstone magic on the grievous wounds of one of her warriors, wounds to which the man had succumbed. Across the room, obviously the scene of a terrific fight, another of the Hou-lei disciples lay dead. The Highwayman was nowhere to be found, but Affwin Wi had his sword and his brooch, and Destros didn't need to stretch his imagination far to imagine the likely scenario that had led to the devastation: Bransen had fought with Affwin Wi's followers and had subsequently been killed by the powerful woman and quietly disposed of.

Destros had never been comfortable with Affwin Wi and the other warriors from Behr. His was not a parochial prejudice, for Destros was far more knowledgeable and tolerant of the traditions—even religions—of the southern kingdom than his monk brethren. He had been to Jacintha, the teeming, colorful, vibrant city south of the Belt-and-Buckle, and truly loved the place and its loud and emotional citizens. The Order of Abelle, like most of the folk of Honce, considered the southerners to be unsophisticated, uncultured barbarians, the "Beasts of Behr." But like the more knowledgeable folk of Ethelbert dos Entel—and Laird Ethelbert himself—Father Destros knew better.

Still, he had little use and even less love for the ferocious Affwin Wi and her small band of mercenaries. He was fairly certain that she had killed the man known as the Highwayman and that it was likely not at the behest of—or even with the knowledge of—Laird Ethelbert.

But the pragmatic monk, who truly wanted this alliance among Ethelbert dos Entel, Vanguard, and his beloved St. Mere Abelle, had no intention of making his suspicions known to the laird or to anyone else.

B y the time King Yeslnik caught up with Prince Milwellis and the Palmaristown garrison in the small town of Weatherguard, down the long grassy hill from Chapel Abelle, the siege and assault preparations were already well under way. Lines of men bearing great logs streamed into the town, which now had far more invading soldiers living in tents than residents in more permanent structures. Huge piles of stones grew daily.

Milwellis stood in the command tent before a large topographical map spread wide on a table. On the map were lines of models of the catapults and small, carved markers to represent cavalry units and archer brigades.

"Do not begin your bombardment of the fools until the harbor is secure," Yeslnik instructed as he entered.

"My father's fleet will see to that presently," the prince replied.

"His warships are in the gulf, yes," said Yeslnik. "But beware, for if the monks determine that they must flee, they will go out in great numbers armed with their devilish gemstones. Before the weight of magical fire and lightning, even our greater ships will prove vulnerable."

Yeslnik and his wife, who stood just behind him, noted a wry smile on the ever prideful Milwellis's face.

"They will not get out of their harbor," the prince assured his liege. "They protect their docks with a narrow channel between high cliffs. There is but one approach between rocky reefs."

"Still, one boat armed by the great magicians of the order might break through that gauntlet," said Yeslnik.

"They waited too long," Milwellis replied with obvious confidence. "You will see the value of your loyal subjects of Palmaristown in the dawning light of tomorrow."

Yeslnik looked to Olym, who could only shrug.

"We awaited your arrival," Milwellis explained. "We did not feel it necessary to move with expedience since the monks and their visitors from Vanguard show no apparent haste to be free from their walled prison. They hold to the notion that their chapel will withstand all that we can offer, and they may be correct."

"But when the rest of the world, Vanguard included, bows to King Yeslnik, that security will seem as a prison," said the king, and the Prince of Palmaristown smiled and bowed respectfully.

"You will leave here for Ethelbert's city with all confidence that Palmaristown controls the gulf coast and that your enemies will not escape Chapel Abelle," Milwellis assured Yeslnik.

The king did not sleep well that night, but not for any lack of confidence that the plan was going along splendidly. He was agitated and excited by the surprise Milwellis had promised him, and so when the prince's man came to rouse him at first light, he was already awake and dressed. He and Queen Olym met with Milwellis on a bluff overlooking the dark gulf waters. A stiff wind blew in from the sea, but it was not cold, and lines of whitecaps crashed in against the rocks far below.

Milwellis nodded to the left, where a large ship was just coming into view. "An old cargo barge," the prince explained. "Refitted with many tall sails and with great posts running deep below her, far below her keel."

The ship turned, making straight for the narrow approach to the gap between the high cliffs, a thousand feet below the walls of the great chapel. Through that gap, unseen from this angle, sat the docks of Chapel Abelle, accessible to the chapel complex high above only through long tunnels.

"You are attacking by sea?" a confused Yeslnik asked, for the defensible nature of Chapel Abelle's docks had been made quite clear to him and it seemed impossible that any force could break through that way. "How many warriors are aboard that ship?"

"None," said Milwellis, smiling still. "And only a handful of crew."

Yeslnik looked at him curiously but said no more, instead watching as the large ship passed from sight into the cliff gap. Almost immediately there came the sharp retort of Abellican lightning, flashes of fire and bursts of thunderous magic as the monks defended their docks.

Then came a tremendous explosion, and though Yeslnik did not know it, this one was self-inflicted on the ship, a blast calculated to take out her starboard hull just below the waterline.

Yeslnik looked at Milwellis curiously.

"The ship is sunk," the prince said, and he seemed quite pleased by that.

Yeslnik just stared at him for many heartbeats.

"In the shallowest and narrowest part of the approach," Milwellis explained. "Where her wreckage"—he held his hand up diagonally before him—"will block the entrance or egress of any sizable boat. We reinforced every corner of the barge with thick metal. It will take the monks weeks of difficult work to clear enough of the flotsam to have docks accessible to anything larger than a small, rowed craft."

"Brilliant!" Yeslnik exclaimed as the situation became clear. "You have just freed many of our warships from the duties of blockade so that they may run wild along the Vanguard coast. Or even all the way to Ethelbert dos Entel should I need them to finish that troublesome laird."

"You have entrusted us with the most important duty of all," said Milwellis, and in that moment of victory Yeslnik allowed him his exaggeration. "Dame Gwydre and Father Artolivan will not escape Chapel Abelle. They will exit only under a flag of surrender to King Yeslnik of Honce."

King Yeslnik could hardly contain his elation. Behind him, Queen Olym clapped excitedly. Half of his plan for victory, the isolation and irrelevance of Dame Gwydre, Father Artolivan, and the forces of Chapel Abelle, seemed assured. Now all that he had to do was push Ethelbert into the sea. Bannagran would command a force that could accomplish the task.

Yeslnik merely had to stay alive to be assured the absolute and uncontested kingship of Honce.

It was a good morning.

Brother Pinower of St. Mere Abelle crawled from a vertical chute, climbing into the early-morning air on a small ledge halfway up a giant rocky cliff face, one of the guardian cliffs sheltering the bay that held the chapel's docks. The young brother noted his fellows on the cliff across the way who had crawled from similar tunnels. One of the first things the monks had done after the initial construction of the chapel more than half a century before was to catacomb these two cliffs to create lookout points and attack perches, and now, for the first time, it seemed as if they would need them.

Pinower could hardly believe his eyes as the huge ship glided into view, moving easily across the choppy water. The deck was not crowded with archers, nor were any ballistae or catapults evident. Did they think they could just sail in to the docks uncontested? Pinower looked back to the chapel walls looming in the distance more than two hundred feet above his perch. He pictured the four great catapults set behind them.

The warship executed her last turn around the reef and headed straight between the cliffs. Pinower could only imagine that the large craft's hold was full of warriors. They would try to weather the beating. Pinower squinted and tried to gauge the plating on the ship.

It seemed absurd. The Palmaristown sailors had to know that they could not withstand the power of St. Mere Abelle!

"Put up a flag of truce," Pinower quietly whispered to the unseen enemy sailors, thinking this had to be an attempt at parley. How relieved would he, would any of them, be if such a deal could be struck!

The ship moved to the mouth of the cliffs.

St. Mere Abelle's catapults fired in rapid succession, four huge stones in the air at the same time. The catapults hadn't been used in years, though, and despite careful sighting, the stones splashed down into empty water, three in front of the approaching ship and one to the side.

Calls rang out across the cliffs, and Pinower reached his hand forward, grasping a graphite, the stone of lightning.

"Raise your flag of truce!" the monk demanded. Across the way the first lightning bolt thundered down at the sails, tearing one asunder. A second bolt from Pinower's cliff, just below the monk, thundered into the mainmast, and the top of the shaft began to burn.

Pinower heard the sound of the catapults again, and that prompted him to fall within his own graphite. He felt the energy building, his fingers tingling with power, and he let fly a considerable blast that blinded him as it flashed down upon the ship, lighting fires on the mainsail.

A boulder plopped into the water right before the ship, a second sailed over, but the remaining two both struck home, crashing through the deck.

Pinower winced, expecting to hear cries of pain and fear from below.

But there was nothing, just the damaged ship sailing in toward the docks, one sail burning and another hanging torn.

The monk noted movement then on the aft deck, a handful of men scrambling over the taffrail.

But they weren't running in terror; their movements were precise and practiced.

Pinower understood, and his eyes widened. He started to call to his brethren to hold their lightning and for the catapults to cease, but even as he started to yell the thunderous retort of a lightning bolt drowned his words. More ensued, a cascade of blue-white lightning reaching down from the cliffs and battering the craft with such brilliance that Pinower had to avert his eyes.

He looked back just as the starboard side of the great ship exploded, a great bubble of water and a flash of flames reaching forth.

"No, no, no," Brother Pinower mouthed, and he noted a small rowboat moving away from the warship, pulling out into the gulf. Almost directly below him, the warship listed and swirled to a stop.

Pinower scrambled back down the chute and rushed along the narrow tunnels to inform his superiors. He heard other monks in the tunnels cheering their victory, but he knew better.

The enemy had achieved their goal this morning.

He found all the principals gathered in Father Artolivan's quarters. The masters of St. Mere Abelle were there, along with Father Premujon of Vanguard's Chapel Pellinor, Dame Gwydre herself, and, of course, Father Artolivan.

Pinower slipped in quietly and took his seat off to the side of the leaders.

"Their boldness speaks of desperation," Artolivan remarked, his voice very shaky this day, his eyelids heavy and his every movement filled with obvious discomfort.

"Uncoordinated," one of the masters remarked. "They did not employ archers to keep our brothers low on their cliff perches, nor did any catapults of other warships send forth their missiles."

"The ship is stopped?" Dame Gwydre asked. She looked at Pinower as she spoke, as did many others.

"Exactly where our enemies wanted it to sink," the brother replied glumly.

Father Premujon started to question that, but he stopped short, catching on.

"It was no attack," Pinower explained. "But merely flotsam for a blockade."

"Clever," said Father Artolivan, but he did not seem overly concerned. "The strait is blocked?"

"It was a large ship and seems as if designed to sink at an angle," Pinower explained. "I doubt that any vessel of considerable size could cross in or out."

"They try to seal us into a place from which we have no intention of leaving," said Father Premujon. "And in doing so, they minimize their own avenues of attack."

"They mean a long and full siege, then," Artolivan reasoned, and again he did not seem bothered.

Why should he, Pinower realized, since the monks hadn't planned on breaking out of the chapel anyway and were very confident that they could withstand a siege indefinitely. Pinower did note, though, the very concerned expressions of Dame Gwydre and Father Premujon, their visitors from Vanguard, whose road home was across the gulf. Gwydre in particular seemed none too pleased with the events of the morning.

Artolivan noted that, too, apparently, for he looked right at the Lady of Vanguard when he declared, "Brothers will go out to the wreck under cover of night to determine how it might be cleared away. They will weaken seams and attach ropes so that if we choose we can pull the wreck apart at our convenience.

"This is not ill news," the old father said to the wider audience, raising his voice, though it hardly sounded strong. "We have known from the moment of our proclamation of disloyalty to the claims of Yeslnik that our success rested upon the work of our emissaries to Laird Ethelbert. St. Mere Abelle stands as a solid monument of defiance, but our influence is limited beyond our walls."

"I fear for the people of Vanguard," Dame Gwydre remarked. "Would that I could go home to lead them in this dark time."

"We will find a way," Father Artolivan promised even as Father Premujon began to reply. "As I am confident that your man Dawson will find a way to get back to us with word from the south."

Brother Pinower brought a hand to his mouth. He had an idea.

There was no moon that night, and under the cover of darkness a handful of monks gathered on the docks of St. Mere Abelle. They each carried a malachite, the stone of levitation, and a graphite, a serpentine, and a ruby. A pair also held curved iron bars two feet in length, one end of each set with potent lodestones, the stone of magnetism, which were useful in pulling metal nails.

They dropped their woolen robes and moved to the very end of the wharf. "Remember, do not disassemble it," said the monk leading the group. "We are merely inspecting the wreck, weakening it so that we can be rid of it in short order should the need arise to clear the strait." The young brother was not the most senior monk of the group, for Brother Pinower, clad in only a loincloth, stood among them, malachite in hand and assorted other stones in a small pouch tied on one hip. He also carried a large backpack full of supplies and common clothing.

Enacting their gemstones, the brothers stepped down to the water and walked upon it in single file. They made the wreck without incident and went to work, letting those with engineering expertise thoroughly examine the craft. Pinower stayed with them for a short while, for he, the most versed in gemstones, knew the potential troubles of enacting magic underwater. A graphite, for example, might throw a line of lightning across a field, but underwater, it would more likely produce a globe of energy that could easily sting, stun, or even kill a careless user.

The team worked with typical monkish discipline, the engineers pointing out critical joints and support planks that could be removed, and the monks diving to the spots to loosen nails and pegs. Using clever teamwork, they managed to utilize a serpentine shield that allowed them to isolate areas of wood that could then be scorched with the magical fire of rubies.

"Are you certain that you should venture forth this night?" the leader asked Pinower as they stood together on the water near one of the protruding and angled masts. "Our flashes are muted by the waves, but some are visible nonetheless, and light carries far across dark waters."

"I will find my way safely," Brother Pinower assured him. "Now is the time for men to step forward bravely, as Father Artolivan has done in defying Yeslnik. He has chosen principle over expedience and has reminded us that there are bigger things than these corporeal, mortal bodies. On my first day at Chapel Abelle—St. Mere Abelle—those many years ago, the inducting brother bade us to consider our physical form as no more than a wagon carting us along a road much longer than this life span in this world. The secret, he said, is to leave this leg of our eternal journey with our hearts pure, integrity intact. Principle over expedience, brother, and let the consequences be accepted as they fall, as we can only control that which is in our hearts. Father De Guilbe chose expedience. Since Yeslnik appears so near to victory, he reasoned that the order should accede to his demands and offer fealty. To Father De Guilbe's thinking, we could thrive under King Yeslnik.

"But Father Artolivan knows better and understands the truth of who we are and why we are here. He chooses the way of principle. I have never been more proud of our order, and my only fear as I venture forth is not for me but for those I would leave behind should I fail in this task."

The other monk smiled at Pinower and nodded, his expression full of appreciation. "You'll not fail, brother," he said. "You walk with Blessed Abelle. Your steps are sure because you know they are upon the right road."

Pinower was glad for those words. He smiled in reply and patted the younger monk on the shoulder. Then he splashed his foot upon the water to accentuate his point as he quipped, "Even if that road is the surface of the sea!"

And with that, Brother Pinower jogged away from the brother and the shipwreck, straight for the southern coast of the Gulf of Corona, moving east of St. Mere Abelle. He knew that he would have to cover many miles before finding an accessible beach, and knew, too, that the distant beach would be only the beginning of his journey. He felt the great weight of responsibility on his shoulders as he jogged across the water, but that weight didn't drag him down. Quite the contrary, Brother Pinower kept putting one foot in front of the other, and his gemstone magic did not fail because he knew that so many depended upon him getting far to the east and finding Dawson McKeege's *Lady Dreamer.*

He tried not to think of the consequences should he be caught, for Brother Pinower had never been a brave man, never a warrior. He remembered the scene outside St. Mere Abelle, when Brother Fatuus and the other captured monks of Palmaristown's chapel had been brutally murdered because they would not renounce the church of Father Artolivan.

Brother Pinower fully expected that the same brutal fate would befall him.

But he ran on anyway, as Brother Fatuus had continued to the gates of St. Mere Abelle even dragging several spears behind him. He thought of that monk's ultimate courage, his refusal to break faith even in the moment of his death, and Brother Pinower drew strength.

He ran on across the waves, past the swells breaking on sharp rocks or thundering against the tall stone cliffs. With his malachite magic flowing strong and keeping him atop the water, the currents couldn't drag him in, but every wave lifted him up high and dropped him down behind it.

Not far to the east of St. Mere Abelle, the night growing long, the eastern sky beginning to brighten, Brother Pinower saw the dark outlines of sails. Palmaristown warships, he feared, full of archers with longbows. He felt vulnerable then when the swells lifted him, knowing that his silhouette might be spotted against the solid cliffs, knowing that if he was spotted a rain of arrows would soar out at him.

But still Pinower ran, and when the morning light peeked over the eastern horizon, brightening the coast, he moved in tighter to the cliffs, darting behind the many rocks and continuing on whenever no enemies were nearby. Finally he found a place where he could move away from the water and onto a long, sloping field. Pinower wasted no time in dressing in his peasant's clothing. Only then did such a fit of great weariness, both from his long run and from his continued use of gemstone magic, overwhelm him that he found a sheltered nook among the tall rocks and settled in for a nap.

He awoke long after noon, rose, and looked back to the west and his chapel home. He prayed to Blessed Abelle for his mission's success. Not for himself but for all of those who were counting on him, and, truthfully, if someone had offered Brother Pinower a deal, the cost of his life in exchange for delivering the message to Dawson, he would have taken it.

Because this wasn't about him at all. It was about St. Mere Abelle, about the integrity of Father Artolivan's decrees, about the autonomy of the church, and about the defeat of several men who had shown themselves to be unworthy of the titles they had so recklessly claimed.

It was about the prisoners at St. Mere Abelle and in chapels all around Honce. It was about a higher plane of justice and of truth, and, without that place, then for what was life worth living, anyway?

He prayed to Blessed Abelle and he prayed to Brother Fatuus.

Brother Pinower would not fail.

The first of Milwellis's catapults let fly the next morning, throwing a huge stone to the field just before the towering stone walls of St. Mere Abelle. Inside the chapel courtyard, the ground shook, and more than one man upon the wall cried out in alarm.

Dame Gwydre walked resolutely across the courtyard, a lone figure, tall and thin with her light brown hair cut short and fashionable and a smart but simple wrap pulled tight about her. Around her the monks and the attendants, who were mostly former prisoners of one side or the other in the ongoing war, rushed to and fro, calling out orders and crying for everyone to take cover.

Dame Gwydre ignored those shouts, and when the next rock soared in, this one clipping the top of the chapel's front wall, then skipping up and over with a line of debris behind it, the woman did not flinch in the least. The Dame of Vanguard was no stranger to war. Entire villages under her domain had been sacked, every person and animal within murdered by the hordes of goblins and trolls inspired by the vicious Ancient Badden. She had smelled the stench of death, had witnessed the mutilation, and had lived for years on the very edge of disaster. It would take more than a few haphazard catapult throws to rattle Dame Gwydre.

She walked to the parapet ladder and gathered her wrap to free her legs, calmly climbing even as shouts announced a third missile was on the way. The blast hit the wall not far from where Gwydre climbed, and her ladder bounced back dangerously before settling once more into place.

Again, the woman didn't flinch as she climbed to the parapet. She looked out over the long, sloping field toward Weatherguard, shielding her eyes so she could better discern the line of catapults.

"Dame, I beg of you, seek cover!" one monk exclaimed as he rushed to usher her away.

"Only a coward would throw from afar," she replied. A fourth stone rose into the air but fell far short, bouncing about the turf and rolling to within a few strides of the wall.

Dame Gwydre laughed at the pathetic shot. "I do not fear cowards, brother," she said to the monk and turned to face him directly to let him see her serene smile.

The man straightened his shoulders and returned her smile. From him emanated the same sense of calm that became infectious about the courtyard. The brothers and attendants went about their chores with rocks arching through the air, setting watchers along the wall, calling shots and yelling to those in an area of imminent peril. But the disruption had been minimized, as Gwydre had hoped, and morale had been fully restored to the point where a playful betting pool erupted about where each subsequent stone might hit.

Dame Gwydre spent most of the morning on the wall, even placing a few bets with the brothers, until Father Premujon scrambled up the ladder behind her.

"Artolivan is not well this day," he informed her. "He will likely not rise from his bed."

"Has he named anyone to speak in his stead?" Gwydre replied.

"Brother Pinower is out to the east. Brother Jurgyen, perhaps?"

"Has Artolivan named a successor?"

"Dame, he is not dying!"

"We are all dying, father," she calmly replied. "He should name a successor."

"Fathers of the order are selected by committee, not as an inheritance," Premujon explained.

"I know, and I know, too, that such a gathering of leaders could not be brought about easily." She turned to look over the field, for the monks were calling to her of danger. She spotted the boulder immediately where it arced and spun end over end, almost as if it were flying slowly, as if all the world were moving in half time.

"Dame!" Father Premujon cried. He grabbed her and tried to pull her aside.

Gwydre resisted his tug. The enormous rock plummeted at the last and hit the wall below; the shock wave nearly knocked them both from their feet.

"I win!" Gwydre cried in elation, and a great cheer went up about the courtyard. She winked at Father Premujon. "I do make such an inviting target."

"Lady?" the monk gasped.

Dame Gwydre walked by him to the ladder and started down. "Gather the masters," she bade the father. "Let us dine together this day."

"Where are you going?"

"To speak with Father Artolivan."

The dame caught up with Premujon and the other monks, all the masters of St. Mere Abelle, as the meal was being set out in the chapel complex's great dining hall. She waited for the attendants to finish bringing the food and drink before standing at the center of the long table and lifting her flagon in toast.

The others stood and lifted their cups in reply, but all were glancing around with confusion, not quite sure what to make of this impromptu gathering. The rocks had been flying at St. Mere Abelle all morning long, and a couple of men had been injured, though, thankfully, none seriously.

"I have spoken with Father Artolivan," Dame Gwydre explained. "He is well. Let us toast to his continued health."

"Huzzah!" the monks cheered and drank, and more than a few started to sit once more. But Dame Gwydre remained standing and kept her flagon high.

"But in the event that his health should worsen," she said, "Father Artolivan has named a successor, a steward to the leadership of the Order of Blessed Abelle."

Now the whispers began, some soft, some loud, as the brothers all began chattering with surprise.

"Should God take him from us, Father Premujon of Vanguard will steward the chapel and the order," Gwydre said.

"This is unprecedented," one monk remarked. He looked to Jurgyen, whom many considered Father Artolivan's most trusted advisor. Many other gazes also fell upon Jurgyen as the brothers took their seats.

"Father Artolivan has decreed this?" Jurgyen asked.

"He has, and I trust you will go and confirm it presently," Dame Gwydre replied.

But Jurgyen surprised her, showing the strength of his character. "No need, good lady!" he said with great exuberance. "We all trust the messenger." At that, Jurgyen stood and lifted his mug, and everyone followed suit. "And who can disagree with the wisdom of Father Artolivan's choice?"

There was nothing but sincerity in the young man's voice, and almost everyone in the room was nodding in agreement. There would be no argument here; the brothers had decided to work toward the common and most important goal, their personal pride put aside.

Dame Gwydre looked to Father Premujon. The man fidgeted and seemed quite out of sorts. But in the end, he smiled back at her and joined in her toast. Dame Gwydre had facilitated this. They all knew it. She had gone from the wall to Father Artolivan's bedroom and had demanded that he name a successor and that the successor be the man of her choosing, the father from Vanguard whom she had known and trusted for many years.

When Father Premujon asked—accused, actually—Gwydre of this after the dinner, the woman didn't deny her role in the least.

"He needed the responsibility lifted from his old shoulders," she explained. "And I needed someone in place who would remain strong through the trying days ahead. I needed you, Premujon, a fellow of Vanguard, who has known great hardship and who will not flinch when King Yeslnik comes calling."

Father Artolivan, confident in Gwydre and their mutual selection of Premujon, rested very well that night, sleeping more peacefully than he had in years, since the war between Ethelbert and Delaval had commenced.

He died quietly the next morning.

CHAPTER 8

The Heart of the Matter

"And so our young hero has found a cause," Master Reandu said to Bransen when the Highwayman ventured to Chapel Pryd later that same day.

Bransen eyed him curiously, not pleased by the sarcasm in his tone.

"Bransen will fight for . . . Bransen," Reandu said. "I am surprised that you did not bargain harder with Bannagran. Perhaps you might have added some gold to the purse for your services."

Bransen continued to stare at the man to try to take a measure of this sudden change. Hadn't Reandu begged him to "accept the deal" offered by Bannagran? And now he seemed quite perturbed that Bransen had done exactly that. They locked stares for some time.

"Are you angry with me, Brother Reandu?" he asked. "Or with yourself?"

"With both," the monk replied. "And with all the world."

"A few hours ago you bade me accept the deal and help be done with this war," Bransen reminded. "What has changed?"

Reandu rubbed his face, looking very weary indeed. "In helping Bannagran, you aid Yeslnik."

"Yeslnik or Ethelbert," said Bransen. "They are one and the same. Equally worthless."

But Reandu shook his head, slowly and deliberately.

"What has changed?" Bransen asked again.

"King Yeslnik's advance guard came in this day. The king is not far behind," said Reandu. He got up and moved about the room, peering out every exit to ensure that they were alone. "King Yeslnik has declared war against St. Mere Abelle."

"St. Mere Abelle?"

"Chapel Abelle," Reandu explained. "Abelle has been declared a saint by word of Father Artolivan and the masters, and so the chapel has been renamed in deference to Abelle's holy station. With the declaration has come a determination of defiance against King Yeslnik, and he, in turn, has declared the church outlaw. Do you know Father De Guilbe?"

Bransen scoffed at the mention of the unpleasant man.

"Then you do," said Reandu.

"He has brought trouble," Bransen reasoned. "That is no surprise."

"He will arrive here with King Yeslnik in the morning."

Reandu went quiet, and Bransen sat back and digested the bits of information. "So if King Yeslnik has declared the church outlawed and yet Father De Guilbe travels with him . . ." He paused and looked at Reandu, who was nodding slowly.

"Then De Guilbe is now outside the order," Bransen finished.

Reandu frowned. "The Church of the Divine King."

"No," Bransen corrected, "the order, your order, is now led by De Guilbe and not Artolivan."

The weary Master Reandu rubbed his face and looked away.

"So it does matter to you now which side proves victorious," Bransen said. "Before, you were interested merely in ending the war, but now the stakes have been raised. Now it has become a personal trial for Master Reandu."

The monk looked back at him, and there was no disagreement in his solemn expression.

"Do you wish to recant your advice to me, your humble servant?" Bransen asked, unable to resist a bit of smugness at that confusing moment. "Should I betray Bannagran and flee to Ethelbert's flag? Or should I simply surrender to Bannagran once more and go back to his chains and blades?"

"No, of course not," Reandu said. "No, Bransen. My advice to you would not have changed."

"But you do not wish Yeslnik to win," Bransen said bluntly.

Reandu's eyes widened, and he glanced all around nervously. Then he growled, angrily, and began breathing heavily, and Bransen could see that the man was torn here, was mad at himself. Did Reandu, perhaps, not like what he was learning about his own courage and convictions?

"When the war was merely about the torn flesh of peasants, Reandu cared less," Bransen stated. "But now, over some silly allegiance to a sainted dead man and a meaningless church, Reandu has come to care."

"I always cared, Bransen," Reandu replied, his voice showing the wound. "Always did I wish to alleviate the suffering. . . ."

"If the war was declared over this very day, Yeslnik the victor, De Guilbe the new religious head of Honce, would Reandu accept the verdict?"

The clever question had the monk wincing in pain and embarrassment.

"I would not have advised you differently, even had I known the escalation of enmity between St. Mere Abelle and King Yeslnik," he said, strength returning to his voice. "My duty is to advise you to do that which is best for you and for your family. I would not have Bransen executed by Bannagran before King Yeslnik's throne, nor would I demand of you that you find in this war a higher context and mission."

"Even as you are faced with exactly that?"

"Perhaps," the monk said and shrugged. "I see no clear path before me, but I will seek the correct road for myself and for those who look to me for guidance."

"De Guilbe or Artolivan?" Bransen asked. "Hardly a difficult choice."

Reandu looked around once more as if he expected the royal guard to swoop down upon them at any moment. "What do you know?"

"De Guilbe is a wretch," Bransen said. "A merciless brute quick to punish any who disagree with him. You know of his history?"

"I know that he went to Alpinador at the request of Father Artolivan."

"Where he imprisoned those who would not bend to his demands of conversion and warred with those who came to rescue their imprisoned brethren," Bransen replied. "Murdering them at the base of his fortress walls. Do you think that a proper use of the holy gemstones? And when one of the brothers in his charge could not stand the needless bloodshed any longer and thus freed the captured Alpinadorans, bringing peace to the island, De Guilbe ordered the monk beaten unconscious and cast out in a boat to die. But he did not die—indeed, he rescued me in the cold north, and that man, that monk Cormack, is of great character and conscience, a man your order should revere and not torture!"

Bransen's own volume gave him pause, and he was surprised to realize how much he had emotionally invested in the fight between Cormack and the church. He couldn't help but give a little self-deprecating laugh at his own unexpected passion. "I was in the north at the demand of Dame Gwydre of Vanguard," he explained.

"Yes, to battle Ancient Badden. The details have come to Chapel Pryd. Your exploits were no small matter to the Order of Blessed Abelle, I assure you."

"And when I went to battle Ancient Badden, I went with many allies, including the monk De Guilbe had cast out to die. But De Guilbe was not beside me, nor were any of those under his command. Nay, he fled the field."

Reandu stared at him.

"And when Dame Gwydre pardoned the monk De Guilbe had banished, and when Father Premujon of Chapel Pellinor supported her edict, so began the battle between the church and Father De Guilbe. In Chapel—St. Mere Abelle, Father Artolivan, too, opposed De Guilbe, strongly."

"And you believe that his defection to Yeslnik is self-serving and not necessarily rooted in the call of his conscience," Reandu reasoned.

"It is rooted in his wounded pride," Bransen assured him. "And nothing more, unless it is his realization that his actions have cost him the succession of old Artolivan's seat."

Reandu took a moment to digest this information before stating the obvious, "You are not pleased with Yeslnik's choice of De Guilbe, and never were you pleased with Yeslnik himself, as I recall. Has this news given you pause over your agreement with Bannagran? Will you betray him and simply run away?"

"No," Bransen answered without hesitation. "For I have seen the alternative, Laird Ethelbert, and am no more impressed by him. My fight is personal with Affwin Wi; she stole my sword and the star brooch Father Artolivan entrusted me with. I ride with Bannagran but care nothing for the larger questions of the day. There is no right and wrong to be found there in my heart."

"I don't believe you," said Reandu.

Bransen started to rebut the monk but held his tongue. Something about the manner in which Reandu was looking at him told him the truth of the monk's accusation: Reandu didn't believe him because Reandu expected more of him.

That notion shamed Bransen. He wanted to deny that Master Reandu's opinion held any meaning to him. He reminded himself of his years living in the hole in the floor of Chapel Pryd, when Reandu and Bathelais and the other brothers had practically imprisoned him and had given him the most humiliating and filthy duties. He had carried chamber pots for this man, Reandu, and given the unsteady legs of the Stork, he had often worn their contents.

He brought back all of those unpleasant memories then in an attempt to defend against the pangs of guilt, but one truth kept peeking through the wall he was constructing: Reandu had cared about and for him, and in the critical moment when Master Bathelais was about to strike Bransen dead—as Bransen tried to rescue Cadayle from the rape of Laird Prydae—Reandu had stopped Bathelais.

"I'll not betray Bannagran," Bransen said. "My fight is with Affwin Wi. Your own choice is more important to the ways of the world."

"Many look to the Highwayman with hope."

"Your order is fractured and is choosing sides," Bransen reminded. "The Highwayman is but one man." He paused and lowered his eyes, closed them, and closed his heart. "The Highwayman is but one dead man, killed in the east by warriors from Behr."

B rother, begin the process," Father Premujon ordered.

"It is no small matter," Brother Jurgyen replied with obvious exasperation.

"It is necessary."

Jurgyen shook his head. "We cannot affect the fate of Vanguard's ports. Whatever information we may garner would be cursory and would not alter our course. . . ."

Father Premujon closed his eyes, his face growing very tight, and Jurgyen wisely quieted.

"Brother," Premujon said after taking several deep breaths, "the gulf teems with Palmaristown warships—likely Delaval ships, as well. Lady Gwydre is cut off from her people, and those people may well prove critical in our battle with King Yeslnik."

"We cannot affect the fate of—"

"Information is power!" Premujon interrupted. He raised his voice for effect and not in anger, grabbing Jurgyen by the shoulders. "We have in our grasp the greatest weapon of all. We can see events far removed and know the outcomes weeks before our enemies can adjust accordingly. We will be the quicker!"

"Father Artolivan did not agree with you," Jurgyen dared to reply. "You tried to make this argument with him, no doubt, and yet he did not assemble the brothers and hand them soul stones that they might go forth in spirit alone. The edicts of our order—"

"And yet even as you argue with me, you would have sent the brothers forth in spirit to inform the other chapels of the passing of Father Artolivan."

"There are times for such risks," Jurgyen admitted. "We sent word of the canonization of Blessed Abelle. We came to you in spirit in the far north of Vanguard with word of the war."

"And so you shall go to Vanguard again with news of the war and with words of rally," Premujon explained. "And to gather information from the northern holding that Dame Gwydre can rest easy as she continues her battle with Yeslnik."

"You ask for more than a single, simple journey and for more than the communion with prepared brothers on the other end."

"I do."

"The risks are unprecedented! Many will die!"

"I know."

"Yet you persist in this madness all so that Dame Gwydre can rest easy," Jurgyen remarked.

"He would," came a voice from the door. The speaker, Dame Gwydre, entered the room.

Brother Jurgyen closed his eyes and lowered his head.

"For that and so that we might learn of events in the gulf," Gwydre went on. "Events that may well determine our course here at St. Mere Abelle." She looked to Father Premujon and nodded her chin toward the door. The monk caught the cue and promptly left them alone in the room.

"Pray speak your mind," Dame Gwydre said to the brother. "Bluntly."

Jurgyen looked at her skeptically.

"I have been at war for more than a year, brother," Gwydre said. "I have witnessed utter carnage in Vanguard villages, where every man, woman, and child was slaughtered by vile trolls. I stand here now amidst a rain of catapult throws. I promise you your words will not hurt me."

"We should not risk the spirit walking so casually as I was commanded," Jurgyen said. "To send brothers out across the gulf on so regular a schedule is madness."

"It is necessary."

"And this is why you elevated Father Premujon to the leadership role," Jurgyen accused.

"Father Artolivan selected his replacement, as is acceptable in times when a formal Council of Masters cannot be convened."

"Father Artolivan acceded to your request," Jurgyen accused. "Dame Gwydre asked him for Father Premujon."

"You heard such a thing?" she asked.

"I deduced such a thing," the monk admitted.

Gwydre laughed helplessly. "Had you been in attendance, I admit you would have heard such a thing."

Jurgyen's eyes went wide at the unexpected confession.

"The choice was logical," the woman explained. "None here have more experience than Father Premujon. None have served the order more loyally, and none have shown such nimbleness."

"Nimbleness?" Jurgyen asked, perplexed. Only for a moment, though, as he considered the history of Dame Gwydre and the Order of Blessed Abelle. Her war with the Samhaists hadn't begun out of whole cloth, and one of the precipitating events to Ancient Badden's turn against her was her intimate relationship with a monk. Gwydre had fallen in love with a brother of Chapel

Pellinor, and Father Premujon had known about it from the beginning. "Nimble," he said aloud with a little smile. He thought it a good word.

"He understands me," said Gwydre. "And he complements my decisions appropriately."

"And he follows your orders, obviously."

"Nay," Gwydre replied without hesitation. "Not that stubborn one!"

"He has ordered me to prepare rooms of meditation and to send many brothers to the corners of the world, particularly across the Gulf of Corona, to gather the information you desire."

"Because he knows it is the correct tactic. We are trapped in here, brother, as Ethelbert was trapped in his city. Our enemies run across the land and sail across the seas. We must know the result of their movements if we are to properly counter."

"And you must know of your beloved Vanguard."

"I want to know," the woman admitted. "Wouldn't you?"

The simple honesty and logic hit Jurgyen hard and shamed him for his obstinacy. Truly he felt the fool for having so accused this woman of nefarious plotting!

"But you would not have us impart the word of Father Artolivan's death?" he stammered, finding suddenly that he wanted to change the subject.

"Oh no," she replied. "We cannot do so. Not while Yeslnik holds so visible an advantage. Such news will strengthen the hand of Father De Guilbe in this dangerous time. If Father Artolivan is no more, then those brothers at the many chapels across the land may well turn De Guilbe's way. He has King Yeslnik's sword. He is the easier choice."

"You have little faith in the brothers," Jurgyen scolded.

"I understand human weakness, brother. I understand that even brave men may need a measure of hope to facilitate their course to battle. Now is a time of great uncertainty in the chapels of Honce, a time of confusion and difficult choices. Now is not the moment to herald the death of Father Artolivan, who has stood so bravely against the tyrant Yeslnik."

Jurgyen considered for a few moments, then nodded his agreement to all of it. "You would have most travel across the gulf even though the more immediate events lie to the south?" he asked.

"This was not my fight, and I am unknown to many of the folk in the southern holdings of Honce," Gwydre explained. "But it is my battle now, and by Father Artolivan's own design I will be presented as a possible alternative ruler to both lairds, Yeslnik and Ethelbert. Is this not true?"

"It is."

"And so our ultimate hope rests in the security of Vanguard, for if Yeslnik claimed that land in conquest, then with what title might I presume to climb the throne of Honce? I am Dame Gwydre only because that northern holding, Vanguard, is my domain. Without it, I am merely Gwydre."

Once more Jurgyen felt his cheeks flush with embarrassment. He had thought that he was correct in his arguments against Dame Gwydre's course, mainly because he had presumed the woman had not thought through her plans.

In a strange way, though, when his embarrassment wore away, Jurgyen was comforted by the forethought and calculation of Dame Gwydre. He even viewed the promotion of Father Premujon in a new light, more complimentary to this woman. Yes, Gwydre had manipulated Father Artolivan, had lobbied him hard for her preferred successor, but truly, given his experiences with the kind and wise father from Chapel Pellinor, Jurgyen could not disagree with Father Artolivan's decision.

The brother argued no more. He assembled the brethren of St. Mere Abelle that very night, choosing from their ranks those most powerful with the gemstones and most seasoned in the act of spirit walking. He delivered Father Premujon's orders—Dame Gwydre's orders—with all the zeal as if they were his own.

"Information is power," he told the brothers. "A weapon we will use to bludgeon this pretend King Yeslnik and the traitor De Guilbe."

They began assembling that weapon in the dark of night, insubstantial spirits moving through the shadows with not a whisper of sound.

A t Bannagran's insistence Bransen stayed in Chapel Pryd and out of sight the next day when King Yeslnik and his grand entourage entered Pryd Town. Yeslnik rode in splendor in a coach bedecked with sparkling jewels and leafed in gold. Trumpeters announced his arrival, their sharp notes rousing the townsfolk while guards filtered throughout the side avenues, demanding the villagers rush to the main thoroughfare and cheer for their king.

The army of Delaval marched behind Yeslnik's coach, eight abreast and stretching for miles down the road, more than twenty thousand strong. They kept their formations tight, their boots stomping the cobblestoned road in sharp cadence, in time with the drummers set at intervals among their ranks.

Master Reandu stood beside Bannagran before the gates of Castle Pryd. The monk stiffened. His discomfort was not lost on Bannagran as the glittering coach wheeled to a stop just outside the gates. Attendants scrambled to the door to pull it wide and place a short stairway before it to help King Yeslnik and then Queen Olym descend. Others carried the royal chairs, but Yeslnik waved his away and started toward the waiting laird even before Olym had taken her seat.

"Laird Panlamaris and Prince Milwellis have besieged the traitors inside Chapel Abelle," the king said before Bannagran could even offer a greeting. "Land and sea. The treacherous Artolivan and that beastly Dame Gwydre will sit in their hole and witness the birth of my kingdom all around them."

Bannagran respectfully bowed to acknowledge the important news, but he didn't look down as he did, instead watching as four bearers—slaves captured from Ethelbert's army—carried the powdered and vain Queen Olym. Behind her came a large monk, tall and wide, a giant of a man perhaps ten years Bannagran's senior but showing little sign that he was past middle age in his steady and strong gait.

"This is Master Reandu?" the large monk asked, his voice stern and loud.

"It is," Yeslnik answered, a wry smile on his face as he motioned the monk to take the lead in the conversation. The giant man didn't hesitate moving right up to Reandu, standing tall and imposing over the man.

"Father Artolivan has betrayed Honce," he announced.

Reandu didn't blink. He knew enough of the story to realize that this was Father De Guilbe.

"Chapel Abelle—"

"St. Mere Abelle, they call it now," Reandu corrected.

De Guilbe fell back a step though hardly cowed and even looking as if he was winding up for a charge. "They shame Abelle with their exploitation of his name at this time."

"You do not think our founder worthy of sainthood, father?" Reandu asked innocently.

"That is a process, master, and one ignored by Father Artolivan for no better reason than to separate himself from King Yeslnik. We both know why this time was chosen for Abelle's ascent to sainthood. The cynicism of that premature proclamation shames the memory of Abelle."

"We should discuss this in private, father."

De Guilbe scoffed at him. "The business of the church is the business of Honce," he replied. "All that we do, we do in the name of divine King Yeslnik."

Reandu didn't even try to hide his shock. "Divine king?" he echoed.

"It is providence that has brought this great victory and circumstance," Father De Guilbe explained. "Abelle, great Abelle, started the process, and here, less than a century later, we find Honce soon to be united." He turned and motioned to Yeslnik. "Under this man, this divine king. And we as ministers of the word must accept that truth and embrace it. Artolivan believed that it was time for the order to evolve, and he was right, though his direction was the past and not the future. It is time now for the Church of the Divine King to stand behind this man who has won Honce and united her. All the land will know peace if we stand strong."

"The Father of St. Mere Abelle and all the masters within would not agree with you, father," Reandu said.

"They have made themselves irrelevant by their obstinacy and their treason!"

Reandu wanted to shout at the fool to be silent, but he held his words and looked to Bannagran for some support. But the Laird of Pryd slowly shook his head, urging Reandu to silence.

Reandu took a deep breath to steady himself. He reminded himself that his words would affect all of the brothers under his guidance and the future of Chapel Pryd itself. His heart told him to fight De Guilbe's assertions, to stand proud and strong on principle, but his mind easily calculated the ultimate cost of such a stand. To what gain?

"So as with the lairds of Honce, the chapels, too, are pressed into choice," said King Yeslnik, and he motioned for Father De Guilbe to move back beside him. "Where will Chapel Pryd stand when Bannagran leads my armies to the gates of Ethelbert dos Entel, this time to destroy the outlaw laird?"

Reandu looked to Bannagran again, and the Bear of Honce stepped out before the king. "Master Reandu and his brethren will march beside me, of course," he stated flatly. "Their gemstones will serve the men of Pryd as they have without question and without reservation these long months of trial."

"Indeed," said Yeslnik, seeming hardly convinced. "And tell me, regarding my edict on the disposition of the prisoners—"

"Those prisoners taken from the field who were once loyal to King Yeslnik serve in my ranks," Bannagran assured him.

"And those loyal to Ethelbert?"

"Eliminated to a man," Bannagran lied. "Your orders were explicit. There are none loyal to Laird Ethelbert in Chapel Pryd or in all of Pryd Town."

"That is good," said Yeslnik. "Then the choice by Master Reandu has already been made and made correctly."

"We will march with Laird Bannagran, my king," said Reandu, but he was staring at Father De Guilbe as he spoke the words. De Guilbe's returned glare showed that he did not believe his fellow monk.

"I add ten thousand to your ranks, Laird Bannagran," Yeslnik said. "March east and not south. The southland has gone wild, and no supplies will be found there. I charge you with the defeat of Ethelbert. Claim his city for me, and I will widen your holding greatly."

Bannagran bowed and did well to hide the contempt on his face. This assault should have been accomplished months before when the combined armies of Yeslnik, Bannagran, and Milwellis had converged on Ethelbert dos Entel. Still, with ten thousand extra soldiers, Bannagran didn't doubt that he could win the day and the city.

"Beware Ethelbert's assassins," Yeslnik continued. "The Highwayman—"

"The Highwayman is not in Ethelbert's employ, nor has he ever been," Bannagran interrupted.

Yeslnik stared at him incredulously. "He killed King Delaval!"

"Nay, my king, we were mistaken."

"His blade broke off in my uncle's chest! I gave that very blade to you!"

"Nay, my king, it was not his blade," Bannagran continued. "It was the sword of Affwin Wi, a murderess hired by Laird Ethelbert."

"How can you know this?"

"I am closer to Laird Ethelbert's lines," Bannagran explained. "Affwin Wi's exploits and those of her mercenary band have been whispered all about, and I do not doubt them. The broken blade you gave me surely resembled the sword of the Highwayman, but the patterns carved into the silvery metal were wrong. On closer look Master Reandu informed me of this."

He looked to the monk as he finished, as did Yeslnik and De Guilbe and every man and woman near the castle gates.

"It is true," the monk reported. "We have confirmed it. The assassins who killed your uncle were in the employ of Laird Ethelbert, but Bransen Garibond, the man known as the Highwayman, was not among them."

Behind the gaping King Yeslnik, Queen Olym gasped and fanned herself with obvious relief. Yeslnik shot her a dangerous look, and she reached out and grabbed his arm for reassurance as he turned back to face Bannagran and Reandu.

"The Highwayman is still wanted for other crimes," he said. "You would do well to drag him to me or deliver his head, at least."

Reandu's eyes widened as Bannagran nodded.

"There are few in the world who understand this murderess from Behr," the monk blurted. "Perhaps the Highwayman—"

Bannagran cut him short with an upraised hand.

"The Highwayman is a blood enemy of this Affwin Wi creature," the laird explained. "She and her order are not in the favor of the cult he claims as his own. He will likely kill her and solve our problem for us."

King Yeslnik eyed him suspiciously. "You seem to know a lot about him."

"You charged me with finding him," Bannagran reminded. "To do that, I needed to learn all there is about him. Knowing one's enemy grants power. I know where he is and I know where he is going, and that path will lead him to do battle with Affwin Wi. Whatever the outcome of that fight, our position—your kingdom—is strengthened."

"You let him go once, and I forgave you," said Yeslnik. "I will not forgive you again if the Highwayman escapes."

Bannagran nodded.

"I grant you ten thousand of my soldiers to strengthen your own five thousand," Yeslnik said. "Secure every village between Pryd and Ethelbert and then lock the wretch in his city by the sea. I will join you at his gates, and we will push him into the sea and be done with him."

"It will be my pleasure, my king," Bannagran replied. "But I would ask of you a short respite for the soldiers."

Yeslnik's face screwed up with curiosity. "What do you mean?"

"A week of rest and plentiful food here in Pryd Town. We have been marching from coast to coast. Many have feet so swollen they cannot tie shoes upon them."

"A week? A week for that dastardly Ethelbert to strengthen his defenses! No, I say! Go and kill him! Go straightaway, I say!"

"The forward scouts will be out this very night," Bannagran promised.

"And the rest of you?"

"As soon as I can organize the forces appropriately."

"Tonight!" Yeslnik demanded. "Tomorrow morning!"

"That would be a disaster," Bannagran said coolly. "I know not your men or their leaders. To simply march off without the proper precautions would risk attrition and even skirmish within our own ranks."

"I would have Ethelbert," Yeslnik demanded.

"Indeed," Bannagran agreed. "And with two days' preparation, my march will be swift and strong."

Yeslnik looked as if he wanted to stamp his feet like an angry child, and he even crossed his arms over his chest. But Bannagran would not back down. In the end the warrior laird got his way.

King Yeslnik was back on the road to the west soon after, leaving behind a tent city of soldiers now under the command of the Laird of Pryd. To Reandu's great relief, Father De Guilbe departed with the king.

"You'll not kill Bransen," Reandu said when he was alone with Bannagran.

"We have a deal. Once he has dispatched Affwin Wi—"

"King Yeslnik will still demand his execution."

"He will charge me with that, but alas, I will never quite catch up to the Highwayman."

"You told him that he could live in Pryd Town with his family."

Bannagran gave a little laugh. "What would you have me do, monk?"

Reandu wanted to shout that Bannagran should defy Yeslnik, should demand that Bransen's name be cleared, but he offered no more than a simple, frustrated sigh. For there was no answer to Bannagran's question. King Yeslnik would not be persuaded by any sense of justice.

With a curt bow the monk left the castle, but before he got out the door Bannagran called after him. "Tell Bransen to shadow our march in disguise and to speak only with you or with me directly. Three days from now, perhaps four."

Reandu paused and brightened a bit at the surprising defiance Bannagran was showing to the impatient young king. But he did not look back. With ten thousand of Yeslnik's soldiers in the march and likely their own orders concerning the disposition of the Highwayman, Bannagran's call for disguise seemed quite appropriate.

It fits you well. It fit your father well," Reandu said to Bransen after the young man put on the brown woolen robe the monk had offered. "Even in your days with us so long ago, I never imagined that I would see Bransen in the robes of an Abellican brother."

"They are as uncomfortable as they are impractical," Bransen replied.

"More uncomfortable to you because of what they represent, no doubt."

"As they will become to you when Father De Guilbe claims supremacy over your church."

The retort obviously stung Reandu, his shoulders slumping almost immediately. "Few will follow him," he replied, but there was little strength or conviction in his tone.

"Fewer will follow Reandu to King Yeslnik's gallows," said Bransen, refusing to let the monk get away so easily. "I am no longer amazed by how quickly a man will justify his change of heart when a spear is leveled his way."

"Your cynicism is inspiring," the monk deadpanned.

"Only because you know it to be well placed."

Reandu stood straighter suddenly. He moved to the small room's single door and pushed it closed, then turned back on Bransen and asked, "Do I?"

Bransen shrugged as if the answer should be clear.

"I am afraid," the monk admitted. "I fear that De Guilbe will win and those at St. Mere Abelle will pay for their courage with their lives."

"It seems a likely outcome. But not all, I promise you. Cadayle is there, and Yeslnik will not have her."

"Because she is something for which the Highwayman will fight."

Bransen narrowed his eyes.

"But the rest of Honce be damned?" Reandu asked.

Bransen snorted. "The rest of Honce is beyond my influence. . . ."

"The women and children of Honce, the helpless elderly of Honce," Reandu continued, his voice rising, his shoulders squared, "all of them can be trampled under Yeslnik's armies or Ethelbert's armies, and Bransen cares not. Those miserable peasants who suffer under the horrors of this war are not Bransen Garibond's concern. The thousands of Garibond Womaks who try to simply live their lives without upset are not your problem."

"You cannot place that burden upon me," Bransen replied sharply.

"I should not have to," said Reandu. "The Bransen I knew would take it upon himself." He shook his head and opened the door, motioning for Bransen to leave.

Bransen didn't move immediately. He stood there, staring after Reandu, wanting to shout at the monk for his blindness to the obvious truth of the matter. There was nothing Bransen could do, that these events were beyond him, were beyond any man, and were, indeed, the wretched truth of mankind. What did it matter who won this foolish war? What did it matter which noble, be it Delaval or Ethelbert or even Gwydre, assumed the throne of a unified Honce? What did it even matter that Honce be unified? Certainly Gwydre would be the best choice, but to what end?

For she could be no more than a temporary light to curb the darkness of human reality.

But Bransen didn't shout at Reandu. Silently, garbed as an Abellican monk, the Highwayman left the small room in Chapel Pryd, and three days later walked with the fifteen thousand whose boots shook the ground of Pryd Town on their march to the gates of Ethelbert dos Entel.

Bannagran stared out the eastern window of his room in Castle Pryd overlooking the chapel. Once again the Highwayman had come into his life, and once again he had not killed the outlaw.

Why would he show such mercy to this one? He could claim pragmatism in each instance, but he knew that doing so would only half answer the question. What was it about the Stork that had so often stayed Bannagran's hand? Respect?

Perhaps, for none could question that the resilient young man had overcome tremendous obstacles in his life, as none could question the prowess of the warrior. But it was more than simple respect, Bannagran believed, though he had never taken the time before this moment to actually sit back and try to sort it all out.

The last candle went down in Chapel Pryd across the way, its small windows going dark. Reandu and the brothers had retired for their last night in Pryd Town, perhaps forever, Bannagran knew. He hadn't actually lied to King Yeslnik when he had declared that Reandu would be by his side for the march to the east or that Reandu and the brothers would serve well the army of Pryd and Delaval.

But neither had he told King Yeslnik the whole truth, for Bannagran knew Reandu well enough to understand that the monk would never betray the Order of Abelle for this new Church of the Divine King that the brutish De Guilbe had proclaimed. No, Reandu and most of the brothers (certainly those who had joined the chapel only to erase their status as prisoners doomed for execution) would not remain in Pryd Town under that option. They would flee to St. Mere Abelle or somewhere else beyond the immediate reach of Yeslnik.

That thought troubled Bannagran deeply, and he was surprised to realize that truth as he mulled it over. He had no wife, no family, and, indeed, no friends other than Reandu. Yes, Reandu was his friend. Not a friend like the sycophantic and opportunistic young noblemen who followed him about his court, laughing at his every joke with too much enthusiasm. Not a friend like the many women Bannagran took to his bed, all eager to steal his heart and claim a place as the Dame of Pryd. Reandu wanted nothing from him, though in many ways, the brother demanded more of Bannagran than any other person alive. Yeslnik ordered Bannagran to follow his orders, but Reandu always reminded Bannagran to follow his heart, which was the more difficult course by far.

The laird thought back to the scene in the dungeons the previous day. Would he have killed Bransen had not Reandu intervened? Certainly he was moving with that intent, and certainly he was angry enough with the Highwayman to do so. But no, he realized, he would not have killed Bransen. He did not want to kill Bransen.

Why was this one so different from all the others who had errantly crossed Bannagran's path and inspired his wrath? Why this man whose actions had led to the death of Bannagran's dearest friend, Laird Prydae?

A wistful look came over the face of the Bear of Honce. He felt a kinship to Bransen, for, like himself, the young man was a victim of his physicality. Bransen's infirmity had trapped him as the Stork for most of his life, had determined his course in life. So it had been with Bannagran. At the age of fifteen, young Bannagran had been stronger than any man in Pryd, and his proficiency in the fighting arts had caught the attention of Laird Pryd. And so Pryd had summoned him to the castle and had enlisted him to befriend his son, Prydae.

Thus had Bannagran's life path been set in motion. He and Prydae had trained together, had ridden together, and, when they were still teenagers, had gone to battle together. Bannagran the bodyguard had become Bannagran the trusted friend, and so he had spent the whole of his adulthood in Castle Pryd beside the prince, who became the laird.

He had achieved a great reputation through great exploits. He became known as the Bear of Honce, the champion of Pryd, and lairds from all around Honce had taken note of him in the powrie wars in the east.

It had been a grand life, full of adventure, full of wine and women and rousing cheers.

So why, now, did he feel so empty? So without purpose? He was the Laird of Pryd Town, a community flourishing under his control. He was the commander of King Yeslnik's main force, and his men loved him and would follow him to the gates of the demon dactyl's lair if he so asked them.

Strangely, he didn't care.

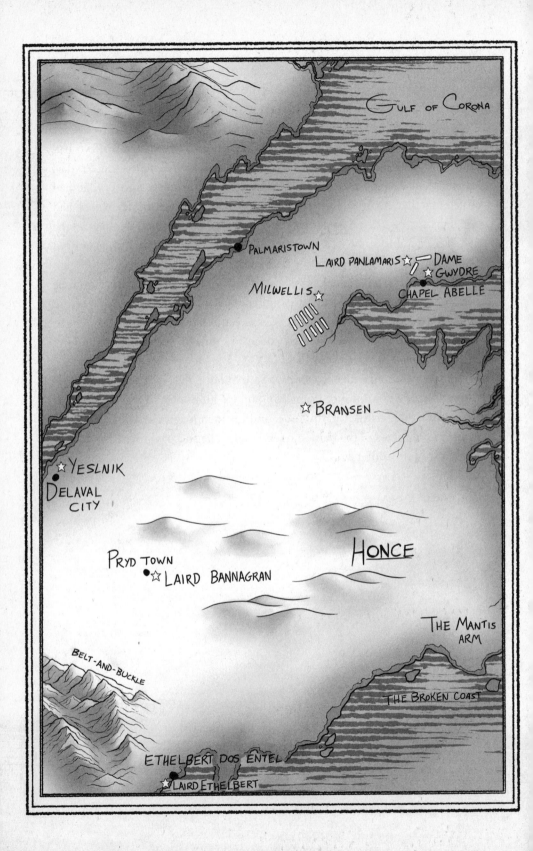

PART TWO

The Three Roads of
Jameston Sequin

*D*espair. It is a trap or it is the awful truth, the stark and undeniable realization of ultimate futility.

My legs are now strong, but I stand on shifting flats of mud. I am straight now in posture but crooked in vision, for I have glimpsed the horizon, and it is a dark place. Not for any dactyl demon, not for any goblins or trolls or powries, but dark by the incessancy of mankind's foibles.

In Weakness . . .
In Pride, they will call themselves god
In Envy, they will kill their neighbor
In Wrath, they will lay waste to the fields
In Sloth, they will let their neighbors starve
In Avarice, they will steal all unto themselves
In Greed, they will horde excess
In Lust, they will damn consequence.

The Book of Jhest was my companion, words copied by my father, wisdom garnered by the generations of Jhesta Tu mystics over the centuries, their reflections of the simple truths of the world. The book, my companion, resides in me still with passages I had thought unraveled but which reveal to me new secrets as my experience grows. Once I read "In Weakness" and saw a world not worth redeeming, and then I was the Highwayman. Then, with Cadayle by my side, I considered the passage as a warning against my own limitations and darker potential.

Now I fear it as inevitability.

For I have come to profoundly fear that there is no lasting goodness, nor can there be. With great hope did my father return from Behr, the Book of Jhest in hand, the song of the Jhesta Tu on his lips, and Sen Wi beside him.

They killed him for his optimism, for his idealism, for his hope that there was a better way.

How many hours, how many days, how many weeks, how many months, did he toil to copy those words? How many times was a page discarded because a single symbol was penned wrong?

The permanence of wisdom etched on fragile parchment so easily lost. And will the concerted effort of a future king collect them all and destroy them? And will all the followers, the Book of Jhest etched into their thoughts, be gathered and slain?

Inevitably so.

And what then is left?

What worth art and the just swing of sword
What small steps might man move forward
When a single man of ill design
Of lust and greed may just consign
To the ashes the work of those before
And halt their march forevermore?

That is my despair, that the accumulation of justice and goodness is an illusion, a temporary stay. One King Yeslnik will erase the gains of Dame Gwydre; one Father De Guilbe will chase away the call of Cormack's justice. A Gwydre or a Cormack might win, but eventually will a Yeslnik claim the throne or will a De Guilbe steal the church. And then the darkness settles, and justice is scattered, and the memory of Sen Wi dies with me, and the memory of Bran Dynard is lost in the ashes of Garibond Womak.

Is it no more than a circular road? Can the work of good men do no more than stretch it to the shape of an ellipse? For so long I dared not believe so, but now I see no other possibility.

In that case, then what is the point?

I do not know. The mud shifts below my feet. In Pryd Town, the Highwayman was a selfish man. In the cold north, under the tempting optimism of Dame Gwydre, the Highwayman found wider purpose.

But on a road in the east, in the death of Jameston Sequin and the betrayal by Affwin Wi, I was reminded all too clearly of the circle that is the fate of man.

The mud shifts again.

I know that I want my mother's sword. For that I will fight. I know that I demand the brooch Father Artolivan entrusted to me. For that I will fight. These are my two immediate certainties, and my third, Cadayle, awaits. Would that I could fix the world!

But another Yeslnik will claim the throne.
And another De Guilbe will steal the church.
And the flames of an Abellican ruby consume the Book of Jhest.
Sometime, somewhere, out there just over the dark horizon.

—BRANSEN GARIBOND

CHAPTER 9

The Moment of Courage

"Just piss yer pants," Engren the soldier grumbled as his tent companion crawled over him on his way to the exit. "It'll keep ye warm."

"It's summer," the third man in the tent argued. "And I don't want him stinking worse than he's already stinking!"

"Shut yer mouths, the both of ye," Cawley Andadin scolded, and he pushed aside the tent flap and crawled outside. "Tired o' being an animal, I am."

"It's what we be," said Engren. "Ye're a soldier, a dog. Thrust yer spear and wear yer enemy's blood and stink like piss and mud all the year long."

"We'll be back to Comey Downs in a month," Cawley replied, referring to their home village, just northeast of Delaval City. He was not a young man, and the ground was unforgiving to his old bones. He pulled himself up to one knee with great effort and then with a grunt heaved himself up to his feet. "Home, and with it all done. With Ethelbert done and Yeslnik the King of Honce and no more fighting. Me wife's not liking the smell of piss much."

"A month, yeah," said Engren in his typically dour tone. "A month, and we'll be getting slaughtered outside Ethelbert's gates. And if the Bear finds us a way to win, our reward will be a march to Chapel Abelle. Dodge the spears of Ethelbert. Dodge the lightning bolts o' the monks. All's the same and not to end. I'm thinking that dying might be th'only escape."

Cawley wasn't listening any longer. He was miserable enough without letting Engren's constant complaining weigh him down even further. He had spent a good few weeks in Comey Downs with his wife and five children. While going out on the road had been emotionally troubling, Cawley had mitigated his despair with a reminder that this was likely the last march. They were going for Ethelbert, King Yeslnik had told them, and would be under the guidance of the great Bannagran the Bear. All the way to Ethelbert dos Entel to end the war, with Cawley's group and ten thousand Delaval soldiers backing the legendary five thousand veterans of Pryd. Given the reputation of Bannagran, whose name was whispered reverently by ally and enemy alike, Cawley believed that they would do just that, that this time, the thorn of Laird Ethelbert would be eliminated.

And they had the monks with them, almost all of them, led by Master Reandu himself. Rumors also spoke of another ally, a small man many believed to be the Highwayman.

This time the assault was for real, Cawley told himself, and not like that inexplicable retreat they had executed all the way back to Delaval. This time they would end it.

He moved away from the dying campfires into the brush to relieve himself. He caught a movement out of the side of his eye a moment later and thought it must be another of the soldiers coming out for similar reasons.

The man was fastening his pants when the hood went over his head, his legs kicked out from under him. A fine cord went around his throat, stopping his breath, and preventing him from crying out. He tried to reach up and loosen the cord, but fingers knifed into one armpit, then the other, and for some reason that Cawley did not understand his arms seemed to simply die, all strength gone.

He was down on his face in moments. He tried to kick and thrash, but someone fell atop him, and a soft, woman's voice began whispering in his ear, "Sleep, sleep."

He felt the cord loosen some time later, felt the ground under him as he was dragged along. He stood on the edge of unconsciousness for a long time, too weak to call out but not quite escaping the sensations all around. His captors sat him up against a tree and tugged his arms hard behind him, his wrists bound around the other side of the tree trunk.

The hood came off, and Cawley saw her in the moonlight right before his face. The second he realized she was a Beast of Behr, with her almond-shaped dark eyes and black hair, he knew he was doomed.

Many whispers had spoken of Laird Ethelbert's vicious assassins.

She smiled at him, disarmingly, then slapped him hard across the face. He started to respond but went silent, feeling a clawlike implement, like the head of a garden rake, come up tight against his groin.

"If you yell out, I will make your death hurt," the woman promised in her odd accent.

Cawley stared at her, his eyes wide, licking blood from his split lip.

"Do you understand?"

Cawley nodded, eyes wide.

"Where is your army marching?"

Cawley licked his lip again, and she slapped him even harder.

"Where is your army marching?"

"East!" he gasped.

She slapped him again, and the world began to spin before Cawley. He could hardly believe this tiny creature could move so quickly and hit so hard! To make matters worse, she also pressed in with the claws against his scrotum.

"To Ethelbert dos Entel?" she asked.

Cawley groaned and nodded.

"You march to kill Laird Ethelbert?"

"No," the man gasped. "I'm just a soldier. I do what they tell me."

Behind the woman, a man spoke in a language Cawley did not understand.

"How many soldiers?" the woman asked.

Cawley stammered, "Lots."

The woman hit him again, and again.

"Five thousand o' Pryd," he blurted, and she backed off momentarily. "The rest're from King Yeslnik."

This time she punched him square on the nose, shattering it and jolting his head back against the tree. It took Cawley a few moments for his eyes to stop spinning, and he tasted the blood running from his broken nose.

"Yeslnik is not the king. Ethelbert is the king," she corrected.

"I'm not for caring who's the damned king," Cawley said, finding strength and courage in the certainty then that he would soon be dead no matter what he said.

The woman stepped back and stood up straight. She glanced over her shoulder at the man Cawley could not see and said something again in the language he could not understand. Then she turned back, and her smile—her awful smile—told him.

His eyes widened; he started to cry out.

The woman turned sidelong as she dropped low into a crouch that seemed almost as if she were sitting on the ground. Out snapped her leg, perfectly aimed, her foot slamming into Cawley's throat with jarring force. He rebounded off the tree again, and a strange tingling, a sensation of utter numbness, began to flow out to his limbs. He considered that curious sensation for some time before realizing that he could no longer draw breath.

He saw the man then, dressed in black like the woman, walking past him. He didn't understand, didn't feel anything, but he noticed that his arms fell freely at his sides and that the ties had been cut as he began to tilt to the side.

Cawley felt nothing as he fell over. He kept trying to draw breath, but none would come.

The man moved above him—he sensed that he was about to be finished off—but the woman intervened, speaking to him harshly but more to Cawley in his own tongue.

"Let him die slowly," the woman said. "Let him know that he's dying."

Cawley heard the words and watched the man and woman walk away, but that offered little encouragement to the suffocating, paralyzed man. He thought of his wife and their kids. He dreamed of working the fields with his sons, of going home that night to hot pumpkin pie, or apple pie—yes, apple, he decided, for none in Comey Downs could make an apple pie better than Maisey Andadin. . . .

The starlight faded to black.

Bransen sensed something. . . . He couldn't be sure of what, exactly, but he had come out of his meditation certain that something unusual was afoot in the dark and quiet night. He unwound himself from his cross-legged position and came to his feet in perfect silence. Bransen narrowed his gaze and scanned the dark forest beyond the campfires.

He thought of the gem-encrusted star brooch then and the cat's-eye agate that allowed him to see in the dark. How he wished he possessed such a gemstone now!

Bransen closed his eyes and recalled the stone and the sensations of its magical emanations. He could nearly levitate without malachite, so when he opened his eyes he tried to mimic the cat's-eye magic and found to his surprise that the dark was not nearly as absolute. Off he went at a swift pace. He started to discard his uncomfortable monk robes as soon as he moved out of sight of the tents, but he changed his mind; if he were caught here by Bannagran's men it would not do well for them to recognize him as the Highwayman.

Even in the bulky woolen garment the Highwayman moved with grace and silence, gliding through the shadows with ease, hearing every sound about him, smelling the scents of various animals. He wasn't sure what had stirred him from his contemplation, and his direction seemed random to him on a conscious level, but he continued on, trusting in his instinct.

He found a soldier lying in the dirt, very still.

Bransen soon discerned that a single blow to the throat had felled the man, though he had been beaten somewhat before that mortal strike. Blood had started to cake on his face from the broken nose. A glance at the tree, at the hair and blood stuck on its bark at less than waist height, informed Bransen even more of what had just occurred here.

The fallen man was not breathing. Bransen grabbed the man's windpipe and gently massaged it, glad for the soul stone Reandu had offered. He used that magic now, sending waves of warm breath into the soldier, repairing his crushed throat and calling his spirit back to his broken form.

A long while slipped past, but Bransen did not stop his work. He sensed the slightest bit of breath in the man's throat, so he reached for the gemstone magic even more furiously.

It wasn't until the man began to cough that Bransen realized his own emotional disconnect throughout this process. He had seen a man in trouble, and his instincts had taken over. He had put himself in a vulnerable position, falling into the swirl of hematite out here in the forest and with enemies so obviously near.

He knew with certainty that only one person would have done this, and that gave him great pause. Why was this man still alive? Affwin Wi didn't make such mistakes, and so Bransen knew then that it was likely not a mistake.

Was she baiting him, trying to lure him into the open?

He looked at the poor soldier, sent his thoughts through the hematite one last time to give the man a bit more relief. And as he did, the Highwayman laughed at himself and his stubbornness to ignore the world around him.

For such was the truth of who he was, no matter how hard the Highwayman tried to deny it. He could lie to himself and insist that he hadn't fallen over the wounded man to save him for the sake of the man's life, but to save him so that he, Bransen, could possibly gain some important information.

That not-so-subtle distinction was not lost on the young warrior, and when the soldier at last opened his eyes to look upon the man in monk's robes who had brought him back to life, he found that stranger scowling severely.

The soldier recoiled and curled defensively, coughing still.

"Who are you, and who do you serve?" Bransen demanded.

"Cawley o' Comey Downs, for King Yeslnik and marching with Laird Bannagran!" the man rasped through his raw throat.

"Rest easy, man, the danger is passed," Bransen assured him. Gradually, Cawley unfolded and looked at him directly.

"Two o' them, at least," Cawley gasped. "A woman, Beast o' Behr. She caught me and kicked me."

"What was she wearing?"

"Black—like the Highwayman . . . like you—" Cawley bit off the word and averted his eyes, and Bransen realized that the monk disguise was probably the worst-kept secret in the ranks.

Within moments, Cawley was stumbling back into the encampment, holding his sore throat and happy to be alive. Bransen was long gone behind him, into the forest, his monk robes soon looped over a branch.

He was hunting now. He was the Highwayman, a mask over his eyes. He knew now why he had come out of his meditative trance and understood the sensation that had alerted him.

It was indeed Affwin Wi. It was his mother's sword and the brooch Artolivan had given him. His blood and breathing ran hot with adrenaline as he moved through the forest, trying desperately to pick up the woman's trail.

A lways correct," Merwal Yahna said to Affwin Wi as they noted the Highwayman slipping through the trees below the hillock they had climbed to garner just such a view. "He saved the soldier no doubt."

"And the soldier sent him on his hunt for us."

Merwal Yahna pulled out his exotic weapon. "Shall we go and be done with the impudent man?"

Affwin Wi was shaking her head. "He will be of use to us in dissuading Ethelbert from any rash decisions."

"He is dangerous—" Merwal Yahna bit that thought off short when Affwin Wi scowled at him.

"You wish to fight him again," the man accused. "One against one."

"I will kill him when I must," Affwin Wi assured him easily.

"Such misplaced honor is Jhesta Tu, not Hou-lei," Merwal Yahna reminded.

"Honor?" Affwin Wi said doubtfully, and she added, "Sport."

B ransen was still moving, his footsteps coming more slowly, when the eastern sky brightened and the first ray of the sun peeked over the horizon. He ran up a tall tree then, scanning the countryside.

But she was gone. He knew it in his heart.

Bransen lay back against a branch, considering his missed opportunity. Rage bubbled inside him, for he wanted nothing more than to face this Hou-lei woman and retrieve his sword and brooch. And to kill her, he admitted to himself, for what she had done to Jameston Sequin.

But his anger was tempered by thoughts of Cadayle and their unborn child. Could he beat Affwin Wi? Alone, even, although he knew that it was unlikely he would ever get the chance to fight her without Merwal Yahna at her side?

He had vowed revenge, vowed to get his items back, but sitting there in the tree as dawn brightened the eastern sky, Bransen questioned his determination and his confidence. For all the value he placed in that sword, was it worth the price of his life—and not just his life, but the well-being of Cadayle and his child?

Somewhere in the distance to the northwest a horn blew, and several others responded. The army was awake and soon to be moving. Bransen looked back the way he had come, estimating the miles between his current position and his monk disguise. He shook his head and started away, not to retrieve the robe, but to intercept Bannagran's march.

As the Highwayman.

Cormack and Milkeila entered Laird Ethelbert's chambers cautiously, still not quite sure of what to make of the elderly but energetic laird. The summons had been brought by one of Father Destros's monks, which gave the couple some comfort, but the young monk's demeanor, his level of urgency, had also brought trepidation.

They entered the room to find Ethelbert sitting with his three generals, Father Destros, and another monk to one side and Affwin Wi and Merwal Yahna standing before the throne. At the sight of the dangerous mercenaries, Cormack and Milkeila, holding hands, both squeezed more tightly.

Ethelbert turned a stern glare over Destros, promptly dismissing the monk who had accompanied the couple.

Cormack felt Affwin Wi's stare boring into him as he walked up beside her to stand before the laird and his court.

"Your plans fall like the rain and run to the sewers, it would seem," Laird Ethelbert greeted.

"Laird?"

"You would have us parley with Bannagran of Pryd, but this man they call the Bear marches now to destroy us," Ethelbert explained.

Cormack looked at Affwin Wi.

"She found him less than a week's march from here along with an army of many thousand, perhaps three or four legions," said Ethelbert. "Most of them are Yeslnik's soldiers. There will be no parley with Laird Bannagran." His voice lowered as he added, "Just the blood, so much blood."

"So much Delaval blood," added Myrick the Bold. "We will slaughter them at our gates!"

Cormack tried to digest it all as cheers for the city of Ethelbert dos Entel came from the generals and the two monks. Through it all, Ethelbert, Affwin Wi, and Merwal Yahna stared hard at the emissary couple.

"Perhaps you should ride north to rejoin your Dame Gwydre at St. Mere Abelle," said Ethelbert. "If you remain here you will be expected to join with all your heart in the battle against the invaders."

Cormack wasn't quite sure what to say at first, but he was shaking his head, his instincts telling him that this news was not as unwelcomed as Ethelbert believed. "No, I pray you, laird," he said. "Does King Yeslnik ride beside Bannagran?"

He looked to Affwin Wi as he asked, and the woman shook her head. "He has run back to his castle," she replied. "Else we would have left him dead on the trail."

"Then this is our chance," Cormack blurted, his gaze darting from Ethelbert to each of his generals in turn. "We must go meet Laird Bannagran. With all speed, to engage him as far from the gates of Ethelbert dos Entel as possible!"

"You have gone mad, young brother," Ethelbert replied, his headshaking generals in obvious agreement.

"No, laird, this is our opportunity," Cormack pressed, growing more determined as he sorted through all of the options. "Outside of Pryd, far from home, Bannagran will find his army much less eager for engagement."

"You would have me leave my city defenseless against him, while I chase an army more than twice or even thrice the size of that which I might muster?"

"It would be sheer madness to abandon our walls," Kirren Howen remarked. "Let the Bear of Pryd Town come on. We will hold him to the field and rain death upon his army day upon day!"

"Even if what you say is true," Cormark replied, and he shifted his tone and his intended reply quickly as the scowls came back at him, "even if we hold and slaughter Bannagran's men, to what gain? What is our plan from there? How shall we seize the initiative from Yeslnik and turn back the pressing tide?"

"Perhaps your Dame Gwydre and Father Artolivan will have that answer, yes?" asked Ethelbert. "If your suggestion is to take such a risk as to ride forth and face them on the open field, then you are mad."

Cormack looked to Milkeila for support, and the woman took his hand and squeezed hard again. "We knew this would be a great risk, Laird Ethelbert," the barbarian woman said. "If not on the field, then we would have had to go to Pryd Town to find Laird Bannagran, and that would have been no less difficult. His march may offer us the option of retreat if we prepare the place of meeting correctly."

"We've the walls and a protected bay," said Kirren Howen. "I can think of no better place to make our desperate offer to Bannagran."

"Desperate," Cormack echoed. "And it will seem so if we do it with Bannagran's army camped outside." He turned his attention to Laird Ethelbert directly. "I pray you, laird, do not tarry. Meet Bannagran before his goal is in sight, and before he can surmise that your offer of alliance is made of desperation alone. If he believes this to be a last chance for Laird Ethelbert to save his life and his title, then know that he will not be merciful and will not betray King Yeslnik.

"Go out and meet him, I beg. Bargain from a position of power, not desperation."

A wail from the shadows at the back of the room turned all eyes that way, and Cormack crinkled his face as he recognized Palfry, Laird Ethelbert's beloved attendant. The waiflike man scrambled from the shadows and rushed across to the room's other door, holding his mouth as if he might throw up with every step.

"You will go and speak for Dame Gwydre?" Kirren Howen pointedly asked.

"I will."

"Even if we do not?" the general pressed. "If we remain in Ethelbert dos Entel, Cormack and Milkeila will still go forth to meet Bannagran?"

"I . . . we will."

Kirren Howen laughed at him. "He will cut you in half with that massive axe of his."

Cormack shifted uncomfortably from foot to foot. "All that I have heard of Laird Bannagran paints him as a severe but honorable man. An honorable man will adhere to a flag of truce."

"You will be killed before you get near to Bannagran," Affwin Wi said, drawing all eyes to her in surprise. She drew out her sword, Bransen's sword, and held it up near Cormack. The man held his breath, confused and wondering if her claim meant that she intended to slay him then and there.

"The Highwayman," she said. "The man you call Bransen. The man you call friend." She shifted to face Laird Ethelbert. "My agents run Bannagran's line, as you ordered. I am not surprised by their words that this man, the Highwayman, walks among the soldiers."

Like all in the room, Cormack's eyes widened with surprise; Milkeila clutched his hand even more tightly.

"We welcomed him as an ally and a student," Affwin Wi said sternly to Cormack. "He has betrayed us."

Kirren Howen cursed under his breath and banged a fist on the table.

"The Highwayman knows much of our defenses. And now Laird Bannagran knows, as well."

"What have you to say to this?" Laird Ethelbert asked Cormack.

"Bransen is from Pryd Town," the man replied, his voice shaky. He stammered, trying to continue, trying to find some explanation for this unexpected news—and trying to put it into context with his previous fear that Affwin Wi had murdered Bransen to take the sword and brooch.

"He would not know," Milkeila interrupted in sudden epiphany. Everyone looked to her to see her face as puzzled as their own expressions. "About the offer of Dame Gwydre to Laird Ethelbert," the woman explained.

"Yes, yes," added Cormack. "Bransen left St. Mere Abelle before our plans were crafted and even before Abelle was sainted and Chapel Abelle was renamed. He would not know that you, Laird Ethelbert, have agreed to an alliance with Dame Gwydre and Father Artolivan."

"He marches with my enemy," Ethelbert said.

"He will kill you in the forest before you get near to Bannagran!" Affwin Wi spat.

That preposterous line solidified the ground under Cormack's feet. "No," he replied. "Bransen would never take up arms against me or Milkeila at the request of any laird or dame or king or father. Nor would he choose battle against Father Artolivan, and certainly not to side with Father De Guilbe. No, I know Bransen much better than to even think any of that a possibility for a moment."

"He marches with my enemy," Laird Ethelbert said again, dryly, and his tone gave Cormack pause.

Once more, the former monk looked to his beloved Milkeila, and as if she read his mind, the Alpinadoran shaman smiled and nodded for him to press on.

"This is the time for men of great courage, Laird Ethelbert," Cormack said. "Better that Bannagran is marching east, further from Yeslnik's influence, when we go and meet him. He will honor a flag of parley, and we should all hope that Bransen has engendered his trust. Because Bransen will join with us—of that I am sure. And Bransen is no small voice among the people of Pryd, where he is considered a hero, and among the brothers of Pryd, including Reandu, the master who presides over Chapel Pryd due to Father Jerak's illness."

Ethelbert glanced over to Father Destros at that.

"Father Jerak's spirit and thoughts have long left his body, it is rumored," the monk replied.

"No better opportunity will we find," Cormack added, growing excited and letting that emotion filter into his voice.

"And no further east and no further removed from the fool Yeslnik will

Laird Bannagran be than on the day he arrives on our field," Kirren Howen reminded.

"Where your parley will be viewed as no more than the desperate last plea of a doomed laird and a doomed city," said Cormack. "Laird Ethelbert, I beg of you. Now is the time. Let us speak with Bannagran and convince him that the winds have changed and that there is a better goal for Honce than the rule of Yeslnik."

Again Kirren Howen moved to respond, but Ethelbert silenced him, silenced them all, with an upraised hand. The old laird sat there for a long while, mulling, then stood up from his throne and stepped from the dais to address Cormack eye to eye.

Cormack saw it, and so did Kirren Howen, as the general held back his two younger and more anxious counterparts, Myrick and Tyne. Something changed in Laird Ethelbert's demeanor, like a great sigh and a nod of ultimate acceptance.

"I cannot bring my army forth from these gates," the laird said. "For Bannagran is a clever general who would know our strength and weakness and would ensure that he destroyed us out on the field before we were ever able to return to the protection of the city's walls. What a terrible laird I would be to my people to leave the good and trusting folk of Ethelbert dos Entel so defenseless in the face of the ruthless Yeslnik."

"Bannnagran will honor a parley," Cormack dared to reply.

"Indeed, he would. But he would, at the same time and quite morally, position his force to defeat our escape should the parley come to no agreement. And I think it will come to no agreement."

Cormack started to reply but bit it back when he saw that Ethelbert meant to continue.

"It is a desperate plan Dame Gwydre has concocted and no less so than the stubborn and just defiance of Father Artolivan," the laird said. "I assure you that their courage is not lost on me. How much easier would it have been for both to simply agree to the notion of King Yeslnik. Had Father Artolivan followed the command of Yeslnik to free his men and execute mine, across all the chapels of Honce, then the war would likely near its end with Yeslnik's vast army sitting outside my gates at present if they had not already broken through!"

"My laird!" Myrick the Bold protested, but Ethelbert turned and laughed at him and motioned to Kirren Howen.

"You know," he said to his older and wiser general, and Howen had to nod his agreement of the laird's dark assessment.

"I am grateful to Father Artolivan," Ethelbert continued. "His courage and defiance have given hope to my good friend, Father Destros, there. And I am intrigued by Dame Gwydre. I cannot bring my army forth, for I fear the plan desperate. But yes, young Cormack, the plan is worth the attempt."

"You will allow me to go forth?"

"I will go with you," said Ethelbert, to a collective gasp from all in the room.

"No, my laird!" Myrick and Tyne cried together.

Again Laird Ethelbert turned away from Cormack to face them, his gaze settling on Kirren Howen, who sat with his hand on his chin, taking a good measure on the surprising Ethelbert and passing no obvious judgment.

"I and a select group of trusted guards," Ethelbert went on, "a small but capable accompaniment."

Both Affwin Wi and Merwal Yahna nodded, but Cormack saw trepidation there. They did not agree with Laird Ethelbert's choice, but it was not their place to disagree.

"I would proudly ride with you, my laird, my friend," said Kirren Howen, and both the younger generals looked at him incredulously.

"And I would be better for having you!" Ethelbert said, and it occurred to Cormack that the old laird was growing much more animated, almost jovial, as if he had suddenly seen a path to heave aside all the weight from his tired old shoulders. He was even standing straighter!

"But that cannot be," Kirren Howen said quietly. He nodded, as the two seemed to hold such complete understanding of each other. The respect in Kirren Howen's eyes was clear to see. Yes, Cormack thought, something had changed here. Suddenly, even Kirren Howen was surprised by Ethelbert's announcement, and, Cormack suspected, so was Laird Ethelbert himself.

"Our two young protégés are promising, you agree?" Ethelbert asked, and Kirren Howen smiled and nodded yet again. "But they are not tempered well enough to deal with King Yeslnik should he come a'calling."

"I would fight him to the bitter end," boasted Myrick, and the two older warriors, laird and general, laughed at the irony of their point being made so clearly.

"Young and proud Myrick, if I am gone, there will be no need," said Ethelbert. "Ever was this fight between me and Laird Delaval, not between Ethelbert dos Entel and Delaval City. Never was there enmity between our lands. Nay, it was the arrogance of Delaval that started this war, and it is the unbridled ambition of his idiot nephew that perpetuates it. The focus of his ire, the obstacle he seeks to remove, is Ethelbert the man, not the city. I will parley with Bannagran as our friend Cormack here delivers the desperate plan. Should that parley fail I will try to return to my city, for it is there I wish to die and not on the fields of some other holding. But that is of no consequence."

"My laird," Myrick said, his voice cracking as if he would break down in tears.

"You should live to be as old as Ethelbert," the old laird said.

"I would go, as well, my laird, if you would allow," said Father Destros, stepping forward. "Father Artolivan has made a brave choice, as you said, and a sorry emissary of my order I would be if I remained here with this important—"

"Granted," Ethelbert said. "Chapel Entel should be represented. But I charge you now with softening your words should the parley fail."

"Laird?"

"I'll not have the fate of Ethelbert dos Entel and the bargaining position of Steward Kirren Howen compromised because of a stubborn monk." He cast his glance back at Cormack and slyly added, "It would seem as if I have one stubborn monk to contend with already."

"I am not of the order, laird," Cormack replied.

"So you say," Ethelbert replied, obviously unconvinced.

"He will not be king," Merwal Yahna said to Affwin Wi when they were alone in their wing of the castle. "He hasn't the stomach for the fight."

"The wind blows from many different directions," Affwin Wi replied. "But all the breeze is against him."

"Will you go and dance for him this night?" Merwal Yahna asked, and there was no missing the venom in his voice. "That he might drift off to dreams of who he once was, that he might escape the truth of the weakling he has become."

"He is old."

"Too old."

Affwin Wi looked at him curiously. "And what would you advise?"

"We are done with this place," Merwal Yahna insisted. "This land, where our inferiors look upon us as if we are beasts."

"You speak like one who hasn't the stomach for the fight."

"Ethelbert will not ascend whatever his course!"

Affwin Wi smiled wickedly. "Why would you think I am speaking of Ethelbert?"

Merwal Yahna started to respond, but the words didn't come forth as the implications of clever Affwin Wi's words sank in.

They would find their way to greater power and treasure even if Laird Ethelbert would not. The warrior from Behr was glad to hear such words from

Affwin Wi, such assurances that she had played Laird Ethelbert dispassionately. He silently berated himself for those nagging jealous doubts that had inspired his anger, and he went to Affwin Wi eagerly and swept her into his arms.

When they tumbled to their bed, she, of course, was on top.

A liar I would be if I did not admit my surprise," Kirren Howen said to Ethelbert a bit later when they were alone in the laird's sitting room, sharing some fine drink.

"No less a liar than myself."

"You found Cormack persuasive."

Ethelbert shrugged, unwilling to make that conclusion. "More than ten thousand," Affwin Wi said. "Perhaps near to twice that number."

"And led by Bannagran, the Bear of Honce," said Kirren Howen. "Not by the foolish and cowardly Yeslnik."

"And with soldiers dressed in the fine armor bought by Delaval's endless gold and likely with a fleet of warships working their way around the coast and perhaps with that brutish Milwellis returning as well. Did you believe we could survive that?"

Kirren Howen stared at him.

"In honesty?"

"No, my laird," Kirren Howen admitted. "When Yeslnik ran from the field, I hoped we could parley our position and be done with this war. By all accounts that cannot happen. He is determined now and wise enough to hide while greater men carry out his commands. The Bear will not flee the field, and our walls will not stop his vast army."

"I could send Affwin Wi to murder him."

"She and the handful around her would have to battle through the finest warriors of Pryd and Delaval, perhaps, if she is not lying, with the Highwayman among them, and then with Bannagran himself. You could try that course, but . . ."

"But to what end?" Ethelbert finished for him. "The army of Pryd is well seasoned and layered with leadership—all trained under the eye of Bannagran." He took a deep sip of his potent Jacintha drink and gave a little chuckle. "We cannot win and cannot hold. How did our guest Cormack say it? This is the time for men of great courage?"

"My friend Laird Ethelbert is such a man," said the old general, drawing another chuckle from the laird.

"No man has lived a better life than Ethelbert," the laird replied. "All that

I have known I owe to this city, my home. It has served me through the decades, loyally and with love. A sorry father I would be to Ethelbert dos Entel if I cowered now behind her walls. Perhaps Dame Gwydre's plan will succeed, and all the world will be brighter, but even should it not, my friend, Ethelbert dos Entel will be better for my going. That is the truth I am faced with, and you cannot disagree."

The general sat stone-faced.

"And so I am called to be a man of courage," Ethelbert continued. "And so 'tis the time for Laird Ethelbert to truly serve the city that has served him for so long. I am not afraid and am not saddened. To see these walls broken by the stones of Yeslnik, to see him ride victorious through the gates . . . that, Kirren, would bring me tears."

"I know my role, laird," Kirren Howen assured him. "Should you not return, should the armies of our enemies arrive at the gates of Ethelbert dos Entel, I will . . ." He paused and took a deep breath, then drained his glass. "I will surrender the city to the King of Honce," he finished, and Ethelbert lifted his glass in toast.

CHAPTER 10

The First Road

Is it that you wish to embarrass me? Or anger me?" Bannagran said to Bransen, who was walking in his Highwayman outfit and not wearng the brown robes Reandu had given him.

"You employed the Highwayman, did you not?" Bransen asked a bit too innocently.

"Or like a child, you wish to see how far you may stray before the paddle is applied."

Bransen's bored look almost taunted Bannagran to try just that.

"I am not your subject, Bannagran."

"Laird Bannagran!" one of the Pryd nobles insisted, but Bannagran himself held up his hand for the man to shut up.

"You claim that you wish to make your home in Pryd Town," the laird reminded. "That would make you my subject indeed."

"On this march, I am your . . ." Bransen paused and considered his words carefully here, finally turning to Reandu as he finished, "your mercenary. Yes, that is a good word for it. I found your soldier in the forest and saved his life, so perhaps we should discuss my payment."

Bannagran's grin was not one of agreement, Bransen knew, but he pressed on anyway. "You wish me along because you fear Affwin Wi, as well you should. I wish me along because I have unfinished business with Ethelbert's murderess. That is the extent of my intended service, and truly you have asked no more of me. But there is more, perhaps."

"I have little time for your riddles," said Bannagran.

"I am your mercenary," Bransen explained. "Affwin Wi I will defeat because I must and for my own selfish needs, but I bear no antipathy to Laird Ethelbert's soldiers or to the old fool himself. One laird is as awful as the next, after all. That ambiguity is double-edged, however. I'll not work toward

Ethelbert's defeat out of any sense of loyalty to you or to that idiotic Yeslnik, surely, but that does not mean that I will not work toward Ethelbert's defeat."

"Loyalty to Pryd Town, then," Master Reandu said. "It was ever your home, Bransen, and certainly that means some—"

"It means nothing," Bransen harshly interrupted. "It was the place of my torment and my indenture."

"I don't believe you."

"You hold many false hopes, brother, not the least of which is reflected in those atrocious robes you wear so proudly."

Reandu merely shook his head and sighed.

"So you will not serve laird or king, but will do battle against Ethelbert," Bannagran clarified. "For gold, I expect."

Bransen smiled. "Do you wish their left ears, or the whole head?" he asked. "A king's gold coin for each I deliver. Do not look so sour at the notion, Bannagran. Consider instead the value I bring to your ranks."

"Why would not every man in the ranks demand the same terms?" asked the same noble who had earlier scolded Bransen.

"Why would I care if they did?"

"You are truly a wretched creature," said the noble.

"I?" Bransen asked innocently. "Am I the man who trampled the fields south of Pryd, driving the villagers to the foothills and an existence of sheer savagery? Am I the man who has claimed the land as my divine right, marching armies over folk who want no more than to fill their bellies on occasion and find a warm bed at night? Am I that man?"

"You have not the couth to be called a man, any man!" the noble retorted.

Bransen laughed at him. "Then I am an animal. Do you fear animals?" He stopped when he noted Bannagran scowling at him.

"Consider my terms, *Laird* Bannagran," Bransen said. "I promise you, it will be the best expense of your campaign."

To everyone's surprise Bannagran did not dismiss the notion outright, and his expression and posture revealed his interest. Clearly, he was considering how he might best utilize this mighty weapon known as the Highwayman.

Bransen nodded and started away, but the nobleman stopped him short. "Laird Bannagran has not dismissed you!" he scolded.

Bransen swung about. "Every time that fool speaks to me, add a silver coin to the bounty," he told Bannagran. "Or I will cut the bounty in half if you allow me to deliver his head for the first payment."

An exasperated Bannagran motioned the nobleman to silence and waved Bransen and Reandu away.

On the word of Laird Bannagran himself," Bransen insisted, holding out his hand.

Master Reandu stared at the hand, then back at Bransen, while several other brothers whispered in small groups all about them.

"A sunstone, a malachite, a lodestone, a soul stone, and a cat's-eye," Bransen reiterated when Reandu didn't move.

"I read the laird's note," Reandu replied dryly.

"And yet you hesitate."

"No good will come of this," Reandu said as he fished in his belt pouch for the desired gemstones.

"Was it the mountains of dead soldiers and townsfolk that convinced you? Or the razed villages and ruined fields?"

"Your insufferable sarcasm tries my patience."

"Sarcasm or truth?" Bransen retorted. "Is it that Master Reandu hasn't the heart to open wide his eyes, preferring instead the somber reassurances of chapel artwork?"

"I was not speaking of the war," Reandu said. "Perhaps we are closer in agreement on that matter than you might believe. Nay, I was speaking of your evil pact with Laird Bannagran."

"Evil?" Bransen replied, feigning hurt. "If the laird heard your term for his decision, you might find yourself at the wrong end of a swinging axe."

"Enough, Bransen! I said evil because that is the word I meant to say. You fancy yourself an assassin now? The man I knew in Pryd Town was no assassin."

"And yet I killed men in Pryd Town."

"You defended Cadayle. That is not the same thing."

"And now I will kill enemy soldiers," Bransen reasoned. "Is that not the point of war?"

"That is not the point!" Reandu's volume brought several gasps from the gathered monks and Reandu turned on them angrily and waved them away.

"Then it is the means to the point, yes?" Bransen said more quietly as the others shuffled away.

"It is one thing to do battle on the field of honor—"

"A most stupid description," Bransen interrupted.

"And something completely different to go hunting for victims," Reandu finished.

"As Ethelbert sent his assassins to kill Laird Delaval?"

"Yes! I knew then, immediately so, that the assassin could not be Bransen

Garibond, even when convincing evidence and King Yeslnik's declaration all pointed your way. I knew immediately that Bransen, the boy I knew as the Stork, the young man who grew strong and sure, could not have done such a thing."

"If I thought it would end the war, then I would kill Bannagran, or Reandu, right now," Bransen argued. "If I believed it would end the war, I would kill myself!"

"Ah, then you do care!"

The logic trap put Bransen back on his heels for a moment, but he settled quickly and replied, "Nay, brother, I care only about that over which I might have some control. I cannot end this war, and so I care nothing about it—other than to secure my own future with the gold I intend to collect."

"It is only about Bransen, then?"

"Yes. Only about Bransen and Bransen's family. I cannot stop this madness and cannot save the villagers from the stomp of armies. I cannot return civilization to the now wild southland and cannot breathe life into Jameston Se . . ."

Bransen stopped and closed his eyes and had to work hard to keep himself steady. Master Reandu put a hand on his shoulder. "Is it guilt that drives you to this evil pact with Laird Bannagran?" he asked gently, softly, as if he was again talking to that awkward boy who had carried chamber pots for Chapel Pryd those years before.

Bransen shrugged the man aside. His thoughts were on Jameston, though, on the man who had cared enough to walk beside him down a dangerous road, the man who had mentored him, albeit briefly. The man he had come to call a friend. He thought of Jameston's life story. Jameston had used his great skills in the forest to collect bags of gold in Vanguard and Alpinador. The man was possessed of knowledge valuable to noblemen of great means, and so they paid and paid well. Was Bransen doing anything different than that, truly? And if he had not devised this mercenary plan, would he have gotten the gemstones he needed to have a chance of defeating Affwin Wi?

"The world is at war," he said, his voice steady once more. "Men die in war. I cannot stop that, and so I shall not try to. But if they are to die anyway, then better by my hand, that I might collect some gold for the sake of my family. You are wrong, then, for something good will come of it. I will fill my coffers with gold and will care for my wife and her mother and my unborn child. I'll not live the life of a peasant. Nay, and my family will not be crushed by the march of armies, for those with wealth rarely are!"

Reandu tried to slap him across the face, but Bransen caught the monk's hand and easily held it back.

"Are you any better?" Bransen said through gritted teeth. "Will your brothers not heal Bannagran's warriors so that they can return to the field to die or to kill? Will you not throw bolts of killing lightning at the enemy on behalf of Laird Bannagran?"

"We will heal the wounded—of both armies," Reandu replied.

"You will heal those Bannagran brings you to heal, and they will not be men of Laird Ethelbert unless he wants to torture them when they are whole once more! Your actions support Laird Bannagran and so they support King Yeslnik, who has declared the leaders of your order to be heretics. So in truth, Reandu the coward, you will use the gemstones of Abelle to support the cause of Father De Guilbe, and even by your order's guttural standards he is not a man of character, wisdom, or mercy."

Reandu's mouth moved as if he was trying to find some retort to the hard claims, but Bransen cut him short.

"That is the truth of it, and you cannot deny," Bransen said. "Out of cowardice or moral indifference you have chosen the side that opposes Father Artolivan, and while you convince yourself that you will only be acting as Father Artolivan long ago decreed, you know the truth of it. Your march beside Bannagran aids his cause, aids Yeslnik's cause, and aids Father De Guilbe's cause."

"This discussion is not about me," Reandu insisted. "It is about you and your choice."

"Only because Reandu hasn't the courage of his espoused convictions."

"You are no assassin!"

Bransen stared at him for a few moments, then chuckled wickedly. "Count the ears in the sack before you make such a claim," he said as he walked away.

He moved through the branches like a whisper of wind, running along limbs and lifting himself into great, near weightless leaps to land lightly on the branch of the next tree in line. The night was dark about him, but he could see well enough with his intimate knowledge of the cat's-eye agate. The gemstone's magic magnified the starlight many times, and Bransen quite comfortably ran along the tree branches.

Near the top of a tall pine he came to a high ridgeline, a wide valley opening before him to the south. He spotted the light of a campfire, then another.

"Refugee peasants," he whispered to himself. "Or Ethelbert's scouts?"

A twinkle came to Bransen's eye. He looked back to the northwest, marking his position. It wouldn't be wise to be caught out here alone and lost. Bransen turned back to the south and the valley far and wide below him. He reached into the malachite, seeking its levitation powers. He leaped out from the tree and drifted on the night breezes far, far into the distance.

Sometime later, the Highwayman caught hold of the high branches of a tall oak, pulling himself in close to the trunk and sending a shower of acorns bouncing below him. Several small animals skittered through the nearby brush, but the Highwayman took little note of them, confident that he had floated down here unseen.

He stayed in the trees for some time, again running from branch to branch. Soon after, he spotted the soft orange glow of a dying campfire. He noted a sentry, a woman clad in leather and holding a long-handled, small-bladed axe. She leaned against a tree not far from the one he stood upon. Bransen smiled wickedly. Soldiers, not peasants.

He moved past the woman, giving a little shake to the high branches as he did, just enough of a commotion to get her attention but not enough to alert her to any danger, but just so that she would think it a gust of wind or a squirrel, perhaps.

The sentry's interest passed quickly as Bransen knew it would, and the Highwayman glided past, coming to a perch overlooking the small camp. He noted four soldiers—two men and two women—some clad in pieces of leather armor, one man stripped to the waist, milling about the small fire. One sipped gruel from a bronze bowl; another sat on a log, running a whetstone along a dull and chipped blade.

The Highwayman moved along, walking a high perimeter of the encampment, seeking more sentries. He came back to his original perch, confident that there were only five enemies total.

Five gold pieces.

He moved back into the forest, coming to a branch—silently this time— above the woman sentry. She was still leaning against the tree, half-asleep. Bransen thought back to the Book of Jhest, to the lessons of the assassin, the quick and silencing blow.

He dismissed the malachite fully before he dropped from the branch, wanting to come down hard and fast. He could have cupped his hands before him, down low at his waist, to hook the woman's forehead and drive her head backward with enough force to snap her neck, a quick and easy and very quiet kill.

But he didn't. He landed behind her instead, startling her, but before she could cry out the Highwayman, still carrying the momentum of his fall, drove his middle knuckle hard into the base of her skull.

She dropped straight to the ground with no more than a slight whimper.

Not enough to alert the camp, the Highwayman believed, so when he made his way to the perimeter he was not surprised to see the four milling about exactly as they had been, except that one of the women had crawled into her bedroll.

He scanned quickly, trying to discern the most dangerous of his opponents and to plan an attack route. He stepped back into the woods, closed his eyes to picture the appropriate attack routines, given the position and number of his enemies, as described by the *Book of Jhest*.

Three running strides later the Highwayman leaped up high and grabbed at the power of the malachite to lift him higher and longer.

The woman sipping gruel cried out and dropped her bowl. One of the men, moving off to the side to relieve himself, stopped in mid-stride and glanced over his shoulder. The other man looked up from his sharpened old sword just in time to see the Highwayman land before him. He flipped the blade up to catch it by the hilt but caught a foot instead . . . with his mouth. His head snapped back and he flew, landing on his back at the edge of the fire. How he yelped as flames bit at him!

The Highwayman was already gone, sprinting toward the seated woman. She leaped up, her dagger out in a flash, and she stabbed ahead.

But the Highwayman had gone to the side suddenly, cutting fast and diving into a roll. He came around, not only back to his feet, but springing into the air. Again the malachite gave him lift. He released the magic as he arced toward the woman in the bedroll, who was fumbling with her covers. She managed to throw her arms up defensively over her head as he crashed down upon her, his knees blasting the air from her lungs.

A rain of blows poked through her blocks, slamming her about the face and head with sudden and vicious fury. When she tried to punch back, to simply push him back and slow the assault, he caught her extended arm, squirmed about to plant his leg behind her upraised arm, then drove hard against her wrist, cracking her elbow.

Up he went to his feet, spinning to meet the other woman's charge, but so pained was the shriek of the poor woman he had just attacked that Bransen's knees wobbled and almost buckled beneath him.

"You are no assassin!" he heard Master Reandu scolding in his mind.

The thrusting dagger nicked his forearm, drawing blood, and the Highwayman backed instinctively. And the woman, hearing the wails of her companion, came on ferociously, stabbing again. But before her dagger got close, her opponent somehow kicked his leg straight up, smacking her weapon hand and sending her dagger high into the leafy canopy above.

Still his foot went up until it was directly over his head. The woman warrior really didn't comprehend the significance of that, charging in, growling and shouting for her companions.

Down swept the Highwayman's foot right before the woman's face, the scrape of it stealing her momentum. She brought her hands in to block, but the Highwayman kicked straight up again with only a slightly altered angle, and his foot swept up under her blocking hands and cracked against her chin. Her teeth chomped together hard, several chipping, and blood erupted from her bitten lip.

Dazed and staggering, the warrior fought hard to keep her balance and her hands before her defensively, but she could hardly follow her attacker's movements as the Highwayman slipped his punches through one after another.

Three hard left jabs rocked her backward, stumbling. She caught her balance and punched out hard but hit only air, for the Highwayman was gone. He had dropped to the ground before her in a low, one-legged crouch. He swept his other leg across, catching the woman on the back of the ankle and sweeping her legs out from under her.

Up went the Highwayman, leaping high into the air above her, and he descended to land on one knee atop the woman, blowing out her breath in a great rush.

The Highwayman couldn't finish the move, though. Hearing movement behind him he threw himself back to a standing position and spun about, his hand slapping across before him just in time to knock a thrown knife aside. The man came in furiously behind the throw as if to tackle the Highwayman, who bent to the side at the waist and snap-kicked out to halt that charge with a stunning blow to the ribs. Wincing, the man staggered back a step and lifted his fists as the Highwayman came in.

A left jab led Bransen's way. The man punched both his fists, his hands closing together to block the blow. A second jab brought the same response.

The Highwayman sent out a third, loping left hand, and out came the block. With a brutal and sudden twist the Highwayman put a right hook in hard behind those extended hands, smashing the man across the jaw, his head snapping to the side. He straightened and stumbled back and to the side a step, as if the vicious blow was still exerting force upon him.

The Highwayman matched his stare and saw that it was a vacant thing. Bransen turned away with a laugh. He heard the man mumble something, then felt the rush of air as the warrior just fell facedown to the dirt. The man with the sword was up across the way, lurching over to grab across his chest at his burned shoulder. His eyes went wide when Bransen stared at him, and with a yelp, he turned and ran off.

The silver flash of a reflection caught Bransen's attention, and he looked to the side to see the knife he had kicked high into the trees now lying on the ground. He slipped his toe under it and flipped it into his waiting hand, retracting with a single, fluid motion. He sent the knife out end over end, burying its blade into the back of the fleeing man's thigh. With a grunt of agony the man grabbed at it and bent over, swerving unevenly, half falling, half throwing himself into a bush.

Bransen surveyed his work. The woman with the knife moaned softly and almost breathlessly as she tried to suck in enough air to keep herself alive. The man he had hit with the right hook lay facedown, exactly as he had fallen. The woman in the bedroll, though, had pulled herself up to one elbow and had kicked her covers mostly aside.

The Highwayman surprised her when he grabbed her hard by the hair and tugged her head back viciously. Her eyes widened when she saw Bransen's right hand cocked back behind his ear, fingers stiffened for a killing blow upon her exposed throat.

She stared up at the masked face and knew her doom.

"My baby girl," she mouthed silently, for she knew that her life was surely at its end. Her expression reflected that hopelessness, and her whole body just relaxed in the resignation of ultimate despair.

Bransen Garibond saw it and recognized it, and it shamed him profoundly.

He wanted to be callous enough to drive his fingers into her throat and claim his first gold piece. Only then, behind the emotional fence of absolute ambivalence, could he truly be free of his agony and grief. He let go of her hair and stumbled backward, gagging.

"Damn you, King Yeslnik!" he swore, and he spun away, tripped to his knees. He gagged as he caught himself on all fours and threw up. "Damn you, Laird Ethelbert," he coughed and gasped between puking.

"Damn all of you!" he shouted into the night when he stood straight once more. He threw his head back, his arms out wide to the side, and screamed as loudly as he could manage with all the strength of his emotional agony reflected in every note.

He hated them, all of them, for what they had done to his father and his mother and to Garibond Womack. But mostly, Bransen hated them for what they had done to him, here and now, for the insanity of this absurd war that had brought him out here in the unfitting guise of a murderer.

They had made the Highwayman an assassin, an uncaring, unfeeling tool of murder, and nothing more.

"Damn you," Bransen said to the woman in the bedroll, who was sitting up now and staring at him incredulously.

"Damn them all," he said to her.

She shook her head, her mouth hanging open.

Soon after, Bransen Garibond stumbled through the forest feeling more like the unbalanced Stork than the cocksure and powerful Highwayman. In his hand he clenched a gemstone, a soul stone that he had used to minimize the wounds of all five of his "victims."

He hadn't earned his five pieces of gold; he hadn't taken them prisoner, even (for he feared that Bannagran would likely have executed them); he hadn't even robbed them!

But had he done any good, truly, by following his conscience? Wouldn't they just be out there when Bannagran closed in on Ethelbert, ready to join in the fight and die anyway, or to kill some men of Pryd or Delaval, perhaps?

The questions were way beyond him. Sensibility was way beyond him. He was stumbling more profoundly then, walking with an awkward and clumsy gait, falling more than once. At first he thought it was just his confusion, but as he continued on, ever more slowly, it began to dawn on him that something was very wrong here.

His line of *ki-chi-kree* was not holding. He felt it shivering and splintering. He took a deep breath and stood as straight as he could, and tried to walk.

He was the Stork.

The image of the woman, her head pulled back, her lament for a child she would never again see, haunted him and closed in on him, even as the words of Reandu's protest echoed in his mind.

His personal journey down Jameston Sequin's first road had led Bransen to the edge of a dark and deep hole, and the Stork realized to his horror that he had fallen in.

CHAPTER 11

The Restless Dame

"Aye, lady, o lady!" came the shouts across the waters, echoing up the stones to the back wall of St. Mere Abelle.

"I bid you go back into the chapel," Brother Giavno said to Dame Gwydre when she arrived on the wall, stoically and stubbornly staring out to sea past the wreckage of the blockade boat to the solitary Palmaristown warship in sight between the high cliffs that sheltered the chapel's docks.

Behind Gwydre, Father Premujon reached for her arm as if to give motion to Giavno's reasonable request.

But Dame Gwydre pulled away.

"I need to hear this," she said.

"Yer Pireth Vanguard's burned, lady!" a sailor on the ship called out. "We sacked her good, we did. Now we've yer women, and fine they be, lady! Come and join with us, and if ye're half the ride of yer peasants, then welcome ye'll be!"

"Is it confirmed?" Gwydre asked tersely.

"Lady?" asked a flustered Brother Giavno.

"Pireth Vanguard," the dame replied. "Has it been sacked?"

Giavno closed his eyes and mumbled a quick prayer to St. Abelle. "Aye," he said. "We know not the extent, but one of the brothers sent his spirit across the gulf and saw that Pireth Vanguard has, indeed, been hit hard."

"And their claim of stealing women?"

Giavno shook his head and held his hands up helplessly. "I know not."

"Could it be true?" Gwydre asked, turning to her friend Premujon. The father had no answer, but his sour expression spoke volumes.

"Send forth more brothers in spirit form, across the gulf, the length of Vanguard's coast," Gwydre demanded.

"We are taxing them greatly," warned Premujon. "This is no easy task—

few brothers can so energize the soul stone for such a journey, and fewer still can do so repeatedly."

"I will know the fate of Vanguard," the woman replied in no uncertain terms.

"It is a difficult task," Brother Giavno intervened. "And dangerous."

"I know the risks. But I will know of my home," Dame Gwydre said flatly. She turned back to stare at the distant sails, and when more taunting rolled in with the waves, the lady moved to the ladder and away from the wall.

"It is a difficult time," Father Premujon said to the obviously shaken Brother Giavno. He didn't have to finish his thought, for he knew that everyone at St. Mere Abelle shared it: As difficult as the current situation might be, it was only going to get worse.

Much worse.

Almost on cue, the whole of the courtyard shook as a boulder thrown by one of Laird Panlamaris's catapults slammed into the wall across the way. The opening salvo of a barrage, they knew, and so the brothers followed Gwydre down from the wall and into the strongly fortified chapel structure to ride out the latest rain in an unending storm.

D awson McKeege tore off a piece of smoke-dried fish and chomped it hard, then spat it out onto the deck, muttering with rage. For he, too, heard the echoes of the taunts being hurled from the decks of the Palmaristown warships, aimed at his beloved Dame Gwydre.

"We should put out from our shore running and put the dogs to the water," one sailor remarked, walking past the captain.

"I'll kill 'em four at a time for ye, Captain," another called.

Dawson munched another bite of the chewy fish, grumbling with every movement. How helpless he felt! *Lady Dreamer* had run fast from Ethelbert dos Entel, sweeping past the few fishing boats still sailing along the Mantis Arm and catching the strong Mirianic breezes on their turn into the Gulf of Corona. It hadn't taken them long to recognize the coming problems, however, for the gulf waters were thick with warships, Palmaristown and Delaval City's fleet. *Lady Dreamer* had a short keel, though, and so the coastal shallows served as their sanctuary from the much larger warships, both because they could keep out of reach of the deeper-riding ships in many areas and because the shore provided them with some measure of camouflage. Still *Lady Dreamer* only un-furled her sails under the cover of night, for if she was sighted, she would be shadowed by an increasing fleet of hostile ships and would be boxed in against the shore with nowhere to flee.

They weren't many miles from the cove and St. Mere Abelle's docks now as the crow might fly, but Dawson knew that the treacherous waters and uneven reefs meant more than a day of hard sailing to get in, and he knew, too, that they'd never make it without fighting through at least two warships, each of them twice *Lady Dreamer*'s size. They couldn't get home by sea. It would take at least two days of sailing to find a proper place to debark for a hike to the chapel, and even then, what obstacles, what ranks of enemy soldiers, might they find?

"Man in the water!" came a shout, and sailors began running to the starboard rail, pointing anxiously.

Dawson looked all about in confusion, for no other boats were to be seen. Had one of his men fallen overboard in these calm seas? He understood when he arrived at the rail, but his eyes went even wider in surprise. The description "man in the water" didn't really fit, he decided, for this one was more on top of the water—in fact, running on top of the water.

"Crazy monk," one sailor remarked.

"Brother Pinower!' another said excitedly, for Pinower was known to the crew of *Lady Dreamer*.

Huffing and puffing, the monk reached the side of the Vanguard flagship. "Might I trouble you for a rope?" he asked between gasps.

M akes me glad we got no women," Gnurgle the powrie captain said to the first officer of his barrelboat as they, too, listened to the wicked taunting of the Palmaristown crew. "All them longlegs're ever thinkin' about."

The first mate spat in his open palm and winked lewdly at the captain.

"Ye wantin' to sink the dogs?" he asked.

Gnurgle scanned the waters, noting three other warships within an easy sail of the one whose crew was doing all the shouting. He had only three other barrelboats in his shiver, and these enemies weren't the smaller warships so common along the outer shore.

"Nah, Shiknickel and his boys are waiting for us in the river," he decided. "If we find any o' these sailing alone, we'll put her to the waves and put her boys to the blade, but we're not going against this many afore we've met up with the rest o' the boys."

The first mate spat in the water at that, obviously unhappy, but he kept his grumbling to a minimum. "I'll get us moving, then," he said as he moved back to the hold and the ranks of powries at the pedals. "Sooner we get to the river, the sooner we get to spill some blood. Me beret's going dull."

"Aye, get us moving but keep us wide," Gnurgle ordered, for he knew his bloodthirsty second-in-command well enough to understand that an "accidental" encounter wasn't out of the question here.

Gnurgle really didn't want to engage these particular warships, whose decks were full of archers. Normally he wouldn't have cared much about the odds, but Shiknickel's call had been full of optimism that there would be plentiful bloodletting along those riverbanks.

Patience would make his beret shine all the more.

It took all of Dawson's willpower to keep from screaming several times, particularly when he and Brother Pinower crossed near to jagged rocks with a heavy surf threatening to wash them in hard. Dawson held to Pinower's hand with all his strength, thoroughly uncomfortable with this magical water walking, for that hand-to-hand connection extended the magical powers of the malachite from Pinower to him. If he let go, the cold, dark waters would take him.

By the time the two finally got into the cove near St. Mere Abelle's docks, a predawn glow had brightened the eastern sky, and by the time they got onto the docks themselves, the morning light shone brilliantly.

But no more brilliantly to Dawson than the image of Dame Gwydre and of Callen Duwornay, when he met up with them soon after. He rushed to his lady and kissed her hand, then swept over to Callen and crushed her in a great hug and a passionate kiss that went on so long it had Dame Gwydre giggling and Callen's daughter, Cadayle, blushing.

"I told ye I'd be back for ye," Dawson said when at last they broke the kiss, though neither showed any hint of easing up on the hug.

"I never doubted you," Callen replied.

"You delivered my emissaries?" Dame Gwydre asked, and, finally, the couple shifted side by side.

"Aye, they're with Ethelbert, and it seems we've an alliance," said Dawson.

Dame Gwydre breathed a sigh of relief, as did everyone in the room, including Brother Giavno and Father Premujon.

Dawson noted Cadayle staring at him hopefully, but the daunting question came not from her, but from Callen, standing at his side. "Any news of Bransen, then?"

Dawson tried to appear calm, but his sinking expression spoke volumes to all around before he finally stammered out, "We didn't see him, no, but Cormack and Milkeila will find out where he is, don't ye doubt."

Many exchanged concerned looks at the hesitancy in Dawson's response, and all of those gazes eventually settled on Cadayle.

"You didn't see him, but what word did you hear?" Callen asked, and when Dawson hesitated, she added, "You wouldn't be a smart one to start lying to me now."

The old sea dog rocked back on his heels. "We're worried for him, to be sure, but we heard no word, and, truth be told, we feared to ask too much. Ethelbert's bodyguard, a woman of Behr, is carryin' a sword much like Bransen's. Our guess is that them two met. She's just like him in that Jhesta Tu thing, so we're hoping he's out working for her."

"But you're fearing . . . ?" Cadayle prompted.

"Not for knowing," said Dawson. "Cormack and Milkeila will learn the truth of him, if there's any truth to be known in Ethelbert's domain."

Cadayle started to inquire further, but Callen grabbed her arm and hushed her, nodding toward Dame Gwydre and Father Premujon in a not-so-subtle reminder that there were other matters to discuss, however much they both feared for Bransen.

"So we have Ethelbert with us, and that is no small thing," Dame Gwydre stated. "But our scouts claim that Yeslnik marches once more to Ethelbert dos Entel, and he has us trapped in here by that wretched Panlamaris on the land and a great armada in the gulf."

"And they're hitting at Vanguard, so they're shouting," said Dawson.

"They are," Gwydre confirmed. "The brothers have ventured there in spirit form."

"And we're not for getting to our kin," Dawson remarked.

"Then what are we, here, to do?" asked Gwydre. "We cannot simply sit behind these walls and hope that the events of the world turn in our favor."

"Cormack will approach Bannagran of Pryd, as we proposed," Father Premujon reminded. "He is a fine emissary, and I believe that Master Reandu will support our proposition."

"Bannagran will more likely be swayed if we secure the former alliances of Ethelbert—the coastal holdings east of here," Dame Gwydre reasoned. "Let us bring them into our alliance. Brave Brother Pinower has shown us that Milwellis's net isn't nearly as tight as he believes, after all. My ship awaits not far from here, I trust."

"Sitting quiet in a cove," Dawson confirmed.

"It is time for me to go out," Dame Gwydre decided, to more than a few fearful gasps. "Fear not, for I will not walk openly and will not walk alone."

"If all the brothers and all the former prisoners here at St. Mere Abelle were to accompany you, and Dawson's crew as well, it would not be enough," Premujon replied. "Lady, I beg, you are too important to take such a chance."

"I cannot simply sit here to the drumming of Panlamaris's catapults and the songs of sailors' taunts while the world is conquered around us."

"And if you go out and are caught, then there is no hope against Yeslnik," Premujon reminded. "None."

Dame Gwydre ran fingers through her short hair and had no response. Truly she felt trapped here, helpless against the waves of troubling tidings.

They all did.

B rother Jurgyen yanked open the flimsy door and threw aside the heavy dark curtain, rushing to the side of screaming Brother Auchance, who lay curled on the floor. He couldn't quiet the poor young man, couldn't even uncurl him from the fetal position. He looked into the monk's eyes and saw nothing but a blank stare.

Auchance was looking far, far away.

Jurgyen had seen this before, and so he closed his eyes and hugged the brother close. The man had fallen into the body of another, probably someone a hundred miles away, and had become entwined in a battle of souls for that foreign body. There was no way for a spirit-walking brother to win in that situation, for even a temporary victory would mean possession, and possession could not endure (nor should it, since it was considered among the most immoral possibilities of gemstone magic).

The brother had been evicted. As the magic of the stone had faded, he'd found his way back to his own corporeal body, here in the one of the meditation rooms in St. Mere Abelle. But the experience had broken him, Jurgyen knew from bitter experience.

Other brothers arrived behind him. He backed out of the tiny closet and bade them to take poor, young Auchance to a bed in the rooms of healing. "Tie him down," he instructed, and they nodded, for they all knew that the monk would injure himself in his likely fits of thrashing.

Brother Jurgyen stormed away. Perhaps Auchance would recover, and perhaps he would die. There was nothing that Jurgyen or any of the brothers could do to help with this malady, and that helplessness only infuriated him as he made his way to Dame Gwydre's chambers. He knocked hard on the door and burst through it before the woman had even bade him to enter.

"Brother!" she scolded.

"How many will die for your insatiable need to scour your beloved Vanguard?" he roared. "To confirm the tragedies that the Palmaristown sailors yell at us every day? It is madness!"

"Nay, brother," she replied, keeping her voice very calm and motioning for Jurgyen to take a seat across from her as she sat before the burning hearth. The evening air had a chill, though summer was upon them, for the winds were off the gulf this night.

The monk moved to the chair but did not sit down.

"I am no less concerned than you regarding your brethren," Gwydre assured him. "And I salute their heroism in going forth in spirit form."

"You act as if they have a voice in the matter."

"No more than the warrior who charges the enemy line."

Jurgyen winced at that honest reply as he slid into the chair. He remained determined, though, to hold the edge of his anger. His brethren were depending on him to end this madness of spirit walking, he believed.

"We have lost another one," Jurgyen said to her. "Our ranks thin."

"But you are training more?" Gwydre asked, though her tone made it sound more like an order than a question, as indeed it was.

"Do you mean to destroy the whole of our order?"

"Would you prefer the stewardship of Father De Guilbe and the Church of the Divine King?"

The cutting question settled Jurgyen, and he looked away.

"Dawson McKeege came into St. Mere Abelle this day," Gwydre said. "Brave Brother Pinower's gamble in running across the waves brought to us great news and hope."

Jurgyen reluctantly nodded.

"It is our only hope," Gwydre said to him. "We will know of far-off events before our enemies learn of the situation, and so we will prove more nimble. With the spirit walking of brothers, perhaps our armies will better position for a battle or will learn of traps Yeslnik sets for us. You cannot underestimate the value of that, brother. What commander would not wish to know the movements of his enemy's armies?"

"Nimble," Jurgyen grumbled. "We can barely depart these gates."

Before Gwydre could reply, shouting from the hallway caught their attention and a moment later, an out-of-breath Brother Giavno rushed into the room. "Bass Cove," he said, gasping for air.

"Bass Cove?" Jurgyen echoed with confusion.

"Bass Cove of Vanguard?" Gwydre asked, coming out of her seat. "The fishing village?"

Giavno nodded and worked to catch his breath, and Gwydre wailed, thinking it had suffered a terrible fate at the swords of Palmaristown sailors.

"A victory," Giavno stammered.

Now Jurgyen, too, scrambled to stand.

"A great victory for us," Giavno said again, and finally he calmed enough to stop gasping. "Your warriors set a trap for the Palmaristown ships," he explained. "Many of Pireth Vanguard's refugees found their way to Bass Cove, and so they were prepared."

"How do you know this?" Brother Jurgyen asked, and he looked to Gwydre as he spoke.

"I was there," Giavno explained. "In spirit."

That brought a nod to Jurgyen from Gwydre.

"I told them of the coming of the Palmaristown fleet," Giavno said, barely able to contain his ecstatic giggling. "I—"

"By Saint Abelle," Brother Jurgyen said, and he made the sign of the evergreen.

"Three Palmaristown warships taken whole," Giavno elaborated. "Three Palmaristown crews killed or captured."

"This is fine news," said Gwydre, and when she looked to Jurgyen, she found him nodding his agreement with enthusiasm.

"There is more, lady," said Giavno. "The Vanguardsmen are organizing to sail south, a large armada full of warriors. To their lady's side, they believe."

"They will be sunk in the gulf!" Jurgyen exclaimed. "Even with the three Palmaristown warships at the tip of their flotilla."

"I tried to caution them," Giavno replied. "But I dared not engage too closely without returning to report on the turn of events."

Dame Gwydre nodded and looked to Jurgyen. The monk sucked in his breath, for he knew well the risk of Giavno's act. To walk in spirit form was dangerous enough, but imparting information in such a state would put a brother in close contact with another being—often too close to resist the almost irrepressible temptation of possession. Giavno had gotten away with it once, apparently, but he was risking his sanity in the act.

But Jurgyen couldn't deny the potential here for exactly that which Gwydre had claimed. He glanced at the floor, a smile of self-deprecation creasing his face.

"Go out again when you are able, brother," he told Giavno. "I beg of you. You and many others, myself included."

"You would venture forth in spirit?" Gwydre asked, and Jurgyen looked up at her and let her see his admission that he had been clearly wrong.

"With coordination, we brothers can guide this Vanguard fleet," he explained. "Perhaps they will avoid the warships of King Yeslnik."

"You are our strength," Dame Gwydre said to both monks. "The brothers of Blessed Abelle afford us a power that our enemy cannot know and cannot match. Go with honor, pride, and great care, I beg. We will know quickly what they will not fathom for days or weeks, and that will be our advantage."

CHAPTER 12

The Second Road

Master Reandu looked from the trio of robed "brothers" to the other observer, the Laird of Pryd, who scowled as they moved out the far side of the monk enclave of the wider army encampment.

"He knows," one of Chapel Pryd's lesser brothers remarked to Reandu in harsh and nervous tones.

Master Reandu took a deep breath, then walked slowly across the way, garnering Bannagran's attention as he approached.

"No word from Bransen," he said to the laird.

Bannagran didn't look at him, but kept staring at the departing monks who were not monks at all.

"They are fleeing?" Bannagran asked in a flat and even voice.

"I cannot ask them to go to war with their brethren."

"So you allow them to fight beside their brethren against us?"

"No, laird," Reandu said, patting his hands in the air to calm the volatile man. "No, never that. The battle is ended for them. They will find a chapel. . . ."

"I am to trust that?"

"They joined the order."

Bannagran did turn on the monk then, scowling fiercely. "I allowed you to claim they had joined the order so that we did not have to follow King Yeslnik's demand that all of Ethelbert's prisoners be put to death," he reminded. "You repay my mercy by betraying me?"

"I did not betray—"

"They will flee to Laird Ethelbert's side at first opportunity. They will be given arms and will return to kill your fellow men of Pryd."

Reandu shook his head with every word. "I have their word. The war is over for them. All they want is to return to their families. Surely you cannot disagree with that!"

"You try my patience, monk."

"I recognize your humanity."

Bannagran scowled at him even more fiercely, but then the tension broke and the large and muscular man looked at him more curiously. Reandu found that expression far more unsettling. "Or is it that Master Reandu, too, is thinking of deserting the cause of King Yeslnik?" he asked bluntly.

Reandu rocked back on his heels, not blinking and not replying.

"It is true," Bannagran stated. "You chose to bring those three along and selected the other brothers among the flock of Chapel Pryd because these are the ones who wish to flee the cause of King Yeslnik. You would leave me— would leave your fellow men of Pryd Town—on the battlefield without gem- stone healing?"

"No," the monk stated flatly. "No, we will stay throughout the fight to aid the men of Pryd and all the wounded who come to us."

"But you would deny King Yeslnik?"

"I serve the Order of Blessed Abelle, whose masters reside at St. Mere Abelle in the north of Honce," the monk dared to reply. "I have heard no good of this man, Father De Guilbe, whom King Yeslnik has determined to speak as the leader of this new Church of the Divine King. You cannot ask me to re- nounce my allegiance any more than Bannagran would have renounced his loyalty to Laird Prydae, were he still alive."

"A brave admission," replied Bannagran. "I could tie you to four horses and send them running to the points of the compass for merely speaking those treasonous words."

"I would rather that than renounce Father Artolivan."

Bannagran looked at him as if he had lost his mind but only for a few mo- ments before the large and muscular laird began laughing. He continued to shake his head, then simply turned and started away.

"Laird Bannagran, not I or any of my brethren will desert you in the fight, should it come," Reandu called after him, a promise he intended to keep.

Bannagran didn't stop walking but looked back over his shoulder and said, "And after the fight?"

Master Reandu could only stare at him, letting the words hang empty in the air. He stood there for some time, watching Bannagran as the man receded among the tents and other soldiers. Strangely, Reandu found that he wasn't surprised by the laird's seeming indifference. Bannagran's heart wasn't in this campaign, wasn't for King Yeslnik. Reandu was certain that

Bannagran fairly hated the foppish pretender. Still, Reandu had all but ad-mitted that he would defect to Artolivan, who was now openly opposing Yeslnik. Actually witnessing Bannagran's nonchalance in the face of that was no small thing.

Reandu closed his eyes and reconsidered his course, not for the first time, and he doubted for the last. His loyalty was to Artolivan and the Order of Blessed Abelle—the real one and not the shadow church King Yeslnik was try-ing to create. The monks at Chapel Pryd agreed with that decision almost to a man as they had applauded Master Reandu for cleverly dodging the king's order to execute the prisoners held at Chapel Pryd.

But Reandu's heart was for Pryd Town most of all. Pryd was his home—his family had been there for as long as any could remember, many genera-tions. And Reandu had grown to respect and admire Bannagran as well. How could he leave his home and his laird?

But how could he not, if remaining there meant a declaration of fealty to that awful Father De Guilbe and this new made-up church whose name ele-vated the wretched Yeslnik to "divine"?

"It will all work out," he whispered to himself, nodding and silently re-minding himself that the issue between King Yeslnik and Father Artolivan was far from settled. Likely they would come to an accord since no army could possibly topple the great fortress that was St. Mere Abelle and since, when at last the war between the lairds was over, it would be in no one's best interest to continue a fight between church and state.

The assurance found little hold in Reandu's heart, though, for the master had more than enough personal experience with King Yeslnik to know that the man could not be trusted to do the right thing, particularly as far as the common folk were concerned.

Still, the monk could hope, he supposed.

He heard a call then for "Master!" and from the insistent tone, he realized that the younger brother had likely been shouting for him for some time. He glanced about, finally spotting the monk and others gathered on a knoll, pointing to the tree line. Reandu understood their excitement, and his own eyes widened indeed when he, too, spotted Bransen.

The young warrior looked haggard, indeed, and though no wound was evident upon him, Reandu had to think that he had suffered some type of phys-ical trauma, for he held one hand up to his forehead and walked shakily, not quite Stork-like, but certainly not with the agile and balanced strides of the Highwayman.

Reandu rushed down to him, but Bransen didn't stop or glance at or acknowledge him in any way.

"What is it?" Reandu asked, and he noted that it was indeed a soul stone that Bransen was pressing against his forehead.

"I . . . I . . . I . . ." Bransen stammered in reply. He shook his head, spittle flying, and staggered past.

Master Reandu nearly gagged. The Stork had returned and persisted even though Bransen had a soul stone against his forehead! Reandu rushed to Bransen's side and took him by the arm. He wouldn't let the young warrior shake him away, though Bransen surely tried.

"Bransen, what has happened?" Reandu asked. Other monks came rushing down to help.

"I . . . I n . . . nee . . . need rest," he managed at last as he tried to pull away. But another monk grabbed him by his other arm, and that brother and Reandu ushered Bransen quickly to a tent and a cot and eased him down.

Bransen lay there for some time, staring off to the side, though he was surely looking at things within his own mind and not at Reandu or anything else in the tent. Reandu called to him repeatedly to try to get some explanation, but the young warrior wasn't talking.

Soon after, the exhausted Bransen fell fast asleep.

"A strip of cloth," Reandu instructed the other monk, who rushed from the tent and returned almost immediately with a small square of wool. Reandu rolled it up and tied it about Bransen's forehead, setting the soul stone underneath it to hold it in place, much as Bransen had typically done before Father Artolivan had given him the lost star brooch.

Reandu dismissed the other monks, but he didn't depart with them. He sat beside Bransen throughout the rest of the day, occasionally using a second soul stone to infuse the weary young warrior with warm waves of healing magic. Finally, as the night deepened, Master Reandu stood to take his leave, to gather some dinner before retiring.

"You were ri . . . right," Bransen said as the monk turned away. Reandu spun back to see the young warrior open his eyes. "Does that fill you with pride?" Bransen asked, and his voice seemed steady once more, though surely not nearly as strong as it had been when he had gone out the previous night.

"What do you mean?" Reandu asked, coming back and crouching low over the prone man.

Bransen looked away.

After a moment, Reandu understood. "You could not do it," he said, and a smile widened on his face. "You could not kill them."

Bransen looked back, and he wasn't returning that smile. With a great scowl he said, "Does that please you?"

"More than you can imagine, my friend."

Bransen's frown melted into a look of curiosity.

"Did you think I would cheer your fall from morality?" Reandu asked him. "Did you believe that I would be glad to learn that you, a wonderful and generous soul I have known since your childhood, were as crass and callous as so many of these supposed leaders?"

"Perhaps I am not as brave as I assumed."

"Brave?" Now Reandu couldn't suppress his chuckle. "You are no assassin, Bransen Garibond, nor is this other image of you that you name the Highwayman. You have never been an assassin."

"Ancient Badden would not agree with your assessment."

"In killing Ancient Badden you saved hundreds of innocents," Reandu answered without the slightest hesitation. "In that act you ended a war, and the man was deserving of his end. But this pact you forged with Bannagran . . . No, Bransen, that was not a just and moral agreement. You knew it, and in the moment of truth, when you could not continue your deception of your heart, when continuing would fundamentally and adversely change the man you are, you chose the correct road. I could not be happier."

Bransen stared at him hard. "I am afflicted once more," he said, and his voice remained unsteady.

"What happened? Did you suffer a wound?"

"No."

"When did it occur? Did you engage in a fight?"

"The fight was over, and I won and was not injured," Bransen explained. He lifted his hands before him and stared at them as if they were covered in blood. "I had her," he said, and he clenched his left hand. "Head back and helpless."

It wasn't hard for Master Reandu to piece the rest of it together. The Stork had manifested itself to save Bransen from his worst instincts, the monk master believed, and he was very glad for it. He grabbed Bransen's hands in his own and squeezed them gently.

"And now I am crippled once more," Bransen said, his voice barely a whisper.

"Was it not this Jhesta Tu training that you claimed had freed you of the Stork and of the need to use the soul stone?" Reandu asked.

Bransen looked at him, obviously intrigued and apparently unwilling to admit it.

"What would that discipline say to Bransen in that situation? Are the Jhesta Tu assassins?"

"No," the weary young warrior whispered.

"Is that not anathema to their beliefs?"

"It's all a lie," Bransen muttered and looked away.

He was ashamed of himself, Master Reandu knew. That, the monk believed, was a very good thing.

Reandu said not another word that night and stayed with Bransen for a long while, until the emotionally battered young man fell asleep once more.

Bransen burst from the tent the next morning with the soul stone strapped securely to his forehead and his black silk mask hanging loosely about his neck. He wasn't solid on his feet, though certainly more balanced than he had seemed the previous day.

"You slept well?" Master Reandu inquired, moving to join him.

Bransen nodded.

"That is good, because we have a long march before us by order of Laird Bannagran. If you intend to continue this road, I mean."

"I will retrieve my sword and the brooch Father Artolivan gave me," Bransen replied. "And then I will be gone, far from this place, far from Yeslnik's Honce."

Reandu cocked an eyebrow curiously at that. "You concede the land to him?"

"It is a foregone conclusion."

"So where will you run? Alpinador?" he asked. "To Behr, perhaps, the home of the Jhesta Tu?"

"Or to Vanguard," Bransen replied. "To the wilds of the north beyond the reach of Yeslnik's soldiers. I will gather Cadayle and Callen, and we will be gone across the gulf. To all the world the Highwayman will be dead."

"Dead?"

"Yes."

"That is how you want it?"

"Yes."

"And those who would benefit from the work of the Highwayman should be content with their miserable lot in life, because the Highwayman could not be bothered to champion them?"

"I care not," Bransen declared. "My road is my own to choose, and my responsibility is to myself and to my wife and family."

Reandu grinned just a bit, but did not let it widen to mock Bransen. But in truth, the monk didn't believe Bransen at all here, though he expected that Bransen was sincere about his own blather. Despite his protests to the contrary, Bransen cared for the common men and women of Honce.

Reandu saw no point to pressing the issue at that time, though. Bransen would have to work through this newest self-deception as he had the previous one.

With a curt bow, Bransen walked off to get some breakfast, leaving Reandu to stand alone in the middle of the monk enclave, for though he, too, was hungry, the monk decided that it would be better to give Bransen distance at that time. The young man needed to sort out what was truly in his heart and mind, and only Bransen could provide his own answers.

The army was on the march soon after, and it was a swift march indeed, as Reandu had promised. They continued east around the same ridgeline from which Bransen had levitated two nights previous, then turned southeast, a straight line for the still distant city of Ethelbert dos Entel. The sun disappearing in the west, they had just ended the march to settle in for the night when Bannagran's chariot rumbled into the midst of the monks.

Reandu rushed to greet him. Before the monk could even speak a word Bannagran told him to get into the chariot.

"There will be a parley," the Laird of Pryd explained. "You will stand beside me."

"A parley? With whom?"

"Climb up," Bannagran reiterated.

Reandu motioned to direct Bannagran's gaze to the side near a stretch of thick pines where Bransen loitered.

Bannagran flicked the reins to get his team moving, eight other chariots sweeping in his wake. He didn't continue through the monk enclave, nor did he turn back as Reandu had expected. Instead the chariot veered toward the young warrior standing alone by the pines.

"A parley with Laird Ethelbert's representatives, perhaps including the ones you seek," Bannagran explained to Bransen.

Bransen rushed up, and Bannagran motioned to the next chariot in line, then set his team moving again, this time back the way he had come. Bransen had barely set his feet on the floorboards before the second chariot in line rumbled away.

The remaining seven came behind in a line, the ground shaking under the pounding hooves and rolling wheels. Cheers from the soldiers went up wherever they passed, all splendid in their shining bronze, the world trembling beneath them. Though he was not driving, Bransen felt nearly giddy with power up here. He had never done battle from such a perch, nor had he fought extensively against charioteers, but suddenly he understood why so many footmen fled before such a sight as the armored carts.

They crossed out of the vast encampment at its forward point, the intersection of the eastern and southern roads. To the south they went, Bannagran maintaining the lead.

"He is the laird," Bransen said to his driver, nearly shouting so that he could be overheard above the rumble of hoof and wheel. "Shouldn't he be in the middle or near the rear of the procession?"

"Not Laird Bannagran, nay!" the driver replied. "Never does he shield himself with his lessers. Laird Bannagran is the first to the battle and the last to leave the field."

And so you love him, Bransen thought but did not say. Despite his sour mood and their unpleasant history, he had to admit his own respect for Bannagran. He compared this laird's actions with those of the foppish Yeslnik, who no doubt would have sent others to parley while he himself hid at the rear of his great army, surrounded by elite guards several ranks deep.

And surely Bannagran knew that truth about the fool king as well, and yet, unbelievably, the man showed such loyalty to the crown!

Bannagran pulled his chariot off the right-hand side of the road and onto a grassy lea shaded by the canopy of a line of large oak trees. Acorns of past seasons crackled under the press of the wheels, and dried leaves rustled and flew from the breeze. The three chariots immediately following with attendants turned with the laird, but with practiced precision the next three rumbled along the road right past the meeting point while the remaining two held far back to the north. As his chariot came to a stop, Bransen jumped down and moved out onto the road to watch the lead teams. They climbed a slight incline to the south to the highest point of the road, and there two pulled up while the third turned about to serve as relay for any information to the main encampment.

"Keep them tethered and ready," one of Bannagran's charioteers told the two attendants who had ridden with the third and fourth team. "If Laird Ethelbert has treachery planned we will turn it back upon him in swift manner."

Bransen noted that the man lifted his voice with that last promise to make sure that Bannagran heard, no doubt.

"Laird Ethelbert has no treachery planned," the laird replied with certainty and an obvious bit of annoyance.

The three charioteers began sorting out the proprieties of the planned meeting, while Master Reandu stayed near to Bannagran, who moved to the far side of the line of oaks and was staring off to the southwest. Bransen moved nearer to them, subtly hoping to overhear.

"It will be his surrender," Reandu was saying. "Ethelbert's men have little fight left in them. They know they cannot win."

"Laird Ethelbert is a proud man," Bannagran replied.

"Which is why he will come out to you. Never would he hand his sword to King Yeslnik. But there is no dishonor in surrendering to the Bear of Honce and the army of Pryd, not after the reputation you and your followers have rightly earned in the course of this war. Was it not Bannagran who sent Laird Ethelbert fleeing from Pryd when Ethelbert thought the field was surely won?"

Bannagran didn't respond, but Bransen knew that the sour look on his face was honest humility.

This was the man who had brought such misery to Garibond Womak, Bransen reminded himself. This was the man who came for Bransen to castrate him in some Samhaist nonsense ritual whereby Bransen's genitals would have been sacrificed so that Laird Prydae would be virile once more. And when Garibond had thrown himself down, pleading mercy for Bransen, who was still but a boy back then, Bannagran, this man before him now, had dragged Garibond away.

Later, when Father Jerak of Chapel Pryd had declared Garibond a heretic, Bransen's beloved adoptive father had been burned at the stake. And they were both complicit. Both of them! Reandu and Bannagran had been a part of that execution, if not a part of the decision itself.

Bransen had to keep reminding himself of that truth.

Bransen felt itchy, beads of sweat forming on his forehead. The world was too harsh, too vile, and even these men, to whom he had to admit some affinity, particularly to Reandu, were part of that hardness.

"Never forget that," he heard himself saying, though he hadn't meant to speak aloud, and when he did, both Bannagran and Reandu turned to regard him.

"Forget what?" the laird asked tersely.

"That you have a history of battle with Laird Ethelbert," Bransen stammered, his weakness of voice caused by desperate improvisation and not by the bubbling and babbling Stork. "Laird Ethelbert is an honorable man, perhaps, but he is one who has been bitten hard by the cold iron of Bannagran of Pryd."

"Perhaps? An honorable man, perhaps?" Bannagran pressed.

"His assassins," Master Reandu explained.

"Employing Hou-lei impugns his honor," Bransen declared.

The laird looked at Bransen curiously, then dismissively, before turning away. More interested was Master Reandu, who stared at Bransen and nodded and then, on sudden impulse it seemed, pointed up into the trees.

It took Bransen only a few heartbeats to understand his meaning, and the young warrior nodded and smiled slyly. As Bannagran turned back to regard him, Bransen used his malachite gem to lessen his weight and leaped high, landing nimbly on the lowest branch. He looked down to where the three charioteers were preparing a meeting area, brushing away the slippery bed of acorns. Bransen moved along the branches to a place of concealment just above where they were expecting Ethelbert's emissaries to stand.

He heard Reandu assure Bannagran that he would be safer now, heard the warrior laird scoff in reply.

Both would have scoffed all the more, Bransen realized, if they understood what was in his heart. For if it came to blows in the clearing below him, he doubted he would intervene, and if he did he had no idea on which side he would fight.

Whichever side best suited his own needs, he stubbornly and unconvincingly told himself.

Barely had Bransen settled when one of the forward scout chariots came roaring back down the road, swirling dust and twigs and acorns as it cut sharply onto the lea.

"Laird Ethelbert himself!" the driver shouted. "Laird Bannagran, it is Laird Ethelbert himself who comes to parley!"

Bransen looked to see Bannagran and Reandu exchanging glances, both obviously impressed.

The chariot driver flung his reins to one of the attendants and sprinted to stand before his laird.

"How many with him?" Bannagran asked.

"A contingent of only a handful, but it was old Laird Ethelbert, to be sure, centering their ride."

"Be alert," Bannagran told all around and above him. To the driver specifically, he added, "Fetch the trailing chariots and move them closer, near enough to strike should treachery be shown."

"Aye, laird, but there are only a few with Ethelbert," the driver replied. "A pair of monks, a pair of women, and another man, of Behr, I believe, and dressed in the black silks of the Highwayman."

Above them in the tree, Bransen tensed. He crawled out and strained his eyes to the south road, arriving at his perch just in time to see the contingent cresting the hill and walking their horses slowly between the two remaining forward chariots. It was indeed Laird Ethelbert astride a large white stallion, holding the fiery beast with a sure hand. Bransen noted Affwin Wi and Merwal Yahna, as he had expected from the charioteer's description, trotting along easily beside their laird.

Of the other three, he could not be certain from this distance. A pair of monks, yes, and a woman dressed in the garb of the northland of Alpinador, a woman dressed in barbarian shamanistic clothing, all tooth necklaces and feathers, much as Milkeila had worn.

Bransen found that he could hardly draw breath. It *was* Milkeila, and one of the monks was surely Cormack. Milkeila and Cormack with Laird Ethelbert! Milkeila and Cormack walking their mounts beside the murderess, Affwin Wi, and her vile cohort, Merwal Yahna!

What could it mean?

Bransen searched for shackles upon them, for surely his friends must have been bound to allow themselves such company. But no, he saw, they were not chained, nor did either seem uncomfortable riding beside Laird Ethelbert. Bransen lost sight of them briefly in the maze of branches below, but he heard the horses stop at the edge of the lea and the four riders dismount. They walked over in a line, five holding back a few steps and only Laird Ethelbert stepping out to stand right before Bannagran.

"You look well, Laird of Pryd," he greeted. "And though we are—or were—enemies, know that I have watched you with continued admiration."

"You are too generous," Bannagran replied, his tone too severe for the words.

Laird Ethelbert chuckled at that. "Can we not enjoy the respite in some measure of civility and calm?" he asked, and Bannagran shuffled uncomfortably.

"True enough," Bannagran admitted. "I have not forgotten our journeys together along the Mantis Arm, chasing powries into the sea. Forgive me my sword's edge. I am weary of war."

"As are we all. There is nothing to forgive."

"Most generous," Bannagran said with a bow.

"You are surprised to see me here, of course," said Ethelbert. "And you are surprised, no doubt, that I called for a parley. It would seem as if there is nothing left to say."

Bannagran nodded.

"But the situation has changed," Ethelbert said. He turned to the monk on his right. "This is Father Destros of Chapel Entel." The monk bowed.

"Beside me stands Master Reandu of Chapel Pryd," Bannagran replied.

"Who follows Father Artolivan?" asked Ethelbert.

Bransen focused on Reandu's reaction, noted the frown that momentarily crossed his face, and noticed, too, that Laird Ethelbert didn't miss that scowl.

"The order has broken with Laird Yeslnik," said Ethelbert.

"King Yeslnik," Bannagran corrected. "And only a faction of the church has turned from his certain victory. A foolish move."

"Or a move of principle. What say you, Brother Reandu?"

Ethelbert's discerning gaze made Reandu shrink away, more so when he saw Bannagran turning to scowl at him.

Laird Ethelbert continued, "I am told by both Father Destros here and my visitors from St. Mere Abelle that this alternative church Laird Yeslnik desires will hardly resemble the tenets and truths of the Order of Blessed Abelle. Surely it is more of a political alliance of convenience than any agreement rooted in faith."

"I know nothing of the spat, nor do I care," Bannagran interrupted.

"You do not care?" Ethelbert asked incredulously, almost mockingly. "A powerful faction has joined the ranks of your enemies. Surely that is cause of concern for Laird Bannagran. Nor is this defection just the church, although that defection alone should give you pause. Nay, Cormack and his lovely companion, Milkeila of Alpinador, sailed to Ethelbert dos Entel as emissaries not only of Father Artolivan, who rules the Abellicans at St. Mere Abelle, but of Dame Gwydre of Vanguard."

Bannagran tried not to appear impressed, Bransen saw clearly from above, but for Bransen, it was all he could do to hold his position and not fall out of the tree in the unsettling wake of such overwhelming news. Dame Gwydre and Father Artolivan had allied with Laird Ethelbert? Did they not know that Ethelbert was every bit the scoundrel as Yeslnik? Did they not know that Ethelbert employed murderers and knaves and that Jameston Sequin, friend to Dame Gwydre, had been murdered by Ethelbert's assassins? Bransen had to breathe deeply to steady himself, but too late, he realized, as both Affwin Wi and Merwal Yahna suddenly tensed at Ethelbert's side, the woman drawing her sword—drawing Bransen's sword!—and lifting it his way.

"What?" Ethelbert stammered, fell back a step, and then followed Affwin Wi's pointing blade to see Bransen in the boughs above.

"What treachery is this, Laird Bannagran?" the old laird protested. "I had thought you an honorable—"

He stopped as Bransen dropped from the branches, landing lightly and unthreateningly at Bannagran's side.

"Bransen!" Milkeila and Cormack shouted together.

"No treachery," Bannagran assured his counterpart.

"I will have my mother's sword," Bransen demanded, his voice strong and steady.

Affwin Wi smiled at him so wickedly.

Bransen didn't back down and returned that smile. "I will have that sword and the brooch you stole from me."

"Took from you, you mean," said Affwin Wi. "By right of my superior rank and by right of my victory in battle against you, traitor."

Bransen saw the confused looks of both Bannagran and Ethelbert. At his side, Reandu began quietly imploring him to be silent and step back.

Of more concern, across the way, Cormack and Milkeila seemed at a loss, completely unnerved and unsure, and with such a mix of emotions twisting their features that Bransen could hardly sort them out.

"We feared you dead," Cormack said, "but were told—"

"Lies, no doubt," said Bransen, staring at Affwin Wi as he spoke. "For that is the way of the Hou-lei."

"Does this young man speak for you, Laird Bannagran?" Ethelbert demanded.

"Be silent, fool!" Bannagran scolded, turning threateningly toward Bransen.

"You come to parley, as emissaries of Dame Gwydre," Bransen said past Bannagran, aiming his remarks at Cormack and Milkeila. "To ally with Ethelbert?"

"Control your man, Laird Bannagran," Ethelbert warned.

A much larger man, Bannagran grabbed Bransen hard by the upper arm and pulled him back.

"Would Dame Gwydre be so willing for such an alliance if she knew that Laird Ethelbert's assassins had murdered Jameston Sequin?" Bransen asked bluntly.

Cormack and Milkeila fell back at that, staring alternately from Affwin Wi and Merwal Yahna to Laird Ethelbert. More telling to Bransen was the reaction of the other monk, Father Destros, his face a mask of fear, as if he had known or at least had suspected the dark secret of Jameston's demise.

"This is not about you or your friend, boy," Bannagran said quietly to Bransen as he bulled the young warrior backward to only token resistance. "You were not invited to speak." He ended by shoving Bransen back several steps. Master Reandu rushed up to take Bransen by the arm, whispering desperately for him to be quiet.

"Murderer," Bransen said to Ethelbert, then added, "murderess!" aimed at Affwin Wi. "I will have my mother's sword if I have to pry it from your dying grasp."

Both Affwin Wi and Merwal Yahna started forward at the threat, but Laird Ethelbert bellowed, "Halt!" before they could go very far. With a ferocious scowl upon his old face, the laird motioned the pair back behind him and told Affwin Wi in no uncertain terms to put the sword away.

"These issues are beyond my knowledge," Ethelbert said to Bannagran, though he was obviously aiming his remark at Cormack and Milkeila as well as Bransen, for whatever that was worth. The old laird turned to directly address Cormack as he continued, "We will learn the truth of it all, I promise." His voice grew very old then. "In the confusion that is war many die needlessly."

"What do you want, Laird Ethelbert?" Bannagran interrupted. "You asked for parley, and so I am here. I honor your flag of truce."

"And I, yours," Ethelbert assured him.

"But my patience thins in light of these revelations and in the face of your warriors' threat."

"No threat," Ethelbert assured him. "I did not come to threaten but to offer."

"Then make your offer."

"Join us," Ethelbert said bluntly.

A few steps back from Bannagran, Reandu's continued quiet advice to the Highwayman stuck in his throat at that proclamation, and both he and Bransen turned blank stares at the surprising laird.

"I know you, Bannagran of Pryd," Laird Ethelbert continued. "I have witnessed you in battle, both as footman and as general, and I know that you cannot stomach the likes of that snot-nosed nephew of Laird Delaval."

"Beware your words of King Yeslnik," Bannagran warned.

"King Yeslnik," Ethelbert scoffed. "He is not prepared to lead a single small holding let alone the whole of Honce! Were he a farmer his crops would die and his chickens would starve. He could not throw a fishing line into the Mirianic without falling in behind it!"

Bannagran didn't seem to appreciate the mirth, for a smile did not crease his face. He stared hard at Laird Ethelbert, his expression unreadable.

"It is more than a matter of competence," Cormack interjected, stepping up beside Ethelbert. "It is a question of judgment and morality. Dame Gwydre has chosen to side with—"

"Do you speak for Dame Gwydre?" Bannagran asked.

"I do."

"And for Father Artolivan?"

"He does," Father Destros called from behind.

"I do," Laird Ethelbert corrected.

"We do," was all that Cormack would concede. He and Ethelbert exchanged a quick, but sharp, stare before Cormack stubbornly pressed forward. "It was not Dame Gwydre's intent to take sides in this conflict," Cormack explained. "She sailed south to deliver news of the defeat of Ancient Badden in Vanguard and the ascendance of the Order of Blessed Abelle in those northern reaches. She came to see if she could mediate in this terrible war, to help heal the wounds of Honce."

"A wiser course than the one you have ultimately chosen," Bannagran assured the former monk.

"It was the immorality of Yesl . . . King Yeslnik's proclamation," Cormack explained. "The dactyl-inspired demand that those prisoners who had served Laird Ethelbert be murdered. That foul edict demanded our course and the decision of Father Artolivan."

Bransen had stopped watching his friend Cormack, instead turning his eye to regard Reandu. The master didn't blink through Cormack's explanation, licking his lips as Cormack recounted the meetings that had brought Dame Gwydre and Father Artolivan to the conclusion that the notion of Yeslnik, this young man with such careless disregard for the lives of others, becoming King of Honce was simply unacceptable.

Master Reandu wanted to cheer Cormack's bold stand, Bransen realized, and indeed he thought that Reandu might not be able to contain himself and might do just that! The implications of that obvious truth had the Highwayman screwing up his face with confusion.

"It was not only an affront to those men who had served my army," Ethelbert added, "but one to your own soldiers."

Bannagran didn't look very convinced.

"Would your warriors not face more difficult fights if they marched against an enemy who knew that to surrender was to be put to the sword?" Ethelbert asked. "Is not the offering of mercy and safe return a valuable parley position to a general who has won the field and does not wish to inflict wholesale slaughter upon his enemy?"

"The winds have turned against Yeslnik," Cormack insisted. "All of Vanguard and the brothers of Abelle have thrown in with Laird Ethelbert."

"All of Vanguard?" Bannagran replied with a mocking chuckle. "Palmaristown alone puts more men on the field than your Dame Gwydre can manage, and not all of the brothers have run to the call of the traitor, Father Artolivan." As he finished, Bannagran turned to regard Reandu, who withered under the laird's imposing stare.

"Father Artolivan answers to a higher king than any mere mortal man," said Cormack.

"Does he indeed?" asked Bannagran. "Would Ancient Badden's deluded minions not say the same of him?"

That put Cormack back on his heels, Bransen noted, but the resourceful former monk squared his shoulders and insisted, "It is for the good of Honce, for the good of the common folk of Honce, that Dame Gwydre and Father Artolivan have chosen to oppose Yeslnik."

"They will be buried side by side, then," came Bannagran's sarcastic reply.

"And not for any personal gain," Cormack managed to continue. "Laird Bannagran, I beseech you. . . ."

But the Bear of Honce was laughing at him, so Cormack relented. "It is all for personal gain whether for Dame Gwydre or Laird Ethelbert or King Yeslnik," Bannagran admitted. "Whether for Father Artolivan or Father De Guilbe or Master Reandu there. For all of us, you fool. Spare me your words of greater imperative or nobler cause. A man thrusts his spear into the gut of another for the cause of personal gain and not out of nobility. A laird seeks alliance for personal gain or begins a war to expand his holding. No doubt your Dame Gwydre eyes a foothold on the civilized lands in recompense for her token support of Laird Ethelbert. She will soon come to regret that choice of ally, though." He turned and glanced back to the west. "You have no doubt heard of the scope of my force, and it is but one of King Yeslnik's three great armies. You are sorely outnumbered, outarmed, and outarmored."

"But if you were to join with us . . ." Cormack replied when all recognized that Laird Ethelbert, staring hard at Bannagran, was not about to say anything at that dangerous point.

"The outcome of the fight would be less assured?" Bannagran asked with a laugh.

"For the good of the common folk of Honce," said Cormack.

"For many more years of war, you mean," said Bannagran. "And for the same outcome for those who survive the march of armies, whether Ethelbert or Yeslnik claimed the throne."

Laird Ethelbert stiffened at that, a remark he clearly considered an insult, but again it was Cormack who spoke up.

"It will be neither!"

The force of his declaration did give Bannagran pause, after which he asked, showing only minimal interest, "Do tell."

"When the war is won, Honce will have no king, but a queen."

"A queen? Your Dame Gwydre?"

Cormack didn't blink, his shoulders straight and square, his jaw strong.

"Some huntress from the wilds of Vanguard will conquer Honce?" Bannagran asked, his voice filling with mocking incredulity. He turned to Ethelbert. "And you would agree with this?"

Ethelbert sputtered a bit, shaking his head, and started to explain that the details had not yet been agreed upon, but Bannagran's laughter had him too flustered to make any point.

"How desperate must you be, Laird Ethelbert," the Bear of Honce said. "It pains me to witness you as a broken man. You, who were once a leader among men, and for so long!" He shook his head and laughed again. "I will honor your flag of truce, though I would be doing you a favor to take your head and be done with this foolishness here and now."

Behind Ethelbert, Affwin Wi brought a hand to her sword hilt. Behind Affwin Wi, Bannagran's men similarly moved.

Ethelbert held up his hand to calm his volatile assassin.

"You have revealed your desperation, Laird Ethelbert," Bannagran went on. "Your wisest course—all of you—would be to surrender and accept Yeslnik as king and pray that he have mercy upon you."

Cormack began to respond again, but Ethelbert stepped nearer to him and reached across with his arm, driving the younger man back. "I know you, Laird Bannagran of Pryd. I have seen you in battle. I saved your life once and Laird Prydae's and the lives of many of your soldiers when the powries had you trapped in a gully."

"That was a long time ago."

"But not so long that I have forgotten the Bear of Honce, Prydae's champion," said Ethelbert. "I know your axe and so I know your heart, and that heart cannot suffer the fool Yeslnik who has never bloodied a blade against a man who could defend himself."

It was perfectly quiet then, with all eyes intent on Bannagran—except for those of Bransen, who studied all the others, particularly Reandu. The monk stood completely still, holding his breath.

"I remember that day in the east when Laird Ethelbert did not shy with fear but came on to secure the flank of Pryd," Bannagran replied after a long pause. "Out of respect for that day I allow you to leave now in peace and return to your city. For your own sake, reconsider your foolish course."

"Spend the night in contemplation," Ethelbert suggested. "This is an important decision, friend."

"A night will not change all that has gone before," Bannagran answered.

"As a personal favor to a man who once saved your life," said Ethelbert, "I will return in the morning under a flag of parley."

Ethelbert and Bannagran stared at each other for a few heartbeats then. Ethelbert started away, his entourage turning in his wake.

All but Affwin Wi. "Highwayman," she called after Bannagran, too, had started off in the other direction.

Bransen stepped past Reandu to match her stare.

"Come and get your sword," the woman teased.

Bransen steeled his gaze and started forward, but Reandu rushed up to grab him. That alone would not have stopped the determined Bransen, but Bannagran veered to move right in front of him, scowling fiercely.

"They came holding a flag of truce," the Bear of Honce said. "Do not dare begin your vendetta under the banner of Pryd Town."

"She challenged—" Bransen stopped, seeing that he would get nowhere here. He looked past Bannagran to Affwin Wi, Merwal Yahna standing close behind her.

"Let it pass," Bannagran warned.

"She wants my sword because she broke her own in the chest of your beloved Delaval," Bransen said to unnerve him.

But Bannagran didn't blink, and Bransen turned back to regard Affwin Wi. She was smiling her wicked smile. Bransen knew that no matter the outcome of the war—whatever alliance or terms of surrender or conquest might occur—he and Affwin Wi would have their fight. And only one would survive it.

CHAPTER 13

A Glimmer

On shaky legs the men carried the boulder, the tenth they had brought across the field this morning. Arms ached; fingers had long ago blackened from blood blisters where rocks had fallen upon them. They had to stop but could not, for Laird Panlamaris was ever watchful and full of rage and ire, more than ready to deal out harsh discipline. The catapults had to keep throwing stones, all the day long, and if the porters had to travel farther to gather the stones they needed, then so be it.

Laird Panlamaris's only response to their complaints was to tell them to run faster.

Milwellis watched it all with mounting concern. Day by day by day his father had grown angrier and more obsessed with Dame Gwydre. She was the cause of it all in his bloodshot eyes. She had unleashed the powries upon his beloved Palmaristown.

"Hurry with that missile!" the laird shouted at one crew struggling to get a large, unwieldy boulder up the rise from Weatherguard. "The beam is set and ready to throw! Be quick, I tell you, or you'll feel the cold iron of my sword!"

The flustered and exhausted porters tried to pick up their pace, but they grew uneven in their strides and the support poles moved too far apart, dropping the stone to the grass where it began rolling back down toward Weatherguard.

"Idiots!" Laird Panlamaris yelled, drawing out his sword and starting down the hill.

Milwellis cut in front of him to block his advance. "Father!" he yelled. "Father, no!"

Panlamaris brushed him aside and kept marching toward the crew who were now scrambling desperately, trying to reset their carry poles under the runaway boulder.

"Your point is made, laird," General Harcourt said from the side.

Panlamaris looked to him, as did Milwellis, regaining his balance. When they, too, looked down the hill to see the crew working frantically, finally hoisting the boulder once more and double stepping up the hill toward the waiting catapult, they understood Harcourt's meaning.

"You're thinking that I was making a threat to get them moving," said Panlamaris. "Might be that I was just thinking of killing one of the fools."

"Father, I beg—" said Milwellis, but he stopped abruptly when the laird fixed him with a threatening glare.

"That witch Gwydre set the beasts upon Palmaristown," Panlamaris said in a low and wicked tone. "Upon your home!" He threw his sword down at the ground, where it sank in halfway to the hilt. "Your home! Powrie rats in your home!"

He spun about to see more than a few of his bedraggled warriors staring at him wide-eyed from afar. "Every catapult's throwing!" he cried. "Fill the damned place with stones!"

"I know, Father, but . . ." Milwellis said, advancing, but when he got within reach, he found his voice choked off as the old and large laird grabbed him by the throat with tremendous force.

"Your home!" Panlamaris screamed in his face. He shoved Milwellis back again. "I don't want you begging," he said. "I want the witch Gwydre begging. On her knees and begging. Aye, but I'll take her good then. I'll have her every way a man can, and when I'm done with her I'll spit on her and kick her and cut her open chin to mound." He narrowed his eyes as he stared hard at his son. "Now get those porters running and get those damned catapults throwing, or I'll put you in the damned basket and fling you against the chapel wall."

Milwellis blanched and fell back another step, not knowing what to make of this demon that had once been his father. Truly, he had never seen Panlamaris so out of sorts, so full of outrage. He looked past the man to the always levelheaded Harcourt, and the general seemed almost embarrassed and equally perplexed.

"Go!" Panlamaris shouted, and Milwellis staggered away.

"My laird," Harcourt dared to say a few moments later. He walked up to his old friend and lowered his voice so that no one else could possibly hear. "Prince Milwellis is a fine progeny. He has made a great name for himself and for the line of Panlamaris."

"I will have that witch," the seething laird replied.

"It would not do to embarrass Milwellis in front of the men he has so finely commanded," Harcourt warned, and then he, too, fell under Panlamaris's withering gaze.

But the laird said no more. He tore his sword free of the ground and stalked away. Very soon after he was screaming at another crew of porters he deemed too slow with the stones, though the exhausted men seemed as if they would simply collapse where they stood.

Laird Panlamaris would hear none of it. The catapults kept their frantic pace; that was all that mattered to him.

She was a fair thing, barely past her tenth birthday and full of life and love. Work on the farm was hard, to be sure, even for the child, for her father and older brother were off to war, and she and her mother and her aunts had to keep the gardens tilled and weeded.

But she was happy when she went to her chores in the field outside the small town of Greenmeadow. It was a beautiful summer day in the pretty town of trees and pastures with the silver snake of the Masur Delaval glistening in the west. On a clear day, the high walls of Delaval City could be seen far to the south, particularly if there had been a morning rain and the white stones of the great city glistened with wetness.

Not today, though, for the clouds lay heavy, and every so often a gentle mist drizzled about her.

That didn't diminish the young girl's smile. She skipped across the small field to the far planting, hoping to collect some squash in the basket she carried. She paused before she got there, puzzled by the sight of someone amidst the crops. She thought it another child, perhaps her age, for he stood about the same height as her, though his limbs and torso were much thicker.

"Hey, buy'a'mule," she called, using the nickname her father had often tagged on her, a gibberish word created for the sake of an old joke about silly children running errands to the town's common market.

The other fellow stopped and turned about, and she grew even more perplexed, for he was indeed her height, but his face was hairy like an adult's, and his clothing was most unusual.

She didn't know the significance of a powrie beret. She had never heard of the bloody-cap dwarves.

She was smiling until the very instant a serrated blade cut her throat.

All along the eastern bank of the Masur Delaval the powrie barrelboats slid onto the sand, the eager dwarves pouring forth, knives in hand. Mischief had transformed to open war, and in a powrie war there were no innocents and no civilians.

The goal was to kill anyone and everyone they encountered, to murder people in their sleep, if possible, to chase them down through the fields and forests and slay them, all of them. Their orders were to avoid the large cities of Palmaristown and Delaval and to focus instead on the many small villages, most no more than clusters of three or four homes. Sweep the rural areas of humans, chase them to their great cities, and then slip away to the waters of the great river, the Gulf of Corona, and the Mirianic Ocean. They would strike and strike again, along the river, the gulf, and the seacoast.

They would pay back the humans for staking powries on long poles outside of Palmaristown.

A thousand dead would not sate their bloodlust. Ten thousand dead would not sate their bloodlust. Ten thousand dead human children would not sate their bloodlust.

The counterweight fell, the wheels spun, and the long arm of the trebuchet creaked and groaned and swung, launching the rock through the morning air. The crew cheered as soon as it was away, certain they were on the mark this time. Sure enough there came the sharp retort as the stone exploded against the thick and unyielding wall of St. Mere Abelle. As one the artillerymen turned to regard Laird Panlamaris, who stood, scowling as always of late, and staring at the chapel with hatred etched upon his old face.

Not far away, Prince Milwellis clapped his hands in salute to the crew, the first who had actually hit the distant chapel in more than a day.

"More!" Panlamaris barked. "Knock them into the sea!"

"Easy, my laird," said General Harcourt, standing beside him. "There aren't enough rocks in all of Honce to knock down those walls."

"There are, and we'll bring them," Panlamaris growled at him. "And we'll throw, hour after hour, day and night, until the place falls or fills. I'll have that witch."

"King Yeslnik bids us merely to hold the siege," Harcourt reminded him. For all the day, he and Milwellis had tried to gently nudge the outrage away from Laird Panlamaris. They had never seen the man in such a state, and his anger did not seem to have any end.

"I'll not be taking advice from the likes of the boy Yeslnik," Panlamaris replied. "I'll let him play at king, but only because of the gains to Palmaristown and only because he's better than the witch up that hill and better than Laird Ethelbert. So we'll do as he asks—as long as it's what we're wanting. Now I'm wanting more than to sit here and wait while that witch who sent the powries to Palmaristown rests easy."

"She is not resting easy," said Harcourt. "The siege will play upon her sensibilities, as will the occasional throws of the catapults."

"Occasional?" Panlamaris said incredulously, angrily.

"To weaken their walls and weaken their resolve," the general tried to explain.

"Every day, dawn to dusk and dusk to dawn, like the cadence drums of a tireless marching army," Laird Panlamaris insisted. "When Vanguard falls, what will Dame Gwydre think, I wonder? When Ethelbert is pushed into the sea, how maddening will our thunder sound to Father Artolivan and his fellow fools?"

"Might they come forth?"

Panlamaris shrugged. "If they do, we will kill them. If they do not, we will go in and kill them."

Harcourt winced at that notion, as did Milwellis, who had come over to join the pair. They had both heard the story of the last attempted assault on the chapel, and it had not gone well. With their gemstone magic the monks had turned the Palmaristown charge into a fast and desperate retreat, one that left many Palmaristown soldiers dead on the field.

"Our spearmen and archers could not reach them behind their walls, but oh, how their magical bolts reached down at you," Harcourt dared to remind the laird. "Would you shed more Palmaristown blood against those impregnable walls? Please, laird, I beg of you to let Chapel Abelle be their prison, then, while King Yeslnik conquers the world around them. And let it remain their prison."

Panlamaris began a stream of curses at Artolivan and the monks then and didn't stop until long after, when Father De Guilbe walked over to join them.

"I thought you'd be halfway to Delaval City this late in the morn," Milwellis greeted. The priest had traveled from Pryd only to deliver King Yeslnik's report with plans to be out the next morning to begin organizing the new Church of the Divine King from the streets of Delaval City.

"I do so enjoy watching the great stones thunder against the foolishness of Artolivan," the large monk answered. "When I am properly seated within Chapel Abelle, perhaps I will leave our boulders scattered about the walls and courtyard to remind my brethren forever that the church cannot exist outside of the state, that we are linked by divine providence to the King of Honce."

"You'll be rebuilding the place from rubble," Laird Panlamaris promised.

"Artolivan angered you greatly," Prince Milwellis said knowingly, for whatever institutional and philosophical reasoning De Guilbe tried to put on his betrayal of the church, it was clear that De Guilbe's grudge was personal. Had he been shown the degree of respect he believed he had earned, he would never have left Artolivan's side.

De Guilbe couldn't maintain his scowl against the simple reasoning. "There is that, yes," he said dryly.

A commotion in the distance, down the western road and away from the chapel, caught their attention.

"Your coach?" General Harcourt asked.

De Guilbe just shook his head and continued staring at the approaching wagon, rolling along at great speed. He could tell from the sheer recklessness of the driver that something was amiss.

Even as the wagon crossed the first line of sentries, calls of "powries!" echoed throughout the vast encampment.

"Damn her," Panlamaris muttered under his breath but loud enough for them all to hear.

The three waited as a group that included the driver came running toward them.

"Powries!" one man yelled. "An army of the beasts, crawling out of the river, all the way to Delaval City!"

"By the old ones," Milwellis groaned. "Not again."

Laird Panlamaris shook his fist at St. Mere Abelle and cursed Dame Gwydre.

"You are recalled, laird," the messenger explained. "King Yeslnik would have you sweep the riverbank clear of the beasts, while the warships put down their barrelboats."

"My fight is here," Panlamaris said.

"King Yeslnik . . ." the messenger started to argue, but Panlamaris fixed him with a hateful glare and interrupted.

"If he speaks another word, put him in a catapult basket and throw him at Gwydre," the laird commanded.

The messenger blanched, fell back a few steps, and said no more.

"We must go to the aid of the towns," Harcourt reasoned. "With the armies in the field, they will be defenseless against the bloody caps."

"Palmaristown has a garrison in place," said Panlamaris, for indeed they had left the place defended.

"But the smaller towns . . ."

Panlamaris turned his glower over his old friend, and at first it seemed as if he was going to simply dismiss the smaller towns as unimportant. But then a crack appeared in the mask of rage that was Panlamaris. "Go then," he said to Harcourt and his son. "Leave me with just the catapult and porter crews. Lead the rest to the coast and sweep it clear, Palmaristown to Delaval."

"You will need more than that if the monks come forth," Milwellis interjected.

"They're cowards and they'll hide," Panlamaris replied. "Get me every villager in Weatherguard and every town about and put a helmet on their every head. The monks need not know of your march."

Milwellis looked to Harcourt skeptically, but the old laird shouted at them both, "Go!" and they dared not disobey or tarry.

As soon as night had settled on the land, Prince Milwellis, Father De Guilbe, and more than three-quarters of the eight thousand soldiers who had settled outside of St. Mere Abelle were on the road, marching hard for Palmaristown and the coast. The old and angry Laird of Palmaristown watched them go and then dismissed them. His focus remained on the chapel up the long and grassy hill, and his catapults continued to throw throughout the long night.

He would stay and punish Gwydre and Artolivan.

N ever comfortable in spirit form, Brother Jurgyen willed himself along at great speed, wanting to be done with this duty as swiftly as possible. He ran atop the waters and had no corporeal form out here that could be harmed, of course, but still he imagined great monsters lurking beneath the dark gulf, ready to swim up and devour him.

So it went for a long while as he made his way. He passed some Palmaristown warships, giving them a wide berth as they glided westward in full sail. He thought nothing of it until he came upon a second battle group, similarly rushing back to the west.

Had they, perhaps, discovered the Vanguard flotilla?

Nervous but determined, Brother Jurgyen moved swiftly to catch up to the ships and drifted upward, floating above the taffrail of one. He dared not approach, for several sailors stood there, sharing a drink. He could feel the invitation of their corporeal forms, the soft and dangerous invitation and allure of possession.

He remained cautious but knew that he would not be serving Father Premujon and Dame Gwydre well if he did not try to discern the reason for the Palmaristown westward sail.

Their chatter was mostly the gutter talk of bored sailors, but one phrase leaped out at the spirit of Brother Jurgyen: "The river's full o' powries!"

Jurgyen spent a long time trying to sort that out as he continued north across the wide Gulf of Corona, but when he happened upon a third battle group, this time flying the flag of Delaval, and saw that they, too, had turned westward and put up full sail, it all came crystal clear to him.

The monk reversed his course, flying back toward his waiting body in St. Mere Abelle with all speed. He approached the towering walls in a matter of moments, for the return was always much easier than the journey from the body, but as he neared he instinctively veered aside and moved past St. Mere Abelle.

For Jurgyen remembered the earlier siege and how it had broken.

Brother Jurgyen opened his physical eyes a short while later and pulled himself up from his kneeling position. He turned so fast and exited the small chamber with such urgency that he actually broke one of the hinges on the fragile door and stumbled to one knee in the small hallway.

He didn't care. He ran screaming for Dame Gwydre and Father Premujon.

They all gathered immediately, so important was Jurgyen's tale. It was two hours past midnight, but not a one in the room, not Gwydre, Dawson, Premujon, Giavno, Pinower, or any of the others in attendance, showed any signs of sleepiness.

Not after what Brother Jurgyen had told them.

"This is our chance," Dame Gwydre said, her eyes sparkling with hope.

"A dozen brothers across the water to tell the Vanguard flotilla to sail forth with all speed," said Father Premujon. "If they arrive quickly enough we can shatter the Palmaristown siege."

Dame Gwydre shook her head. "Yes, send the brothers forth," she replied. "And *Lady Dreamer*, too, will sail out, guided by brothers and their gemstones to meet the ships and guide them to a safe berth east of St. Mere Abelle."

Dawson nodded eagerly.

"But we'll not wait the days for the reinforcements to arrive," Gwydre explained. "We've three hundred veterans in our midst and brothers mighty in the use of gemstones."

"Panlamaris is still more than a thousand strong by Brother Jurgyen's guess," Father Premujon replied doubtfully. "We'll be under catapult fire the entire way through the gates and down the hill."

Gwydre's sly smile told them all that she had already figured that problem out. "We'll not walk out the gates, father," she said.

Brother Giavno began to laugh, and all eyes turned his way.

"As Brother Pinower escorted Dawson to us," the monk explained.

Looks of confusion mixed with many nodding heads and grins of understanding.

"You cannot be thinking . . ." Father Premujon started to argue.

"Oh, but I am," said the Dame of Vanguard.

That very night Dawson McKeege bade Callen Duwornay farewell again, took the arm of Brother Pinower, and went across the dark waters to the west. Six other monks accompanied them to ride with *Lady Dreamer* and go forth from her deck as spirit-walking scouts guiding the journey across the gulf. At the same time, Brother Jurgyen and a host of other brothers went out in spirit, running across the gulf to find the Vanguard flotilla and instruct them to sail south and also to mark the movements and positions of the many Palmaristown and Delaval warships sailing westward about the gulf.

When that was accomplished and Brother Pinower returned the next morning with news that *Lady Dreamer* had put out, the more immediate planning went into full swing.

CHAPTER 14

United Against the Other

"You cannot expect me to take him or his proposition seriously," Bannagran said to Reandu. "Ethelbert wears his desperation clearly. He is afraid and knows the war is soon to end, and so he tries to turn us to his cause. He has nothing else to play."

"His cause is Dame Gwydre's cause," Master Reandu reminded.

"Father Artolivan's, you mean," said Bannagran.

Reandu straightened at that, unable to dispute the simple truth of it. His belief in Father Artolivan and St. Mere Abelle was surely his disadvantage in his dealings with Bannagran, but so be it. Master Reandu would not disavow the church whatever the personal cost of fealty.

"You would have me join with Ethelbert," Bannagran accused. "You would have me turn the army of Pryd about and assault King Yeslnik for the sake of Laird Ethelbert and your church."

"Do you think Yeslnik a more deserving king than Laird Ethelbert?" Reandu asked bluntly. "Truly?"

"I think that the ways of the world do not ask my opinion."

"The ways of the world asked neither Delaval's nor Ethelbert's nor Yeslnik's opinion!" Reandu shot back. "No divine angel swept down and told Delaval to claim the throne. No just and good god would ever ask that of the idiot Yeslnik!"

Bannagran's stinging slap staggered Reandu back several steps. He held his balance, somehow, but came up holding his aching jaw and staring at the Bear of Honce incredulously.

Several times Bannagran—who seemed as horrified as Reandu—started to respond, but each time he just growled and scowled and shook his head.

"You cannot speak of the King of Honce such," Bannagran finally explained, though it sounded hollow, even to him. "I have pledged my fealty to him."

"You have often called me friend," Reandu countered.

"And you make it a difficult proposition ever."

"If I am your friend, then I must be able to speak my heart to you," said Reandu. "And I did." He rubbed his jaw again pointedly.

Bannagran glanced around to see a couple of groups looking over at him and Reandu curiously. They couldn't hear the conversation, but they had no doubt seen the slap. The Laird of Pryd scowled at those onlookers fiercely until they retreated beyond the nearest tree line.

"I know the treachery you plan," Bannagran whispered when he was certain they were very much alone. "You are encouraged by the arrival of Laird Ethelbert. I know that you will flee at the first opportunity with those brethren you have brought, and Ethelbert's men will no doubt rejoin him."

"They will not," Reandu replied. "On their word. They are out of the war as they promised. Laird Ethelbert's arrival here does nothing to change that."

"We shall see," said Bannagran. "And if not to Ethelbert, then they will go with you to your home chapel, to the side of Father Artolivan, where your loyalty truly lies."

"I'll not deny that," said Reandu. "Never have I. I am a brother of the Order of Blessed Abelle. It is his path I follow above all others, and that path leads me to St. Mere Abelle and Father Artolivan and not to Father De Guilbe. The man is a godless opportunist, who has placed personal power and glory above the call of the order."

"Many believe that would make him a wise man."

"A coward!" Reandu insisted. "Throughout the short history of our order, brothers have sacrificed their lives before renouncing Blessed Abelle. I expect no less of myself."

"Because you expect a reward in the afterlife for your grand sacrifice," said Bannagran. "The Samhaists would not agree."

"No," Reandu replied. "No, my friend. It is not for the afterlife or the promises of Abelle, great though they are, and indeed I do believe them. No, it is the principle of behavior that I place above even that promise. The greatest gift of Blessed Abelle is the promise of better lives for all men if all men followed the tenets of his order. The greatest promise is brotherhood joined, is common gain for common cause."

Bannagran began to laugh, and that gave Reandu pause.

"You truly believe that?" the Laird of Pryd asked.

"Enough so that if you present me with the choice of abandoning my course or feeling the mortal bite of your great axe, I will suffer the blow."

"So you say until the axe hovers above your neck."

"So I say until my voice is quieted forever." Reandu straightened his shoulders with his proclamation and stared at Bannagran unblinkingly.

For a moment it seemed as if Bannagran would respond, but the powerful man just snorted and walked away, shaking his head with every step.

Master Reandu breathed a sigh of relief.

"He is right, you know," came a voice from above, and Reandu, startled but not surprised, just closed his eyes and sighed.

Bransen dropped to the ground in front of him. "Your idealism is foolish, childish even, in light of the darkness that has come to Honce."

"And without that idealism, my life would be empty," Reandu replied.

Bransen stared at him doubtfully.

"You are to judge me?" Reandu asked. "You, who thought yourself a murderer and nearly destroyed all that you have achieved in that ridiculous self-deception?"

The simple truth of that reminder had Bransen back on his heels.

"Bransen the assassin," Reandu said dramatically, every syllable dripping with sarcasm. "The rogue Highwayman who kills without mercy!"

Bransen pushed past the embarrassment and shrugged off the insult. "Once I believed as you claim," he replied. "And then Garibond was murdered."

Bransen had reversed the conversation and now it was Reandu settling into a defensive posture.

"And I dared to believe again," Bransen went on. "And then Jameston Sequin was murdered. Bitter experience tells me that you chase a fool's road as Bannagran declared."

"Bitter disappointment has weakened your heart and your resolve, you mean."

"You call Father De Guilbe a coward, but you say it from the shadows. Why did Reandu not so declare that to Father De Guilbe back in Pryd Town, I wonder?"

"Because to invite such wrath would be foolish and counterproductive to the cause I serve," the monk replied without the slightest hesitation. "And because other men depend upon me to lead them to safety, and I would not throw that trust to Yeslnik's ill justice. And yes, Bransen, Father De Guilbe is a coward and an immoral opportunist who sees a chance to usurp the power of rightful Father Artolivan."

"And, thus, Bannagran of Pryd must also be a coward," Bransen reasoned.

"A cynic," Reandu corrected.

"They are the same by your definition."

Reandu considered that for a moment, then nodded. "And so is Bransen Garibond, too, a coward?"

"Will he abandon you in your glorious cause, you mean?"

Master Reandu didn't blink.

Bransen considered his own words for a short while, then pulled the soul stone from his forehead and reached into his pouch to collect the other magical gems Reandu had given him. He held his hand out to the monk.

"You cannot bring yourself to profit on the blood of innocents," Reandu replied, making no move to take the gemstones. "And so, since you know that there is no personal gain for you here, you determine that this is no longer your fight. Bransen will run away."

Bransen did not retract his hand.

"You can run from this fight, Bransen," Reandu said. "But you cannot run from yourself. The gemstones are yours, forevermore. I grant them to you without demand, but with expectation that one day you will admit the truth to yourself."

Very slowly, Bransen pulled back his hand. He didn't want to accept the stones, but he knew that without them he would have no chance of defeating Affwin Wi and retrieving his sword or the brooch. Without them he wouldn't likely even traverse the many miles to get back to his wife.

"I am done with this war," he stated flatly. "To you I am a coward, then."

When Reandu didn't immediately reply, Bransen turned and walked away. "You are the bravest man I have ever known, Stork," he heard Reandu say softly behind him, and the weight of that, along with the tender reference to that helpless creature he had been, nearly cut Bransen's legs from under him.

But stubbornly the Highwayman kept going. He didn't slow until he was long out of the encampment, far up the northern road.

W ho is that?" Bannagran asked Reandu as they watched the approach of Laird Ethelbert and his entourage. It was the same group as the previous day but with the notable addition of a man dressed in the colors of King Yeslnik. He wasn't chained, but the look on his face and his position between the dangerous man and woman from Behr spoke volumes regarding his status.

When the group turned onto the lea, the warrior woman grabbed the prisoner hard by the wrist and twisted until a grimace appeared on his face.

Bannagran glanced all around at the many warriors and archers he had prepositioned. Unsure of how Laird Ethelbert would take his refusal of alliance and knowing now that the man had brought his assassins with him, Bannagran had duly prepared for all possibilities.

"A gift?" Bannagran asked. "A prisoner exchange?"

"A man we found wandering the road," said Ethelbert. "Searching for you." He turned to Affwin Wi and nodded, and the fierce woman shoved the poor and obviously terrified man forward.

"To recall you," Laird Ethelbert went on. "He comes with word of a powrie army swarming out of the Masur Delaval and laying waste to the riverside settlements. We had to take him captive, of course. I have a particular fear of spies in these dangerous times. Surely you understand."

Bannagran looked from Ethelbert to the courier. "It's true, Laird Bannagran," the man said with an obvious Delaval accent. "Hundreds of the little rats, and oh, but they've killed a few and more."

"Your King Yeslnik's kingdom is being assailed before it can even be formed," Ethelbert added.

"King Yeslnik bids you return with all speed—and with his army," the courier added. He glanced back at Ethelbert, who nodded for him to proceed. From his belt he produced a rolled parchment and handed it over to Bannagran. The seal was broken, but the two halves very much resembled the wax press of King Yeslnik.

Bannagran handed it to Reandu, who pulled it open and read it quietly to him. ". . . with all haste," Reandu finished a few moments later.

Bannagran paused and let the news sink in. "Convenient for Laird Ethelbert," he said at last. "To turn me away with your city gates nearly in sight."

Ethelbert looked to the courier. "Perhaps the old ones, or Blessed Abelle, favor me," he admitted. "But surely I have no love of powries, and this is not my doing."

"I cannot disagree," Bannagran replied, but he added the caveat, "if this man is who you claim, and if his words are true. Else, it is, indeed, your doing."

"Then you will march back to my gates even angrier," the old laird said sourly.

"There are more couriers, laird," the captured page interjected. "Most riding east along the road. They should reach the end of your long line this very day, if they have not already."

"And then you will turn for home," Ethelbert reasoned. "Only to turn back yet again and come against me once more, I expect. I do believe you will kill half your men simply from marching while my army rests and prepares."

Bannagran stared hard at him but did not respond.

"Or we could march beside Laird Bannagran," Cormack offered. "Joined in common cause against the powrie marauders."

Both Ethelbert and Bannagran looked at Cormack as if he had surely lost his mind.

"Give them a tent and food," Bannagran called to his men, and to Laird Ethelbert he added, "You may remain as my guest while I confirm this tale. Perhaps you will find yet another unlikely reprieve, albeit a temporary one."

With Ethelbert's and Bannagran's permission, Cormack and Milkeila did not remain with Laird Ethelbert and his entourage, going instead with Bannagran and Master Reandu. Cormack did not surrender his notion of joining the forces together in common cause.

"This could be our chance to end this miserable war," he pleaded with Bannagran. "An opportunity for the men of Honce to remember that they are brothers and that there are enough enemies in the wider world without them battling each other."

"Who are you?" Bannagran asked dismissively, and he walked away.

"It is not so misplaced a notion," Reandu said when he was alone with Cormack and Milkeila. "I would welcome such a resolution."

"Your own resolution, that of the church, I mean, might be harder to discover," Cormack replied. "You march with Yeslnik, thus with Father De Guilbe."

"You know him?"

"He led my mission to Alpinador," Cormack admitted. "Indeed, it was his fight with me, his determination that I be banished from the order—even executed for my crimes—that precipitated his wider argument with Father Premujon of Chapel Pellinor and ultimately with Father Artolivan, both of whom judged my cause and course correct."

Reandu stared at him and nodded, recalling all that Bransen had told him of the battle in Alpinador.

"Father De Guilbe is no voice of a just god," Milkeila dared to add.

"I bid you to reconsider your course, Master Reandu," Cormack said. "Father Artolivan and the brothers at St. Mere Abelle have spoken of you as a beacon of light in this dark night."

The skepticism on Reandu's face was clear to see.

"It is true," Cormack insisted. "I was sent to Ethelbert dos Entel to forge the alliance with Laird Ethelbert, but that alone would not suffice. Nay, to Pryd Town I was to go, to speak to you and implore you to show Laird Bannagran the justice of our cause and the injustice of Yeslnik's road. You are a man of honor, so claims

Father Artolivan and Brother Pinower, and, as such, you would understand the truth of Dame Gwydre. Alas, but it saddens me to see you in the service of King Yeslnik and Father De Guilbe."

"I am no friend to De Guilbe," Reandu heard himself replying, and he could hardly believe he was speaking the thought aloud. As telling to Cormack as the words themselves was his pointed omission of De Guilbe's title, something a long-serving master of the order would never do by mistake.

Reandu, so frustrated and teetering between fear and hope, pressed on. "I serve Laird Bannagran. I serve Pryd Town, my home. If they march to war, then my brethren and I are compelled to travel beside them and tend their wounds. But whatever the outcome of this campaign in the east, I deign not to return to Chapel Pryd. My road is to St. Mere Abelle, and how that new name rolls sweetly from my lips! My fealty and that of the monks who have joined me on this march—the whole of Chapel Pryd's brothers—is to Artolivan, Father of the Order of Blessed Abelle."

Cormack and Milkeila both brightened at that surprising and welcomed revelation. "Then speak to Bannagran, your laird and your friend."

"He will not betray King Yeslnik for Laird Ethelbert," Reandu replied, and when Cormack moved to argue, he added, "Or for your Dame Gwydre, whom he does not know."

"But will he allow Laird Ethelbert to bring forth his army to join in the fight against the powries?" asked Milkeila.

"The word of a powrie force is true, then?" Reandu asked.

"The courier was from King Yeslnik, yes," said Cormack. "And by that man's words and not just the letter from Yeslnik, the powries swarm the banks of the Masur Delaval."

"It is rumored that they assailed Palmaristown at the behest of Dame Gwydre," Reandu warned, but Cormack was shaking his head with every word.

"I see doubt on your face, brother," Reandu added.

"In Alpinador, a band of powries fought beside us in our struggle with Ancient Badden, for they, too, would have perished by his hand. It is possible that they are among this force, but by word of the courier it seems that the whole of the Weathered Isles have emptied onto the shores of Honce. This is not the doing of Dame Gwydre—never would she set such a scourge upon the land as that."

"Bransen the Highwayman will support our claims," Milkeila added. "He was there with us when we battled Ancient Badden. The powries of Lake Mithranidoon were the ones who first rescued him after his fall from the glacier."

Reandu's face screwed up incredulously at that strange information. "Bransen is gone," he replied. "To the north, I expect, and his wife at St. Mere Abelle." He paused, shaking his head. "He was there? Beside powries?"

"Common enemies make for unexpected alliances," said Cormack. "Perhaps now again, and with an alliance that will remind the folk of Honce that we are all brothers. Press your Laird Bannagran, I beg. Fate has given us a chance to heal the wounds of a land torn by war."

Reandu looked across the way toward the distant command tent of Bannagran. The monk made certain that he was in that tent with the laird when other couriers came up from along the long line of the marching army to confirm the news and order the recall of Bannagran's forces.

Reandu seized the moment, imploring Bannagran to take the offer of Laird Ethelbert to march beside Honce allies against their common foe.

The Bear of Honce offered a simple and short answer: "Shut up."

Bannagran's turn to the west was immediate, breaking camp that very afternoon.

L aird Ethelbert's troupe rode hard to the south, arriving in Ethelbert dos Entel only a few hours later. Ethelbert immediately convened his generals and explained the shifting situation.

Myrick and Tyne took the same line as Affwin Wi, begging their laird to stay put, to let the powries aid their cause, but Kirren Howen stood quietly, doubt clear on his face.

"You remember those skirmishes along the black rocks of the coast," Ethelbert said.

The old general nodded. "Laird Prydae and his champion Bannagran showed well in the fighting," Kirren Howen replied. "Glad I was to be on their flank, for even then the men of Pryd Town fought better than any others—except our own, of course—Laird Delaval's soldiers included. I am not surprised that Bannagran, the Bear of Honce, has risen to such prominence among the ranks."

"Powries striking all along the river, they claim," said Ethelbert.

"They need us," Cormack dared interrupt. Several hard stares turned on him for speaking out of turn, but Ethelbert didn't look his way and kept exchanging his glance with Kirren Howen.

"Had Laird Bannagran agreed to secure our march, it might have been an opportunity to heal Honce," the general remarked.

"Indeed," was all that tired old Laird Ethelbert could manage in reply. "It might have been."

The finality of his tone stopped the budding protests of Myrick and Tyne before they could begin to mount.

"Then make it so," Cormack tried one last time to press upon them.

"If powries are climbing from the Masur Delaval, then the Mirianic Coast is not secure," Kirren Howen pointed out.

"And without the guarantee of Laird Bannagran, I would not risk a man of Ethelbert dos Entel," Ethelbert added. "Even with Bannagran's word of honor, which he did not grant, I would be a fool to put my garrison on the field near to the superior numbers of treacherous Yeslnik. You see the world with the optimism of a priest, truly, but I view it through the eyes of responsibility."

"If we do not go forth and aid against the powries, when they are defeated Yeslnik will send Bannagran and many thousands back against us," Cormack reminded. "We cannot hope to win."

"Then mayhap we should hope that the miserable bloody caps will kill enough of Yeslnik's men to deter him from that march. Or enough, perhaps, so that we can steal the advantage and destroy them all."

Cormack wanted to argue, and so obviously did he tense that Milkeila grasped his forearm and gently squeezed.

"Your bargaining is not with me, young brother," Ethelbert continued. "You wish to turn Laird Bannagran from the side of the fool Yeslnik. Go then, and quickly, and catch up to his march. If the ways of the world turn the Bear of Honce from the cause of the idiot king, he will ever have a potential ally here in Ethelbert dos Entel. We do not forget the days of yore when Bannagran and Laird Prydae fought on our flank."

He was looking at Kirren Howen as he finished, and the general nodded his complete agreement.

It was something, at least, Cormack silently mused. With Ethelbert's blessing, and that of Father Destros, he and Milkeila started out soon after, back to the northwest.

Two others watched their departure. Affwin Wi and Merwal Yahna did not offer any such blessing or words of encouragement.

"I do not trust this Bannagran," Merwal Yahna remarked.

"Trust?" the woman asked as if the notion was ridiculous.

"If Ethelbert and Bannagran, and thus Yeslnik, unite against the powries, then this young king will demand retribution for the death of Delaval," Merwal

Yahna clarified. "They will only find true alliance through the action of mock justice."

Affwin Wi laughed at him. "Fear not, for Ethelbert will not turn against me."

"He is a desperate man" Merwal Yahna said. "We should leave now. For Jacintha."

But Affwin Wi was shaking her head. "This work is lucrative and enjoyable. You fear these barbarians? We have Jhesta Tu hunting us back in Behr, and I would rather face the whole of Yeslnik's army than hide again in the shadows of Jacintha's streets. We will not leave."

"When a peace is brokered, we will be sacrificed to it," Merwal Yahna warned.

Affwin Wi wore a wicked smile. "Peace?"

"So let there be no peace," Merwal Yahna said, reading her perfectly.

Affwin Wi and Merwal Yahna were called to Laird Ethelbert's side again late that afternoon for a continued discussion of their options.

The three remaining followers of Affwin Wi, led by Moh Li, a man sorely injured by Bransen in the fight that had driven the Highwayman from Affwin Wi's gang, departed Ethelbert dos Entel soon after sunset, following the path of Cormack and Milkeila.

CHAPTER 15

The Third Road

Every step he took moved him farther from his sword, from the artwork, the legacy, of his mother, Sen Wi. That thought nagged at Bransen and pulled against him like an invisible rope, but he stubbornly kept going. He focused instead on what lay ahead, on Cadayle, his beloved, pregnant with his child.

His thoughts were spinning, though. The sight of Cormack and Milkeila and their news of an alliance among Gwydre and Ethelbert and Father Artolivan had rattled him and brought him a level of discomfort more profound than he had expected or understood.

"It is not my fight," he told himself repeatedly, always trying to increase his pace. When crossing a forest he took to the trees, thinking to run across the branches as he had that night he had gone hunting for Ethelbert's scouts.

But he was not nearly as graceful; the gemstone magic was not flowing through him consistently or powerfully. And his line of *ki-chi-kree* shivered. Instances of the Stork pulsed through him, terrible moments when he feared that all of his coordination would flee, leaving him flailing and helpless upon the ground.

Still he kept going. What he lacked in speed he made up for with endurance, walking long into the night and moving again at first light. He didn't recognize the trails this far to the east, though, and so he kept his road straight to the north. To the gulf, he figured, then a turn to the west and St. Mere Abelle. He passed by several villages, not razed like those in the south or those closer to the coast where Milwellis had wound a path of destruction similar to that of King Yeslnik on their respective retreats from Ethelbert dos Entel.

Bransen resisted the urge to go into any of those settlements. He was lonely, to be sure, but that was his way now, he reminded himself. He was walking the second road of Jameston Sequin—the correct road, he now believed, where his focus was himself and his needs, a little corner of the world where he could escape the greater madness of mankind. Unlike Jameston, he would have Cadayle and their child and Callen with him, and what else did they need? What more could the hectic and troubled world offer?

Guided by such an attitude, Bransen felt little guilt on those nights when he did sneak into a village to pilfer food. On one such occasion, he happened upon a large pie cooling in the window of a small cottage. He took the whole thing. It was his, after all, because he wanted it, and what did he care for the desires of those in the house? That's what he tried to tell himself, anyway, as he left, but soon after he had eaten a small slice of the delicious treat, Bransen returned the remainder to the windowsill.

"It wasn't very good," he muttered as he walked away from the windowsill once more, trying to believe the silly justification.

He came upon the coast one bright morning, and he eagerly turned for the west, hoping that he was not too far from St. Mere Abelle and Cadayle. He wanted nothing more than to be in her arms, to be back across the gulf into Vanguard, where he and his family could forget the rest of the world as Jameston had done for all those years.

It had been Jameston's tragic mistake to forsake that reclusive lifestyle, Bransen believed. The scout should have remained in the wilds of Vanguard, the forests he called his home, and let the petty wars of petty lairds solve themselves in blood.

For what did it matter anyway? Whichever laird won; whichever religion, Samhaist or Abelle, had proven victorious in Vanguard; whichever kingdom, Honce or Behr or Alpinador, gained supremacy mattered not at all in the end. Even Dame Gwydre, far better to her people than a selfish fop like Yeslnik, would be only a very temporary reprieve, after all, in the long scheme of the world.

Should Gwydre win, another Yeslnik or Prydae or Ethelbert would soon enough arise to seize the throne and quite likely, yet again, triumph through the spilled blood of peasants.

Bransen couldn't escape his conclusion: It was all a sad, sad joke.

Reports came in to Father Premujon's command room nearly every hour. The spirit-walking brothers of St. Mere Abelle had reached the far shore of the Gulf of Corona and bid the Vanguardsmen to come forth. They had scommanded by Panlamaris as the irate laird continued the siege and bombardment of the chapel.

The spirit-walking brothers knew everything going on in this region of

Honce—the placement of ships and warriors and even the beleaguered condition of Panlamaris's overworked crews.

"They will be more eager to break to the west and run for home," Brother Giavno advised in the command room session that afternoon. "If we fill their eastern flank with the hard assault of gemstone magic and send them in flight, a larger, waiting force in the west will have little trouble in massacring them."

"Is that what you advise?" Dame Gwydre asked him rather pointedly.

Giavno cleared his throat, obviously uncomfortable. "It would seem the prudent military option."

"But is it in your heart, brother?" the Dame of Vanguard pressed.

Brother Giavno took a deep breath but then merely looked away.

"You are a good man," Gwydre said, and many in the room crinkled their brows in confusion.

"I have little desire to massacre Panlamaris's force or any men of Honce," Gwydre explained. "Let us sweep them from the field and send them running, but all quarter will be offered, at all times."

"Lady, I remind you that we will be outnumbered more than two to one," Brother Jurgyen remarked.

"They will be caught completely without their guard," Gwydre assured him. "And every report shows them to be a haggard and exhausted bunch, worked to the point of collapse. Let our initial assault be full of lightning and fire, explosions and great noise and shouts of war. They will break and run."

"Laird Panlamaris will not run," said Jurgyen.

"Then we will kill him," said Father Premujon, and the matter-of-fact answer from the father of the Order of Blessed Abelle, speaking of killing a man as casually as if he was referring to emptying a chamber pot, made more than one monk stare at Premujon with astonishment.

"Let there be no doubt that we have entered the battle, that we now fight in the war," said Premujon. "It is not our preference, surely, but neither was it our choice or doing. Bitter experience over many months has taught us of Vanguard that in such a struggle to the death, the lessening of violence does not lessen the misery. Nay, it is the truth of war that brutal and swift is oft the most merciful way."

"But with all offer of quarter," said Giavno, and Premujon smiled and nodded.

"Then let it begin," said Gwydre. "At dawn tomorrow, the catapults of Laird Panlamaris will fall silent at last."

Every former prisoner residing at the chapel, nearly four hundred men and women, reaffirmed his or her allegiance to the Order of Blessed Abelle, and all were ready and eager to go out and fight under the banner of Dame Gwydre. All the day, they spoke of Brother Fatuus, who had walked from Laird Panlamaris's line, who had suffered the spears of his enemy but had not relented until he had reached the gates of the chapel, whereupon he had gone happily to his just and everlasting reward. They would fight for the order, for Dame Gwydre, and, most of all, for the memory of Brother Fatuus.

The ferrying began that night, two lines of water-walking monks escorting the warriors to the shoreline to the east and west of St. Mere Abelle. Brothers Pinower and Giavno personally escorted Dame Gwydre and promised to fight by her side until they drew their last breath. It went on all through the first hours of quiet darkness. Soon after midnight, the two hundred warriors and forty monks beside Dame Gwydre in the east sorted their ranks and recited their strategy, while in the west, across Panlamaris's line, half of those numbers in warriors and monks dug in to strategic positions, quite confident of the route of retreat.

M oving along the coast long after the sun had dipped below the western horizon, Bransen spotted a dark but definite encampment to the south. At first he thought to simply pass by and continue on his way, for St. Mere Abelle loomed in the west, high in the distance against the starry sky, but not so far away. With the assistance of the cat's-eye agate, he would arrive this night, even if he allowed himself this small detour.

He quickly discerned that it was a military camp, and he glanced often at the distant chapel, guessing that these were enemies intent on that place— that place where Cadayle and Callen slept. He still wanted no part of the war, but certainly he would not allow his stubbornness to endanger his beloved wife and his unborn child.

He decided that he would return to the chapel with much information of this force in the east. He even pulled his mask up, assuming once more that alter ego he had known in Pryd Town. Slipping past the outer guards proved no difficult task for the stealthy Highwayman. Along the ground or in the trees, Bransen's line of *ki-chi-kree* held strong, as did his command of the gemstones. He noted many monks among the soldiers and feared that the wretch De Guilbe had garnered a strong following in short order. He spotted only one fire, small and obviously shielded from distant eyes.

He crept along in the branches, nearing the close perimeter of the few seated about the low-burning flames. And then he lost his breath, as among the few near the fire he recognized Brother Pinower of St. Mere Abelle, Brother Giavno, and none other than Dame Gwydre herself!

Dumbstruck and suddenly afraid that St. Mere Abelle might have fallen, Bransen blurted out an indecipherable sound and, without even realizing the movement, dropped from the branches to the ground. All in the camp stirred at that, reaching for weapons and gemstones, and behind him Bransen heard a pair of guards call out, "Stand or die!"

He held his hands out in a nonthreatening manner. "I am Bransen Garibond," he managed to sputter as the soldiers came up to him, spear tips gleaming in the moonlight.

"Bransen!" Pinower and Giavno said together.

Giavno rushed up beside the Highwayman and clapped him on the shoulder. "A fine night it is, then," he cheered, ushering Bransen through the line of nodding soldiers and monks to join Gwydre and Pinower by the fire.

"And a fine meeting," said Dame Gwydre.

"Blessed Abelle is shining on us this night!" Pinower exclaimed.

"Aye and the old ones are looking to our cause," Gwydre added, just to draw a smirk from both monks, and when those expected looks came, the Dame of Vanguard grinned from ear to ear.

"The chapel?" Bransen asked. "Cadayle and Callen?"

"Faring well behind thick walls Yeslnik cannot breach," Dame Gwydre assured him.

"But you are out here in the open night."

"The alliance has been sealed with Laird Ethelbert," Gwydre explained. "I am out to further our needs. . . ."

"I came from the encampment of Laird Bannagran of Pryd and from a parley with Laird Ethelbert and Cormack and Milkeila," Bransen explained.

"Fine news!" said Brother Pinower. "It is our hope that Bannagran will turn to our cause."

"What said he?" Dame Gwydre pressed.

"He told Laird Ethelbert to go home," Bransen replied dryly. "And better for your cause if you had never allied with that murderous old fool."

All three exchanged glances, then turned their eyes upon Bransen.

"Ethelbert's assassins murdered Jameston Sequin," Bransen reported. Gwydre gasped and put a hand over her mouth, and Giavno called upon the gods by making the sign of the evergreen. Whispers erupted all about the camp and much of the joy at discovering the Highwayman returned washed away in the blink of an astonished eye.

"Jameston Sequin? Murdered? On Laird Ethelbert's command?" Dame Gwydre asked after the few moments it took her to compose herself.

"I know not and I care not if Ethelbert was involved," said Bransen. "I found

Jameston dead in an abandoned cottage, and I have no doubt as to whose weapon struck him down. That man, a warrior of Behr, serves Ethelbert as a mercenary, and he accompanied a fellow assassin from Behr, a woman named Affwin Wi, to murder King Delaval, as well."

"How do you know this?" Brother Pinower demanded.

"I was there in their court," Bransen replied. "The broken sword found in King Delaval's chest was the blade of Affwin Wi, Laird Ethelbert's prime assassin."

Again, Pinower, Giavno, and Gwydre looked to each other blankly, surprised by the news, and out of that stupor came Brother Pinower, eyeing Bransen more closely.

"You wear a headband above your mask," the monk said in a leading manner.

"To hold a soul stone to my forehead."

"But the brooch Father Artolivan gave to you—"

"Was torn from my head by Ethelbert's assassin. She carries it now, and my sword."

Fittingly, considering the mood shift descending upon the encampment, a log shifted in the fire then and rolled away, the already low firelight diminishing greatly.

"I barely escaped with my life," Bransen added. "Affwin Wi is trained as a Jhesta Tu and is surrounded by other formidable warriors."

"Laird Ethelbert meant to kill you?" Dame Gwydre managed to say past the lump in her throat.

"I doubt he knew anything of it," Bransen replied. "It was personal with Affwin Wi."

"This happened at Laird Bannagran's camp?" Dame Gwydre asked.

Bransen chuckled and kicked the fallen log back to the fire, then took a seat beside it. Staring into the flames, he recounted his journey to Pryd Town and to the coast beside Jameston, then detailed the time he had spent with Affwin Wi in the court of Ethelbert. He saw no reason to hide anything from this group.

He told them of his fight and escape and of the journey along the devastated southland that had taken him again to Pryd and to the march with Bannagran and Reandu and fifteen thousand warriors back to the east.

"And so I left them," he finished some time later. "For their fight is not my fight, and I no longer care which side prevails."

"You say that to Dame Gwydre's face?" Brother Giavno scolded. "You have no shame, then?"

"Shame?" Bransen echoed with a mocking laugh. "You who march to war would speak to me of shame?"

"Bransen, what has happened to you?" Dame Gwydre asked. She stood up and motioned for the others to remain silent, then moved beside the young man. "Walk with me," she bade him softly. "Your troubled soul wounds me."

Bransen looked at her doubtfully, but he did stand and walk off arm-in-arm (for he did not resist when she took his arm with great familiarity) with the Lady of Vanguard.

"Laird Ethelbert has joined us in alliance," she said as they moved to the edge of the firelight, the forest thick about them. "It is necessary for both of us to hold any hope of turning back the scourge that is Yeslnik. I will see to it that your sword is returned to you."

Bransen sighed at her, for she simply did not understand.

"And the brooch," she said. "Surely you wish those items returned."

"I do not deny that," Bransen said. "But I care hardly as much as you believe."

"What is it, Bransen?" Gwydre pressed. "What has happened to you? You are not the same man who departed St. Mere Abelle. Indeed, you seem more akin to—"

"The man you first encountered, tricked into your service by your man Dawson?"

"Yes," Gwydre admitted.

Bransen thought long and hard on that observation, for he knew that it was true enough. What had happened to him?

He had dared to care. He had dared to let optimism creep into his vision.

"I am no mercenary," he said, and he chuckled again, sadly, pathetically, recounting his night hunt from Bannagran's camp to collect trophy ears for gold.

"Of course you aren't," said Gwydre.

"Yet you used me as one, did you not?" the young warrior asked. "I served as Dame Gwydre's mercenary, her assassin, to go and slay Ancient Badden."

"You know the truth of Ancient Badden," Gwydre protested. "You know that it was right and good and necessary that he be slain."

"I went for reasons of personal gain," Bransen argued. "As a mercenary."

"And you admitted to me that, had you understood the greater truth of the war in Vanguard, you would have gone of your own volition without need for such reward," Gwydre reminded him. True enough, it sent a jolt through Bransen's dour mood.

"Nor did you go as a profiteer even before you understood the greater good," Gwydre persisted. "You went for the sake of your freedom and for the good of your family, and that is a noble cause, not the crass gold-hunting of a mercenary. Surely, Bransen, your mood cannot be of any fears that you are no better than those who do murder for Laird Ethelbert's gold."

"It does not matter," Bransen replied without hesitation.

"Truly it does!"

"No!" Bransen shouted right back at her. He looked away and pulled away and gritted his teeth, and it was all he could manage to hold back a scream of ultimate frustration. "It does not matter, because none of it matters. The way of the world is war, and the unscrupulous will ever rise to rule."

He kept walking slowly, but Dame Gwydre stopped. When he turned back to regard her, he found her standing straight, hands on hips, scowling after him.

"Not you," he stammered in apology. "I know that you rule Vanguard wisely, and I doubt not that you would serve as a wonderful Queen of Honce and that the lives of your peasants would be bettered by your actions."

"You just said that it matters not."

"Because you are a mortal woman, after all, and so fleeting is life. The cycle of misery can be interrupted, but it cannot be stopped."

"I do not believe that."

Bransen shrugged. He did not care. How could this war—how could any war—be worth the cost for such a temporary gain?

"Our great and glorious cause is a fool's errand," he said quietly, and that defeated tone made it all the more profound and powerful. "Even should Bannagran turncoat against Yeslnik, even should we march to Delaval and seat you as Queen of Honce, there will always be another Ancient Badden or King Yeslnik or Laird Prydae or Father De Guilbe to take it back. I understand now why the Jhesta Tu dwell in a remote mountain fortress far from the politics of men. With their strength and knowledge, they could likely shape the world, but they, too, recognize the futility of it all. Jameston Sequin should have stayed in the northern woods."

"His cause was just," Dame Gwydre insisted.

"Just and hopeless. One good soul against a castle wall topped with unjust enemies."

"We can win the day for Honce," Gwydre said. "I believe that young Yeslnik has erred in his decree to the Order of Blessed Abelle. He has pushed the goodly brothers too far with his demands of execution and betrayal, and they . . ." She paused when she looked upon Bransen, shaking his head as if none of it mattered.

"What road for Bransen, then?" she asked. "I cannot force you to march with me, of course, and trust that you'll never support Yeslnik."

"That you can trust, yes," the young warrior assured her. "I am bound for St. Mere Abelle and the arms of my wife. By our agreement, you will sail me wherever I choose, and I choose Vanguard."

Gwydre started to respond, but Bransen cut her short. "Not to serve you," he explained. "To find a place where I and my family can live in peace, away from the stupidity of the wider world."

"You will run and hide in a forest?"

"It was good enough for Jameston Sequin."

"Cadayle's mother might now consider Dawson McKeege part of that family," Gwydre warned. "For they have fallen in love."

The news caught Bransen by surprise, obviously, but he merely gave his signature helpless chuckle yet again and moved on.

"I cannot get you to Vanguard," Dame Gwydre admitted. "And surely not with a pregnant Cadayle beside you!"

"I have your word."

"You have the Gulf of Corona swarming with Palmaristown and Delaval City warships," Gwydre explained. "There is no safe passage."

Bransen chewed his lip.

"So what then for Bransen?"

"To remain with Cadayle in St. Mere Abelle as long as Father Artolivan allows," he said quickly, not bothering to think it through, for all that he cared about at that moment was making it clear to Dame Gwydre that he had no intention of going to war.

"Father Artolivan is dead," Gwydre informed him, and he winced. "Peacefully and of natural cause. Father Premujon is seated at the head of the Order of Blessed Abelle now, a worthy successor to a fine man."

"And when that successor is not so worthy?" the unrelenting Bransen asked.

"You are running and hiding," Dame Gwydre dared remark, but in a light tone.

"You should be glad that I am and that I am not continuing my bargain with Bannagran to aid in his fight with Ethelbert."

"That is a fight we hope to avert."

Bransen shook his head and hardly cared—or made it seem as if he didn't care, at least. "When I learned of your alliance with Laird Ethelbert, out of deference to you I rescinded my agreement with Bannagran and departed," he lied, and Gwydre's smile showed that she saw right through him.

"And now you are again the same Bransen who first came to Vanguard," Gwydre said. "Full of cynicism."

"Accepting of reality," he corrected.

It was Dame Gwydre's turn to shake her head. "You had grown so much," she said. "Tell me, Highwayman, if we could go back to that time you first came into Vanguard but with all the knowledge you have gained these last months, would you join with me and go after Ancient Badden?"

The old question, Bransen realized. Dame Gwydre's measuring stick for Bransen Garibond's character. "No," he answered, flooding his voice with strength and not bothering to internally sort whether it was the strength of conviction or of simple stubbornness. He didn't blink when Dame Gwydre argued with him, telling him that she did not believe him. This was not the same conversation he had shared with the woman in Pellinor those months ago, when he had then proclaimed that he would have, indeed, enlisted in her cause against the Samhaists, and for the sake of his own peace of mind he could not allow her to believe that this was a replay of that discussion.

"Do you even care that Ethelbert murdered Jameston?" he asked bluntly.

"You do not know that to be true. You, yourself, said it was likely personal with Affwin Wi." Gwydre looked into his stubborn face with great sadness. "Of course I care. The death of Master Sequin wounds me profoundly. He was a great and accomplished man, and I was proud to call him a friend."

"But you would look past it for the sake of this alliance you so desperately need even if you discovered Ethelbert knew of his assassins' work?"

Dame Gwydre blew a weary and pained sigh, and Bransen knew that he was getting to her, wounding her, though to what end or for what purpose, he did not know. She started to respond several times, trying futilely to explain that the circumstances surrounding Jameston's death would indeed have consequence but, finally, admitting that the situation was much larger than the question of Jameston Sequin.

"I am responsible for the people of Vanguard, some fifty thousand souls, all weary of war," she said. "King Yeslnik has already begun his assault on my shores. Would you have me throw away Vanguard's only hope?"

"If Laird Ethelbert is your only hope, then you have already lost," Bransen said dryly.

"The alliance between Vanguard and Ethelbert and St. Mere Abelle purchases leverage," she explained, "to bring more lairds to our cause. Few would follow King Yeslnik if they came to believe in an alternative ruler who might defeat him on the field."

"If you wish to lessen the misery of all, then just surrender to Yeslnik," said Bransen. "Let the war end, let him go back to Delaval as you go home to Vanguard."

"And allow him to claim all of Honce as his domain?"

"Why would you care, if not for foolish pride? Do you believe that Yeslnik the idiot will know enough about the goings-on in your far-distant holding to truly interfere?"

"The people of Honce proper cry out in despair. I cannot ignore that plea!"

"Only those who crave their own power cry out," Bransen argued. "For the rest, be it Yeslnik or Ethelbert, Gwydre or Premujon now, they care not. They only want the war to end."

"And when King Yeslnik, secure in Honce, decides that Honce is not enough?" Gwydre asked. "When he sails an armada to Behr to wage a wider war? When he marches through Vanguard on his way to conquer the Alpinadoran tribes?"

"You do not know he will do that."

"I know that he is without mercy and that he is full of treachery. He would have the monks execute all the prisoners taken from Ethelbert's ranks."

"And all of your own actions are for the cause of the common man?" Bransen asked, his voice dripping with sarcasm. "None of this is for the gain of Dame Gwydre?"

The woman looked at him as if he had struck her.

"A pox on all your houses," Bransen snapped at her, but his voice quickly broke into a stutter as he continued, "If I cared at all which of you won the worthless throne, then perhaps I would fight, but since I do not . . ." It took every ounce of his concentration to even get the sentence out, dragging some syllables along painfully and biting off others as his jaw involuntarily clenched.

"You can lie to me, Bransen Garibond, but you cannot lie to yourself. Listen to your own words, for they speak not to the truth in your heart. That is the source of your malady. That is why you again need the gemstone tied tightly to your forehead. When your heart is not right, so, too, will go astray your body and mind."

"You know nothing of me," he shot right back.

Dame Gwydre looked at him carefully for a few heartbeats. "Perhaps I do not. Perhaps I was wrong to think so highly of Bransen Garibond."

"Perhaps you were. Would you rescind your Writ of Passage, then, Queen of Honce?"

Dame Gwydre wore a sour expression. She shook her head, though in response to his question or simply to show her disgust Bransen could not fathom.

Bransen didn't even follow her back to the camp to rejoin the monks. He just walked off to the north and the coast, then to the west, chewing his lip with rage every step of the way.

He began to see signs of the besieging force as St. Mere Abelle came into clear sight, sitting up on the high and rocky cliff, unscalable from the ocean and a fairly steep ascent from all three other directions. Bransen climbed a tree to gain a better view of the field and the situation. Directly down the hill from the front gates, he saw the line of catapults, and even as he watched, one let fly a large stone. It arced through the air to hit the turf directly before the wall, skipping up to crack against the wall itself. It bounced harmlessly back to the grass, where it lay among dozens and dozens of other boulders.

They were halfway between midnight and dawn, and still Ethelbert's catapults were throwing?

The sight alarmed Bransen, for Cadayle was within those walls.

Another rock went into the air, and he grimaced, imagining her huddled with terror, hugging Callen, as it slammed in hard, shaking the foundation of the chapel complex. A third stone went up shortly after, and this one cleared the wall. Bransen nearly cried out in fear.

A moment later, he was glad that he had not, for movement below him and not far from the tree in which he was perched caught his attention. He froze in place, staring down, sorting out the movement as a small group of soldiers, obviously Palmaristown, patrolled the region. He thought to wait them out, but the report of another stone slamming into the stone of the complex startled him. He had to get to Cadayle!

The Highwayman came down from the tree in a rush, using the malachite to ease and control his fall. He got to the lowest branch before being spotted by a leather-clad soldier some ten strides away—ten strides or one great, gemstone-enhanced leap for the Highwayman. He soared toward the shouting man, who lifted a battle-axe at the sight. The man took his weapon in both hands as he realized to his horror that the Highwayman flew toward him from on high, a leap that no man should have been able to make. Awkwardly, he turned the blade and swiped it upward as his attacker descended.

The Highwayman easily kicked it aside with one foot, landing heavily on the other onto the shoulder of the man, who groaned and lurched and flew to the side. The Highwayman didn't fight the momentum, just threw himself over sidelong, settling in a deep crouch. The man he had landed upon didn't fare as well, though. He stumbled and staggered off balance, grabbing at his wounded shoulder before tripping over a root and tumbling to the ground.

The Highwayman was over him in an instant, but he didn't land a finishing blow. He didn't have to, for in the tangle of his fall the poor soldier had fallen on his axe blade. He writhed in pain, a long but superficial gash running the length of his ribs.

Bransen stood straight and swung about to face another soldier coming in hard, spear extended. Up into the air the Highwayman leaped, higher than any man should, and when he tucked his legs, his feet were up higher than the newest opponent's head. She lifted her spear to try to fend, but the Highwayman went right over her. He landed lightly and sprang up again, lifting above her as she turned and spinning a tight circuit as he went so that he could launch a heavy circle kick that met her squarely at the top of her ribs and the base of her throat as she came around. She flew back as if she, too, had been launched from one of Milwellis's catapults, her spear flying harmlessly aside.

Shouts erupted from the brush as more soldiers closed in on the Highwayman, but he thought of Cadayle and was having none of it. He sprinted off for the distant chapel, his strides lengthening as he fell into the malachite, great bounds like that of a hunting cat or a fleeing deer. He easily outdistanced the pursuit, even outrunning the volley of spears that were thrown his way.

With Cadayle in his thoughts, the Highwayman would not slow, and when he reached the base of the high wall of St. Mere Abelle, the malachite's power flowing through his limbs, he seemed, to those watching from the distant trees and to those monks cheering him on from the parapets, to simply run up the wall.

He shrugged off their shoulder clapping and well-intentioned hugs and leaped down to the courtyard, sprinting across the way to the room he had shared with Cadayle.

His relief at seeing her, eyes and smile wide with surprise and pure joy, was matched only by the sincere sense of calm that came over him when she wrapped him in a great hug. They fell asleep in each other's arms, all tears and giggles, and Bransen felt as if he could stay there, could hide there, forevermore.

It proved a short respite, for barely a couple of hours later, Callen Duwornay burst into the room, calling out and waving her arms frantically.

"It's begun!" she cried. "Oh, it's begun, and a beautiful thing it is!"

Bransen snapped into a sitting position. "What?"

"Gwydre's fight, don't ya know? Sweeping the field, she is! Oh, come and look!"

Bransen and Cadayle scrambled out of bed and dressed quickly, then rushed out of the keep and across the courtyard, to join all of those remaining inside St. Mere Abelle atop the front wall.

Bransen's pulse pounded in his veins, for he heard the shouts of battle before he ever got up the ladder. Horns blew and magical lightning bolts crackled in the early-morning air. By the time he reached the parapet, slowing only to help Cadayle up the last couple of steps, several lines of thick black smoke rose into the dawn's light.

"They're burning the catapults!" said one of the monks on the wall, a young brother who seemed as if he was yet to reach puberty and whose high-pitched voice confirmed his youthful appearance.

The brother kept talking, but Bransen wasn't listening. He moved right up to the wall and peered over intently. The rout was on before him, and, truly, it was a lopsided affair. Gwydre and her force had charged in from the east, from in front of the rising sun; Bransen could picture the spectacle of that, and could imagine the horror of Panlamaris's men as they tried to sort out the enemy assault with the blinding glare behind. He felt a tinge of regret and tried hard to suppress it.

"We've suffered their rocks every day and every night," Cadayle reminded.

Bransen nodded. A large group of Panlamaris's men broke away to the west, in full panic and retreat, and Bransen spied the large man—the laird himself—screaming at them and waving his great sword.

All along the wall the monks and others began cheering wildly, even more so when a group of the Palmaristown garrison rushed their way, scrambling up the hill, all crying and begging for mercy.

"All quarter offered!" several brothers began to shout. "These misled warriors are our brothers and sisters!"

Bransen felt as if the slightest breeze might knock him from his feet.

"Get out there," Cadayle said in his ear, through the tumult rising all around them.

Bransen turned to stare at her incredulously.

"This is your fight," she said. "This is our fight, as surely as any we have ever known."

"I am done with fighting!" he shouted back, and many around them quieted at that, several monks gasping in shock and obvious dismay. This was the Highwayman standing among them, after all, one of the great champions of their desperate cause.

"It doesn't matter," Bransen said. "None of it matters."

"Ye cannot be thinking that Queen Gwydre'll be as ill-tempered as King Yeslnik," remarked Callen, coming over and sounding every bit the peasant woman from Pryd Town. "What fool's got ye, boy?"

"Don't you see?" Bransen asked, pulling away from Cadayle and addressing all of those around him, most of whom were staring at him with open shock, and some with open contempt. "Even should we seat Gwydre on Delaval's own throne, it would be but a temporary reprieve, a short pause of misery."

"Bransen!" Cadayle pleaded.

"It's the truth," he said to her, coming close again and taking her hands in his own. "I've come to know that, and it pains me greatly. The road men walk is a roundabout. There is no better way to be found."

"How can you say such things?"

"Too many who believed otherwise have died in vain. My father and mother . . ."

"In vain, ye say, but yer ma saved that girl ye hold," Callen reminded from behind him.

"Garibond and Jameston," Bransen went on, trying to ignore her. "All dead, and to what end?"

"And what would you have us do?" Cadayle asked.

"Run away to the north. To the forest, once home to Jameston Sequin, and far from this madness."

"To live as hermits in the woods, then?"

"Free of lairds, free of church, free of war," Bransen insisted.

Cadayle stepped back and pulled her hands free, one of them coming up to cover her mouth.

"Dame Gwydre will honor the terms, and will sail us to . . ." Bransen started to say, but he stopped abruptly when Cadayle hit him with a stinging slap across the face.

"You would do that to our child?"

"Cadayle," Bransen whispered.

"Hit him again," said Callen dryly.

Cadayle glanced at her mother for that comment, but only briefly. "Why did you ever get up?" she asked Bransen.

He looked at her perplexed.

"When they knocked the Stork into the mud," Cadayle explained. "Why did you get back up?"

"What nonsense—"

"No nonsense," Cadayle interrupted. "If it all means nothing, then why'd the Stork ever climb out of the mud? If there's nothing to be gained, then why didn't you just lay there and die in the soft black muck of nothing?"

Bransen looked at her dumbfounded and glanced around to meet the hard stares of everyone in the area.

"It's a roundabout!" he declared. "A walk in a circle to the same awful places again and again."

"More of an egg," said Callen, and all eyes turned to her. "And a rolling one, at that. Oh, the road's going back sometimes—too oftentimes—but it's rolling forward so long as men and women of heart and cause are moving it so. The world's a better place than it was when Callen went into the Samhaist's sack o' snakes, don't ya doubt! And 'twas a better place then than when Callen's ma was a girl and half o' Pryd starved to death."

Cadayle grabbed Bransen by the front of his shirt and pulled him to face her directly. "We've a chance now, right now, and it's one worth taking. You go push the road, the roundabout, whatever you may call it, forward! For me and for our baby that's in my womb. And for yourself, my love." She tenderly stroked his face, and though he initially tried to pull away, he didn't fight her touch for long.

"You'll not forgive yourself if you run away."

"Or you'll not forgive me," he said dryly.

Cadayle took pause at that and looked at him with clear love and sympathy and gently stroked his face once more. "I could never not love you, my Stork," she said. "But don't you wallow there in the mud. You get up. This is our fight, all of us, and I only wish I could go with you, weapon in hand and a song on my lips. Dame Gwydre deserves your sword."

"I have no sword," Bransen reminded.

"Get the Highwayman a sword, ye damn fools!" Callen shouted, and several men on the wall rushed away.

Bransen looked at his mother-in-law, and Callen shrugged. Bransen couldn't help but chuckle against the unrelenting woman.

"Father Artolivan's church stood against Yeslnik," Cadayle went on. "They stood for mercy and justice and at great cost. Would you abandon them now?"

The young monk rushed up and thrust a sword into Bransen's hand, nodding hopefully. Bransen turned from the eager young man to Cadayle, who reached up, holding a thin black strip of cloth.

She tied his mask on his face and whispered, "Go." And then she offered him her hand, as she had when he had lain in the mud on that long-ago day.

Bransen took her hand and kissed it softly. Then he nodded to the others, offered a self-deprecating snort, and jumped over the wall.

Many gasped at that, but not Cadayle. She moved to the crenellation and looked at her husband, the Highwayman, as he descended the high wall with spiderlike speed. All about her, the cheering began anew.

G et up, ye damned child!" Laird Panlamaris said, his voice uneven. He tried to kick at the soldier, who huddled upon the ground, but the desperate laird staggered as he did and nearly fell.

The soldier scrambled away, crying and begging for mercy.

Panlamaris spat at him, though that, too, fell far short. The large, old laird spun about, inadvertently drawing a circle in the bloody dirt with his low-hanging sword. He looked for his men, he called for his men, but, alas, there were none about—none who would answer that call, at least.

He had been routed, his army driven from the field around him. Old Ethelbert knew the truth of it. So many times he had seen his enemies in this very predicament.

Not far to the east, the sun now raised above them, Dame Gwydre and her line re-formed. Grim-faced, their banners high, to a man and woman they stared at the Laird of Palmaristown.

"Come on, then!" Panlamaris howled, lifting his sword awkwardly, the movement nearly throwing him from his feet. The blood on the ground about him was his own. Garish wounds crisscrossed his arms and chest, and so bloody was one side of his face that he couldn't see out of that eye. The stump of a broken spear stuck out from his side, waving with his every breath.

"You are defeated, Laird Panlamaris," the Dame of Vanguard replied, and she and those around her advanced to within a few strides of the man. Flanking her left and right, brothers Pinower and Giavno each lifted a hand, presenting graphite—the stone of lightning—Panlamaris's way.

"Ah, ye witch!" the old laird roared, and he reached back his sword arm as if to throw.

Twin bolts of lightning shot out from Gwydre's escort, jolting him, slamming him, knocking him back several strides.

The stubborn old man did not fall over, though. He held his balance, spat some more blood. He looked hatefully at Gwydre and lifted his sword arm yet again.

A black form rushed across in front of him before the monks could even loose their second volley, and the Laird of Palmaristown staggered back again, a look of sheer surprise on his weathered face—surprise rooted more in the realization that he was dead than by the appearance of the Highwayman on the field.

For in his passing, the Highwayman had spun a tight circle, his elbow flying high behind him to score a perfect strike against the threatening old laird's windpipe.

Panlamaris looked at him curiously for a few moments, his arm dropping, his sword falling free of his grasp.

He fell facedown in the bloody dirt, dead at last.

"Welcome home, Highwayman," Dame Gwydre said.

Bransen glanced back at the distant St. Mere Abelle, where Cadayle, he knew, was watching. He was on Jameston Sequin's third road now, the path that had led Jameston to his death.

His wife demanded this of him; his unborn child demanded this of him; the Stork demanded this of him.

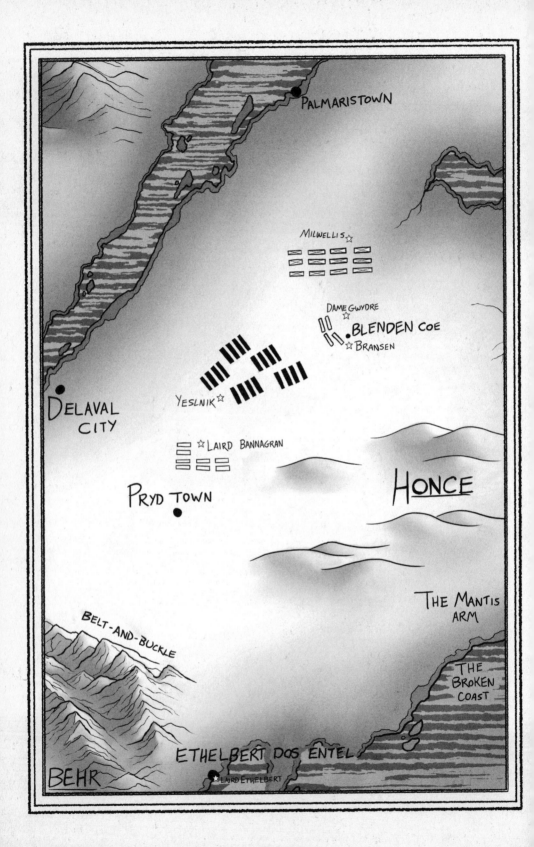

The Forward Crawl
of Humanity

I knew from the moment I opened my eyes—or rather, from the instant my eyes popped wide—that some deep and unexplored thought had forced itself upon me. It took me a few moments to even recall where I was, there in the quiet room in the dark night. What great comfort was Cadayle's steady breathing in the bed beside me.

We were in our room at St. Mere Abelle the night after the rout of Laird Panlamaris. The next day promised to be full of carrion birds and large graves and the awful smell that had become all too common across the breadth of the land.

And then what?

There was talk of a fleet sailing in, full of Vanguard warriors, ready to march beside Dame Gwydre. There was talk of marching in pursuit of Prince Milwellis and, oh, if another such victory as the one of this morning could be achieved, then wouldn't King Yeslnik run and hide in Castle Delaval?

There was talk of war. It was all the talk, brothers and commoners alike, and despite my report regarding the happenings in the south and Pryd Town, Gwydre and Premujon, Pinower, and all the others still held hope that Bannagran would turn to their side. If he did not, given his skill and the fifteen thousand warriors he commanded, he could likely sweep the field of Gwydre and the force from Honce and of Ethelbert, as well, should that laird come forth.

That terrible truth was the catalyst that had led to the epiphany that had so thrown me from my slumber.

Bannagran of Pryd. He seemed such a simple man, strong of arm and straightforward of intent. He was the consummate general, or the consummate footman; it mattered not what role was thrust upon him.

But did it matter, I wondered, which enemy he was asked to slay?

That was my epiphany: that Bannagran of Pryd was not akin to Affwin Wi. They were greatly similar, of course, for both had spent their lives in training for battle and both served their masters ferociously. But while Affwin Wi did so for personal gain, for gold even, the same could not be said of Bannagran.

For Bannagran, serving Laird Prydae or King Yeslnik or any other is a response to a sense of duty, a belief that such was his place in the world, his purpose in the world.

The Hou-lei tradition is that of the pure mercenary and, thus, strictly amoral by definition. The true incarnation of a Hou-lei warrior is the perfection of the physical and the denial of the emotional. Could Bannagran be said to be a Honce version of Behr's Hou-lei?

No.

I do not even hesitate in answering that question. The man has left too many clues to the contrary. If Affwin Wi were the Dame of Pryd, she would not have let me live when I was captured there recently ... or she would have crippled me beyond repair and dragged me to Yeslnik so that he could enjoy my execution.

Affwin Wi would not have allowed the prisoners who were held at Chapel Pryd to don the robes of the order and escape King Yeslnik's sentence of death.

So the question becomes, Why, then, would this man of conscience and honor allow himself to be used as a pawn for immoral men such as Yeslnik?

This dilemma followed me as I slowly crawled out of my bed and moved across the room to the window looking over the chapel's back wall and the dark waters of the gulf.

I found my answer when I first peered out, before I lifted the glass pane and inadvertently viewed my own reflection.

For I see the answer to Bannagran of Pryd when I look into the mirror darkly and honestly.

Always a champion, never a laird, truly, for either of us. We dare to serve and serve extraordinarily well, when duty is thrust upon us, when Bannagran goes to fight Ethelbert and Bransen goes to fight Ancient Badden. But when the path is not determined by someone else of greater authority, then Bannagran balks and Bransen ...

I'll never forget the look on my face as I snickered before that glass in the predawn room at St. Mere Abelle. I was naked, figuratively and literally. In the dark of night, in the long shadows, I had nowhere left to hide.

For in the moment of truth and courage, I had run away. I had abandoned Reandu and Cormack and Milkeila and Dame Gwydre's cause and all that I know to be right, because in that moment I had been a coward.

And in following this wicked and "impetulant," as Jameston labeled him, King Yeslnik, so, too, is Bannagran playing the role of the coward. Never on the field of battle, certainly, neither he nor I, but in the realm of responsibility, so alike are we and so cowardly, both.

Would Bannagran admit the truth of himself to himself, I wonder?

And if he did, could he bring himself to march for King Yeslnik?

From the time of Jameston's death, and despite my protests to the contrary, I meandered without purpose. Through the southland and to Pryd, then east with Bannagran and north to St. Mere Abelle, my paths had been a mixture of self-delusion and self-denial, constantly thumbing my nose at the wider world in a pout of superiority and feigned indifference. For the first time since Jameston's murder, looking at my reflection in that dark room, the sound of Cadayle's steady breathing anchoring me, I knew my road.

And I knew the consequence of failure, to myself and to Honce.

—BRANSEN GARIBOND

CHAPTER 16

Body, Mind, and Soul

Cormack knew better than to question Milkeila's instincts. The shaman had noted something amiss, some movement or sound, perhaps. She paced about their small encampment cautiously, peering into the darkness, holding her solid oaken staff in one hand and the loops of her toothy necklace in the other.

She chanted to the trees and the grass, bidding them to tell her the secrets of those who walked near.

She kept ending her song, though, and turning to Cormack, her expression befuddled. "They tell me of no intruders."

"But you do not believe them?"

"Someone, something, is about," the shaman declared. She swept her gaze across the fields and trees. "I sense it keenly."

She moved to the fire and began chanting again, but this time her call was to the fire itself, strengthening it, brightening it.

Cormack joined her and took out his dagger, though it was more a knife for utility, like cutting kindling, than a serious weapon. "Do you know where? . . ." he started to ask, but he stopped suddenly and spun about, the hairs on the back of his neck standing up.

"You felt that?" Milkeila whispered, turning beside him.

"Or heard it," Cormack said, unsure which of his senses had told him that there was someone or something near.

Brother Cormack, he heard in his thoughts, not in exact words, but a representation of a greeting by a familiar voice. He recoiled instinctively, mental defenses rushing to the forefront to deny the intrusion. Even as he did that, hardly thinking of it, he sorted out the intrusion and knew, then, the source.

"Brother Giavno!" he said aloud, and Milkeila screwed up her expression curiously.

"Spirit walking!" Cormack explained in a harsh whisper. He nodded as it came clearer to him. "He seeks information so that he might report to Dame Gwydre."

"So we must tell him."

"All of it," said Cormack, and he began, paused, and asked a question instead. "Has Dawson returned to St. Mere Abelle?"

Yes, he heard in his mind.

Not knowing where to properly begin, Cormack started recounting their adventures at Laird Ethelbert's side, of the meeting with Bannagran and Bransen and the loss of Jameston Sequin.

"We have not surrendered the notion of a truce with Laird Bannagran yet," he finished after a few moments. "He seems not an unreasonable man, and Brother Reandu does not support the cause of Father De Guilbe—of that, I am sure."

He felt Giavno's approval and a sensation of farewell, and a moment later Cormack looked at Milkeila and announced that they were alone.

But they were not.

Weary from his magical expenditures and from simply resisting the urge to possess Brother Cormack, Giavno's ghost swept out of the encampment. He wasn't sure if he wanted to soar through Bannagran's lines to learn what he might of the powerful laird or return straight to St. Mere Abelle and report on Cormack's progress, perhaps to return the next night.

Barely away from the couple, though, Brother Giavno found a detour.

He sensed them before he saw them, their mortal forms compelling his wandering spirit toward them. Their positioning and posture warned him clearly enough, for they—two forms—crept along branches in the direction of Cormack and Milkeila.

Bandits?

Giavno flew in closer. Though he dared not try to read the minds of either, he felt their malice, and he saw their weapons.

He sped back to the encampment and imparted a fast warning, Murderers! Flee! to both.

Cormack sputtered a question, but Giavno didn't pause. He sent forth the thought again, Murderers! Flee! and willed his unseen spirit back to the forest.

Ishat Parzun crouched on the thick branch, twisting himself about in an effort to gain a clear look at the low firelight ahead. He held up his fist, signaling his companion to halt. He licked his dry lips, knowing that Affwin Wi would not be pleased if he failed in this. Half their band of eight had been killed: one in a fight with Milwellis's knights; two by the Jhesta Tu Highwayman; and one by the tall scout, Sequin.

Affwin Wi would tolerate no further failures.

But this seemed simple enough. Ishat and Wahloon had teamed on successful assassinations several times before, and these two strangers did not seem so formidable. Not compared with the martial prowess of two Hou-lei warriors, at least.

Still, the assassin reminded himself to take it slow as he crept inch by inch along the upsweeping branch, moving closer to the firelight and higher.

The victims were scrambling! They knew!

Ishat Parzun leaped to his feet and waved Wahloon forward. Off Ishat ran, along the branch, leaping to another and taking a circuitous route to the right of the couple. The man, Cormack, yelled out and grabbed at his arm, and Ishat understood that Wahloon had scored a hit with a *shur'a'tu'wikin*, a small throwing star, Wahloon's favored weapon.

Now Wahloon had the attention of the couple, and Ishat rushed along, confident of the kill. To the side and above, he leaped and executed a twisting somersault, catching a branch in his grasp. He swung under but held fast as the branch bent forward under his momentum, then reversed his direction, meaning to let go with one hand and spin around at the exact moment of the branch's greatest swingback, dropping from above onto his victims.

He caught it, swung out, and then came back and started to turn.

And then it hit him, as solidly as if a club had struck him on the side of his head. Ishat Parzun had never been violated in this manner before, and the sudden and vicious encroachment of another soul into his mortal body revolted him so profoundly that he lost all sense of where he was.

Somewhere in the distance the woman shaman screamed a warning. He flew from the branch, tumbling out of control. He landed feetfirst, but falling forward, hooking his toes awkwardly, and the ground rushed up to slam him in the face.

But Ishat didn't feel that impact, or the blood rushing out of his shattered nose, or the sharp pain about one eye from a crushed socket. No, his pain was internal at that awful moment, as a clawing, shadowy form assailed something more profound and sensitive than his flesh, as an invading spirit fought to expel him from his own corporeal coil.

———

Milkeila's cry and her shove were the only things that allowed Cormack to fall out of the way of the flying black-clad form. The back of his arm torn and burning with fiery pain, Cormack stumbled and fell to one knee as the assassin flew past him, landing hard. The man's awkward descent made no sense to Cormack and Milkeila, for they thought these warriors akin to the graceful Highwayman.

The monk didn't focus on that unexplained event, though. Expecting more of the sharp missiles from the man crossing the other side of the encampment, Cormack threw himself into a forward roll and came back to his feet angling to the side. He spied the other assailant, the man's arm up to throw, but before he ever executed the throw, the small campfire exploded, directionally and with the blast aimed right at the star-throwing assailant. Sparks and cinders cut through the darkness, and the warrior launched himself sidelong through the air.

Cormack glanced at Milkeila. Of course she had done that! She faced the fire, chanting to the ancient spirits of the earth, bending the flames.

"Come!" Cormack called to her. "Quickly! We know not how many more are about!" He scrambled to her side, and together they ran into the tree line. A whistle just over his head was the only indication Cormack had of how close the next missile had come.

They had barely reached the trees when Milkeila spun back and raised her staff and necklace, and Cormack noted a wave of energy, like the distortion of a heated surface, roll out from her. The assailant nearest them writhed on the ground, seemingly out of his senses, but the other man had nimbly come back to his feet. He started forward but jerked weirdly, for the grass was grabbing at his feet, and when he tore one foot free, a clump of dirt went flying! He did well to regain his balance almost immediately, but then a branch bent down at him, as if grabbing at him!

And indeed it was. Cormack marveled at his wife's attunement with the plants about them. Strong was Milkeila's magic, and without gemstones, and it remained one of Cormack's greatest laments that his order would not study the mysterious powers of Yan Ossum, would not see them in concert with the powers bestowed by the gemstones of Blessed Abelle.

Now Milkeila went with him into the darkness of the tree line, but barely had they entered when the woman stopped and shook her head, looking back the way they had come.

If Brother Giavno could have seen his own body, far across the miles in St. Mere Abelle, he was certain that his face would be streaked with tears. The tumult and darkness of possession engulfed him and swirled and jumbled everything he had known to be good or evil.

Even so, he could not stop. For the sake of Cormack and Milkeila, perhaps for the success or failure of the war itself, he could not surrender this battle. So he thrashed, losing himself in the fury of the moment, battling for control, muscle by muscle.

The body he had invaded was enough his own at that point for him to feel the grab on his shoulder when the assassin's companion came by, yanking him roughly to his feet.

"Ishat!" he heard the man scold him, and he saw momentarily out of Ishat's eyes to witness the other man lift his arm, a small circular throwing missile in hand.

Brother Giavno tried to yell out, "Cormack," but nothing decipherable came forth from the twisted lips. The monk gained enough control of one arm to lash out, though, his punch slamming his companion in the jaw just as he moved to throw.

The momentum had Ishat stumbling forward into the lurching man—at least until that warrior deftly and powerfully caught his balance and shifted in a twist, throwing Ishat over his hip. Staggering, out of control, both Giavno and Ishat reflexively recoiled as they went face-first into the fire.

Explosions of searing pain assaulted Giavno and Ishat simultaneously, and now the corporeal form did scream out, as the two inhabitants found common agony. Arms and legs began thrashing, desperately trying to get out of the blaze. He—they—hit the dirt and began rolling about wildly to douse the biting flames.

"Ishat!" the other man cried.

The assassin went to his fallen friend, slapping at the flames and trying to roll the wounded man over.

And all the while, Cormack lined up his charge, for Milkeila had assured him that there were only these two.

The black-clad man lifted his friend's arm, then cried out and threw his arms up defensively as Cormack flew in sidelong, a heavy body block. He collided hard and took the smaller Behr man down beneath him, the monk scrambling even as they hit the ground to execute a deadly hold. Cormack was no stranger to battle. His fighting prowess had been the primary reason he had been selected to journey to Alpinador with Father De Guilbe's expedition those years before. He wore a powrie cap because he had, indeed, defeated a bloody-cap dwarf in single hand-to-hand combat, no easy feat for any human!

Cormack didn't know how he might measure up against either of these two assassins in a fair fight, though he suspected the answer to be not very well if either was anywhere near as proficient a fighter as Bransen. With that unsettling thought in mind, his focus from run to leap to body block and now, especially now, remained tight. All that he wanted to do was get his legs wrapped about the man's neck.

And he did, and he clamped down with all his strength. The man reached up at him, or tried to, but the grass grabbed at him once more, further pinning him.

Milkeila was doing that, Cormack knew, and he clamped down tighter, with all his strength, and dared glance back to see his beloved wife rattling her necklace in the air before her, bidding the grass to pull at the man.

"The other one," Cormack growled to Milkeila, for now his leg vise was set and he knew that his battle was at its end.

The downed assailant pulled an arm free and slapped at Cormack's leg, but weakly and too late, and Cormack just rolled himself to the side, bending the doomed man's head back with the turn.

And the former monk of Abelle squeezed and pushed aside his compassion with a continual reminder that this man was as dangerous as Bransen.

The pain did not abate, though the flames were gone, for now it was of a different source, a brutal struggle of muscle against muscles, of muscles against themselves. Brother Giavno and Ishat battled furiously within the wounded body, Ishat instinctively countering every attempt by Giavno to garner any control of any part of the body that belonged to him.

Normally, a possessing brother in such a situation would be expelled; his own reactions to the horror of possession would weaken his willpower enough for the host spirit to throw him far. But Giavno knew the stakes here, and he fought harder and more furiously, pointedly sending his demands to parts of the body where he believed Ishat to be weakest. They thrashed and squirmed, rolled about and kicked and flailed wildly. Fists clenched and the muscles of one arm contracted, biceps and triceps, each pulling against the other to their fullest, so disconnected to each other, so lost in the singular determination of separate wills, that the fibers tore and blotches and bruises erupted the length of the upper arm.

A second battle erupted in Ishat's jaw, with teeth grinding and pressing tightly. At one point, Giavno gained the upper hand, and Ishat's mouth twisted open just enough for Giavno to stick out the man's tongue. Ishat regained control. Hardly conscious of the movement, he clamped the jaw tightly again, biting off the end of his tongue.

And so it went, thrashing and squirming, pain mixing with strain, sharp and dull and weaving in and out as each of the internal combatants wrestled back control. Through all of it, Giavno fought blindly, blackness and pain and his sense of self somehow mingling with, being lost to, the identity of Ishat.

He managed to gain control of the one eye that was not swollen shut just in time to catch a glimmer of Milkeila's form standing over them, of Milkeila's staff fast descending.

A burst of senselessness, an explosion of white fire that quickly dulled to nothingness, sent Giavno spiraling uncontrollably. Again, though, he did not exit the corporeal form, but instead felt a contraction, a pointed tightness and grip in his, in Ishat's, chest.

Then he felt a sudden cold sensation and saw a flood of light, distant and surrounded by blackness as if he was looking through a dark tube. And growing, rushing toward him and he toward it. He felt nothing, he knew . . . nothing.

Brother Giavno—the collection of memories and experiences and thoughts that comprised the consciousness of the man known as Brother Giavno—felt a rush of freedom as his soul flew from Ishat's dying corporeal form.

Then nothing. Emptiness. A void.

Nonexistence.

Brother Giavno's eyes popped open wide, and he reflexively threw himself to the side, crashing into the wall of the small meditation room at St. Mere Abelle. He tried to make sense of what he had seen, to put it in the perspective of Blessed Abelle and the promises of eternity. He tried, but everything jumbled too quickly. He tried to call for Brother Pinower, for Father Premujon, but the sounds that came out of his mouth made no sense, the garbled nonsense of a spirit-walking brother gone insane.

In a brief moment of clarity, Brother Giavno understood the source of his malady and from that deduced the source of this too-common loss of sensibility that occurred with brothers who dared use the soul stone to such dangerous extents.

He couldn't cry out clearly, couldn't form a cogent phrase, because he wasn't alone.

Ishat—some manner of the being that had once been Ishat of Behr—had come back with him and now reflexively, instinctively, battled Giavno for control.

Giavno stood, turned toward the door, and pushed his way into the corridor. Other brothers were around him, he saw through fast-blinking, flittering eyes. They grabbed him and supported him and called his name.

He tried to respond and did manage to call out the name of one brother, but when he tried to expand on his sentence, only gibberish came forth.

He knew, and those around him knew, for they had seen this before.

The struggle was not the same as the one that had occurred in Ishat. There was no fight for control of Giavno's physical form and no danger that he would tear himself apart, muscle against muscle. But Giavno found his every thought stabbed by the raw emotion and unbridled terror of the utterly lost soul of Ishat Parzun.

He had sacrificed his sanity to save Cormack and Milkeila.

W hat was that?" Milkeila asked as she stared wide-eyed at the very still form on the ground below her. She glanced over at Cormack, who finally dared to unwrap his legs from the assailant's neck. "I did not hit him that hard."

"Brother Giavno," Cormack explained. He climbed to his feet and bent over the fallen Behr warrior, bringing his fingers to the man's throat to see if his blood still pumped. "Alive," he said to Milkeila. "Barely." He walked over to join his beloved, then similarly bent over the burned and battered body.

"Brother Giavno," he announced again after a quick inspection, including pulling aside the man's shirt. He nodded as he searched and pulled the shirt down lower, revealing the bruises on the man's upper arm. "He waged an internal war. Brave man. We owe him our lives." Every word came hard to Cormack, for he understood the implications here and knew that Giavno's efforts had likely cost the monk greatly, perhaps irreparably.

He stood up and closed his eyes and was very glad when Milkeila wrapped him in a tight hug.

The other man stirred. Milkeila broke off the hug and moved toward him as he began to cough, and then started to sit up.

She moved to restrain him, but Cormack cut in before her and kicked the man hard in the face, laying him low.

"Cormack!" Milkeila cried.

"For Giavno," was all the disturbed man would reply. He took a deep breath then and rolled the man over, tugging his arms tightly behind his back. "We need some rope or cloth," he started to say, meaning to finish with "or we have to kill him," but Milkeila was already on the task. She moved to a nearby tree thick with climbing grapevines. She whispered to it and stroked the trunk gently and gave a slight tug on the vine, which dropped to the ground beside her. Still talking to it and gently coiling it, Milkeila moved beside Cormack. She placed the vine on the ground beside the man and called on the spirits of Yan Ossum.

The vine began to crawl of its own accord. It snaked up onto the man's back and slithered about his wrists as Cormack fell back in surprise. Winding ever more tightly, the vine wrapped intricately, weaving in and out and about. With the man's wrists secured many times over, the vine's remaining length climbed up his back and looped like a constrictor about the poor fellow's neck.

"He'll not get free," Milkeila assured her husband. "Let us be quick to Pryd and Laird Bannagran."

Cormack looked at her doubtfully. "If Bannagran learns of this attack, if he recognizes our prisoner as he surely will, then how are we to assure him that Laird Ethelbert is trustworthy and deserving of alliance?"

"How are we to believe that?" Milkeila asked.

"For Dame Gwydre, then," Cormack decided. "We will speak not on behalf of Laird Ethelbert."

"For Dame Gwydre and Father Artolivan," Milkeila agreed. "For the good of all the folk of Honce."

The man on the ground began to stir again, so the couple hooked him under the arms and hoisted him roughly to his feet. They set off at a swift pace, pushing their prisoner along.

Two days later, they arrived in Pryd Town, less than an hour after Bannagran's army had settled about the place.

Clear sailing in the gulf, and Dawson will be ashore in three days!" Dame Gwydre said excitedly, rushing into the audience hall of Father Premujon. The woman quieted immediately, though, when she noted the tenor of the place. She brought her hand to her mouth to muffle her gasp when she spotted Brother Giavno laid out on a bench to the side of the dais. Brothers Pinower and Jurgyen crouched over him, with Father Premujon and several of the chapel's masters standing nearby, shaking their heads solemnly.

"What has happened?" Gwydre asked, rushing over.

"The perils of spirit walking," Jurgyen explained, looking up at her and meeting her gaze squarely. She found no contempt there, nor blame, just a resigned sadness. "He has been driven to madness, no doubt through the sin of possession."

"Can you help him?"

Jurgyen shrugged, and Pinower said, "We have sent for Bransen. Perhaps his mystical skills and the power of our gemstones will penetrate the veil Brother Giavno has constructed."

"It is a terrible loss," said Father Premujon. "But it will not be the last we can expect." He stepped over and herded Pinower and Jurgyen away from Giavno's twitching body. "The army of Vanguard approaches," he said to them. "We must make our preparations and be out to the east to greet them. You have a great and vital march ahead of you, brothers. Go now and sleep—it has been a long night."

"The man is my friend," Pinower struggled to reply. "I cannot leave. . . ."

"You would honor him by deserting the cause to which he has so greatly sacrificed?"

Pinower lowered his gaze and gave a great exhale, a great sigh, and seemed to simply deflate. "No, father."

Premujon hugged him and whispered something in his ear, then pushed him away, toward the door.

Brother Jurgyen caught up to Pinower and supported him and also patted Gwydre comfortingly on the shoulder as he walked past her. The two brothers neared the exit as Bransen, Cadayle, and Callen came rushing in.

Bransen moved right past them, sprinting to Giavno's side, and Pinower and Jurgyen paused to watch, both making the sign of the evergreen.

Beside Bransen, who was already crouching over Brother Giavno, Father Premujon waved them out of the room.

"Can you help him?" Dame Gwydre asked, coming over to the Highwayman.

Bransen looked at her doubtfully. Without saying a word he unwrapped his bandanna and took down the soul stone Master Reandu had given him. He clutched it tightly in his hand, feeling its magic keenly, then placed it on the forehead of Brother Giavno. Almost immediately, the man's eyes flickered open and began to twitch.

Bransen felt the spiritual connection to Giavno. He pictured his own line of *ki-chi-kree*, running like a thin line of lightning from his head to his groin. Then, in the swirl of the hematite, he saw Giavno's line and felt the constant interruptions to it, the stabbing outbursts of protest causing it to flicker and spasm.

Bransen broke the connection and fell back, confused. He opened his eyes to find Gwydre and Premujon hovering about him, staring at him hopefully.

"I don't know," was all that Bransen said, and with a glance at Cadayle, who nodded her agreement, he fell back into the stone, seeking again Brother Giavno's *ki-chi-kree*.

It seemed like only a matter of moments, but most of the morning had passed before Bransen again opened his eyes and looked outside the spiritual experience of the soul stone. Gwydre was gone from the room, as were Callen and most of the monks, but Cadayle and Father Premujon sat together on a nearby bench.

"Bransen, what do you know?" a startled Premujon asked when he noticed that the Highwayman had returned from his out-of-body journey.

"Brother Giavno is in there," Bransen heard himself answering, although his concentration remained almost fully upon the task of deciphering all that he had seen, the darkness and the jumble. And then it occurred to him, "But he is not alone."

"Possession?" Father Premujon asked, coming right out of his seat, as did Cadayle beside him. The woman rushed to support her husband.

Bransen shook his head, unsure.

"One of De Guilbe's traitorous monks?" Father Premujon demanded, but again Bransen shook his head.

He wasn't certain. He needed to go back and try again to separate Brother Giavno from this other entity—enough at least to try to gain some information from the monk. But what he needed most of all was to rest.

"After supper," he said. "In the quiet night."

"Dame Gwydre wishes to be out before the dawn," said Cadayle. "You must march with her."

Bransen nodded. He knew that, had pledged that, and, freed of his bout of self-pity and cynicism by the loving slap of Cadayle, intended to fight for Gwydre, for his family, with all his heart. He glanced back at Brother Giavno, though, and knew, too, that he had to come back here, had to go back through the gemstone and Jhesta Tu magic into the realm of the spirit to try to find the lost soul. His friendship to Giavno demanded that, of course, but so, too, did his sense that there was something more here, something important.

I am surprised that you came to Castle Pryd instead of the chapel," Bannagran remarked when Cormack, Milkeila, and their prisoner were marched into the laird's hall. "But I see that you come bearing a gift, at least."

"Demand free me!" said the man from Behr.

Bannagran flashed an amused grin and motioned to a guard, who promptly stepped over and smacked a mailed gauntlet into the side of the prisoner's head. Stubbornly, the warrior began to protest again, but Bannagran warned him to silence with a wagging finger.

"That is one of Ethelbert's hired assassins, I expect," the laird said.

"I believe his name is Wahloon," Cormack replied. "Else, that is a Behr word meaning something else."

"Wahloon, Hou-lei!" Wahloon said proudly, thrusting his chin forward.

Bannagran gave him a sidelong smirk and motioned to the guard, who smacked him again.

"You have seen the truth of the war, then," Bannagran said. "Laird Ethelbert cannot win, and so you have betrayed him to win my graces."

It wasn't a question, but stated as fact, and in a tone growing darker and more intense. Cormack glanced at Milkeila, who merely shrugged. When he turned back to Bannagran, he saw that the man was standing, towering over him, though Cormack was much taller, with a hateful look in his eyes.

"You think to impress me with treachery?" Bannagran fumed.

"Treachery?"

"That you wish to change your allegiance is for your own conscience, but to so deceive a laird—"

"No, Laird Bannagran!" Milkeila interrupted, and Cormack was glad that she did, for he could see that this ball of anger was gathering speed, rolling down the hill like an avalanche. And with Laird Bannagran facilitating that fall, surely it would prove no less deadly.

"We come as emissaries to promote the cause of alliance," Milkeila went on.

"Dame Gwydre beside Bannagran of Pryd," Cormack added, "and with the Order of Blessed Abelle supporting their cause against King Yeslnik."

"Emissaries with a gift," Bannagran said.

"Not gained through treachery," Cormack explained. "Not our own, in any case. This man and a companion attacked us on the road. If there was treachery afoot, it was—"

"Ethelbert's," Bannagran finished for him.

"Laird Ethelbert!" cried Wahloon, and that earned him another heavy slap that staggered him into Cormack.

On a motion from Bannagran, a pair of guards rushed up to the man and dragged him away.

"Laird Ethelbert tried to kill you, then?" Bannagran asked. "Perhaps he is not as fond of your Dame Gwydre as you believe."

"If it was Ethelbert," said Milkeila.

"That is one of his assassins, is it not?"

"It is," Cormack replied. "But it is senseless for Laird Ethelbert to try to kill us, even as we support his cause—likely his only hope—to Bannagran of Pryd."

"Then what?"

"I know not," said Cormack.

"Ethelbert's court divided?" Bannagran asked, and Cormack could only hold up his empty hands.

Bannagran gave a wicked little chuckle. "We will learn soon enough," he promised, and he waved the guards to drag Wahloon to the dungeons.

"Laird Bannagran, I protest!" said Master Reandu, coming in the door just as Wahloon was being taken out.

Bannagran dropped his face into his hands and sighed.

"They come to us as emissaries, under a flag of truce!" Reandu continued, rushing forward to Cormack's side.

"Truly, he squeezes the blood from my heart," Bannagran whispered to Cormack and Milkeila just before the sputtering Reandu arrived on the spot.

"You remember Cormack and his wife, Milkeila," Bannagran said before Reandu could launch into another diatribe. Reandu glanced at the couple and still seemed ready to erupt, but his expression soon enough changed to one of curiosity as he clearly saw that the two weren't bound.

"We brought the assassin in as a prisoner," Cormack explained.

Master Reandu turned his curious expression to Bannagran.

"It is a long tale they can tell to you at your chapel," Bannagran said, and he waved for more attendants to escort them all out.

"Laird, I beg you to reconsider your course," Cormack pleaded. "Dame Gwydre is noble in heart and mind. The cause of the Order of Blessed Abelle is just."

His voice rose as he was pulled back from the throne.

"My laird, please," Cormack called.

"My course is to kill powries, monk," Bannagran called back at him. "There is no course more just than that!" To Reandu he added, "Keep them in your chapel. I will call for you shortly, as soon as I have spoken to the prisoner."

"Spoken to?" the monk asked suspiciously, for he had seen Bannagran's dungeon.

"With all the respect due an assassin, I promise," said the laird, and before Reandu could answer, another guard, acting on Bannagran's wave, shut the heavy oaken door in his face.

As soon as his spirit entered the realm of Brother Giavno, Bransen found himself enmeshed in a spinning and confusing jumble of opposing thoughts and wants and emotions. It wasn't an internal argument, of the kind every man experienced, and not based in simple puzzlement or torn loyalties

or fear of unexpected consequences. No, this jumble was more akin to swirling thoughts and demands, unrelated to and seemingly unaware of contradictory notions moving right beside them, even merging with them.

Chaos, Bransen thought. Pure and unblemished chaos. He tried to search
further but found himself distracted, and when he tried to examine the distraction, he found himself distracted again, in an entirely new direction.

Bransen rushed back through the soul stone portal, back into his own
body, and opened his eyes. He stood and rubbed his face and shook his
head.

"What do you know?" Brother Pinower asked, startling Bransen, who was
unaware that the monk had entered the dark room. "What did you see?"

Bransen took a deep breath and tried to formulate some cogent response.
What had he seen? He had sensed the identity of Brother Giavno, a man he
knew fairly well from their travels in Alpinador and Vanguard, inside the
tumultuous swirl of discordant thoughts.

Images of blowing desert sands and dome-topped shining marble structures, pink and white and some covered in gold, flashed in Bransen's mind—
little specks of the southern kingdom of Behr, he knew, for he had seen the
same type of architecture, on a far lesser scale, in Ethelbert dos Entel.

"Had Brother Giavno traveled to Behr?" he asked aloud, though he was
speaking to himself.

"To Alpinador but never south of Pollcree that I have heard," Brother
Pinower replied, and again his voice somewhat startled Bransen.

"Spiritually," Bransen clarified. "Is it possible that he flew his soul all the
way to the desert lands?"

Brother Pinower's face screwed up for a moment. He shook his head but
then merely shrugged. "He was not assigned to any such thing. His mission
this night was to find Cormack and Milkeila and learn, perhaps, of their progress. Nothing more."

Bransen considered the words and thought of the last time he had met
with Cormack and Milkeila. They accompanied people who would know of
such sights as those he had found inside the spinning memories within Brother
Giavno. Was it possible that there truly was another entity trapped inside the
mind of the mad monk? He stared at the troubled man across from him.
Giavno was asleep, but it was far from a contented respite. He trembled and
shook, occasionally cried out and waved his arms defensively.

"Dueling spirits," Bransen whispered.

"How so?"

Bransen turned to Pinower. "Or pieces of consciousness," Bransen tried to explain. "They fight for control of the man's mind—one other consciousness at least—and that battle manifests itself as Brother Giavno's madness."

"How could this be? Is it the mind of another brother who was out spirit walking? Surely not Cormack!"

"No," Bransen said repeatedly. "I believe that Brother Giavno possessed someone—likely someone far in the south—and he has inadvertently taken a piece of that person back with him to St. Mere Abelle. Both of them trapped in his one mind, vying for supremacy, though they likely are not even aware of the other." Bransen's face lit up with cognition. "Perhaps that is always the way with the madness that sometimes results with spirit walking. In the act of possession, you are aware of your dalliance, and surely your target understands and recoils immediately from the intrusion. And so it is a furious and desperate battle of willpower, but one with singular identities. This, brother, this is true madness, an oblivious mingling of two minds, two spirits, two souls. I cannot—"

He stopped as Brother Pinower made the sign of the evergreen, and even in the dim light of predawn, he could see the blood drain from the man's face.

"Does the mind that is still Giavno know anything about the progress in the south?" Pinower meekly asked after a short pause.

Bransen glanced back at the man.

"Dame Gwydre will be out within an hour," Brother Pinower reminded.

Bransen nodded and sat down again beside the dreaming and restless monk.

"No, Bransen!" Brother Pinower scolded. "You came forth in fear. Do not risk your own clarity again in the madness that is Brother Giavno!"

"I know what I will find in there now," Bransen calmly answered, and he flashed a confident smile.

A smile that was a complete façade, for Bransen was truly afraid of entering the swirl of discordant and jarring sensibilities.

But he had to.

CHAPTER 17

The Angry Young Laird

They swept down from the high ground, across the grassy banks, crying out for vengeance, waving their weapons, and banging their shields. In the small town before and below them, where every man, woman, and child lay dead or dying, threescore powries adjusted their bloody caps, glowing with fresh blood, and grinned wickedly.

To the side of the rise and the main charge, Prince Milwellis stood in his chariot, expecting this fight to go as had the previous two. His losses would be significant, he expected—perhaps as many as two hundred men—but in the end, the powries would be eliminated.

"There is fear in their eyes," one horseman nearby remarked, and everyone knew he was speaking of the Palmaristown garrison and not the unshakable dwarves.

"Hold steady," Milwellis said to all. "Our footmen will not flee the field." Many nods came back at him, for that was the crux of their strategy this day, as in the previous fights. The footmen, peasants mostly and expendable, would swarm the town, flushing out all of the enemies, and only when their sheer numbers facilitated a powrie retreat would Milwellis and his veteran riders and charioteers sweep in from the sides to claim ultimate and final victory. They had a thousand men descending upon this hamlet; the powries might kill them fifteen to one and still be massacred in the end.

The end, Milwellis was cunning enough to understand and callous enough to accept, was all that mattered.

Sounds of battle joined; the ring of iron and bronze and the screams of pain and terror and hatred filled the air. The horses nickered and pawed the ground in nervous anticipation, proper extensions of their riders and drivers, Milwellis knew. No matter how many battles he fought, no matter how many enemies he defeated, this prebattle feeling—the sweat, the churning stomach, the fear—never changed. Milwellis thought of his first fight, a skirmish with a tribe of wild savages across the river from Palmaristown. The river was deeper and calmer on that western bank, more favorable to the larger ships being constructed, and his father had proposed building a second set of docks and a new section of the city over there. Also, the high ground directly across from the current Palmaristown seemed a perfect gateway to the great trees coveted by the shipbuilders and the open and fertile lands that could make Palmaristown the first city of Honce instead of the second.

A very young Milwellis had led that expedition, though in truth, the prince now had to admit to himself, he had been no more than a figurehead and, perhaps, the entire mission had been designed simply to enhance Milwellis's standing in the city proper. The "battle" on that day really wasn't much of a fight, and not a man was killed on either side before the savages had fled into the forest, but Milwellis keenly remembered his fear and the sweat. He had thought those a sure sign of his cowardice and failure, but to his surprise, his father had assured him that any man who did not experience that discomfort before a fight wasn't as brave as he was stupid.

An especially piercing shriek rent the air and pulled the prince out of his contemplation, and he chuckled quietly, for he seemed to mentally replay that first fight before every impending battle.

"Powries out to the west," the spotter in the trees above informed them. "They're breaking."

"And sails?" Milwellis called up to him.

"North," the man replied. The prince nodded, for the trap was in place.

"Ride with the smell of burning Palmaristown in your noses!" Milwellis called to his men. "Ride with the sight of ruined buildings and murdered children in your eyes! Ride with the blow of the horn of Panlamaris in your ears and know this day that these dwarves we trample under hoof and under wheel will never again spill the blood of our families!"

A great cheer went up, and horses strained against the holds of their disciplined riders and drivers.

"Hold, Milwellis!" came a call from the back. The prince turned to see a soldier rushing toward him, waving his arms frantically. Behind the man, coming at a slower pace, marched Harcourt and some others.

The leading soldier gasped for breath as he verily fell against the side of Milwellis's chariot. "General Harcourt bids you to send forth your legion as planned," he sputtered. "But for you to hold and await his arrival."

"What foolishness is this?" Milwellis countered, and he glanced at the riders around him, all staring incredulously at the disheveled courier. Milwellis was making his reputation as a leader who actually led the way into battle, after all, and such courage had earned him the great respect of his legions. "Stand aside or be run down!"

"No, my laird," the man said, and Milwellis growled and took up his reins as if to proceed, but then held back as the word "laird" registered. He turned a shocked expression at Harcourt's courier.

All around and behind Milwellis, horses began to trot and chariots to roll as General Harcourt, rushing forward as fast as his old legs would carry him, prodded the horsemen and charioteers to begin their charge.

"What did you call me?" Milwellis said to the man, who blanched and seemed as if he was about to faint.

By the time Harcourt reached Milwellis's side, most of the cavalry was away, thundering along their predetermined course to intercept the powrie retreat. Milwellis still stood there, staring at the courier, unblinking, his mouth hanging open.

He was still in that pose and posture when Harcourt finally managed to join him. "Milwellis, my friend, ill news from the north," he said.

"My father?" Milwellis mouthed quietly, still staring at the courier.

"His force was overrun by Dame Gwydre," Harcourt replied. He reached up to put a hand on Milwellis's shoulder, but the prince shrugged him off. "My friend, my laird," Harcourt said, "Laird Panlamaris of Palmaristown is slain."

Milwellis growled and roared and plucked a spear from the bucket of his chariot, and only Harcourt's fast reaction stopped him from throwing it into the courier!

"No!" Milwellis roared. "This cannot be! That damned witch of Vanguard!"

Harcourt motioned for a couple of the men who had accompanied him to hustle the terrified courier away and turned his full attention to the volatile young man. "You are the Laird of Palmaristown now," he said, his voice mostly calm but with a measure of consternation in it. "You cannot behave in such a way. The men must fear you but they must love you as well, or you will not receive their finest efforts."

"They are peasants, and I will do with them as I please."

"These are soldiers, my laird. Not simply peasants. Soldiers who run and ride under your banner into the lines of powries and Ethelbert's traitors. My laird, they loved your father. Their pain at hearing his death will be little less than your own."

Milwellis began to argue, but when he looked at Harcourt he noticed the moisture rimming the old general's eyes. Harcourt had been by Panlamaris's side for decades, for longer than Milwellis had been alive, and never once had the man shown anything but love for Panlamaris.

"Pray offer my apology to the courier," Milwellis said somberly. "Then discharge the man back to Palmaristown with a bag of coin for his troubles."

"Wisely done, young laird."

"And now, get you to your team. Let us ride in together to bring ruin to these filthy dwarves, that I might turn my army back to Chapel Abelle and exact revenge upon the witch of Vanguard."

"Your safety is paramount for the next few days, my laird," said Harcourt. "The city cannot lose two beloved lairds so near in time to each other."

"Your concern is touching," Milwellis responded with obvious sarcasm. "Truly. Now get to your team, and let us slaughter some powrie marauders."

Harcourt nodded and called for his chariot.

"Sails north," Bikelbrin said to Mcwigik, the pair rolling along as fast as their short and bandy legs could carry them. Their caps shone bright this day, and three of Milwellis's soldiers had been taken down between them, although they argued with every stride about who struck the killing blow on the last human. But while powries could be as savage as any creature on Corona and as stubbornly brave as the demon dactyls, they weren't outright suicidal . . . usually.

"And lots o' them," Mcwigik replied. "Won't be easy getting out."

"Worth trying, even?" asked Bikelbrin. "Sure that our hearts'll be harder to find at the bottom of a river."

"Ye're wanting a stake up yer bum, then?"

Bikelbrin just sighed. "Last kill was me own."

"Ye hit a corpse," Mcwigik retorted. "Too slow with yer hatchet."

"Yach, but when we're done killin' the fools here, know that I'll spill yer own blood, Mcwigik o' Cingarron Lea."

And there it was, spoken openly, as clear an admission that they were surely doomed as any powrie would ever utter.

Mcwigik's breath blew out then, and he let out a little yelp and staggered forward.

"Spear!" Bikelbrin explained when he glanced his friend's way, to see the shaft of a javelin dragging behind Mcwigik. His eyes widened as he looked past Mcwigik, and Mcwigik, too, turned about to note a chariot bearing down on them, the red-haired man driving it, all bedecked in bejeweled shining bronze armor and hoisting another javelin to throw.

Mcwigik was flying then, thrown out of the way by his friend Bikelbrin. He bounced sidelong over the banking to tumble and bounce through the grass, cursing with every painful twist. He landed facedown in the mud by the riverbank, half in and half out of the flowing water.

He tried to get up.

Above him, he heard Bikelbrin gasp in pain.

Mcwigik struggled to his knees and elbows.

Above him, horses whinnied furiously, their hooves pounding the ground like thunder, and a shriek from one of the beasts told Mcwigik that his friend had gotten in a strike or two. Bikelbrin grunted again and cursed and Mcwigik heard the chariot rock and bounce as it passed over him. Then it pulled up short, and Bikelbrin cursed some more.

"Come on, ye blood-haired son of a fisherman's whore!" the powrie cried, his voice thick with pain.

Mcwigik knew his friend was dying. He forced himself up higher and reached back, grasping the spear shaft with one hand. He closed his eyes and cried out as Bikelbrin shouted his final curse and yanked the spear free, dropping it into the dark water beside him. He tried to stand but couldn't get higher than one knee, and when he lifted his head upright, the world began to spin before him.

He saw his enemy, though, through the dizzying blur. The red-haired human approached in a straightforward and fearless manner, sword in hand and dripping blood.

Bikelbrin's blood, Mcwigik realized.

The powrie threw his short iron sword, and the man yelped and stumbled back. He didn't fall, though, and when he straightened again, the side of his face covered in blood, he began his determined march against the now unarmed and badly weakened Mcwigik.

"Yach, but ye're a boot-stomped frog!" Mcwigik said, his sentence truncated by the heavy, two-handed swing of a broadsword.

He didn't feel the water as he splashed facedown into the Masur Delaval.

The last thing he heard was a distant human voice calling out, "Your face, my laird!" to his killer.

H old your course," Harcourt whispered repeatedly to Milwellis over the next few days. Scouts returned from all parts, assuring the new Laird of Palmaristown that there was no enemy force congregating anywhere near his already battered and wounded city.

Milwellis grimaced with every repetition, always looking north along the river, always looking home. "He should come forth," he replied several times, referring to the King of Honce, who, by all accounts, was holed up in his walled city, surrounded by tens of thousands of soldiers.

"His hesitance is your gain," Harcourt answered on a foggy morning along the riverbank. "We are more than halfway to Delaval City from Palmaristown and have swept the land and the river clear of powries through all of that populated region."

"The people sing praise for the King of Honce," Milwellis reminded.

"They sing louder for the savior Laird of Palmaristown. For you. And King Yeslnik hears those songs, do not doubt. Your march has been as brilliant as courageous, and all the folk are taking notice. You'll hear few songs to Bannagran now and many to Milwellis."

"King Yeslnik will come to see me as a rival," Milwellis remarked.

"He will come to realize that you are his only hope."

"And yet, this Bannagran peasant controls more of his army than I."

"Where is Bannagran?" Harcourt asked. "The threat is here, the bloody caps, and Bannagran has not arrived on the field. King Yeslnik values his own safety above all else, and you, Laird Milwellis, secure that. With every victory you strike, with every powrie force massacred and drowned, Palmaristown stands taller."

"My father was defeated by Yeslnik's enemies," Milwellis stated flatly.

"All the more reason for you to hold to your course and secure the whole of the Masur Delaval," replied Harcourt, and his voice did crack a bit at the painful reminder. "You must climb upon your father's broad shoulders and stand taller than he. Your actions now, for Honce and not just for Palmaristown, secure your place as the second of Yeslnik. All the coast for Palmaristown, from our city across the gulf and down the Mantis Arm all the way to Ethelbert dos Entel. That was your father's dream, and will be your reality."

Milwellis stared at loyal Harcourt for a long while, truly appreciating the man. He knew that Harcourt was hurting badly—as badly as he was—by the loss of Laird Panlamaris. He knew that Harcourt, like he, wanted nothing more than to turn back for Palmaristown and then march east to Chapel Abelle to repay the traitors. But Harcourt never once wavered, his eyes and words and vision locked on the mission at hand, solidly for the benefit of Palmaristown and, now that he was laird, for the benefit of Milwellis.

"We come into lands where Bannagran should arrive," Milwellis said. "Narrow the line nearer to the riverbank and let us increase our pace. If any powries have moved farther inland, let Bannagran have them. I wish to see Delaval City before the week's end."

Harcourt considered the orders for a moment, then nodded and smiled at the young laird. "Wisely decided," he said.

"King Yeslnik will see the flag of Palmaristown before he spies the banner of the peasants of Pryd," Milwellis assured his general. "He'll be knowing who it was that kept him safe in his high walls."

Harcourt's smile was genuine. His heart stung for the loss of his old friend Panlamaris, but it lifted with hope anew at the cunning and ambition of the man's red-haired son. Laird Panlamaris was dead, but Palmaristown would know a stronger and brighter day.

Laird Milwellis would rise now, above all others. Of that, Harcourt was confident.

CHAPTER 18

Daring the Consequences

Bransen felt as if he were sifting through a tangle of roots, as if two willows had joined in battle, their supple appendages whipping and wrapping and twisting until it became impossible to know where one tree ended and the other began. For such was the tangle within poor Brother Giavno's mind.

Every now and then, Bransen could get a sense as to which branch belonged to which tree, Giavno or Ishat (he knew the man's name to be Ishat), but even then the challenge for his disembodied spirit remained, for he, too, was now a willow in the wind, trying to control his own thoughts, trying to keep his own supple mental appendages from grappling with and being entwined with those of Giavno and Ishat. He knew what he wanted to do, though; if he could manage to help Giavno regain a sense of self, a foothold in time and space and a realization that this was his body and place, perhaps the monk would have a fighting chance of expelling the man from Behr.

Bransen had no sense of time in here, for the thoughts piled one above the previous in rapid succession. Most of those moments were spent in mental dodging, pulling away before being caught and held. Every now and then, however, Bransen did find a distinctive thread, a piece of consciousness he knew to be Brother Giavno. On those occasions, he silently screamed at the man to stand firm, to know his sense of self, and to recognize that this was, indeed, his place. And as the surprisingly clear streams of Giavno's consciousness flitted and dispersed, Bransen always warned him that there was no other place to be found, that if he could not win here, he was doomed to nothingness.

Bransen opened wide his eyes and fell back to the side, sliding right off the chair and barely catching himself before staggering several steps. He stood up straight, gasping and trying to find some easy rhythm to his breathing, reminding himself repeatedly of who he was and where he was and what he had just, of necessity, done.

A long while passed as Bransen just stood, deciphering some of the information he had come away with. He was truly surprised to realize that he had learned so much, for when it was being imparted he had barely been aware of it!

He knew of Cormack and Milkeila's latest mission to Bannagran and of the attack by the Hou-lei assassins. Brother Giavno had saved his friends in the south, surely. Giavno had sacrificed himself for the sake of his old friend Cormack. Bransen had felt the intersecting notions of altruism, of greater good, and of compensation within the mad monk, for he knew the tale of Giavno and Cormack and of how Giavno had betrayed Cormack to the sentence of Father De Guilbe in faraway Alpinador. Indeed, Giavno had been the one to carry out the sentence, whipping Cormack nearly to death.

"You are redeemed," Bransen said to the monk, who sat across from him, his head lolling stupidly from side to side. Bransen glanced out the window and noted the sun. Gwydre and Pinower were long out of St. Mere Abelle, moving east along the southern shore of the Gulf of Corona to an assigned spot where they were to meet up with Dawson McKeege and the Vanguard flotilla.

The thought of saying goodbye to Cadayle yet again stung Bransen as he considered his course, but his wife had made her own feelings on this very clear, after all. It was their war, too, hers and Bransen's, and a war worth fighting and worth winning.

"Fight well, Brother Giavno," Bransen said, and he respectfully bowed to the monk and rushed from the room.

"You, as well," Giavno replied, though not loud enough for Bransen to hear. The monk blinked his eyes a few times, taking in his surroundings.

"St. Mere Abelle?" he said, or started to say, but then Ishat attacked again in his mind and his head rolled and he began to babble, and all the world became again a knot of supple appendages and discordant thoughts.

It was a kiss of promise, a kiss of hope and desperation, a longing for quiet times ahead—but, Cadayle insisted, quiet times under the rule of a goodly queen.

"Bannagran is key," Bransen said when at last their lips parted and he moved back a finger's breadth from his pretty wife.

"He seems uninterested," Cadayle replied, for Bransen had told her of the news from the south.

Bransen smiled. "I know him. I know who he is."

Cadayle backed off a bit more and looked at Bransen with puzzlement.

"I know his fear," Bransen said. "That is the key to it all, for all of us. Fear is the emotion that most guides our actions."

Cadayle appeared unconvinced.

"In the Book of Jhest, the ancient wisdom of the Jhesta Tu insists that it is fear of death, of that greatest unknown, that guides most lives. Whether moved to goodly deeds or to heinous ones—as with the Samhaists toward your mother—it is that overriding fear of nothingness that allows a man of good heart to rot. Bannagran watched your mother put into the sack with the snake. He allowed it. Master Reandu allowed it."

"They could not stop it," Cadayle replied.

"Half the townsfolk of Pryd watched it and cheered it and allowed it! Perhaps some of them thought it justice, though Callen's crime was hardly worthy of such an awful retribution. Nay, most endured it and embraced it because they were afraid, not of reprisal at that time, but of eternal damnation or nothingness had they not supported the evil Bernivvigar. That was his hold, and as he commanded death itself, so his hold grew stronger."

"You think Laird Bannagran, the Bear of Honce, the greatest champion alive, is afraid of dying?" Cadayle asked skeptically.

Bransen half nodded, half shrugged. "Not exactly that," he replied. "But in many ways, the hero Bannagran is less brave than Laird Delaval or Laird Ethelbert, or even the idiot Yeslnik."

"Yeslnik cowers and shrieks like a child when threatened," Cadayle argued. "Bannagran smiles and attacks."

"Without responsibility," said Bransen. "For that is his fear."

Cadayle spent a long while digesting that and trying to make some sense of it, but in the end, she just conceded the point and asked, "And you believe that you can turn him to our cause?"

Bransen thought, Or to his own, but he kept that to himself and answered, "If I cannot, then the best we can hope for is a retreat to Vanguard, where we will all be so far away that Yeslnik will not think it worth the trouble to pursue us. Even if I do convince Bannagran that our cause is correct and just, Yeslnik holds the upper hand."

Cadayle smiled and came forward, tightening her hug on her husband. "Nay," she whispered. "Gwydre does." She kissed Branson softly. "For Dame Gwyd—Queen Gwydre has my husband at her side, and woe to any who dare to challenge the Highwayman."

She kissed him again, and again, and it seemed to last forever while it was happening, a deep and inviting and warm blackness. But when it ended, all too soon, Bransen felt as if hardly a heartbeat had passed, and, truly, he never wanted to leave Cadayle's side ever again. He let his hand slide down as they embraced, to feel her belly, to feel his child in her womb. What an extraordinary year it had been!

When Bransen rushed out of St. Mere Abelle's front gate a short while later, he understood clearly the stakes in this dangerous game he played: the promise of happiness weighed against the potential of utter ruin.

Just outside, he fell into the malachite again, lessening his weight, using those giant running strides, lifting and floating and propelling himself past any obstacles to cover a tremendous amount of ground in short order. He focused on this task, speed, most of all, finding the limits and balance of the gemstone magic to perfectly complement his powerful strides, with minimum physical and mental effort.

He felt like he could run like this, effortlessly, the leagues rolling out behind him, for all the day long.

Gwydre and her force had left before the dawn, Bransen had exited the gates of St. Mere Abelle with the sun already low in the western sky, and still, his steps greatly exaggerated and elongated by the gemstone magic, he came in sight of Gwydre's camp before darkness fell.

The soldiers and the monks greeted him warmly, even by a round of cheering at one point, and it struck him in this moment, in this mood, with this plan, poignantly. A self-deprecating chuckle escaped him as he came in sight of Dame Gwydre—and no doubt, she viewed it as his typical humility in the face of public applause.

But Bransen wasn't thinking himself unworthy at that moment, he was laughing at his inability to accept the role such accolades had afforded him in all the weeks and months before. He was the Highwayman, a hero to the people, not because of his physical prowess, though that was surely a vehicle for his ascent, but because he had taken up their cause against the injustices of callous lairds. And he had not been able to bring himself to accept such accolades, not out of humility, but out of cowardice, for to admit them was to take responsibility for them. To admit the cheers was to accept responsibility for the man who was cheering.

"How fares Brother Giavno?" Brother Pinower asked him as he approached Gwydre.

"He is in there, fighting," Bransen replied. "I tried to unravel enough of his thoughts to allow him a grasp of identity. But the entanglements are vast, I fear, and only Brother Giavno can truly find his way through the knots.

"But I did garner much information from him," Bransen announced, turning his attention to Gwydre.

"Good news from the south?" she asked hopefully.

"Possibly," Bransen answered. "And certainly I learned of critical developments that teeter on the edge of victory and disaster. I have come for you," he added, holding out his hand.

"St. Mere Abelle?" she asked, obviously not understanding.

Bransen shook his head. "South."

"Dawson will dock in two days, my army behind him."

"There is no time for delay, and no need for your army at this time. Indeed, in this instance, bringing your army would likely do no more than ensure its destruction."

"What is this about, Bransen?" Brother Pinower asked.

"It is about Bannagran of Pryd and about Cormack and Milkeila and their valiant efforts to turn him from the side of King Yeslnik."

"Bannagran has turned?" Gwydre asked, and Pinower sucked in his breath in desperate hope.

"No," Bransen answered. "But I think he will."

Gwydre looked at him curiously.

"You would take our leader to Bannagran's court when he has not yet deserted the ranks of King Yeslnik?" Brother Pinower asked incredulously. "When he has not proclaimed a truce or allegiance to Dame Gwydre? A fine prize you would deliver!"

"Yes," Bransen answered. He turned to look directly into Gwydre's eyes. "Yes," he repeated. "I will protect you, there and back again. I know Laird Bannagran, and, for all of our battles, I know that he is a man of honor. He will accept our offer of parley, honestly and honorably. And I believe that when he sees the truth of our cause and of our queen, he will recognize the folly that is Yeslnik. Now is our moment."

"She cannot go," Brother Pinower declared. "I have been charged with her safety and I will not allow it."

"I went to the glaciers of Alpinador to do battle with the most dangerous man in the world on your behalf," Bransen reminded Gwydre. "I delivered the head of Ancient Badden to you, for your sake and for that of your people. And I support your cause now—you know that."

"I do not question your loyalty."

"It is your judgment we question," Brother Pinower added.

Bransen flashed Gwydre a wry little smile. "I am correct in this. I know

Bannagran. I have a message for him, and that message is you, and I will deliver it with a mirror."

"You speak in riddles!" Brother Pinower protested, but Dame Gwydre held up a hand to silence him.

"You trusted me to win your war," Bransen reminded her.

Dame Gwydre took his hand, and Brother Pinower protested loudly.

"How long will we be away?" Gwydre asked.

"A matter of days," Bransen promised.

"Pryd Town is a week's hard march from here!" the agitated monk argued. "At least!"

Bransen winked at him. "You should learn how to better manipulate your gemstones," he said, leading Gwydre away.

"Are you ready to fly, milady?"

"Fly?"

"Well, perhaps 'bounce' would be a better description."

"Bounce?" Gwydre repeated again, as Bransen fell into the malachite and transferred its levitation powers to her as well. Still holding fast to her hand, he leaped away, soaring ten strides from Brother Pinower, touching down lightly, and springing away once more, an even farther leap.

All witnessing the deerlike movements gasped, some giggled, and more than one, Pinower included, made the sign of the evergreen.

By the time Dame Gwydre caught her breath, the campfires of her forces were long out of sight. Bransen had asked her if she was ready to fly, and she thought that a perfect word for this experience. For she barely touched down at the end of each stride and felt weightless even then. Away they flew, another ten long strides in one great bound.

The moon rose in the east, a cloudless night, and still they ran on. It rose up above them, just south of their position, hanging in the air before them and dulling the multitude of stars with its glow, and still they bounded across the miles.

"How far have we come?" Gwydre asked Bransen when finally he stopped, along a line of thick pines that offered shelter.

"A long way," he replied.

"Are you not weary?"

"It is late, and I need to sleep, yes, but the effort is remarkably light. Blessed, indeed, are the gemstones of Abelle. Each step is easy . . . and far."

"I could move my armies across the miles, surround King Yeslnik," the Dame of Vanguard mused.

Bransen grinned at her. "Our movement is as much a matter of my Jhesta

Tu training as the gemstone magic," he said. "I doubt you would find five brothers, nay two, who could so manipulate the malachite to travel as we have."

"Your humility is endearing," Gwydre said sarcastically, but she was smiling back at Bransen. He bowed.

"When will we arrive in Pryd Town?" Gwydre asked.

"Probably not tomorrow, but the next day, I expect."

Dame Gwydre nodded and chewed her lip.

"Bannagran will honor a flag of parley," Bransen assured her. "As he did with Ethelbert."

"He refused Ethelbert, you said. He mocked the man and sent him away with a promise that he would soon tear down the walls of Ethelbert's beloved city."

"All true."

"He is going to dismiss me out of hand . . . if we are fortunate."

"It is possible," Bransen replied. Gwydre looked up at him curiously with obvious disappointment, letting Bransen know that she was hoping he would disagree with her. But he didn't. He just smiled and shrugged.

"You are irascible," Dame Gwydre said.

"Sleep well, milady," said Bransen. "We have a long . . . bounce tomorrow." He held up a low-hanging branch, inviting her into the cavelike hollow beneath it.

"Out here, under the moon and the stars," Gwydre said, waving him away and turning from the pine tree shelter. She moved to a grassy patch and lay down on her back. She folded her fingers behind her head and seemed so very much at ease.

Bransen just stared at her in admiration. There was so much simple truth about Dame Gwydre. He thought of Bannagran, he looked at Gwydre, and he was certain that the Laird of Pryd would have a harder time sending her away than he had Ethelbert.

They were out again soon after dawn, moving even faster than on the previous leg of the journey. For now, the sun bright in the sky above, Bransen didn't need to waste any of his magical energy on the cat's-eye agate, the gem which allowed him to run in the dark. He could plan his steps better and— even more important—plan his landings better. Also, Dame Gwydre was less a passenger this day and far more involved in coordinating her movements with Bransen's. She laughed to him that this journey reminded her of games she used to play as a young girl, skipping and dancing.

In the early afternoon, Bransen had a good idea of where they were exactly, recognizing the small town just three days' normal march north of Pryd. They crossed fields now, open and level, and heard the cries of onlookers.

They just ignored those commotions and kept right on bounding along, knowing that none of the concerned citizens could hope to catch up to them.

They ended earlier that night than on the previous, for Bransen knew that they were but a couple of hours north of Pryd Town, and he didn't want to go in under cover of darkness.

"Nor do I wish us exhausted," he explained to Gwydre as they settled in under the stars once more. "We must be sharp and rested for our parley with Bannagran, for convincing him will be no easy feat."

"But you think it possible?"

"If I didn't, I would never have so inconvenienced you." He tossed her a wink and lay back on his natural bedding.

"Bransen, why?" Gwydre asked him before he had even closed his eyes. He sat up to his elbows.

"Why?"

"Why this change in you, so full of hope and determination?"

"I told you when I returned with Badden's head—"

"That was a long time ago," Gwydre interrupted. "Not so long in months, perhaps, but ages in terms of what we have experienced since. And even then, when I saw that you had come around to the notion of a just cause and a greater good, you were not nearly as animated as this warrior I see before me now."

"You disapprove?"

"Hardly that!"

Bransen laughed. "Three good women, Dame Gwydre," he answered.

"Your wonderful wife, surely."

"And her mother."

"Dawson would agree."

"And you," Bransen added.

Dame Gwydre did not blush, but neither did she reply.

"The difference between you and Yeslnik, particularly regarding the lives of those you would rule, is too great for even stubborn Bransen Garibond to dismiss," Bransen explained. "When winter fell deep in Pellinor, you brought your subjects into the warmth of your home. You fed them and gathered wood for them and made sure that they were safe. In such a state, I expect a hungry Yeslnik would eat his subjects."

"Bransen, no!"

"He would feed them to his wife, at least," the Highwayman replied. His grin disappeared after a moment, his expression reflecting the seriousness of the situation. "Honce will be united under a single ruler. Of that, I have no doubt. The brutality of the war between Delaval and Ethelbert has assured that outcome—few holdings could hope to stand on their own any longer, even without the deep resentments that have been fostered from land to land and laird to laird. If Yeslnik is king, his rule will be marred by almost continual war, for the people will suffer and the lairds will face uprisings. Even the church will turn against the common folk, for Father De Guilbe, I assure you, is an unpleasant and wicked man."

"I have seen enough of him to know the truth of your words. But I assure you that such is not the case with Father Premujon."

Bransen nodded his agreement, then lowered his gaze, considered his own words, and shrugged. "This is worth the fight," he said quietly. He looked up at Dame Gwydre. "This is worth dying for."

CHAPTER 19

King's Favor

Powries!" Yeslnik screamed. He threw a pillow across the room. "Always it is something to deny me my glory! Can they not all just accept God's proclamation and let me have my due?"

"Soon, my love," said Queen Olym, who sat at her vanity powdering her cheeks and nose.

"It is unpleasant!" Yeslnik whined.

Olym dropped her powder box to the vanity with a clunk and swung her ample form about to better view her husband. "It always will be," she said. "There will always be a powrie, or a peasant, or a nasty laird to cause mischief. That is the way of it, and that is why you have Bannagran and Milwellis. You need not bother with the details of order, just the luxuries that order brings to you—to us—as King and Queen of Honce. So there are powries running the river coast, killing peasants. Oh dear, but it pains my heart!" She fluttered her eyes and mockingly grasped her chest, but came out of the pose with a stern and fixed look. "Why do I care and why does King Yeslnik? The silly dwarves cannot harm us behind these walls. I did hope to summer in Palmaristown this year, but the city is still damaged anyway, and next year will suffice."

Yeslnik gave a deep breath and slouched his shoulders, his whole body relaxing. He walked over to his wife as she turned back to her large mirror and retrieved her powder box. He grasped her thick flesh at the base of her neck and began kneading it with his fingers. The woman paused in her powdering.

"You always know what to say to make it better," Yeslnik said quietly, bringing his lips to Olym's ear and nuzzling there as he finished speaking.

Olym went back to powdering. "Yes, my king, and you always seem to need reminding," she answered somewhat distantly.

"I should be quick and away this morning," he said. Olym's eyes widened, and she looked at his reflection in the mirror curiously.

"I shan't allow Bannagran and Milwellis to have all the fun in killing the little beasts," said Yeslnik, and as a smile widened on Olym's face, he added, "I do so love the smell of blood on my sword."

For a large woman, Queen Olym could move with speed and grace, and she did so then, rising and spinning out of her seat to bull-rush Yeslnik half-way across the room where they tumbled together onto the cushiony bed.

Sometime later, King Yeslnik ran along the wall of Castle Pryd, excited by the news. He came to the northeast tower and took the stairs to and three at a time, finally gaining the roof, where his lookouts greeted him, pointing excitedly to the northeast, where a large encampment could be seen just off the riverbank.

"Laird Bannagran has come," Yeslnik said with a wide smile.

"No, my king," a lookout corrected, and Yeslnik snapped a glare over him.

"It is Prince Milwellis of Palmaristown, King," another man explained. "He has swept the riverbank clear of powries as his fleet has scoured the river." The man pointed upriver, directing Yeslnik's gaze to the flotilla of warships barely visible in the foggy distance.

"Milwellis?" Yeslnik murmured, trying to make sense of the distance and the trials the man must have conquered to have come so far so fast. "Prepare my coach, prepare my army! We march this day!"

He rushed from the tower, and what a glorious morning it had been! He could hardly wait to tell Olym of the news, and he wondered if he had enough time before the arrangements for departure were completed to enjoy the company of his wife once more.

He didn't, for his army, bottled up inside of Delaval City all these days while reports of powries swept in from all along the Masur Delaval, was more than ready to march. The eastern gates of Delaval City swung wide and the grand parade flowed forth, endless lines of horses and chariots and marching footmen. In their midst rode Yeslnik and Olym, inside a gilded and armored coach, surrounded by the finest horsemen of the king's army, their bronze spear tips shining brightly in the morning light. Right behind that group rode Father De Guilbe in a coach no less decorated, monks flanking him on either side, chanting with every step.

As they neared the encampment, soldiers all about buzzing that it was indeed Milwellis, whispering with awe that he had come so far and so fast and had so thoroughly dispatched the wretched powries, Yeslnik bade his coach-men to drive on harder. Before the sun had crested overhead, Yeslnik found himself seated beside his wife on the top of his ornamental coach, where a pair of thrones had been set. From on high they watched Milwellis's approach, the man riding up in a fine chariot, General Harcourt driving a second by his side.

"I would not have thought you could travel so far south so fast, battling powries along the way," Yeslnik bade his general as Milwellis and Harcourt dismounted and handed their reins to attendants.

"They are insignificant gnats to the army of Palmaristown," Milwellis answered as he arrived at the side of the coach, before and below the king and queen. Father De Guilbe moved up to stand beside him, offering a slight nod of greeting. "We slaughtered them every step and left them rotting by the riverbank, or"—he glanced to his right, out toward the Masur Delaval and the many warships shadowing his march—"drowned in the dark and cold waters."

Milwellis again glanced all around, hiding a smile, it seemed. "My king," he asked, "do you think it wise to be so prominently displayed?"

Yeslnik's face screwed up with confusion. He glanced to Olym, who snapped at Milwellis, "Should he grovel with the peasants?"

"No, of course not, my queen," the Laird of Palmaristown answered. "It is just that an enemy archer might spy him from afar up there, and yourself as well."

That had the two nobles shifting nervously, and Yeslnik calling for a ladder.

"And I am keen to prevent such loss," Milwellis went on, though Yeslnik wasn't really paying him much heed.

"You said that the powries were slaughtered," Yeslnik scolded, gingerly making his way down the ladder, pointedly before his wife.

"They are."

"Then what archers need I fear?"

"Word from Chapel Abelle has not reached this far south," Harcourt remarked to Milwellis, and that had Yeslnik and Olym exchanging concerned glances and made De Guilbe shift and turn to face the pair from Palmaristown directly.

"Dame Gwydre has come forth, my king," Milwellis reported.

"What?" Yeslnik stuttered. "I told you to keep them imprisoned in their walls! Can you not perform the simplest of duties, Prince of Palmaris—"

"Laird of Palmaristown," Milwellis dared interrupt, and the weight of his words did, indeed, excuse the indiscretion.

"Where is your father?" Father De Guilbe demanded.

"Dead before the walls of Chapel Abelle," said Milwellis. "We turned as you ordered," he added, looking back to Yeslnik. "To the river and the powrie threat. And soon after our departure, the witch of Vanguard struck."

"She coordinated the assault with her powrie minions!" De Guilbe insisted.

Yeslnik growled, Olym gasped, and Milwellis nodded, not about to disagree. "My father was slain before the walls, his force overwhelmed."

"Surely you do not blame me!" King Yeslnik demanded, and he even stamped his foot to accentuate his point.

"No, of course not, my king," Harcourt interjected.

Milwellis was glad of that, glad that his advisor had given him the moment to compose himself before he had uttered something ungraceful to the King of Honce.

"The powries had to be defeated," Milwellis agreed. "It was the only course, particularly since Bannagran of Pryd has not found his way to the river." He glanced at Harcourt as he finished the sentence, and the older man gave him a wink of approval.

"I rode from Chapel Abelle to protect Palmaristown, to serve the minions of my father and my king, and to protect the walls of Delaval City," Milwellis went on. "The death of my father is the doing of Dame Gwydre alone, and I will have her head in recompense. As the Laird of Palmaristown, I demand no less."

"Yes, it is your city now, I suppose," Yeslnik replied. He paused and tapped his fingers to his lips, nodding and thinking. "Your father was a great man. My uncle, the King of Honce, spoke of him often as a fine ally and friend."

Milwellis knew the phony ploy for what it was, of course, but he accepted the truth of Yeslnik's words, inadvertent though it might be. Given Milwellis's ambitions for the glory of his city, it was good to have the King of Honce speaking of Panlamaris in such a positive manner.

"And so my father oft spoke of Laird Delaval," he replied.

"King Delaval," Yeslnik quickly and sternly corrected.

At Milwellis's side, Harcourt gave a curt bow. "Even before he wore that mantle, King Yeslnik," the general explained. "For many years, Laird Panlamaris viewed your uncle as a great and powerful ally."

That seemed to satisfy Yeslnik, but Milwellis remained tensely staring at the foppish man.

"Where is Laird Bannagran?" Milwellis asked. "My march has been full of enemies and battles at every mile, yet all that Bannagran has faced before his great army are the miles of empty land!"

King Yeslnik answered him with a long silence and stare, one that revealed nothing of Bannagran, but much of Yeslnik's own displeasure that the Laird of Pryd had not yet arrived.

"What good my march, then?" Milwellis pressed. "We risked the wrath of our most powerful foes in their fortress of Chapel Abelle. Laird Panlamaris paid for that risk with his life, as he rushed to sweep clear the river and bank of the wretched powries. Palmaristown paid dearly for the good of King Yeslnik's kingdom, while Bannagran and Pryd Town sit quiet and content."

For a moment, it seemed as if King Yeslnik meant to lash out verbally at the malcontent Milwellis, but he calmed quickly.

"As soon as Laird Bannagran is finished with Ethelbert, I will pull back my legions from him," Yeslnik said.

Milwellis waved the thought away. "Forget Laird Ethelbert at this dark time," he advised. "Your more dangerous foes are Dame Gwydre and the monks of Chapel Abelle. The prisoners incarcerated there have joined their ranks, so say those who fled the field, and the witch of Vanguard has more tricks to play, I am sure. Ethelbert is in his hole, and there he will stay. Send a fleet to blockade him so that no supplies or mercenaries come to him from Behr but eliminate the more immediate threat, I say."

"Laird Ethelbert guided the assassin who murdered my uncle!" Yeslnik argued.

"And you have punched him back into his hole," Milwellis replied. "Command the center, my king. You cannot safely stretch your line with Dame Gwydre running free so near to Palmaristown, to Pryd Town, and to Delaval City."

That last reference had the always nervous Yeslnik stiffening a bit.

"The brothers of Abelle can weaken your high walls with their gemstones, do not doubt," Milwellis continued.

"We have brothers to counter!" Yeslnik shouted at him, and the king turned to the hulking Father De Guilbe for support. Indeed, De Guilbe was all too glad to stick out his chin and cross his large arms over his large chest.

"If you gathered all of the brothers loyal to Father De Guilbe of all of the chapels across Honce, they would not come near to matching the magical prowess of Artolivan's skilled monks. Most of the older brothers have fled or gone into hiding, their old loyalties to Chapel Abelle holding firm. And not all the other chapels of the world combined have near the quantity or quality of the gemstones at Chapel Abelle. This I know from the brothers of the Chapel of Precious Memories, and this you, too, know, Father De Guilbe."

King Yeslnik seemed quite taken aback at being spoken to in so blunt a manner. He looked to De Guilbe again and saw that much of the man's puffery was no more. Father De Guilbe seemed smaller in that moment of truth, for, indeed, Milwellis had spoken truly, and all there knew it.

"And so you believe that these few hundred brothers and prisoners, led by a witch from Vanguard, will threaten the power of my kingdom?" Yeslnik asked with as much skepticism as he could manage.

"Preposterous!" Father De Guilbe added.

"I believe that they can cause great mischief," Laird Milwellis replied coolly. "No more than a few hundred powries crawled out of the river, and they brought great distress to Palmaristown and to every port between my city and your own. Gwydre and Artolivan are smarter than powries—and more dangerous—with a host of monks and their gemstone magic. They won't slaughter haphazardly and send more folk running to King Yeslnik for safety. Nay, they will carefully pick their fights, perhaps against the lairds most loyal and the chapels turning to Father De Guilbe's vision of Abelle. And as they defeat those chapels, how many converts will they win and how many more gemstones will they place in their arsenal? Your course, our course, is clear, my king," he finished dramatically. "The garrison of Palmaristown is on the march, as is the army of Delaval City. The witch has come out of her hole, and so we must put her back into it and then tear the walls of Chapel Abelle down around her."

A long pause ensued, with Milwellis staring at Yeslnik, not blinking at all. More than once did King Yeslnik avert his eyes, and more than once did he bring his fingers to his lips, tapping nervously.

"I gave Laird Bannagran two legions," Yeslnik said at length. "To you I give three—four! Four of my eight remaining, to hunt down Dame Gwydre and be done with her and to tear Chapel Abelle to its foundation so that Father De Guilbe might rebuild it in my image."

Despite his impassive façade, Laird Milwellis could not help but gulp at that surprising and most welcomed proclamation. Four legions! Twenty thousand soldiers to join his Palmaristown thousands! He would sweep the land with such a force, overwhelming any and all who came before him.

Even Chapel Abelle. When he had made the demand to destroy the place to Yeslnik, it was more symbolic than realistic—could any army tear down the fortress of Chapel Abelle?

Milwellis didn't know, but with more than twenty-five thousand warriors at his command, suddenly it seemed quite possible.

"Finish the powries, if any remain," King Yeslnik commanded him. "Then win the war, however you need do it. Kill the witch Gwydre. March to Vanguard if you must to finish her! When you see the moment of triumph before us, go to aid Laird Bannagran and finish the dog Ethelbert. Crush Chapel Abelle! These are the charges I give to you, General and Laird Milwellis. You are my most trusted commander now. You have proven your worth against the powries and the loyalty of your city in the great cost it has endured for the sake of my kingdom. While Bannagran tarries, Milwellis shines as brightly as the sun. I put in your charge the garrison of Delaval City, the mightiest army the world has ever known. Win the war, Laird Milwellis, and your reward will be as great as anything you can imagine."

Beside Milwellis, General Harcourt nearly swooned. He stared at his young laird, this man who had so expertly manipulated King Yeslnik to the gain of Palmaristown, with open admiration. He knew at that moment that the time of training Milwellis had ended, that Prince Milwellis had truly become Laird Milwellis, and, he suspected, that Laird Milwellis would outshine even Laird Panlamaris.

"But leave no enemies a clear march to Delaval City," Yeslnik added.

Harcourt did well to hold his chuckle at that typical Yeslnik reaction. The man still had more than twenty thousand warriors surrounding him, behind walls as tall as those of Chapel Abelle itself. And yet, with the foppish Yeslnik, for all his legions and visions of total conquest, ever there remained the fear.

No matter, Harcourt thought and Milwellis agreed, indicating so with a smirk to Harcourt. To both men, it seemed clear that Palmaristown's greatest glories lay right before them.

CHAPTER 20

The Art of Compromise

The Highwayman and Dame Gwydre entered Pryd Town late the next morning, without fanfare, without much recognition. Bransen even took care to disguise his revealing clothing for the sake of Dame Gwydre, nervously walking at his side.

He noted that Gwydre, too, had retreated to a disguise (though, of course, none in these parts knew her at all, anyway), putting up the hood of her traveling cloak so far forward that it covered not only her hair, but much of her profile, as well.

How could she not be nervous? Bransen asked himself as they crossed the northern fields, through an endless sea of tents.

"How many?" Gwydre asked quietly from under the hood. "Pryd is more powerful than I had imagined."

"Most are from Delaval," Bransen explained. "I learned that Yeslnik granted Bannagran a sizable force so that he could rid the world of Laird Ethelbert."

"So many," Gwydre said, her voice full of trepidation.

Bransen took her hand and she squeezed his tightly.

"If every man and woman of Vanguard took up arms, I could not hope to lead them to victory against such a force as this," Gwydre said. "So many! I could not imagine . . ."

"Yeslnik can muster several times this force," Bransen heard himself reply, and when Gwydre squeezed his hand tighter, he felt foolish, indeed, for divulging that disturbing truth.

"We cannot win," Gwydre whispered.

"We have to win," Bransen whispered back. He stopped walking and looked at Gwydre, drawing her gaze to his own. Silently, they stared and nodded, "tying iron to their bones" as the old saying went.

"Surely this force could sweep Laird Ethelbert away," Gwydre remarked when they began walking again.

"The city is well defended, and by desperate men with their backs to the sea. Bannagran would defeat him, but it would not be without great cost to this army, large as it is. Of course, if we have our way, Bannagran will never again march to the Mirianic."

"Why did they turn? Why are they are back here in central Honce?"

"Recalled because of the powrie fight, so revealed Brother Giavno. Resupplying and preparing to march again, but to the west and the river, not east."

"You believe this to be a good thing for our cause? The coming of the powries, I mean."

Bransen had no answer for her, but he doubted that Bannagran was thrilled at being pulled back from a campaign. They would know soon enough, he reminded himself as they crossed onto the main road of the town proper, Castle Pryd looming before them.

"Here, but I thought you had run off from us, Highwayman," said one of the four sentries at the front gate, which was open but imposing nonetheless. "Not that many wanted you along for the march."

"Hardly that," Bransen lied. "There were more important matters to attend."

"So said Laird Bannagran?"

"There was no time to tell him," said Bransen. "I return now with important information. Announce me, I beg, and send a courier to Master Reandu."

The man looked at him suspiciously for a few heartbeats, but then nodded to his companions and disappeared inside. Just a few moments later, Bransen found himself entering the audience hall of the Laird of Pryd yet again.

Bannagran smirked and shook his head at the sight of him. "You are like the wart I keep cutting from my toe," he said.

"Forgive my absence," Bransen said.

"Forgive? Do you think I was angry at hearing that you had fled the lands once more?" He snorted derisively. "I thought that I could put away my knife and that my toe would know relief, and this time, perchance, forevermore."

Bransen caught Gwydre's concerned look beside him and so he tossed her a reassuring wink.

"And who is this that you have brought? One of the Duwornay women?"

Gwydre's expression remained concerned, but Bransen motioned to her, and with his reassuring nod, she pulled back her hood.

Bransen turned to Bannagran, sitting halfway across the room, to gauge his reaction, and, indeed, the man started, leaning back with his eyes wide, then coming forward, certainly interested.

"Callen Duwornay?" he asked and started to rise.

"A forward scout," Bransen corrected, "come to accept Laird Bannagran's agreement and word that he will honor a flag of parley."

"Parley? What are you babbling about, Stork?"

Bransen took the insult in stride. "I have returned ahead of the most important meeting Laird Bannagran might ever know."

"Ethelbert again?"

"Nay," Bransen replied, and he painted a wry smile on his face to heighten the laird's curiosity.

"Father Artolivan, then," Bannagran reasoned, and if he was at all impressed with that possibility, he didn't show it. "I would have thought him too old—"

"Father Artolivan is dead," Dame Gwydre interrupted.

That silenced the man. He came forward a step, looking Gwydre up and down, clear interest on his dark face.

"Will you offer your word of honor?" Bransen asked.

Bannagran eyed him suspiciously but gave a slight nod.

"Dismiss your guards," Bransen bade him. "All of them."

Bannagran stared at him hard for a moment but then motioned for the sentries to leave the room. Bransen followed them to the heavy oaken door and shut it behind them.

"Artolivan is dead, you say?" Bannagran asked the woman.

"Father Premujon of Vanguard now leads the Order of Blessed Abelle. It was he who blessed the army, my army, when we swept Laird Panlamaris from the field before St. Mere Abelle."

Bannagran's eyes widened, indeed!

"Laird Bannagran, I present to you Dame Gwydre of Vanguard," said Bransen, walking up beside his companion.

"You come here, to the court of your sworn enemy, unarmed?" Bannagran asked.

"I have the most dangerous weapon in the world beside me," Gwydre assured him. "And I have the word of an honorable man, do I not?"

"That remains to be seen, perhaps," said Bannagran. "But what I am not is a foolish man. You come to me championing the cause of Laird Ethelbert, whose murderers tried to assassinate the couriers you sent to him. Is that your meaning of 'honorable'?"

A sharp knock on the door interrupted the conversation, followed by the voice of Master Reandu. "Laird Bannagran! I would speak with you and Bransen."

Bransen looked to Bannagran for permission, and the laird just laughed at the ridiculousness of it all and waved his hand toward the door. "I will enjoy his expression when you tell him his beloved Father Artolivan is dead," he said to Gwydre, but before he could begin to revel in his cleverness, Dame Gwydre shot back, in all seriousness, "No, you won't."

Bransen opened the door and Reandu, Cormack, and Milkeila rushed in, and before they could even begin to properly greet Bransen, Cormack identified Dame Gwydre and all three stared in silent confusion.

Bransen closed the door behind them.

"Ah, yes, and back to our discussion of Laird Ethelbert," Bannagran started again. "Ask your emissaries, lady. Ethelbert's assassins tried to kill them, and these same assassins murdered King Delaval, who was ever a friend of Pryd. And you come here in the hopes that you would convince me to fight for his cause?"

"No," said Gwydre. Bannagran's volume had increased by the word, and he had moved much closer to Gwydre, an obvious attempt to make her feel smaller. But she didn't back away an inch. "For Honce!" she said right in his face. "I come here in the hopes of convincing you to fight for what is right."

"And for Bannagran," Bransen added, but no one paid him any heed, all eyes locked on Gwydre and Bannagran, these two most impressive and powerful figures, standing barely a hand's width apart and staring at each other with such intensity that if someone had dropped kindling between them and it had spontaneously ignited, not a person in the room would have been surprised.

"For Honce," Gwydre said again. "For the people of Honce. For all of those who have been forgotten in the march to personal glory."

"For the peasants?" Bannagran asked dismissively, and Gwydre fiercely scowled.

"What choice was offered to the people of Honce, peasant and noble alike, in the decision of these two lairds, Delaval and Ethelbert?" Gwydre asked.

"The choice of which."

"Merely that?"

"That is more than they deserve."

"You do not believe that."

"You do not know me," Bannagran reminded her, but Gwydre's ensuing smile took a large measure of the certainty from his rigid expression.

"By what right?" she asked. "Ethelbert and Delaval and now this wretched Yeslnik after him claim the throne of all the land simply because they presume themselves the strongest. It is not by edict, not by the request of the lairds, and not for the good of the holdings. Nay, it is the temptation of power and nothing more. To be the king is what they, all three, demand and desire. To expand their personal powers and nothing more, and for their folly tens of thousands have been pecked by the carrion birds and the crops fail and the young and old sit hungry and cold. Tyrants, all three."

"And Gwydre is different?"

That evoked a hard and angry stare from the woman, her eyes flashing dangerously.

Bannagran's dark eyes flashed as well in response. A smile creased his face as he took a deep breath—took a deep breath because Gwydre had obviously just taken his breath away.

"By Abelle," Bransen heard Reandu whisper.

"You will find that I am someone who does not like to be mocked, Laird Bannagran," Dame Gwydre said in a low and even voice. "I came here in good faith to appeal to a man of character."

"You came here hoping that I would bow before you and lend you my thousands so that you could steal victory from the weary and warring lairds and thus claim Honce as your own," Bannagran replied. "Do not pretty it with pretty words, lady. The blood smells the same."

"And yet, the church supports my claim."

"If you believe that will impress me, then perhaps you should scold your scouts who told you of my affinity for the church, Abellican or Samhaist. I'll not weep for dead Father Artolivan, I assure you." He looked at Reandu as he finished, and the man blanched as Bannagran's words truly registered.

"Then you are not as wise as Bransen, who championed your character to me, believes," said Gwydre. "For Artolivan was a wise and temperate man, blessed with generosity and wisdom in amounts far greater than those of this foolish young king you slavishly follow."

The word "slavishly" had proud Bannagran standing up straighter, squaring his shoulders and narrowing his eyes.

"O wondrous Laird Bannagran," Gwydre taunted. "The great Bear of Honce, sniffing the heels of foppish King Yeslnik."

"Beware your words, lady," Bannagran said quietly.

"How many victories will you have to win on the field, Bear of Honce, to repair the legacy of any man who would whimper at the whip of sniveling Yeslnik?"

"A victory that strikes dead the Dame of Vanguard should suffice."

The four onlookers shared alarmed expressions, but Gwydre didn't blink.

"You disappoint me," she said evenly, and of all the words launched that day, those seemed to strike Bannagran the hardest. Mostly it was her tone, Bransen and the other onlookers knew, for it was full of honest remorse.

Bannagran didn't reply, didn't blink, and quickly erased his wince.

"Am I permitted to remain in Pryd Town this night?" Gwydre asked. "Or should I be away at once?"

"I would be within my rights to take you prisoner."

"Laird!" Reandu gasped, and Bransen took a step forward, more than ready to intervene, with lethal force if necessary.

But Gwydre disarmed them both by lifting her hand to the side to ward them away. "There is more to the character of Bannagran than Bannagran is brave enough to admit," she said.

Bannagran laughed at her. "You may stay in the castle itself, of course," he said. "I would have it no other way, Lady of Vanguard. I'll honor your parley." He turned to Bransen. "But that one will be the guest of Master Reandu at Chapel Pryd. I need no assassins in my midst."

"I'll not leave Dame Gwydre," said Bransen.

"Yes, you will," Gwydre corrected, and when Bransen stared at her hard, she responded in kind and bid him to be gone.

"I will have an attendant show you to your room, lady," said Bannagran. "You will be gone with the sunrise."

"Gladly away," she agreed.

Below the side kitchen area of Castle Pryd, in smoke-filled rooms of mud and stone, where the rats ruled and the cockroaches served as commoners, the few miserable human intruders, guards and prisoners alike, lost all sense of time and humanity.

Beaten and starved, Wahloon dangled by his wrists, the iron collars digging painfully into the base of his hands.

Painful, but only when the disciplined warrior allowed it to be. Wahloon had trained under Affwin Wi in the ways of Hou-lei, the ways of the warriors of Behr. Like the training of their descendants, the Jhesta Tu, the discipline of the Hou-lei was all encompassing. It strove for harmony between mind and body within a specific philosophical framework that balanced the relationship in the realms of the physical and tactical by disregarding the emotional—in the Hou-lei's case, the elimination of conscience, for conscience was viewed as weakness in a warrior. That was the distinguishing feature between Jhesta Tu and Hou-lei, for a Hou-lei warrior was an instrument of war. Nothing more and nothing less. A perfect, disciplined weapon.

Mind and body joined. Mind over body when necessary.

Wahloon did not feel the pain, not the whip gashes in his back, not the bruises on his face, not the cuts along his hands and wrists, not the strain of hanging suspended from the floor. He allowed his shoulder muscles to stretch and twist appropriately so that they did not resist the weight.

He tried several times to writhe and squirm his wrists out of the bracer-like shackles, but to no avail. He had no footing, no balance with which to manipulate the items. He needed something to stand on.

Torchlight stung his eyes and alerted him of movement. One of Banna-gran's troglodytes entered the chamber, a hunched and twisted man, bearded and filthy, with two twisted yellow and green teeth and only one good eye. He was a diminutive fellow, hunched and round, his broken form accentuated by a sleeveless woolen sack he wore from neck to knees. He carried a plate of food, rotten and maggot-ridden. Even that meager and wretched meal wasn't for Wahloon, though, but for the gaoler, who grinned evilly as he dipped his greasy fingers into it and shoveled a writhing mass into his mouth.

"Oh, but are ye hungry, smelly one?" he asked.

Wahloon's response came in the form of a kick, weak and pathetic, but effective enough to clip the plate and upend its contents into the gaoler's face.

Wahloon groaned and let his legs fall limp, seeming weak from agony and hunger.

The gaoler howled in rage and stepped forward to pummel the helpless man, who was not so helpless after all.

Up snapped Wahloon's legs, around the troglodyte's neck. The warrior locked his ankles together. Suddenly strong, Wahloon twisted his hips over one way, then back the other and the flailing gaoler turned with him, lurching side to side. The troglodyte tried to yell out, but it came forth as a gurgle. He slapped and pinched at the warrior's legs, but Wahloon felt no pain. He tried to bite at the legs, but Wahloon had his shin under the man's chin and would not allow him to squirm free at all.

Wahloon flipped right over, crossing the chains, so that he was facing the wall, and bent hard at the waist, pulling the gaoler forward and down beneath him. To the troglodyte's surprise, the prisoner then released him, planted his feet on the back of the hunched man's shoulders, and snapped his lower body forward, ramming the gaoler into the stone wall.

The gaoler caught himself enough to avoid splitting his bald head wide open, though he was bleeding badly. As Wahloon shoved away from him, he tried to scurry to the side, but before he had gone a stride, in came the warrior's bare foot, knifing hard against his throat and slamming him again against the wall. Now he was gurgling and lurching, and Wahloon swung level before him and began pumping his legs, knees rising to smash the troglodyte in the face repeatedly.

He went down to his knees, and Wahloon let himself twist back the other way. He used the momentum of that swing to bring his legs up and over, inverting in a hanging roll and straightening with all his strength and speed as he came around so that he double-stomped the kneeling gaoler's shoulder and head, throwing the man facedown to the floor.

He groaned and tried to rise once, but just once, before he fell flat and hard and lay still, making little mewling and gasping noises.

Wahloon flipped back the other way and stood atop him, finally releasing the pressure from his weary shoulders. He stomped hard on the back of the man's head a couple of times to ensure that he wouldn't roll away, and then he used his newfound leverage to begin his work on the shackles—not a difficult task for one who had trained in the ways of Hou-lei.

He thought for a moment of donning the gaoler's bug-ridden wool smock but grimaced in disgust and shook his head. Besides, he understood the pathetic martial prowess of the sentries in the area. If they recognized him, they would quake in terror, and that would only make killing them more pleasurable.

"The days are dark," Cormack lamented back at Chapel Pryd.

"There is no sunrise," Reandu agreed.

"Come with us, brother," said Cormack. "To St. Mere Abelle. We will follow the will of Blessed Abelle, protected by high and thick walls King Yeslnik cannot breach."

"The army of Vanguard will arrive presently, if they have not already, and you would surrender to your despair?" Bransen said from across the room, where he sat on the sill of an open window that faced Castle Pryd.

"Ethelbert will not come forth," said Cormack. "Indeed, after his assassins assailed me and Milkeila outside of Pryd, I am not sure that I want him to leave his city! And you witnessed the response of Bannagran."

"I thought that the meeting went better than I could have hoped."

All three in the room turned curious stares Bransen's way.

"Dame Gwydre was not taken prisoner," Bransen explained. "Nor was she turned away. Nor did she back down from Bannagran's snarl—indeed, her bark was louder than his own, and made him take notice."

"Did you expect that Laird Bannagran would have imprisoned her?" Milkeila asked.

"It was a possibility."

"And still you brought her here?" Cormack asked and scolded.

"I don't deny the desperation of our situation. I know about Ethelbert, though I wonder if he was aware that the assassins hunted you. I do not believe he has as tight a leash on Affwin Wi as he believes."

"We're talking about Bannagran and Dame Gwydre and your decision to bring her from the safety of St. Mere Abelle," said Cormack.

"She brought herself out from behind the walls, first to sweep aside Laird Panlamaris and his catapults and then to march east to meet with the Vanguard flotilla. I merely persuaded her to come to Pryd Town to meet this general whose aid she so coveted. And, as I said, I think it went quite well . . . better than I had hoped."

"He refused her," Cormack reminded.

"And she is in his castle, as his guest," said Bransen. "Did you not see it?"

"See it?"

"Dame Gwydre intrigued him," Master Reandu explained. "Her wit, her courage, her presence." He nodded at Bransen. "Yes, her words cut the man deeply, else he would have sent her away, at best."

"Intrigued him," Bransen repeated, returning Reandu's nod. "At the very least, Dame Gwydre's blunt words have given Bannagran pause and made him less comfortable with his role as the foolish Yeslnik's foolish pawn."

"He'll not likely turn traitor," said Cormack.

"Not now, perhaps," said Bransen. "Some seeds take time to grow."

"And in that time, Yeslnik will conquer the world."

"No," Bransen said, smiling serenely. He moved from the window to regard the others, to make sure he had their complete attention. "King Yeslnik will govern only where his armies remain."

"He will push Laird Ethelbert into the sea, surely," Cormack argued.

"And I hope that the man cannot swim," Bransen replied. "I've no doubt that King Yeslnik's armies are beyond our power to battle, but we have a weapon that he does not." He paused to watch the curious trio lean forward with anticipation. "We have the spirit-walking brothers," Bransen explained. "We will know where Yeslnik's armies are and where they are marching. And so let him chase us futilely the length and breadth of Honce. Whenever his armies conquer a holding and then depart, we will walk in behind them and bid the people to hold hope. And if ever his armies leave open a flank or send out lesser forces, we will meet them and crush them. And all the time, St. Mere Abelle will remain undaunted and unconquered, a beacon of hope against King Yeslnik. Time will work against him as his warriors grow ever wearier with their endless marching and as his general Bannagran continues to realize that the man is a fool and continues to mull the words and promises of Dame Gwydre."

"You believe that?" Cormack asked.

"I do," said Bransen. "And more than that, I believe it to be the worst of the possible scenarios. This meeting with Bannagran is not over. I did not carry Dame Gwydre halfway across Honce to so easily let Bannagran avoid facing the truth of his decisions."

Bransen smiled wryly, walked back to the sill, and swung his legs out the window. "In fact, I think I will pay our Laird of Pryd a visit at this very late hour."

"Wait!" Reandu called as Bransen started to slip outside. "What has happened to you?" Reandu asked. "When last we parted . . ."

Standing on the lawn before the window then, Bransen turned to regard the master. "In the midst of a war, I have found peace," Bransen replied. He left it at that, though many more thoughts streamed through his mind. His voice was strong and he felt strong, though he wouldn't take the chance of removing the soul stone strapped to his forehead; too much was at stake for him to risk the return of the Stork. That strength of body reflected his inner calm, he knew, his newfound purpose and understanding.

It was worth it. He believed that now. With a nod to his friends, he started off across the courtyard, not to the front gate, but to the side wall that separated the grounds of Chapel Pryd from those of Castle Pryd.

Bransen considered the structure before him as he silently came over the wall. Castle Pryd was not large, really just a solid and thick central keep with a trio of smaller one-storey wings about it. Bransen knew the building fairly well, particularly the keep itself. He noted a light burning in a narrow window on the third and top floor and recognized that as the room once belonging to Laird Prydae and to Laird Pryd before him. Bannagran would have taken it as his own, Bransen surmised, and so he moved quiet as a whisper across the courtyard to the corner where the two nearest wings met at the base of the keep. There, he fell into the malachite magic and began his spiderlike climb, first to the roof of one of the low wings, then, when he was confident that no sentries were looking his way, up the tower itself.

He picked his way along the cracks in the stone, his strong grip easily finding handholds sufficient to support his nearly weightless body. He went beside a window about halfway up and glanced in, noting the stairway where he had once, long ago, pursued Laird Prydae, where Master Bathelais had tried to lash at him with gemstone lightning, but had been stopped by the courage of Reandu.

It seemed like a lifetime ago to the young man who had known such an adventurous and interesting year.

"A year," Bransen mouthed silently. "Just a year." How much had changed!

His nostalgia flew away then as he noted a figure climbing the stairway. He quickly moved back from the window so that he would not be noticed, a dark silhouette against a lighter sky, for the man carried no torch.

He carried no torch. . . .

Why would that be? Bransen tried to find a logical explanation for that. The stairs were steep, dark, and treacherous. Why would anyone climb them on a dark night without a source of light?

Bransen held his breath, hearing footsteps, very light, made by no boot. He dared move his head back to get an angled look at the window and just noted the man's passage, seeing no more than the back of his pant leg.

Silken and black.

Bransen had to remind himself to breathe. He thought of going right into the window behind the Hou-lei, but he scaled the side instead, rushing up hand over hand. All notion of stealth fled in his rush, and before he had gone five feet he heard shouting from the courtyard below. He ignored it and pressed on until he was staring into Bannagran's room on the keep's top floor.

Bannagran slumped in a wide chair before the hearth, an open and nearly empty bottle in his hand. He might have been asleep, and certainly he was near to dozing. Behind him, directly across the room from Bransen, the door eased open and the black-clothed assassin slipped in. The Hou-lei warrior paused right there, for beside the door sat a rack of knives.

He took one and eased his way toward the clueless Laird of Pryd.

Bransen could hardly register the scene unfolding before him. His mind darted in a hundred different directions all at once. Would the death of Bannagran benefit Dame Gwydre and Honce? Was this acceptable justice for the man who had murdered his father? Should he allow it? Could he stop it?

By the time he blinked the myriad questions aside, Bransen figured that he had been stupefied for too long, that the choice had been taken from him. His hesitation had decided his course.

Or not.

"Bannagran!" he shouted, flinging himself through the window, a forward roll that brought him back to his feet and in a dead run at the seated Laird of Pryd.

Bannagran's eyes went wide with terror, and he threw his hands up before him as Bransen roared in . . . and leaped above him, diagonally over his wide chair. Bransen landed before the assassin, who lashed at him with the knife. Instinct alone saved the Highwayman, as he pulled up short and threw his head to the side, leaning away just out of reach.

The assassin reversed his grip smoothly and chopped a backhand. The

Highwayman again ducked his head and shoulders back, but this time he snapped his right arm up vertically inside the reach of the knife so that it connected, forearm to forearm, with the assassin. At the same time, Bransen brought his left arm across his chest, then swept it before him as he shoved a backhand with his right, a powerful crossing motion of his arms.

His satisfaction as the knife went flying lasted only as long as it took him to realize, at the painful end of a lifted foot, that the assassin had surrendered the knife willingly in exchange for the clean strike.

Bransen staggered backward, trying to stand straight and keep his defenses up. Tears welled in his eyes as explosions of pain and waves of numbness washed over him from his smashed groin. His opponent saw his vulnerability and came on hard, striking with open palms, kneeing and kicking.

Sheer terror stole the pain from Bransen, and he worked furiously to counter and block, falling fast into a smooth rhythm. Many heartbeats passed before he even realized that he had caught up to his opponent's swift and accurate moves.

The Highwayman could hardly believe that he had suffered no serious or debilitating strikes as the two settled into a more measured and balanced routine. Wahloon was good, very good, and kept the initiative, pressing forward, fingers stabbing. He swung a right hook and kept going around when the punch didn't land. It seemed almost as if he were screwing himself into the ground, for as he spun, he went down low in a crouch.

Instinctively, Bransen hopped, and just in time, as Wahloon's leg swept harmlessly under him. Bransen landed gracefully and in a powerful pivot position, left foot forward. Immediately, he rotated his hips and kicked out with his right, but the assassin, rising fast, had his hands in place to double block, and it was all Bransen could do to stop from having his foot grabbed and caught. Still, as he brought his foot in, he kept his presence of mind enough to reverse his momentum and go forward with his upper body, jabbing left and right with a flurry of strikes.

Wahloon leaned back out of reach, his open hands blocking and slapping at the punching Highwayman, who kept coming forward, for Bransen was determined to press his advantage while he had the assassin backing and somewhat off balance.

Wahloon launched into a backflip, kicking out as he turned horizontal, a surprising strike that clipped Bransen high on one arm and slowed his pursuit. Over went the assassin to land on his feet, and he bounced away into a second somersault, this one sidelong and high and right over another of the cushiony chairs.

Bransen dismissed his surprise, even admiration, at the graceful and balanced retreat, and went in fast pursuit. He lowered his shoulder and barreled into the chair, sending it skidding and tumbling at the assassin, who promptly leaped and somersaulted again, tucking tight in a forward roll that landed him right back in place, the chair now behind him and his opponent rushing in.

Both men struck with fury and amazing speed, hands and feet becoming a blur of motion, slapping and snapping against each other with great force.

Sobered by the commotion and the shock, Bannagran circled the combatants. He tried to follow their movements but found himself standing with his mouth agape at the beauty and power and ferociousness of the dance. He heard the slaps more than he actually saw them.

Down went the Highwayman in a spinning descent, his leg stabbing out at the Behr warrior's knee. Wahloon barely turned his leg enough so that the kick didn't shatter that joint. As if he hadn't even been hit, the warrior came forward over Bransen as the Highwayman tried to rise, his hands jabbing down hard like the talons of a hawk, stabbing and grabbing.

Bannagran stumbled to the side, circling back in front of the hearth and hoping to get around to the door. He heard shouting and knew his guards were on their way.

He knew, too, that the Highwayman had just saved his life.

Bransen's hands worked in tight, circular patterns above and before him as he stood back up, deflecting the many strikes of Wahloon. The assassin's continuous straightforward angling surprised him, for surely the man could have arced a hook or two around his hands to score a painful hit. But Wahloon remained strangely focused, every strike going for Bransen's forehead.

Every strike or every grab?

That notion hit Bransen hard as he finally came up even, the two resuming their furious exchange. The assassin kept going for his forehead. The assassin was trying to strip away Bransen's bandanna and gemstone!

Wahloon leaped and somersaulted again, twisting about as Bransen turned sidelong to the left and went over the other way, the two crossing paths upside down in midair, both punching out as they did. As soon as he landed, Bransen pivoted around backward, launching a circle kick.

So did Wahloon, the two kicking feet slamming together. Bransen hopped off his right foot and rotated his hips, sending that foot out behind him as he landed on his left, and when Wahloon did likewise, the two hooked their right legs at the ankles. Both tugged and they came together hard, clawing and striking every inch of the way. And again, Wahloon went for Bransen's bandanna.

Bransen let him. The Highwayman fell into himself, into his *ki-chi-kree*, and mentally separated himself from the soul stone even as Wahloon's grasping hand ripped the bandanna and stone away. Bransen staggered, seeming out of control, and Wahloon struck, a leaping circle kick that would have smashed the side of Bransen's head with enough force to snap his neck.

Except that in the instant it took Wahloon to leap and spin, the Highwayman wasn't there. Bransen had dropped straight down into a crouch, so low that his butt brushed the ground. He could feel his line of life energy twitching—it wanted to break apart—but he held it firm and came up and forward with tremendous power and speed, punching out with a strong right, burying his fist into the descending Wahloon's groin. The assassin jerked out and back and somehow, with great effort and discipline, managed to land standing.

But that was a mistake, for Bransen continued to drive upward, and when he was standing, he threw himself into the air, flipping over and double-kicking out as he came around. He hit Wahloon with both feet, soles crashing in against the man's shoulders and throwing him backward into the side of Bannagran's chair.

Even worse for the dazed assassin, he landed right before Laird Bannagran, who had reached into the hearth and produced a smoking log from the low-burning fire.

Bannagran met the falling assassin with a heavy swing, the log cracking Wahloon's skull, snapping his neck, and stopping cold his momentum. He swung about weirdly, twisting and collapsing to the floor in an awkward heap. And there he lay very still.

Bannagran looked up at Bransen, looked past Bransen to the guards bursting in the door. He held up his hand to keep them at bay as they leveled their spears at the Highwayman's back.

"I suppose you expect my gratitude," Bannagran said to Bransen.

Out of breath, hurting in many places, and trying hard to keep his line of life energy from scattering, Bransen could only shrug before he sank down to one knee.

"Get this fool out of my sight," Bannagran instructed the guards, who lifted their spears and rushed to flank Bransen, left and right. "Not that fool," Bannagran scolded, and he kicked the dead assassin in the side of the head. "This one!"

They rushed over and began dragging Wahloon's body away, and Bannagran tossed the log, its bark red with blood and bits of brain matter, back into the hearth. The laird shook his head as Bransen managed to pull himself back to his feet. He glanced to the side and noted Bransen's bandanna, the gray stone sitting on the floor nearby. Never taking his eyes off the dangerous Highwayman, Bannagran walked over and picked up the stone and cloth.

Bransen reached out for them from across the way, but Bannagran scoffed and held them close.

"He . . . h . . . he would have killed you," Bransen reminded, his voice unsteady, Stork-like.

"I've saved a thousand men, and a hundred have saved me," Bannagran replied. "That is the way of war. You betrayed Ethelbert's assassin because it benefitted you; do not pretend any friendship or kinship to me as the cause."

Bransen closed his eyes and tried to regain his steadiness.

"Do you have anything to say before I have my guards drag you away? Or should I just throw you back out the window and be done with you?"

"Did you deserve my efforts here?" Bransen answered with a question of his own. "Is the life of the Laird of Pryd worth fighting for?"

"What idiocy?"

"Is the life of the man who murdered my father worth my time or effort?" Bransen asked. He opened his eyes and glared at Bannagran. "Are you the beast you so stubbornly insist that you are, Bannagran of Pryd?"

"Your father? Garibond Womak?" Bannagran snickered. "Are we back to that, Highwayman?" He snorted with clear derision and walked over to retrieve his great axe, which rested against the side of the hearth. "Too long have I suffered your whimpers. Your father, my friend Prydae—it would seem that we have little to say, then. So come on and be done with it. I will be rid of you at long last, or I will—"

"Be dead," Bransen finished for him. "And that does not strike fear into the heart of Bannagran the brave, does it?"

"We're all dying, fool."

"Aye, but your lack of fear is not because of Bannagran the brave. It took me a long time to understand that about you."

"Back to idiocy, I see," Bannagran said, and he maneuvered his chair back into place, which put it between himself and Bransen.

"You are not afraid of dying because you are a coward," Bransen accused.

"Do tell," the laird replied, amused.

"I know you, Bannagran, because I know myself. You look at me and you stare into a mirror."

Bannagran scoffed even louder.

"Cowards, both," Bransen insisted. "Neither of us has ever found the courage to lead. We are servants because we are afraid."

"I am the Laird of Pryd. I thought you knew that."

"You are the servant of Yeslnik, as you were the servant of Laird Prydae and of Laird Pryd before him. You can lead armies, but you are no leader."

"You babble."

"And I can outfight almost any man in Honce," Bransen went on. "But like Bannagran, when I serve no laird or dame, I serve only myself. The Highwayman of Pryd Town held no responsibility for the folk he claimed to champion. In truth . . ." He paused, lowered his gaze, and gave a self-deprecating chuckle. When he looked back up, he was somewhat surprised to find a look of interest on Bannagran's face. Perhaps it was the liquor, perhaps the rescue, but whatever the reason, Bransen knew that he could not let this slim opportunity pass. "In truth, I cared nothing for the injustices served upon them by your friend, Laird Prydae. How many maidens did he drag to his bedroom? And not one did the Highwayman rescue other than Cadayle, my love. Even when I stole food and money and gave it back to the folk of Pryd, I did so only to anger Laird Pryd."

"I could have you executed for this admission."

"You could have taken my head several times, Laird Bannagran, with or without cause, and always with the blessing of King Yeslnik. In fact, it is exactly your hesitance that has led me to this place and this time, with Dame Gwydre beside me."

"On a fool's errand."

Bransen shook his head. "You are better than this role you have played, like the palace dog doing tricks for the spoiled child that is Yeslnik."

"We are back to this," Bannagran interrupted. "I already gave my answer to the woman who holds your leash. Your desperation shines darkly on your cause. Did you really think to march into Pryd Town and turn me to your side, to trade one master for another?" He held up his hands and closed his eyes, then shook his head fiercely and glowered at the Highwayman. "I have told you more than once to be gone from this place, on penalty of death."

"Hear me, Laird Bannagran, I beg," Bransen pleaded. "I just saved your life and ask only that you hear me out fully."

"I know everything you mean to say, and it bores me, as you bore me. You want me to turn against King Yeslnik in the desperate hope that we might put Dame Gwydre on the throne of Honce—Dame Gwydre, who knows nothing of the land and people south of the Gulf of Corona, and they know nothing of her. Dame Gwydre, who is just a name, after all. King Yeslnik has won the day.

You know it to be true. The best advice you might offer to your precious lady is that she sue for peace and beg forgiveness. Her cause is lost."

"That she will never do," came a woman's voice from the doorway, and both men turned to see Gwydre herself standing there, wearing nothing but a simple nightshirt, her short hair rumpled as if she had just awakened.

"Then you do a disservice to those you claim to champion, lady," Bannagran said. "I have more warriors here in Pryd Town alone than you and Ethelbert together might muster, and my force is a third of what King Yeslnik can put on the field against you, less than a third!"

"It matters not at all," the unshaken woman replied. "I follow the cause of justice. I can march no other way, and justice demands the defeat of King Yeslnik. This is not about me, Laird Bannagran, nor is it about you, nor about Bransen. It is about the people of Honce, the farmers and the fishermen, the children and the elders so full of wisdom. They call out in voices thinned by the thunderous march of armies, but I hear them. And Bransen hears them. Does Bannagran?"

The Bear of Honce laughed and walked over to stand right before her. "For them, Dame? Or should I call you Queen Gwydre?" he asked sarcastically.

"It is not about me," Gwydre said quietly.

"Is it not?" Bannagran shouted in her face. "You feign humility and generosity and will send a thousand more to their graves, and all, and only, so that you can be queen!"

Gwydre slapped him across the face, and Bransen sucked in his breath.

Bannagran laughed, though, and Gwydre moved to slap him again, but this time, he caught her by the wrist. Undaunted, the woman slapped at him with her left hand, but again, Bannagran caught that one, too, in his iron grip, and with a quick tug, he brought Dame Gwydre right up against him.

And then he kissed her.

Bransen tried to shout in protest, but he had no voice with which to yell. He started forward just as Gwydre finally managed to pull back from Bannagran.

She held her hand up to stop Bransen.

"Get out," Bannagran called over his shoulder to Bransen, and he tossed the bandanna and the soul stone to the floor near the wiry man. "The same way you came in."

"I'll not leave Dame Gwy—"

"Bransen, go," Gwydre bade him.

"And you, lady, would do well to get yourself back to your room, lest one of my sentries see you with your charms so exposed and . . . well, do what a man will do."

"It is not about me, Laird Bannagran," Gwydre said as she moved to the room's door, where, indeed, a sentry stood and stared at her with a rather lewd smile. Dame Gwydre just ignored him.

"I'll not make you the Queen of Honce, lady," Bannagran assured her.

"Then make yourself the King of Honce," Gwydre said and exited.

Bannagran had no response to that. He stood staring at the open doorway, and behind him stood Bransen, frozen in place with his hands tying the bandanna about his head.

Finally, Bannagran managed to turn about and fix Bransen with a glare. With a tapped salute, Bransen slipped out the window and disappeared into the night.

The Highwayman wandered for more than an hour, ending up at the lake, not far from the house where he had lived with Garibond. He looked back at that dark structure now and thought of all the good times he had shared with Garibond. Fishing, reading the secrets of his father's Book of Jhest, just those moments of quiet and serenity sitting across the table from his adoptive father, a man who needed little and asked for nothing.

The distraction of that pleasant memory could not hold, however, and Bransen found himself staring across the dark waters, wondering what in the world had prompted Dame Gwydre's parting remark to Bannagran.

"King Bannagran," Bransen said aloud, just to hear it, just to try to absorb it.

He couldn't. No matter how many times he whispered the name, it sounded discordant in his heart—a heart still broken from the loss of Garibond, a heart still stung by the actions of Bannagran. Bransen had thought that he had put most of this behind him. Had he not come here, Gwydre in tow, to make peace with the man, after all? Had he not come here to teach Bannagran the truth of Bannagran, for it was, in many regards, the same truth Bransen had finally come to know about himself?

So why had Dame Gwydre's words so unsettled him?

Because he had come to enlist Bannagran in the cause of Dame Gwydre, a goodly cause. He had come to Pryd to give Bannagran a chance at redemption and perhaps a greater opportunity to follow a more just road going forward. But this was different, for if Bannagran fought for the cause of Bannagran there was no altruism, no penance, no redemption, and in that void, how could Bransen ever consider the man worthy of the title?

And in that regard, could Bransen really fight for Bannagran as he had chosen to fight for Dame Gwydre? He had no answers to those unsettling questions, none at all. But he had to find them. He stared at the water, reached up, and untied his bandanna with one hand, dropping his soul stone into the other.

Bransen took a deep breath, then another, afraid of the journey before him. He thought of Giavno, forever wounded, and reminded himself that Bannagran, though untrained in the magic of the sacred gemstones, was a man of great discipline and fortitude.

But Bransen had to know.

He closed his eyes and brought his clenched fist and the soul stone right between his eyes, focusing on its teeming energy, seeking its inviting depths. In the gray smoothness, Bransen found release, his spirit drawing from his corporeal form and flying free into the dark Pryd night.

Straight for Castle Pryd, he flew, up high along the keep's sides and to the same windowsill through which he had charged earlier that night.

Snoring, Bannagran lay sprawled in his cushiony chair before the now dark hearth, his arms hanging out to either side, legs straight out before him. He still wore his muddy boots and had his great axe near at hand, leaning on the side of the chair. Two bottles lay on the floor, one empty, one nearly so.

Bransen built a picture in his mind—a scroll Father Artolivan had shown him of the order from Yeslnik that all of the prisoners from Laird Ethelbert's forces be executed. Bransen wasn't sure of the exact wording, but he formulated the thought clearly—Ethelbert's men were to be executed—and used that solid notion to lead the way into the spirit of the sleeping man.

Bannagran snorted and stirred, and an image of Dame Gwydre in her revealing nightshirt—more revealing than Bransen remembered it by far!—flashed in Bransen's consciousness. More images of the woman flitted about, but Bransen didn't pause to reflect upon them.

He stabbed at Bannagran's dream—Execute the prisoners!

A wall of anger came back at Bransen, accompanied by a jumble of thoughts: that it would outrage the peasants, that such an action would dispirit their own soldiers, that such an edict would push the one ascendant church away, and, finally and most important to Bransen, that it was simply wrong.

The order was an action without honor.

There the Highwayman had his answer, so quickly and so concisely, that Bannagran, the great Bear of Honce, the fearless and ferocious warrior who had cut so many enemies down, was, as Bransen had guessed, possessed of some measure of honor.

A great measure, considering the anger that continued to roil in the man. Bransen felt drawn deeper into this complicated mind. He thought of

Giavno again, briefly, but couldn't help himself as Bannagran's dreams invited him in.

Yeslnik! Bransen's thoughts shouted, for he wanted to capture an unvarnished response, a sense of the man's gut, before the inevitable moment when Bannagran recognized the horrific intrusion and instinctively fought back.

Yeslnik!

Bransen felt the roar of revulsion as intimately as if it were his own, and, for a brief moment, he thought it was aimed at him, at his intrusion. But no, he realized, Bannagran hadn't yet registered the possession for what it was, and so the revulsion was aimed squarely at the would-be King of Honce.

Gwydre! Bransen fired at him, and the images flowed freely, and Bannagran stirred again, even physically thrashed a bit on the cushiony chair. Bransen felt the warmth there . . . no, not warmth but heat.

He thought of Cadayle; he couldn't help but think of Cadayle!

And then there was Bannagran, thoughts afire, but not about Gwydre, nay, about the horror of this nightmare, of this intrusion.

Bransen retreated and ran away. With every bit of discipline he could muster—with every memory of lost Giavno playing loudly—Bransen resisted the primal urge to remain and to possess, the temptation that had destroyed so many monks, and he ran away. His spirit flew out the window and across the castle courtyard, over the wall, and out to the lake in the east, to the beacon of light that was the soul stone.

He came back to physical consciousness sitting on the rock by the lake, his hands trembling and mouth agape, gasping for breath. Reflexively, he glanced back toward the distant castle, as if he expected Bannagran to be exiting the gates, leading an army to find him and kill him for his violation.

Gradually Bransen calmed and sorted through the tumult of thoughts and images, the revulsion at the order of execution and at Yeslnik himself, and the strength of arousal at the notion of Dame Gwydre!

Bransen didn't return to Chapel Pryd that night but found some sleep right there beside the quiet lake, whose stillness so contrasted with the turbulence that roared in Bransen's spinning thoughts.

The next morning, Dame Gwydre found Bannagran sitting on his throne in the main hall of the ground floor of Castle Pryd, his bearded chin in his hands and a look of great consternation on his dark face.

"You will honor the agreement and flag of parley?" she asked. When he didn't answer, she added, "I will be out to the north and rid of Pryd Town this very morning."

Bannagran lifted his head and looked up at her, appearing as if her words had not at all registered.

Gwydre eyed him curiously. "The flag of parley?" she asked.

"Go where you will."

"Laird?"

"He's turned me back to the east," Bannagran replied, which only made Gwydre's puzzled expression screw up even more.

After a moment of consideration, she asked, "King Yeslnik?"

"I'm not needed along the Masur Delaval," Bannagran informed her. "And so it is back to Ethelbert dos Entel for my forces. There you have it, lady, get your Vanguardsmen to Laird Ethelbert's side and perhaps you can sting King Yeslnik's smaller force, far from home for both of us."

"Why would you tell me . . . ?" Gwydre's voice trailed off. "You were sent there to vanquish Laird Ethelbert, then recalled, and now, so soon, you are being turned about once more?"

"I lose ten men for every league we march," Bannagran replied. "Provisions have grown scarce from our passage, there and back, and the folk of all the towns between Pryd and Ethelbert dos Entel now flee when they hear word of an army, any army, drawing near—they flee, and quite efficiently, leaving little behind for hungry scavengers."

"You would tell this to King Yeslnik, but he wouldn't hear."

Bannagran snickered helplessly.

"Would General Bannagran advise this march at this time?" Gwydre asked.

"No."

"But Laird Ethelbert is a dangerous foe."

"Be gone, lady," Bannagran bade her.

"You know that this man you follow is not worthy to be king," Gwydre said. Bannagran looked up to glare at her, but she didn't back down. "You know it. Indeed, you know that his reign will be disastrous throughout its length, short may it be."

"Be gone, lady," Bannagran said again, this time with an ominous tone in his voice, one that told Gwydre that she was pushing him too hard.

"Perhaps I will return to you in the coming weeks," she said, and Bannagran looked at her as if she were insane. "When you can better judge my actions against your King Yeslnik. When you see the truth of who I am and what I do and how I do it. Will you honor my flag of parley again, Laird Bannagran?"

Bannagran snorted, shook his head, and chuckled helplessly. "If you have something to say worth hearing, lady."

Gwydre smiled coyly. "I always do."

She bowed and moved away, out the castle doors and across the courtyard. She arrived at Chapel Pryd, standing before Master Reandu, at the same time as Bransen arrived from the lake.

"The parley is ended," she told the monk.

"Profitably, I hope."

"We shall see," Gwydre started to say, but Bransen interrupted with a sly, "Yes."

Gwydre and Reandu looked at him curiously. "What do you know?" the Dame of Vanguard asked.

"I know Bannagran," Bransen replied cryptically, and as the others stared, he offered no more.

Finally, with a shrug, Gwydre addressed Reandu. "I may return in time."

"That would be advised," said a still smiling Bransen, and again the other two looked at him curiously.

"We may be gone," Master Reandu replied. "There are rumors afoot that Laird Bannagran has been ordered back to the east to do battle with Laird Ethelbert."

"He has," Gwydre confirmed. "But I doubt he'll go. The events in the heart of Honce will change quickly, and King Yeslnik will find that he needs Laird Bannagran right here in Pryd Town to protect his flank."

"We are all weary of the road and the war," said Reandu.

"Not all," Bransen said with a grin.

"Come," Gwydre bade Bransen. "We have much to do."

They set off to the north, bounding across the fields in great, gemstone-enhanced strides.

CHAPTER 21

Scout and Speed

"They are eager," Dame Gwydre said to the gathered leaders. She and Bransen had returned to the gulf coast to find Dawson and the Vanguard flotilla moored offshore, unloading a force of nearly five thousand Vanguard warriors. As they had then marched west to a position south of St. Mere Abelle, word had come of Milwellis's new march, back north along the river with a force much larger than the one he had commanded when he had left the field before St. Mere Abelle.

And so the brothers had gone forth spiritually over the next few days to monitor the young laird's progress and to follow the Palmaristown fleet as well, which was sailing hard out of the river, no doubt to blockade and bombard St. Mere Abelle yet again.

Every one of those spirit-walking monks had returned to his body shaken by the sight; several legions marched with purpose and good cheer, singing songs with every stride.

"I can get the boats loaded and back to sea," Dawson offered. "Might that we sail our boys all the way to Ethelbert's city but ahead o' them Palmaristown ships at any rate."

"We can fight them at sea," one of the captains said, and others agreed. These were the former leaders of the isolated Vanguard towns and really seemed more akin to Alpinadoran tribal chieftains of their respective followers than the lairds of Honce proper.

"We got only three ships that can fight one of theirs," another of the leaders chimed in. "And we've never sailed a ship that big into a battle. I'll fight 'em on land, not to doubt, and my boys will take down two, nay three, for every one I lose. But not at sea, Dawson. Not even for yourself, and we're all knowing that there's not e'er been a better sailor catching the following seas than Dawson McKeege."

Dame Gwydre looked to Dawson to respond.

"We cannot fight them at sea," Dawson admitted. "Might be that the powries'll hit them again, and so be it."

"Their warships concern me not at all, other than their role in delivering warriors to land," Gwydre concurred.

"So we brothers watch them," Brother Pinower offered, and Dame Gwydre nodded.

"Our more immediate concern is Laird Milwellis and his great force," Gwydre told them.

"Their front ranks have already turned from the river," said Brother Pinower.

"Toward St. Mere Abelle, no doubt," Gwydre replied

"It will take more than he has at his command to break the walls of St. Mere Abelle," Pinower asserted.

Bransen laughed at that, and all eyes settled on him.

"We won't go back in there," he said. "Not if we hope to win. Not if we hope to gain important allies in our cause. With you and your spying brethren supporting us," he said to Pinower, "and a cause we know to be just, we can move about much more easily than Milwellis's cumbersome force."

"And with much less attrition," Gwydre agreed. She shared a look with Bransen that spoke of confidence to those gathered about them, as if they had foreseen this march and now were prepared for it, even welcomed it.

"Particularly if we aid in that attrition," said the Highwayman, and he pulled his mask over his eyes as he finished. "I return after sunset."

"I will keep my candles burning," Dame Gwydre promised.

With a tap of his hand to his forehead, Bransen turned, fell into the magical energy of the magical hematite, and bounded away like a fleeing deer.

"Mobility," Dame Gwydre remarked quietly, and all around her leaned in as she elaborated. "Mobility and information. We will know our enemy's movements, but he will not know ours. We can catch him as we please, but he cannot catch us." She paused and let her gaze drift about the gathering.

"That is why we will win."

They are stretching their line, Bransen mused with a knowing smile. The spirit-walking monks had reported as much. By all reports of the commoners, the young laird's march to the river and all the way to Delaval City had been brilliantly executed. He had carved the riverbank like a grid, methodically and swiftly, and cleared each segment. The fleet sailing the river had coordinated all; the powries had been killed and chased away in short order.

But the Book of Jhest had taught Bransen that confidence could be a leader's important ally or his worst failing. In the days since his turn to the east, Laird Milwellis had allowed the growing excitement to get the best of his formation. Apparently expecting no enemies lying in wait, he had erred in allowing those front ranks to get out too far ahead of the main body of his vast army—an army that stretched for miles along the flat stones of the road. All of Milwellis's forward scouts had been spotted by the spirit walkers and caught by the Highwayman. The vast army was running blind into the ambush.

Lying on his belly at the top of a small hill north of the road, Bransen and a score of gemstone-wielding monks watched those front ranks march past. Down the hill behind Bransen, a hundred handpicked warriors lay in wait among the tall grasses, the strongest and most ferocious of the Vanguardsmen and some of the prisoners taken from the lines of Laird Ethelbert, men seething with hatred at the carnage this man, Milwellis, had inflicted upon their homes and their brethren.

The monk lying beside Bransen stirred, but Bransen motioned him to hold still and directed his gaze to the east, where a small cluster of farmhouses lay quiet amidst the rolling fields.

Gwydre's army was there, ready for a fight.

"Alone? Are you sure?" the monk beside Bransen whispered to him, and it was not the first time the man had expressed his concern.

Bransen glanced just west of his position, to the thin line of trees reaching down to the road and resuming again not far on the other side. He nodded and smiled, knowing that they had picked their spot very well. "Fast and hard and with a show of explosions," he whispered in reply. The monk nodded and both turned their heads back to the east to see the front ranks of the marching soldiers nearing the farms.

Another smile from Bransen and a definitive nod sent the monk into motion. On his signaling wave, the warriors began their quiet ascent up the back side of the hill. Bransen shifted to the west, inching toward the trees.

Gemstones in hand, the monks led the charge. A great shout went up from the hill, and from on high came the brothers and the warriors, banging their weapons and screaming with every stride.

Milwellis's soldiers on the road began to scramble into position; horns blew a haphazard warning song. The first bolts of lightning reached down to the road, heightening the confusion more than inflicting any real damage. Milwellis's soldiers farther to the east predictably turned and then predictably turned again at the sound of the charge of Gwydre's army.

Bransen watched it all unfolding, measuring the progress and reminding himself to be patient. His timing was the most critical here. He rolled the two gemstones, serpentine and ruby, around in his right palm and keenly felt the connection to the malachite held in his left hand.

Milwellis's forces began to regroup quickly, a testament to the seasoned fighting force. All except for those on the road directly before the charge of the monks and the handpicked warriors, just below Bransen, just to the east of the tree break. More warriors came in, east and west, to try to bolster the battered area.

Bransen tapped his closed fists to his forehead. By the time he brought them down, he was glowing softly, a blue-white hue. He leaped away, a great, malachite-enhanced bound, landing right before the trees nearly a third of the way to the road. As he touched down, he brought forth the power of the ruby, a great, fiery blast that flew out from him in all directions, setting ablaze branches and grasses.

He bounded again, and the fires exploded as he landed. He lifted off in his third great leap and saw Milwellis's warriors on the road before him, screaming in terror and scrambling for their lives. Some desperately threw spears as they fled, some drew their blades and set their feet.

This time Bransen enacted the ruby's power as he descended, just out of reach of the swordsmen, blowing a fiery gap in Milwellis's marching line. He touched down lightly, trying to ignore the screams of men aflame, and leaped away again to the south, extending the firebreak to the other side of the road.

Three jumping strides later, far from the road and the enemies, he turned back. His smile now was grim, but he was indeed smiling, for the influx of reinforcements had been halted and Gwydre's army charged in from the east, overwhelming all before them.

The monks and the lead force held their ground. Bodies piled around them, but they sang and they stabbed, and explosions of lightning crackled and thundered repeatedly. The Highwayman ran to them to bolster their position as the hundreds of enemies who had marched past that spot came rushing back, fleeing Gwydre.

For a long while, Milwellis's men had no organization to their retreat and were cut down with ease. As soon as a determined group had formed and begun its charge, Bransen again leaped out, evoking the largest fireball of all in the road before them. The vise closed as their coordination shattered in that moment of shock.

Most fled haphazardly only to be slain. Others just threw down their weapons and fell to their knees, begging mercy.

"Now turn!" Bransen yelled to the monks and the strike force, for Gwydre's army was upon them and the fight to the east in full control.

From the west, Milwellis's force streamed into battle through the firebreak, but the Highwayman and his allies met and turned them back, pushing right to that choke point between the burning lines of trees, and in that smaller bottleneck their fury and magic could not be withstood.

More than a mile back from the fighting, Laird Milwellis, riding beside Harcourt, heard the commotion brewing in the east. He kicked his mount to a trot, pushing through those footmen marching before him until he met up with the fleeing forces and saw the burning trees across the fields before him.

"Dame Gwydre!" men shouted.

"Monks of Chapel Abelle!" others keened in terror.

"We are routed!" yelled one.

Milwellis turned to Harcourt, panic evident on his young face.

"Now is your moment, laird," the general advised.

And so it was. Milwellis had seen enough combat to understand the implications of a rout, the potential catastrophe suffered by a force turning and fleeing in terror. He had used such tactics to turn the enemy forces at Pollcree; those enemies had never recovered.

Gwydre could do real damage here. He didn't believe that she had a sizable force, but that wouldn't matter.

Milwellis drew out his sword and lifted it high in the air to catch the light of the morning sun. He called for his trumpeters to blow loudly as he kicked his mount into a gallop off the road to the south, then swung about to the north.

"This is our moment!" he shouted in his booming, resonant voice. "Our foes have left the walls of their chapel prison! They cannot match us! They cannot withstand us! Charge, o you from the west! Form your groups and charge! Bang your shields and know that we win the war here and now!"

He looked to Harcourt as he finished, motioning his chin back to the west. The general kicked his mount into a run to help the formations and organize the waves of metal and flesh.

But Milwellis did not ride to join him. Determined that Dame Gwydre would not inflict a major wound on his army, the Laird of Palmaristown rode the opposite way, to the east, rallying the fleeing men to his wake as he went, calling for defensive squares upon every piece of high ground, reminding the warriors of who they were and who they served.

The Highwayman led the charge through the firebreak, running down flee-ing soldiers and turning more in terror before him.

But then he saw Laird Milwellis upon his steed, rallying his forces. How he wanted to rush out and engage the man then and there, to decapitate this invading army so soon into the campaign!

But he could not take that risk, for beyond Milwellis came the dark cloud of an army more vast than anything Bransen had ever imagined possible, roll-ing across the fields like a swarm of locusts with such girth and depth that Bransen could not understand why the earth itself did not collapse beneath their boots.

"To the firebreak! To the firebreak!" he called to monk and warrior alike, charging to and fro, collecting brothers and warriors and turning them back. He kept glancing at the distant Milwellis as he did, though, hoping for some opportunity for a personal battle to present itself.

It didn't, and Dame Gwydre and Brother Pinower were waiting for him when he came back through the firebreak.

"We must be gone from here at once," Bransen said to her. "The fires burn low, and Laird Milwellis will vigorously pursue."

No argument came back at him. This had already been decided long ago, a quick strike and a quicker retreat.

Dame Gwydre directed his gaze to the northeast, where a sizable force was already fleeing the field. "The prisoners, many score, to St. Mere Abelle," she explained. "We must hold here long enough for them to be safely away."

Bransen looked to Brother Pinower.

"Do you wish to attempt it?" the monk asked, and Bransen nodded.

Pinower immediately began rounding up the many brothers. "Graphite!" he instructed them, forming a long line just back from the firebreak while Dame Gwydre and Dawson set up a shield wall at the breach itself.

Milwellis's bulging front line came on, stopping short and filling the air with spears. Up went the shields, but still many men fell screaming, monk and warrior alike.

With a roar, the army of Palmaristown and Delaval came on.

The shield wall re-formed but seemed a puny thing before that massive charge, seemed as if it would surely be swept aside like parchment in a gale. At the last moment, Dawson shouted the command and the shield wall collapsed—just fell to the ground—and the line of monks, Bransen at their center, all joining hands left and right, leaped forward past them.

As one, the brothers fell into their graphite stones, building the charge and sending the lightning forth before them. Bransen improvised, reaching his own lightning out, angled left and right. His bolts intersected those of his companions, crossed them and caught them and turned the whole of the barrage into more of a net of lightning than a series of sharp bursts.

"Continue!" Brother Pinower cried. "Let the magic of the stones flow through you!"

And they did, and if one faltered, another rushed in to take his place. Bransen did not falter, though. His energy was the binding force here, the cross-link of the web, and the crackling air fanned out before them, engulfing Milwellis's front ranks as they neared.

Men stumbled, others toppled, and even those who somehow held their feet could not move forward with any force or determination. More warriors piled in behind, but the stubborn net of lightning did not dissipate, and they, too, were stopped short, shaking, teeth chattering, as they fell to the ground.

Behind the monks, Gwydre called for the retreat to the southeast.

Bransen fell into his soul stone at that call, sending his thoughts out left and right, connecting with the brothers. He felt the magic coursing through them, exiting their hands to fill the air before them. He heard Brother Pinower call for them to run away behind Gwydre's retreat. He heard Pinower call for him, the monk's voice growing distant, for he, too, obviously, had fled. But the Highwayman held his ground and somehow held the web of lightning intact. It seemed to him for many heartbeats as if he were somehow keeping that energy of his brethren left and right alive, as if he had stolen their magic with his own.

And, indeed, he had. He couldn't hold it, of course, not for any length of time, but when he at last released it in one final burst of power, he opened his eyes to see piles of trembling, shaking men, lines of disoriented and fallen soldiers so deep that those pressing in had to pick their way, their long way, to come at him.

A hundred spears did reach out at him, thrown in frustration by those behind the cluster of fallen attackers, but they landed harmlessly, for Bransen reached again into his malachite and sprang away ahead of the barrage, leaping far to the southeast.

He caught up to Pinower and the trailing brothers almost immediately, Milwellis's force coming in fierce pursuit. The lightning web had killed no one, Bransen knew, but he thought himself quite clever, indeed, for when they had laid out the battlefield plan, they had determined their retreat through a small forest surrounding some hills to the southeast.

Now that forest loomed before them, and they knew if they could get into it, Milwellis could not catch them.

For the last ones in—Bransen and Brother Pinower—set the woods ablaze.

O n his mount in the fields before the firestorm that engulfed the forest, Laird Milwellis could only stare hatefully at the blocked trail.

"We will catch them, laird," Harcourt assured him. "We have seen their tricks, and they flee away from Chapel Abelle, their only possible refuge."

"They are small and fleet."

"But we will ensnare them, do not doubt."

Milwellis looked to his trusted friend and nodded. "Send a long arm straight east," he instructed. "They are not to gain a northward march—cut them off from Chapel Abelle."

Laird Milwellis was not discouraged when he went back to the road and the original battlefield. He had lost about three hundred men, but no matter, for his enemy had played her hand, and now she was removed from Chapel Abelle's strong walls.

It was only a matter of time.

T he man stumbled but held his balance, clutching his face all the while, blood running from between his fingers.

Seated before him, Bannagran knew that he shouldn't have slugged the messenger. The poor sot was just a messenger, after all. But since King Yeslnik was far away, the messenger had to suffice.

Bannagran looked down at the crumpled parchment in his hand, the newest order from King Yeslnik. The fool had recalled him again. *Abandon the march to Ethelbert dos Entel!* the note read. *Return to Pryd Town and hold the center region as brave Laird Milwellis catches our enemy Gwydre and destroys her.*

Bannagran threw the parchment to the floor and turned an exasperated expression on Master Reandu, standing beside him. Reandu backed away a step. He, after all, had read the note to Bannagran. Judging by the man still stumbling before the throne, the news had not been well received.

"Do you think that Yeslnik even knows that we never left Pryd Town after his last reversal?" Bannagran asked.

"I think that many things are happening, and quickly," Reandu answered. "The king is reacting to a shifting situation."

"He is purely reacting," Bannagran replied contemptuously. "His plans shift with the change of the wind."

"Gwydre came forth from St. Mere Abelle," Reandu reminded.

"And the brave Laird Milwellis will hunt her and kill her."

The sarcasm and anger in Bannagran's tone was not lost on anyone in the room, and many cautious looks came back at him. He laughed at himself, shook his head, and pointed to the trembling messenger. "Heal the man!" he ordered Reandu.

The monk hustled to do just that, while Bannagran focused again on the crumpled parchment. Why had it so angered him, particularly given his decision that he wasn't marching to Ethelbert dos Entel anyway? The stupidity disturbed him, surely, for this was Yeslnik's third reversal of the marching order. But no, it was more than the typical failings of Yeslnik, Bannagran had to admit, particularly in light of his inadvertent tone when he had spoken of Laird Milwellis. For a long while now, Bannagran and Milwellis had been viewed as competing for the favor of King Yeslnik, and while Bannagran had mostly avoided any confirmation of that seemingly ridiculous notion, the building rivalry was obviously in his thoughts.

Did he really care about Yeslnik's favor, or was this simply an expression of his pride and determination in bettering his perceived rival?

"The brave Milwellis," he muttered under his breath, and he remembered a day during the campaign in the east when he had arrived at Yeslnik's encampment with a large group of prisoners. Yeslnik had ordered him to execute them, and when he had balked, the king had turned the duty over to the other arriving general, then Prince Milwellis of Palmaristown. Milwellis had done the deed, gleefully, so Bannagran had heard.

Bannagran spat at the parchment. He rubbed his bearded face and closed his eyes, only to find an image of Dame Gwydre waiting for him.

CHAPTER 22

King Yeslnik's Long, Hot Summer

They found the town of Pollcree deserted that hot early-summer day. They had expected as much, for the approach of an army—any army—struck sheer terror into the hearts of the beleaguered Honce citizens after these brutal years of war.

Fortunately for the folk of Pollcree, though, this was Dame Gwydre's army, with no intention of causing mischief. Even more fortunately for Pollcree, the spirit-walking monks knew precisely where the townsfolk had gone to hide.

By design, Bransen was first to that spot, a series of well-hidden caves more than a mile to the south of the town itself. He approached silently and in the shadows, taking a lay of the ground and noting several disguised entrances. He went to the largest, near the center of the line along a long running ridge.

"Belay your spears," he called as he neared. "I am no enemy. I am the Highwayman of Pryd Town, sick of war and of lairds who claim dominion over lands they do not own."

There was no movement from the shadows behind the brush that had been piled before the opening, but Bransen knew that guards watched him from within. Still he approached openly, confident that he could dodge any spear or arrow coming forth.

"Will you greet me, or will you cower?" he asked. "For I know you are in these caves, hiding from the march of another army."

He shuffled forward slowly, hands up before him unthreateningly. He heard a whisper, "Kill him!" followed by some tussling and objections.

"What will you gain by killing me?" he asked, straightening. "I come to you unarmed and in peace, with information and to serve as your prisoner if you so determine that necessary."

He was right at the brush by then, where he paused and listened. But no sound came forth, and he could well imagine several guards just inside the cave, holding their collective breath.

"Your leaders will wish to hear what I have to say," he remarked and began to pull brush away from the pile.

"No!" came a call from above and to Bransen's right. He looked up and tried to hide his surprise when he saw two guards—a man and a woman—standing on an outcropping barely fifteen feet from him. The man held a sword, the woman a bow, leveled his way.

Bransen held up his hands.

"Not through there," the man instructed, waving Bransen up to him.

For a moment, Bransen considered falling into his malachite magic and leaping the fifteen feet to stand before the pair, but he wisely decided against that course, realizing that it might bring a frightened shot from the archer. So he climbed up agilely instead, wiping the dirt from his hands as he stood before the pair.

"The Highwayman of Pryd Town?" the woman asked, seeming unimpressed.

But the man added, "I have heard tell of you."

Bransen bowed politely.

"Why have you come?" the woman asked sharply.

"With information. To tell you of the army that approaches—one you need not fear—and of the momentous happenings in Honce."

"We know all too much of those," said the man.

Bransen bowed again.

The woman motioned with her bow to an opening in the hillside, barely visible behind a large stone. With the bow still trained on him, Bransen led the way in.

As his eyes adjusted to the dimness of the cave beyond, with few torches burning and only a few openings letting in meager bits of daylight, he noted a sight that had become all too familiar about Honce: the beleaguered civilians of an awful war, mostly very young and very old, their faces haggard, eyes full of fear. But fear tinged with deep resignation, Bransen noted, and that made it all the more heartbreaking.

He noted, too, many weapons leveled his way.

"I am not your enemy," he said.

An old woman shifted through the crowd. She was thin, very thin, with a hunched back, but despite her advanced age—Bransen figured that she had to be near to ninety years old—her hair was still dark and barely tinged with gray.

"Then why are ye here?" she asked. Bransen's scrutinizing gaze prompted her to add, "Eireen's me name, and Pollcree's me town."

"The Dame of Pollcree?"

"Bah, but Pollcree's not a holding, just a town," she corrected. "Part o' Laird Binyard's lands, but he's dead now, o' course, and his garrison's scattered and the lands are in ruin."

"The Governess of Pollcree, then," Bransen said with a bow.

"As good a title as any, for what any're worth."

"I am here as the advance messenger for the army of Dame Gwydre of Vanguard, who has joined with the brothers of St. Mere Abelle. . . ."

"Brothers o' what?"

"Chapel Abelle," Bransen clarified. "Now St. Mere Abelle. The monks who serve the memory and desires of Father Artolivan."

"Memory? He dead, too?"

Bransen nodded. "Peacefully so, and with his successor picked, and with a new mission for the brethren." He stepped back to take in more of the audience as he finished. "To oppose the war and the men who claim dominion at the end of a spear. The brothers are to serve the townsfolk, not to support the armies that march and ravage the land."

"Didn't ye just say ye was in front of an army, then?" Eireen asked.

"But an army that has entered Pollcree in peace, good governess. Not to burn your buildings but to repair them." That brought more than a few whispers about the cave, and more and more people gathered around.

"Do send your scouts to confirm my words. Five thousand men and women, repairing homes and finishing the work in the fields . . . well, as much as two days will allow, for that is all that we have, with Laird Milwellis and a vast force in pursuit of us. We wish to be away long before he nears, that he'll turn aside from Pollcree and not march through your fair town.

"And Dame Gwydre herself will arrive here soon. Yes, we know of this place, and it was not happenstance that brought me here. She will come with brothers carrying gemstones to heal the wounds of your people and with stocks of food for the people of Pollcree. Our hunters have been busy of late, the game surprisingly plentiful."

"At what cost?"

"None."

Eireen looked at him skeptically, as did many others.

"Dame Gwydre will defeat Laird Milwellis and Yeslnik, who calls himself king," Bransen assured her. "And she will rule Honce as she has ruled Vanguard, a servant of her minions, who would see to their health and well-being in the knowledge that such will promote a stronger and more prosperous land for all."

"Ye said ye were against war."

Bransen shrugged. "Some stubborn people simply will not surrender, I fear."

"Ye're crazy."

"I have been called that and worse." From outside the cave came word that a small force of soldiers and porters and monks neared the hillside. "But no matter," Bransen finished. "For Pollcree, the present is good, whatever the ultimate result. Come and meet Dame Gwydre, I bid you. Have your sick and injured gather and prepare your cooking fires for a meal long overdue and long deserved."

What choice did the folk of Pollcree have? They were no army, and the few among them who could fight would have been slaughtered to a man and woman had they attacked even the fraction of Dame Gwydre's army that accompanied her to the caves that hot summer day. And any thoughts they had of resisting, even of doubting, diminished quickly, as the monks went to the task of using the soul stones on the sick and injured and as piles of food—good and fresh food—were set before the caves.

Eireen did send scouts to the town proper, and they returned excited and grinning widely, with reports of ongoing repairs to roofs and walls and many crops being put in. Suddenly what had seemed assuredly a disastrous harvest was given promise, though much of the season was past.

The critical moment of the entire encounter came as midday passed, when Bransen happened upon a secret back chamber of the cave and found within a group of nearly fifty men and women, young and healthy.

"Dame Gwydre," he called. "You will see this." Many of the twoscore and ten before him put their heads down in despair. Some wept, for they had been through this before.

Gwydre, Brother Pinower, and Dawson arrived beside a protesting Eireen and with scores of townsfolk behind them.

"Well now, what have we here?" Dawson asked.

"Deserters," Bransen reasoned.

"Ye're not to take them!" Eireen yelled sharply at Gwydre, but the younger woman held up her hand, and her commanding presence set Eireen back on her heels.

"You have tired of war, and who can blame you?" Dame Gwydre said to the frightened group. "I'll not ask which side you fought for, for it hardly seems to matter now." She turned to the monk. "Brother Pinower, fetch your brethren and tend to these poor souls."

"I'm not fighting!" one woman yelled from the back.

"No," Gwydre said before others could chime in. "Nor do I ask that of you. You have nothing to fear from me and mine. We come not as conquerors and surely as no press-gang! But do come forth from this hole. There is food aplenty!"

"At what cost?" one man near to Gwydre asked sharply.

"I charge you with continuing the work here at Pollcree," Gwydre answered without hesitation. "Your weapon is a plow or a hoe or a mallet, if need be. That is the price I place upon you, if you are to partake of the healing magic and the foodstuffs. What say you?"

They said little and moved tentatively, as did the other off-balance towns-folk, for none had expected anything quite like this. For years, they, like many of Honce's other towns, had been battered by the march of one army after another, their healthy, young adults whisked away to fight for Ethelbert or for Delaval or for Yeslnik—it mattered not at all.

But Dame Gwydre kept her word, and for two days her monks and soldiers tilled and planted, hammered and split wood, healed and gave food, and then, with Milwellis turning toward her from the north, she bid Pollcree fare-well and marched her army off to the southwest.

Indeed, she and her forces were planting more seeds than those in the fields.

And they continued to sow, day after summer day, in villages across the north-central region of Honce.

Sweat beaded on Laird Milwellis's sunburned face as he surveyed the rolling fields before him. Dame Gwydre was supposed to be here. Every report had indicated that her march would take her to this very spot and in a time frame that allowed Milwellis to arrive first.

But she wasn't here.

"I assured King Yeslnik that battle would be joined in this time and place," the laird said quietly to Harcourt, riding at his side.

"Her force is smaller and more nimble," Harcourt replied.

That did little to comfort Milwellis. For weeks now, as summer had passed its midpoint, he had been in pursuit of the elusive dame. Time and again, Mil-wellis had marched into a town to discover that Dame Gwydre's army had passed through only a few days—once, only a few hours!—prior and then had vanished like ghosts into the countryside.

Every ambush he had set had been missed or ambushed in turn, and always in that hit-and-run style, a quick skirmish with little real damage to either side, though with more to Milwellis's ranks, invariably.

Milwellis glanced around at his vast army, at the tired and sweaty faces. The damage he saw there, not measured in blood, was all too real.

"Do you think Gwydre grows as weary of this as I do?" he said.

"Do you?"

Milwellis looked at Harcourt directly and grimly and shook his head. "The townsfolk grow to love her and supply her forces and cheer their passage."

"And so we must continue to make examples of them as traitors!" declared Father De Guilbe, riding up to join the pair. Obviously uncomfortable in the brutal heat and astride a horse, the giant man huffed and puffed with every word.

Milwellis fixed him with a stern stare. De Guilbe had only recently rejoined them, sent as an emissary from the impatient Yeslnik.

"You should have burned every house in Pollcree to the ground," the monk went on undeterred. "And more than a few with the families still inside! They gave comfort to your enemy."

"You have that backward, good father," said Harcourt.

"Nay," Father De Guilbe argued. "Their relationship is mutual. In accepting the hand of Gwydre, they reject the hand of King Yeslnik, and so they must be punished. Every villager of every town in Honce must know that the arrival of Dame Gwydre portends doom. We must teach them to shun her or even to fight her."

"Enough, De Guilbe," said Milwellis. "We did punish Pollcree."

"The only villagers executed were the four brothers of Chapel Pollcree!" the monk reminded. "A fitting example."

"You walk a thin ledge here," Harcourt warned the monk. "You would have us batter King Yeslnik's subjects while Dame Gwydre feeds them?"

"What is your more gentle recourse gaining you? When Gwydre moved through Pollcree those weeks ago, you did nothing to warn her away, and, alas, the witch returned through the town to cheers!"

The simple statement of fact left Harcourt at a loss, and he turned away. With a superior expression stamped upon his wide, tanned face, the monk not so gracefully turned his gelding about and bounced away.

"The taste of that man grows more foul with every word," Harcourt grumbled.

"But perhaps there lie beads of truth within his uninvited sermons," Milwellis replied, and he was almost as surprised by his statement as was Harcourt, whose eyes widened and mouth hung agape.

"He would have us attacking Chapel Abelle while Gwydre runs free!"

"Not that, of course," said Milwellis. "But regarding the villagers."

"Pollcree?"

"When De Guilbe executed the four brothers of Pollcree, did not the fifth and sixth join his ranks?" Milwellis asked.

"Oh, and I'll be counting upon their loyalty when the arrows fill the air," came the sarcastic reply.

Milwellis dismissed that obvious retort with a glare. "Where is she?" he asked his general, turning back to the field and the question of Gwydre. "She should be here, and yet, her forces are nowhere to be found. And so we continue our run through the heat and the mud, losing men at every turn in the road."

"Gwydre runs, too."

Milwellis shook his head, having none of it. He understood the difference here and, indeed, could see it clearly within the two factions of his own army. The Delaval contingent, war-weary and too long from home, marched because they had no choice in the matter. Some spoke around their campfires in nostalgic whispers about Laird Delaval, but these were men and women too long from home and detached from any real sense of purpose out here.

They were in stark contrast to Milwellis's Palmaristown garrison, men and women who had seen their homes burned and their neighbors murdered by the most foul powries and who blamed Dame Gwydre personally for that heinous attack. All they wanted, all Milwellis wanted, was to take the field against Gwydre and repay her for the assault on Palmaristown. They were hot and tired, of course, but their purpose remained strong, and, to a one, they would stay out here for as long as it took to defeat the witch of Vanguard.

Milwellis wasn't worried about losing his Palmaristown soldiers to attrition, and, he feared, neither was Gwydre regarding her fresher Vanguard contingent.

Across the fields later that same afternoon, Laird Milwellis marched into a hamlet, just a cluster of about a dozen houses and a single common room. He blamed them, loudly and publicly, for aiding Dame Gwydre and accused them of warning her of his approach. No denials rang loudly enough to defeat his accusations.

He burned the town to the ground and killed every male villager he found, the very old and the boys who could barely be called men.

"So be it," he remarked to the fuming Harcourt as they rode out of the hamlet. "Let us try Father De Guilbe's way."

I trust that you will honor the flag of parley," Bransen said when he entered the castle.

"Are you going to ask me that every time you bring Dame Gwydre to Pryd?" Bannagran replied.

"Protocol."

"Bring her in and be gone," the laird said and waved his hand. But he was smiling, as he had been over the last few weeks on every occasion that Bransen had brought Dame Gwydre for a visit. And over the last three weeks, since the passage of midsummer, those visits had grown much more frequent.

"There is more this time," Bransen said. "More that I must ask of you."

Bannagran looked at him with a mixture of curiosity and concern. Bransen was glad to see that concern!

"I must be gone this night," Bransen explained. "And I fear that I may not return. Should that happen, I would ask you to deliver Dame Gwydre back to her forces."

"Where are you going? Is this some plot to murder Yeslnik or Milwellis?"

Bransen shook his head. "It is a personal quest, one that I have avoided and wrongly so. If I succeed, then I should return by this time tomorrow. If not, then know that I languish in Laird Ethelbert's dungeon or, more likely, that I am dead."

"You're going for your sword."

Bransen didn't blink.

The Laird of Pryd began to laugh. "All your talk of service to Dame Gwydre and service to Honce is a lie, then," he chided.

Bransen stiffened his spine but didn't respond. He understood Bannagran's reasoning, of course, and had battled it mightily in his own thoughts for many days now.

"Why would you do something so dangerous when the cost to Dame Gwydre's cause would be very high and the gain, if there is one, is to Bransen and not to Honce?"

Bransen didn't see things that way. There was more to that sword and the brooch than the personal comfort of having them returned would bring. With those items, he would surely better serve Dame Gwydre's cause. More than that, though, Bransen knew now that he needed to do this to complete his journey.

And it was past time to sort out this uneasy relationship with Laird Ethelbert.

"The night is uncomfortable," came Gwydre's voice from the doorway. "The biting bugs relish the heat."

"Do enter," Bannagran said.

Gwydre walked up, but stopped short, looking from the laird to Bransen. "Have I missed an important conversation?"

"No," said Bransen, but Bannagran interjected, "Your man here was telling me that he will be off at once to hunt Laird Ethelbert's assassins."

Dame Gwydre's eyes opened wide, and she gawked at Bransen.

"We must learn of Laird Ethelbert's intent," he said.

"He sits and waits and watches," she replied, "like many of the lairds." When she finished, she put a sly look over at Bannagran, who merely shrugged. "Our progress has been strong. Laird Milwellis and King Yeslnik grow more frustrated and foolish by the day. The countryside is turning against them. You would risk—"

"The countryside is full of old women and children," Bannagran interrupted. "Your dance around Milwellis's force has been impressive, I admit, but if he catches you, he will destroy you."

"Only if the other lairds of Honce are too cowardly to stand for that which is right for Honce," Dame Gwydre retorted without hesitation.

"A mouse who steps aside from a charging horse is no coward," Bannagran replied.

"I see a town possessing a vast army with a general they adore," said Gwydre. "Hardly a mouse, sir."

Their stares grew more intense with each word, and Bransen realized that this was not a new discussion, that, more likely, they threw these words back and forth with each of Dame Gwydre's visits, like a ritual . . . a courting ritual.

"I will not go if you deny me permission," Bransen interjected.

Both dame and laird turned to him, and both seemed almost surprised to find that he was still there.

"What do you intend to do?" Gwydre asked.

Bransen blew a deep breath and offered an almost sheepish shrug. "To speak with Ethelbert, to try reason with him again, both for his allegiance and for the return of those items wrongly taken from me."

"And if he denies you? Do you intend to do battle with the garrison of Ethelbert dos Entel to get to this assassin woman?"

Bransen shook his head—an honest answer—for he knew that it would never come to that. Affwin Wi would not need to be cornered to engage in a duel with him. She would welcome it. It was her way, the way of the warrior, the way of Hou-lei and of Jhesta Tu.

"You have earned my trust in your judgment," Gwydre said. "I owe you this, at least—and indeed, much more. Be temperate and be wise, my young friend. Honce cannot afford to lose the Highwayman at this time."

Bannagran snickered at that, but Bransen ignored him and offered a nod and an appreciative smile to Gwydre.

"Return to me as soon as is possible," Gwydre commanded. "I charge you with that task above all."

Bransen nodded again and took his leave, fully intending to adhere to that order.

M y dance about Honce impresses you?" Gwydre asked as soon as Bransen had left them alone.

Smiling, Bannagran rose from his seat and moved to stand before her. "So much about you impresses me," he said quietly, and they kissed.

But Bannagran pulled back from that embrace and, grinning wickedly, added, "But I still think that King Yeslnik is going to kill you."

Gwydre fell back as if slapped, but only for a moment. "Only if Bannagran is a coward," she retorted, and the mighty laird laughed all the louder.

CHAPTER 23

Full Circle

Merwal Yahna stayed in the deepening shadows as the courier chattered excitedly to the guards escorting her in from the gate.

"From Behr," the woman said, her accent showing her to be from central Honce, likely Pryd Town itself. "And Laird Bannagran held one in his dungeon." She turned, wide-eyed, to the guard on the other side. "But the man escaped and tried to kill Laird Bannagran himself!"

"Laird Ethelbert will hear of this," that guard assured her. "And he will answer Bannagran's demand of accountability!"

Merwal Yahna glanced all around. The castle was in sight, just up the road. He drew out his weapon. He leaped from the shadows.

Just a few moments later, he dragged three bodies into the back of a storage shed and covered them with sacks of grain.

Sleep, my tired love," Affwin Wi whispered into Laird Ethelbert's ear, at the same time her index finger pressed expertly at the artery along the side of his neck.

The old man opened his eyes and tried to sort through this mystery. He had made love to her that night, the first time he had been able to perform such an act in a long, long while. Affwin Wi had given him a drink of powerful herbs to facilitate the act, and they had worked marvelously.

But now, afterward, Ethelbert lay in his bed, his body numb, his arms and legs not answering the call of his thoughts, unable even to speak, to question, to protest.

"Sleep, my tired old lover," Affwin Wi said, a wicked grin on her beautiful face.

Ethelbert stared at her, his expression asking the question he was unable to voice.

"Your day is past," the woman explained. "You have surrendered your ambition. There is nothing more for you." She pressed her finger in harder, and Ethelbert's vision blurred.

"I do this for you," Affwin Wi said.

Ethelbert stared at her for the few heartbeats he had remaining of consciousness.

When he lay still, Affwin Wi knelt, leaned back, and stared at him for a long, long while.

Finally she slipped off the side of the bed and slowly dressed. She was surprised at the heaviness in her heart, pointedly reminding herself that Ethelbert had been a tool for her gain and nothing more.

She had to be done with him now, she stubbornly told herself. He had indeed surrendered his ambition. However the greater war fell out, Laird Ethelbert was determined to be no more than a minor player.

"We should not have pursued the emissaries," Merwal Yahna said, entering from the shadows at the side of the room. He glanced from Affwin Wi to the naked form of dead Ethelbert upon the bed. "You made love to that wrinkled old beast?" he asked, scrunching up his face as if someone had dangled a hill skunk carcass in front of his nose.

"He was a great man, once," the woman replied. "He deserved as much before he died."

"He could have been a great man again had we let him join with Bannagran of Pryd."

Affwin Wi shook her head. They had been through this already, in the discussion that had led her to Ethelbert's chamber that night, aphrodisiac and paralyzing poison in hand.

The pair were running out of options. No doubt other guards at the gate had heard bits of the woman courier's claims.

"I do not wish to return to Behr," Affwin Wi stated.

"Then where? To Bannagran after our minion tried to kill him? To King Yeslnik? Does he know that your sword took the heart of his uncle?"

"Perhaps Kirren Howen will prove more ambitious than Ethelbert," Affwin Wi said. "Perhaps he will seek greater glories, and, if not him, then Myrick or Tyne."

"And when they find the bodies? And when they hear the tale of Ishat and Wahloon?"

"Your good cheer serves me well this night when a man I cared for lies dead before me," the woman sarcastically replied.

Merwal Yahna didn't reply, just stood staring, as did Affwin Wi. Had they truly wound themselves into a corner from which there was no gain to be found? Was the only road left to them a journey back to Behr?

Gradually, Merwal Yahna found himself looking to Affwin Wi for an answer, as he always did for guidance. When a wry smile at last spread upon her face, the man's expression grew anxious.

"The courier," Affwin Wi said. "Deliver her body to this room."

Merwal Yahna's smile was immediate, as the plan came clear to him, for it all made perfect sense. The treachery of Bannagran, sending an assassin in the guise of a courier, would serve them well with Kirren Howen, particularly if they wanted the man to go forth to seek greater glories.

It would take a caravan longer to travel from Pryd Town to Ethelbert dos Entel than to St. Mere Abelle, but only because of a winding road through difficult terrain. For Bransen, freed of such impediments through use of the malachite magic, the journey was much easier. Long before dawn, he saw the distant lights of Laird Ethelbert's large seaport, smelled the Mirianic, and heard the crash of waves.

As he lay down to sleep, nestled in the mossy roots of a large tree, he reminded himself of how blessed he was to enjoy such freedom. He, the poor Stork who could barely escape the confines of Chapel Pryd's small courtyard, could now run the breadth of Honce in a matter of days! He, the awkward and unbalanced youth who could be knocked over by the slightest push of a bully, could now challenge the likes of Affwin Wi.

He put his hand into his pouch and felt the various gemstones, connecting with their magic just long enough to identify them, as he tried to sort through the tactics he would need to balance the fight against the woman. Even if Merwal Yahna did not join in—and Bransen believed that he would—Affwin Wi had the advantage here, in no small part because she was in possession of Bransen's own sword. And the brooch. How much had she learned of the gemstone powers? What level of mastery had she attained?

The magical aspect of their upcoming battle was his advantage, he told himself as he drifted off to much-needed sleep.

He awoke early but did not immediately go into the city. As he considered his course, he understood that he didn't want to fight Affwin Wi in there. Too many of her allies could be about him, unseen and waiting for the moment to strike. And even if he won, in Ethelbert's city with so dramatic a victory at hand, he might then have to battle with and escape from half the garrison! Even worse, if he defeated Affwin Wi before so many witnesses—perhaps before Ethelbert himself—then how would he subsequently speak with the laird regarding Dame Gwydre? That, he reminded and scolded himself, was no small part of this mission to the southeast.

Soon after midday, he picked his careful way closer to the city walls, moving steadily east, north of the city, until he came to the rocky shoreline, with the docks in sight south of his position. Laird Ethelbert had relaxed his defensive posture, Bransen recognized all along the way. The immediate threat of Bannagran and Yeslnik had been removed, and so the people of Ethelbert dos Entel had returned to the more mundane and necessary duties of life: working the fields outside the city walls and fishing the waters of the Mirianic. Bransen had spotted few armed soldiers along the wall.

He removed his backpack and produced clothing typical of the region: loose-fitting, well-worn, and weathered. His darker skin tones would serve him well here, for many of Laird Ethelbert's subjects could trace a branch of their ancestry to the southern land of Behr.

Using the malachite to cross inlets of water and to navigate sharp outcroppings of stone, he easily managed to stay far from the occasional fisherman along the shore. Bransen slipped around the corner of the wall, rushed a few steps across the water, and then scrambled up the dock posts to join a throng of fishmongers and customers. Without incident, he arrived at the wing of Ethelbert's castle housing Affwin Wi and the remnants of her dwindling band.

And there, Bransen stood frozen by his doubts. Could he beat this woman, this assassin of Behr? And how could he be taking such a risk as this, with Dame Gwydre, her entire cause, depending upon him to perform those tasks as only the Highwayman could? Who else could deliver Gwydre to Pryd Town so secretly and swiftly week after week?

All of those disturbing notions swirled in Bransen's head and heart until even more profound risks bubbled up in his thoughts. What of Cadayle? What of their child? How could he be so selfish as to take this risk, at this delicate time?

"It is necessary," he whispered quietly. "This must be settled, for the sake of Gwydre's kingdom, for Ethelbert's place." He went silent, but his thoughts continued, *And for me.*

That was the crux of it. Bransen knew that he could not serve Gwydre, serve the cause, to his fullest ability while this sword—his sword—hung over him, casting dark shadows on all that he had to believe was true.

Like a raindrop on a windowpane, Bransen felt as if he was rushing, rushing downward to an inevitable and inevitably futile end. He could believe in Dame Gwydre's Honce, even in Bannagran's Honce if it came to that. He could take joy in the potential future of his life with Cadayle and their child and with Callen and Dawson, no doubt nearby.

But those were merely pieces in the larger scene of the life of Bransen Garibond, the purpose of his existence, the demands of his heritage. He could not be true to himself, to the identity of the Highwayman, and to the promise of his mother and father—both fathers!—if he did not settle this. He took a deep breath and steeled his resolve, but before he could take a step, a voice from on high assailed him.

"You!" Affwin Wi shouted. Bransen looked up just in time to see the woman lift his sword and leap from the balcony a score of feet above him.

On pure reflex, Bransen flipped sidelong into a cartwheel, then a second, coming around just as Affwin Wi landed in a graceful roll. All around them people turned to watch, and up above Bransen heard the cry of Merwal Yahna.

This is not the place! his thoughts screamed at him, but when Affwin Wi came on he met her charge ferociously. He leaped into the air, leg snapping out once and again. He barely dodged the stab of her sword, as she barely ducked away from the double-kick as she tumbled past him.

He landed and spun, lifting a circle kick as he went to keep her at bay, for the nimble woman was back to her feet almost immediately, reversing her momentum to strike at him again.

Bransen turned and dove back to a garden beside the porch of Affwin Wi's castle wing. He rolled across the dirt between two small trees and came to his feet with the larger trunk, the width of a forearm, separating him from the pursuing Affwin Wi.

She slashed his sword across powerfully, felling that tree.

As Bransen had expected.

As the sword sliced cleanly through, he launched a spinning kick against the severed trunk, knocking it aside. As he came around to face Affwin Wi, who was all too eager to charge into him, he thrust forward his hands, left and right, and launched two fistfuls of dirt into her face.

Bransen retreated into the alley. He leaped up against the side of the castle wall, touching with his right foot, then springing away at an angle to climb higher on the perpendicular city wall, where his left foot found a quick brace to spring him back to the right. Back to the left, right again against the castle wall, and then left yet again, put him to the top of the castle wall.

He had meant to go right over, but a sentry to the left caught his eye, the man just drawing his sword. A leap landed Bransen right before him, too close for the man's reactive swing to gain any momentum. Bransen's left hand caught the man by the wrist, while Bransen punched straight out with his right, his open palm thumping hard right into the center of the poor sentry's chest. The man staggered backward, all strength gone as he tried to draw breath, and Bransen deftly stole his sword.

He heard Affwin Wi in fast pursuit and did not doubt that she would scale as easily as he, though the malachite had enhanced his strides, and so he didn't dally any longer. With a nod of apology to the stunned sentry, he leaped from Ethelbert dos Entel to the foothills and then bounded along with great, floating strides. Shouts went up behind him, arrows flew. But he was too swift, his leaps too erratic, and soon he crossed down to the western plains before the city.

Affwin Wi pursued.

He saw that, welcomed it as he continued to the north in full stride, past the gawking farmers, past the shouts of the city guards, and beyond the reach of the occasional spear or arrow. All pursuers fell far behind save Affwin Wi, and even she could not keep up with his exaggerated leaps, except that he wanted her to. Bransen went around to the north of the city, to the higher and more familiar ground, and eventually came to a bluff from which he and Jameston Sequin had once looked down at Ethelbert dos Entel.

This was the spot, this was the time of Bransen's choosing.

He reached into his pouch and produced his gemstones, sorting them, feeling them, teasing their magical energies. He noted Affwin Wi's determined approach and a second figure, similarly dressed, running hard to catch her.

The doubts began to rise, but Bransen dismissed them.

He was no raindrop wearily dying on a pane of glass; he was the Highwayman, the son of Sen Wi and Bran Dynard, the child of Garibond Womak, the student of Jhesta Tu and of the gemstones of Blessed Abelle.

"You were a fool to come," Affwin Wi said as she cautiously approached.

"You tried to murder Cormack and Milkeila, even Laird Bannagran himself," Bransen retorted. "For so long now I have been wondering about that. What gain, after all, Laird Ethelbert might find in killing two emissaries from Dame Gwydre."

Affwin Wi grinned at him.

"Because it was not Laird Ethelbert," said Bransen. "Not with Cormack and Milkeila, and not with Jameston Sequin. It was you, the murderess of Behr. For a long time that made no sense to me." He tilted his head to regard her curiously. "Why?"

The woman just kept grinning.

"Because you feared the end of the war?" Bransen reasoned. "Because if the alliance had been forged, then both Bannagran and Gwydre would have stood taller than the laird who protected you? Is that why you tried to kill them?"

"And now I will kill you," Affwin Wi promised, and she charged forward, the Jhesta Tu sword leading the way with mighty slashes, weaving and cutting with practiced unpredictability.

The Highwayman cartwheeled to his right, coming up in a defensive posture, his sword back in tight near his shoulder, held vertically, his left hand out in front.

Affwin Wi dove into a roll as he disappeared to the side, came up to her feet, positioned perfectly to execute a swift turn, and closed immediately, cutting at Bransen's leading hand.

He dropped his hand easily under the swing and thrust his sword forward, but with a softened grip so that it caught Affwin Wi's swinging blade as a man might catch a thrown egg. As soon as the blades lay parallel before him, Bransen worked his wrist over, trying to hook his mother's sword and throw it from the woman's grasp.

But Affwin Wi rolled her wrist as well, opposite his, thus engaging the blades more swiftly than Bransen had anticipated, and so her own twist and slide nearly wrenched the sword from his hand!

That he held on was a credit to his strong grip, but Affwin Wi continued her riposte as if expecting that move all along, cutting short the follow-through of the sword throw and stabbing forward, twisting her delicately curving blade deftly to slip it past the cross hilt of Bransen's sword.

The Highwayman felt the sting and saw the blood, but again, his reaction was not far behind the move, and he avoided any major gashing. He reangled his blade and batted it across, rapping Affwin Wi's sword harmlessly.

On she came, cutting and thrusting in a wild and furious routine. The Highwayman fell into his crouch and worked his own blade with equal fervor, metal ringing against metal repeatedly, so quickly that it seemed like the chime of one long bell.

For a short while against the continuing barrage, Bransen tried to recognize the pattern to her movements, tried to sort it among the many routines he had learned in his perusal of the Book of Jhest. Turning his full attention away from the fight was his mistake, he realized when he missed one block and got nicked again on his forearm, then missed a second deflection as Affwin Wi thrust at him.

Bransen ducked desperately, angling to the side, but Affwin Wi's fine blade—his own mother's magnificent sword—sliced the outside of his left shoulder. He stumbled aside and she pursued, and again the swords collided with an impossibly frantic pace.

No longer was Bransen seeking recognition in his opponent's movements. No longer was he thinking of the Book of Jhest. No longer was he thinking at all! Now it was instinct and reaction, a back-and-forth stab and block and slice and parry that had the both of them moving about in hops and starts, forward, sidelong, and back.

Affwin Wi came across with a mighty cut, but the Highwayman's sword was there, vertically blocking.

But the Highwayman was barely holding it!

A look of confusion on her always confident face, Affwin Wi tried to reverse her cut as the blades connected, sending Bransen spinning end over end. Not to fly away, though, but to loop in place in the air, for the Highwayman had cleverly exerted just enough counterpressure on the hilt. He stepped his left foot out to the right before him, half turning, and caught the hilt of the spinning sword with a reverse grip in his left hand. Without hesitating, thinking he had won the day, he stabbed a backhand at the woman.

To his amazement, she was out of reach. Recognizing his vulnerability, the Highwayman did well to hide and dismiss his surprise that his clever move had scored him nothing. Not even aware of the action, he fell into the magic of the malachite and sprang up into the air, tumbling sidelong, tucking not at all, and still easily clearing not only Affwin Wi but also the reach of her overhead stab.

As he landed, shifting to face Affwin Wi directly, he found her in a similar spring and twist, now going above and beyond him, her downturned head a dozen feet from the ground.

"The brooch," Bransen heard himself whisper. He was not pleased to learn that Affwin Wi had so mastered the gemstones already!

He leaped again, so did she, and as they passed in midair, higher than a tall man's head, they brought their weapons crashing together, the force of the blow sending both of them spinning sidelong through their descent. But neither stayed on the ground for long, springing away, for now the fight had taken an extra dimension in its deadly dance.

They leaped and somersaulted, spun and lay out horizontally, floating past each other at various angles, striking out at each other each time to the ring of metal and with enough force to turn the combatants.

On one such pass, Bransen, flat out and facing downward after the twist from Affwin Wi's parry, tucked and flipped as he neared the ground. He planted his feet strongly and leaped backward as fast as he could manage, thinking to catch the woman before she could get fully into her subsequent launch.

But Affwin Wi hadn't jumped. As if she had, yet again, been one step ahead of Bransen, the woman landed and released the magic of the malachite in her brooch, grounding herself and coming about, perfectly positioned to catch him in his next flight.

The Highwayman noted it at the very last moment and released the malachite magic, dropping him short of the mark. He managed to lift his sword before him to block another mighty swing, but that, again, was exactly what Affwin Wi wanted. For she wasn't swinging at Bransen but at his blade.

The Jhesta Tu sword hummed as it came across, a thing of beauty, of delicate and powerful silverel metal, wrapped a thousand times over itself so that it only sharpened as it wore down. The Highwayman had no choice but to attempt a powerful block, and the rigid posture and powerful stance worked against him as Affwin Wi cut across with all her considerable strength. He heard the crash of metal; he saw a spark as the blades collided and instinctively blinked and recoiled. He opened his eyes to find himself holding a stub of a blade, two-thirds of its length spinning through the air to the side.

Affwin Wi presented her sword before him, claiming victory. Bransen heard laughter; he glanced sideways to see Merwal Yahna standing there, hands on hips.

Bransen retreated but quickly ran out of room as he came to the backside of the ridge, a sheer drop of twenty feet or more behind him.

"Yes, you can leap away," Affwin Wi said to him as she slowly approached. "But know that I will catch you and kill you!" As she finished, the woman came on with frightening speed, lifting the sword high for a strike that Bransen couldn't hope to dodge or block.

But neither did he retreat. He lifted his hand from his pouch, drawing forth the power of the gemstone as he went. Stronger and stronger, he coaxed that magic forth, charging the stone powerfully by the time his hand was up before him. And then he let it loose. The lodestone, magnetite, snapped from his grasp, propelled by its attraction to the target, the hilt of Affwin Wi's sword. As it struck, the sword went flying, spinning end over end, and three of Affwin Wi's fingers went flying as well. Shock on her fair face, the woman staggered backward. Merwal Yahna cried out but was too far away to help her.

Bransen started forward but stopped short, for Affwin Wi dismissed her shock and pain in an instant, throwing it all out in a primal keen of outrage.

She was glowing, too, in a serpentine shield, reversing her footing and charging ahead once more.

Bransen understood her intent and ran away. With the malachite, the Highwayman leaped from the ridge, landing lightly on the nearest branch of a large tree. He caught his balance and turned to see Affwin Wi charging, blazing with the flames of a ruby gemstone! She seemed a living fireball, and elemental creature of searing flames. There could be no escape . . . certainly none in the flammable branches of a summer tree!

Bransen used his soul stone to stab at her consciousness, to try to distract her in her concentration. At the same time he sent forth a burst, a pulse, like a magical dart, from the antimagic sunstone. But Affwin Wi was still a living fireball, still leaping high in the throes of the malachite, and still screaming. All Bransen could do was drop from the branch in desperation.

Even as he collided with the next lowest branch, not so gracefully twisting about to avoid any serious injury, he came to understand that the pitch of her scream had changed. Only after he negotiated the branch to fall clear of the others and land on his feet beneath the tree did he come to recognize the true source of her new yell.

Agony.

The fiery woman sailed past where Bransen had been standing, collided with the tangle of the tree farther on, and thrashed about insanely as she crashed through that tangle to land at last hard on her back on the ground below.

Bransen's desperate strike with the sunstone had stolen only one bit of magic, the serpentine shield, and now the fires of the brooch's ruby chewed at her furiously. She rolled about on the ground, screaming in agony.

Horrified, Bransen ran to her, desperately patting at the last stubborn flames. He fell into his soul stone and tried to impart waves of healing magic, but when he placed his hands upon the shivering woman, her skin just slipped away.

Bransen fell back in horror and disgust.

A scream so outrageous, so primal, so feral, shocked Bransen back to his sensibilities just in time to see Merwal Yahna charging at him, nun'chu'ku lifted high above his head, its deadly strike bar spinning furiously.

There was no reason to be found on the man's face, no pause and no sanity. In the split second he looked up at Merwal Yahna, Bransen knew that the man, overcome with rage and anguish, meant only to kill him, to smash him dead where he knelt beside the shivering and dying Affwin Wi.

Bransen spotted his brooch and snatched it up from her bubbling skin even as he fell into his own malachite and launched himself away, leaping backward and up into the air, spinning a somersault and landing on a branch some fifteen feet from the ground.

Merwal Yahna ran right to the base of the tree, sputtering curses with every step. Like a crazed animal, he began lashing at the large trunk with his exotic weapon, back and forth, chipping bark with every strike.

"Come down! I kill you! Come down! You die!" he roared.

"Enough!" Bransen shouted back at him after a few moments, during which he placed the brooch against his forehead and felt its magic connecting with him once more. Hardly shifting his hand, he pinned it in place, and he felt its magic coursing through him, energizing him. "This is ended, Merwal Yahna. It is time for us to place our differences behind us and work for the good of our respective lairds and for the good of Honce—"

"Come down!" the bald man shouted, and he rapped the tree repeatedly, his ire showing no sign of relenting. "I kill you!" He kept shouting and swinging. Bransen tried to reason with him, but to no avail.

Finally Merwal Yahna started to climb, and Bransen knew that he would have to fight the man. He shook his head and watched Merwal Yahna's progress. As soon as the warrior reached the base of the branch upon which Bransen stood, Bransen sprinted the other way along it, lifting himself with malachite as he went so that the branch did not bend. Nearing the ridge upon which he had first joined in battle, the Highwayman leaped with all his strength. If he could only get over that ridge, he thought, and back to his sword . . .

He didn't make it. Despite his great leap, despite his concentration in the gemstone, the distance was too far. Bransen collided with the side of the cliff facing, held on and tried to climb, but the jolt had him dazed a bit; he slid down near to the ground before he finally caught himself.

Too late, he knew, when he heard Merwal Yahna's roar close behind him.

Bransen's focus went to the brooch set on his forehead, focusing on the backing that held the six gems in place. As he turned, Merwal Yahna barely two strides away, the moment of his death surely upon him, Bransen lashed out with all of his magical energy, a complete orgasm of magical release.

The lightning bolt blinded and shocked him as surely as it must have shocked Merwal Yahna. The screams of rage disappeared in the blink of an astonished eye and in the thunderous explosion of power that reverberated for what seemed like seconds. As his vision returned, Bransen saw that the man was no longer before him.

Other than his silken shoes, which lay upon the ground exactly where they had been when Bransen brought forth the stroke. Bransen's eyes scanned back, and there lay Merwal Yahna to the side of the tree trunk, some thirty feet away, smoking and twitching wildly.

Overwhelmed, Bransen staggered to the man's side, and knelt over him, determined not to let this one die. Merwal Yahna would go with him to Laird Ethelbert's Court, Bransen decided, as a witness to the attacks on Cormack and Milkeila, as the murderer of Jameston Sequin.

Yes, he nodded, but even as he did, Merwal Yahna snapped his left hand up and across, cracking Bransen's jaw and throwing him back to the ground. The Highwayman struggled to catch himself and get back to his feet, knowing Merwal Yahna was surely coming on. His right hand grabbed something solid and smooth . . . a wooden pole, Merwal Yahna's fallen weapon. He rose to a sitting position and jumped to his feet as Merwal Yahna stood on unsteady, trembling legs . . . but legs steady enough for the raging man to launch himself at Bransen.

Bransen leaped, too, higher and somersaulting and twisting as he went. As he lifted from the ground, he flicked his wrist and sent the nun'chu'ku spinning. He caught the free pole in his left hand, both hands down low as he spun over the stumbling Merwal Yahna. Passing over the man, Bransen crossed his hands violently and powerfully and threw his right shoulder under as he came around, speeding his spin as he fell straight to the ground, taking Merwal Yahna over backward behind him.

For a moment, Bransen thought that a thick branch had broken nearby. Only when Merwal Yahna's heavy, lifeless body fell atop him did he realize that cracking sound was the man's neck breaking under the momentum of Bransen's descent and in the twist of the exotic weapon.

Bransen wearily pulled himself out from under the man and climbed to his feet. He surveyed the two fallen warriors for a long while, deep regret washing over him. How much good might these two have accomplished? Such grace in battle, such skill. He thought that perhaps he should bury them side by side.

Bransen's expression went cold a moment later, though, when he thought of Jameston Sequin. Merwal Yahna had killed his friend and in a most dishonorable way. Not in a duel, and not even face-to-face. Merwal Yahna had punched his nun'chu'ku through a wall and through the back of Jameston Sequin.

Bransen looked down at that exotic weapon now, swinging at the end of his right arm. He slipped one side under his rope belt and put his hands on his hips, again looking from Merwal Yahna to the charred corpse of Affwin Wi.

He remembered Jameston Sequin.

He left them for the vultures.

Using the powers of levitation, the Highwayman went up the cliff facing, back to the field. He found his sword easily enough, but when he bent to pick it up, he stopped fast. For there, too, was the lodestone, set into the weapon's hilt, locking a crushed and torn finger in place. Bransen found a stick and managed to pry both gemstone and finger loose. He held the sword up before his eyes, staring at the marvelous hilt, an intricate design of ivory and silver fashioned into the likeness of a hooded serpent.

It was marred now by the impact of the lodestone, a deep blemish on one side of the serpent's tapering neck. Pangs of loss flooded Bransen, to think that he had damaged his mother's perfect sword, this devoted and loving work of art.

He grasped the blade as he would in battle and moved it through a series of thrusts and defensive parries, blowing a great sigh of relief to realize that the balance remained perfect. He could feel the indentation, but it was a smooth dent, one that cradled his middle finger perfectly as he swung the blade about.

He had put his mark on his mother's sword.

Bransen looked back toward the city of Ethelbert dos Entel. Now it was time to put his mark on Dame Gwydre's budding kingdom.

T hank you for seeing me, but I would speak with Laird Ethelbert directly," Bransen said as he stood before the general, two younger commanders flanking him and a phalanx of sentries ready to swarm on his word.

"You claim to have knowledge of the war's events and to speak for Dame Gwydre," Kirren Howen replied. "Why would we not entertain you?"

"I left your fair city under less than perfect circumstances."

"You were chased out," said Myrick, one of the younger generals, and Kirren Howen and the other general, Tyne, flashed scowls his way, pointedly reminding him to remember his place here.

"And now I have returned to you," Bransen replied, staring at Myrick through every word. He turned back to Kirren Howen. "To Laird Ethelbert. You have heard of Dame Gwydre's many victories in the north?"

"I have heard that she manages to stay one stride ahead of Milwellis of Palmaristown. I have heard of no decisive victories other than her defeat of Laird Panlamaris."

"A series of minor wins, since then," Bransen admitted, "but accumulating into something more profound. The name of Dame Gwydre is whispered from the lips of every villager in the north of Honce now and always with joy and reverence. Milwellis of Palmaristown grows more frustrated every day, his army more weary and homesick. But not so for Dame Gwydre's army, for they believe in their cause, in her cause."

The generals absorbed the information, but all three seemed strangely detached to Bransen.

"She will win," he said confidently.

"Laird Bannagran refused our offer of alliance," said Kirren Howen. "You were there, as I recall, among his ranks."

Myrick and Tyne crossed their arms over their chests at that remark, and for a brief moment, Bransen almost expected the three to charge at him.

"And so I was surprised to hear that you had returned to our city, speaking for Dame Gwydre," said Kirren Howen. "Do you fight for both sides, then?"

"I am Gwydre's man, fully," Bransen asserted. He didn't know it then, of course, but that proclamation had just saved his life that dark day in Ethelbert dos Entel. "The situation with Laird Bannagran remains unclear," Bransen went on.

"Yet you marched with him, coming toward our city." There was no missing the accusatory tone.

"I marched for reasons personal and surely not for King Yeslnik, whom I despise."

"And we are to trust you?"

Bransen smiled and bowed. "The situation in Honce has changed. I came to inform you of those changes, for know that Dame Gwydre will win this war. Where will Laird Ethelbert and your city fit in when that occurs, I wonder? But of course, that is for him to decide."

"Where is Bannagran?"

"In Pryd Town with his thousands. He does not march forth."

"Where is Gwydre?"

Bransen had to hide his grin, for he almost blurted out (simply to see the looks on the faces of the younger generals) that she, too, was in Pryd at that time. "Laird Milwellis would ask that same question, for she is everywhere and nowhere all at once."

"You will answer his question!" Myrick demanded.

"I have delivered my message to you, though I wished to speak directly with Laird Ethelbert," Bransen said.

"That we cannot allow," Kirren Howen insisted.

"Then relay my message, and, with your permission, I would take my leave."

"Your message?" the general echoed skeptically. "You came to tell us that Milwellis was chasing Gwydre all about the northland, and that we already knew."

"I came to tell you that the war is turning in Dame Gwydre's favor. You should know and understand that. She offered you friendship and alliance, and you accepted. Such a bargain demands reciprocity."

"What? She would have us come forth while Bannagran sits in Pryd Town with a force thrice our garrison?"

Bransen shrugged. "I have delivered my message. I will go." Before anyone could respond, the Highwayman bowed and quickly took his leave, and though a couple of the sentries near to the door bristled as if to impede him, Kirren Howen waved them to stillness.

Bransen was glad to be out of there, and very glad that he had left the sword and brooch hidden beyond Ethelbert dos Entel's walls. All he had wanted to do was to put a whisper into Laird Ethelbert's ear to entice him to look more closely at the war, perhaps even to entice him forth that he could bring more pressure on King Yeslnik's forces.

That's what Bransen tried to tell himself as he crossed through the city. He couldn't help but grin, for the cryptic reference to personal reasons for his march with Bannagran was not by accident.

He wanted Laird Ethelbert to know. Surely the man was wondering even then where his assassins might be, given that Bransen was back in town, and surely the man had heard some tales of the pursuit by Affwin Wi and Merwal Yahna that had driven a strange man from town earlier that same day. No doubt Ethelbert had realized him to be the fugitive in question when he had so unexpectedly appeared at the man's court.

Ethelbert's generals had done well not to tip their hand. They hadn't mentioned the rumors of a chase, nor had Kirren Howen brought his assassins into the conversation at all, but surely they all were wondering.

Yes, Bransen could say with a good measure of honesty, he had gone to Ethelbert dos Entel for the good of Dame Gwydre's cause, but he wouldn't hide from the personal pleasures the visit had offered to him. When they found the bodies of Affwin Wi and Merwal Yahna, not so far from the city walls, he wanted Laird Ethelbert to know that he, the Highwayman, had slain them both.

He retrieved his items and purposely moved again near to Ethelbert dos Entel's western gate, even saluting one guard with the fabulous, famous sword, tipping it to his forehead where he had replaced the brooch.

Bransen smiled when the guard rushed back into the city, no doubt to shout the news.

He wanted Laird Ethelbert to know.

By the old ones, it is a dark day," Tyne said when Bransen had gone. "He did it, along with the woman," Myrick asserted. "We should catch him and flay the skin from his bones! Such treachery should not—"

"Enough, Myrick," Kirren Howen said. "Affwin Wi slew the woman even as she murdered Laird Ethelbert. The Highwayman was not there. Do you believe that he could have eluded Affwin Wi so completely?"

"And where are Affwin Wi and Yahna?" Myrick demanded. "Chasing someone from our walls, yes? The Highwayman?"

"If it was the Highwayman, then Affwin Wi would have dragged him back to the city at the end of her sword," Tyne insisted.

Kirren Howen rubbed his face, feeling very old and very tired. He hadn't even buried his beloved laird yet, hadn't even let the word go forth that Ethelbert was dead, and the nonsense of so many possible conspiracies did not sit well on his shoulders at that grim time.

"Enough of this useless conjecture," he told them both. "We must decide what is best for Ethelbert dos Entel. Laird Ethelbert would demand no less of us."

A guard burst into the chamber. "General!" he cried, gasping for breath.

"What is the meaning of this?" Myrick asked.

"He has her sword!" the guard exclaimed.

"What?" all three commanders said in unison.

"The Highwayman," the guard explained. "He has Affwin Wi's sword!"

Kirren Howen's face went blank. The world had just grown more confusing and more dangerous.

CHAPTER 24

Loyalties

Kirren Howen looked at the charred body of Affwin Wi, so disfigured as to be nearly unrecognizable.

"The Highwayman did this," Myrick the Bold said. "There can be no doubt."

"So it would seem," Kirren Howen replied.

"And so he was part of the plan to murder Laird Ethelbert!" Myrick exclaimed. Kirren Howen flashed him an angry glare, reminding him to keep his voice down. They had come with a dozen sentries and the peasant woman who had discovered the bodies. All stood nearby in the shade of the same tree into which Bransen and later Affwin Wi had leaped.

Both generals glanced that way now, to see curious looks coming back at them, but it seemed clear that Myrick's words hadn't fully registered to the group. Kirren Howen breathed a sigh of relief at that. He wasn't sure how he wanted to proceed here. They hadn't let news of Ethelbert's death spread from the castle yet, and Kirren Howen preferred to keep it quiet until he could figure out exactly how the laird's demise had come about. Something about the obvious story, about a woman from Bannagran sneaking in and murdering the man, rang hollow to him.

Where were the guards who had left the gate with this assassin, reportedly taking her to see Ethelbert? What of Bransen, the Highwayman, who had arrived to speak with Ethelbert on the morning after the laird's death? Had that been but a ruse so that he wouldn't be implicated in the murder? But if that were the case, then why had the Highwayman shown his face at all in the city? Certainly he could have gotten out of the city as quietly as he had apparently gotten in!

Now this, the two greatest warriors in all of Ethelbert dos Entel, lying dead on a field outside the city's walls. Little of it made any sense to Kirren Howen.

"What are we to do?" Myrick asked more quietly. "Do we march to Pryd Town to avenge our laird?"

"Avenge? You presume much. To think that we could even go to war with Bannagran is folly."

"Then what?"

"We learn the truth of this crime."

"We know the truth!" the impetuous and hot-blooded Myrick insisted.

"We know nothing," said Kirren Howen. "But we shall."

I told him where you went and what you did," Dame Gwydre said to Bransen as they departed Pryd on the morning after his return.

Bransen looked at her skeptically, as if determined to remind her that he really didn't care what Bannagran might think of him. "He said that we lost valuable warriors for our cause, no doubt, should Ethelbert turn to our cause."

Gwydre laughed, showing Bransen that he wasn't far off the mark. "There is that," she admitted. "But more so, Bannagran appeared impressed, both by your simple act of defeating those two warriors and that you went to such lengths to avenge a fallen friend."

"Without reminding you that he hadn't avenged his fallen friend by executing me?" Bransen asked sarcastically, and Gwydre laughed again. Indeed, she seemed to be in a fine and joyous mood this morning.

"Bannagran thinks highly of you. He respects your journey and the place it has taken you."

"Now I feel guilty for all the fantasies I've had of killing the brute."

"There is no end to Bransen's sarcasm, I see."

"Would you have it any other way?"

Dame Gwydre stared at him.

"I am here, am I not? I led you here, in fact! Is that not enough of a show of faith in Laird Bannagran?"

Gwydre let it go at that, and the pair bounded across the countryside. To Gwydre's surprise, though, Bransen headed for the east, and not directly north toward her forces. When she finally found the moment to question Bransen of their course, he said it was time for her to meet Laird Ethelbert.

"You trust that he will not kill you for what you did to his warriors?"

"You think me foolish enough to give him the opportunity?"

Kirren Howen brought his hands up to tousle his hair as he leaned back against the wall of a storage shed not far from the city's main gate. Two guards lay dead on the floor before him, ostensibly the victims of the same woman assassin who had murdered Laird Ethelbert.

The crafty old general noted that these two had been bludgeoned, one's neck snapped, while Ethelbert had been slashed across the throat. More and more curious. Myrick postulated that the Highwayman likely killed these two, while the woman murdered Ethelbert.

Father Destros and Tyne argued with him on that point, and it was obvious to Kirren Howen that Destros was sharing his doubts about the whole theory. They had interviewed the other guards who had been at the gate when the woman had arrived, and the snippets she had told them spoke of an altogether different kind of treachery here aimed at Bannagran.

"Take them to the chapel and study their wounds more closely," he instructed Destros. "Then come to me in the castle when you are certain of the type of weapon used and when you can guess at the expertise required."

Myrick started to protest.

"You are a fine commander, Myrick the Bold," Kirren Howen interrupted, "but you show your inexperience with every word you utter. You are speaking of the fate of a city here . . . of a city that is now fully our responsibility. To run off impetuously is to risk disaster. Nay, our course is to remain calm and to learn."

"But—" the man started to argue.

"I know your pain, friend," said Kirren Howen. "And I would see Laird Ethelbert's assassin dead in the most painful manner I can determine, do not doubt. But many important decisions lie before us, and we have not nearly the information we need to make them properly." He glanced at Destros and nodded. The monk rushed outside to summon fellow brothers to help him carry the dead sentries to Chapel Entel.

Kirren Howen had barely returned to the castle when the excited Destros rushed in to speak with him. "The Highwayman returns," he blurted.

Kirren Howen stared at him dumbfounded. "He is here?"

"Soon."

"How can you know this?"

"He came to me, spirit walking, and bade me to speak with Laird Ethelbert, to arrange a parley this day at sunset."

"He will be taken when he enters the city."

Father Destros shook his head. "He wishes a parley outside the gates in an abandoned cottage at the edge of the forest not far from here."

Kirren Howen narrowed his eyes threateningly.

"He brings Dame Gwydre to speak with him."

Kirren Howen's eyes opened wide at that! "He asked for Ethelbert?"

"He does not know that our laird has been slain."

"Or he is a practiced liar."

Destros shook his head. "Spirit walking and communicating in such a form is a joining of minds and of souls, my laird. . . ." He paused and looked at Kirren Howen curiously, and the general, too, was caught off guard by the reference to a title that he surely would call his own.

"In such a state there can be no deception," Father Destros concluded. "The Highwayman was not lying. He does not know that Laird Ethelbert has been slain."

Kirren Howen wasn't truly surprised by that bit of news when he paused to consider it. So much of the assumed story had kept him off balance, with nagging doubts regarding the tiny details at the edges of the tale.

"We will go and meet with the Highwayman and Gwydre," the new Laird of Ethelbert dos Entel said.

"Perhaps you should send someone in your stead."

"Would Laird Ethelbert have done so?"

There was no need to answer that question, of course, particularly considering that Ethelbert had personally traveled to the edge of Bannagran's army, ultimately vulnerable.

Still, both Destros and Kirren Howen breathed a sigh of relief to find only Bransen and Dame Gwydre waiting for them in the appointed rendezvous, a ruined cottage not so far from the city, the same cottage where Jameston Sequin had been slain.

"I would speak with Laird Ethelbert directly," Dame Gwydre said.

"I speak for the city," Kirren Howen replied.

"I would not have my words misinterpreted when they reach Laird Ethelbert's ears."

Father Destros shifted nervously, a move Bransen noted. When Dame Gwydre continued, Bransen stopped her with an upraised arm. Staring hard at Destros, he asked, "What is it?"

"Your man here need answer some questions," Kirren Howen said, deflecting the inquiry and causing Bransen to turn and face him directly. "Concerning a man and woman from Behr."

"Affwin Wi and Merwal Yahna," Bransen replied. "I killed them. Both of them."

Father Destros gasped and put a hand to his mouth. Dame Gwydre turned to Bransen sharply, but Kirren Howen didn't blink.

Bransen pointed to the back corner of the single-room cottage, to a hole in the wall about a foot off the floor. "Jameston Sequin was murdered in that spot," he explained, and Dame Gwydre gasped this time.

"My companion," Bransen explained. "Dame Gwydre's friend . . . indeed, a friend and legend throughout the Vanguard Holding. Merwal Yahna killed him on the word of Affwin Wi. She took from me my mother's sword and this brooch"—he pointed to the star brooch set on his forehead—"entrusted to me by Father Artolivan. I went to retrieve them, and she fought me in fair combat, as did Merwal Yahna. They are dead."

His matter-of-fact tone did much to defeat any protest coming from Kirren Howen, and it was obvious from his reaction to both Bransen and Gwydre that the man hadn't been overly fond of Ethelbert's assassins.

"Laird Ethelbert named them as champions of Ethelbert dos Entel," Kirren Howen warned. "You should take care of your admission."

"Then are we to presume that Laird Ethelbert sent them to murder Cormack and Milkeila, as well as Laird Bannagran?" Bransen retorted.

Kirren Howen winced at that. It was the same story he had heard from the guards who had been at the gate when Bannagran's "courier" had arrived.

"This is true, then?" he asked.

"It is," said Bransen. "Another friend paid dearly in that unwarranted attack."

"If you thought pursuing Bannagran would bring safety to your city, then we can ignore that indiscretion," Dame Gwydre added. "We have all been pushed to desperate measures in these trying times. But I would speak with Laird Ethelbert directly. The events in the north will change swiftly—"

"He is dead," Kirren Howen said bluntly, and to their astonished stares he added, "murdered in his bedchamber. I know not by whom, but we found a courier from Bannagran dead at his bedside, killed by Affwin Wi, who found her over Laird Ethelbert's body."

Bransen and Gwydre looked to each other blankly for a few moments, but then Bransen softly chuckled and said, "Convenient."

"What do you mean?" Kirren Howen asked.

"Did you, did Laird Ethelbert, send Affwin Wi's assassins on the road after Cormack and Milkeila? Or after Bannagran himself?"

Kirren Howen's silence spoke volumes, and both he and Bransen knew that they were drawing the same conclusions here.

"So you speak for the city now, wholly so?" Bransen said.

Kirren Howen nodded, and Bransen stepped aside with a nod to Dame Gwydre.

"I have not much time," Gwydre started. "Laird Bannagran wavers in his support of King Yeslnik. I know not if he will turn against Yeslnik, but I do not believe he will fight in support of the man. Great armies will clash in the north. Now is not the time for the warriors of Ethelbert to remain behind their walls."

"Or is it precisely that time?" Kirren Howen retorted. "To let others spill blood while we strengthen our defenses?"

"The fate of Honce hangs precariously," Dame Gwydre replied. "Should Yeslnik win the day, do you think your walls will hold him at bay? For no matter how hard I sting him in the north, you know that the victor of that conflict will come out stronger."

"So if Dame Gwydre wins, will I need my walls, good lady?"

Without hesitation and with a wide and sincere smile, Dame Gwydre replied, "No. The warriors of Ethelbert dos Entel have earned their place and their peace many times over. All of Honce is grateful that Laird Ethelbert stood strong against the darkness that is Delaval City."

"I will hold you to those words, Lady, whether we come forth or not," said Kirren Howen. Dame Gwydre nodded.

"We take our leave," the dame announced. "There is much astir in the north." With appropriate bows, she and Bransen strode from the cottage.

"Following seas, Lady of Vanguard," Kirren Howen said, tipping his heart if not his hand, for that expression, shared by sailors the world over, was the most sincere of well-wishes.

Hand-in-hand, gemstone magic flowing through them, Bransen and Gwydre bounded away to the north to rejoin the army of Vanguard, to begin again the wild flight about the holdings of Honce. The summer had deepened now and, with the heat, so, too, had deepened the misery of Milwellis's futile pursuit.

Both Gwydre and Bransen knew that the time to finish the war was nearly at hand.

If Laird Bannagran is settled in Pryd Town, we are not forced to remain here," Kirren Howen said to Myrick, Tyne, and Destros soon after Bransen and Gwydre had departed.

Myrick shook his head in protest.

"Do speak your doubts," said Kirren Howen.

"Our charge is to protect the city, for the memory of Laird Ethelbert."

"You would have us join with Dame Gwydre against the masses of King Yeslnik?" Tyne asked, his voice thick also with reservations. "By all accounts,

Yeslnik and Milwellis and Bannagran all command many legions of skilled and well-armored warriors. The power of Delaval City is not to be discounted."

"And I do not do so," Kirren Howen replied.

"But you would have us join with this desperate plan of Dame Gwydre's. Are we to believe that she was not a party to the murder of Laird Ethelbert?"

"Yes," Father Destros interjected in answer to the latter conclusion.

"Perhaps join with her," said Kirren Howen. "Perhaps not."

"Laird?" Myrick and Tyne asked together.

"Which side will we join?" Kirren Howen asked rhetorically. "Why, which-ever side will win, of course. We know that we'll not have the kingdom to claim as our own . . . not now, with Laird Ethelbert lost to us. And we haven't the re-serves any longer to entertain any such notions. We are for Ethelbert dos Entel now. Nothing less and nothing more. And so we will enter into a treaty with whichever side will win the day, and always we will march with a clear road back home behind us."

Father Destros bristled at that.

"Your church will choose as you and your brethren see fit," Kirren Howen assured him. "I will take no actions against you and, indeed, will help facili-tate your retreat to St. Mere Abelle should it come to that." He looked to the others and lifted a glass of wine in toast.

"This is not our fight, Gwydre and Yeslnik," he explained. "But, for the good Laird Ethelbert and for Ethelbert dos Entel, perhaps we can make it our fight when the moment of victory is upon one or the other and, in joining, become the tipping point to a crushing victory.

"Our numbers double, and our importance multiplies many times over in such a situation," he explained. "For not only will we be joining in the cause of Yeslnik or Gwydre, we will not be joining in the cause of their opponent. And so we will very likely be able to dictate terms favorable to our city in return."

Smiles spread on the faces of the two younger generals, and both lifted their glasses in agreement.

"Take heart, my friends," Kirren Howen proclaimed. "If the Highway-man's confidence is at all justified, and King Yeslnik has reason to be worried, then we will profit. Let us assemble a swift and agile force. I'll not have us caught outside our walls and not engage in any battle until and unless it is of our choosing."

"For Ethelbert dos Entel!" Myrick the Bold said and lifted his glass once more.

"For Laird Ethelbert!" Tyne added and corrected, tapping his glass against that of his friend.

De Guilbe's Epiphany

"They are nowhere to be found, my laird," the scout reported.

"Go away," Milwellis said to him, and when the scout tried to further respond, the laird fixed him with a threatening glare. Bowing ridiculously, the scout ran away.

"Always the same," said Harcourt. "She is a clever one."

"Too clever," said Milwellis. "Always too clever! How is this possible? How can the witch so anticipate our every move, our every ambush, and our every feint? Do we have spies among us?"

"Do continue," came a third voice, and the pair turned to see Father De Guilbe walking over, nodding with every long stride.

Both men, particularly Harcourt, fixed him with a hard stare, for he wore a wry, little smile, as if he was enjoying their frustration. Given the inevitable growing rivalry within the court of Yeslnik, where several prominent figures, Milwellis and De Guilbe among them, would constantly vie for the king's favors, the moment grew more tense with every stride the loud and arrogant monk took their way.

"It is a source of constant discussion in King Yeslnik's court," De Guilbe said, when neither man moved to speak. "You need not hide your folly here."

"Do tell," said Harcourt.

"Surely it is no secret that Dame Gwydre has run you all about the ways of Honce," said De Guilbe. "When you departed Delaval City with so grand a force at your call, we had thought—we had all thought—your task to be a matter of days in completing, not weeks and surely not months, and yet the summer grows old and Gwydre runs free."

Harcourt and Milwellis exchanged concerned looks.

"And, of course, that unfortunate situation forces King Yeslnik to hold fast his other force, Bannagran's force, and offers comfort and reprieve to the defeated Ethelbert," De Guilbe went on dramatically. "Your failure sends discontent across the kingdom."

Harcourt glared at the man and seemed ready to spring upon him, but Milwellis caught something else here, some background motive to De Guilbe's nattering.

"What do you want, monk?" the Laird of Palmaristown asked bluntly.

Harcourt looked at Milwellis curiously, while De Guilbe feigned surprise. "Want?"

Milwellis held up his hand to silence the monk immediately.

"You have come to fashion a report for King Yeslnik," Milwellis reasoned.

"King Yeslnik's patience thins."

"And so will that report be favorable to Laird Milwellis or favorable to Laird Bannagran?" Milwellis asked.

"What has Bannagran to do with this matter?" Harcourt interjected, but his face lit up with revelation as he regarded the grin of Father De Guilbe.

"You would use us against each other to Father De Guilbe's gain," Milwellis stated.

"That is a harsh accusation, laird," said De Guilbe.

"It is a logical assumption, for I would do the same, were I you," said Milwellis, and De Guilbe grinned all the wider.

The monk's expression grew grim almost immediately afterward, though. "I want Dame Gwydre defeated," he said. "I want Father Artolivan thrown down into the mud and all his followers with him."

"You want your seat at Chapel Abelle, no matter how grand the promise of a mother chapel in Delaval City," said Milwellis. "Should King Yeslnik empty every quarry in Honce of stone and build you a chapel so huge as to dwarf the Belt-and-Buckle range, you would still prefer the seat at Chapel Abelle."

De Guilbe looked to Harcourt, his smile returned. "How can one so young show such insight?" he asked the general.

"What do you want?" Milwellis demanded.

"To press King Yeslnik's favor to the side of Laird Milwellis?"

The laird didn't respond at all, didn't even blink.

"I want to know that you agree with me that Chapel Abelle must be defeated and that I must be installed there, not in Delaval or anywhere else, if the Church of the Divine King is to hold sway over the outland chapels," the monk said, his voice very serious and even.

"Nothing would please me more than to enter the courtyard of Chapel Abelle and avenge my father."

"I know," said De Guilbe. "And that is why I have come to you at this time. Not as a spy for King Yeslnik but as a friend."

"A friend?" Harcourt asked doubtfully.

"An ally," De Guilbe corrected.

Milwellis nodded, figuring it all out. "When Dame Gwydre is defeated and Laird Ethelbert is pushed into the sea, the brothers in the fortress of Chapel Abelle will pursue diplomacy."

"What choice will be left to them?" asked De Guilbe.

"And King Yeslnik will be advised to heed that call, his armies weary, the length and breadth of the land battered," the laird went on.

"But would he be wise in heeding that call for peace?"

"For him, yes," Milwellis admitted. "But for you, no."

"And for you?"

"No."

"Then we are agreed?" De Guilbe asked and extended his hand, which Milwellis accepted.

"Chapel Abelle and Palmaristown will be fine allies," the monk remarked.

V ery little surprised or shook Father De Guilbe. The man had traveled the world, had battled powries and barbarians, and had led his brothers through the harshest of climes. The Order of Abelle had never known a tougher man, often cruel and pragmatic, a man who would not spare the whip (as Cormack could surely attest!) and who accepted the death of soldiers, fellow monks, and innocent civilians with hardly a shrug of care, so long as the outcome of such conflict moved toward his vision of order.

More than a few of his colleagues through the years had remarked that he was more akin to the Samhaists in temperament than to the brothers of Abelle, and De Guilbe knew that in many ways they were surely correct. His split with Father Artolivan had been as philosophical as incidental; to De Guilbe, the church had grown soft under Artolivan's gentle guidance, and that could only spell the ultimate doom of the order.

The order.

That was the key to it, after all. It was the duty of the church, whatever church stood dominant, to impart a sense of order and discipline upon the fearful rabble. When it had become obvious that Yeslnik would be King of Honce, that Delaval City would prevail over Ethelbert dos Entel, the Order of Abelle had to abandon its stance of neutrality and throw in with the winner.

Whether Yeslnik was a moral and good man was irrelevant, to De Guilbe's thinking. Whether his order to execute the prisoners taken from Ethelbert was right and just was not important. Not in the long run. Not for the future of the church that would remain in the kingdom Yeslnik had claimed.

Still, for all the hardness that encrusted the character of Father De Guilbe, he found himself gasping for breath when at last he had unraveled Dame Gwydre's awful secret.

"What do you know?" demanded Harcourt when the obviously shaken monk walked into the tent of Laird Milwellis that dark and rainy night.

His face ashen, shaking his head with every word, De Guilbe announced, "They have thrown off all bounds of morality and decency. They have abandoned all caution in their desperation."

Milwellis lifted his palms, his posture and expression showing him to be completely baffled.

De Guilbe held up a gray stone, a soul stone. "Spirit walking," he explained. "It is—it was—a rare practice, a dangerous practice, an often immoral practice. In the more disciplined church before the rise of Artolivan, spirit walking was used only in cases of extreme emergency, when the mother chapel needed to impart some edict or warning of utmost importance.

"Utmost, I say! A brother wandering lost in the forest on a freezing winter night was forbidden to exit his corporeal form through use of the gemstones, even at the cost of his own life."

"We've little time for church history, brother," said Harcourt, but Milwellis hushed him quickly, staring at De Guilbe with clear interest.

"King Yeslnik was correct in granting you his legions," the monk said. "Your march to Delaval City was tactically flawless, as the many dead powries can attest, and your work out here has followed that same course. I have spoken with your commanders, and not one finds a moment of doubt or a parcel of fault for the tactics you have employed these months. But still you have not caught the witch."

He held up the soul stone again, and Laird Milwellis's eyes went wide.

"The answer is that simple?" Milwellis asked incredulously. "Their monks have been floating about us, disembodied? Hearing our plans and intended movements?"

De Guilbe nodded. "It is the only possible answer."

"You just now came to this conclusion?" Milwellis asked. "How could you, or the other monks who have marched with me these weeks, not have solved the simple riddle? If they knew of this possibility, how could they remain quiet? And why did De Guilbe not send word of warning from Delaval City weeks ago?"

"Because I—and certainly these lesser monks!—did not entertain this possibility," the father answered with confidence and calm. "You cannot understand how extraordinary, how extreme this is. . . . I did not expect Father Artolivan, for all of his obvious faults, to so quickly devolve to such madness."

"Madness? Can we doubt their effectiveness?"

"Madness," Father De Guilbe insisted. "In the saner church of yesteryear, brothers were instructed to refrain from this unholy and insidious practice. There was no exception."

"You just said that there were exceptions," Harcourt reminded.

"In the most extreme circumstances and with very specific and limited use. Now they abuse the practice beyond all comprehension."

"And in so doing, they survive," said Milwellis. "Your older church does not sound like a saner church. Without this cleverness, I would have slaughtered them weeks ago."

"Better that!" De Guilbe shouted. "For them, better that! For you do not understand the implications of spirit walking nor the temptations. A disembodied spirit desires, yea, even demands, a corporeal coil and will thus force a brother's spirit to engage in the evil and damning act of possession. I can only guess how many of Chapel Abelle's brothers are now dead or forever insane for these desperate and diabolical actions. Soulless and insane or dead for their evil efforts and answering now in the fires of the old ones."

"The old ones?" Harcourt asked, his eyes wide at the monk's reference to the Samhaist gods.

"They have their place," De Guilbe replied. "And it is no place a true follower of Abelle would wish to venture."

Harcourt started to respond again, but Milwellis cut him short. "If all that you say is true, then how do you come to believe that the witch Gwydre is using this spirit walking?"

"It is the only explanation," the monk replied with all confidence.

"And you can confirm it?"

De Guilbe nodded and held up his soul stone yet again. "Only in the most extreme circumstances," he said. "Such as this one."

A sly smile widened on Milwellis's face, white teeth showing behind the red of his beard, which had grown quite unkempt of late. He turned to Harcourt.

"Then we have them."

He knows," Bransen assured Dame Gwydre, Dawson, Brother Pinower, and several other leaders at the same time Father De Guilbe was conveying his revelation to Laird Milwellis. "He was out there in spirit. Father De Guilbe recognized our spies."

"None of the brothers concur," said Pinower.

"They do not disagree with me," Bransen replied. "They only admit that they cannot confirm my report. I would not have expected any of them to have noted De Guilbe. He was careful and clever."

"But you recognized him?" There was doubt evident in Pinower's voice, but Bransen took no offense.

"I bring a dimension to the gemstone magic that you do not, Brother Pinower," Bransen said matter-of-factly. "They are a part of me now, more intimately than you could ever imagine."

"Because you're Jhesta Tu?" the monk asked, his voice growing sourer, as he obviously considered Bransen's remarks an attack on his beloved order.

"Because of my unique relationship with them, particularly the soul stone," Bransen corrected. "You might use the stone to heal another or occasionally to be free of your mortal body. I use it to sustain my very being. This stone"—he tapped the soul stone at the center of the brooch set on his forehead—"is set as the apex of my life energy, which the Jhesta Tu call *ki-chi-kree*. It is not a foreign or separate part of the Highwayman."

Dame Gwydre looked to Brother Pinower, but the monk had no more questions and no reason to doubt Bransen's claims about the stone or, more important, about Father De Guilbe.

"De Guilbe knows," Bransen assured them both. "Milwellis knows."

"Then the game's ended," Dawson McKeege remarked. A general look of despair ran through the gathering as the implications of De Guilbe's discovery, of the loss of their secret tactical information gathering, settled in upon them.

"Good," Dame Gwydre said, surprisingly. She walked past her gawking commanders and stared out to the southwest. "I grow tired of playing the mouse to Milwellis's cat. The summer nears its end, and I have many who need return to their families in Vanguard to prepare for the onslaught of winter."

"You will simply flee the field and leave Honce to Yeslnik?" asked an astonished Brother Pinower.

Gwydre's responding look was no less incredulous. "Hardly. We have wearied them, we have worn them, and we have broken their spirits. Now is the time to fight them, in a place of our choosing, and be done with this nonsense of war."

"Five to one," Dawson warned. "And that's just Milwellis. If Yeslnik comes forth, it'll be more than ten against our every one."

"Good," said Gwydre and all raised their eyebrows. "Then it will be finished in one place, at one time."

"What're ye saying?" Dawson replied, the salt coming back into his accent.

"Are we to run headlong to our slaughter?" Brother Pinower added.

Dame Gwydre smirked at both of them, silencing them. "Plot our run, twixt Milwellis and Pryd Town. Find a place not so far from Pryd that will favor us in the fight."

"Yeslnik's got fifteen thousand in Pryd," said Dawson.

"Does he?" was all that the smiling Gwydre would answer. She walked off then, motioning for Bransen to follow her.

"You take a great risk," Bransen said as soon as they were away. "You have no commitment from Bannagran."

"Father De Guilbe knows our advantage now, so you said. And so our advantage is no more."

"Honce is a wide land, and we can move more swiftly than—"

"To what end?" Gwydre asked.

"The people of town after village after town have come to love you," Bransen reminded. "They speak your name with hearts full and curse Milwellis . . . indeed, many curse King Yeslnik all the louder!"

"The people you speak of are not warriors and many have felt the painful consequences of their sympathy toward us. It occurs to me that this Laird Milwellis, whose brutal reputation is well earned, will grow even more frustrated and more angry if we continue to flee him and will raze every village that shows us a pittance of kindness or even those that do not rise up and fight against us as we approach. Would you have that dark stain on your heart, Bransen Garibond? Because I would not."

"You put great stock in Bannagran. Has he earned it?"

"Have I a choice?"

"We could flee to Vanguard straightaway. They will never get their warships in place and coordinated in time to stop our flight. If they follow, it would be to their utter ruin, with winter closing in. Few in Honce have felt the bite of a Vanguard winter."

"Yeslnik is a fool, but Milwellis is not. Were we to take sail, he would align his warships to protect the mouth of the Masur Delaval and march his army to besiege St. Mere Abelle and urge King Yeslnik to send another army to be rid of Laird Ethelbert. And in that event, how could I expect the courage of Bannagran . . . ?" She paused and sighed.

"Twixt Milwellis and Pryd Town," Bransen replied with a grin and a sly wink.

Deliver that," Bannagran bade the captain of the Delaval forces under his command.

The man, tall and lean, looked down at the rolled parchment suspiciously.

"I seek to put an end to this miserable war," the Laird of Pryd explained.

"So does King Yeslnik," replied the captain. "So does Dame Gwydre, I would expect!"

"Do you think my army wishes to march all the way back to Ethelbert dos Entel?"

"If King Yeslnik demands it of us!"

Bannagran snorted and waved the man away, growling, "Deliver it."

But the captain stood resolute. "You must tell me what it is, specifically."

"Why?" Bannagran asked with a knowing grin. "Because you fear that if it is not what your precious King Yeslnik wishes to hear, he will cut off your head?"

The captain tried to remain stoic, but his blink and a slight slump of his shoulders betrayed him.

"And this is the man you would have me die for?" Bannagran asked. "And this is the king you would die for?"

"My laird!"

"Deliver the message," Bannagran said in threatening, even tones. "Or I will chop your head off, stuff the parchment in your mouth, and have your head deliver it for me."

The captain blanched and stormed out.

"See that he takes the leaders of his troublesome legion with him," Bannagran said softly to Master Reandu, who stood beside his throne.

Reandu nodded. "And send the next brigade in to speak with Laird Bannagran?"

Bannagran nodded. "Your monks are on the roads east and north with the same message?" he asked.

"I wrote three copies for you, did I not?" Reandu replied with a smile. "I will fetch the brigade, but they all know your rousing speech by now, of course," Reandu said.

"And most welcome it."

The monk patted Bannagran's strong shoulder and scurried out the door. Bannagran settled back in his throne and rubbed his weary face, stopping short when he heard clapping from the back corner of the room. He turned and stared at the flutter of some drapes, and then the Highwayman strode into plain view.

The few sentries in the room bristled, but Bransen ignored them as he walked over to stand before the Laird of Pryd.

"Do you ever bother with the announcement of your arrival anymore?" the laird asked.

"I wished to view your efforts without influencing them."

"Where is Gwydre?"

"That's what I came to tell you." Bransen took a seat on the hearth bench to the side of the throne. "I have been all through Pryd Town this morning," he explained. "You have welcomed those forces given you by Yeslnik as if they were citizens of your holding. And you have split them among your own ranks and among the homes of the townsfolk."

"You came here to state that which you have witnessed for weeks now?" Bannagran asked. "Was I to field them in hot tents through the summer, while Yeslnik ordered me to march and to stay, to march again and to turn about?"

"None of which you have done."

"In the end, I am where Yeslnik decided he most needs me."

"You need not worry over Laird Ethelbert," Bransen said.

Bannagran tried not to show that he cared.

"Ethelbert is dead," Bransen explained. "His generals believed that the messenger you sent was the culprit."

Now the laird looked truly perplexed.

"Dame Gwydre and I met with them when last we left you," Bransen explained. He laughed at the absurdity of it all, but as soon as he heard a commotion out by the small castle's door, his expression grew deadly serious. "You weaken their loyalty to King Yeslnik and strengthen their love for Bannagran and for Pryd Town."

Bannagran didn't disagree, didn't even blink.

"How many have left for Delaval City over these weeks?" Bransen asked. "A third?"

"Less."

Bransen smiled and brought his hands up to clap his approval quietly. Then he melted away behind the draperies as a group of forty Delaval soldiers was escorted into the room.

Laird Bannagran's sermon sounded as music in the Highwayman's ears. Bannagran didn't quite demand fealty and didn't quite threaten imprisonment, but his point was unmistakable as he assured these warriors—men and women who had come to trust him as their leader—that they were now fully considered as soldiers of the garrison of Pryd Town.

"We are the greatest legion that has taken the field in this war," Bannagran said to them, and though not so long before the proud Delaval warriors might have taken that assessment as a slight, now they were honored by their inclusion in the elite legion.

"I have watched you carefully these months," Bannagran went on. "Through dispiriting marches that lead not to battle but only to further marches! But you did not waver and did not falter. I am blessed to have been given the finest of legions to make my own.

"Do not doubt," he said suddenly, sharply, and he rose from his chair and stabbed his finger at them, "that if I deemed you unworthy, I would have sent you away, as others have gone. There is no room in Pryd's garrison for the weak or the weak of will. But I accept you and am honored to lead you."

Peeking out from behind the drapes, Bransen couldn't contain his admiring smile, for he could see the truth clearly displayed on the faces of every warrior standing before Laird Bannagran.

They would fight for him.

They would die for him.

Not for King Yeslnik, but for Bannagran.

CHAPTER 26

Convergence

 Even as Bannagran's courier departed Pryd Town, a second messenger arrived in Delaval City, this one from Laird Milwellis.

"The riddle of Dame Gwydre's elusiveness is solved," proclaimed Milwellis's man. "The Laird of Palmaristown has discovered her immoral treachery, wasting the souls of spirit-walking monks as she flees, ever flees, in fear of him."

"And what does this mean?" King Yeslnik demanded, trying to hold back his enthusiasm . . . for surely the courier was nearly jumping out of his boots with excitement.

"The glorious Laird of Palmaristown will have her now, in short order, and the northland will be secured. We have her!" the man declared, his grin nearly taking in his ears. "Now that we know her tactics, we have tricked her into a grave mistake. She believes that we have left our flank exposed and so she runs to our south and west, toward this very city!"

Yeslnik's eyes went wide at that, more out of fear than anticipation.

"She intends to pass Laird Milwellis by in a swift flight and then turn north to try to strike at Palmaristown," the courier quickly clarified, "for she has not the strength of forces to do battle with Laird Milwellis and surely not to threaten the high walls of Delaval City."

Yeslnik tried not to show it, but all in the room saw his clear relief.

"So Laird Milwellis will turn and catch her at last," Yeslnik said, trying to recover his composure. "It has taken him far too long to be rid of the inconvenience that is Gwydre."

"She is fleet, and though we will use her secret sight against her, we cannot fully blind her," the courier replied.

"What does that mean?"

"Catching her will be no easy task for one large force, and Laird Milwellis does not wish to split his legions too thin against a dangerous enemy."

"You claimed that you had her," Yeslnik scolded.

"We do, my king, when you come forth."

Wearing a perplexed expression, Yeslnik had no response.

"Come forth in all your glory," Milwellis's man explained. "A straight march along the course described." He held up a parchment and unrolled it to reveal a map of Honce, complete with representations of the major forces in play: Milwellis, Yeslnik, Gwydre, and Bannagran.

"She is trapped," the man went on. "As she passes, likely this very day, Laird Milwellis will turn his force and lengthen his line north and east of her. When you come forth, so, too, will the western route be blocked. To the south lie Pryd Town and Laird Bannagran. Dame Gwydre has nowhere to run."

Before Yeslnik could respond, Olym blurted from behind, "All glory to King Yeslnik!"

He turned to regard his plump wife.

"This is your moment, my beloved champion," she said quietly. "Gwydre will be ensnared before all of Delaval's power, with nowhere to run. She will surrender or be slaughtered to a warrior, and word of your victory will spread throughout the kingdom, and none will dare oppose you!"

"Cannot Milwellis finish this witch?" Yeslnik asked, as much to Olym as to the courier.

Olym rushed from her chair to Yeslnik's side and whispered into his ear. "Beware, my love! If all glory is to Milwellis, will he claim more for Palmaristown and for himself? He is your general. Do not make of him a king!"

Yeslnik blanched at that notion and turned back to the courier. He composed himself quickly and looked past the man to his commanders, standing in lines to either side of the carpet leading from the door to his dais.

"Prepare the legions!" he commanded in regal and powerful tones, and a great cheer went up in the great hall.

The courier's smile widened even more, and he bowed again and again, repeating, "My king!" with each genuflection.

Separate holdings once more?" Bransen asked incredulously. "That is your message to King Yeslnik and Milwellis and Ethelbert dos Entel?"

"Fewer and greater holdings," Reandu answered for Bannagran, who sat staring coldly at Bransen.

"Independent kingdoms for Yeslnik, for the Laird of Ethelbert dos Entel, for Gwydre, and for Milwellis?" asked Bransen, shaking his head with every word.

"Bound by the common Church of Blessed Abelle," Reandu was quick to add.

"Bound only by gamesmanship and fear of alliance," said Bransen. "And as it sorts, who will march first and against whom? This is no end to war but merely a pause as each king decides which rival he might most easily topple."

"King Yeslnik will never accept it," Master Reandu said.

"Then why would you propose such nonsense?" Bransen started to ask, but he let the end of the question drift away as it began to make sense.

"Because Laird Milwellis is an ambitious man and Laird Ethelbert, or his successor now, a nervous one," Reandu explained.

Bransen paused and let that settle in his thoughts for a long while. "You seek to drive a wedge between Milwellis and Yeslnik," he said. "Do you expect to prompt Milwellis to treason or just to force Yeslnik to see him and you in a new and threatening light?"

"Either would serve," Bannagran answered.

"Then you do not expect your proposal to prove acceptable."

"Of course not."

"But why?" Bransen asked simply. Bannagran stared at him as if the answer should be obvious, and indeed it was, but Bransen wanted to hear it aloud.

"Dame Gwydre has already begun her run," Bransen said. "I doubt I could be by her side in time to turn her away from this course she has chosen, as Milwellis will be quick to cut off her escape."

"You should have informed me of her run before it began," said Bannagran, and it was obvious to Bransen that he, too, was struggling to find a way to sort through this dangerous conflation of contradictory plans.

"We had no time. Milwellis had our advantage revealed, and, were we to delay, he would come to suspect that we knew of his revelation, and he would become suspicious of our every movement." Bransen paused and blew a sigh, trying to find a way to resolve the awkwardly converging plans. "I could turn her south, perhaps, that she could run through Pryd Holding and out to the open south ahead of Milwellis and Yeslnik."

"You believe that Yeslnik will come forth from Delaval City?" Bannagran asked.

"Milwellis knows that he cannot catch us alone. The bait is clear and the hook disguised."

Bannagran looked to Reandu, then stared off into the distance, plotting.

"You quickly travel great distances with Dame Gwydre," Bannagran said to Bransen.

"A trick of gemstone magic and my Jhesta Tu training," said Bransen.

"Can you catch up to Reandu's monk on the north road?"

"Brother Castingay," Reandu added. "He left this morning."

Bransen shrugged. "I believe I can with ease."

"Can you deliver him quickly to Milwellis's camp?" asked Bannagran.

Bransen, his expression curious, did not respond.

"Do so," Bannagran bade him. "And tell Brother Castingay to inform Laird Milwellis that King Yeslnik has received the same offer and that I expect the king will accept, though he will surely recall all his legions from both Milwellis and Bannagran."

Bransen, puzzled but starting to figure it out, looked to Reandu.

"Brother Castingay is traveling openly along the road," the monk explained.

"And when I have done this?" Bransen asked Bannagran. "Would you have me return to you? To Gwydre? To turn her south to Pryd Town?"

"That option always remains," Bannagran replied, and his voice was full of confidence again, and the hints of a smile grew at the edges of his mouth. "But not yet. Return to me in time but first scout well the road to Delaval City. Let us see if Yeslnik comes forth to Milwellis's call. Let us learn if he has the belly for a fight."

"And what will Bannagran do?" Bransen dared ask.

"I will decide where I want to win the war," the Bear of Honce replied.

Delaval City had not seen so grand a procession in the memory of anyone alive. Trumpeters lined the main boulevard all the way from the castle to the city's eastern gate. Every rank, every line, marched in perfect harmony, boots stomping the cobblestones in cadence.

A legion of foot soldiers led the way, twenty abreast and three hundred deep. Then came the elite cavalry in shining bronze, horses and riders armored, spear tips gleaming in the morning sun.

The rolling thunder of the chariots followed, their ranks separated by a line of gilded coaches, the king himself in the most decorated one of all. He sat atop its roof on a throne glittering with gold leaf, occasionally tipping his hand in recognition of the thousands who lined the wide street to bid him farewell.

From the high balcony of Castle Delaval, Queen Olym watched them all go, and Yeslnik made sure to acknowledge her, and when he did, any in the crowd who did not cheer wildly were sure to be reminded of their place by the many soldiers who roamed about the gathering, iron poles in hand.

Behind the king and the coaches of his entourage came the rest of the chariots, and behind them three more legions of footmen, their long lines interspersed with an endless stream of wagons full of salted fish and other supplies. By the time the last of Yeslnik's army passed through the city gates, the sun was low in the west and the king was long out of sight of the city, miles along the road.

As soon as he had crossed under the gates, Yeslnik had retreated inside his armored coach, and his personal guards, several score of veteran warriors, stayed close to him in the march and formed an iron ring about him in the encampment that night. His day of final victory was at hand, and he would take no chances.

Despite the many sentries, though, he was truly a lonely man. He missed his wife terribly. She had been his strength these last weeks, prodding him on to greater heights of glory, rewarding him for his courage with memorable nights of lovemaking. This was the first time they had been apart in months, the king realized as he settled in to sleep and found that he could not.

Olym was his only friend. He had sent for her coach; he needed her beside him, lending him courage through this great battle, but she would not arrive until the next day, at the least.

She was his only friend. That unsettling thought followed him to his bed. He recalled his uncle's court; Laird Delaval had surrounded himself with trusted and loyal warriors, with men and women he called his friends. Not so for Yeslnik. His two primary generals, Milwellis and Bannagran, were lairds of their respective holdings. Should he bring them to Delaval City? Garrison Commander Bannagran, perhaps?

No, rather Milwellis, he decided, for Bannagran was too old and surly to share in the benefits Yeslnik might know as uncontested King of Honce. For all of his love for Olym, the thought of the pleasures of many pretty young ladies was not unpleasant. Yes, when this business with Dame Gwydre was finished, he would invite Milwellis to Delaval City as his chief advisor, as his garrison commander, and as his friend.

He wanted a friend . . . many friends, he decided. He would gather a court of nobles, young and randy, and together they would enjoy the pleasures of a bevy of young and pretty ladies.

An image of a scowling Olym rattled his senses as he lay in his bed.

But King Yeslnik shook that away. He was the King of Honce. His every desire would be met and by whomever he chose. Olym would have to accept that.

He was the King of Honce.

But he was a lonely man.

That was most amazing, Highwayman!" Brother Castingay said to Bransen when they ended their bounding run, the vast encampment of Laird Milwellis in clear sight in the valley below. "Would that Master Reandu had afforded me a malachite, that I might attempt such a prance back to Pryd Town when my duties here are finished!"

"We would not have Milwellis and Father De Guilbe learning of this property of the gemstone," Bransen said. He thought, but didn't add, that Castingay would do well to never attempt such a prance on his own. Only Bransen's unique combination of qualities and training afforded him such freedom. Any other monk running as he did, with those great and high leaps with every stride, would surely shatter his ankle upon landing or smash into a tree or a thick wall to a crashing demise.

"You know your duty here?" Bransen asked.

Brother Castingay held up the rolled parchment, sealed in wax with the crest of Pryd. "And King Yeslnik will accept the proposal of Laird Bannagran," he said.

Bransen nodded, though he still wasn't quite certain of Bannagran's intent here or of how it might all play out.

"Am I to remain with Laird Milwellis or return to Pryd?" Castingay asked.

Bransen considered the likely road ahead for Milwellis. "Be away from this camp as soon as you are able," he replied. "The next week will be filled with battle and death. Follow the stench of rotting bodies if you choose to join in or find a small village nearby to house you through the chaos. But do not stay with Milwellis unless your heart is for Father De Guilbe and unless you have the call to do battle with your own brethren of Pryd."

"Do you believe that Laird Milwellis will war with Laird Bannagran?" Castingay asked breathlessly.

Bransen just smiled and shrugged. He wasn't sure, but he hoped that it would come to that. Indeed. He left the man with a clear road to Milwellis's lines and bounded away to the southwest, traveling many miles before settling beneath the low-hanging branches of a wide pine for a good night's rest . . . in sight of a second vast army, the garrison of Delaval City.

Still, and to his surprise, Bransen did sleep soundly. All the parts of Honce were moving, he knew, converging to the great battle of his age. But, strangely, he was not agitated or afraid. He thought of the promise of Gwydre and of his beloved Cadayle and of their coming child. He had, indeed, found a road worth walking . . . a bloody and difficult one, to be sure, but one that was right and just. This was Gwydre's promise to him.

That night, Bransen affirmed his belief in the future—his own and that of the beauteous land he called his home.

If he could only survive the battle . . .

CHAPTER 27

Blenden Coe

K ing Yeslnik sat atop his coach, tapping his fingers on the oaken arms of his gilded throne. On the ground before him stood Captain Descarde of the Seventh Legion, one of the battle groups Yeslnik had granted to Bannagran. Beside the king stood a nobleman of his court, an advisor who had read the note from Laird Bannagran, and atop the nearby wagon to Yeslnik's right sat Queen Olym, arrived at last from the city.

"It is good that you have come forth," Descarde said, stumbling over every word as he tried to unsaddle himself from the burden of having delivered the obviously unwelcome proposal. "I might return with all haste to Laird Banna . . ." His voice trailed off as Yeslnik began talking to Olym, ignoring him fully.

"Did you hear that, my queen?" the king asked. "An end to the war, so says Bannagran, this man you think so grand a champion."

Around him, unnoticed by Yeslnik, several men shifted nervously, for there could be no question of the impressive nature of the Laird of Pryd, whose exploits in the war were legendary throughout the ranks of Delaval's garrison.

"We simply stop! How marvelous!" Yeslnik chided. "And since my victory is at hand, assuredly, now is the time for me to divide my kingdom among several smaller kingdoms. Oh, my, but how wonderful, with Bannagran getting his own!"

The advisor at Yeslnik's side strained to laugh at the mocking tones.

"Alas, but he has seen too much of the war," Queen Olym replied. "I have heard of such things, where mighty warriors become cowardly. It is a great loss, but no matter, for our kingdom is at hand. Indeed, my husband, perhaps it is better that a once-mighty laird so nearby to Delaval City has lost his loins for the fight."

King Yeslnik chuckled and nodded, fixing his stare back on Captain Descarde.

"You would have me return to Laird Bannagran and tell him that his offer is refused?" the man asked.

"Oh, more than that," Yeslnik said dramatically. "I would have you go back to Pryd—take extra horses and ride through the nights!—and tell my subject of the situation. Dame Gwydre and her pitiful forces flee straight at my army, trapped north and west by the great General Milwellis and with Bannagran and the thousands I gave to him blocking her way to the south. Tell him to come forth and join in Gwydre's slaughter, or I will remove him from the seat of Pryd in disgrace. Perhaps he can yet salvage a place among my generals, perhaps I'll even allow him to join in the rout of Laird Ethelbert, but I'll not tolerate his hesitance. Not now."

The captain bowed.

"Go!" King Yeslnik, so full of pride and power and glory, yelled at him.

"Bannagran needs to be leashed and lashed," Yeslnik remarked to his queen.

Olym tittered and arched her eyebrows at that, and Yeslnik scowled at her, fully understanding where her lewd mind had run off to.

An interesting proposal," Harcourt said to Milwellis.

Milwellis didn't immediately respond, considering more carefully the implications of Bannagran's curious and unexpected ploy. Surely Yeslnik would be outraged . . . particularly at this moment, with one of his prime enemies about to be utterly destroyed.

Of course, Bannagran likely did not know that. "We must move more quickly," he instructed Harcourt. "I would catch and destroy Gwydre even before she encounters the Delaval garrison, if that is possible."

Harcourt looked at him curiously, obviously expecting more.

"And since Bannagran will not likely come forth . . ." Milwellis said.

"All glory to Palmaristown," Harcourt finished, now nodding.

"And who better to absorb the Holding of Vanguard than Milwellis of Palmaristown?" the laird asked. "With our ships dominating the gulf and securing the trade routes."

"Bannagran's hesitance plays for us," Harcourt agreed. "Might he even evoke war between Delaval City and Pryd Town?"

"A marvelous possibility," Milwellis said. "But one stride forward at a time, my friend. Let us crush Gwydre and quickly, that none share in our glory.

Then we will let King Yeslnik determine our course, be it to Chapel Abelle or even to distant Ethelbert dos Entel. I will be the good and loyal prince." He glanced down at the parchment from Pryd Town. "While Bannagran pauses to irrelevance."

A wry smile spread across Milwellis's face. He looked to the south, toward the distant army of Vanguard, soon, perhaps even this fine day, to be conquered.

"An interesting proposal," he repeated back to Harcourt, who nodded in silent applause to the obvious inner workings of Laird Milwellis' mind.

T his will be the field of battle," Dame Gwydre decided as the great force pursuing her grew closer throughout that day. She stood on a ridge, looking east across a descending slope to a wide field interspersed with small copses of maples and elms.

"Blenden Coe," said one of the nearby monks, a man from the region. "There have been other notable battles here."

"I had thought we would find higher ground, more rocky and defensible," Brother Pinower remarked.

So had Gwydre, but the choice had been forced by the proximity of King Yeslnik's forces in the other direction. She had walked into the trap determinedly and knowing all the while that any chance of survival hinged on the magical prowess of Pinower's monks and any chance of victory on the decision of Bannagran, whose forces sat immediately south of her position.

She looked that way as she considered the Laird of Pryd, and her turn did not go unnoticed.

"If he does not come?" Pinower asked, the question that was on the minds of all, save Bransen.

"Then we flee to him," Gwydre replied. "He'll not stop our run."

"Bannagran will come," the Highwayman assured them all. "He goaded Milwellis forward with a message and gave King Yeslnik pause. That was his intent, and only because he would have us fight them separately."

Dawson's sigh turned the lady and Bransen his way, her expression one of surprise and curiosity.

"There's no telling what a man like that'll do when his world's on the line," Dawson said. "He's all a friend to ye when you visit, to be sure, but how might that friendship hold when fifty thousand warriors are chasing you to his town?"

Gwydre held her hand up in concession, and, for a brief moment, she appeared very old and tired to those around her. She had taken an awful risk here, and now, faced with the converging armies—either of them far outnumbering her own—she couldn't help but second-guess her gamble. She could have left her five thousand in Vanguard, far from Yeslnik's reach. Surely, he could not have so easily sent tens of thousands against her in that remote and forbidding wilderness. She could have left the prisoner army and the brothers inside the thick walls of St. Mere Abelle, for would any army ever breach that mighty fortress?

"This is not about us," Bransen interjected, and he stepped up beside Gwydre, who was glad for his support. "We are here for the people of Honce and the misery they will surely know if we desert them to the whims of King Yeslnik."

"This will be the field of battle," Dame Gwydre said again, more resolutely. "Prepare it quickly, for Milwellis will come on eagerly and will not pause to wait for King Yeslnik. All glory to him, he believes, and Yeslnik is a day's march away at the least."

"The rise is for me and my brethren to defend," Brother Pinower explained, pointing halfway down the descent.

"Their horsemen will break into a charge at the base, no doubt," said Bransen.

"And that is the time to hit them the hardest," Pinower agreed.

"What else?" Dame Gwydre asked Bransen when Pinower scurried away. Bransen's surprise at her obvious uncertainty was clear. "This is not the type of battle we fight in Vanguard," the dame admitted. "Rarely do armies there number in the hundreds, and here we face thousands with thousands."

Bransen swallowed hard, realizing only then the responsibility that would be his. He thought of the Book of Jhest, that marvelous tome he had memorized in his youth. Much of the book was devoted to personal fighting styles and philosophy, but there were many verses regarding the great battles of the great wars.

Bransen looked around at the landscape, picturing the battle in his head, playing it out as a bird might witness it. "Logs," he said.

"Logs?" Gwydre and Dawson asked together.

W ord traveled fast along King Yeslnik's line: Dame Gwydre had stopped and turned to face Milwellis before the jaws of their trap could engulf her.

"Faster, then!" demanded Queen Olym when the word reached the pair, riding atop their respective coaches. "I would see their blood!"

"Drive on!" King Yeslnik agreed. "And where is Bannagran? Bid him come forth! There can be no escape for the witch of Vanguard!"

Within an hour, King Yeslnik had his answer, for across the wide fields to the south appeared an army more than half the size of his own and flying the wolf-emblazoned pennants of Pryd Town.

"Gwydre's end!" Yeslnik proclaimed at the sight, and he flailed his fist into the air, overwhelmed with joy. Where could she go, caught between three forces, each far superior to her own?

Soon after, a contingent of heavy war chariots rumbled across the fields, and cheers for Laird Bannagran preceded the man's ride to Yeslnik's coach.

"I feared that I would have to ride all the way to Pryd Town to pry you from your hole," the king greeted the laird. Yeslnik seemed quite pleased with himself as he looked down at Bannagran from on high.

"I sent you a courier, an offer," Bannagran replied, and he didn't bow and didn't refer at all to Yeslnik's title, as protocol demanded.

Yeslnik sputtered, trying to find a reply.

"Five holdings and an end to the war," Bannagran clarified.

"The war ends this day!" Yeslnik screamed back at him. "Dame Gwydre will fall to Laird Milwellis right before our eyes and to our blades as well, if we do not tarry."

"Even were that so, it would only preface a continuing war."

"Ethelbert?" Yeslnik said with a dismissive snicker.

"And the brothers of Abelle and Vanguard itself." Bannagran paused and stared hard at the King. "And . . ." he hinted.

"What do you say?" King Yeslnik demanded.

"I have your answer?" asked Bannagran.

Yeslnik sputtered again. "My answer?" he shouted incredulously, angrily.

"I ask you one more time," Bannagran said calmly, "abandon this war and divide Honce accordingly."

King Yeslnik trembled with rage. "Honce is mine!" he screeched. "Mine! From Delaval to Ethelbert dos Entel, from the Belt-and-Buckle to the forests of Vanguard. Mine! How dare you? Honce is mine!"

"We shall see," said Bannagran, and on his nod his practiced brigade whipped their teams into a gallop and rumbling turn.

"What?" Yeslnik yelled behind them as they rumbled away. "Treason!" he shouted. "Stop them!"

And, indeed, some of the king's men moved to do just that, with one in particular barking commands at his soldiers and at Bannagran to surrender.

The Laird of Pryd lifted a spear from the bucket at his feet. His throw was true, as usual, and strong, the spear plunging through the commander's chest and driving behind him to the ground, pinning him in place. He was still standing, but his arms swung limply at his sides, for he was also quite dead.

With Bannagran at their tip, the wedge of his skilled charioteers thundered through the scattering ranks of confused Delaval soldiers, back to the south and their lines.

"My king?" more than one of Yeslnik's commanders pleaded with him back at the coaches.

"Fight them! Kill him!" was all that the stunned and terrified Yeslnik could demand. He leaped from his throne and scrambled down the ladder at the side of his coach, disappearing inside and slamming the armored door behind him.

More than one commander raised an eyebrow at that, but these were skilled warriors, men who had trained and fought under the able command of Laird Delaval. They scattered to their respective battle groups, turning the lines, readying the archers, and forming defensive squares as the fields south blackened with lines of warriors marching under the flag of Pryd, not Delaval, then charging without hesitation to the command of the Bear of Honce.

The ground shook when they came on, driving into King Yeslnik's flank, led by Bannagran and his devastating wedge of veteran charioteers.

The sky blackened with arrows.

The fields reddened with blood.

The air filled with the screams of battle, of rage, of agony, of terror.

There was no shortage of second-guessing on the ridge west of the low field known as Blenden Coe when all the higher ground north and east darkened with the soldiers of Laird Milwellis. Shoulder to shoulder and many ranks deep, their sheer numbers mocked Dame Gwydre's plan or any rational hope that she could win the day.

Those enemies in the north held their ground, planting their long spears in the turf and standing at ease, while in the west, the great force began to move, spilling down the northern slope into the bowl of Blenden Coe, forming into squares.

"How many to each?" Gwydre asked Dawson McKeege, who stood beside her.

The old sailor snorted. "Five hundred? A thousand?" he said as square after square rolled over the eastern crest and marched down into Blenden Coe. Three squares across and five deep, fully fifteen were in sight.

"Beware the line in the north," Gwydre warned.

"The ground up there is difficult, and we've archers and monks ready to sting them if they try to run about us," Dawson assured her. He left it unspoken, but his ending snort told Gwydre that he was thinking the same thing as she: With the overwhelming force marching straight at them, what need did Laird Milwellis have of any tactical flank?

Fittingly, the sky darkened as storm clouds rushed on brisk late-summer winds and stole the late-morning sun.

"If we sting them hard enough, be prepared to break and run," Gwydre said to Dawson and to all the other commanders about her. "To the south and Pryd Town."

"If Bannagran won't come to us, we'll go to him," Dawson muttered under his breath, and, like Gwydre, he looked to the south.

Milwellis's leading squares were halfway across the mile-long field by that point, all shields and spear tips and the rattle of armor and the thunder of marching boots. The storm clouds above seemed to mirror their approach, the sky darkening as the field darkened with cavalry groups, few chariots, but scores of riders, positioned between the second rank of squares, riding about the lines and tightening the formations, barking orders and encouragement.

"Come on, then," Dawson muttered when the first line paused just beyond the slope at the western end of Blenden Coe. He glanced back over his shoulder at the second contingency, and he noted a rider fast approaching along the western road.

Dawson tapped Gwydre's shoulder, and when she turned to regard him, he motioned to the distant man. Both were still looking on curiously, back to the west, when the storm broke in the east, the leading three squares coming on with a howling charge.

"Let fly! Let fly!" the commanders shouted to the lines of archers up on that ridge, and lines of Vanguardsmen bent their bows and sent their killing darts into the air.

But the shield walls stopped most of that with only minimal damage.

Behind the leading squares, groups of Palmaristown archers rushed into place and tried to return the volley, but from the lower ground, they couldn't yet reach Gwydre's position. Seeing that as their enemy's only advantage, Milwellis's commanders urged those first squares on faster.

Up the slope they charged, screaming wildly and beating their weapons against their shields.

And a second storm broke, a thunderstorm, and not from the skies above, but from the ground before them, as the brothers of St. Mere Abelle popped up from their concealment and blasted Milwellis's ranks with stunning bolts of graphite lightning.

And most powerful of all, centering the line of Dame Gwydre's monks, came the magical explosions of the Highwayman, and while many men fell wounded to the lightning of the monks, those who fell to the power of the Highwayman did not rise up.

Stroke after stroke crackled into the tight formations, scattering electrical charges across the iron-banded shields like the interconnected strands of a spider's web. Men staggered and stumbled as the focused assault became a confused and faltering jumble.

More lightning came forth, and atop the ridge Gwydre called for more arrows. Again the sky filled with deadly darts, and this time, with the enemy formations compromised, with much greater effect.

"Let fly! Let fly!" Gwydre and all of her commanders implored their archers, for the only hope for the brothers below, who were now running up the hill and stopping only occasionally to launch a weak lightning stroke, was continued confusion among Milwellis's front ranks. The Highwayman bounded among the fleeing monks, helping brothers to their feet and shoving them along their way. When he stopped and turned and let fly a blast of lightning, all pursuit in that region simply ceased.

Still, arrows chased those monks up the hill, and several brothers fell thrashing to the ground. From the ranks below came riders, just a few, galloping up the turf, braving the hail of arrows to catch a wayward brother and cut him down.

And farther below, the second rank of squares methodically marched past the retreating first groups, continuing up the hills.

"They're not all up," Gwydre said to Dawson when he turned to shout out more commands.

Dawson turned to her, shaking his head. "Now or not at all," he said. "And sure if not at all, then we're all lost."

Dame Gwydre closed her eyes and tried to steady herself with long, deep breaths. She thought herself a fool for continuing her march; she should have returned to St. Mere Abelle . . . or to Vanguard!

Come along and ride hard," Milwellis said to Harcourt and Father De Guilbe as they watched the second rank of squares ascend the hill, victory all but assured. "I wish to be there when Dame Gwydre begs for her life."

The two shared a laugh at that long-awaited prospect, and both were just about to kick their mounts into a run when over the crest of the far western ridge came a curious sight: several burning logs in a long line. At either end of each stood runners, holding ropes affixed to those clever barriers. The runners didn't hesitate and didn't slow, charging down at the marching enemies, pulling the logs between them. With their fires raging along their oil-soaked lengths, those logs gained momentum and outran their pullers, bouncing and rolling down the hill.

How the soldiers of Milwellis scattered before that conflagration! More logs appeared atop the ridge and followed the first barrage down the sloping ground and more after that.

Running beside that third wave of rolling firebombs came the brothers of Abelle once again, gemstones in hand, and with the ranks confused and dodging and scattered, their lightning strokes sent many men shuddering to the ground.

"The beasts!" exclaimed Father De Guilbe.

Laird Milwellis let out a growl of outrage. "Onward!" he bade Harcourt, as if he meant to turn the tide all by himself.

Harcourt grabbed Milwellis's mount's bridle and held the laird back. "Swashbuckler's flash," the general explained, referring to a sea term to describe the technique of a particular type of swordsman, who used exaggerated movements and flair to disguise often ineffectual maneuvers. "Be at ease, laird. Their display is far more impressive in appearance than effect, I am sure."

So they waited and watched, and Gwydre's forces pressed from the top half of the ridge with volleys of arrows and magical explosions. The screams of pain echoing in Blenden Coe were those of Milwellis's men, then and for what seemed like a very long while.

But it was not, and, as Harcourt had predicted, nothing dramatic changed in the greater scheme of things. Gwydre's ploy had killed many of Milwellis's men—a couple of hundred, perhaps—but the swarm of the laird's army continued their indomitable march, and even those shattered formations worked fast to regroup and begin again the press.

"Swashbuckler's flash," Milwellis said back to Harcourt, great relief in his voice. "How many more tricks might Dame Gwydre have to play?"

"Not enough," Harcourt assured him.

CHAPTER 28

The Swirling Tides of Battle

His actions toward strengthening the loyalty of his soldiers, particularly those given to him by the very king they now battled against, had worked handsomely, Bannagran knew in the first confusing moments of that collision of armies. He had worked hard to make them view Pryd Town as their home, had given them land on which to build houses instead of living in tents, and had invited their families to join them. Well-rested, well-fed, and fighting for a man they had come to love and for a town that all of them could now call home, the legions of Pryd slammed hard into Yeslnik's flank, determined to be done with this miserable fighting once and for all.

But these were seasoned Delaval soldiers opposing them, in superior numbers, and Yeslnik's men did not break and run.

And so Bannagran and his charioteers had to be everywhere at once, omnipresent on the battlefield, thundering in wherever the line of Pryd seemed most shaky and vulnerable. None could withstand those powerful charioteers and their godlike leader. None dared remain on the field before the Bear of Honce.

But the enemy line was long and disciplined and turning in to flank the smaller Pryd force, east and west. Even if they won the day, Bannagran knew that he would have little in reserve to meet Laird Milwellis on the field.

In the height of the fighting, with men dying by the score, horns began to blow and every warrior, Delaval and Pryd alike, turned to see a new force entering the fray, charging hard from the northeast.

"Milwellis has come! Milwellis has come!" those men and women around the coaches of Yeslnik and Olym cried, and the foppish king dared come forth and climb again to the roof of his carriage. His smile nearly took in his large ears as he peered to the northwest, to see a great legion rushing in, sure to slam against Bannagran's exposed flank.

"They will split our enemy asunder!" one of the nearby commanders shouted. "Even the great Bannagran cannot hold his line together! Swiftly will come the end of Bannagran!"

"Death to the Bear of Honce!" another commander shouted.

"Milwellis has come!" King Yeslnik cried, and all about him cheered. "And so you die, Bannagran the traitor!"

All along the line of Delaval, the cheering heightened, for who else might it be but Laird Milwellis of Palmaristown?

The force closed, the cheering continued, and King Yeslnik hopped about with glee . . . and such relief. But gradually, interspersed with those cheers, came questioning remarks from Yeslnik's commanders.

"Light horses?" one asked.

"Milwellis is armored," another added.

King Yeslnik's smile dissolved as he looked around at the gathering, some commanders in trees, others atop wagons, and all peering intently to the northwest.

"Laird Milwellis was wise enough to lighten a force to come to our cause," Yeslnik said after many more comments and doubts filled the air about him.

"It is not Laird Milwellis, my king," one commander dared remark, and Yeslnik fixed him with a look of surprise and anger and fear.

"It is Laird Ethelbert!" another added, as the first shrank back from that dangerous look. "He has come forth in all his power!"

The blood drained from Yeslnik's thin face. He turned fast to look to his wife for support, to the woman who had given him such courage and daring in these last months.

But she stood staring wide-eyed, her hands up before her gaping mouth, and when she noted Yeslnik's look, she let out a ghastly screech and retreated fast again to the sanctuary of her armored coach.

Yeslnik looked back to the approaching force.

He trembled. He sweat. He tried to call out an order to his commanders to regroup and tighten their lines.

But all he could do was squeak.

Friend or foe?" the driver of the chariot beside Bannagran asked when the identity of the new force entering the field of battle became clear.

"The men of Ethelbert dos Entel hate Yeslnik," another driver insisted.

"They hate Laird Bannagran, too," said the first.

"Follow!" Bannagran commanded, and he swung his chariot around and charged away from the raging battle, straight toward Laird Ethelbert's approaching line. He lifted his great axe high above his head as he came in clear sight of the group and began waving for them to turn north, a course that would veer them from Bannagran's flank and toward the approaching eastern edge of Yeslnik's forces.

Across the field, horns blew—not the typical trumpets of Honce, but more exotic and rich wind instruments whose sharp notes often graced the wide avenues of Jacintha in Behr. Kirren Howen appeared, astride his charger and surrounded by his trusted generals. He lifted his sword in salute to Bannagran and turned his force to the north, as directed.

It occurred to Bannagran then that this Dame Gwydre was a most remarkable diplomat. And the Highwayman, too, though it pained him to admit it!

A cheer went up all around Bannagran, who wasted no time in reversing his direction, and now, with unexpected allies ready to turn the tide of the battle, the Bear of Honce drove even more furiously back into King Yeslnik's ranks, spears flying, his armored team churning men into the mud, the spiked wheels of his famous war chariot cutting enemies apart, his great axe clearing groups of men with a single powerful swipe.

None stood before Bannagran and his team; more fled than fell, and the integrity of King Yeslnik's line weakened along its entire center.

East of that press, Ethelbert's charge overwhelmed the spur of Yeslnik's line, speeding to battle, launching volleys of spears from shoulder-held atlatl, swift cavalry cutting through the lines of confused footmen, and, within minutes, it was Yeslnik in danger of being flanked, not Bannagran.

Oh, the treachery!" King Yeslnik cried dramatically when it became clear not only that his archenemies had come to the field in support of Bannagran but also that the eastern city's forces would make short work of Yeslnik's northern flank.

"Go forth, my king!" one of the nearby commanders implored him. "Now is the time when great men may recapture the press of battle."

"What?" Yeslnik asked him incredulously.

"Our lines are breaking," another commander explained. "The peasants are confused by the betrayal of Bannagran and the arrival of this new and furious enemy. They need to see you riding among them, rallying them back to the cause of King Yeslnik."

"Your presence will strengthen them and turn them back to the battle," a third added.

"And we will win?" Yeslnik asked, somewhat meekly, his gaze drifting across to Olym on her wagon as he spoke. The severity in her expression was not lost on him.

The three commanders looked to each other.

"Or we will die in glory," one finally admitted, and Yeslnik let out a little shriek.

"My wife is here on this field of death," he said, more to cover his own fear than anything else.

"The queen to Delaval City!" a commander yelled, and men began hustling all about, putting fresh horses to Queen Olym's wagon and ordering an escort for the desperate run.

"Now, my king," said the first commander. "Our lines are falling. It is time to ride forth." Behind him came a stableman, pulling Yeslnik's armored white charger, the horse he had typically ridden onto battlefields after the fighting had ended.

Yeslnik blanched. "No, not here," he stammered.

Many sets of eyes settled on him.

"No, behind our walls. The high and thick walls," Yeslnik went on, improvising for all his life now, for he knew with certainty that if he rode out on that field, the Bear of Honce would cut him down. "Yes, yes. To Delaval City we go. All of us. We will regroup and hold these traitors at bay, and Laird Milwellis will come in from behind and crush them against our walls!"

His great enthusiasm was not met in kind, not from the commanders and not from Olym, who stared at him hard from the next wagon over. How many times had poor Yeslnik seen that look!

"Go and save the day," the queen even called to him.

"Shut up, woman!" he heard himself yelling back at her, and he could hardly believe the words as they left his mouth. It didn't matter, though. Not this time. Not with the Bear of Honce running wild out there and vile Laird Ethelbert and his assassins so near at hand.

"To Delaval City!" Yeslnik commanded all around him. "Turn about and flee!"

"My king, if we do so, we will be routed, surely," said the first commander. "Half of our men will die on this field or scatter to the corners of Honce, and less than a quarter will ever return to the city."

"Go! Go!" Yeslnik shouted back at him, disappearing into the wagon and slamming the door.

Across the way a short while later, Laird Bannagran was not surprised to see the rising dust of frantic retreat as King Yeslnik fled the field.

Time to run, lady," said Dawson McKeege as the latest ploy of fiery logs burned themselves out and the vast army before them, stung but not terribly wounded, regrouped and once more began their inexorable march.

Dame Gwydre reflexively glanced to the south, as if she expected a great army led by Bannagran marching to her aid.

But there was nothing, and she turned back to Dawson and resignedly nodded. She knew the peril here; while she and some of her forces might escape, the battle would prove disastrous to her cause. And now, if Bannagran had not come and would not come, her cause was lost.

Shouts from Brother Pinower turned them both around, to see the monk running toward them and escorting a pair of riders, Cormack and Milkeila.

"Bannagran has come forth!" Cormack cried. "He battles King Yeslnik down the western road!"

"There's our course," Dawson said, and Gwydre nodded, a bit of hope returning to her dark expression. "We get to him, and we'll fight them all!"

"How fares he?" Gwydre asked.

"We know not," said Milkeila.

"We were sent straightaway before the fight was joined," said Cormack. "But joined it was, for we heard the first ring of battle as we rode hard to find you."

"Then let us be gone and quickly," said Gwydre. "Perhaps the outcome is not yet decided."

"No," another voice joined in, and Bransen walked over to the group. He nodded at Cormack and Milkeila and managed to grasp Milkeila's hand as he walked past her to stand before Dame Gwydre. "Not yet," he said. "We have not hurt Milwellis enough." His voice was strangely calm, the timbre of it more intriguing than the surprising words.

"If we retreat to Bannagran, so, too, follows Milwellis," Bransen went on, "and with Yeslnik's thousands bolstered by this massive force before us, our loss will be complete."

Hopeful smiles turned fast to dour expressions, for it was hard to argue that assessment with so great an army marching up the rise at them.

"Then what would you have me do?" Dame Gwydre asked him, calmly and reasonably.

"I would have you tell me that this war is worth all the misery," Bransen replied, and many eyebrows arched at that. "I would have you promise me that your ascent is worth the price of so many innocent lives and the agony so many families will know when this day is done."

"Bransen," Dame Gwydre stammered in response, "what would you have me say? How might I weigh the price of such misery?"

"By promising me that Queen Gwydre of Honce will be as Dame Gwydre of Vanguard," Bransen said, and he grasped her by the shoulders and locked her eyes with his own. "You will care for them, all of them, throughout your reign. You will make their lives better, subjects of every remote corner of this land. You will end these miserable wars and seek peace among the lairds and among the kingdoms."

"You're rambling, boy," said Dawson.

"No!" Bransen yelled at him. "No. I will hear it. I must believe it. I must know it before . . ."

"Before?" Dame Gwydre asked.

"I have killed so many men and women this day," Bransen lamented. "Common folk who did not deserve to die. Men and women who are here because they were given no choice in the matter, to fight for a cause they neither understand nor endorse. Whether the misplaced rage of Palmaristown warriors or the helpless victims of Yeslnik's press-gangs, they do not fight to support the cause of an evil king. Nay, they fight because if they did not they would be put to the stake."

"It's the nature of things," Dawson remarked.

"No more!" Bransen shouted, and he turned fiercely on Dame Gwydre. "Promise me!" he shouted at her, tears streaming from his eyes. "We will win this day, here and now, and many, many will die, but only if Dame Gwydre is who I have come to trust her to be."

Again Dawson started to chastise Bransen, but this time Dame Gwydre held up her hand to silence him. She stared at Bransen, hard at first, but then her visage softened as she reached up to gently stroke his young and innocent face.

"I am," she whispered. "For myself I seek nothing. For Honce I seek everything."

"And it is worth the pain and the misery?"

"Who can know, Bransen? But surely it is a better outcome by far than that of a crowned King Yeslnik."

"I need more than that."

"The hand is played—the ugly hand—but there is a difference in victory or defeat. A profound difference for all the folk of Honce."

"Promise me."

"I promise." She leaned in and kissed Bransen on the cheek.

"For Cadayle," he whispered.

"I promise," Gwydre replied.

Bransen stepped back and took a deep breath. He turned to all of them. "Do not flee. You will know when your victory is at hand." He moved away, leaving Dawson, Pinower, Cormack, and Milkeila staring at each other incredulously, and both Pinower and Dawson lifted their open palms helplessly, completely befuddled.

"What's it about?" Dawson asked Gwydre.

The woman turned and faced Blenden Coe, where Milwellis's forces dangerously neared, three intact squares already moving steadily up the rise and with nothing substantial to oppose them, no tricks and not nearly enough forces.

"About honor," she replied. "And decency. And the demands of conscience and the strength of sacrifice."

Bransen looked down on Blenden Coe. He thought of Affwin Wi, then, strangely. What secrets had she learned from her time in the Walk of Clouds among the Jhesta Tu? Were the answers of his life, of his freedom, there in that distant and mystical place?

A tinge of regret stung the young man. Perhaps he should have gone south with Cadayle and Callen when first they had left Pryd. Perhaps he should have been stronger in his convictions and more determined to follow his father's footsteps to learn if that wondrous book he had so revered as a child, that wondrous tome that had guided his life, was the hint of something great or if he, in his desperation, had attributed to it more promise than the actual truth of the Jhesta Tu.

He glanced over at Dame Gwydre, at Queen Gwydre.

Or was this his destiny? He silently replayed her promises in his head, her assurance that the gain would be worth the price.

Bransen fell into the magic of his brooch, more fully and deeply than ever before. The serpentine glow came up around him, and flames engulfed him, angry, furious, white-hot flames. He drew forth his sword, his mother's sword, and held it high, and then, with the magic of Abellican malachite lifting his body, the Highwayman leaped from the ridge.

He glided down the slope from on high, a soaring beacon of hope for Dame Gwydre and, soon, a flaming harbinger of doom for the men of Laird Milwellis.

He landed on the field before the center square, a tremendous blast of flames rolling out from his feet. Those front ranks cried out and ducked as the wave of heat washed over them, and several threw spears.

But the Highwayman was already gone, leaping into the air again, clearing those tightening front ranks and crashing down in the middle of the tight formation. Again came an explosion of flames, this one engulfing many men near to the Highwayman's landing.

Screams and chaos shook the square, multiplying many times over as the Highwayman rushed about, flames bursting from him, his sword stabbing with deadly precision at terrified man after woman after man trying desperately to get out of his way.

His ruby magic exploded again, and many died, and he leaped to the back of the square and turned, aiming his sword along a line of archers moving between the center square and the one to the north, and from that sword tip came a stroke of lightning.

As one, the line of archers fell to the ground.

From the other direction came a volley of arrows, as Bransen turned on the second archer line. The missiles flew all about him, but he did not feel their sting, so deeply was he into the magic of the brooch.

A second lightning bolt laid that line low.

The Highwayman bounded away, to the north, leap after leap that ended each time in a devastating fireball.

On one descent, he saw a spear set before him, but he could not sway. And so he cried out in rage and denial, impaling himself as he landed and blowing away all those around him, including the warrior holding the spear. The Highwayman leaped away immediately, trailing no blood, for as the spear had pierced his flesh, so, too, had it punctured the serpentine shield, and the hot flames had cauterized the wound as soon as the Highwayman had leaped back off the bloodied weapon.

He felt no pain. The soul stone in the brooch kept him strong. He bounced back the other way, assaulting the third square.

Up above, Dame Gwydre saw her moment and began her charge.

The old ones!" came a cry.

"They fight for the witch Gwydre!"

"Oh, we are doomed!"

"It is Abelle himself, come from the grave!"

The shouts grew more desperate along Milwellis's lines. Those leading formations evaporated, scores of men burning and dead on the western slope, dozens of archers thrashing in the death throes of killing lightning, scores more cut down by the fiery blade of the Highwayman.

That retreat did not halt at the next grouping of military squares, for with the fleeing soldiers came the Highwayman himself, in full, burning glory and power.

"Stop him!" Father De Guilbe shouted from behind Milwellis, who sat beside Harcourt.

"Stop him!" De Guilbe shouted again as another fireball exploded, scattering men, some aflame, all fleeing in abject terror. The monk shouted again as more cried of the old ones or of Abelle himself rising up in support of Dame Gwydre.

Milwellis turned and yelled, "How?" in the monk's face, his frustration clear and consuming. He turned to Harcourt, who had no answers, for the general, like the laird, the monk, and all the men on both sides of the battle, had never seen anything like this display of sheer, unbridled magical power. Godlike, the Highwayman bounced about the field, making his way through the ranks and leaving mounds of bodies in his devastating wake.

"It is magic!" Milwellis shouted, turning back on De Guilbe. "Your magic! You stop him!"

Harcourt grabbed Milwellis by the shoulder and shook him, and Milwellis looked back at the man with shock . . . until he noted that Harcourt was pointing frantically ahead.

For on came the Highwayman, in all his terrible splendor.

"Archers form! Around me!" yelled Milwellis, and so commanding was his roar that many archers and spearmen heeded his command.

"Fill the air! Shoot him dead!" Laird Milwellis screamed, and a scattering of arrows flew away.

"No! Together, you fools! A barrage to lay him low."

Fully engulfed by the magic and the fury, the Highwayman moved without direction but with great purpose. Wherever he saw a concentration of enemies, he bounded and exploded, and darted about, stabbing and killing.

Every blast, every strike, killed a bit of his own soul, he knew, but he held to the promise of Gwydre, the promise of Honce renewed.

Up into the air he went, and only then did he see the great black volley swarming his way. He threw forth a fireball there in midair, the force of it deflecting many missiles aside and disintegrating many others.

But some got through the conflagration, and Bransen felt the iron tips and wooden shafts sliding into his body.

He landed unsteadily, but instinctively sprang away again, veering to the side, trying to get away from the biting arrows, for another volley was in the air. He landed and leaped into a copse of trees.

Confused and with his line of *ki-chi-kree* wavering, trying hard to fall fully into the soul stone and enact healing magic upon himself, Bransen slammed hard into a tree trunk. He managed to grab on and hold his place some twenty feet from the ground, but the only fires burning then were those in the trees behind him, lit by his flaming wake.

He tried to fall more fully into the one stone that could save him, for now he felt, most profoundly of all, the serious wound from impaling himself. His gut was torn, his line of life energy shivering, breaking. The pain threatened his concentration.

He thought of Cadayle.

Behind him he heard the horns of Gwydre's countering charge. He hoped he had done enough.

B reak off!" Bannagran commanded his forces repeatedly. He led his chariot group along the lines, pulling back his men.

For the rout was in full now, with King Yeslnik fleeing the field. His army crumbled behind him, men throwing down their weapons and running away, or falling to their knees and begging for mercy.

Mercy that Bannagran was determined to show, for that was what Gwydre had taught him and that was what filled his awakening heart.

As his orders multiplied throughout his forces, warriors and commanders echoing the call for quarter, Bannagran swung back to the east and lashed his team into a full gallop.

"Relent! The day is won!" he shouted as he neared Kirren Howen's legion, and it was strange, indeed, to hear these men of that eastern city cheering for him as he passed among their ranks. He pulled up fast before the three generals.

"All quarter given," he told Kirren Howen.

"You ask much," the new Laird of Ethelbert dos Entel replied. "The day is won, and my men, so long at war, will have their revenge."

"No, laird!" Bannagran demanded. "This is for Honce. All of it."

Kirren Howen and his two generals stared at Bannagran as if he had reached over and slapped the laird across the face.

"Yeslnik is through," Bannagran explained. "He cannot survive this day. It is time to heal the land of Honce."

"Is this mighty and merciless Bannagran I hear before me?" Laird Kirren Howen asked.

The great warrior, the Bear of Honce, smiled and shook his head. "Perhaps it is Dame Gwydre," he admitted. "But it is right, and it is for the best for what will follow this day."

Kirren Howen straightened in his saddle as his generals and his men looked at him curiously. "You will be king, yes?" he asked.

Bannagran didn't flinch.

"And Gwydre your queen?"

Again, the Bear didn't respond.

"What for Ethelbert dos Entel, then?" the laird asked.

"A shining and wondrous city on the Mirianic Coast, with the full support of Delaval and Pryd and Vanguard and the Order of Blessed Abelle," Bannagran promised.

Kirren Howen paused and considered the words for a long while. "My trusted generals and friends," he said at length, and both Myrick and Tyne leaned toward him. "Do spread the word that all quarter is to be given."

For what seemed like a thousand heartbeats, not a sound could be heard about Laird Kirren Howen and the stunning proclamation.

"And tend the wounded," he continued, and he looked at Bannagran as he finished, "of both sides."

Bannagran walked his chariot beside Kirren Howen's horse and held forth his hand. "I have not forgotten our alliance in the east against the powries," he said.

"Nor have I," Kirren Howen replied, and he took Bannagran's hand.

As if from very far away, Bransen heard the cheers around Milwellis, heard the laird himself calling for more volleys into the copse.

Bransen held on tightly and concentrated on his soul stone, holding steady his life energy. He managed to glance about, the branches crackling with flames behind him and skipping arrows all about him. He noted the carnage he had wrought this ugly day.

He had killed hundreds and wounded hundreds more.

He held to Gwydre's words, her promise, and the thought of the world his child would come to know. He had to believe that the price was worth the gain. He winced as another arrow invaded his body, driving deep into his shoulder, but the soul stone magic was there, keeping him alive.

He heard one voice above all others, though, and the message that it carried wounded Bransen more profoundly than any dart ever could. For it was Milwellis, rallying his force.

"The demon is dead," Milwellis proclaimed. "And now comes the witch in folly!"

Bransen couldn't see much of the battlefield through the pain and the tears and the smoke and the tumble of smoking leaves, but he quickly came to understand that Laird Milwellis had somehow held his force together. He managed to glance back behind him, toward the western slope, toward the horns of Gwydre. Down the hill she came, he knew, and knew, too, that he had weakened Milwellis's line enough for her to drive hard through those first ranks.

But as he swung his gaze back, Bransen realized that it wouldn't be enough. Not hardly. For those thousands around Milwellis stood firm, and the laird himself sat tall above them, forming them into a countercharge and heartening them with every word.

Bransen's shaking hand reached into his pouch, and he brought forth his fist, clutching a gem.

The soul stone protested as he turned his focus, and he knew then that to relinquish his concentration from the healing magic was surely to die.

He knew it, but he knew that Gwydre was doomed.

The price. The gain.

And now she is ours!" Laird Milwellis insisted. He lifted his mailed fist before him in a punch of victory, and all the men began to cheer.

The sharp crack of air interrupted that, though, and just as he started to shout the command to charge, Laird Milwellis felt his own fist, his own gauntlet, smash into his face with tremendous force.

And from that gauntlet, through that gauntlet and through his hand, came a screeching projectile, crushing through bone, tearing through brain, and blowing the back of Milwellis's skull and helm away.

The laird flipped backward from his horse, falling facedown to the mud, quite dead before he ever landed.

"Laird!" Harcourt cried after the moment of shock. "Father, tend him!" he started to yell at De Guilbe, but when he looked at the monk, his words failed.

For De Guilbe sat on his horse behind Milwellis, a strange look in his eye, a weird chuckle escaping his lips. He looked down at his own chest, where blood widened under his brown robes and streamed out the hole made by the lodestone.

He looked at Harcourt curiously.

"I am dead," he said.

And he was.

In the tree, Bransen could not see his handiwork, for his sight had turned inward. He pictured Cadayle, beautiful Cadayle, reaching down to him as he lay in the mud, the poor Stork who had been bullied to the ground yet again. He felt her warmth, her kiss . . . her love. He felt the brush of her brown hair on his face, a gentle place to hide from the pain.

He heard Gwydre's promise.

And he knew, somehow he knew—perhaps it was the cries around him, the calls of Abelle or the old ones themselves come to Dame Gwydre's call.

Somehow he knew that his sacrifice had not been in vain.

He left the battlefield with hope.

CHAPTER 29

The Royal Procession

 Yeslnik stared out from the high window of his keep, beyond the walls of Delaval City to a field blackened by a great and combined army. He had less than two legions, no more, for in the rout many had died, many more had fled, and many, so said the rumors, had turned against him, joining the ranks of the Bear of Honce.

"Milwellis," he whispered, he begged to the wind, praying for the Laird of Palmaristown to come forth and crush the army before his gates. He looked to the river, where an armada of his warships and those of Palmaristown had gathered, but they remained far out in the river, out of range of Bannagran's archers.

He rubbed his face.

"He will come," Olym assured him when he turned around. "Harcourt will tell us."

She referred to the news that had come to Yeslnik's chambers only a few moments before, an announcement that General Harcourt of Palmaristown, Laird Milwellis's second, had somehow managed to bypass Bannagran and Gwydre's tens of thousands and enter Delaval City.

"When will Milwellis attack?" Yeslnik demanded of Harcourt as the man was escorted through his door.

The general stopped his march and cast a curious look Yeslnik's way. "Laird Milwellis is dead," he replied. "And his army scattered before the rage of Dame Gwydre and some demon dactyl known as the Highwayman."

"What?" Yeslnik screamed, coming out of his throne and trembling. "I lent you legions!"

"The carrion birds feast well in Blenden Coe," Harcourt replied. "The army was broken and the battle ended, even before Laird Bannagran arrived with thousands more to bolster Dame Gwydre's cause and with the warriors of Ethelbert dos Entel beside him to bolster the cause of both."

"But surely you have something left?" Yeslnik pleaded. "I see the armada in the river!"

"Crewed thinly," said Harcourt, "and by no force that might do battle with the Bear of Honce."

"But you got in here, and so we can escape," Yeslnik said, grasping at any hope he could find.

Harcourt laughed at him. "Laird Bannagran, who has my sword in surrender, sent me in," he explained, and Yeslnik fell back into his throne. "He demands that you yield. Delaval City, all of Honce, is his, is King Bannagran's." He paused and drew a deep sigh. "And Queen Gwydre's, curse her name."

"No!" Yeslnik screamed, slamming his fist on the arm of his oaken throne. "No! We must kill them! You must kill them!"

Harcourt looked at him with an expression of pity . . . not pity for feeble King Yeslnik but for all of Honce, it seemed. "All is lost," he said somberly, and he bowed and exited the room.

Yeslnik sat as if frozen for many heartbeats, then finally leaped from his throne and rushed out of the room, to the top of the long stair.

"You cannot leave me!" he screamed at the man now far below. "You cannot! I command that you kill them!"

Yeslnik felt a strong grip on his shoulder, and he swung about to see Olym before him. "You do it!" she screamed at him, pounding on him frantically. "Strengthen your army! Hold strong the walls until they are gone! You feeble fool! You should have stayed on the field as your generals demanded, to defeat Bannagran out there!"

"While you fled?" Yeslnik screamed back.

"I am your queen! You must protect me!"

She hit him, but now, for the first time in his life, Yeslnik was having no more. He balled his fist and slugged Olym hard in the face, then repeatedly slapped and punched her, and, when that did not suffice to satisfy his rage, he grabbed her by the hair and tugged hard, taking out not only a handful of strands but a hairpin as well.

He struck with it, stabbing it into Olym's chest. Again and again, Yeslnik pumped his arm, all of his fury playing out with every invasion of his wife's flesh.

She screamed, she begged, she threw herself against him.

But Yeslnik merely growled, glad that he had mortally wounded her.

He kept growling until he realized that he couldn't support her great bulk against him and that his heels were against the top step of a long staircase.

Cormack and Milkeila had not marched that afternoon with Gwydre and Bannagran back to Delaval City. As soon as the battle had ended, Bannagran and Gwydre had swung about in pursuit of Yeslnik, to be done with this all. But they had left many behind to tend the wounded, to pile and burn the dead. So Cormack and Milkeila remained about Blenden Coe, with so many wounded to tend and so many questions still unanswered.

It wasn't until two days later, the same morning that Harcourt arrived in Delaval City, that the pair at last discovered some credible witnesses who led them to a burned and scarred copse of trees. The couple made their way among the many trunks and roots, and, of all the treasures that would be looted from the carnage of Blenden Coe in the aftermath of that battle, none shone more precious than the sword Milkeila found on the ground in the leaves beneath one tall maple.

The woman paused a long while, steadying herself, before she dared look up.

To the tree-borne grave of the Highwayman.

He's dead," the young and pretty woman said to Harcourt when he rushed back to the stairs to view the broken body of King Yeslnik. "They're both dead!"

"What do we do?" another attendant asked in despair, and, indeed, the gloom spread wide and far and fast.

"We open the gates," Harcourt said, and all eyes looked upon him. "And pray that our conquerors are beneficent."

The gates of Delaval City were opened that day, as the sun sank low in the western sky, as, in a field far away, Cormack and Milkeila knelt and cried and kissed the hero who had won the day in Blenden Coe.

Harcourt of Palmaristown met the royal procession at the gates as they marched. He presented King Yeslnik's sword to Laird Bannagran . . . nay, to King Bannagran.

Bannagran took it and looked to Queen Gwydre at his side. Then he glanced at Master Reandu and at Laird Ethelbert, following right behind, who nodded his agreement.

Bannagran accepted Yeslnik's sword but in turn gave Harcourt back the sword the general had surrendered in Blenden Coe.

And in that moment, the horns of Pryd began to blow, and the horns of Delaval City replied, and the horns of Vanguard resounded, and the horns of Ethelbert dos Entel joined in, and from the ships in the river came the horns of Palmaristown, and in that moment of confusion and fear, there came to Delaval City, hope.

Unlike so many who had left Blenden Coe, traveling straight to Delaval City to attend the formal wedding and coronation of Bannagran and Gwydre, Cormack and Milkeila took a more roundabout route, moving north and west to the bank of the Masur Delaval not far south from Palmaristown.

It seemed a fool's chase, even to Cormack, who had insisted upon it, but he was determined to at least try. He owed his unlikely friends that much.

Whether it was some magic in the powrie beret he wore or a matter of good information gleaned from some of Milwellis's soldiers or simply dumb luck or some combination of the three, Cormack did not know, but walking along the river, the monk recognized the familiar face immediately, though it was bloated in death and well along in rot.

But he knew this dwarf, without doubt.

"And Bikelbrin's up here," Milkeila called a few moments later from the rise just off the river. "I cannot believe that we found them!"

Cormack stood hands on hips, looking down at the powrie who had befriended him. The weight of all world fell on his shoulders in that one moment, and tears escaped his eyes. Tears for Mcwigik and Bikelbrin, tears for Bransen, tears for Jameston Sequin, tears for all the dead and all the maimed and all the grieving.

"Bury them?" Milkeila asked, for she was not sure why Cormack had insisted on this expedition.

The monk shook his head. He drew a knife from his belt and crouched down over his dead powrie friend.

"Cormack!" Milkeila yelled at him when he started cutting, but he did not stop, and by the time the woman arrived at his side, he stood up and showed her Mcwigik's heart. Methodically, the monk went to Bikelbrin and similarly cut out his heart.

"What are you doing?" Milkeila asked repeatedly as Cormack found a clear spot in from the river, a place suitable for his needs. He placed the hearts down gently and began to dig with his knife.

"Help me," he said.

"You bury their hearts?"

"And then we sing," Cormack said. Milkeila paused and stared at him suspiciously.

She went to her work, though, and they finished the hole and placed the hearts of Mcwigik and Bikelbrin within.

Cormack tapped down the replaced earth, then grabbed Milkeila by the shoulders and bent low in a huddle. He began the cadence of the song he had learned long ago in a place far away, and Milkeila dutifully chanted along, though she did not know the words.

It didn't matter, Cormack thought, for what did he know of this ritual anyway? Would two new dwarves, offspring of his friends, actually come forth?

"That is Sepulcher?" Milkeila asked when they were done.

Cormack nodded.

"Why?" the woman asked.

"I don't know," Cormack answered honestly. "A debt repaid?"

The couple stood holding hands above the graves, the womb of Mcwigik and Bikelbrin, for a long, long while.

And there they put the past behind them and turned south toward Delaval City, toward the future.

Epilogue

Bransen Garibond, Prince of Pryd, cast his line into the still waters of the lake and rested back against the stone. This was his favorite fishing spot in all of Pryd Town, a small outcrop that jutted into the water beside the old house, the childhood home of his father and namesake. From the window of that house, his house now, his father had often watched his adoptive father, Garibond Womak, similarly casting.

At least, so claimed his mother and grandmother, and Bransen could well imagine it. He felt connected to this place, which, along with Castle Pryd, had been his home for all his thirty-five years. Here he was at peace. Here the world was as it should be in the kingdom known as Honce-the-Bear in God's Year 111.

"Father!" he heard a call from his teenaged son, and Dynard came into view, sprinting past the house toward Bransen. On the porch, Callen McKeege stood up curiously, but old Dawson, well into his nineties now, hardly seemed to notice the disturbance.

"Word from Ursal!" Dynard exclaimed, referring to the throne of Honce-the-Bear, a city once known as Delaval.

Bransen knew what was coming before Dynard even spoke it.

"To the castle," he instructed his son, and Callen and even old Dawson followed.

They found Cadayle, the longtime Dame of Pryd, tending one of her many gardens. Her smile had not diminished with age, though the sparkle in her eyes had never quite returned after the loss of her beloved husband.

"The king is dead," Bransen told his mother.

Cadayle closed her eyes and took a deep and steadying breath. Like Bransen, she wasn't surprised by the news, for all in the kingdom who knew well the old Bear of Honce knew that he wouldn't long survive after the death of his wife, Queen Gwydre.

"What now?" young Dynard asked.

"It is good that they had a child," said Cadayle. "Prydae will be king. He is a good man, I think," she added hopefully.

"You have not seen him in eleven years," Bransen reminded. "Not since the Abellican Centennial."

"He is near to your age," Cadayle replied. "You knew him best of all. Do you think me wrong?"

Bransen shrugged.

"He's got his father's size, to be sure," said Callen.

"Aye, but has he his mother's good heart?" old Dawson added, and that was the rub, after all. For more than three decades, the land of Honce-the-Bear had known peace and prosperity. For one brief shining moment, all the people of the land had mattered, not the king and queen. And no lairds, not Dame Cadayle of Pryd nor Laird Cormack and Dame Milkeila of Vanguard nor any of the many lairds of Entel in the east nor any of the many lairds of the lesser holdings, had hoarded their treasures while the peasants had suffered. For that was not the way of King Bannagran and Queen Gwydre's Honce, and only once in all the years had an upstart laird in Palmaristown defied them.

And even there, in the city that had once blamed Dame Gwydre for the murderous attacks of powries, the garrison and peasants of Palmaristown had refused to fight for the treasonous laird when Queen Gwydre and her fleet had arrived.

But that was all a different age now as the reign of Gwydre and Bannagran had come to an end.

"Prydae will be his mother's fine son," Bransen said, nodding his head. "Or I will become my father's son and put to use my grandmother's shining sword."

"Don't talk like that, boy!" Callen scolded, but Cadayle hushed her.

"No, do," the Dame of Pryd told her child. "If the world is ever in need of you, then answer that call."

Bransen, son of the Highwayman, nodded, and though he believed his prediction about the reign of King Prydae, so, too, did he believe his claim about his own determination, for he was his father's son, and his mother's, and he would fight if ever the need arose.

As long as the price was worth the gain.

At St. Mere Abelle, Father Abbot Reandu, the leader of the Church of Blessed Abelle, received the news of Bannagran's passing with great sadness.

He had known the king longer than any man alive and had witnessed the great growth of the Laird of Pryd in the months leading up to his ascension to the unified throne.

Honce-the-Bear would not easily recover from the loss of Queen Gwydre and King Bannagran, so close together, and his own role in assuring that the light of their reign did not darken in the coming days would not be a minor one.

Reandu had been in Ursal when Queen Gwydre had died, passing peacefully among loved ones and dear friends, including Laird Cormack and Dame Milkeila, who had sailed all the way from Vanguard upon hearing of her illness.

Reandu stared out his window, in the same office that had belonged to Father Premujon and Father Artolivan before him, and let the tapestry of his life play out before him. He thought of Cadayle and of Bransen, the Highwayman— the little Stork—a damaged child living in a hole and carrying chamber pots, who had so unexpectedly come into Reandu's life and had so unbelievably come to play the most important of roles in the great struggle of his day.

A moment of regret brought a wince to the Father Abbot, but it passed quickly. They had done great things. They had made the world a better place, and, in the end, it could not be denied, in cottages across the length and breadth of Honce-the-Bear, that the price had been worth the gain.

"And so our work goes on," Reandu said.

"It ever will, father," Master Pinower said behind him. "It ever will."